I0771443

WELCOME TO THE NEXUS

THE PLANAR GATES: BOOK ONE

NATE GILLICK

NEW ATARAXIA PUBLISHING LLC

Copyright © 2025 by Nate Gillick

Published by New Ataraxia Publishing LLC

All rights reserved.

Paperback ISBN: 978-1-968406-00-4
Ebook ISBN: 978-1-968406-01-1

No part of this publication may be reproduced, distributed, or transmitted in any form or by any means, including photocopying, recording, or other electronic or mechanical methods, without the prior written permission of the publisher, except as permitted by U.S. copyright law. For permission requests, contact nate@nategillick.com.

The story, all names, characters, and incidents portrayed in this novel are fictitious. No identification with actual persons (living or deceased), places, buildings, and products is intended or should be inferred.

Cover design by MiblArt.

Visit the author's website at www.nategillick.com

Join the Planar Gates Reddit community at /r/PlanarGates

Dedicated to Dr. Bernard Harrison

This book would not exist if you hadn't been there for me when I needed you.

The world is a better place with you in it.

PART 1
WELCOME TO THE NEXUS

CHAPTER 1

JONAH'S MONSTER

If anyone disturbs my peace today, I'll murder them.

Serena held a cup of tea under her nose, savoring the scents of lemon and lavender. On the table before her, she held open the pages of the only novel in town she hadn't read yet. The tension between her shoulder blades eased as she sipped her drink. Songbirds sang to each other as a gentle breeze ruffled the leaves. *Solitude and quiet. At last.*

"Serena! SERENA!" The all-too-familiar voice came from the opposite end of the village's central courtyard. Jonah. Of course.

She downed the rest of her tea in one long swallow, then slammed the cup down with enough force to snap the handle off in her hand. Whoops. She placed a couple of coins on the table to cover replacement costs. It wouldn't be the first time she'd broken one in Jonah-induced frustration, and she wanted to stay in the tavern keeper's good graces. She imagined herself strapping Jonah to a litter, dragging him into the woods, and leaving him for wolves. Or tying him up and leaving him dangling over crocodile-infested waters. Why did it always have to be her? Couldn't he just *once* let her delegate the task to another hunter?

No use delaying the inevitable. What nonexistent beast would she be contractually obligated to hunt today? "Over here, Jonah," she lifted an arm in a lazy wave.

Jonah took a seat across from her, oblivious to both the shattered cup and her barely restrained temper. He fidgeted. Stood and danced back and forth like he had to relieve himself. Ran his hands through his hair. Sat back down and bounced his leg up and down.

"Use your words," Serena said. "What is it this time?"

"A monster killed one of my cows." He looked ready to jump out of his skin, glancing all over the place like a nervous squirrel. Same as any other day. Why would such a nervous man choose to build a life on the frontier?

They'd had some version of this conversation many times over her four years in Valencia. Besides serving as the lead hunter and trapper for a village of a hundred people, it fell to her to deal with threats like wolves and bears.

And monsters, if such things still existed.

"Where's the body?" Serena asked, expecting him to tell her it vanished. Jonah's constant reports of monster sightings never included conclusive evidence.

"What's left of it is in my cattle pen."

Serena's interest perked up. Maybe, for the first time ever, a visit from Jonah wouldn't be a complete waste of time. The man saw the work of monsters in everything. The morning after strong winds rolled through the region, he'd insist a monster pushed on his fence posts, causing them to lean. Monsters drank from his ponds, causing them to run dry. It had nothing to do with a drought. Monsters, not mice, inhabited his barns at night. He needed mental help, not a hunter, but her contract required her to investigate all claims of predatory activity in the area. She didn't want to give the church any reason to terminate her contract early and not pay her completion bonus.

"Did you see the monster itself, or just the remains of the cow?"

"Only the mutilated remains," Jonah said. "Wolves didn't do this. It's not a bear either."

Serena stood and stretched, then picked up her book. "This is the first day off I've had in a month, Jonah. I'll take a look at your dead cow. I'll walk the perimeter of your land. If I don't see anything, I'm calling it a day and will resume the investigation tomorrow."

Jonah opened his mouth to complain, but froze under her withering glare.

The pair stopped by her tiny log house long enough for her to leave the book and retrieve her bow and a quiver of arrows. She wore a knife at her hip. Each of her boots had a throwing knife tucked into the lining. She didn't expect to encounter anything, but it would be unprofessional to go unprepared.

At the edge of the village, Jonah paused next to the mysterious statues that inspired the founding of Valencia. Five years ago, explorers working their way north stumbled upon a pair of life-size statues in a region with no known history of human settlement. Each looked like they'd been carved from marble the day before, with no signs of dirt, erosion, or corrosion. One depicted Alainna, the All-Mother, creator of all life on Alterra. The other statue, ten feet away and facing the same direction, depicted an unknown male. Both had their arms at their sides with their hands turned out in a gesture of greeting. The church considered the statues holy relics. Valencia served as a base for clergy and archeologists to investigate their origin.

A village so far from civilization needed farmers to provide food security long-term, which led to Jonah and a handful of others joining the project. They needed meat and furs, which Serena and other hunters provided. At the end of her five-year contract, she'd return to civilization with enough coin in her pocket to take several years off if she wanted to. The church had rich backers funding this expedition.

While Jonah prayed to Alainna, Serena removed an arrow from her quiver, kissed it, and placed it in the hands of the unknown male. She'd retrieve it when she returned.

"Why do you always do that?" Jonah asked, his prayers concluded.

"Alainna gets all the love. Why aren't people more curious about the identity of our male friend? Is he a god too? Alainna's lover? The first person to accept her teachings and spread the gospel of the All-Mother?" Serena wasn't a devout follower of the church, but she loved a good story. She suspected there was an epic behind the origin of the statues. She gave the male statue an affectionate pat on the side. "Whoever this is, I hope he takes it as a sign of respect that I ask him to bless an arrow and keep it safe for me."

It took twenty minutes walking along a dirt road to clear the forest and arrive at Jonah's farm at the edge of the grasslands. Serena knew at once something strange had happened here. This wouldn't be yet another example of Jonah crying wolf and dragging her out here for no reason.

His surviving cows huddled at the far end of their pen, pressed up against the fence. In the middle of the enclosure rested a mutilated corpse. Not seeing anything else moving in the immediate area, Serena climbed over the fence to take a closer look. Jonah followed but kept a healthy distance, as if concerned the corpse carried diseases.

A diagonal slash ran from the cow's shoulders down to its rear legs. The cut was deep and clean, as if rendered with a sword. Smaller puncture wounds dotted the edges of the cut near missing chunks of flesh. "You're sure a monster did this?" Serena asked. Wolves and bears would have left behind claw and bite marks. Though flesh was missing, it didn't resemble any carnivore's feeding pattern she'd ever seen or read about.

"What else could it have been?" Jonah asked.

"Nothing in nature cuts this cleanly. This is the work of a blade." She tried not to sound too pleased with that. Human crimes fell under the jurisdiction of the town guard. Let those lazy bums deal with it. "Do you have any enemies, Jonah? Can you think of anyone who would wish you harm?"

"Not at all."

She believed him, which made the cow's death more perplexing. Though Jonah jumped at shadows and saw monsters everywhere, he only annoyed her about it. He was generous with his time and resources with his neighbors, ensuring they all had thriving properties. He drove her insane, but everyone else loved him.

"Wait, what's this?" Light reflected off an object protruding from one of the puncture wounds flanking the main cut. Serena squatted down and pried it loose with her knife. The black metallic object looked more like a crocodile's tooth than a broken blade. It extended from the tip of her middle finger to the base of her hand.

This might be her problem after all.

Serena tossed the object to Jonah, who bobbled it several times before it fell to the ground. "Do you recognize that?"

He made no move to pick it up. "You don't? I thought you were the monster expert."

She'd read every book in the capital's library on known animal species, monsters of antiquity, and mythological beasts as a teenager. She liked to think of herself as a walking encyclopedia of animal facts. It proved very helpful in securing her contract. Since they were setting up a village in uncharted territory, the church wanted a lead hunter with as broad a knowledge base as possible.

Out of an abundance of caution, Serena pulled an arrow from her quiver to have one ready. "If it's a monster, it's not documented in any lore I know."

Jonah's surviving cows shuffled closer together, pressing hindquarters together to create a defensive ring with their calves in the center. They sensed something. She thought she did too, as if an unseen predator had her in its sights.

An attack could only come from two directions. Anything large enough to leave behind such a lengthy slash would be too large to hide amongst Jonah's cabbages across the road to her left. Behind her was Jonah's house and miles of grazing land. Any monster nearby would be hidden in the rows of corn a hundred yards to her right, or in the forest in front of her. She nocked an arrow and scanned the tree line for any signs of movement.

Wood cracked and splintered as something massive landed on the roof of Jonah's house.

Serena turned and squinted against the sunlight to see what looked like a horse-sized praying mantis on the roof. Its arms looked like reaper's scythes, gleaming in the late morning sun. A mass of writhing tentacles hung where mandibles should be, each ending in a sharp tooth similar to the one she'd found lodged in the dead cow.

Definitely my problem.

"Don't move, Jonah." She didn't want the monster chasing him if he fled like a spooked rabbit. No guarantee she could protect him if he did. *There's no guarantee I can protect him NOW.*

If Jonah heard her, he gave no sign.

The mantis creature turned its head slowly, its multifaceted eyes lingering first on Jonah, then Serena, then the cows. Was it choosing its next victim? Deciding if any of them were threats?

Jonah's roof buckled under the creature's weight as it pounced. Serena let an arrow fly. She missed low. She dove to the side to avoid a slash that would have bisected her at the waist, then rolled to her feet while reaching for another arrow. The mantis ducked under a shot aimed for its head and charged her again.

Goddess, that thing is fast. Wolves moved like tortoises in comparison. Hoping to throw off its timing, she dropped her bow and charged it in turn, sliding at the last second. It slashed harmlessly over her head. She drew her knife and stabbed its thorax three times. Green blood dribbled from the wounds.

Serena stuck close to the monster's flank to hinder its ability to slash her. Since she'd dropped her bow, she tossed aside her quiver as well. The mantis moved too fast for her to get a clean shot. She'd never be able to outrun it. If she wanted to keep herself and Jonah alive, she'd have to get creative with her knife.

The mantis spun in circles several times, trying to orient itself to attack Serena. She never gave it the chance, staying close and stabbing into its sides and hacking at its legs as fast as she could. Each attack against its exoskeleton felt like stabbing into a watermelon with a blunt dagger, but she persisted. It might flee if she wounded it enough.

Changing tactics, the mantis crouched and pounced across the enclosure towards the ring of cows. One of them charged the mantis. The giant insect decapitated it with a swift, brutal swing. Panicked at the sight and smell of fresh blood, the rest of the herd slammed against the fence in an attempt to knock it over and escape. Ignoring them, the mantis turned to face Serena.

The two combatants stared at each other. Serena felt like a matador facing down an enraged bull. When the mantis charged, she'd have to react quickly. Anger, terror, and adrenaline coursed through her, creating an unfamiliar sensation of heat in her chest. Anger at having to fight on a rare day off. Terror that the monster might win. Adrenaline at the thrill of battle. She'd defeated a dire bear and survived multiple encounters with wolves. None of her prior experiences with predators prepared her for a giant, lightning-fast insect with razor-sharp arms.

"Run, Serena!" Jonah shouted. "We should get the town guard!" He stood at the edge of her peripheral vision, as still as a potted plant. A conspicuous stain darkened the front of his pants and ran down his legs. He made no move to heed his own advice.

She didn't bother responding. Never taking her eyes off the mantis, she sheathed her knife and squatted to retrieve the throwing knives in her boots. It continued to stare at her. For reasons Serena couldn't understand, she felt like an unknown third party was also watching.

Jonah's fence broke under the weight of a dozen cows. The terrified cattle stampeded out of the enclosure, some cutting themselves along sharp edges of splintered wood or tripping over fallen railings. It was a miracle none of them broke a leg.

The mantis pounced. Serena strafed left, throwing a knife at the insect's multifaceted eyes. She missed low, the blade instead digging into one of the writhing tentacles surrounding its mouth. She threw her second knife without aiming, making an instinctive adjustment based on the oncoming enemy's speed. As if guided by the goddess's hand, it struck a bullseye with the insect's left eye.

Partially blinded, it flailed at empty air. Serena used its distraction to unsheathe her knife and rush it. She used one of its legs as a stepstool to leap onto its back. Holding her knife in a two-handed grip, she stabbed into the back of the monster's neck with all her strength. The mantis bucked and thrashed as it tried to shake her off. Serena squeezed her legs tight and held on for dear life, stabbing and sawing her way through the creature's neck. Green gore splattered her face, chest, and hands.

Just die already! Her legs and core muscles screamed their protest at the effort of staying mounted on the enraged monster. At the moment her strength gave out, she struck something vital. The mantis bucked Serena loose in its death throes. She twisted her ankle in an awkward attempt to land on her feet. She fell backwards, creating just enough separation to avoid being crushed under the mantis's bulk as it collapsed.

The sensation of heat in her chest faded as she took one deep breath after another. The adrenaline surge took longer to fade away. Flat on her back, she watched a single cloud drift lazily overhead. She felt sore and bruised, but otherwise unharmed.

"Are you alright?" Jonah asked, offering a hand to help her to her feet.

"I'll live." Serena accepted his help, gingerly testing her twisted ankle. It hurt, but she could walk if she had to. "How are your cows?" She wiped a sweaty strand of auburn hair away from her eyes, smearing mantis blood across her forehead in the process. Fantastic.

Jonah saw his own hand was tainted from helping her and wiped it across a dry section of his pants. "I can't round them up when they're this agitated. I'll let them roam until they've calmed down and we've got this mess cleaned up," he gestured broadly to include his dead cows and the mantis corpse.

"By 'we' I hope you mean the town guard," Serena said, limping over to her fallen adversary. "I was supposed to have the day off." She took her knife and severed one of the mantis's arms.

"What are you doing?" Jonah asked.

"Taking a trophy," Serena said. "If we go back to town and tell everyone we were attacked by a giant bug, do you expect anyone to take us seriously without proof?" She wrenched the arm free. "Besides, I'd like the blacksmiths to take a look at this and confirm it's metal. That seems unnatural."

The mantis's body shuddered. Its legs twitched as if looking to find their footing. More death throes? Could it still be alive, even though she'd cut halfway through its neck? Not wanting to take chances, Serena sheathed her knife, adjusted her grip on the mantis scythe, and decapitated the giant insect with its own arm.

Jonah turned away and vomited into the grass. "I'll tell the clergy you deserve several days off for this," he said when he could.

"I would appreciate it," Serena said. Keeping her weight on her good leg, she cast her gaze skyward and did a slow turn. Not seeing anything unusual, she did a second, slower spin to study the forest, Jonah's fields, his retreating cattle, and his damaged roof. Though she didn't see any signs of danger, she couldn't shake the lingering sensation of being watched. Probably just post-battle nerves.

Jonah picked up Serena's bow and quiver and handed them back to her. They didn't bother hunting down her stray arrows or throwing knives. That could wait. Once she had her weapons slung over her shoulder, she allowed Jonah to wrap an arm around her for support, then the two started the slow trek back to Valencia. With her free hand, she held the mantis scythe like a club, keeping the sharp end as far away from her as possible.

CHAPTER 2
GRIM TIDINGS

Serena and Jonah took a detour on the way back to Valencia to bathe themselves in a nearby river and wash their clothes. She didn't want to return covered in insect blood. He didn't want to arrive reeking of piss. He helped Serena keep weight off her ankle as she picked her way down the rocky shore and made sure she was comfortably situated in the water before walking a hundred yards downstream and around a bend to tend to himself. He stayed in shouting distance until she signaled she was clean, dressed, and ready to move on.

By the time they reached the statues at the edge of town, Serena's ankle felt better, allowing her to walk unassisted. She retrieved her arrow from the male statue's hand and gave him a thankful nod. It felt like a blessing to be home with all her limbs intact.

On the far side of the village, dozens of people loitered around the stairs leading into the church. It was a popular place to wait for the weekly supply wagons from the capital, which carried letters from home, official church communications, and any items villagers ordered that couldn't be grown or produced locally. The wagons represented the remote village's only connection to civilization. They should have arrived by now. She'd have to ask about it after she got the town guard to help Jonah deal with his cow carcasses.

"Don't make a scene," Serena said, placing a hand on Jonah's shoulder. She feared after finally being right about the existence of a monster, he'd repeat his performance from earlier, running around the courtyard shouting about it.

"I wouldn't dream of it." Jonah's chagrined expression suggested he'd been about to do just that.

"Let's take Left to avoid the crowd."

Valencia had only three streets, dubbed Left, Center, and Right, each named by their position relative to the gaze of the mysterious statues. Only Center was wide enough to accommodate horses and wagons. It included the town's central courtyard. Left ran behind Serena's house and terminated at the modest barracks the five members of the town guard shared. Tucked away in the back corner of the town, it was a simple one-story wooden structure which took up five times the footprint of individual homes. It contained the permanent living spaces for the guards, supply closets, a front office, and three jail cells to hold unruly drunks until they'd sobered up.

Serena pounded her fist twice on the front door then opened it and stepped inside without waiting for an acknowledgment. She found all five guards sitting around the table in the front office, engrossed in a game of poker. "What the hell is this?"

Like her, they'd all signed five-year contracts with the church. The closer they got to their end date, the lazier they became. Playing cards when they should be helping with crowd control and unloading the wagons upon arrival was a whole new level of apathy for them. They hadn't even left someone outside as a lookout while they ignored their responsibilities. It was like they *wanted* to get fired. Or they thought the clergy wouldn't go through the hassle of letting them go and bringing in replacements ahead of schedule.

"Let the townies take care of it themselves for once." Karl, the head of the guards, waved a hand dismissively. "Clergy and scholars rarely exercise. They're all soft. Unloading their goods will help toughen them up."

Serena scoffed. "Don't try to put a virtuous sheen on your laziness." She took a breath to tamp down her anger, keeping it simmering just below its boiling point. "This was supposed to be my first day off in a month, but I've still been working. Do *not* test my patience. Jonah needs your help. Send two men to tend the wagons, have the rest help Jonah, and we'll forget we walked in on you gambling while on duty."

"We will?" Jonah asked, stunned. He spent so much time on his farm that he lacked any notion of the depths of the town guard's uselessness. Lucky him.

"We will. And they'll agree, because they want their bonuses as much as I do. Between doing an honest day's work and facing a misconduct review, I know what choice I'd make."

Karl made no effort to disguise his animosity. With Jonah as a second witness, he couldn't try to play off a formal complaint from Serena as baseless lies. "Short stacks tend the wagons," he growled. The two men with the smallest stacks of chips stood up and left without a word, casting nasty glares in Serena's direction on the way out. Their haste to obey suggested this wasn't the first time they'd decided who did what based on a poker game.

"Thank you for your cooperation," Serena said with exaggerated politeness. She allowed herself a moment of petty satisfaction — Karl unknowingly assigned himself the worse of the two options. He started gathering cards and chips to hide the evidence of their transgression. Serena tossed her trophy onto the table, sending chips flying in every direction. Karl made a rude gesture and went to his knees to clean up the mess.

"What's this?" One of the remaining guards leaned forward to examine the scythe blade.

"I carved that off the monster I killed at Jonah's farm," Serena said.

"Monsters are your department," the third guard said, unimpressed by the amputated limb on their poker table. "Deal with it yourself. Ain't that why the church pays you so much?"

Of course one of them would bring up the pay gap between her and the guards. They almost always did when she asked them to do their jobs. Like it was her fault the church considered hunting a much more valuable service than interceding in the rare instance of disorderly conduct.

"I kill the monsters, you dispose of their remains," Serena said, reminding them of a clause in their contracts she'd never had to invoke. She picked up the mantis blade and turned for the door. "I'm leaving Jonah in your very capable hands." She managed to not sound sarcastic. "He can fill you in on how we spent our morning. I have to report to the church and let them know about this creature."

Disorder and confusion greeted her at the courtyard. The wagons arrived during her argument with the town guard. She only saw two, when there should be three or four. Two drivers operated each wagon, taking turns handling the reins. They looked like they hadn't slept in days. One rocked back and forth with the despondent, dissociative look of a man in shock. Some of the villagers took it upon themselves to start unloading the wagons to help the beleaguered drivers.

Deciding it best not to get involved while carrying a weapon of strange origin, Serena skirted the crowd to take the steps to the church's entrance, where Pastors Amanda and Kristoff watched the scene unfolding below them with wait-and-see attitudes.

"Kristoff, can I borrow you for a moment?" Serena asked, not addressing the man by his title. The church preached that all people were created equal. In a village this small, the pastors felt that being addressed by their titles elevated them improperly over the people they served. Though they held all the power in the village, they liked to pretend they didn't.

"Of course," Kristoff said, casting a wary gaze at the mantis scythe. "Why don't we step inside."

The interior of the church was a far cry from the architectural majesty of the Radiant Temple of the All-Mother in the capital. A dozen rows of benches ran down either side of an unadorned room, with a wide aisle down the center. The back of the room held a stage the pastors spoke from, to better be seen by their congregation. There was no altar. Along the top of the back wall *YOU ARE LOVED* was painted in flowing golden letters with red borders.

Kristoff led Serena to the edge of the stage and took a seat so he could face the door. Serena set the mantis scythe against a bench in the front row and joined him.

"I've never seen a weapon like that before." Kristoff nodded at Serena's grisly trophy. "It looks metallic, but it's... connected to flesh? Have you been working on your day off?"

Serena smiled despite the circumstances. Kristoff seemed to always know when someone did or didn't want small talk, and never wasted someone's time. Serena appreciated that about him. "Not by choice." She filled the pastor in on her battle at Jonah's farm. "It was fast and lethal. I only saw one, but that doesn't mean there aren't others."

Kristoff nodded. "What do you recommend we do?"

Evacuate Valencia, Serena wanted to say, but knew the church wouldn't give up their holy mystery and the revenue they could bring in when Valencia expanded into a full-blown pilgrimage site. They'd say she was overreacting. Such decisions should wait until they knew if there were more of the creatures. Best to offer a plan that brought in reinforcements to move things in the direction she wanted. "Write to the capital. Convince them this is a real, manticore-level threat. Ask them to send at least a platoon of soldiers to help me and our other hunters canvas the forest."

"Is that really necessary? The military will balk at sending troops so far afield."

"So we send them the mantis arm as proof. I managed to kill one, but I can't promise you that I'd succeed again. It would be a mistake to assume me and our other hunters are sufficient to kill more of these things," Serena admitted. Successful hunters were often known for their egos as much as their kills. She couldn't afford pride here. She wouldn't be the only one hurt by underestimating the danger.

Shouting from outside interrupted their conversation. The church's door rocked as something heavy banged against it. One of the guards unleashed a string of profanities sure to earn him a reprimand later, then the doors opened. All four wagon drivers entered, followed by one of the town guards, and finally Pastor Amanda.

"What's going on?" Kristoff asked, his eyes taking in the scene with an alertness that reminded Serena more of a bird of prey than a clergyman.

"If the drivers are to be believed," Amanda said, looking like she'd aged twenty years in as many minutes, "the capital has fallen."

"That doesn't make sense. We've been at peace with our neighbors for generations."

"It wasn't people," the most lucid-looking of the drivers said. "It was an unholy legion of demons from the blackest hell."

"Our friend here has a poetic tongue," Amanda said. Did she detect fear underneath her irritation? "And because of it, the whole village is panicking. I'll work on calming our flock while they fill you in." She helped a vacant-looking driver take a seat in the back row of benches, then exited the church with the guard following close behind. Two of the other drivers collapsed on benches and fell asleep immediately.

Only the driver who'd spoken remained on his feet. He had the bearing of a military man, like he'd served before retiring to courier work. His clothes were disheveled and filthy, as if he'd worn and slept in them for multiple consecutive days. Serena observed these details in the background, her focus locked on the man's eyes. They had the vacant look of someone who'd lost all reason to continue living.

"My name is Kevin Kleimann," the driver said, advancing down the aisle to stand before Serena and Kristoff. "I've been a driver for Continental Express for almost ten years." He spoke in the no-nonsense manner of a man delivering a report to his superior officer, but there was no heart in it. Simply a man falling into old habits as a coping mechanism. "We were preparing to set off for Valencia when the capital was attacked."

"By demons from the blackest hell." Serena said, pushing herself off the stage. It felt wrong to be seated for a conversation like this. "Could you give us a more literal description?"

"Insects the size of horses. Like praying mantis, but thicker thorax, sturdier legs. Tentacles around their mouths. Arms like a scythe, capable of cutting a man in half with a single swing. Fast as a bird of prey when diving in for the kill. It sounds unbelievable, but with the All-Mother as my witness, it's true."

Blood drained from Serena's face at the description. How could legions of insects that size remain so well hidden that nobody knew they existed? If the most heavily fortified city on the planet couldn't hold them off, what hope did she have of protecting this tiny village?

Her parents lived in the capital, as did her extended family. Were they dead? Could they have gone into hiding, or escaped in time? Serena clenched her fists, her fingernails digging into the palms of her hands almost hard enough to break the skin.

She couldn't afford to dwell on *what ifs* right now. "I believe you. I've seen one too." Serena pointed at the mantis arm draped against a bench to Kevin's right.

Before he could comment, Kristoff asked, "What happened in the capital? How did you escape?"

He had to ask a second time before Kevin turned his gaze away from the severed arm. "We had the wagons loaded and were heading out when we heard a loud buzzing in the air. I looked up and saw hundreds of them blocking the sunlight. The next instant, they were rampaging through the streets, slaughtering anyone and anything in sight. They cut down the horses and drivers of the rear wagons when we hit a snag in traffic. The way cleared, and our panicked horses took off. The monsters could have finished us, but pedestrians were easier targets. We saw hundreds of people hacked apart by the time we cleared the outer wall."

"This happened three days ago?" Amanda asked. Under normal circumstances, it took that long for caravans from the capital to reach Valencia.

"Indeed. Not knowing what else to do, I insisted we complete our delivery so we'd be with other people when we decided what to do next. I thought if those monsters were after people, they'd be more likely to migrate south than come this way." He looked again at the mantis arm. "I thought it'd be safer here."

"Thank you for letting us know what happened," Kristoff said. "The tavern has some rooms on the second floor. Take your men and get some proper sleep. You're safe here."

He spoke with such conviction, Serena almost believed him.

"Suggestions?" Kristoff asked once they were alone again. The commotion outside had died down. For now.

Serena's mind returned to her original opinion. The one everyone would hate. "Evacuate Valencia at dawn. Load the wagons with all the food and building supplies they can haul, and then venture as far north as we can endure. Most of us will have to travel on foot. If these monsters behave like normal insects, they won't like the cold. It's our best bet until we know..." She trailed off, unsure how to finish that sentence. *The fate of the capital. If anyone survived. If we're the only people left on all of Alterra. If the All-Mother herself will save us.*

Kristoff's gaze drifted over Serena's head to the *YOU ARE LOVED* text on the back wall. His shoulders drooped in resignation. "Why don't you go home and get some rest? I'll call for a town-wide meeting tonight. I'll need you, Jonah, and Kevin to testify to what you've seen, or people will never go along with an evacuation. Leave the mantis blade here. May Alainna save us."

Serena exited the church, her eyes unfocused and her mind running in a million directions at once. If she hadn't faced one of the monsters herself, she'd never have believed Kevin's tale. She still couldn't fathom there being enough of them to overwhelm the capital. Were they a form of divine retribution for humanity's sins? That didn't seem likely when the three kingdoms had been at peace for centuries. She recalled ancient myths of evil creatures emerging from underground to cause chaos. Could this have happened before in their distant past?

When she returned home, she lay on her bed and closed her eyes, hoping in vain that she could take a nap. Her imagination swirled with violent imagery of the capital's citizens meeting brutal and merciless ends. Her parents were probably dead. She didn't want to believe it, but they weren't anyone's definition of monster hunters or survivalists. Her father was a librarian, and her mother a tailor. Neither of them understood her desire to learn to shoot a bow, explore uncharted wilderness, or put herself in harm's way against dangerous wildlife. Her mother in particular hadn't wanted her to go "get herself killed" on the frontier.

How horribly ironic that, for the moment at least, the frontier seemed the safest place to be.

She doubted it'd stay that way for long.

Stop thinking about it. Serena forced herself to stuff the fear, anger, and grief in a deep corner of her mind and forget it. She could mourn once they'd fled further north. They had to hope the climate would be too cold for the bugs to follow. *Mom and Dad would want you to survive, Serena. So survive.*

CHAPTER 3
THE SWARM

S everal hours later, Serena stood on the roof of the church, watching the villagers scramble to load their belongings into wagons, saddlebags, or the packs they carried. People who finished moved on to help their neighbors. Serena hadn't needed long. Everything she owned fit in a single trunk. With her needs tended to, she'd volunteered for the first shift watching for monsters in the sky. Only the church stood tall enough to allow her to see over the canopy.

As expected, nobody wanted to evacuate. Despite testimony from three witnesses, they refused to accept the reality of the situation. Frustrated, Serena had grabbed the mantis arm, walked across the courtyard from the church steps, and demonstrated the strength and sharpness of the monster's blades by hacking into her own house. The edge bit into the dense, old-growth logs as if they were rotted scrap wood. On the third strike, the blade broke loose from the flesh part of the arm, leaving it stuck deep in the wall. It didn't take an expert to see that her strikes could have decapitated someone. At that point, they finally listened.

The exodus would begin at dawn.

"When you defeated that monster, I thought we were safe. I never would have thought we'd be abandoning the town." Jonah stood at Serena's side. He'd returned to town when summoned for the emergency meeting, and since then hadn't done anything for the evacuation effort but lighten the tavern's kegs.

A dozen people kneeled around the statue of Alainna, offering one last prayer to the goddess before saying goodbye to the representation of the All-Mother, perhaps forever. In a rare moment of professionalism, the town guards helped others pack without complaint, though that assistance irritated some. A shouting match broke out between one of the guards and a scholar who insisted his journals about the soil and rock surrounding the holy statues were essentials worthy of the limited wagon space. Two junior members of the clergy stuffed a horse's saddlebags with every hymnal in the church's possession.

"How far north do you think we'll need to go to be safe?" Jonah asked.

Serena found herself agreeing with Karl's uncharitable opinion of Valencia's permanent residents. They *were* too soft, too used to relying on their hired tradesman and hunters to get the hard work done. Even now, they couldn't separate *needs* from *wants*. Fleeing north would teach them hard lessons. They probably wouldn't all survive, even if they never faced monster attacks.

"I hear Karl wants the town guard to have authority over the hunters during our march, instead of how it's always been," Jonah said.

Nobody had their eyes turned towards the church roof, yet Serena couldn't shake the feeling of being watched. Hours after leaving Jonah's farm, the sensation still lingered.

"You with me, Serena?" Jonah asked, waving a hand across her vision.

"Shouldn't you be packing?" Serena shook her head in an attempt to clear her mind and reset her focus. Had he been talking the whole time?

Jonah took a long pull from a flask. "It'll be fine. A dozen people are helping me strip my farm tomorrow and load up wagons. We'll meet up with everyone at the first night's rest. Why? Are you trying to get rid of me?"

"For once, no." Not being alone was a comfort while waiting for what felt like the end of the world. "I just don't want to see you get left behind, or your crops go to waste. You see a monster one time, and now we're all fleeing."

"I've seen monsters many times," Jonah insisted. "This is just the first time you believed me."

Serena walked to the other end of the roof to survey the surrounding forest. The setting sun bathed the canopy in an orange glow that extended to the horizon. Under other circumstances, it would've been beautiful.

A hundred yards from the edge of town, the canopy shuddered. Dark shapes emerged into the twilight sky. A pair. Then six. Then a dozen. A dull thrum filled the air as they surged towards the town.

"We're under attack!" Serena shouted, drawing her bow. Her first shot impaled a mantis in its thick thorax. Her second pierced another in the abdomen as it flew overhead. Neither monster seemed aware they'd been shot. They stayed in formation with the rest of their group to fly over town and land by the statue of the All-Mother and her companion.

Her warning never reached the worshippers around the statues. A trio of bugs cut through them as they tried to rise to their feet. The other monsters fanned out to run down fleeing villagers.

Serena fired arrow after arrow into the insect swarm. She scored a lethal headshot on one before it could bisect a man fleeing for his front door. Another arrow rendered a mantis unable to swing its left arm. One stubborn mantis took five shots to the thorax and abdomen before collapsing in the center of the courtyard. They were much easier to hit when they weren't charging her.

Karl rallied the guard. Outnumbered two to one, they still rose to the occasion and fought valiantly. Serena did what she could to help them, aiming for headshots where possible, but more often settling for shots with the best chance of crippling an arm or leg. Other hunters lent their bows to the effort, as well. The monsters had poor peripheral vision and a strong preference for focusing on one target at a time. The guards took advantage of that, keeping one mantis focused on them while positioning themselves so a second wouldn't be able to attack.

After a few minutes of furious fighting, they'd evened the odds, but Serena was running out of arrows.

"Serena!" She spun at Jonah's cry. The roof shook as a mantis landed and charged him.

The poor farmer never had a chance.

The monster impaled Jonah with both arms faster than Serena could draw an arrow. It lifted him to its tentacle-lined nightmare of a mouth and crushed his head like a watermelon. Jonah's abruptly silenced scream would fill her nightmares for the rest of her life, assuming she survived the next few minutes. Nobody deserved to die like that.

Distracted by its meal, the mantis gave Serena the time she needed to steady her shaking hands. She shot an arrow into an eye the size of a serving platter. When that didn't kill it, she took her last arrow and repeated the trick with the monster's other eye. The mantis crumpled, pinning Jonah's remains to the roof under its bulk.

The church shook beneath her feet as a mantis hacked apart the church's entrance. Moments later, Pastor Kristoff's screams joined the chorus of terror and pain playing out below. It didn't take a strong imagination to picture his fate.

A second wave of monsters flew overhead and spread out to land at the edges of town, forcing fleeing villagers back towards the central courtyard. Serena forced herself to tear her gaze away from what remained of Jonah. Nothing she could do for him now. She had to get more arrows and defend the living.

She raced to the nearby ladder and slid to the ground. Staying low, she crept up to a wagon parked in front of the church. Pieces of the wagon drivers were scattered in the vicinity. Anger commingled with terror in her chest as she shifted Kevin's body enough to retrieve the spare quiver she'd placed in the wagon an hour earlier.

Kill, or be killed. It's them or me. And if it's me, I intend to rack up a body count on the way out. Bloodlust was a new sensation for her. She didn't hunt for the thrill of a kill, she wanted to provide people with meat and furs for warmth. No part of an animal went to waste on her watch. She had no malice towards predators living according to their natures, even when they attacked or tried to poach her kills.

Nothing about these insects felt natural.

Serena nocked an arrow and stepped out of cover. It wasn't hard to find targets. The remaining villagers huddled together in the central courtyard like a school of fish surrounded by sharks. Only three guards remained.

The insects stood still for a moment, then four pounced at each guard with perfect coordination. No matter which way the guards dodged or spun, scythe blades awaited them. Karl struck a mortal blow against one of his assailants before succumbing to a slit throat. Their deaths triggered a collective hysteria within the huddled mass of humanity. Villagers took off in every direction.

That kicked off the feeding frenzy.

The monsters surged into the crowd, slashing wildly. Screams and cries filled the air. The scent of blood grew ever stronger. Serena fired continuously, but had no more success stopping the massacre than she would have dousing a raging house fire with a single glass of water.

One of her neighbors crawled in desperation for the false safety of his house, his legs gone below the knees. A mantis jumped down from a nearby roof to finish him off.

I'm dead. The heavy thud behind her could only be one of the bugs landing. She'd been too distracted by the carnage in front of her to stay mindful of her surroundings. *Rookie mistake.*

The insect rammed her with its head, sending her stumbling towards scattered bodies. Before she could regain her balance, it hit her again. She slid and landed hard on the blood-slicked pavement. As she rolled to her feet, she found herself alone amongst the dead. A dozen insects surrounded her. She felt like a baby seal surrounded by hungry orcas.

Serena tossed her bow and quiver aside. This close to so many of the monsters, she'd never get off a clean shot. Instead, she unsheathed her knife. When one of the monsters came at her, she'd dodge, hug their flank, and stab like she had the mantis at Jonah's farm. She just had to repeat that trick twelve times in a row. No problem.

The monsters didn't attack.

"Scared of me?" Serena asked, trying to track every monster at once. If she could get by one and escape to the tree line, perhaps she could lose them. Those odds sucked, but it had to be better than fighting them all.

One of the monsters charged her. Serena took her chance. She slid under a high swipe that didn't look right. Had it tried to swat her with the flat side of its blade? She sprinted for her tiny window to freedom, only to take a blow to her side from another mantis.

That one had *definitely* been the flat of the blade. Her legs were still connected to her torso. A third insect rammed her chest with its head. Serena tripped over a severed arm and landed on a heap of corpses.

The monsters backed off and began feasting on the bodies closest to the edge of the courtyard. Their behavior made no sense. Why hadn't they killed her?

When she stood, a mantis dropped its snack and knocked her down again. She regained her feet, only for another mantis to ram her. Serena crouched, then took off like a sprinter. Ten feet later, a third of the insects plowed into her and sent her into a wild, uncontrolled tumble.

With each hit, Serena's rage intensified.

She thought of Jonah, the man who saw monsters in every shadow. He'd always been convinced a monster would kill him. He'd been right. She thought of Pastor Kristoff, who lived to make everyone feel valued and cared for, ripped apart under the words *YOU ARE LOVED*. She even lamented the loss of Karl, who shirked responsibility at every opportunity, but stood tall with his men when it mattered most.

These monsters slaughtered the people she was meant to aid and protect. Now they had the nerve to rub her face in her failure?

Why have they not killed me yet?

Refusing to be cowed, Serena stood again. She took a blow from behind and slid on her chest through a pool of blood.

Something inside her snapped.

"Enough!" Serena roared, surrendering to her rage. Power unlike anything she'd felt before coursed through her veins, as if a dam holding it back had burst. In an instant, she became a human inferno. It felt like the most natural thing in the world. Flames coated her arms, causing her sleeves to burn away in seconds. The knife in her hand melted under the intense heat. She tossed the ruined weapon aside and stood. Despite the heat, she felt no discomfort. Her flesh didn't burn. The flames felt like an extension of her will. Directing their flow was as simple as breathing.

When a mantis tried to knock her down again, she acted on instinct. A jet of flame erupted from the palm of her hand, catching the insect in the face. The acrid odor of melting flesh filled the air. Her victim flailed at nothing, took two steps forward, and collapsed into a spasming heap.

She hurled a fireball at the next closest insect. It exploded against the monster's thorax and coated it in oily flames. That mantis cut down its nearest neighbor in its death throes.

Serena took off in the only direction open to her. Alainna's statue caught her eye like an improbable offer of salvation. Three insects landed in her path to cut her off. Their coordination remained perfect. As if with one mind, they spread their arms out to form the widest possible barrier.

Without conscious thought, Serena channeled power into her hands. She wanted to lash out and inflict pain and death upon anything that stood in her way. *They. Will. Burn.* Fireballs appeared above each upturned palm. They started out the size of apples. As the line of bugs stepped forward, they swelled to cantaloupe size. She smashed the fireballs together, merging them into one that ballooned to the size of a watermelon as she continued pouring power into it.

A mantis pounced.

Serena threw her fireball with an underhand toss. It caught the insect in the abdomen and exploded, sending chunks of monster flying in every direction. One of its blades missed her by a hand span. She ran at the remaining two in her path, spraying each with a jet of flame. A heavy buzzing filled the air as the remaining bugs took to the air, as if panicking that she had a straight shot for the statue of the All-Mother.

She'd never sprinted so hard in her life. Her legs felt leaden and stiff, like they would lock up on her at any moment. A deep fatigue pressed down on her, and she had to will herself to keep moving. The flames that once coated her arms were now a low flame dancing across the back of her hands.

As Serena drew close, Alainna and her counterpart emitted a hum which crescendoed into a *pop*. With a flash, an iridescent ribbon of light appeared. It stood as tall as the statues, filling the entire ten-foot gap between them. The way colors swirled across its length reminded Serena of soap bubbles. She couldn't see through it. For all she knew, she could sprint through the light and into the waiting blades of a mantis on the other side. But if this wasn't divine intervention, she didn't know what else it could be.

The buzzing of wings filled her ears. Monsters were right over her head. She saw more closing on her in her peripheral vision.

There was no choice.

The statues offered salvation, or death.

Trusting her fate to the goddess, Serena sprinted through the ribbon of light.

CHAPTER 4
THE NEXUS

Serena slipped at the abrupt transition from hard earth to a smooth tile floor. The last flickers of flame disappeared from her hands as she landed hard on her butt. After falling down or getting knocked down so many times in the last few minutes, part of her wanted to remain on the floor. She forced herself to rise and check for pursuers.

A ribbon of light like the one she'd run through hung between two featureless metal poles. Eight golden runes floated in the air above the iridescent light. With a faint popping sound, the light disappeared, taking the runes with it, leaving behind only the metal poles and a drab white wall.

Nothing came through after her.

She took deep breaths, fighting to get her racing heartbeat under control. Adrenaline coursed through her so strongly she thought she might be sick.

"You're safe now." The voice belonged to a middle-aged man in a navy blue uniform that reminded her of the capital's civil peacekeepers. A symbol was sewn onto it over his heart. It looked like the number eight kicked onto its side, then squished. He stood in the middle of the room, inside a round desk with seating for two. He looked her up and down with undisguised concern. "Do you need medical assistance?"

"Where am I?" Serena asked, confused by the abrupt change of scenery.

"You've arrived in the Nexus." Never taking his eyes off her, he gestured around the room, drawing her attention to similar pairs of metal poles lining the walls. "This is an Emergency Recall arrival zone. Do you need medical attention?"

"I'm fine." Noticing his gaze lingering on her chest, Serena looked down and noted the villager's blood smeared all over her. "The blood isn't mine. Where am I?" She asked again, not understanding his original answer.

The man opened a waist-high gate to exit the circular desk. "I'm unarmed," he said, doing a slow spin to show he carried no weapons. "May I approach you?" His caution poked a hole in her confusion. Was he scared of her? Did he think she'd killed someone?

He didn't look threatening, so she nodded her consent, but stayed alert for any sign of attack. He did a circle around her, checking for cuts and lacerations. Not finding any, he ran her through a concussion test, which she submitted to with the grace of a spooked animal that couldn't decide if it should freeze or bolt. Her brain just shut down in the whiplash of fleeing a massacre and arriving in a sterile white room.

"The Nexus is vast. It can be hard to understand at first." Apparently satisfied she wasn't hiding any injuries, he stepped back. "It's your first time here, isn't it? Do you want to talk about what happened? Or would you like to get cleaned up first? We have shower facilities and can provide you with a change of clothes."

His questions got her brain working again. How could he be so calm? Didn't he understand what was happening? "What about my village? They're under attack! They need help!"

They're gone, Serena. There's nobody left to save. She clenched her fists and fought to silence such thoughts.

"I'm sorry, truly." He looked away from her, as if embarrassed or ashamed. "The system detected Vohr on your world and initiated the quarantine protocol to shut down the Gate. The Vohr cannot be allowed to spread to other worlds or infiltrate the Nexus. Your world was sealed off from the rest of the Planar Gate network. I'm afraid they're on their own... and you won't be able to go back." His haunted expression implied this wasn't the first time he'd delivered that news to someone.

"Liar!" Serena shouted. "People are dying back there, and you're going to do nothing? Send an army!"

"I'm afraid that's impossible."

"Then send me back, coward!" The defiance was reflexive. To go back alone would be certain death, but *someone* had to slay the monsters and look for survivors.

"I can't do that." A note of sorrow cracked through the man's facade of aloof, bureaucratic politeness. "The quarantine protocol is automatic, and irrevocable. You're lucky you made it through before the Gate shut down."

I can't go home.

He won't send help. Deflated, Serena staggered over to a row of chairs beside the circular desk and sat down heavily. Her footsteps tracked blood and dirt across the white tile floor. She didn't care. The last of her fighting spirit left her. What had happened?

Everyone I've ever known is dead.

I failed to protect those people.

NOBODY could have won that fight.

...I have magic? Only one in a thousand people on Alterra displayed any kind of power. Abilities usually manifested during puberty, not when someone was in their twenties.

She wanted to scream, but had no energy left. Fatigue weighed her down like a heavy blanket. She wanted to sleep for a week.

"Can I get you something to drink, or a snack? I have bottled water in a cooler below my desk, and some crackers. It's not much, but it can tide you over until you're situated in the N.E.S.T."

Serena ignored him and squeezed her eyes shut, desperate to hold back the tears that wanted to burst forth. One they started, they wouldn't stop. She couldn't lose the last shreds of control she had left. Not while she had no idea where she was or what would happen to her now.

Why didn't the monsters kill me? She played back the final moment of the massacre in her mind. They'd deliberately pulled their punches, attacking to incapacitate, rather than kill. And they'd tried to keep her away from the... What was it called? A *Planar Gate?* Did they know what it was and what it could do? How smart were they? The things could fly, but they'd stayed below the canopy until the last moment, as if they knew they needed to stay low to avoid detection. That implied a certain level of cunning. But they fought like mindless killing machines outside the moments where they moved like they shared one mind.

The man returned to his desk and spoke into a cylindrical object whose purpose eluded her. Her mind drifted, not paying attention to his words. At least he wasn't pressing her to talk. She knew she'd have to do something. Eventually. Her eyes unfocused as she stared off at nothing, her mind running the same thoughts over and over in a loop.

"An Orientation officer will be coming soon to take you to the N.E.S.T," the man behind the desk said a few minutes later. "Can I show you to our shower facilities so you can clean up? Or at least offer you a change of clothes? I don't think you'll want to leave here…" He left the sentence hanging, studiously not asking how she got covered in blood. He'd referred to the monsters that ravaged her world as *Vohr*. If he knew their name, he probably knew enough to picture what had happened to Valencia.

"Ok." Serena followed him through a door along a side wall and down a long hallway. Glass doors on their left and right slid open automatically as they passed, revealing well-lit rooms with flat tables in the middle. She didn't recognize any of the equipment, but guessed it was medical in nature. "What is this place?"

"You're in this sector's Emergency Recall Response Facility. Planar Gates have the ability to detect nearby magically gifted beings in distress and open a doorway to a Nexus facility like this one. We get a lot of people fleeing violent circumstances who arrive injured. This building serves as an Emergency Room and hospital. Our staff tends to patients on the floors above us until they're called down for an emergency."

"If you know violent things could come through the Gate behind me, why are you alone?" Serena asked.

"Oh, trust me, that room is *very secure*," the man said. "Safety measures would have kicked in if needed. But when they're not, a single friendly face is less intimidating to new arrivals."

She'd take his word for it. "What's that nest thing you mentioned?"

"The N.E.S.T is the Nexus Emergency Shelter and Training facility. For beings who arrive in the Nexus with nowhere else to go, they provide long-term housing and a basic education on the nature of the multiverse. They also provide trauma and grief counseling, financial assistance, and employment resources to help people determine how to start the next chapter of their lives."

The last door on the left took them into a tiled room with benches running down the middle. Glass doors along the walls led to small, enclosed rooms. Each had a metal spigot above head height and a shelf holding several kinds of soap. Serena was shown how to operate the shower, and how to toggle a switch that locked the door and rendered the glass opaque. Finally, her guide opened a closet and fished out a unisex black cotton shirt, socks, and pants in her size, setting them on a bench beside the showers. He had no replacement for her boots. "You can leave your old clothes here," he said. "We'll have them professionally cleaned and sent to your room in the N.E.S.T."

"Burn them," Serena said. She couldn't imagine ever wearing them again, no matter how clean they were. Nothing would ever remove the memory of the horrors she'd endured in them. Her guide nodded, seeming to understand.

"Meet me back in the arrival room when you're done. Take all the time you need." Satisfied she had no questions, he made his exit.

Serena had no idea how long she stood in the shower, letting warm water rain down upon her. Where did the water come from? Could it run out? She washed her hair, scrubbed dirt and blood off her skin, and cleaned her boots as much as possible, all while fighting to keep her mind blank. She didn't want to think about Valencia, or the capital, or giant bugs, or anything else. The shower's water was infused with some form of magic she'd never heard of before. Its waters soothed and eliminated her scrapes and bruises from the battering the mantis monsters had given her. The overwhelming sense of fatigue she felt lessened, though she still felt exhausted.

An indeterminate amount of time later, she returned to the arrival room. The man behind the desk had his back to her as he spoke with an angel. Though he lacked wings and halo, she couldn't imagine the newcomer as anything else. He wore the heavy brown robes of a monk, with intricate decorative white stitching webbing its way throughout. Light danced across the smooth splendor of his dark skin and shaved head. Were he human, he'd be in his late forties or early fifties. The angel radiated an aura of casual competence, like a man who knew he could handle any challenge thrown at him. A living personification of *everything is going to be fine*. In spite of everything, she found herself relaxing in his presence.

"My name is Orlan," he said. "I'm Head of Orientation for this sector of the Nexus, and I'm here to show you to the N.E.S.T. What's your name?"

Unprepared for the overpowering aura of calm that Orlan radiated, she needed a moment to remember how to speak. "Serena."

"You're the third survivor of a Vohr attack to arrive today," Orlan said. "The others have been given housing as well. It's late, but you'll be able to meet them tomorrow." How did he know Alterra was attacked? Were angels psychic? No, the man at the desk must have told him. "Are you up for a walk?" Having no idea what else to do, Serena nodded.

Orlan led her through a large sliding glass door at the far end of the room and into an area unlike anything she could have imagined. The entire village of Valencia would fit within it with room to spare. They stood at the edge of a vast, stone tiled courtyard. Dozens of merchants had stalls set up, reminding her of a flea market. Hundreds of feet overhead, a floating ball gave off artificial sunlight. Illusion magic created a convincing facsimile of sky and clouds, but couldn't completely hide the grid structure of metal beams supporting a roof. The courtyard was surrounded on all sides by a building twenty floors tall. Stores took up the ground level, while the higher floors looked like apartments. Laundry hung from clotheslines on some balconies, while on others, families looked down on the hustle and bustle of commerce below.

Humans were a distinct minority amongst the hundreds of beings going about their business. Satyr street performers juggled balls of fire, delighting crowds of children. A cyclops tried on various hats from a rack set up outside a storefront, while a wolf-man described the materials used for each. Dice clattered against a table outside a cafe where a gnome, dwarf, and leprechaun engaged in a game of chance.

Everywhere she looked, she saw beings she'd thought existed only in mythology. It should have been a wondrous sight. She felt too numb to appreciate it. Dozens of species interacted peacefully with each other, like it was just an ordinary day. Why not? They still had their families. They could go home.

"We stand inside the heart of all creation," Orlan said. "You'll hear many words used interchangeably for the different places life hails from. Universes, worlds, realms, planes, dimensions, realities... they all mean the same thing, really. The Nexus is the hub through which all are linked. Planar Gates serve as the doorways by which someone can walk from one reality into another, or come to the Nexus."

They walked past a giant salamander selling grilled spiders and millipedes impaled on sticks to a clientele of bipedal frog-people. At a nearby table, a figure in black robes sat alone. A deep hood covered their face, making it impossible to guess their species.

"One of the Planar Gate pillars on Alterra looked like Alainna, the goddess who created our world," Serena said. "None of our scholars suspected it was some kind of transportation device."

"Every Planar Gate looks different," Orlan said. "Some take the form of gods and goddesses. Others represent known historical figures or iconic animal species. Whatever form they take, it's always of symbolic significance to that world. You're not the only one to discover what you thought were ancient or holy relics are a doorway to the multiverse."

He saw something in her expression and paused. "You thought the Gate opening for you was divine intervention." He said it as a statement, not a question. "I'm not an expert on religious matters. We have theological counselors available in the N.E.S.T if you'd like to talk to one. Some religions handle the reality of the multiverse well. For other traditions, it's a struggle. Please don't take what happened to you as a sign your beliefs are false. A crisis of faith is common with Vohr survivors."

Just how many people like me has he met?

"I'm fine," Serena said. Orlan's expression suggested polite skepticism, but he didn't press the matter. "I take it that means you're not an angel?"

He laughed, the sound warm, rich, and free of condescension. "I'm as human as you."

Serena fumbled for another question to ask. If she kept her focus on gathering information, she wouldn't have to think about anything else. "Who created the Nexus?"

"The origins of the Planar Gate network and the Nexus remain a mystery. Some people believe both were created by a god or gods. Others believe we stand in an artifact created by an ancient, highly advanced species that has since disappeared. Your guess is as good as anyone else's." Orlan pointed to a set of marble steps to their right, which lead up to the first level above the courtyard.

As she crested the steps, she realized the entire floor was marble as far as she could see in either direction. Marble columns acted as structural supports for the floors above. The opulence of the construction put even the most decadent Alterran mansions to shame. She had the impression the locals didn't consider it anything special.

Orlan must have sensed the gist of her thoughts. "This marble was wood and stone, once upon a time. A team of volunteer mages transmuted it over the course of a decade as part of a community beautification project."

"It's certainly impressive," Serena made an all-encompassing gesture, "but it seems small for the hub of all creation."

"Oh, this isn't the whole Nexus. The courtyard and floors above us make up one cube. Think of a cube like one wood block in a box packed with many other neatly stacked blocks. The Nexus is made up of billions, perhaps trillions of interconnected cubes like this. Some serve as transit hubs to and from different realities, or to facilitate rapid movement from one cube to another. Others are used as residences or commercial districts. This one is a mix of all of that."

"Billions?" He couldn't be serious. The scale of such a structure defied comprehension.

"Indeed," Orlan said. "You could ride a train for a week in any direction and not reach the edge of the Nexus. Believe me, I've tried."

Straight ahead and a hundred feet from their position at the top of the stairs, a large set of glass and gold doors slid open. A shirtless, orange-skinned, heavily tattooed man levitated toward them. His body was a cyclone of fire from the waist down. "That's Estus, the majordomo of our sector's N.E.S.T," Orlan said. "He's an efreet. He may look a little scary, but he's a total softie."

The temperature rose as Estus came within arm's reach, but not nearly to the degree she'd anticipated. "Greetings Orlan," he said, bowing to each of them in turn. "I got the notice we had another first-timer come in by Emergency Recall. I'm assuming that would be this lovely young woman in your care?" Orlan nodded his confirmation.

"Serena, tomorrow I'll have a meeting with you and the other recent Vohr survivors. I'll be happy to answer any additional questions you have about the Nexus, the multiverse, and the N.E.S.T's resources to help you build a new life," Orlan said. "Since Estus is here, I'll have him help you settle in. He's very good at his job. You're safe in his care. If you need any food or drink, let him know."

"It was evening on Alterra when..." Serena didn't finish the sentence. "I just want to sleep."

"I'll take you right to your room," Estus said.

Serena mirrored Orlan's bow with one of her own as they said their goodbyes and he went ahead into the N.E.S.T.

Estus took her hand and kissed it like she imagined a knight would when meeting a princess. The gesture felt both charming and ridiculous. A brief flicker of heat kindled in her breast at the efreet's touch. "A Daughter of the Flames," he said. "It's been a long time since I've met a kindred spirit."

"Daughter of the Flames?" Serena asked, falling in stride beside him. It sounded like a title. She heard the capital letters.

"An elemental entity like myself can sense similar power in the souls of others."

"I've never displayed any magical aptitude before today."

"You're a natural pyromancer, no doubt about it," Estus flashed her a broad smile. "Efreet are never wrong about such things. The first days are the hardest. You may lack control over your power now, but it will come in time."

A rainforest greeted Serena on the other side of the gold and glass door. In the back of the lobby, a reception desk of thick wood logs stood in front of a waterfall. Stone bricks led the way through beds of exotic flowers. A rich canopy blocked out much of the overhead light, giving the lobby a calm, evening atmosphere. "We try hard to make the N.E.S.T. an island of calm in the chaos of the multiverse. So much of the Nexus can feel artificial, making green spaces like this important." Estus motioned her to the left, towards a pair of small doors, which had a single button in the space between them. When the efreet pressed it, one of the doors slid open. They stepped into a small, cramped space. "This is an elevator," he explained its purpose and operation as the doors closed.

"Do many people arrive in the Nexus with no knowledge of this place?" Serena asked.

"It's rare, when you consider how many universes are out there, and how many beings inhabit them. Still, given the scale of creation, it happens often enough to merit having facilities like these to house folks with nowhere else to go, who need help and guidance."

The elevator opened to a basic hallway lined with doors. Wood floors met log walls, with lighting provided by torches that gave off no smoke. It felt homey, familiar, not unlike the inn in Valencia. Halfway down the hall, Estus pointed to a door on the right. "Room 618 will be yours for the time being. Please place your palm in the red square on the door."

Serena placed her hand in the square, located at chest height. She felt a faint vibration run up her arm, then the red paint turned green and the door swung open. She once again struggled with the casual opulence on display. Only the Alterran elite would build like this... and this was an *emergency shelter*? The room was twice the size of her little cabin in Valencia.

A fireplace roared to life when she crossed the threshold. Stained glass lanterns splashed warm color across a bed big enough for three people. Plush carpeting made her feel lighter on her feet. On the opposite side of the room from the bed, she saw a fully stocked kitchen. Another door led to a washroom.

"The room scanned you to determine your needs when you touched the door. Everything in here was then created to be as comforting for you as possible. It's very, very expensive magic. We have a few merchant lords to thank for the donations that made it possible." Estus followed her inside, floated over to a bedside table, and fished a book out of a drawer. "This is the single most important item in here," he said, handing it over to her. Curious, Serena flipped through it, seeing only blank pages. "It's a Nexus Personal Encyclopedia. They manifest in a form their user will find familiar. Ask it a question, and you'll find your answer in its pages."

She wanted to crawl under the sheets and sleep, but her inner bookworm couldn't resist such an invitation. "Tell me about efreet." She watched as an illustration of an efreet appeared on the front page, followed by information on their physical characteristics, typical magical capabilities, native dimensions, and more. The book automatically flipped pages as needed to make way for more writing.

"Oh, you want to know more about me? You flirt." Estus winked. "That book will be an invaluable tool to help with your learning, just know it only works in the Nexus. You'll have to leave it here if you venture off to other planets, but otherwise, feel free to use it as much as you want." He levitated over to the door. "I'll stop by in the morning when it's time to meet up with Orlan for your first Orientation session. If you need anything before then, let the book know. It also serves as a communication device and will appraise me of your needs. Don't be shy about using it. Seriously. You wouldn't be inconveniencing me. I love helping people." The efreet bowed and floated over to the door.

"Welcome to the Nexus, Serena. We're happy to be of service, though it's a shame your arrival comes from such tragic circumstances. Daughter of the Flames, I wish you restful sleep." Estus bowed again and closed the door behind him.

Serena sat at the edge of the bed, a fresh wave of exhaustion threatening to overwhelm her. Before she could sleep though, she had one final task. She flipped to a blank page. "Tell me about the Vohr."

REQUEST DENIED.

"Those monsters killed everyone I know. Tell me about the Vohr."

REQUEST DENIED.

"Do it, or I'll burn you in that fireplace!" Serena pointed at the fireplace as if the book could see it.

REQUEST DENIED. THREE RESTRICTED QUERIES HAVE BEEN LOGGED. NEXUS PERSONAL ENCYCLOPEDIA WILL NOW IGNORE ALL INFORMATION REQUESTS FOR A PERIOD OF EIGHT HOURS. FURTHER ATTEMPTS TO ACCESS RESTRICTED INFORMATION UPON REACTIVATION WILL BE FLAGGED FOR SECTOR COUNCIL SECURITY REVIEW.

Serena hurled the useless book at a wall. Alone and surrounded by impossible luxury, the dam of her emotions broke. All the dark thoughts she'd tried to suppress roared to the surface. Everyone she'd ever known was gone. She could never go home. Her survival was nothing but outrageous luck. Why did she get to live, and nobody else?

She hugged a pillow close and sobbed until she fell into a deep, dreamless sleep.

CHAPTER 5
KNOW THY ENEMY

A knock at the door jolted Serena awake. She'd fallen asleep in her clothes atop the covers. Panicked, she patted her hips, looking for the knife she no longer had. She checked her boots for throwing knives before remembering she didn't have those either. If the monsters broke down the door, she had nothing to defend herself with.

"Serena, it's Estus. May I come in?" The efreet's voice brought her mind back to the present. Neither Orlan or Estus had given her any reason to believe they meant her harm. She took a moment to calm herself before giving him permission to enter.

Estus opened the door and floated in carrying two sets of clothes, both in the same no-nonsense black. "These are just something to get you started." He shuddered as he set them down on the bed as if they were the ugliest things he'd ever seen. "You'll be given some spending money later on to purchase something more to your taste. Would you prefer to make yourself breakfast here, then meet with Orlan in the lobby in an hour, or have me take you down to our cafeteria, where you can meet one of our other Vohr survivors early?"

"The N.E.S.T. can create fully stocked kitchens in the rooms, and they have a cafeteria? Is everything in the Nexus so fancy?" Serena asked.

"This N.E.S.T. is much better funded than most," Estus said. "Besides our budget allocation from the sector government, we've received generous donations from a few merchant lords, and a massive endowment from an Akakami who lost a bet. Charity doesn't come to them naturally."

"What's an Akakami?"

"A synonym for parasite, if you ask me." He picked up her Personal Encyclopedia from the floor and handed it to her. "You may want this for your meeting with Orlan." He didn't ask how it had gotten so far from the bed.

"Why wouldn't it tell me anything about the Vohr?" Serena asked.

"I should have warned you about that. Orlan will explain why during your session. Now, on the subject of breakfast, would you prefer to eat alone here, or venture down to the cafeteria?"

Serena noted Estus wouldn't provide direct answers to her questions, but set that aside to ponder his proposition. She didn't have any desire to cook for herself, and wasn't sure what she'd ask the Personal Encyclopedia about if she spent her time alone. Talking to someone sounded like the better option. "I'd prefer the cafeteria, thank you. I thought there were two other Vohr survivors?"

"There are. Ivy's a dryad. Most of her dietary needs are covered through photosynthesis, so she's taking care of herself. I'd introduce you to Cypher. Like you, he's human."

Estus stepped outside to give her privacy to change into fresh clothes, then they took the elevator back to the bottom floor. They went left down a hallway that ended in a set of double doors. Inside, the cafeteria was arranged like a buffet. Three rows of food stations ran down the middle, while tables took up the rest of the space. At maximum capacity, the cafeteria could serve several hundred people. Of the dozen beings there at the moment, only one was human. Estus floated over to the man and bowed. "Cypher, this is Serena. She arrived about eight hours after you checked in. She's also come to us under *unpleasant circumstances.* Would it be alright if she joined you for breakfast?"

Cypher looked to be in his early thirties and come from a world very different from Alterra. His right arm and both legs were an obsidian colored metal she didn't recognize, criss-crossed with fine lines that hinted at hidden functionalities beyond the obvious. Alterrans knew how to create basic prosthetics, but they weren't nearly as advanced as Cypher's appeared to be. Blue highlights accented his dark hair. He wore a tight-fitting blue shirt under a leather jacket, and black shorts that ended at the knee. Both the jacket and shorts featured an outrageous number of pockets. Prosthetics aside, his appearance reminded her of gangsters and thugs, but he carried himself with the relaxed and curious air of a scholar. He studied her with alert and intelligent blue eyes.

"Pleased to meet you," Cypher said. He stood and offered her his left hand. "On my planet, we shake hands when meeting someone. It's usually with the right hand, but most people feel nervous about the prosthetics until they get to know me."

Serena accepted the offered hand and stumbled through his greeting ritual. She wanted to know how he'd lost an arm and both legs, but that didn't feel like an appropriate question for a first meeting.

He gestured towards the buffet lines. "Can I walk you through the options? I'm pretty sure most of this is not meant for human consumption."

"Have fun, you two," Estus said, bowing. "Orlan will meet you in the lobby in an hour."

Serena grabbed a plate from the end of the buffet line and followed Cypher's recommendations. He wasn't wrong. For every item she recognized, she saw bizarre concoctions that she wouldn't serve her worst enemies. Fried insects. Severed tentacles of unknown origin. Boiled snakes. Live worms and maggots. A soup that contained floating eyeballs.

"Are we pariahs or something?" Serena asked when they'd returned to their table. She'd made the safe choice and selected bacon, eggs, and toast.

"What do you mean?" Cypher asked.

"Nobody wants to discuss what happened to us. Estus referred to the death of my world as 'unpleasant circumstances' before he left. My Personal Encyclopedia refused to provide any information on the Vohr. Even the guy in the Emergency Recall room seemed happiest avoiding the subject. Was it the same for you? It's like Orlan is the only one allowed to say anything, and everyone else wants to pretend the Vohr don't exist."

"I noticed that too... What's an Emergency Recall?"

Serena stared at him, surprised at the question. "I was told that the Gates respond to magic users under duress and can open a doorway to emergency services in the Nexus. Isn't that how you got here?"

"Nope." Cypher shrugged. "I have no magical talents whatsoever. I don't think Mallozzi has any magic at all, with the exception of the Planar Gate. Ancient mythology suggests we once did, but a cataclysm destroyed it. In its place, our people pursued technological advancements." He paused. "Do you really want to hear how I escaped to the Nexus?"

"Please," Serena said. "If you're willing to talk about it."

Cypher nodded. "To make a very long story short, our government was on a crusade to erase all history going back more than two hundred years, with an emphasis on eliminating any mentions of magic. I'm the type of person where if you tell me I'm not allowed to know something, I immediately want to learn everything I can on the subject. I came to call myself a techno-archeologist, hunting down old data chips, memory implants, computers, flash drives, DVDs, floppy disks, email archives, and more. I wanted anything that might contain useful information and predate the government's purge."

Serena nodded along, not understanding the specific technologies he referenced, but intuiting his research methods. It sounded like his government had conducted the equivalent of book burning on a grand scale. "And somewhere along the way, you learned about the existence of Planar Gates?"

"Yes. The first documents I found referred to ours as the *Indestructible Object.* The government built a high security research facility on top of it to keep it out of the public eye. I eventually learned where it was, and that it was believed to be a gateway between worlds. I also learned how to activate it." His enthusiasm grew as he told the story. He looked more like an excitable junior professor than a man who'd lost his world.

Cypher grabbed a bottle of syrup and poured a pattern onto his plate. It looked like the knocked over and squished number eight she'd seen embroidered on the Emergency Recall man's uniform. "This is the symbol for infinity. A symbol with no beginning and no end. I traced it in the air in front of the Gate, and it activated for me."

"How did you get to the Gate if it was in a high security facility?" Serena asked.

"I have the Vohr to thank for that. The attack blindsided everyone. Portals to some hell dimension opened all over the city. Nasty, fleshy tunnels in the earth that belched out hellhounds. Imagine a direwolf with no fur and wicked spikes growing from its flesh. Hundreds, maybe thousands of them spread out across the city, slaughtering anything that moved. At the same time, fluorescent jellyfish drifted through the skies, flying into buildings and exploding on contact.

"The military deployed to combat the threat, but they couldn't keep up with the number of monsters pouring in. When new tunnels opened up in military compounds, the troops found themselves flanked and overwhelmed. I figured my only hope of survival was to get to the Gate, which was pretty easy with security forces dead or distracted. I had to hack my way through a couple locked doors, but government security protocols stopped being a challenge for me years ago. I had a few close calls dodging hellhounds rampaging through the corridors, but nobody stopped me from getting to the Gate.

"I emerged in a transit cube, a terminal full of Planar Gates for mass travel to other worlds. Nearly had a panic attack at the sight of so many fantastical creatures. I thought maybe the Nexus was under attack too. A kind minotaur calmed me down and led me here when she realized I had no idea where I was."

Cypher leaned back in his seat and took a bite of buttered toast covered in cinnamon. "That's my story. Are you willing to share yours?"

She opened her mouth to deflect the question, then changed her mind. Why not discuss what happened with someone who would believe her? He'd shared his tale. It'd be rude not to reciprocate. She provided a sanitized account of her battles with the mantis monsters and the discovery of her pyromancy.

"Hopefully Orlan will give us real answers about the monsters that attacked us," Serena said. "I won't be civil if he intends to talk about employment and housing in the Nexus and then just send us on our way."

"Agreed. I plan to keep digging into the matter on my own time, too." Cypher reached into one of his many pockets and pulled out a clear pane of glass slightly larger than a deck of cards but less than half as thick. It lit up at his touch, displaying an array of text too small for her to read from across the table. "Whatever security protocols they have on these Personal Encyclopedias won't hold me back for long." He sounded excited at the prospect of a new challenge.

"You don't seem too broken up about what happened to your world." Serena couldn't quite keep a hint of judgment from her tone.

"Innocent people didn't deserve to die, but you're right, I'm not sad I'll never be going back," Cypher admitted. "Mallozzi was a horrible place. It was a surveillance state where the government did their best to monitor and control everything people did. Dare to express a thought out of line with official government policy and you'd be punished. *Reeducated* at best. Executed at worst." His prosthetic arm twitched. A nervous habit, or gesture with deeper meaning? "Everyone I ever cared about was gone long before the Vohr showed up."

Cypher leaned forward, a gleam in his eye. "You said you can control fire, right? Can I see?" The abrupt change of subject lacked any subtlety, but Serena didn't hold it against him. She doubted he was as unbothered about Mallozzi's fate as he tried to appear.

"I'll try." Serena held out a hand, palm up, imagining a small fireball hovering over it. Nothing happened. She snapped her fingers, hoping a flame would appear at the tips of her thumbs. Nothing. Serena sighed with frustration. "It might have been a fluke. I don't know how I did it in the first place."

"Don't worry about it." Cypher smiled encouragingly. "I may not know anything about magic, but I do know there's no such thing as instant mastery of a skill. You'll figure it out. You discovered this power less than a day ago, right? Give it time."

"Thanks, professor."

At the appointed time, they returned to the N.E.S.T's rainforest-inspired lobby to wait for Orlan. A lone woman stood in the middle of the aisle running from the entrance to the reception desk. Her head was upturned toward the artificial sunlight filtering in from outside. Leaves grew like feathers from her arms, which she spread wide like tree branches. She was naked, save for a separate layer of leaves that covered a minimal amount of her chest and hips. Prairie grass hair spilled halfway down her back. Her skin was a pleasant green that reminded Serena of a well-manicured lawn.

"Are you Ivy?" Serena asked, stopping a respectful distance behind the dryad. If her experience with the Vohr had been anything like Serena's, she might be jumpy.

"Indeed." The leaves along Ivy's arms retracted into her skin as she turned to face Serena. If dryads aged at the same rate as humans, she'd be in her early twenties, a couple years younger than Serena. Ivy's green eyes stared into her own with unnerving intensity. "You are a Vohr survivor."

"I am. I'm Serena." She turned her arms to the side, palms forward, and bowed in the traditional Alterran greeting. "Cypher and I have been swapping notes." She gestured to him, leaning against a tree nearby. "Can you tell us about the attack on your world?"

"I do not wish to discuss it," Ivy said, her tone making clear further questions on that topic would not be welcome. She probably didn't want to discuss such a traumatic subject with a total stranger. Fair enough.

Serena fumbled for a safer topic. "Is this your first time in the Nexus? I'd never heard of it until I arrived here."

"I knew of the Nexus, but this is my first time visiting it."

Serena waited for an elaboration that didn't come. "So, people from your world visited and traded with others?"

"Yes."

Serena thought she'd have a more fulfilling conversation speaking to a potted plant, and was about to say as much when Cypher spoke up.

"Leave her be, Serena," Cypher said. "If she's not up to talking, don't force her."

Not wanting to concede defeat, she made one last attempt at initiating a conversation. "How are we able to understand each other? We're all from different worlds. It's hard to believe you'd both know my native tongue."

"They don't," Orlan said, appearing from another hallway connected to the lobby. He wore the same style of brown robes with white web-like stitching as he had the day before. "The Planar Gates imprint an enchantment on travelers, enabling them to understand the written and spoken languages of almost every being who has ever traveled through a Gate. Some languages still need additional translators. Your brain alters your perception to understand everyone as if they're speaking your preferred language. When speaking to someone who's never traveled through a Gate, they'll hear you speaking their language, as long as one person who knows it has ever gone through a Gate. Quite useful, isn't it?"

"It is," Serena conceded, vaguely uncomfortable with the thought of an enchantment being stamped on her without her knowledge or consent, no matter how beneficial.

"If you concentrate really hard and think about languages, you can turn it off," Orlan said, seeming to sense her discomfort. "I'm not sure why you'd want to though. It's harmless. I'm grateful I can talk with anyone I want to. Cultural and species differences are enough of a challenge to navigate without adding languages into the mix." He pointed back in the direction he'd come from. "If you'd all be kind enough to follow me, I'll be happy to answer as many of your questions as I can."

The interior of the N.E.S.T. made an abrupt transition from a tropical lobby to stone blocks that reminded Serena of castle walls. Orlan led them down a hallway and into a conference room with a single table dominating the middle. There remained enough standing room around it to accommodate beings the size of centaurs. Orlan took a seat at the head of the table. Serena and Cypher took seats on the near side, while Ivy walked around to take a seat facing the door.

Orlan slid a finger along the glass surface of the table. A collection of text and symbols appeared before him. He touched one, causing the words *RESTRICTED BRIEFING* to appear in the air over the center of the table above *Continue?* and boxes marked *Yes* and *No*. "There are many topics we could cover here today, but I assumed you'd all want to start with what happened to your homes, is that right?"

Serena, Cypher, and Ivy all nodded in turn.

"Very well." Orlan touched something on the table. The warning disappeared, replaced by charts and graphs. "I am authorized to give you this information as direct survivors of Vohr attacks, but it is not meant for general public consumption. *Vohr* is the official designation for a variety of monsters of unknown origin. How they're able to travel across the multiverse without using Planar Gates is also unknown. They're a taboo topic, I'm afraid."

"Why?" Serena interjected before Orlan could continue. She'd assumed as much, but wouldn't let that fact pass unchallenged.

"Sector governments are afraid news of Vohr attacks will cause panic and disrupt travel and trade across the multiverse. It could cause violence, civil unrest, supply shortages, hoarding." Orlan had the professional but unenthusiastic tone of someone who'd had to repeat official policy many times, despite disagreeing with it. "Until the government can determine how to predict where they might appear and develop reliable countermeasures, they would prefer to downplay the threat and limit access to information, though survivors are allowed a briefing."

"How generous of them," Cypher muttered.

Orlan ignored the comment. "Thus far, roughly three hundred worlds have fallen to the Vohr, averaging one every two weeks. Your worlds mark the first time multiple realms were attacked in such close proximity."

"This has been going on for more than a decade and nobody knows how to stop it?" Cypher asked, needing no time to do the math.

"Three hundred worlds." Serena's stomach twisted at the thought of the horrors she'd endured being visited upon so many civilizations. "How is there not already mass panic? Why isn't defeating them everyone's top priority?"

Orlan held up his hands placatingly. "There is no pattern or apparent logic behind when and where the Vohr appear. Most sectors of the Nexus represent one to two thousand realities, and up to now, no sector has lost more than two, so the collective will isn't there to invest a lot of resources into understanding and defeating the threat."

"Your superiors are fools," Ivy said.

"There are billions upon billions of different realities across the multiverse. I'm sorry to say three hundred worlds aren't even a rounding error in the grand scheme of things. Sector governments decided a quarantine protocol to keep the monsters from spreading through the Planar Gates or infiltrating the Nexus is the best course of action at this time."

"Which also prevents evacuations of innocent people, the deployment of military reinforcements, humanitarian aid, or research teams," Serena said.

"The safety of the Nexus and the Planar Gate network have been deemed of paramount importance," Orlan said.

Serena clenched her fists as her anger intensified. The government had known about the Vohr for over a decade and done nothing of substance to fight back. Worlds like Alterra were acceptable losses. Great message to give to folks who'd just lost everything. *Welcome to the Nexus. We're very sorry to hear everyone you ever loved died horribly. Please accept a complimentary stay in our lovely rooms. Don't tell anyone what happened to you, OK? That could be really embarrassing for us.* Did the authorities seriously expect them to keep their heads down, smile, and move on with their lives?

She didn't have it in her to shrug and walk away. Screw that. How could she have any kind of a normal life knowing that every two weeks or so, a monstrous horde would wipe out an entire civilization? How could she sleep knowing government officials were aware of the ongoing deaths of millions, perhaps billions, and did nothing?

Alterra deserved vengeance. She wanted to turn every mantis monster into a pincushion for arrows, douse their corpses in oil, and set them ablaze.

"Serena," Orlan said.

"What?" She snapped, his voice yanking her from her thoughts. Flames coated her clenched fists.

Ivy sprang back from the table, terror in her eyes. Bark armor emerged from her skin, covering everything but her face. A bamboo staff started growing in Ivy's fist. Serena had no doubt the dryad would bludgeon her with it if she walked into its range.

"We're all friends here," Orlan said.

"Wrong," Ivy said. She held the staff in a death grip.

"Serena, do you intend Ivy harm?" Orlan asked.

"Of course not." The flames coating her fists blew out like candles as she spoke. She'd melted two indents into the glass. How had she done it? And why was Ivy's reaction so violent?

"I can't begin to imagine what you've been through, Ivy, but we're all friends here," Orlan oozed kindness and empathy. "You're safe, Ivy. Nobody wants to hurt you. Please sit down and let's continue the briefing."

Ivy sat down, but stared at Serena like she was a tiger that would pounce the instant the dryad dropped her guard. The bark armor she'd coated herself with retracted back into her skin. She clutched her staff close to her chest like a security blanket.

For the next hour, Orlan advanced his premade presentation, bringing up images of the various horrors that made up the known Vohr bestiary and discussing what survivors reported they could do. There were the mantis monsters she'd faced, dubbed *manti*. They were dumb, but numerous. Cypher's hellhounds were known as shredders, by virtue of their speed and numerous sharp claws. *Dumb name. Cypher's was better.* Ivy's skin paled at the sight of the reapers, eight foot tall bipedal reptiles with crocodilian faces and hands that had three brutal blades extending from between their knuckles. No doubt she'd seen them herself. Their tough hide protected against magical attacks.

The list went on and on. Explosive jellyfish. A writhing mass of tentacles. A reptile with a spike-covered shell and a tail that ended in a mace. One of the monsters was just a giant, floating, alligator-like eyeball. She couldn't find any logic or unifying theme to their appearance. They looked like something a child might draw after waking from a nightmare.

The group sat in silence when Orlan reached the end of the briefing. Serena had wanted to know everything she could about the Vohr, but nothing she'd learned made her feel any better.

"I must remind you everything you saw here is confidential," Orlan said at last.

"What happens if we talk about it in public?" Cypher asked.

"I wouldn't recommend it," Orlan cautioned. "I've seen sector governments denying and discrediting witnesses. You don't need the negative attention while you're trying to establish new lives for yourself."

"Unbelievable," Serena said. "You're telling us the powers that be would rather inflict further harm on survivors to hide their own laziness and incompetence than do the hard thing and bring people together to fight back."

Cypher raised an eyebrow. "You're surprised?"

"Not really." The major kingdoms of Alterra all had histories of bureaucratic ineptitude and indifference. So much for the Nexus being any more efficient or enlightened.

"There are a couple paths forward from here," Orlan said, forcing the conversation back in the direction he wanted. "The standard path would be to remain here in the N.E.S.T to complete a two week training program. You'll learn about the nature of the multiverse and many of the species that inhabit this sector of the Nexus, including their cultural norms and how they prefer to be treated. You'll also be given assistance in finding work in the Nexus, or we can help you find a new planet to emigrate to."

"And we all live happily ever after." Serena said. "What's the other option?"

Orlan tapped a few icons on the surface of the table. The image of an elven woman appeared in the air. "This is Queen Annea Vantalos of Kimori. She's a friend of mine." Annea wore a regal purple dress that ran down to her ankles. She wore all the jewelry one would expect on a monarch. A crown of gold and sapphires. Bracelets of gold and diamonds. A necklace of rubies and emeralds. She stood tall and confident, with pale green skin and dark hair pulled back into an elaborate series of braids.

"The queen has heard of the Vohr. She's offering refuge to survivors, hoping to learn from them as much as possible about the threat Vohr pose to the multiverse," Orlan said. "You'd have free room and board for six months, which should be more than enough time to integrate yourself into their society. Annea is an extraordinary fighter, and might be willing to train you in combat and magic if you ask nicely. She's a very... hands-on instructor."

Was he blushing?

"Kimori is widely considered a utopia," Orlan quickly added. "Beautiful scenery. No crime. Great food and music."

He was offering them a chance to meet with a ruler who wanted to know more about the Vohr, right after he'd told them not to talk about the monsters. Mixed signals aside, the offer sounded good. In theory. "Has anyone else you've talked to gone to Kimori?" she asked.

"You three are the first to arrive since she made the offer."

How convenient. She had no idea how to verify that. She studied Orlan. The man had a decent poker face, but she sensed he wanted them to take Annea up on her offer. He shifted subtly in his chair and looked away from her gaze like someone masking a lie, but the aura of calm he radiated surged in strength. Did his superiors know he was working with a foreign monarch? Or was he, in his own quiet way, defying orders he didn't agree with? Was this offer really Annea's idea, or his?

She'd take his words at face value. For now. "How long do we have to decide?"

"Take all the time you need," Orlan said. "You could even complete the N.E.S.T's two-week course before heading to Kimori. Feel free to research Kimori using your Personal Encyclopedias."

He stood and opened the conference room's door. "Let's take a twenty minute break. When we return, we'll cover some basic interspecies etiquette. For example, furry species often don't appreciate it when humans try to pet them."

As soon as Orlan was gone, Ivy rounded the table, bamboo staff still in hand. For a moment, Serena feared the dryad would use it. Better to address whatever this was now. Serena started to rise from her seat. "I'm sorry if I—"

"Do not speak to me," Ivy pressed her staff down on Serena's shoulder, driving her back into her chair. Rude. The dryad hurried on and left the room without another word.

"I don't think she likes you," Cypher said.

"How could you tell?" Serena rubbed the spot where the bamboo touched her. "I'd always imagined dryads would be nurturing and kind. Sweet, flowery personalities. I would not use any of those words to describe Ivy."

"We have no idea what she endured to get here. We can assume it was pretty bad. She's probably still scared, and Orlan's briefing wasn't what I'd call *uplifting*. Maybe it's best to give her some space for now."

They left the N.E.S.T. and stood next to a marble column where they could watch the hustle and bustle of commerce on the cube's lowest level. Serena tried to clear her mind by cataloging the species she recognized from folklore. Centaurs. Elves. Lamia and naga. Three different varieties of lycanthrope. A dozen species of fae. A winged serpent. A white, horse-like creature she suspected was a kelpie. The red-skinned woman with curved horns, bat's wings, and a whip-like tail could be a succubus.

Her knowledge of mythology couldn't cover the hundreds of species before her. She saw a purple, flightless bird the size of an ostrich haggling with a four-armed orangutan for a basket of fruit. A pair of bipedal rabbit tailors climbed up scaffolding to take measurements of a reptile five times their size. Six-winged birds fluttered around the artificial sun overhead, singing to each other.

A staggering variety of beings called the Nexus home. Rather than clear her mind, watching them all overwhelmed her senses. And this cube was just one of *billions*, maybe *trillions*, if Orlan spoke the truth. Serena felt small. Insignificant. Unimportant. *Three hundred worlds aren't even a rounding error in the grand scheme of things,* Orlan had said. Serena closed her eyes against a brief but intense surge of panic.

"Are you OK?" Cypher asked, sensing her distress.

"Not really," Serena admitted. "I'm feeling..."

"Agoraphobic?"

"That's the fear of unfamiliar environments or large, wide-open spaces, isn't it? Sounds about right." Serena opened her eyes and locked her focus on Cypher. It felt safer than observing the civilized chaos of the marketplace below. "I'm used to exploring uncharted forests. The unknown shouldn't scare me. I can't explain it."

"Do you spend much time in crowds of people?"

"I spent the last four years in a village of a hundred people."

"That would be a no, then," Cypher said, smiling. "You're going to take Queen Annea up on her offer, aren't you?"

"I think I have to," Serena said. "Spending two weeks here sounds miserable. I need to be *doing* something, not sitting around in classes for days on end. How about you?"

"I lived in the most densely populated city on Mallozzi. I can handle crowds." Cypher ran his prosthetic hand through his black and blue hair. "My place is here."

"What will you do?"

"Frustrate the hell out of a government determined to hide important information from the public. Hack their servers. Or magic crystals. Or whatever. Same thing I've been doing for years. Tell me I'm not allowed to know something and it becomes the only thing I want to know."

Serena laughed. She understood that attitude. "I get it. Tell me I can't do something, and I'll be hellbent to prove you wrong. Good luck. Don't get arrested, okay?"

"I'll be fine. Maybe I'll even be the one to find a pattern to Vohr attacks. I hope things work out for you Serena, but if you find yourself coming back to the Nexus sooner than anticipated, seek me out, OK? We Vohr survivors have to stick together."

"Deal."

CHAPTER 6
THE TRANSIT CUBE

After spending her evening reading up on the world, Serena knew venturing to Kimori was the right decision. The Personal Encyclopedia had nothing to say about the queen, but characterized the world as full of happy people living lives dedicated to artistry and agriculture. An ideal environment for centering herself while she figured out what to do next. Especially if Annea would help her learn how to control her magic.

Unfortunately, she wasn't going alone.

Ivy waited with her in the rainforest lobby for Estus to arrive and lead them to the transit cube. Her bamboo staff was gone, replaced by a staff of darker wood that branched out in several directions at the top. She'd probably picked it up while shopping. It didn't look like she'd purchased anything else.

When Serena learned Ivy also planned on leaving the Nexus, she'd suggested they go shopping together. She'd hoped the invitation would give her a chance to learn more about dryads, and help them move on from their rocky first meeting.

Ivy replied, "Spend your time on preparation, not fraternization." A real ray of sunshine, that woman. If Serena had to put up with the dryad's constant wary glances much longer, the two of them were going to have a problem.

Estus arrived in time to defuse the tense silence before it boiled over. "Good morning, ladies!" He floated to a position midway between Serena and Ivy. "I'm delighted to have the opportunity to help you find Kimori's designated Gate in the transit cube. I've never been there myself, but Kimori's elves have a reputation for knowing how to throw a party. I'm sure they'll make you feel right at home."

Ivy showed no negative reaction to the efreet's arrival. Did that mean she wasn't afraid of fire? After thinking about it, Serena had assumed that was what triggered Ivy's panic in the conference room. Estus was a perpetual cyclone of magical fire from the waist down. Wouldn't he be more terrifying than her?

"Do you both have all your belongings? Nothing left behind in your rooms?" Estus asked.

"I'm all set." Serena patted the satchel at her hip that contained a week's worth of clothing, a new bow and quiver of arrows, some snacks, and a book. Goddess bless the enchantment that allowed it all to fit in there. Magic bags didn't exist on Alterra. She never wanted to be without one again. She'd purchased hiking shoes and thrown away her old boots, happy to be rid of the last tangible reminder of the night she'd lost everything. The Personal Encyclopedia she left behind in her room.

"We can proceed," Ivy said.

As the trio made their way across the courtyard to the far end of the cube, Serena waved to the pair of rabbit folk who'd sold her clothes, as well as a basic leather vest to provide her torso modest protection. She'd wanted clothing more colorful and durable than the black shirts and pants the N.E.S.T. provided. "Our wares look lovely on you!" they shouted as Serena passed.

"Ingrid and Rex are the best tailors in this sector," Estus said. "You'll be grateful for the quality of their wares if you do any training with Queen Annea."

"That would mean more coming from someone who wore clothes," Serena said.

Estus laughed. "I'll have you know there are situations where even *I* have to manifest legs and put pants on," he said. They reached the edge of the cube and stepped onto a giant elevator platform. Despite his light tone, Estus shifted his gaze away from her. His cheeks flushed. He stared at the elevator controls as if they were the most fascinating thing in existence.

"I'd like to hear that story," Serena said.

"Always leave them wanting more," Estus said. The elevator began to rise. "Perhaps another time."

Minutes passed in awkward silence. Several times, the elevator came to a stop to pick up or drop off passengers. A faun got off. Two beings cloaked in black robes got on. After reaching the top level of their cube, the elevator carried on through an opening in the ceiling to the next one up. This one felt like an arid desert, complete with wind-blown sand. After that came a humid cube with pools of water everywhere, populated by dozens of species of amphibians. The third cube had to be an aviary, given the many perches at various heights. Every being in sight had wings.

Serena's eyes needed a moment to adjust when they arrived at the transit cube. Iridescent light from hundreds of Planar Gates filled the cavernous space. It felt like standing amongst a thousand roiling rainbows, the light show punctuated by flashes as various Gates opened or shut down.

Unlike the featureless Gates of the Emergency Recall room, every set of connecting pillars here had their own distinct designs. She saw dragons and gargoyles, plants and animals, and men and women of many different species represented. Every Gate also displayed its own combination of eight different runes. The walls to the left and right of the elevator were lined with Gates, with an additional two rows running down the middle of the area. Walkways or queue lines took up the remaining space, marking departure or arrival lanes.

It was a utilitarian floor plan, with no extraneous decorations or concessions to creature comfort beyond some benches. The soulless efficiency of the transit cube's design clashed with the masterful artistry of the Gate pillars, to say nothing of the light show put on by the Gates themselves.

There were thousands of beings represented amongst the many queue lines. A quick scan of the room suggested every world had different rules or procedures for admission. Some Gates let people walk right through, while others had security agents inspecting baggage before allowing entry.

"This... this is amazing," Ivy said. "So much light. So many colors. It makes my skin sing." Her eyes welled up with tears. "I wish my sisters could see this." She made it three paces before her emotional dam burst. Ivy collapsed to the floor, curling into the fetal position as her body spasmed with uncontrollable sobs.

Serena didn't know what to do in the face of such obvious agony. Ivy hadn't said a word about what she'd experienced before arriving in the Nexus. What could she say other than generic condolences? Would Ivy even want such sentiments from her?

Ivy offered no resistance when Estus picked her up as if she weighed no more than a pillow. He carried her to a nearby bench and set her down with a gentleness at odds with his brawny and vaguely demonic appearance. Serena picked up Ivy's staff and hung back a couple paces. "You're among friends," Estus said. "Do you want to talk about it?"

For several long minutes, the force of Ivy's grief rendered her unable to speak. Estus rubbed her back as she rocked back and forth. Her sobs drew the attention of passersby, who hurried on, not wanting to involve themselves in the emotional distress of a stranger.

"My sisters are dead. All fifteen of them," Ivy said. Her voice was husky and ragged. "They died, one after another, protecting me from reapers as we fled our village."

Fifteen sisters... As an only child, Serena couldn't comprehend the scope of Ivy's loss. She shuddered as her mind conjured up images of the massive reptiles ripping dryads in half.

They sat in silence, letting Ivy take the time she needed to process her thoughts. She didn't elaborate. Estus and Serena didn't ask for details. Gradually, Ivy's sobs subsided and her breathing steadied. She stood and took back her staff from Serena. "I must give their sacrifices meaning," Ivy said, her emotional walls sliding back into place. The dryad straightened her posture. Squared her shoulders. Settled her expression into a neutral mask. "I regret my outburst. It will not happen again."

Estus directed them to the left wall of Planar Gates. They carried on for several minutes before the efreet pointed out their target. While most Planar Gates had matching pillars, Kimori's did not. Representing the two dominant species of the realm, one pillar depicted a giant ant, while an elf adorned the other. The Gate was inactive when they approached. Nobody stood in the queue to wait. If this realm was such a utopia, shouldn't there be tourist traffic? Who wouldn't want to visit paradise? Nothing she'd read cast Kimori in a negative light.

Estus stepped forward, pointing to the eight runes on the wall above and behind the Gate. "Activating a Gate to go to a specific destination is easy enough," he said. "Especially when they have the address for you right there. Just reach out with a finger, concentrate, and draw those symbols in the air."

Some of the runes looked like letters, others pictographs. One looked like a symbol for a mathematical equation. Serena started drawing them. Her writing remained visible as gold script floating in the air, even after her finger had moved on. When she had completed her best approximation of the eight runes, the writing disappeared, and the Planar Gate flashed to life.

Despite the grim circumstances that brought her here, Serena felt a rush of excitement. One step through that ribbon of light and she'd be on a whole new world. Sure, she'd done it once already to get to the Nexus, but this was different. Intentional. Venturing into the unknown...

"I wish I'd brought my camera," Estus said. "The look of wonder on your face is priceless."

"We should not keep the queen waiting," Ivy said, grabbing Serena's wrist and dragging her the last few paces to the threshold.

"Wait! What's a camera?" Serena asked. She found herself on the other side before she finished the question. Real sunshine filtered through a lush canopy to warm her face. A gentle breeze caressed her hair as the Planar Gate shut down. Serena's eyes latched onto the incredible sight before her.

Kimori represented the peaceful coexistence of two very different species. An anthill miles long and hundreds of feet tall formed the world-city's base. On top of it grew a tree so tall the top couldn't be seen through cloud cover. The tree's roots wrapped around the anthill like structural supports before eventually burrowing into the earth. Branches of the great tree extended to the horizon in every direction. Many curved down from the trunk to come within fifty feet of the ground before straightening out. Light and smoke spilled out of window openings in branches, suggesting they were hollowed out and elves lived inside. Massive vines linked branches together. Carriage compartments ferried passengers back and forth across them.

"Is this the greeting we were expecting?"

At Ivy's question, Serena brought her attention to ground level... and the thousands of ants that stood between them and the open gate built into the front of the anthill. Each was the size of a hunting dog. Their mandibles looked strong enough to chew through humans and dryads without issues.

Their silent stares were unnerving.

Behind them, the Planar Gate remained inert. Did that mean they weren't in danger?

If the ants attacked, Serena and Ivy would be dismembered in less time than it took to trace a simple infinity symbol in the air. Serena forced a smile and prayed to Alainna they hadn't walked into a trap.

CHAPTER 7
ARRIVAL ON KIMORI

A moment passed. Then another. The ants hadn't moved. Good. Ivy wasn't panicking. Also good. Serena decided to take the initiative. "Hello! My name is Serena, this is Ivy. We're here at Queen Annea's invitation. Could someone take us to her, please?"

The ants cocked their heads to the side and froze, as if waiting for instructions. Nobody spoke. Several seconds ticked by in awkward silence. Had they understood her? How could she convince them of her peaceful intent if they hadn't?

<WELCOME.> A thousand voices spoke in unison, the word seeming to come from everywhere and nowhere at once. Their message delivered, the ants turned and marched back towards their colony.

Two ants fought against the current of their brethren returning to the anthill, at times climbing on top of their fellow ants and walking across bodies as they struggled to get closer to the new arrivals. Red bodies dancing through an ocean of black ones, Serena had no trouble tracking their progress.

<Greetings travelers! Oof...> The red ant got head-butted by a black one as they returned to the ground from an extended body surf. <Let me through, you useless waste of a thorax.> Hit by a charge from two other black ants, the red ant lost their balance and found themself flipped on their back, then trampled by a dozen black ants before the stampede moved on.

The other red ant jumped, danced, and weaved their way through the horde, nimbly bouncing between them as if they were not there. They reached the end of the horde and kept coming, stopping a body length away from Serena. <Welcome to Kimori. I am Tik-Tik.> The ant wore a collar studded with gems which strobed as they chittered. She assumed the collar translated the ant's language into something non-insects could understand. <My clumsy sibling is Pik-Pik. We are Annea's aides.>

Pik-Pik, still on their back, flailed their legs uselessly in the air. <Yes, yes. Greet the visitors. Don't mind me, egg-mate. I'll just squirm here until you deign to flip me over.>

Tik-Tik let out an exasperated sigh the collar didn't need to translate, then walked over to their counterpart and did as asked.

<The timing of your arrival is fortuitous,> Tik-Tik said. <Annea has us watch the Planar Gate for an hour or two every day. We were already on our way when you arrived.>

<Annea needs some quiet time,> Pik-Pik explained, <or else she'd kill us.>

<Not really.>

<She might.>

<You know she wouldn't.>

<You're probably right. We're delightful.>

<Please follow us.>

Serena and Ivy exchanged a glance, then fell in stride behind the ants as they headed toward the main gate.

<I'm sorry if you felt unwelcome when you arrived.> Tik-Tik twisted their head in a gesture Serena interpreted as apologetic.

<Drones are dispatched for any unscheduled activation of the Planar Gate, to determine if there is a threat to the city,> Pik-Pik said. <We rarely get visitors.>

"Orlan said that Queen Annea wanted to meet Vohr attack survivors. Are we really so unexpected?" Serena asked.

<He didn't send advance notice,> Pik-Pik said. <How could we know when guests would arrive?>

<You can't see the future? Every day you find new ways to disappoint me, Pik-Pik.>

The ants led them inside and through a winding series of featureless tunnels, all lit by bioluminescent fungus on the walls. As they walked, Pik-Pik and Tik-Tik played the part of cheerful tour guides, bombarding them with trivia about Kimori. Elves could live for a thousand years, but ants rarely lived more than twenty. The ants outnumbered their elven friends by more than a hundred to one. The ant colony continued underground for many miles in every direction. The ants had two queens, and a caste system of drones, scouts, and soldiers. Serena tried to ask questions, but struggled to get a word in with the babbling insects.

I think I know why Queen Annea wanted quiet time, Serena thought. *These two never shut up.*

She did her best to keep track of all the turns, but doubted she'd be able to find her way back to the Planar Gate without guidance. Her calves burned from the constant uphill climb by the time they reached an indoor plateau. The ant colony made up the floor and walls, with a gnarled roof of wood overhead — the base of the tree.

At this point, their path branched in three directions. To the right, the path curved back down into the colony. The center path ended in a thick double door with carvings of an ant and an elf on it that matched the appearance of their Planar Gate. Pik-Pik and Tik-Tik led them to the left, up a wooden ramp, and through an opening carved into the tree root.

"What were those other paths?" Ivy asked, her first words since they'd entered the anthill.

<The right path eventually splits. Each path leads to a queen. They like to live far apart so invaders can't easily kill them both.>

<And so they don't kill each other.>

<The middle path is the Grand Chamber of Rule, for times when elf and ant must meet to discuss state emergencies.>

<It's rarely used.>

<This path takes us to Annea's royal reception chamber.>

<It's *also* rarely used.>

<Rarely used for its intended purpose, that is.>

Serena lost track of which ant said what as she scanned the room. Queen Annea's reception chamber wasted no effort on pomp or grandeur. It had no decorations or furniture whatsoever. The cavernous hollowed-out root was lit by sunlight coming through holes carved into the ceiling. In the back, a wide staircase spiraled up and out of view. The reception chamber could be a dance hall for how large and empty it was.

The space had a single occupant, an elf holding a handstand. She wore a sleeveless purple silk shirt tucked into loose-fitting pants designed to allow a maximum range of motion. She transitioned to a one-handed handstand, spreading her legs in an admirable demonstration of balance and control. After maintaining the pose for a handful of seconds, she pushed off with her arm and flipped onto her feet. "Pik-Pik, Tik-Tik, you're back early. I see you've brought guests. Welcome to Kimori, travelers."

The elf stood over six feet tall, with the lean muscle of a natural gymnast. Dark hair flowed past her shoulders. She wore no jewelry. Were she human, she'd be in her thirties, but who could tell with elves? She bent to grab a weapons belt off the floor nearby and cinch it around her waist, then approached the group with the lithe, easy body confidence of a panther.

"We seek Queen Annea," Ivy said.

"You found me." The woman frowned at Ivy's skeptical expression. "Not what you were expecting?"

Ivy described the image they'd seen of an elf in a regal purple dress, draped in jewelry, and sporting an elaborate hairstyle.

Annea laughed, her mirth echoing through the reception chamber. "You've met Orlan. I'm glad he hasn't entirely lost his sense of humor since joining the Weavers."

"I do not understand," Ivy said.

"Orlan knows I'd sooner skin myself with a dull knife than act like a posh, spoiled monarch. He showed you a fake image to tease me." Her expression turned curious. "It's also a code we agreed upon when he needs to call in a favor. Why did he ask you to meet with me?"

She didn't know? So, Orlan had lied to them. Fantastic. "Have you heard of the Vohr?" Serena asked.

Annea's eyes narrowed. "Only through vague rumors, why?"

"Orlan told us you wanted to meet Vohr attack survivors. He said you'd provide room and board for us. Possibly combat training too."

Annea opened her mouth. Closed it. Turned her gaze on Ivy and gave the dryad a thorough looking over. The last traces of good humor faded from her eyes as some mental calculations clicked into place. "What is your name?"

"Ivy."

"Are you Ataraxian?"

"Indeed."

"I spent a year on your world," Annea said. "It's a beautiful place."

"It was."

"Any other survivors?"

"None."

"How many —"

"Fifteen."

Annea stepped forward and bent to swallow the smaller woman in a tight embrace. Ivy stood stiff as a board and didn't return the hug, but did not resist either. How much information had Annea gleaned from so few words? Releasing her squeeze on Ivy, the queen turned to Serena. "You're not Ataraxian. Were you there as well, during the attack?"

"No, Your Maj—" Annea cut Serena off with a finger to the lips.

"None of that. My name is Annea. I find titles pretentious. You don't need to address me by any honorific. Understood?" Annea left her finger on Serena's lips until she nodded.

Serena introduced herself and provided Annea the same sanitized recap of the hell she'd endured that she'd given Cypher. Ivy's skin paled when Serena spoke of her awakened pyromancy. That familiar wary, threatened look appeared on her face, and she took several steps away. At least Ivy didn't try to attack her with her staff.

Annea studied the dryad's skittish reaction. If she had any opinion about it, she kept it to herself. "You've both been through a lot, so I won't bombard you with questions until you're ready," Annea said. "I will honor the terms of the deal as Orlan described them to you. You're welcome to reside here for as long as you wish, so long as you don't cause trouble."

Serena sighed with relief. Orlan had lied, but the part about him and Annea being friends seemed true enough. Annea had heard her tale and wasn't ordering her back to the Planar Gate. That was a start.

"Why don't we go upstairs and set you up with some guest quarters?" Annea said. "After that, I can give you a tour of the world tree."

"Don't you have servants for that?" Serena asked, surprised a queen would volunteer for such a mundane task.

Annea smiled. "Being a queen on Kimori is very different from how it works on other worlds. You'll understand soon enough." She motioned for them to follow her as she turned for the stairs.

"Combat training happens right here. It's a great space. Nobody bothers me here, except for these two." Annea stooped to give Pik-Pik and Tik-Tik head scratches between their antennae. The ants stood taller, taking her comment as a compliment.

The group only made it a few steps before Annea signaled everyone to stop. "Silence."

To Serena's surprise, the ants obeyed. Not seeing anything unusual, she closed her eyes and focused on her other senses, trying to get some sense of why the queen ordered them to stop. She felt the faintest of vibrations in her feet as the ants nervously circled the group. Heard a gentle rustle of grass as a breeze coming through the carved openings above caught Ivy's hair.

Claws scratching at the walls...

"Here? Seriously?" Annea sighed, pulling a pair of throwing knives from her belt. "Arm yourselves, ladies. We are not alone."

CHAPTER 8

LESSON ONE

Annea turned and hurled her knives at a spot on the wall above and behind Serena. Both dug into the wood with a solid *thunk*. The air shimmered not far from the impact point. The wood of the tree root looked how it should, but when Serena focused, she saw slight blurring and imperfections. The creature's camouflage was incredible — far superior to anything on Alterra — but not flawless.

After years of hunting around Valencia, Serena had a sixth sense for when a predator had its eyes on her. She dived to the side a moment before the shimmering mass pounced at her. The creature's disguise couldn't keep up with its rapid movement, allowing her a clearer glimpse of its form as she rolled to her feet.

She cataloged details as best she could before it became nearly invisible again. *Reptile. Binocular vision. Can walk or climb on two legs or four. My height when standing. Twelve feet from snout to tail. A large sickle claw on each foot — probably its main weapon.* Its form reminded her of skeletons she'd seen of ancient, extinct animals known as dinosaurs.

<IT'S EATING MY FACE!> Having missed Serena, the beast went after the easiest available victim. Pik-Pik or Tik-Tik — she couldn't tell which — bucked like an angry horse, trying to throw the reptile off their back. Fangs ground against carapace as it tried biting into the ant's neck. The other ant dashed up the stairs and out of the chamber, chittering untranslatable gibberish the whole way.

Annea pulled a pair of kukris from her belt and rushed to the ant's aid.

Bark grew over Ivy's skin, covering her chest, arms, and legs. Her back remained exposed. She pointed her staff at the growling, shimmering creature. Vines sprouted from the floor, wrapping themselves around its neck and legs. Like a fisher hooking her catch, Ivy yanked her staff up. The vines constricted and withdrew, dragging the beast off its prey and pinning it to the ground. Annea darted in to slit its throat.

"There's never only one," Annea said, scanning the room.

Serena reached into her satchel and pulled out her bow and quiver of arrows. She hadn't even needed to look. All she had to do was think of the item she wanted, and the satchel placed it in her hands. Never needing to rummage around for something ever again? That kind of magic was *life changing*. The gorgon that sold it to her had acted like it was a simple parlor trick.

Serena nocked an arrow and turned slowly, her eyes alert for any oddities with the lighting that might indicate camouflaged predators.

"Nice of you to dress for the occasion." Annea gestured with a kukri to Serena's bow. She never stopped scanning the room for enemies.

"A bow is not clothing," Serena said.

"Without a weapon or magic to defend yourself, you might as well be naked."

"Says the queen of a utopia?"

"I've never called Kimori that."

Serena sensed movement above and fired off a shot towards the ceiling, getting a roar of pain for her efforts. Her arrow pierced a leg. The beast lost its grip and fell thirty feet, bones snapping in one of its ankles when it landed wrong. Ivy tried to snare it with fresh vines, but it limped free before they could gain a hold. Serena loosed two arrows at it in rapid succession, aiming for center-mass. The creature's camouflage made more specific targeting too difficult.

The reptile staggered forward three paces before dropping. Its camouflage fell away as it died, giving Serena her best look at the creatures yet. White scales. Red eyes. Teeth as long as her fingers. Her shots punctured a lung, for sure. Possibly also the heart. If asked about it in a tavern, she'd insist the shots were pure skill, borne from years of studying animal biology. In the heat of the moment, they felt more like luck.

Ivy screamed. A third predator pounced and knocked her flat on her back. The impact knocked the staff from Ivy's grasp, sending it clattering out of reach. Claws raked at Ivy's bark armor, trying to strip it off to get at the vulnerable flesh underneath.

Before Serena could take aim, something tackled her from behind. Her wrist snapped against the unforgiving wood floor. She clenched her teeth and willed herself not to scream. *Forget the pain. Fight back!* Easier said than done. A sickle claw pierced her leather vest and dug into her shoulder blade. Her body jerked as its owner tried to drag its foot to cut her open. The leather held firm.

Hot, damp breath caressed the back of her neck. It smelled like blood and rotting meat. She suppressed the urge to gag as she reached for an arrow with her uninjured hand. Could she find an angle to stab the carnivore before it crushed her skull in its jaws? Only one way to find out...

Thump thump. Thump. The concussive force of impacts traveled through the dinosaur's body and into Serena. The smell of scorched flesh hit her nostrils before her enemy fell onto its side. With its weight removed from her back, Serena stood and checked to verify it was dead. Cauterized gashes in the dead animal's side marked where whatever struck it exploded on impact.

"I require assistance," Ivy said, her breathing labored. She remained flat on her back. A copse of bamboo grew around her and *from* her. It impaled her assailant in half a dozen places. Unfortunately for Ivy, that left her trapped under its dead weight.

Annea made her way towards Ivy, but stopped as another shimmering form charged her. An aura of purple energy appeared around the queen. She made a slashing motion in the air with each kukri, leaving behind a trail of energy in the shape of the slash patterns. Annea flicked her wrists, sending the slashes of energy flying like lightning bolts into the bloodthirsty predator. Deep gashes opened across its chest at impact. It died instantly, its momentum bringing it to rest at Annea's feet.

Once she was satisfied they were safe, Annea asked Ivy, "What do you want us to do here? Cut the bamboo? Can you make it disappear?"

In response, bamboo shoots not impaling flesh shriveled into dust, one at a time. Ivy seemed worried removing the wrong ones would free more weight to crush her. "Lift this creature off me. Please," Ivy said.

"Pik-Pik, would you mind?" Annea asked.

The ant got in position over Ivy and poked their head into the gap between Ivy and the dead reptile. Pik-Pik lifted their head several times, as if testing the creature's weight. In the span of two seconds, Pik-Pik bit through four bamboo shoots connecting the dryad and the dinosaur, then thrust their head up, lifting the carcass off the remaining shoots and sending it flying ten feet.

The ants of Alterra could lift many times their body weight, so Serena assumed the ants of Kimori could too. That intellectual knowledge hadn't prepared her for the reality of Pik-Pik flinging around a carcass more than twice their size and weight with no apparent effort.

With the body clear, Ivy retracted the remaining bamboo shoots and absorbed her bark armor back into her body. "That was unpleasant," she said, stretching. She nodded to Pik-Pik. "Thank you."

Annea paced the room, inspecting the bodies. "Sorry about that. Chameleosaurs are an invasive species. Elven biologists wanted to study their cloaking abilities in hopes of crafting new camouflaging armor. The ant queens wanted to learn about their climbing abilities and running speed in hopes of enhancing drone genetics for greater productivity. Naturally, the imported specimens got loose, started breeding, and here we are."

"You sound pretty nonchalant about it," Serena said.

"Do I?" Annea sounded surprised. "I'm furious. Huge swaths of territory to the south of the world tree are uninhabitable now. Queen Ruta is supposed to have drones patrolling the exterior of the colony at all times to keep chameleosaurs from infiltrating the colony or the tree. Kimori's defense is her primary job. Her sloppiness could have gotten us killed."

"Shouldn't you have bodyguards?" Serena asked. Even if she was a competent warrior in her own right, a queen had to have guards, right?

"I have two. Inara and Pavi have the week off. Pik-Pik and Tik-Tik are not fighters, as Tik-Tik displayed when they ran away screaming."

Two. The queen of an entire civilization felt she only needed two bodyguards. And she felt safe enough to let them both be off duty at the same time. Orlan wasn't kidding when he said Kimori had no social unrest.

"You are hurt," Ivy said, pointing to Serena's broken wrist. "May I take a look?"

Serena nodded her consent. A green aura enveloped Ivy's hands. She wrapped both hands around Serena's broken wrist and applied gentle pressure. Serena felt intense pressure out of proportion to Ivy's movements, but the pain didn't worsen. When Ivy removed her hands, Serena felt fine. She rolled her wrists and felt no discomfort or pain at all. It was like she'd never been injured.

"Thank you," Serena said. "I'm impressed. The healers of my village couldn't fix a broken bone nearly so fast."

"Healing magic runs in my family," Ivy said. "It has for generations." Her eyes lost focus at the mention of family.

Fearing Ivy was heading towards another emotional breakdown, Serena presented her injured back to the dryad as a distraction. "Are you able to fix this too? One of them punctured my armor... and my flesh." She felt an intense itch as the wound shrunk, then disappeared. "Thanks. I appreciate it. I didn't think you liked me."

"I do not," Ivy said. "I was taught to show compassion to the injured. Even enemies undeserving of it."

Serena had hoped her comment would get Ivy to lighten up a little. Maybe provoke her into offering some explanation for why she seemed determined to keep away from her as much as possible. But *enemies?* What the hell?

Before Serena could demand an explanation, Annea rejoined them. "Congratulations to both of you on surviving an impromptu first combat lesson," she said.

"Lesson" implies you taught us something. Serena opted to keep her mouth shut.

Annea looked at Serena like a teacher disappointed in her pupil. "Your archery skills are impressive, but what about your pyromancy?"

"In the heat of the moment, I went with what I know," Serena said. "I haven't been able to summon flames since that first time."

Ivy took a couple steps back. She tried to play it off as going to retrieve her staff, but Serena saw Ivy's discomfort every time pyromancy came up. Annea saw it too, her eyes following Ivy's movements. She frowned, but kept her own counsel.

"Let's have a private session tonight, Serena. I'll bet I can help you discover how to ignite the fire inside." Annea led them up the stairs leading deeper into the tree. "I'll have the ants clean up our mess. Should be enough good scale between the lot of them for a few sets of armor."

The stairs opened up into a cozy lounge space. There was a dining table with chairs, a fireplace, and a stocked bar. A bookshelf beside the bar held dozens of books. Doors on either side of the lounge led to small bedrooms. Potted flowers lined the walls, with more pots hanging from the ceiling. The same bioluminescent fungus from the ant colony provided soft lighting. A half-dozen steps along the left wall led to exit doors. A staircase along the right wall curved its way up and over the bar before ending at an ornate wooden door inlaid with gold filigree.

"Guests of the queen reside here. Pick any room you wish, they're all empty," Annea said. "My private chambers are up there." She gestured to the door above the bar. She walked over to the exit, then paused. "I'm afraid I'll have to postpone our tour of the city for now. I need to find Tik-Tik. Feel free to bathe, grab a bite to eat, or take a nap. You're also welcome to explore the city on your own, if you'd like. You'll find my people love to chat up visitors, since we have so few.

"Pik-Pik, please provide Serena and Ivy any assistance they need. When I've returned with your sibling, I'd like you both to haul the chameleosaur carcasses down to the entrance of Queen Ruta's domain."

Pik-Pik's antennae lowered in agitation. <Is that wise?>

"Don't worry. You can come home as soon as you're done. You don't have to see her or talk to her. I'll handle that myself."

Pik-Pik's relieved chittering needed no translation.

"Serena, I have some homework for you while we're gone. Think back to that night in Valencia. See if you can determine how you tapped into your power. Try to summon it again. Trust me, you can't hurt the world tree. If you can find any measure of control on your own in the next few hours, tonight's session will be much less painful for you."

Serena picked a bedroom at random and sat down on the bed, wondering what Annea meant by *much less painful.* She focused on the memory of the warmth in her chest and tried to will that feeling back into reality.

Nothing happened.

CHAPTER 9

LIGHT THE LAMPS

Despite her desire to explore the elven city built into an enormous tree, Serena spent the afternoon in her room, trying in vain to conjure fire. What good was having magic if she couldn't use it when she needed it? If she'd had control of it, Annea might not have had to save her during the chameleosaur fight. Without mastering pyromancy, how could she fight back against the Vohr in any meaningful way?

She imagined a horde of manti flying at her, blades ready to hack her into bloody pieces. Faking a fight-or-flight situation didn't stir her magic. She tried stretching, jogging in place, and punching the air. Physical exertion didn't kindle any sensations either. Growing increasingly exasperated, she sat on the bed and tried to clear her mind and picture fire in her hands.

Nothing happened.

This is a waste of time.

She felt like an abject failure. While she'd never encountered anything that could camouflage itself as well as the chameleosaurs, she could have done better. She'd failed to detect three of the five. Her skin prickled at the memory of rancid breath against the back of her neck. If she wanted to survive, she had to become better, stronger.

For the briefest moment, Serena felt a flicker of heat in her chest. It faded away as Annea knocked on her door and poked her head in.

"Any luck?" Annea asked.

"None whatsoever."

Annea stepped inside. She'd changed into a silky red dress with long slits on each side that ran up to her thighs. A dress allowing the range of motion necessary for acrobatic dancing. Or delivering a roundhouse kick to your enemy's head. From what she'd seen of the elf so far, Serena thought both scenarios equally likely.

"You're naked," Serena said, recalling Annea's comment during their fight. *Without a weapon or magic to defend yourself, you might as well be naked.*

"Nope!" Annea smiled, parting the right side of her dress enough to reveal a band of slender throwing knives strapped to her thigh. Her liveliness made Serena even more aware of how worn-down she felt. "I met a couple pyromancers in my travels before ascending to the throne. I have a theory about your magic I'd like to test out, if you're in the mood."

Having achieved nothing on her own, Serena wasn't about to pass up potential help. "Sure. Let's do it." She fell in behind the queen, expecting they would be heading into the city or back down to the royal reception chamber. Instead, Annea made a straight line for the stairway leading up to her bedroom.

No way we're training there. "Did you need to get something before we start?" Serena asked.

Annea flashed her a devilish grin. "No, this is our destination. I don't invite just anyone into my bedchambers, you know." She gave her voice a seductive, silky tone. "You're in for the hottest evening of your life. I'll make you *burn* for me."

Serena paused on the stairway, uncertain if Annea was making pyromancy jokes, sexual advances, or both. She didn't mind banter, but what would she say if the queen was serious?

Annea winked and spared her the need to puzzle it out. "There's a meditation chamber attached to my bedroom that we're going to use. The bloodstains haven't been removed from the reception chamber's floor yet, and that space is too big for what I have in mind."

"I see," Serena said, resuming her march up the stairs.

"I'm sorry if I made you uncomfortable. My sense of humor skews towards innuendo, and humans are so easy to wind up. I can't help myself sometimes. If I had genuine amorous intent, you'd know. I'm not subtle about such things."

Serena doubted Annea was big on subtlety in *any* area of her life. They had that in common. To show she hadn't been offended, Serena asked, "You at least put the throwing knives away before rolling into bed, right?"

Annea smiled, winked, and didn't answer the question.

The scents of roses and lavender filled the bedroom. Specimens of both plants lined the walls. Half a dozen other varieties of red or purple flowers grew from large pots spaced throughout the room. Keeping with the theme, Annea's canopy bed had silky sheets and curtains of the same colors. Natural light filtered in from an opening in the ceiling. A set of double doors on the far end of the room stood open, revealing the meditation chamber on the other side.

Serena had expected a small, intimate space with a few pillows and candles. Instead, she walked into an open, circular space almost as large as the bedroom, with three unlit lamps hanging from the ceiling. Annea did have pillows and candles piled up near the door... as well as two wooden batons, each as long as her forearm. "Sit," Annea said. She tossed two pillows into the center of the room, then lit the lamps overhead. Before taking a seat herself, Annea closed the doors, leaving the lamps as the sole source of light.

"Can I ask you something before we begin?" Serena asked, suddenly nervous. She knew nothing about Annea. The Nexus Personal Encyclopedia's entry on Kimori talked about elven art, music, and how they leveled the surfaces of some tree branches to turn them into farmland. It said Kimori was respectful of visitors with peaceful intent, but that they preferred to keep to themselves and discouraged tourists. It said nothing about their monarchy in general, or Annea in particular. She'd feel better knowing more about the queen before submitting to her training.

"What would you like to know?" Annea asked.

"Elves can live for a thousand years, right? You seem pretty young to be queen. Can I ask what happened to the last one?" Serena didn't realize until after she'd asked that the question might be offensive.

Annea appeared unbothered. "Kimori's queen isn't decided by heredity, nor is it a position someone takes on for life. It's a title with a term limit. My predecessor reigned for two hundred years. After I've done the same, another promising young woman will be selected to take my place."

"Does that mean your parents —"

"They're still very much alive," Annea said. "But they're not on Kimori. Tradition dictates that a queen's parents spend her two-hundred-year term living on other worlds, so they cannot attempt to influence the queen's decisions or be taken as political hostages. I think it's an antiquated and nonsense policy, but unlike me, my parents are sticklers for tradition. After my coronation, they left without telling me where they're going."

"When will you see them again?"

"In about a hundred and forty years. They should live another five hundred after that, so we'll still have plenty more time together."

She'd be long dead before Annea saw her parents again. Elven lifespans felt hard to comprehend. "Is that what you meant earlier when you said being a queen on Kimori is different from other worlds?"

Annea shook her head. "It's more than that. Kimori has one law: As long as what you're doing isn't harming yourself, the environment, or anyone else, it's fine. Millennia of history have established the boundaries of appropriate social conduct, what constitutes 'harming someone,' and the appropriate restitution for different offenses. As such, Kimori needs almost no government. We get along and keep society functioning without the need for authorities. While I can issue commands and set policy, my role as queen is more aspirational and symbolic than administrative. I'm the woman elevated to represent the best of what we can be, who has the skills necessary to take charge should our world ever be threatened.

"I'm a glorified cheerleader for my people. I officiate weddings and funerals. I celebrate the naming of newborns. I mediate disputes when they arise. Whenever one of our theaters opens a new musical or play, you can count on me being there opening night. In my personal time, I offer combat and magic training because I enjoy it. It's a good life."

"How were you chosen to be the queen?" Serena asked.

Annea tilted her head, her expression bemused. "You're nervous. I get it. I hope learning a bit about me helped, but that's not why we're here. Would you rather hear my life story, or learn how to access your magic?"

No use putting it off any longer. "Magic," Serena said, wondering what the elf had in mind.

"Your talents first appeared when the Vohr attacked your village, correct?" Annea asked.

Serena nodded.

"I want you to think back to the moment it happened. Focus on your thoughts and emotional state at that time."

Serena pictured the dismembered bodies of her neighbors. Recalled the smell of blood. The terror. The overwhelming sense of powerlessness she'd felt while the manti pushed her around. "I don't remember," Serena lied, stuffing down the memories. "That night was pure chaos."

"And in that chaos, you dug deep and found the power you needed to survive. You didn't give up. Why did you want to live?"

Because who wants to die in their twenties? I was building a life for myself. I was respected as a hunter. The Vohr took all that away from me. They killed everyone. I wanted to see them suffer for it.

"Are you a therapist as well as a queen? What is the point of this?" Serena asked.

"Some magic users draw on emotions to harness and control their power. From what I've seen, that's especially true for pyromancers."

Serena said nothing. Since her escape through Alterra's Planar Gate, she'd been trying hard to avoid feeling anything at all. She took every chance available to distract herself so she wouldn't have time to dwell on her thoughts. What good would that do? The Nexus wouldn't send anyone to help Alterra. They made sure nobody ever could. And the greater multiverse didn't know, or didn't care. If she wanted to see the Vohr burn, she needed to *do*, not *think*.

"Your world is dead, along with everyone you've ever known. How does that make you feel?" Annea asked.

"Hollow. Empty. Adrift." Serena felt her temper rising and stuffed it down. Was Annea trying to twist the knife? "How am I doing? Do you have any ink blots you want me to look at while we're at it?"

Annea stared into Serena's eyes with the unblinking intensity of a predator sizing up prey. Serena stared back, defiant. She felt naked under that gaze, as if the queen could see into her soul and understood everything she'd left unsaid. Such a stare could drive a person to confess their deepest, most private secrets. Serena liked to think she was good at reading people. She knew enough to realize Annea was far better at it than she'd ever be.

Unable to endure the scrutiny further, Serena looked away.

"Now I'm certain you're emotionally activated," Annea said. "I have a good idea what triggers you."

"Care to enlighten me, Master?"

"Introspection is key to controlling your power." Annea snapped her fingers. The lamps extinguished themselves, leaving the meditation chamber in absolute darkness. "You'll never be able to access your power as long as you're emotionally dishonest with yourself."

"I don't understand what you want from me."

"Recall your emotions on the night the Vohr attacked. Recreate them, and you will know how to summon your power at will. Denying, deflecting, and suppressing your feelings will never awaken your magic. We're staying in here until you relight those lamps."

"Then we will be here all night," Serena said.

"No," Annea said, her voice certain, "we won't."

Serena did everything she could to avoid recalling the attack on Valencia. She didn't want to think about manti batting her about like cats playing with a mouse, knowing they could make the kill whenever they wanted. She'd never allow anyone or anything to make her feel powerless like that again. She'd bleach that memory from her mind if she could.

She lost all sense of time in the darkness. How much time had passed? Five minutes? Ten? Annea asked for the impossible. She felt no closer to accessing her magic than she had in her room.

"I tried the easy way first." Annea's voice came from behind Serena. "It's not my fault you're stubborn."

When had she moved?

Serena felt the tap of a wood baton on top of her head. She stood. "Annea, what are you doing?"

"I'm giving you a push."

Serena jumped when she felt another tap, this time at the back of her knee. She doubted Annea would limit herself to taps from the batons for long. "How do you expect me to think when..." *Whap* — that one to the butt. "...When you're poking and prodding me."

"Don't think, *feel*," Annea said. "How does it feel to be Alterra's sole survivor? Everyone counting on you to protect them died."

WHAM. Serena bent forward, air rushing from her lungs as she took a punch to the gut. Just as she started to get her breath back, Annea swept her legs back, toppling her face-first to the floor. "You're not helping!"

"I'll stop when you light the lamps, so get on with it."

Serena rolled to get some distance from Annea. *Thunk.* She cried out as a sharp kick caught her on the side and ribs. Could elves see in the dark? How did she know where Serena was at all times?

I'm not putting up with any more of this bullshit. She took another blow to the legs as she pushed herself to her feet. A familiar warmth filled her chest. Flames sprang to life in her hands. Their light allowed her to see Annea taking another swing at her. *Crack!* Pain surged through her arm.

Serena snatched the batons from Annea's hands. "How do you think it felt to watch monsters slaughter my neighbors? To see people I'd known for years hacked apart and eaten? I arrived in the Nexus drenched in their blood." She felt no pain as the batons burned to embers and ash in her grip.

Flames traveled up her arms, then spread across her entire body. "Alterra is gone. So are three hundred other worlds. But is anyone doing anything to stop the Vohr? No! Why lift a finger to help out someone else's reality? We were told not to talk about it. Wouldn't want anyone panicking now, would we?"

The flames coating Serena's body flared outward, forcing Annea to take a step back. Goddess, the power coursing through her felt so good. "Oh, and then I arrived on a world I'm told is 'basically a utopia,' only to get attacked within the first few hours. You had the nerve to call that a *lesson!* What did you teach us exactly, Your Majesty?"

"You can stop now," Annea said.

Stop? She'd never felt more alive. Power roared through her. She was a living inferno. A fire goddess. "Every two weeks or so, an entire civilization is wiped out, and you want me to sit down and discuss my *feelings?* Am I supposed to sit there, smile, and engage in a pleasant chat about the worst night of my life? Do we settle down by the fireplace afterward with a nice cup of tea? Enough. Coming to Kimori was a waste of time. I'll slaughter the Vohr by myself if I have to, and when I'm done, I'm going after every person in power in the Nexus who knew about them and did nothing."

"Serena, you need to stop." Sweat beaded Annea's forehead. She pointed at the lamps overhead. Wax from melted candles dripped to the floor, while the metal casings glowed like they'd just been pulled from a forge. Surprisingly, neither the floor nor ceiling charred or burned against such heat.

Why should I care about a few ruined lamps? She expanded her flaming aura even further, driving Annea to the back wall. "If you're not going to help me, then get out of my way." Serena cast her gaze around the room, looking for the door.

"Serena, please stop. That much power will burn you up if you don't let it go. You. Will. Die." There was no mistaking the alarm in Annea's eyes.

Rage. My magic is fueled by rage. Annea's fear blunted her anger enough that reason begin to reassert itself. Annea *had* pushed her into finding the key to her power. Serena took a deep breath, then another. The rage melted away, replaced by overwhelming fatigue. *Rage is my fuel... what does that say about me?*

As the flames sputtered and died, she realized that although her magic hadn't burned her, everything she wore was ash at her feet.

With the magic gone, she felt hollow, like her soul had blown out with the flames. Her knees buckled. Annea dashed forward to catch her before she hit the ground.

"Thanks," Serena said.

She blacked out.

CHAPTER 10
SERENA'S NIGHTMARE

Serena found herself inside the Radiant Temple of the All-Mother, one of the most famous buildings on Alterra. She'd only been there once, a decade ago, but the majestic architecture left an indelible impression on her mind. The Radiant Temple housed the world's largest stained glass window. Fifty feet tall by eighty feet wide, it depicted the goddess Alainna in a flowing white dress, her long black hair caught in the breeze. Around her stood an array of disciples representing all the world's cultures. She had her arms spread wide in a gesture of welcome. The words YOU ARE LOVED filled the top of the window.

"THIS IS WHAT YOU WORSHIP? PATHETIC." A deep, gravelly voice came from everywhere and nowhere at once.

Serena spun, casting her gaze around the church. Ten thousand people worshiped here during major holidays, but there wasn't another soul in sight now. Sunlight poured in through the massive window behind her, and yet the lighting in the church felt... off. Like it wasn't reaching the vaulted ceilings how it should. The shadows in the corners and under pews felt too deep.

"Hello?" The church's acoustics amplified her voice to fill the space.

"YOURS IS A FALSE GOD. YOUR PEOPLE GOT WHAT THEY DESERVED."

"Show yourself!" Serena shouted. Her own words echoed back to her a dozen times over. That couldn't really happen here, could it? She reached for the knife she kept at her hip, only to realize she didn't have it. She wore the same plain black clothes she'd received upon her arrival in the Nexus.

The Nexus… Memories of the last few days returned to her in a rush. Alterra was gone. This couldn't be real.

"YES," the voice said a few moments later. "YOU'RE NOT IN YOUR REALITY ANYMORE. YOU'RE IN MINE."

Glass shattered behind her. Serena turned again. A manti cannonballed itself through the stained glass window. In a blink, the monstrous insect closed the gap between them and cut her in half at the waist. Her legs fell one way, her torso another. Pain bathed her like the heat of a thousand suns. She landed hard on her back, not understanding what happened. The manti bent down and used the tentacles on its head to lift her severed legs up to its mouth.

She wished that hadn't been the last thing she'd ever see.

The world spun.

Warm afternoon sunlight caressed Serena's face. Surprised, she opened her eyes to discover her body was whole again. She stood outside the public library she'd frequented most of her life, the one her father worked at. Like the church, there wasn't another soul in sight.

Adrenaline surged through her. She looked around frantically, assuming an attack could come from any direction at any time. How was she still alive? This was all a dream. It had to be. It wasn't possible to be bisected one moment and completely fine the next. But it felt indistinguishable from reality. She'd had plenty of vivid dreams before, but nothing like this. In her dreams, she never felt the sunlight or the breeze. She couldn't smell the roses planted around the library. She couldn't feel the brick walls.

"What do you want?" Serena asked.

The voice said nothing.

Not knowing what else to do, she went inside the library. This was one of her favorite places. When she walked between the rows of shelves, she felt like she'd stepped into another world. These books could teach her anything she wanted to know. They could captivate her imagination with grand adventures.

Her gaze landed on a framed drawing set on the librarian's desk, positioned so patrons could see it. She'd drawn it for her father when she was five. It showed her and her father standing side-by-side, except she stood on top of a big pile of books to make their heights the same. As a teenager, she'd begged him to get rid of it, finding it embarrassing to see such a crude illustration every time she came in. He'd always refused. "It's evidence my daughter loves me," he said. "Why would I ever want to get rid of that?"

As if thinking of him summoned him, her father emerged from a back room, his arms loaded with returned titles he'd be logging back into the library's inventory and then restocking. When he saw her, a broad grin spread across his freckled face. "Serena! I didn't think I'd be seeing you again so soon. How was life on the frontier?"

"Fine," Serena spoke without thought, her mind buzzing with uncomfortable tension. He looked completely real. But he couldn't be. She wanted to give him a hug, or apologize for not writing more often, or warn him about the manti and urge him to take Mom and flee far from the capital. What good would any of that do now?

"What's the matter?" her father asked. "It's never a good sign when you're giving one word answers."

Serena ignored him and did a quick lap of the library. She felt like a deer moments from being ambushed by wolves. The lighting wasn't right in here either. It was too dim for this time of day. Shadows seemed to suck in the surrounding light. Her sweep of the library turned up nothing. No monsters. No apparent threats of a more mundane nature either. Serena and her father had the place to themselves.

Once again, soon after having a thought, reality responded to it. When Serena returned to the librarian's desk, a reaper stood behind her father. The bipedal, eight-foot-tall reptile stood motionless and silent.

Her father was oblivious to the danger. "With how go, go, go you can be, it still surprises me sometimes you're able to sit down and read at all. What's the matter? It's not like you to hold out on me."

The reaper punched her father in the back, impaling him with the three long blades that grew between its knuckles. It lifted him off the ground. "You've got something you need to get off your chest, I'm sure of it." Her father spoke as if nothing had happened. As if he hadn't just received a mortal wound. "It's a slow day. Why don't I close the library for a while and we can go grab a late lunch and talk about it."

The reaper did to her father exactly what she imagined they'd done to Ivy's sisters. Gore splattered the librarian's desk. Serena turned away and fell to her knees. She couldn't breathe. Tears blurred her vision.

"THAT'S NOT THE RESPONSE I EXPECTED," the phantom voice said. "I'M DISAPPOINTED."

The world spun again.

Serena remained on her knees, but now found herself in Valencia's central courtyard. The town was a ruin. The church's roof had collapsed. Most homes had at least one destroyed wall. Bloodstains covered the cobblestones around her.

She wasn't alone.

A lone figure stood ten feet away. He wore black pants and a leather vest, which was open to display intricate patterns of ritualistic scars across his purple skin. A black horn spike grew from his forehead above each of his eyes. His cruel smile revealed two rows of shark-like teeth. He didn't have any hair. A pair of manti stood behind him.

"I'm surprised," he said. Face to face, his voice was still a gravelly rumble, but nowhere near as loud as it had been. "When a fish slips the net, they're smart enough not to jump back in. And yet, here you are."

Serena forced herself to stand and confront the demonic-looking presence. "I don't know what you're talking about."

The man shrugged. "You will, soon enough. I have eyes on many worlds. Which one did you run off too?"

She felt a sensation like worms burrowing through her brain. It was profoundly uncomfortable, as if an external force fought her for control over what she could think about. It felt like an attack, but she had no idea how to counter it. "Who are you? Why are you doing this?"

"My name is Korahshka. I command the Vohr. It's an honor and a privilege to have hundreds of thousands of creatures responding to my every whim." Korahshka snapped his fingers. Behind him, the two manti started... dancing? They bobbed up and down, shimmied side to side, and flailed their bladed arms around in a grotesque parody of art. At a wave, they returned to an inert, motionless state.

Korahshka frowned. "I'll ask again. Where are you?"

The pressure in Serena's head mounted. Her brain felt like an apple being eaten from the inside out. "You don't really think I'd tell you that, do you?"

"Not voluntarily," he agreed. He rushed forward and reached for her neck. Serena batted aside his first attack, but failed to stop the second. He grabbed her by the throat and lifted her off the ground like she weighed nothing, then carried her across the courtyard and bashed her into the front wall of the church once, twice, three times. Thick logs cracked and snapped behind her before her head punched through the wall and she caught a brief glimpse of the church's ceiling.

Her vision blurred. She felt sure she had a concussion. The force of those blows should have been fatal though, not merely painful. More dream logic at work. The worms burrowed in ever deeper. None of this made any sense. She wanted to write it all off as a nightmare, but a primal sense of self-preservation told her it wasn't.

"Why... are you doing this?" Serena asked. Keep him talking. Focus on the here and now.

"I'm working my way across the multiverse to set right ancient wrongs. Bring order to chaos. Discipline to the unruly."

"Good for you."

Korahshka nodded, taking her sarcastic words at face value. "Along the way, my eyes mark targets with rare and exceptional magical gifts, so I can claim those abilities for myself."

"I'm flattered."

"You should be." He spun and threw her away. Serena hit the cobblestones at a bad angle and felt something snap. She couldn't move her left arm. "My eye sensed your latent powers. My manti pushed you into awakening them. But there's more to you than mere pyromancy. I had hoped attacking you or the memory of your father might draw it out of you, but you're being stubborn. Show me your true power."

The worms in her brain whipped into a frenzy, sensing she stood on the precipice of making a critical mistake and giving away information Korahshka wanted to know. She told herself she had no magical abilities. And if she did, she had no idea how to access them. She focused on the pain in her arm. The discomfort in her mind. She cataloged her wounds. It helped keep her away from topics she didn't dare think about.

That wouldn't work for long. The only way to win Korahshka's game was to not play.

She stood, overcome with a sudden, insane idea. If it worked, she'd be free. If it didn't, she'd be dead – but at least she'd die without putting anyone else's safety at risk.

"You want to see what I can do? Fine." She staggered towards Korahshka as best she could with a busted shoulder and many flavors of head pain. "It only works at close range though."

"You can't hurt me here, so show me what you wish to show me." Korahshka threw his arms wide, inviting her to approach. His pet manti moved in behind her to block her from fleeing.

Serena kept walking. If she paused, she'd lose her nerve. She'd only get one chance at this. She had to be decisive. Earlier moments in this nightmare showed Korahshka could pick up her thoughts. The fact that he hadn't already tried to stop her suggested a delay between her thinking something and him knowing it. She couldn't squander that window of opportunity.

"You wanted to see my power? Here it goes!" Serena jumped and headbutted Korahshka as hard as she could, braining herself on his horns.

CHAPTER II
IVY'S TRIAL

<Is she dead?>

<We've been here for hours and she hasn't moved at all.>

<It's almost mid-day. She's probably dead.>

<How do we know for sure?>

<I don't know. I'm not an expert on human biology.>

<Should we get a healer?>

<Annea had two tend to her last night. It wasn't enough. She's definitely dead.>

<We should ask Annea what she wants done before we dispose of the body.>

"I'm not dead. Would you both please shut up." Serena felt like her brain was boring its way through her skull and out her forehead. If she coughed or sneezed, it felt like her chest would explode from the inside out, sending rib shrapnel flying across the room. Every muscle ached from overuse. She couldn't recall another time in her life where she hurt everywhere, all at once. But hey, this was reality. Korahshka couldn't hurt her here. She hoped.

She opened her eyes to find herself in bed, with Pik-Pik and Tik-Tik staring at her like a pair of six-legged puppies. She started to lift the sheet, stopping at the sight of her naked body. She *had* incinerated all the clothing right off herself last night...

<Annea asked us to bring you to her when you woke up.> Was that Pik-Pik or Tik-Tik? How did Annea tell them apart?

<I'm glad you're not dead.>

"I'm going to need a minute to put some clothes on," Serena said.

<That's OK, we'll wait.> The ants stayed right where they were.

"I'm not wearing anything right now."

<That doesn't bother us.>
<We have no feelings about the nudity of other species.>
<We are genderless, sexless drones.>
<We can help you dress, if you'd like.>
"Get. Out." Flames flickered across Serena's fingers. The ants took the hint and left. Serena stood awkwardly, as if she'd aged sixty years in a night. Her muscles screamed in protest as she struggled to fit her arms through the sleeves of a loose-fitting shirt. Perhaps she should have let the ants help, even if that help came with constant commentary. Pride forced her to carry on. That, and she didn't want to know how ants would help her put pants on.

She did everything she could to avoid thinking about the nightmare that wasn't a nightmare. She needed a breather before trying to process how someone or something could invade her mind and desecrate her memories like that. Had there been a point to it, beyond casual cruelty? That sadistic asshole had her world slaughtered. Though she couldn't be certain, she felt confident her mad, suicidal stunt had kept her from revealing her location. That would have to be victory enough for now. If he wanted her power, he'd show himself again. She'd need to talk to Annea about the dream.

That could wait until she felt like a functional human being again.

After five minutes of struggle that felt like an hour, Serena opened her bedroom door. She grabbed her bow and a quiver of arrows, more to avoid comments from Annea about walking around unarmed than from any expectation she'd need to use them. Someone left a spread of bagels and pastries on the lodge's bar. She wolfed down one of each before asking the ants to lead the way.

Pik-Pik and Tik-Tik led her up multiple stairways, some carved into the tree, others built onto the exterior. Every step hurt, but walking helped stretch her out. It kept her grounded. They reached a cavernous hollow in the tree that served as a marketplace. There was a clear logic to its organization, with foods on one side, household goods in the middle, and high-end crafts, clothes, and weapons along the far wall. The market was so packed that Serena would lose the ants in the crowd if she didn't stay close. Elves took the wares they wanted, thanked the shopkeepers, and left without paying. She'd almost shouted about theft until she noticed everyone was doing it. None of the shopkeepers' faces showed any signs of concern.

"Does money not exist on Kimori?" Serena asked. What should she do if she came here later and found something she wanted?

<Not amongst elves.>

<They trade freely amongst each other. There is no exchange of currency. No keeping score.>

<Everyone helps each other out, knowing the kindness they bestow upon others will be shown to them in turn.>

That sounded pretty utopian, despite Annea not thinking of her world as such. "Does that apply to guests from other worlds, as well?"

<In your case, yes.>

<Feel free to take anything you need.>

<But be sure to thank the shopkeepers!>

<It's extremely rude not to.>

<Shopkeepers refuse to serve people who don't properly appreciate their hard work.>

<You could say our economy runs on compliments.>

"What do elves do for money if they want to go to other worlds?" Serena asked.

<There is a global fund for that.>

<Anyone is welcome to take what they need.>

She could think of a thousand ways humans would abuse a system like that. "Are there limits? What's to stop someone from taking a fortune and disappearing forever?"

The ants laughed. They didn't answer the question.

The trio carried on to a series of stairways and walkways built into the exterior of the tree. A light breeze ruffled her hair as they passed balconies where artists painted portraits of their clients. They passed a branch that had a deep groove carved into it which served as a broad avenue. Homes were carved into the branch on either side. Serena had to ask her guides to stop multiple times along the way so she could catch her breath and stretch. It would have been an easy enough climb, if not for her current condition.

<We have arrived.> After more than a half hour of working their way higher up the world tree, they came upon a walkway that terminated at an outdoor amphitheater. The ants took positions at either side of the walkway, as if guarding the place. She sensed it was more about giving the queen privacy than protection.

She almost cried with relief at the sight of rows upon rows of wooden benches. Ivy stood alone on a large, rectangular stage. Eight different kinds of plants grew up from the front edge of the stage, as if Ivy was building the horticultural equivalent of a curtain. As Serena made her way further inside, the dryad set to work on growing a ninth. Annea sat five rows up from the stage. They had the whole place to themselves.

Serena hobbled up the stairs to take a seat next to the elf. "What's happening here?" She asked, watching a fresh sprout break through the stage floor.

"Ivy asked me to take her on as an apprentice and train her as I see fit. This is her first lesson. You may observe, but please do not interfere. I have asked her to produce examples of twelve different plants native to Ataraxia."

"I can't make plants appear from nothing, so it shouldn't be hard to stay out of her way," Serena said. Ivy's new plant stretched up several feet before spreading out across a half dozen branches.

"That is not the true test. I spoke with her this morning while you slept. She said little. What she *didn't* say spoke volumes. I've lived amongst her kind. I believe I understand the nature of her pain. Her trial will be every bit as difficult as yours was, in its own way," Annea said, never taking her eyes off Ivy. When the branches of plant number nine sagged under the weight of blue and purple berries, Ivy moved on to starting number ten.

"How are you feeling?" Annea asked.

"Like I got ripped apart and sewn back together. Would it have killed you to pull your punches a little?" Serena asked. She wouldn't be surprised if Annea had cracked her ribs with a kick. "Pik-Pik and Tik-Tik said you had a few healers tend to me, but if so, why do I still feel so bad?"

Annea turned her gaze away from Ivy's actions on stage. "I instructed them to only heal the injuries I caused, and stabilize you enough that you wouldn't suffer organ failure. The pain you're feeling right now is self-inflicted. I didn't let them heal everything because you need to understand the consequences of your actions."

Self-inflicted? How? She'd felt like a goddess before she'd become too exhausted to carry on. "I don't understand."

"Magic is a bit like breathing," Annea said. A tree sprouted on stage with a dense spread of branches from the canopy all the way to the ground. "Like air, magic is all around us. Like air, we draw that energy into ourselves. However, lungs have a finite capacity — you can only inhale so much before you must exhale. With magic, it is possible to keep inhaling and inhaling until your body breaks down from the strain. That, Serena, is why you're in so much pain. You nearly killed yourself last night."

She *had* killed herself last night. Kind of. Sort of. But not really. *Stop thinking about the dream,* she commanded herself.

Thousands of red and pink flowers burst forth from Ivy's tree with such explosive force that some of the flower heads went flying off the stage.

"How do I know how much magic I can handle?" Serena asked.

Annea shrugged. Not a gesture Serena wanted to see. "I'm not sure yet, in your case. Most of us feel the strain in our bodies as it's happening, like you would feel during a long run or while lifting heavy weights. That sense of strain is enough to keep most people from going overboard. We feel our limits and improve them with practice and training. Our bodies shut down or our magic stops working before we overuse it to a dangerous degree. You possess a rare talent for channeling large amounts of power quickly, but seem to lack any of that natural feedback on what you can handle. That's a dangerous combination. What you did last night is the magical equivalent of deadlifting ten times your body weight without ever having trained. It shouldn't be possible. I certainly wasn't expecting it."

They sat in silence for a time, watching Ivy tend to her plants. Annea's fear in the meditation chamber made sense now. Drawing energy into herself had felt effortless. Could she really do it faster than others? What good was her magic if she risked killing herself every time she used it? How could she ever hope to increase her limits if she couldn't tell what they were in the first place?

Annea leaned forward as Ivy got on her knees and placed her hands against the hardwood floor. "I think Ivy is wrapping up."

Ivy lifted her hands and spread her arms. As she did, vines poked through the floor, chasing the path of her hands ever higher. Ivy stood, and the vines continued to grow in accordance with her hand movements. She created a couple twists in the vines before bringing them together over her head. Through an intricate series of gestures, she got the two vines to tie together in such a way that, when she released her spell, both vines remained standing, each supported by the weight of the other. One vine was orange, the other yellow. Their leaves looked nothing alike. She'd made plants eleven and twelve at the same time.

Showoff.

"Artfully done," Annea said, applauding. "Perfect timing; I see our guests have arrived."

Pik-Pik and Tik-Tik walked into the amphitheater, each leading a line of a dozen elven children. Serena couldn't be sure with elves, but guessed them all to be ten years old or younger. Walking in an orderly fashion she'd never seen in human children that age, they filed into the first two rows of seats, center stage, placing themselves between the queen and Ivy. The curiosity and excitement in their chatter indicated they'd never seen a dryad before.

Ivy's skin paled, her telltale sign of anxiety or fear. She looked at the children as if any one of them would jump onto the stage and bite her.

The children quieted as their queen stood. "Ivy, I'd like you to teach our young students here about the plants of Ataraxia, using the examples you have created," Annea said.

"That would be pointless. Ataraxia is gone. These children would never use that information," Ivy said.

Annea shook her head. "You still live. You've demonstrated excellent control over your ability to create plant life. Kimori is a fertile plane. We might be able to grow these plants here. A piece of your world could thrive again."

"These are poor imitations of the real things. They are unlikely to survive for long, even in ideal conditions." As if to prove her point, one of her first plants — some kind of shrub — bent forward as its stem snapped.

"We won't know until we try. Now, please teach these children about the fine specimens you've made."

Ivy raised her chin in defiance. "I will not comply."

The children squirmed at the tension in the air. Serena couldn't blame them. Ivy had been standoffish and antisocial for all the brief time Serena had known her, but she didn't seem the petulant type. Why be so stubborn? Plants seemed like the safest possible topic to discuss with a dryad.

"What would your sisters think if they saw you here, the sole survivor of your family, unwilling to speak to children?" Annea asked. Her tone was calculated, precise. The sentence was a verbal dagger, and Annea knew it. *Her trial will be every bit as difficult as yours was, in its own way,* she'd said.

Ivy's expression remained neutral, but Serena could feel the anger simmering behind that mask. *I wouldn't be happy either after a cheap shot like that.* It wouldn't surprise her if a pair of vines emerged from their benches to choke the elven queen. What was Annea trying to accomplish?

"That was cruel," Serena whispered. The image of Ivy sobbing over the loss of her sisters was fresh in her mind.

"Sometimes you have to be cruel to be kind," Annea kept her voice low so Ivy wouldn't overhear.

"Bullshit."

"I will not explain myself to you right now. For what it's worth, I feel horrible about it, and hope this is the only time I ever speak to her this way."

Annea turned her attention back to Ivy, who remained silent and still on the stage. "My request is simple, Ivy. Please teach the children about the plants you've created. If that request is beyond your capabilities, then Orlan was misguided to send you to me. You may wish to consider returning to the Nexus and seeking guidance elsewhere."

Ivy remained silent a beat before nodding. "Very well." She covered herself in bark armor. Serena worried she would attack Annea. Or storm off the stage. Instead, the dryad motioned the children to approach. "Please come forward children, to better see the flora of my world." The young elves looked back at Annea, who nodded her approval. They crept towards the stage with obvious apprehension. Nobody wanted to be the one closest to the stage.

With cold, clinical detachment, Ivy started from the beginning of the line and rattled off a few facts about each plant before moving on. She covered their physical characteristics, optimal environmental conditions, growing seasons, and if they had practical applications. She kept her focus always a couple inches over the children's heads.

Ivy stopped at the ninth plant, the squat tree loaded with berries. "This is an *alucinatus* tree. Its berries are used medicinally to improve concentration and knowledge retention. Over time, they have also been known to improve vision."

"I want to try one!" One of the children reached out and snagged a berry before Ivy could stop him.

"Do not do that." Ivy's warning came too late. The boy was already chewing.

He turned back to Annea, his face lit up with pleasure. "These are delicious!"

"Do not eat the berries. I do not know their impact on elves." Ivy stepped in front of the tree, gently slapping away the grasping hands of a dozen children, but she couldn't stop them all. Two more children managed to grab berries and eat them.

Ivy started growing bamboo near the children's feet, not fast enough to hurt them, but enough to get them to back away from the stage. Unfortunately, that wasn't what stopped the kids from going after berries.

It was the sight of their three berry-eating classmates, all staring up into the sky, screaming.

CHAPTER 12

ALTERED PERCEPTION OF REALITY

S erena scanned the sky for any sign of what terrified the children, but saw only tree branches and puffy clouds. Annea raced down the steps to examine and comfort the kids. Ivy just stared, dumbfounded.

At the sight of their queen, the children stopped screaming. They wrapped their arms around her in desperate hugs. "What's wrong?" Annea asked.

"It's staring at us," said a young girl, her voice muffled as she buried her face in Annea's side.

"What is?"

"The eye." The first child to take a berry pointed up at an empty space in the sky.

"There's nothing there," Annea said, stroking his hair.

Serena limped down the stairs to join everyone else. Going down was definitely harder than up, and she had to pause a couple times to adjust her balance.

Annea called in Pik-Pik and Tik-Tik. "Class is over early today. Please make sure they find their way back to their parents." She indicated all the children but the three clinging to her like their lives depended on it. Scared but obedient, they formed lines behind the ants and followed them out of the amphitheater.

As they left, Ivy absorbed her bark armor into herself. She hopped down from the stage to gently place a hand on the shoulder of the girl. Green energy radiated from her hand into the young elf. "The berries are acting as a hallucinogen. I am unable to detoxify an effect like this."

"Then we'll bring them to our healers. There's a clinic a few levels up," Annea said. "We can each carry one."

"I'm in no condition to carry anyone," Serena said, plucking a few berries off the *alucinatus* tree and stuffing them in a pocket. "I can barely walk as it is."

Ivy placed a palm on her back. Warmth flooded her weary muscles.

"Your injuries are extensive," Ivy said. "It would take me hours to heal you. You were not in this condition when I last saw you. How did you acquire this damage?"

"During my training session with Annea, I took in too much power."

"You are a fool. You could have killed yourself."

"So I've been told." Would Ivy even care if she had? She'd made it clear they weren't friends.

"I can walk," the boy said. "Will you hold my hand?"

Serena felt a small hand poke at her side. The boy looked up at her with a mix of hope and worry in his big brown eyes that melted her heart. She'd fight a swarm of manti bare-handed to protect him, if she had to. "What's your name, little man?" she asked, taking his hand and giving it a gentle squeeze.

"Ryul."

"Nice to meet you Ryul. I'm Serena."

As they made their way out of the amphitheater, he kept looking past her. All three children had their gazes locked on the same spot. They couldn't all be having the same hallucination. They saw something. She followed their gaze and felt a familiar sense of being watched settle over her. The same undefinable sensation she'd experienced on Jonah's farm when she fought the manti. It was harder to notice this time, perhaps on account of her injured state, but it was there.

I have eyes on many worlds... Korahshka's words echoed in her mind. When Orlan showed them different monsters in the Vohr armada, one had been a giant, floating eye. Forcing down her rising sense of dread, Serena decided talking with the elf boy might be the distraction they both needed. "What do you like to do for fun, Ryul?"

"I like to practice shooting my bow," he said. "When I get bigger, I want to be even better with it than my mom and dad."

"That's awesome! I'm a hunter too." The two of them lagged behind the others as Serena limped along. Annea gave the little girl a piggyback ride, while the third child walked at her side. Neither of them wanted to be carried by Ivy. There weren't any other pedestrians on the path at the moment to be concerned about, so Serena handed her bow to Ryul. "What do you think?"

He ran his hand across the glossy green wood. The minotaur who sold it to her said it was made from *kassuk* trees from a world called Titanus, and claimed it was "utterly fireproof." Sooner or later, that claim would be put to the test. Hopefully later. "Can I give it a try?"

Serena took a deep breath and looked over the edge of the walkway. The anthill was at least three hundred feet tall, and they were at least that far above where it met up with the world tree. If she fell, she'd have a long time to think about her error before the final *splat*. There weren't any balconies or branches on the way down for a stray arrow to hit. Satisfied no harm could be done, Serena smiled and handed Ryul an arrow. As she had hoped he would, he aimed for the invisible eye. His arm trembled with the strain of holding the string taut. His shot flew off left of his aim, going about a hundred feet before beginning its long descent to the ground.

"Not even close. This bow is too hard for me." Ryul's shoulders slumped.

Serena took the bow back and gave him a pat on the head. "It was brave of you to try. You'll get there eventually," she said. They resumed their walk to the clinic.

"What's the scariest thing you've ever hunted?" Ryul asked, clearly eager to speak about hunting with someone other than his parents.

"I had to hunt a dire bear once, when it decided my village was its territory. Everyone else was too scared to do it. Dire bears are twice as big as a normal bear, fast, and extremely aggressive towards any perceived threat. They have a thick hide, so arrows aren't very effective."

"So what did you do?"

"I decided if I couldn't take it in a fight, I'd outsmart it. I convinced my neighbors to make tar. Dozens of barrels of the stuff.

Dire bears are nocturnal, so we went into the forest by day and dug a deep moat around a tree. Before it was complete, I hunted a couple deer and left their carcasses next to that tree. We filled the moat with tar and covered it with leaves. I stayed alone overnight to monitor the pit. As we hoped, the dire bear couldn't resist an easy meal, and walked right into the trap. Even a dire bear can't muscle its way out of a tar pit if it's deep enough. At that point, it was an easy mercy kill." She omitted that she'd still had to dodge a few desperate claw swipes before she could slit its throat.

As she concluded her story, they arrived at an opening into the tree. Inside, a wide hallway ran several hundred feet before it angled down and out of sight. Ivy stood outside a door with the word HEALERS painted above it. She motioned for Serena to step inside, but didn't follow her in.

The clinic had twenty examination tables, split into two even rows. No walls or curtains separated them, suggesting elves weren't concerned about privacy. Aside from the children, only two other tables had patients. Every table had a bioluminescent mushroom growing from the ceiling above it. Their flexible and extendable stems allowed doctors and nurses to focus light where they wanted it. They could even adjust the brightness by stroking up or down on the stem. A few cases of medical equipment and potions were tucked into a corner, but most of the wall space was taken up by paintings of the world tree, parts of the city, or of ants going about their daily work.

Ryul walked over to an empty examination table and jumped backwards to sit on the edge. The nurse who attended him was the oldest elf Serena had seen so far, with gray hair showing only the faintest streaks of black. How many centuries had she lived?

The nurse placed a palm on his forehead. "What ails you, child?"

"I'm seeing funny colors. And there's a giant eyeball following us around." Ryul said.

The nurse tilted his head up and looked into his eyes. "High temperature. Dilated pupils. Would you follow my finger please? Move only your eyes, not your head." She moved a finger back and forth across Ryul's field of vision. "Difficulty tracking objects. Did you eat the same berries as the other two?" He nodded.

Annea stood between the examination tables, holding the other two children's hands. Both lay on their backs, bodies enveloped in an aura of green energy as nurses set to work purging the berry's hallucinogens. The queen whispered encouraging words to them.

Satisfied the kids were being tended to, Serena hopped onto an examination table. Her vision blurred with the wave of agony that cascaded through her when her butt landed on the hard surface. She bit back a scream. Annea's point was well made. She wouldn't forget the consequences of using too much magic any time soon.

"What troubles you, miss?" Two male nurses approached. One appeared middle-aged, while the other could pass as a teenager.

"Everything. Literally everything," Serena said. If they had to ask, they weren't the healers that attended to her last night.

The older nurse placed a hand on her shoulder. Warmth flowed through her as his energy rippled up and down her body. "Oh my. You have a major case of magic over-saturation. Lie down please."

As she did, the younger nurse placed a hand on her leg. His magic felt less refined, creating a sensation like being rubbed down by a dry towel. "Torn muscles, liver and kidney damage, immune system compromised... How are you not dead?"

"Kelvin, what have I told you about bedside manner?" The elder nurse gave Serena an apologetic shrug.

"It was a legitimate question."

"Pure stubbornness, probably." Serena closed her eyes and let the elves do their work. Her muscles relaxed as their power coursed through her. It felt calming and pleasant, like lying down and soaking up sunlight. Time melted away, her whole world shrinking down to the systematic march of healing magic up her legs and across her chest. By the time awareness of her surroundings returned, the children were healed and gone.

Her healers looked exhausted, the younger one barely able to stay on his feet. He walked over to a chair along the wall and sat down. "I'm going to need to rest up for a bit."

Serena took all but one of the *alucinatus* berries out of her pocket and gave them to the elderly healer. "These are what the kids ate. I thought you might want samples to study."

Annea and Ivy awaited her as she stepped out of the clinic. Ivy stood even further apart than usual. "I told her about our training session last night," Annea said, explaining Ivy's behavior.

Why would Annea do that? She seemed to understand Ivy feared her. She might even know why. Wouldn't explaining what had happened just make it even worse? She doubted Ivy had asked out of concern for her welfare.

Once they returned to the exterior walkway, Serena asked the group to stop. "Annea, could you do me a huge favor?" She pulled out the *alucinatus* berry she'd kept. "Would you eat this for me? I don't think the kids were hallucinating. I'm convinced they saw something, and I'm hoping you can confirm it."

"I'm not sure that's a good idea," Annea said.

"If anything bad happens, we're right by the healers," Serena said. "Please."

Annea reluctantly took the berry and popped it in her mouth. The results were almost immediate. Her pupils dilated. The muscles in her face relaxed. "So many colors. It's like the world is bathed in rainbows. Did you know your aura is *pink*? I thought for sure it would be red, because of your pyromancy." She turned to Ivy. "I can see your skin soaking up sunlight, your every exhalation a puff of white gas."

"The effect appears stronger for adults," Ivy said.

"Annea, we need you to focus. Do you see anything out there?" Serena gestured to the sky beyond the walkway.

It took Annea a moment to process her request, but she eventually turned her attention skyward. "That's interesting. I see a single, floating eye. It's an ugly, reptilian looking thing. A diameter as wide as I am tall. Maybe larger. It seems quite interested in you, Serena."

A chill ran down Serena's spine. She looked to Ivy for confirmation, and got a nod. Annea's description matched something they'd seen in their briefing in the Nexus. The Vohr eyes. Orlan hadn't said anything about them being able to turn invisible. Maybe he didn't know.

"I might be able to render it visible." Ivy kept her voice calm, unconcerned. "Annea, could you point at it?" While Annea tracked it with a finger, Ivy produced a giant purple dandelion head in her hands and blew on it, sending spores drifting off in the direction indicated. "We call these paint spores. They grow every autumn." Her voice cracked. "My sisters and I would chase after flying spores and compete to see who could cover themselves in the most paint. We found it hilarious. Our father did not." She created a second plant and repeated the process, providing a larger area of coverage.

For a moment, it looked like nothing would happen. Then the spores exploded into large globs of purple paint when they struck something in midair. The eye rolled, shaking off globs of paint, but enough stuck to the sphere to keep it visible.

"That's a neat trick." Serena loosed arrows at the disembodied eyeball. It dipped and spun away from her shots. Realizing it was exposed, the eye changed course and flew away. It increased altitude and moved with the curve of the tree, using branches as cover wherever possible. Grateful to be feeling like herself again after the elves' healing, Serena dashed after it with everything she had.

She couldn't allow it to escape and give away her location. If it did, Kimori would be next in line for invasion. *Korahshka CANNOT know I'm here.* Ivy kept pace with her. She understood the threat the eye represented.

"Why are we running?" Annea did her best to keep up, but lacked the life-or-death urgency that helped Serena and Ivy wind their way up the tree at a full sprint.

Up and up they went, dodging pedestrians and muttering apologies. The higher they went, the sparser foot traffic became. They kept going until they passed through a layer of clouds. No branches grew this high up. Uninterrupted sky stretched out to the horizon, but Serena couldn't enjoy the view. The walkway narrowed. Broken or missing planks made it clear this part of the world tree seldom saw visitors. Thankfully, they'd manage to keep pace with the eye. They had the smudge of purple paint in view all the way to the end of the path, before it flew through an opening in the tree.

A ten-foot-high metal gate barred access. Despite its height, it only went two-thirds of the way to the top of the tree's opening, allowing the eye to fly through the gap at the top. Serena pushed at the gate. The lock wouldn't budge.

"Wait," Annea said when she caught up with them. "The Forest in the Sky is beyond that gate. We can't go in there, especially while I'm intoxicated. It's a death trap."

"We have to. He can't know I'm here." Serena placed her palms on the lock, imagining what would happen if the Vohr raided Kimori because of her. She pictured sweet little Ryul, impaled on a manti's blade. It couldn't be allowed to happen. *The eye dies. Right here. Right now.*

"Who can't know you're here?" Annea asked.

Serena didn't answer. Metal liquefied in the face of her overwhelming urgency. With Ivy's help, they forced the gate open wide enough to squeeze through. Good to know that Ivy could work around her aversion to pyromancy in the face of a bigger threat. Serena ignored the queen's warning and passed through the gate. No risk was too great. The eye couldn't escape.

Nothing else mattered.

CHAPTER 13

THE FOREST IN THE SKY

Serena scanned the area, taking in her surroundings while looking for the Vohr eye. They stood in a hollow that encompassed the entire diameter of the world tree. The exterior of the tree grew another couple hundred feet before giving way to open sky. Despite being hundreds of feet above ground level, she felt like she'd fallen into a pit.

Straight ahead, an unnaturally well preserved avenue of short grass bisected dense forest. It ran from one end of the hollow to the other, ending at a life-size golden statue of a dragon, its wings spread wide. It looked as clean and pristine as the day it was made. Unlike any dragon Serena knew from mythology, it sported antlers like a mature buck.

The eye flew down the grass avenue on a direct line for the dragon statue. Serena took off after it, with Ivy not far behind. It moved faster when it didn't need to change altitude or worry about evading arrows, which meant they gained ground on it slowly. Much too slowly. Serena's lungs burned and her heart hammered in her chest. She couldn't remember ever running this hard for this long. At least nothing stirred in the forest or attacked them as they ran deeper into this so-called death trap.

When they got within a hundred yards of the statue, she felt close enough to take a shot. Her aim wobbled. She struggled to focus while catching her breath, causing her first shot to sail wide of the target.

FOCUS Serena. You can do this.

Taking extra time to concentrate and lead her shot appropriately, she loosed another arrow. Black ichor sprayed from the eye. She'd hit the mark. Not taking any chances, she fired off two more shots, each scoring a hit. The eye wobbled in the air for a moment before dropping like a stone.

"Think it's dead?" Serena asked, stepping around the ichor pooling on the grass around the eye.

In response, Ivy picked up the pointed remains of a broken branch nearby. She raised it overhead and thrust it like a spear into the massive pupil. "It is dead," she said, leaving the branch in place.

"Could the two of you please explain why it was so important to come storming into this evil place?" Annea asked, gripping a kukri tightly in each hand. She stared at the trees on either side of the avenue like she expected to be ambushed at any moment.

Serena thought she was in excellent physical condition, but while she puffed and wheezed, Ivy and Annea acted like all the running they'd done to get here was just a light warm-up jog. They weren't even sweating. Could dryads sweat?

"The eye is a Vohr spying tool," Ivy said.

"I think…" Serena paused to take a breath. "I think it was going for that." She pointed towards a tunnel at the base of the dragon statue. It looked organic — a tube of pinkish flesh that throbbed as if it had a pulse. It stank like rotting meat. The tunnel burrowed into the earth for as far as she could see. Serena had to back away before nausea overtook her.

"I've been here once before, when I was young and stupid," Annea said, walking up to the pulsing tunnel entrance. If the smell bothered her, she didn't show it. "This was not here back then. You're suggesting this is some kind of Vohr tunnel into our reality?"

"I know it is." Serena provided a shortened version of Cypher's account of his escape from Mallozzi. He'd seen them with his own eyes. She had no reason to doubt his sincerity. "We should destroy it before anything else comes through."

"I'll handle it. You two keep an eye on the trees." Purple energy flowed from Annea's body into her kukris. Her dilated pupils and uneven balance indicated she still hadn't sobered up from the effects of the *alucinatus* berry, but she had clear control of her magic.

She plunged her kukris into the roof of the tunnel and stepped inside, dragging them through a half dozen paces worth of flesh before sweeping her arms out to cut down the sides. Purple energy flashed along the lines of each cut. Annea hurled herself out of the tunnel, rolling to her feet just in time to avoid a shower of blood and gore as her energy exploded from within the wounds, rupturing the walls of the tunnel.

Like an enraged snake, the tunnel shot up out of the ground, sending chunks of its own flayed flesh flying as it writhed and thrashed about. The dead Vohr eye burst like a melon when the tunnel smashed it. Ivy hid behind a tree. Annea took cover underneath the dragon. Serena retreated down the central avenue. As she prepared to throw a fireball at the living tunnel between realities, its spasms ceased. The fleshy mass faded away as if it never existed in the first place. The ground all around the dragon statue looked pristine, showing no signs of any tunneling activity.

"That was... unpleasant," Annea said. She brushed herself off and returned her focus to the surrounding trees. "I have more questions, but they can wait until we're out of here. The locals may have gone dormant for lack of food, but all that thrashing had to have woken some of them up."

Serena walked up to the base of the dragon's statue. Its head and distinctive antlers were at least a hundred feet over her head. It had to weigh tons. If the statue was pure gold, she could understand why the elves wouldn't want anyone inspecting it. Alterrans had fought wars over much smaller fortunes than what the dragon represented. There was a plaque set on a pedestal between its front legs, made up of two lines. The top line was a single word: BALOR. Below that were eight symbols she assumed to be a Planar Gate address.

"Who or what is Balor?" Serena asked.

"I'll tell you on the way out. We need to move." Without waiting to verify they were following, Annea started jogging back to the entrance, her weapons still in hand. Serena didn't want to do any more running, but fell in behind the queen anyway.

"Legend has it that the dragon god Balor ruled over Kimori many thousands of years ago, enslaving ants and elves alike. He would work us to death farming, mining, or logging the forests surrounding the city. All of those goods would be sent through the Planar Gate to feed troops and build war machines for armies fighting Balor's wars on other worlds. Millions of ants fought and died in those wars. Balor also forced our ancestors to create that statue in his image.

"Following the statue's completion, Balor created the Forest in the Sky — his sick idea of a game. Slaves who were sick, dying, under-performing, or had otherwise displeased Balor or his taskmasters were brought here. They were told Balor would grant freedom and eternal life to whoever could make it to the statue and touch it. In reality, he just liked watching elves get ripped apart and eaten by the monsters he stocked the forest with.

"Eventually, there was an uprising. Elf and ant banded together to defeat Balor and his minions. The dragon god fled and has never returned."

If the statue was an accurate depiction of the dragon's size, and not the product of a massive ego, how could he fit through a Planar Gate? A more important question came to her. "Has anyone tried to go to the location written on that plaque?" Serena asked.

"I attempted it after I escaped this place as an adolescent — nothing happened. As far as I can tell, that plane has been sealed off, no longer exists, or never existed." Annea slowed.

There was movement in the trees.

No, that wasn't right. The movement *was* the trees.

A pair on each side of the avenue uprooted themselves and moved to block their path, the flailing of their roots reminiscent of the chaotic movement of an octopus on land. Wood snapped and popped as they reconfigured dozens of branches from straight wood into multi-jointed arms. Bark fell away near the bases of their trunks, exposing hinged mouths like a nutcracker, lined with saw blade teeth. They didn't have any eyes.

"It was too much to hope that we'd be out of here before Balor's Sentinels woke up." Annea's kukris glowed purple with magic waiting to be unleashed.

"How many of these things are there?" Serena heard more carnivorous trees coming up behind them. The creaking of wood grew louder and louder as one in every four trees came to life. They creeped closer from every direction at once. They weren't fast, but that hardly mattered given their size and their numbers.

They had to be weak to fire, right?

"Don't set them on fire!" Annea said, anticipating her intentions. She slashed the air, converting her movements into lines of energy that she launched at a Sentinel. The attack severed a few arms but didn't slow its advance.

"Why not?" Fire danced across Serena's palms, waiting to be given form and direction.

"They give off toxic fumes when they burn, which will drift down into the city. We'd have torched this place millennia ago if we could."

"Then what do you expect me to do?"

"Dodge their attempts to grab you, and run like hell." Annea dived through the gap between two trees, narrowly avoiding the clutches of multiple arms. She didn't get far before being cut off again by another group.

Serena ducked as several Sentinels swiped for her head. "Ivy, you're the plant expert. Do you have any fancy tricks for this?"

"No."

"Straight to the point. No wasted words. I respect that."

Ivy used a thick stick to parry attempts to grab her arms and legs. As she backed away from one assailant, she walked right into the arms of another. Wooden fingers clutched her waist in a vice-like grip, lifted her from the ground, and ushered her towards their owner's open and waiting mouth.

"No!" Serena imagined herself blasting apart the Sentinel. Her body responded. She became the epicenter of an explosion that ignited everything within a ten foot radius, including Ivy's grassy hair. The concussive force of the blast shocked the Sentinel into dropping Ivy. It and its companions took involuntary steps backwards. Flames flickered and danced along Serena's skin. Holes opened up in her shirt as the material burned.

Ivy stared up at her, naked terror written across her face, like her darkest nightmares had come to life. Serena extended a hand to help Ivy to her feet. The dryad crawled backwards, towards the same monster that had just tried to eat her. "Stay away from me!"

She shook her head with enough force to blow out the flames working their way up her hair towards her scalp.

They didn't have time for this! "What are you more afraid of? The woman trying to help you, or the trees trying to eat you?" Serena shouted. "Get off your ass and *run*."

Annea took advantage of the Sentinel's distraction to climb up the side of one and jump from tree to carnivorous tree, working her way towards Ivy. She used her kukris to sever burning limbs before the flames could spread. The Sentinel's leaves disintegrated into a noxious green smoke as they burned. It wasn't until she hopped onto her fifth Sentinel that the plants realized they had an intruder rampaging through their canopies. Gnarled fingers grabbed Annea's ankles and whipped her into the ground, sending her kukris flying from her grip.

She didn't get up.

Roots dug into the dirt and ripped up grass as the Sentinels shook off their surprise and advanced. Ivy twisted out of an attempt to grab her shoulder and crawled towards Annea. Wooden fists pounded into the dirt behind her. Annea offered no resistance as one Sentinel grabbed her arms, and another her legs. They lifted her up and pulled, each trying to steal the elf for themselves.

Serena took a deep breath, pulling in all the air and energy that she could. This was going to hurt. She exhaled. As the air left her lungs, she pushed her magic outward, turning the low flame coating her body into a roaring fire. She projected the flames out as far as she dared. If she couldn't make kindling of the carnivorous trees, she'd settle for letting them starve. She marched forward with purpose. The Sentinels fell back. Annea's captors dropped her and retreated into the cover of the forest.

"Ivy, we need to run," Serena said. "You'll have to carry Annea. I can't when I'm like this."

The dryad just stared at her.

Serena knew how she must look. A walking inferno. A *naked*, walking inferno. The last scraps of another set of clothing drifted to the ground as her flames burned them away. She couldn't let that become a habit. Her bow was indeed fireproof. Her quiver and arrows weren't. It didn't matter. If they got out alive, it'd be worth it. But to do that, Ivy had to conquer her fear. Right now. "This is a weaker version of what I did last night, Ivy. I have no idea how long I can maintain this. We have to go now, please."

Ivy blinked, as if waking from a dream. She still lacked any sense of urgency.

Serena felt the weariness creeping in. Her legs grew heavier. "I'm not going to abandon you two. We leave together, or we die here. I'm not your enemy."

Ivy grew bold enough to look Serena in the eyes. Serena stared back, praying the dryad would see her sincerity. Ivy nodded, her expression hardening as she found her resolve. Vines emerged from Ivy's wrists, which she used to bind Annea's ankles together. She stood and ran, dragging the queen behind her. Annea was significantly taller and heavier than Ivy, which made the dryad's pace even more impressive. Serena wouldn't make the mistake of underestimating her capabilities again. She followed Ivy as closely as she could, maintaining a delicate balance between staying close enough to deter the Sentinels and far enough back that she wouldn't burn her companions. All while maintaining a blaze that would kill her if she kept it up much longer.

It felt like it took a thousand years, but they made it to the gate without further harassment from their arboreal assailants. Ivy dragged Annea out first. Serena killed her flames and followed behind. Ivy set Annea down and helped Serena pull the metal gate closed.

Metal rang under the impact of a hundred fists as Sentinels reached the gate and tried to force their way out. Additional arms reached out over the gap at the top, but lacked the length and flexibility to bend down and strike them.

Serena was starving. Her body felt leaden. Her knees trembled. If she hadn't already passed into dangerous territory for using so much power, she'd be there soon, but she couldn't stop yet. She had one final task to complete. "Go on Ivy, I'll be right behind you." Serena's hands glowed blue as she concentrated as much power as she could into the tip of her index finger. She attempted a hasty weld to seal the gate shut.

Her knees buckled before she could finish. She caught Ivy running back for her in the second before she passed out.

CHAPTER 14
HEART TO HEART

Serena lay on her back on the dining table of the guest lodge outside her bedroom, staring up at the bioluminescent fungus on the ceiling. After waking up in her own bed, she'd decided to get dressed and relax for a while. If Annea, Ivy, or the ants didn't turn up within an hour, she'd go looking for them. They might be in their bedrooms right now. She hadn't checked. How long had she been out? Was it even the same day?

She thought through what she could remember of the events following their escape from the Forest in the Sky. She had the vague fever dream memory of her body wrapped in a giant leaf. Ivy's doing, no doubt. Had she single-handedly hauled both her and Annea back to civilization? Serena didn't feel like she'd survived a beating, so healers must have tended to her at some point.

The wooden creak of the main door opening brought her out of her head. Ivy stepped into the communal space and stretched. Leaves grew like feathers on her arms and legs. They rustled as she twisted and turned, cracking her back in a series of loud pops.

"That sounded satisfying," Serena said.

"That table is for eating, not resting," Ivy said, absorbing the leaves into herself as she walked over to take a seat at the head of the table.

"What's with the leaves?" Serena asked, ignoring Ivy's comment and returning her gaze to the ceiling.

"I create extra foliage to better capture light when I need more energy than my skin can absorb on its own. I dragged you and Annea a significant distance before finding anyone who could help. It was not a pleasant experience. That was eighteen hours ago. I still feel weak."

Eighteen hours. They'd be into their third day on Kimori. Serena felt like she'd spent half that time incapacitated.

She let out an appreciative whistle. Between herself and Annea, she estimated Ivy would have been dragging close to three times her body weight. She'd been very wrong to assume dryads were soft, flowery beings. "How did you do it?"

"I improvised sleds out of leaves to reduce friction. I could not move quickly. It took more than an hour to find help."

Serena rolled onto her stomach. She placed her chin in her hands and set her elbows on the table so she could make eye contact with Ivy. "Thanks for the save. I'm sure I would have died if not for you."

Ivy looked away, her cheeks taking on a pink tint Serena took for embarrassment. Why be embarrassed of her heroism? Perhaps she wasn't used to praise. Maybe with fifteen sisters, she blended into the crowd and wasn't used to the personal attention.

Since Ivy hadn't rebuffed her efforts to talk to her so far, Serena decided to take a risk. They needed to clear the air between them. "I'm sorry if this is a sensitive topic, but I have to know." She paused and took a breath. She didn't want to aggravate the woman who'd just saved her life, but they couldn't carry on like they had been. "What is your problem with pyromancy? Every time the subject comes up, you become scared or hostile. Your panic attack in the Forest in the Sky nearly got us killed."

Ivy flinched. Would she remain tight-lipped about her phobia?

Ivy surprised her by answering. "My people almost went extinct because of pyromancers," she said. "Five hundred years ago, a majority-human pyromancer cult known as the Cleansing Flame invaded Ataraxia. Humans can survive on planes with little or no ambient magical energy. Dryads cannot. Because our existence *requires* the presence of magic, we were deemed abominations. They wanted to conquer Ataraxia and purge it of magical creatures. The pyromancers culled our population by ninety percent before we eliminated them. We adopted aggressive breeding goals after that to rebuild our population.

"We see pyromancy as the magic of evil, cruelty, hatred, and destruction. Those who wield it are harbingers of death. Our naughtiest children are told a pyromancer will come and burn them alive if they do not behave. Do you understand now? Your brand of magic murdered my ancestors. You represent everything we are taught to hate and fear."

Serena's eyes watered up. She rolled over and hopped off the table before Ivy could see a pair of rogue tears flowing down her cheeks. It wasn't possible to be liked by everyone. The town guard of Valencia had actively despised her. But never before had Serena experienced someone hating her for a part of herself she had no control over. She hadn't asked to be a pyromancer. She just was. The knowledge that people like her had inflicted so much suffering on others made her sick. No wonder Ivy feared her.

"Have I upset you?" Ivy asked, breaking the silence that settled over their shared living space.

Serena wiped her eyes and faced Ivy. "I appreciate your honesty. I had no idea." She spread her arms wide. "Do I seem evil to you? Have I said or done anything that would make you think I want to hurt you?"

"No," Ivy admitted.

Thank the goddess. She didn't know what she'd say if Ivy had said yes. "I want us to be friends. We've both been through hell. We've lost our homes and loved ones. I'm sure you want to see the Vohr wiped out as much as I do. We need to work together. That's going to be hard if you panic every time I use magic. I promise I'm not your enemy."

"I see that now." Ivy offered her hand, and Serena took it. The dryad's posture relaxed, as if she'd finally freed herself from a major source of anxiety. "I judged you without knowing anything about you. Our people suffered much at the hands of pyromancers. It is not an easy prejudice to overcome."

Acting on impulse, Serena pulled Ivy into a tight hug. Ivy surprised her again by returning the embrace.

"You're a badass, you know that, right?" Serena said. "Intentional or not, it was *your* magic with the *alucinatus* berries that led to discovering the Vohr eye. *You* had the solution to help us track it to the Forest in the Sky. *You* ran with me, without hesitation, into the most dangerous place on this planet, because you knew the Vohr had to be stopped. After everything went wrong, *you* had the strength to haul the dead weight of two grown women back to civilization. I'm honored to know you."

"You flatter me," Ivy said. The pink blush returned to her cheeks as she withdrew from the embrace. "I contributed nothing in the fight against the Sentinels. You made an extraordinary physical sacrifice to buy us a window of opportunity to escape. You did not abandon me to save yourself when you could have. You are an honorable woman. From now on I will judge you on your own merits, and not make assumptions because you are a pyromancer."

"Friends?" Serena asked.

"Friends," Ivy agreed.

The door leading higher into the world tree opened. Annea stepped inside, with Pik-Pik and Tik-Tik following close behind. The queen looked haggard, but smiled at the sight of Serena and Ivy in such close physical proximity. "I take it you two have resolved your differences?" Annea asked.

"We have," Ivy said.

"You knew this whole time why Ivy was afraid of me, didn't you?" Serena asked. "Why didn't you say something?"

Annea raised her hands in a placating gesture. "You're both adults. I expected you to act like it and talk to each other. I'm glad you have. I'd have forced the issue in a few days if you hadn't worked it out on your own." Coming from Annea, *forcing the issue* would probably not mean a fun time for anyone involved.

Pik-Pik and Tik-Tik ran up to Serena. They bounced up and down in a way that reminded her more of excited puppies than insects. She found it strangely adorable. <You're still not dead.>

<It was a close call.>

<We carried you back here when the healers finished with you.>

<They don't like you very much.>

That wasn't a surprise. She'd undone all their hard work almost immediately.

<Do you want to know what they had to heal this time?>

She didn't, but figured they'd tell her anyway, so she nodded for them to get on with it.

<You had brittle bones.>

<Hundreds of micro tears in your muscles.>

<Your kidneys and liver shut down.>

<You burst blood vessels in your eyes.>

<You had internal bleeding.>

<Your aorta was ripping itself apart from the inside out.>

"Stop! I get it." She sensed the ants weren't halfway through the litany of injuries she'd caused herself. "It was a desperate situation. I promise not to make a habit of it." She meant it. Twice in as many days she'd almost destroyed herself. She wouldn't make that mistake a third time.

Annea took the chair Ivy vacated at the head of the table. "Sit down, both of you. We need to talk." Her words held a parental air of *I'm not mad, just disappointed.* The sharp gazes she gave them both reinforced that impression.

"Your antics have caused quite a stir in the community," Annea said. "You've now seen for yourself why the uppermost reaches of the world tree are uninhabited. We don't want anyone venturing into the Forest in the Sky. My people want an explanation, and I intend to give them one. So please explain to me what that eye was and why you two were so hellbent on chasing it."

"We already told you; the eye is a Vohr spying device. It couldn't be allowed to report back what it had seen," Serena said.

"That's only half of the truth. Before we entered the Forest in the Sky, you said *'He can't know I'm here.'* What did you mean by that? Who were you referring to?"

Serena looked into the queen's eyes, seeing the unflinching focus of a predator conducting a threat assessment. Lying to her would be a Very Bad Idea. Annea might think her crazy, but she hadn't planned on keeping Korahshka's threats a secret. Now was as good a time as any to share what she knew. She described everything that happened the night before. "I'm certain it wasn't just a dream. It was far more vivid than anything I've ever experienced. He claimed I'm capable of more magic than pyromancy, but didn't seem to know what that actually means. He wants to steal my powers for himself. I thought if the eye escaped, he'd know I'm here and Kimori would become their next target."

"What did he look like?" Annea asked. Serena described Korahshka. Annea swore. "I'm sorry I asked."

"You know what he is?"

"Unfortunately. It might be easier to show you than tell you." Annea closed her eyes and leaned back as if lost in thought. Silence stretched on for an uncomfortably long time. Pik-Pik and Tik-Tik lay on the ground to either side of her. They'd know if something was wrong with her, right? Ivy looked as uncomfortable as Serena felt. Should they say something?

"My understanding was that the Vohr are a collective of mindless monsters," Annea said at last. "Dangerous as hell, but not very bright. You're telling me they have a command structure, and that their general is a dream walker, a wraith, and some kind of telepath." She looked at Serena and Ivy like they should understand what that meant.

"Could you try that again for those of us who never left our homeworlds until a few days ago?" Serena said.

"Dream walking is the ability to enter and control the dreams of another person. Magic doesn't work across realities though, so I'm not sure how he could reach out to you — through the tunnel, maybe? Telepaths can push speech or thoughts from their mind into someone else's, which must be how he controls the Vohr. Wraiths... Well, the word *wraith* has many meanings across the multiverse, but the one that applies here is a being that consumes the soul of another, acquiring the abilities of the consumed."

"Delightful."

Annea stood, a look of resolve on her face. "We have to proceed under the assumption that Korahshka will eventually notice he's missing a tunnel and figure out that it led here. Your actions bought us time, but it would be foolish to believe we're safe. We must prepare for war."

"No offense, but how do you prepare a bunch of artists and musicians for invasion by fifty flavors of evil?" Serena expected the elves to be the type to evacuate, not stand their ground.

"We live a peaceful existence, it's true, but you'll find there's a lot of steel in our hearts. Don't underestimate the ants, either. Together, we defeated a dragon god. And we won't be alone — I know people who owe me favors. Big, *big* favors." Annea stood and made her way to the stairs leading to her bedroom, pausing about halfway up.

"I doubt Orlan had this situation in mind when he sent you here. I won't think any less of either of you if you wish to return to the Nexus and find a safer place to be. Fate is cruel to place you both in the Vohr's path again."

"I'd rather stay with you," Serena said. "If Korahshka really wants my power, I don't expect him to stop hunting for me. I'm not going to just run and hide. My best bet for survival and revenge is with you."

"I will stand with you as well," Ivy said. "I am not a warrior, but I will support you however I can. I think it is what my sisters would have wanted."

Annea nodded and resumed climbing the steps to her bedroom. "I need to grab something, then we'll take our first step in preparing Kimori's defense. We're going down to the Grand Chamber of Rule, where you'll meet the other queens of Kimori."

CHAPTER 15

THE SWORD OF KIMORI

An hour later, Pik-Pik and Tik-Tik greeted Serena, Annea, and Ivy outside the open doors of the Grand Chamber of Rule. They stared at the floor, their antennae drooped low. If Serena didn't know better, she'd have thought someone kicked them.

<The queens will see you now,> they said, motioning with their heads for the group to step inside. Ivy went in first.

"I'm sorry," Annea said, bending low to stroke their thoraxes. "I never would have asked you to talk to her without me if it wasn't absolutely time-sensitive and vital. You were very brave. I'm proud of you." She stepped into the chamber.

Serena held back. The ants had always seemed happy, as far as she could tell. They weren't now. "Are you two okay?"

<We are not.>

<We had to talk to Mother.>

<Mother hates us.>

<She is very mean.>

Serena stared at them, expecting more. There was always more with these too, but not this time. Not knowing what to say, she patted each on the head and followed her companions into the meeting space.

The Grand Chamber of Rule was a wide hall with two rows of columns, which alternated between wood from the world tree and the cement-like material of the ant hive. Bioluminescent mushrooms and moss grew all over the columns and ceiling, bathing the chamber in light equivalent to thousands of candles. While most of the chamber had natural, organic curves to its design, the rear wall was flat. It featured a mural so breathtaking and violent, Serena didn't even notice the ant queens.

The mural depicted thousands of elves and ants battling Balor in the fields to the north of the Planar Gate. Lightning surged from the dragon's antlers, chaining through dozens of elves, illustrated as silhouettes with exposed skeletons. Blood coated the dragon's golden scales as hundreds of elves and ants crawled across his neck, back, and legs, stabbing with swords or digging in with mandibles. Broken and bleeding bodies of both species littered the ground. Other elven warriors clashed with tall, purple skinned men who looked just like Korahshka. Surely, the mural is what Annea wanted her to see.

The ant queens stood to either side of the mural. Each had a door behind them that led deeper into the colony. They were larger than horses. Each had a gold crown on their head and bands of diamonds around all six legs. Their black carapaces seemed to absorb the light around them, making their jewelry shine brighter from the contrast. Like Pik-Pik and Tik-Tik, they wore gem-studded translation collars around their necks.

<It has been a long time since we had a formal meeting, Annea. What do you wish to discuss?> The queen to their left dipped her head in greeting.

<Was it necessary to send the mistakes as your messengers?> The other queen glared at Pik-Pik and Tik-Tik, her loathing coming through loud and clear in the translation. <Their presence is an insult.>

"Queen Ruta, Pik-Pik and Tik-Tik are my wards, and you will treat them with respect," Annea said. "Someday you'll see they are your greatest successes, not mistakes, mutants, abominations, or whatever other petty insults you're in the mood for."

Pik-Pik and Tik-Tik's antennae waved in silent appreciation of Annea's words. They stood a little taller. Though they still wouldn't look at their mother, they stopped staring at the floor.

"With the pleasantries out of the way," Annea didn't hide her sarcasm, "Queens Chibi and Ruta, allow me to introduce Serena and Ivy. Their worlds were destroyed by various species of monsters known collectively as the Vohr. One of my former apprentices, Orlan, recommended they come to Kimori to share with us their knowledge of the threat the Vohr represent.

"Together, they discovered the monsters had a surveillance presence on our world, scouting us as a target for invasion. We would never have known the threat we face if not for them. Ivy in particular was instrumental in developing a method to detect their spies."

"That is not an accurate representation of my involvement," Ivy said.

Before the ant queens could interrupt with questions, Annea described how they'd chased the Vohr eye to the Forest in the Sky and discovered the tunnel between realities. "We still know little about our enemy, and even less about how they can reach Kimori without using the Planar Gate. We don't know if they'll notice we destroyed their tunnel. If they do, will that make us their next target? Will they move on to easier prey? If they plan to return, how long would it take them to make another tunnel, or tunnels? We must assume the worst and plan accordingly. Serena has informed me that the Vohr act under the direction of an intelligent commander."

At Annea's request, Serena told the ant queens of her experience with Korahshka. When she finished, Annea stepped forward and pointed at the mural. "Based on her description, I am forced to assume Korahshka is a Davoh'rei," she said.

<Impossible,> Ruta said. <We drove them off Kimori with their master millennia ago.>

"What's impossible about it?" Annea asked. "We drove them off. We didn't kill them all."

<They've had thousands of years to invade us since the end of the Lost Epoch. They have not.> Ruta sounded determined to disbelieve everything they said. <Why would they attempt it now?>

"We could speculate all we want, but I don't see that accomplishing anything. We need to deal with the problem at hand."

<If this alleged Davoh'rei dream walker wants the human female, we should hand her over or send her back to the Nexus. You cannot offer her sanctuary here. I forbid it.> Ruta stabbed a foreleg in Serena's direction. Her antennae waved in agitation.

"That would be a knee-jerk reaction," Annea said. "We were already a potential target. Unless you believe the Vohr have informants in the Nexus, there's no way they could have known Serena was coming here. We have to operate under the assumption invasion is inevitable. Since we don't know how much time we have, we should begin preparations right away."

Ruta huffed and stamped her feet like a child throwing a tantrum.

<What would you have us do?> Chibi asked, clearly the more well-mannered of the two.

"We need more drones, scouts, and soldiers," Annea said. "As many as the colony can produce and sustain. Drones will need to fortify the colony and assist with the movement of materials as we build defenses on the world tree."

Annea paused and took a breath. "To give us the best chance at victory, I must resign my position as queen. Queen Chibi, I would ask you to coordinate matters of state with the elven Queens Emeritus until my replacement is chosen. Round up promising candidates and start the trials as soon as possible. Waive the Wandering Decade."

<I don't envy you that chore, Chibi.> Ruta said.

"Sorry to butt in, but this foreigner has a question." Serena gestured to herself. "Annea, what are you thinking? Who says 'prepare for war' and immediately resigns?"

"It is foolish to create a power vacuum at a time of war," Ivy agreed.

Annea placed a hand on Serena's shoulder and offered her a weary grin. "I told you, Kimori's queen is a glorified cheerleader to her people."

"Someone with the skills to take charge if Kimori is threatened," Serena said, brushing off Annea's touch. "I was listening. It sounds to me like you're quitting at the first sign of trouble."

"That isn't what I'm doing." Annea's expression turned sad. "Queens can't leave Kimori during their term. That's one tradition I won't break. We need a strong leader here. But we also need to venture to other worlds to collect on those favors people owe me."

Annea got down on one knee and lowered her head in deference to the ant queens. She reached into the deep pockets of her loose-fitting pants and fished out an ancient-looking tiara fashioned to look like braided vines. "With the consent of the ant civilization, I would name myself the Sword of Kimori." Annea raised the tiara with both hands, as if making an offering to a deity.

<That title hasn't been bestowed upon anyone since before the Lost Epoch.> Chibi stepped forward to tower over Annea. <Are you sure you want this? You understand the conditions and responsibilities that come with that title? We would hold your life in our hands.>

<And I'm quick to dispose of those who displease me.> Ruta cast a meaningful glare at Pik-Pik and Tik-Tik.

"I'm aware of the responsibilities and potential consequences," Annea said. "Do you consent?"

<If you say the Vohr pose a dire threat to this world, I will trust your judgment,> Chibi said. <Your character during your trials, your actions during your Wandering Decade, and your conduct since becoming queen all show your selfless nature. I formally recognize you as the Sword of Kimori.> Chibi bowed and turned her head, touching the tiara with her antennae. It glowed in response to the touch. Chibi stepped back to her original position.

<I don't think you're stupid enough to manufacture a threat as a power play.> Ruta stepped forward and repeated the gesture. <Queen Ruta reluctantly recognizes Annea Vantalos as the Sword of Kimori.> The tiara's glow intensified. <Remember that absolute power can be taken away just as easily as it was granted.>

Annea brushed her hair away from her ears and donned the tiara. A bright flash of light forced Serena to close her eyes. Annea screamed. The smell of burning flesh filled the air. When Serena's vision cleared, she saw wisps of smoke wafting up from Annea's scalp. Pik-Pik and Tik-Tik rushed to her side, but she kept them at arm's length. She swayed back and forth a moment before standing.

<Annea Vantalos, Sword of Kimori, we wish you success on your journey. Return to us swiftly with aid. We shall ensure you still have a home to return to,> Chibi said.

<If you can't find us allies in the Nexus, don't come back,> Ruta said.

Serena hadn't considered going back when Annea offered her and Ivy the choice. It dawned on her now that doing so could be a huge mistake. "We can't go to the Nexus!"

The group stared at Serena, surprised by her sudden outburst. "Are we absolutely sure there aren't any other Vohr on Kimori? When I arrived in the Nexus, they could detect Vohr on Alterra. They immediately shut down all Planar Gate access to it. Nobody else could leave, and no help could be sent. If we try to go to the Nexus and they sense Vohr here, Kimori would be sealed off from the rest of the multiverse forever." She prayed nobody had used the Gate in the last few days, and that it would still work. If it did, that meant the tunnel had appeared after their arrival. Kimori seemed like a lovely place so far, but she didn't want to feel trapped here forever.

<She makes a valid point,> Chibi said.

<The risk is unacceptable,> Ruta agreed.

<An intermediary must be used.>

"An intermediary?" Serena asked, not following.

"She's suggesting we travel to another world and use their Planar Gate to go to the Nexus," Annea said. "We'll keep that in mind, but the Nexus isn't our first destination."

<Where will you go?> Chibi asked.

"The Kingdom of Z'han, on a world called Torbakhal. They're a military powerhouse. They'll have personnel and weapons to spare, and they owe me big time."

"Why is that?" Serena asked.

"I died for them." She said it as if it were as trivial as commenting on the weather, but she couldn't mask the pain that flashed across her face. Annea bowed to the ant queens once more. "Thank you for your support. We'll leave for Torbakhal in the morning." The ants returned her bow, then exited through their respective doors into the ant colony.

Ivy stepped forward, green healing energy at her fingertips. She tried to move the tiara to get a better look at the burned skin on Annea's forehead and temples, but it wouldn't budge.

"It's one of the conditions of the title," Annea said. "*Sword of Kimori* is a title only granted in times of war. This tiara is the symbol of my station. It's welded to my skull until the day I die. Or the war is declared over by unanimous vote of myself, the ant queens, the queen replacing me, and the Queens Emeritus."

"And the other terms?" Ivy ran fingers along the edges of the tiara, soothing and healing burned flesh.

"Hold on, are we just glossing over Annea saying she *died* last time she went to Torbakhal?" Serena asked.

"It's a long walk from the Planar Gate to Z'han. There will be plenty of time for stories," Annea said.

When Ivy finished tending to Annea's burns, they exited the Grand Chamber of Rule. "I now have absolute power over all of Kimori, ant and elf alike. I am the tip of the spear advancing Kimori's interests both within and outside our realm. My word is law. Disobeying my orders would result in a death penalty if I wished to invoke it. Neither of you are citizens of Kimori, so you're exempt from that.

"The power comes with a failsafe. If any of the queens whose power I have usurped think I'm not acting in Kimori's best interests, they can revoke their consent for me to have this title. If they do and I'm on Kimori, I will die. If they did it while I'm elsewhere in the multiverse, I'd die as soon as I returned."

"Queen Ruta made sure you knew she wouldn't hesitate," Serena said.

"There's a reason elf-ant relations run through Queen Chibi." Annea forced a smile. "We have plenty to do yet before we leave. We need to brief the Queens Emeritus and explain the situation to the public. I'm counting on you both to make them understand what we're up against."

Annea led the way back up to the world tree, a picture of confidence and purpose. Serena didn't buy the act. She looked too unconcerned for someone whose life depended on the ongoing approval of the other powers of the realm — one of whom clearly didn't like her.

She suspected Annea would rather walk barefoot across broken glass than visit Torbakhal again. She didn't like that one bit.

PART II
TRIALS ON TORBAKHAL

CHAPTER 16

THE WELCOMING COMMITTEE

As the sun rose over the horizon, Serena sat with her back to the elven half of Kimori's Planar Gate, admiring the beauty of the ant colony and world tree. She'd hoped Kimori would be a place of refuge, where the Vohr threat could be ignored until she'd gained enough control over her pyromancy to hold her own against the monsters. Yet here she was, about the venture off to another world in search of allies to help save Kimori.

I won't let them share Alterra's fate.

After an exhausting day of high speed war planning, she just wanted to get on with it. They'd met with the Queens Emeritus, the four living elves who'd held the title before Annea, where they again shared their Vohr horror stories. Two of the Queens Emeritus would work with Queen Chibi to oversee candidate selection and the trials for Annea's replacement, while the other two would coordinate strategic defense planning with Queen Ruta, using what information Serena and Ivy could provide on the Vohr bestiary. As if that wasn't enough talking, Annea held multiple assemblies for the elf population. They hadn't had to speak at those, and thank the All-Mother for that, but Serena didn't enjoy being used as a prop to drive home Annea's warnings and instructions.

"I will never, ever be a diplomat," she complained after their eighth hour of meetings and assemblies. "This is torture."

"Do not complain," Ivy said, following Annea towards a tree branch designated for agricultural use. "Your work is complete. I must still make hallucinogens." Annea wanted guard pairs patrolling the city at all times, as well as pairs of scout ants with elven riders surveying the surrounding countryside. One person would be under the influence of *alucinatus* berries to scan for Vohr eyes, while the other would be their sober guide. The patrols would destroy any tunnels they found, or call for reinforcements if needed.

Though she couldn't make out the words at this distance, a familiar cadence of back and forth babble drew Serena's attention to the open door into the ant colony. Pik-Pik and Tik-Tik were first to exit, with Annea and Ivy following behind. Both ants were saddled with numerous bags and pouches, but they didn't appear inconvenienced by the weight. Annea wore simple purple garb of the same style as the day they'd met. She had a new set of kukris. Ivy carried only the staff she'd acquired in the Nexus.

"Good morning," Annea said. "How did you sleep?"

"One hundred percent nightmare free," Serena said. "I think you're right about Korahshka needing open tunnels to harass me."

"How long have you been waiting?"

"About an hour." Serena stood, brushing dirt off the seat of her pants. She picked up her bow and the new quiver of arrows she'd set beside the ant-shaped Gate pillar. "A drone was kind enough to escort me through the ant colony. I wanted some time alone."

"That's fair. You've been through a lot. Torbakhal will be a shocker too. Z'han is a human kingdom, but I doubt you've seen anything like it on your world."

"How so?"

"They have a unique way of blending magic with technology," Annea said. "It serves them well, but since most of it requires two species to operate, they don't export their creations to other realities."

"How does something take two species to operate?"

Annea smiled mischievously. "You'll find out soon enough. I wouldn't want to spoil the surprise."

"You're evil." Serena nodded to the mostly-naked dryad. "Is Ivy's wardrobe going to be an issue? Some human cultures are very prudish about exposed skin."

"Green skin always draws eyes," Annea said. "I would know. As for the amount of skin? She'll blend right in. We're the overdressed ones." Annea tapped the brand-new leather vest covering Serena's torso, then walked up to the Planar Gate. Golden light followed Annea's finger as she traced eight symbols in the air. Each completed symbol hovered in place as she moved on to the next. When she'd completed the set, the Gate flashed to life, its signature ribbon of light connecting the two posts. "Shall we?"

Serena stepped through the Planar Gate to find herself in the middle of a dense bamboo forest. The stalks grew at least thirty feet high. Their leaves blocked out much of the midday sun. She didn't know why she'd expected a different world's time would match Kimori's, but the instant shift from sunrise to afternoon lighting unnerved her in a subtle way she couldn't articulate. A narrow dirt path cut through the forest for as far as she could see.

"Welcome to Torbakhal," Annea said as the rest of the party crossed into the new reality. "It's a long hike to Z'han. We'll have to keep a brisk pace if we want to get there before nightfall."

"Shouldn't there be a welcoming committee here, or something?" Serena asked. She did a slow spin to confirm nobody hid nearby.

"Like Kimori, Torbakhal does not have much contact with the greater multiverse," Annea stepped away from the Planar Gate as it shut down. Torbakhal's Gate pillars looked like sedimentary rock layers — a much plainer design than most Serena had seen so far. "We're unlikely to see anyone until we're out of the forest and reach the farmland outside the city's wall." The dirt path was only wide enough for them to walk two across. Serena and Annea took the lead, with Ivy in the middle, leaving the ants in the rear.

If they had a long hike ahead of them, Serena didn't want to spend it in silence. Never waste an opportunity to gather more information. Especially if there's nothing else to do. "Annea, you mentioned you were here before as part of a Wandering Decade, right? What is that?" It seemed like a safer conversation starter than "*How did you die?*"

"Before she can ascend to the throne, every potential queen must complete a Wandering Decade," Annea said. "We visit ten different realities, living in each for a year. Additionally, each must be a plane that hasn't been visited by prior queen candidates. The idea is to give future rulers of Kimori perspective on the greater multiverse, while bringing back knowledge that could benefit our people. Ataraxia was my first stop, Torbakhal and the Kingdom of Z'han were my last."

"You said you died here. Explain." Ivy, direct as always.

Annea looked to the skies as if weighing whether or not she wanted to share that story. Finally, she spoke. "Shortly before my time here ended, I helped broker a peace treaty between the Human-Octari Alliance of Z'han and the fairies of this world, bringing a halt to a war that had raged for centuries."

"If humans and fairies were at war, surely the humans were the aggressors. Why help them?" Ivy asked.

"Rude," Serena said, giving Ivy a wink to show she wasn't offended. Considering what humans did to her world, it wasn't surprising Ivy would think that way.

"The fairies of Torbakhal are not tiny tricksters or keepers of nature's balance," Annea said. "This species is known as Kroen, and they're as tall as you or Serena. They don't know the meaning of words like kindness, benevolence, empathy, or consent."

"Consent?" Ivy asked.

"All Kroen are female. They must mate with a male of another species to reproduce. Their mating process leaves the man a gibbering idiot for the rest of his short life. Given the loss of sanity and dramatically reduced lifespan, Kroen rarely find willing participants. Do I need to elaborate?"

"You do not."

Serena shuddered. That sounded like the recipe for a war that would only end with the Kroen's extinction or humanity's enslavement. "How did you get them to stop fighting?"

"Both sides suffered heavy losses over the years. I brokered a deal neither side liked, but would tolerate to prevent further bloodshed. The Kingdom of Z'han would turn over male criminals to be mates to the Kroen, who would in exchange cease all kidnappings and attacks on human territories. The Kroen got guaranteed reproductive partners, and the humans didn't have to fear random attacks.

"To seal the deal, the warring factions devised a signing ritual brutal enough that each party would feel assured of the other's sincerity if they went through with it. Representatives from each side had to drink a cup of *salamir*. It's a poison that sends your pain receptors into a frenzy. It leaves a victim begging for death in minutes, but takes hours to run its course. Your skin feels like paper ripping itself over and over. Every breath is like inhaling shards of broken glass. Eventually, blood vessels burst, and the lucky ones bleed to death and die ahead of schedule. As the person who brokered the deal, I had to drink the poison, as did the Kroen queen and the king of Z'han."

How vicious must the war have been for that to seem like a reasonable way to ratify a *peace treaty?* "That's horrifying," Serena said.

"Indeed," Ivy shooed a fly away from her face. "How are you alive now?"

"A small number of Kroen have the ability to restore life to the recently deceased. Like the poison, it's an ordeal. I cannot articulate to you what it feels like to feel your soul leave your body, only to be violently stuffed back inside moments later." Annea made a show of checking that her kukris were secure in their sheathes, probably to avoid looking at either of them. "Kroen resurrected the dead, while human healers dealt with the internal injuries caused by *salamir*. Both sides had to cooperate or the whole ritual failed."

Silence descended on the group. What did a kingdom have to endure to chose to willingly sacrifice their own people, even if they were criminals? What crimes merited what amounted to capital punishment? Murder, for sure. But what about getting in a bar fight? Tax evasion? Stealing a loaf of bread? What had Annea seen here to think it'd be an acceptable option?

"Z'han has known sixty years of peace," Annea said, perhaps trying to reassure herself it had all been worth it. "All the same, I'm hoping we don't encounter the Kroen while we're here."

"Do they have orange skin and butterfly wings?" Ivy asked.

Annea came to an abrupt halt, her hands drifting to the handles of her kukris. "Where are they?"

Ivy pointed at a gap between bamboo shoots, where two Kroen hovered in the air near the canopy, staring down at them with swords drawn. The rust and corrosion on their blades was obvious even from this distance.

"The best way to deal with Kroen is to be the bigger bully," Annea said. She shifted her attention to the figures in the air. "We see you up there! Stop following us like timid babies on your first hunt. If you want to talk, get your asses down here. Otherwise, go home."

"Why would we want to talk to you?" The pair fluttered over the dirt path and cut their altitude in half. "We don't appreciate strangers trespassing in our territory." As they got closer, Serena saw they wore necklaces of teeth around their necks. Human teeth. Their clothing was tattered, ill-fitting, and filthy. Their greasy hair looked like it hadn't been washed in weeks. They reminded Serena more of harpies than fairies.

"Cut the crap. This forest and all land up to the Tigris River belong to Z'han by treaty. I doubt the kingdom will take kindly to your intrusion. Fly home while you still have wings."

"We will, but not empty handed. Mother Superior's never going to believe The Deceiver came back."

Serena spun at the sound of bamboo bending and snapping. Another half dozen Kroen weaved their way through the forest behind them. The Planar Gate had a welcoming committee after all. They'd waited to show themselves until the Gate was too far away for an easy retreat, then blocked that escape route anyway. Serena had to admit it wasn't a bad setup for an ambush.

"Would you to prefer to come back with us as living prisoners, or fresh corpses?" the Kroen asked. "We're fine either way."

CHAPTER 17

BATTLE IN THE BAMBOO FOREST

"Deceiver?" Annea unsheathed her kukris. "I didn't think I'd be adding another title to my collection today. It feels like a misnomer though. I never deceived anyone."

Serena reached for an arrow, forsaking any thoughts of using pyromancy. No sense in starting a forest fire. The six Kroen behind them spread out. Two stayed on the path, the other four flew into the bamboo to take flanking positions. Like the lead pair, they looked filthy, ragged, and malnourished.

"You tricked our former queen into making a bad deal! Z'han didn't provide enough males. We killed each other in competition for mates, hurting our population even more. Mother Superior will restore us to glory!"

"I don't know your Mother Superior, but based on the look of you sorry fools, I very much doubt it," Annea said.

"Don't disrespect your betters. Your head will be a fitting addition to Mother Superior's throne."

"Only if you can take it." Annea launched herself at the Kroen doing all the talking.

For a moment, nobody reacted, fairies and foreigners alike stunned at Annea's speed and agility. She shot ten feet forward and fifteen feet in the air to reach her target, whom she decapitated with a single swing of a kukri. With a flip and a twist, Annea landed on her feet, facing back the way she'd come.

The Kroen's head and body crashing to the earth stirred everyone into action. Serena took a shot at the other lead Kroen, hoping to clear the path so they could run. The shot sailed through empty air as her target dived after Annea. She didn't like taking aim at sentient beings, even in self-defense.

A blow to the head cured her of any sentimentality she might have for the mangy fairies. If the Kroen wouldn't play nice, neither would she. Serena staggered forward into several bamboo shoots. She ran a hand through her hair and came back with bloody fingers. A rock whizzed past her head. The Kroen responsible for it fluttered through the bamboo nearby, reloading a slingshot. Knowing she wouldn't be able to return fire in time, Serena dived to the side to dodge the next missile.

A Kroen swooped down to grab one of the ants. She failed to wrap her arms around their thorax, but managed to lift them off the ground by grabbing one of the packs they carried. She didn't get far though, as her intended victim bent their neck back and bit into her skull with their mandibles, crushing it like a ripe melon. A Kroen diving for the other ant peeled off at the sight of the carnage.

Serena dragged herself to her feet. Wood snapped and cracked behind her. Risking a look, she saw Ivy had her staff raised high. The normally rigid bamboo shoots surrounding her rubberized and writhed like a pack of snakes awaiting a command. With a flick of her wrist, Ivy set them loose, forcing Kroen to dive, weave, and roll like mad or get swatted out of the air. Two Kroen crashed into each other in midair. Bamboo stalks hammered them into the ground and clubbed them into a fine paste. Ivy may claim she wasn't a warrior, but she sure had solid instincts for weaponizing nature.

The dryad's attack convinced the pair of Kroen nearest Serena to retreat deeper into the forest. A rock ricocheted off a stalk nearby, missing her cheek by an inch. The other Kroen in the pair carried no weapons. She extended her arms towards Serena, with each thumb and pinkie finger touching its match. Orange energy flowed from her fingertips into a ball between her palms. Knowing an attack when she saw one, Serena dived back onto the path as the fairy unleashed her magic. The ball of energy cut through swaths of bamboo without resistance, hit the ground, and exploded where she'd stood a second before. Dirt and plant matter flew in every direction. Serena rolled to her feet, brushing dirt off her arms, face, and hair.

"Stand down!" Annea shouted, addressing the Kroen. "We've killed half your number. Don't throw your lives away pursuing glory."

A sword-wielding Kroen flew high into the air, turned, and dived. Annea spun away from the trajectory of the attack, crouched, then launched herself twice her own height into the air. Spinning with a dancer's grace, she cut through the fairy's wings as she descended. Unable to decelerate or change course, the Kroen hit the ground with bone-shattering force, twitched twice, then lay still.

"Five dead. I tried to warn you," Annea said.

The Kroen that unleased a magic attack at Serena emerged from the towering bamboo shoots. She had another orb of orange energy ready to fire. Serena shot first. Her arrow scored a direct hit on the energy ball. It exploded on contact, disintegrating the Kroen and blasting apart several rows of bamboo behind her. Divorced from their bases, the severed portions of bamboo clattered to the ground at random angles.

With six of the eight attackers dead, and no real harm done to Serena or her party, the survivors took to the sky and retreated.

"Is everyone alright?" Annea asked, sheathing her kukris.

"I am uninjured." Ivy pointed her staff at the bamboo she'd enchanted. It straightened out and stiffened back into its original form.

"I took a blow to the head, but it's minor. I'll be fine." Serena allowed Ivy to wave a hand over her scalp to heal the wound. She stared at the severed head of the first Kroen. "Are they all like this?"

"No, we got off easy," Annea said. She walked over to one of the ants and planted a kiss on the top of their head. "Tik-Tik! You stood up for yourself! No running away screaming this time. I'm very proud of you."

If an ant could blush, Tik-Tik would right now. Their antennae waved in a mixture of happiness and agitation. <I was so scared. I didn't want her to hurt me.>

"You were very brave."

"This was getting off easy?" Serena asked.

"This group was young and undisciplined. They wore no armor. Their weapons and knowledge of magic were crude, except for that one," Annea pointed to where the magic-using Kroen had disintegrated. "I'd wager they were outcasts looking for a means to curry favor with those in power. They set up camp near the Planar Gate, hoping something of value would come through. Z'han would not have been at war for so long if all Kroen could be defeated so easily."

"What do we do with the bodies?" Ivy asked, gesturing with her staff at the corpses strewn about the trail.

"Leave them," Annea turned her back on the carnage and started walking. "Their bodies will serve as a warning to any other trespassers."

Serena fell in behind the elf, uncomfortable leaving bodies to rot. "You really hate them, don't you?"

"I pitied them, once. Perhaps they're cursed. Their biology doesn't make sense. I don't understand how evolution could demand a species prey on other species like they do to survive. But then I came to know them better. They're the personification of malice. Cruelty is more important to them than self-preservation. The peace treaty was a rare moment where their desire to stave off extinction triumphed over their baser instincts." Annea closed her eyes and took several deep breaths, not needing to see to maintain her balance on the flat and straight dirt path. "The quicker we can convince Z'han to supply us with weapons and troops, the happier I will be."

She hid it well, but Serena saw the tension in Annea's shoulders. Her stride lacked its usual fluidity. The raptor-like intensity of her gaze had softened, as if she couldn't quite give anything her full attention. She kept at least one hand on a kukri at all times. Setting foot on this world was ripping open old wounds for her.

What a merry band of adventurers we are. Serena felt her own grief bubbling to the surface and shoved it back into a dark corner of her mind. *Nope. Not going there today.*

She turned her attention to the ants. If anyone could keep her distracted, it would be those two. "Pik-Pik, Tik-Tik, can I ask you two a personal question?"

<You may ask us anything you like.>

<We have no secrets.>

"I'm sure it's a touchy subject, but... Why is Queen Ruta so mean to you?"

<We are mistakes.>

<Abominations.>

<Mutants.>

<Freaks.>

"Stop that," Annea said. "I've raised you better than that. You are beautiful miracles." She slowed her pace until the ants caught up to her. She patted both on the head, then pulled a flask of water from one of their packs. "Stop repeating your birth mother's slander."

<Yes, Annea.> They bowed their heads, chastised.

The duo turned their attention back to Serena. <As we are sure you have noticed, there are no other red ants on Kimori.>

<When we hatched, Ruta saw our color and did not want us fed in our larval stage.>

<She considered us an unwanted mutation which would harm the colony.>

<Ruta enforces conformity in her brood. She wanted us killed.>

<Annea was touring the hatcheries that day and made an appeal for our lives.>

<Annea took full responsibility for raising us, and agreed we would not interact with other ants unless operating under her orders.>

"Best decision I've ever made," Annea said, offering the flask of water to Ivy and Serena, who each took a pull. "Pik-Pik and Tik-Tik are much smarter than the average drone. Typical drones have little individuality. They exist as an extension of Queen Ruta and Queen Chibi's will. Pik-Pik and Tik-Tik have personalities and can think for themselves. They're quick witted and fiercely loyal. One day, I will get their narrow-minded mother to realize the ants could achieve wonders if all drones were like these two."

Both ants waved their antennae in appreciation of the compliments.

Serena felt better as the ants regaled them with tales of their lives as Annea's assistants. They chattered away for hours, but saved their best story for last. Annea decided to give her friends Inara and Pavi a hard time by letting Pik-Pik and Tik-Tik give them official job interviews to retain their roles as her bodyguards. The ants took great joy in making it as awkward as possible, asking them questions about their hobbies, favorite sex positions, favorite animals, the appropriate number of days to mourn if Annea died horribly, their favorite time of year, their preferred method of execution as punishment for the dereliction of duty that lead to Annea's grisly murder, where did they see themselves in two hundred years... And, of course, if they wanted to assassinate the queen, how would they do it?

"It was so hard not to laugh," Annea said. "They were absolutely inspired. I've never seen Inara and Pavi look so confused. It was a fair test though. Realistically, social awkwardness is the most dangerous thing most elves face," her expression darkened. "That'll change when the Vohr arrive."

If Annea's comment hadn't killed their rising spirits, the view that greeted them when they exited the bamboo forest certainly did. The sun sat low on the horizon. It would disappear within the next hour or so. They stood atop a hill with an uninterrupted view of the countryside all the way to the ocean. The stone wall of the Kingdom of Z'han showed evidence of damage and poor maintenance even from miles away. Built across a peninsula, the kingdom had an outer and inner defensive wall on its inland side, but no apparent defenses against anything coming from the ocean. Four of the ten defensive towers along its length were heaps of rubble.

Fields of corn and wheat filled the distance between them and the kingdom, though there was also grazing land for cattle near the ocean to their right. To their left, a raging river marked the end of Z'han territory, with untamed wilderness on the other side.

Hundreds of farmers working the fields closest to the river raced for the city gates. Explosions of green and orange energy sent plumes of dirt into the air and ignited crops.

Two Kroen fluttered overhead for every Z'han farmer fleeing for their lives.

"They'll be massacred," Serena said.

Where was this great army of Z'han that Annea wanted to recruit?

CHAPTER 18

THE PEOPLE WITH THE OCTOPUS TATTOOS

Annea's hopes that peace had endured disintegrated faster than Z'han's crops. How many years of peace had her death bought? Was Z'han any better off from her efforts, or had it all been for nothing? She'd expected to see a flourishing kingdom, not beleaguered defenses.

Hundreds of people sprinted through the corn and wheat fields towards the open gate to Z'han. Kroen shouted war cries and gave chase. They wore green scale armor designed to absorb the energy discharged by Z'han rifles. Half of them wielded swords, the other half attacked with magic.

"We have to help them!" Serena said.

"Wait." Annea held out an arm to stop Serena from charging into the fray. Something about the situation felt odd. Farmers usually worked in teams when tending their fields. Safety in numbers. These people were spread too far apart, and they maintained that distance as they fled. It looked too disciplined — not at all what she'd expect from terrified civilians. "There's a world of difference between fighting in self-defense and charging into a military engagement."

"I see no military," Ivy said.

"I think you will in a moment," Annea said.

Supposedly vacated corn and wheat fields rippled with movement. Moments later, the sky flashed with the intensity of a monsoon season thunderstorm. Rifle fire lanced up from the ground into the unsuspecting Kroen. Their opening salvo killed dozens before the Kroen raised protective shields of blue energy around themselves. It took Annea's eyes a few seconds to adjust to the brightness enough to tease out the well-hidden forms of soldiers in the fields. Had they used their own people to bait a trap?

Under the relentless torrent of fire, the Kroen's shields shattered like glass. Their armor only saved them for another second or two before becoming overwhelmed. True to form, the fairies continued hurling explosive energy at any human they could see, prioritizing slaughter over their own survival.

Wood snapped and cracked as dozens of trees collapsed on the far side of the river, revealing a half dozen mechanical walkers hidden under the canopy. Each walker had two cockpits, one for a human pilot, the other a water-filled capsule for their Octari. The bipedal constructs stepped into the river and opened fire with projectile weapons attached to main arms the human pilot controlled. Eight slender arms fanned out from the walker's back. Each of those independently tracked and shot Kroen with an energy beam more powerful than the standard infantry rifle.

These death machines were new. New was bad. New meant Z'han felt threatened enough to develop even deadlier weapons than they'd had sixty years ago. Such complex constructs would have taken years to design and perfect. Was the whole peace treaty a sham? Had there been any meaningful break in hostilities?

The Kroen dived to bring the fight to closer quarters. Sudden, strong updrafts of hot air kept them from descending to within ten feet of the ground. The army of Z'han took ruthless advantage of their enemy's confusion, pouring fire into one fairy after another. Their constructs forded the river to assist with mopping up the remnant.

"We can advance now, this will be over soon," Annea said. Serena was right. It was a massacre, just not the one she'd expected. "Keep your arms held out to your sides, palms front. Kroen never show enemies empty hands, so it's the easiest gesture to avoid potential misunderstandings."

"Our lack of butterfly wings isn't enough?" Serena asked.

"Scared soldiers with itchy trigger fingers can make poor snap decisions. Especially with the adrenaline pumping after a battle like this," Annea said, thinking of close calls she'd had with the Z'han army on reconnaissance missions. "Therefore, we should look as nonthreatening as possible as we approach." She started off down the hill, choosing her footing carefully on the steep slope.

The few remaining Kroen went into suicide warrior mode. Some of them conjured balls of energy twice their size and hurled them at Z'han's massive death machines. Most of their attacks were hit with rifle fire and exploded prematurely, incinerating any Kroen in the area, but one survived the shots fired into it and plowed into a walker. It exploded with a deafening boom, sending shards of metal flying in all directions. Moments later, there was a secondary explosion as whatever powered the thing detonated.

Other Kroen cut each other's wings off, allowing them to plummet under the strong updrafts so they could fight at ground level. Armed only with their energy rifles, the Z'han soldiers weren't prepared for melee combat. But at that point, it didn't matter. Z'han's greater numbers cut down their remaining enemies with ruthless efficiency.

The fighting concluded by the time the travelers from Kimori reached the base of the hill. Annea and her party approached the main gain through a lane between wheat fields, trying to make their presence as obvious and nonthreatening as possible.

Two men approached as they neared the main gate. Neither wore a shirt, but Z'han men rarely did. The legs of their loose-fitting cloth pants stopped above the knee. Each had a holstered pistol and baton strapped to their waist. Both had a lifelike depiction of an octopus covering the majority of their chests, which looked like white body paint over dark skin.

It wasn't body art, of course.

But she wasn't about to tell Serena or Ivy that.

"You've come at a bad time, travelers. State your business," the older of the two said.

"Greetings, I am Annea, queen of Kimori." That was a lie, but it would be easier for strangers to understand than the nuances of her new title. "I travel with Serena and Ivy, refugees under my protection. Pik-Pik and Tik-Tik are my stewards," she gestured to each in turn. "We seek a meeting with your king. I apologize for our unfortunate timing. I thought the war between the Human-Octari Alliance and the Kroen was over."

"Over?" The younger of the pair, most likely a teenager, looked at Annea like she'd crawled out from under a rock. "We've been at war my whole life!"

"Relax Kendrik, don't embarrass yourself," the older man stepped forward, an early hint of gray peppering his hair. He studied her as if checking her appearance against an image in his memory. "Did you skip *all* of your lessons? Annea is the reason your dad lived long enough to meet your mom. If she wants to meet with the king, we'll see that she does." He bowed. "My name's Darius."

His words implied that while the peace was gone, there *had* been a time of peace. It hadn't all been for nothing. "How long has the fighting been going on, Darius?" Annea asked. "Have we met before? You don't look old enough to have been alive during my first visit to Torbakhal."

"There are many paintings in your honor across the kingdom, celebrating the peace you helped us achieve. It lasted almost forty years, but the fighting's been going on long enough now that an entire generation of young men like Kendrik have grown up never knowing peace." He gestured for them to follow him through the main gate. They filed in amidst several groups of soldiers wearing suits of wheat stalks or corn leaves as camouflage. Everyone else in sight wore only shorts and shoes. Women had their chests wrapped.

Everyone had an octopus covering their skin.

"You used your own people as bait," Ivy said.

"Volunteers only," Darius said. "We've spent weeks cultivating an air of social dysfunction, hoping to bait in a swarm like that. This victory should give us a couple months of breathing room before they try anything again."

"How big are their numbers?" Annea asked. "How big are *yours*?"

Darius spoke candidly. "We're hurting. Our population has declined every year since the war reignited. As I'm sure you've noticed, that makes defending and maintaining the kingdom... challenging. We've had to become more unconventional with our tactics."

They moved to the side of the road to make way for a caravan of mounted horses leaving the city. Each horse pulled behind it a wagon holding a sealed container of water with a hose attachment, which they'd use to douse the fires in the fields. Their rapid pace indicated they expected people to move or get run over.

Unlike the outer wall, the interior of Z'han looked much like Annea remembered it. Wide cobblestone roads allowed for the easy movement of troops, materials, and Z'han's new walking war machines. This close to the gate, all buildings would be martial in nature, storing weapons and ammunition. Past that stood rows of blocky, windowless stone buildings that served as factories for the production of energy weapons and other tools of war.

"Why does everyone have an octopus on them?" Serena asked. "Are those tattoos? Body paint? They're incredibly realistic."

"Neither," Kendrik said, "they're Octari."

"Ok... so what's Octari?" Serena shrieked and jumped like a startled cat when the octopus across Kendrik's chest *moved*. It crawled across his skin to reposition itself on his back, facing her. A single tentacle pushed out from the teen's body, transitioning from two-dimensional art into physical flesh as it did so. It tapped Serena on the shoulder before she could jump out of range, waved, and retreated back onto the boy's body to become flat once more.

"*That's* an Octari. There's no need to be afraid, Derek just wanted to say hi."

"Derek? The magical octopus is named *Derek*?" Her initial shock gone, Serena stared at Kendrik's back with undisguised fascination.

"Some Octari prefer to take human names since they're easier for us to pronounce," Darius said. "My partner's name is Pythagoronaughtusvantarialtero."

"Derek's a fine name," Serena leaned forward to examine Derek. As she leaned from side to side, the two-dimensional creature mirrored her movements. "I have so many questions. Can he talk? Do you feel it when he moves? How does he shift from flat to, well, to being *real*."

Annea smiled. Serena's reaction to the Octari closely matched her own when she'd first learned the creatures were living beings, not body art.

"Our relationship with the Octari is complex," Darius said. "If you'd like, after your group meets with the king, I could ask one of the palace stewards to give you a more detailed account of our history and symbiotic relationship."

"I'd love that!" Serena radiated a sense of childlike wonder. She held out a hand near Kendrick's back. Sensing what she wanted, Derek extended a tentacle to give her palm a gentle smack before flattening out against the teen's body again. Anything that could make the young woman smile and take her mind off the horrors of the last several days was a blessing.

Ivy cast Annea an accusatory glare. "You did not tell us about the Octari on purpose."

"Guilty," Annea admitted. "You wouldn't want me to ruin all the multiverse's surprises, would you?"

"I would not object."

After several blocks, they reached an open plaza with a large fountain in the center. Within the rectangular pool, three Octari sculptures had their tentacles pointed at various angles. Water flowed from the tips of their limbs. Young boys and girls ran through the water, laughing and splashing each other. Older men and women sat at the edge, some without an Octari on their skin. Their partners had detached to go for a swim.

"Is that volleyball?" Serena pointed to a deeper pool connected to the fountain, which had a net strung up across it. A human versus Octari game was in progress, with two men and a woman playing against their partners. The Octari could not reach high and spike the ball like a human could, but with eight limbs, they proved adept at reaching the ball no matter where the humans tried to place it. The human team struggled to slosh through the water fast enough to respond to the Octari's expertly placed hits.

"It is," Darius said. "Every once in a while, Octari need exercise in their physical form. We find play helps strengthen the bond between Octari and host."

"Host?" Serena asked.

"The person wearing them in their two-dimensional form."

"How can anyone play while your kingdom fends off an attack?" Ivy asked, her eyes on the farmers and soldiers dispersing throughout the city. Several sported severe burns from close proximity to explosions.

"When you've been at war for as long as we have, and suffered what we have suffered, you learn to make the time for entertainment and joy. The alternative is to go insane." He pointed to a rack of rifles standing within a couple paces of the pool. "We're always ready to fight at a moment's notice."

As they neared the palace, Annea noticed more and more eyes on their group. Two green-skinned beings, a fully clothed human, and a pair of giant ants would be quite the sight to people who had little interaction with the Nexus or civilizations from other realities. She was used to the attention, having been stared at plenty over the course of her Wandering Decade. After being away from Z'han for sixty years, she hadn't known what kind of reaction to expect upon her return. How many people would even remember her?

Annea forced herself to focus as they climbed the hundred stone steps to the palace's front doors. Z'han wasn't the peaceful kingdom she'd hoped it would be. Here they were, struggling to survive, and she'd come looking to syphon off weapons and troops for a war of her own — resources they wouldn't be pleased to part with. Perhaps *couldn't* part with.

She'd find out very soon just how grateful the kingdom was for those forty years of peace...

CHAPTER 19

THE KING OF Z'HAN

They entered the palace through massive hardwood doors featuring carved depictions of humans and Octari. The doors opened on an unfurnished chamber large enough to house a thousand people for a banquet or ball. Everything in sight was white marble, from the floors and support columns to the steps at the back leading up to the second floor and throne room. Doors along the sides of the hall led to the kitchen, pantries, wine cellars, and servant's quarters. Larger doors to the left and right of the steps were open and led to a courtyard.

Despite the palace's importance, the entry hall stood virtually undefended. The people of Z'han had no fear of an attack from within, and knew the Kroen would have to go through many waves of defenders to get to this point. A lone guard stood at attention inside the door. The vast space was otherwise uninhabited.

"Is King Lordran available?" Darius asked. "He has guests from another world here to see him."

The guard looked to Annea, eyes going wide with recognition. "He is in the throne room. Wait a moment while I see if he's available to see you." Without waiting for a response, the young guard took off across the hall, up the stairs, and into the throne room.

They didn't have to wait. The onyx and gold doors to the throne room opened by the time the rest of them reached the stairs. "Space is limited," the guard said apologetically. "I'm afraid your stewards will have to wait outside." Kendrik and Darius said their farewells and returned to their posts, while Annea, Serena, and Ivy went inside. Pik-Pik and Tik-Tik took up guard positions outside.

The founding king of Z'han believed public business should be conducted out in the open, and so deliberately designed the throne room to be suitable for little more than small private meetings. The average bedroom in an inn had a larger footprint that Z'han's throne room. Each wall had a mural depicting a moment from the kingdom's history. There was the moment humanity and the Octari cosigned the Declaration of Unity, establishing their intent to live together as a united society. Another depicted Z'han's first contact with Torbakhal's merfolk.

"Annea... That's you, isn't it?" Color drained from Serena's face as she pointed at the mural covering the back wall. This one was new. Once again, *new* meant *bad*. Gone was artwork representing Z'han's discovery of their Planar Gate. In its place was a depiction of the peace treaty signing which marked the end of hostilities with the Kroen, breathtaking in its brutality... and accuracy. Annea's stomach twisted at the sight of it. This was no idealized scene of enemies sitting across the table from each other, sipping tea and signing a document. No, it explicitly depicted the horror of the ritual, with Annea, King Ethys of Z'han, and Queen Tilanda of the Kroen all sprawled out, dead on the ground as blood leaked from their eyes, ears, and noses, staining the surrounding grass crimson. White, ghost-like figures representing their souls hovered over their bodies, each wearing a different expression of anguish and misery.

Annea wanted to stab her kukris into it. Repeatedly.

They'd done what they had to. To glorify it like this felt obscene.

King Lordran sat on a throne of intricately carved wood which depicted humans and Octari building the kingdom's defensive walls. Both races held hammers or stone in their respective limbs. "Queen Annea," the king nodded in respect as he set down a stack of papers on a small table beside the throne. "I did not expect to see you again in my lifetime. You've barely aged at all."

"And you've managed to live a full life," she replied, trying to reconcile the man in front of her with the Lordran she'd known. He'd been a ten year-old boy when she last saw him, an energetic youth third in line to the throne, whose insatiable curiosity led him to bombard Annea with questions about the multiverse. Now in his seventies, he looked frail, with thinning white hair and little muscle hanging on his bones. A stiff breeze could knock him over. He wore no crown — the ornate walking stick propped up against the throne served as his symbol of rule, a gold Octari handle with its limbs wrapping around a shaft of redwood.

"Aye, and more than half of it at peace, thanks to you." He paused. "My apologies about the artwork. It was my father's idea. He felt depicting the truth of the ritual would make clear that the peace agreement was a brave act to establish a brighter future, not a cowardly retreat from the fight."

"King Ethys faced a lot of criticism for the decision. It makes sense he'd want others to understand the sacrifices involved," Annea said diplomatically. Ethys had been a stubborn asshole with too much pride and a fixation on glory. Of course he'd want to appear the martyr over an event he hadn't organized or negotiated. His involvement had been participatory at best. At least he *had* gone through with it, in the end.

"What brings you back to our war-torn corner of the multiverse?" Lordran asked, turning the conversation away from his father and the struggles of the past.

Annea braced herself, anticipating her request for military aid would not be well received. "My world faces imminent invasion," she said, "from a monstrous force that has already destroyed over three hundred worlds. I have come to you seeking military assistance to bolster our defenses."

King Ethys, were he still alive, would have laughed in her face. *"The pacifist wants to play at war now, does she?"*

His son had more tact. "What makes you think we have any resources to spare? We're warring against beings with no sense of self-preservation, who seem able to largely shrug off losses like the blow we've dealt them today."

"I was not aware of your situation when we arrived," Annea said. "I gave your father Kimori's Planar Gate address when I left, you know. How could I know you were at war when nobody ever contacted us?"

"Why would we? I still remember the bedtime stories you told me as a child, Annea. The people of Kimori don't involve themselves in the affairs of other realities."

"The mural behind you suggests otherwise," Ivy said.

Annea clenched her teeth to suppress a bitter laugh.

Lordran turned his attention to the dryad, fixing her with a disapproving glare. "I don't believe we've met."

"My name is Ivy. The Vohr destroyed my world. Kimori will meet the same fate if you do not provide support."

Thanks for the vote of confidence, Annea thought.

Unprompted, Ivy and Serena described their experiences with the Vohr. Ivy spoke in a detached, near-monotone voice, narrating her experiences as if they happened to someone else. She spoke in broad terms and never mentioned her sisters. Serena, whether she intended it or not, fed on Ivy's energy. Like one hunter speaking to another, Serena described the manti's anatomy, behaviors, and attack patterns. To Lordran's credit, he paid close attention and didn't interrupt.

"I wouldn't be asking if our needs weren't dire. I died for this world," Annea said. She hated to play the guilt card, but she wouldn't let pride hold her back from pulling every possible lever to ensure her appeal's success. "Surely four decades of peace is worth something."

A far-away look came over the king's eyes while he consulted his Octari partner.

"Octari and their hosts communicate telepathically," Annea whispered to Serena and Ivy, not wanting either of them to speak into the awkward silence and interrupt the king's deliberations.

"Linneasorbolorenti says we'd dishonor ourselves if we don't make a sacrifice for you in your time of need, after the sacrifices you made for us." Lordran gestured to the Octari centered on his chest. "We have nine Shrike units in service, and three more nearing completion. I can loan you two, with their human and Octari pilots. That's the best I can do. We don't have conventional troops to spare anymore."

"Shrikes? Are those the tall mechanical walkers we saw fording the river as we approached?" Annea asked.

"Indeed, but there's a catch."

"Of course there is," Annea sighed, rubbing her forehead.

"Come with me," Lordran stood, grabbed his walking stick, and escorted them down the stairs. Annea gestured for Pik-Pik and Tik-Tik to stay put. The king led them around the corner, through the doors leading to the courtyard.

Two Shrikes stood in the middle, facing a large metal gate that served as a side exit to the palace. Z'han's newest bipedal death machines stood fifteen feet tall. Legs as thick as tree trunks supported a barrel chest that gradually tapered towards the cockpits at the top. The human's cockpit occupied the top third of the machine's torso, while the water-filled Octari cockpit sat above and behind it, like someone had replaced a head with a fishbowl. The eight thin arms on the back that the Octari controlled were folded up like a closed umbrella. The human-controlled arms ended in multiple rifle barrels welded around a fixed point. Annea suspected they rotated at a high speed while discharging projectiles. Bullets? Flechettes?

Z'han technology usually looked like a marriage of human practicality with Octari elegance. Not the Shrikes. She'd never have imagined the Octari would participate in the creation and use of such brutal, ugly, and merciless machines.

"These are the units I would loan you," Lordran said. Both were powered down and undergoing maintenance by a human and Octari pair. The humans worked on the unit's legs or arm guns, while their Octari crawled around on the machine's back checking all the arm connections. Lordran circled around to the rear of the constructs. A hatch door hung open where the base of the shoulder blades would be on a person. Inside the hatch, they could see a mold meant to fit a sphere-shaped object triple the size of a volleyball. "Shrikes are powered by leviathan pearls, which are extremely dangerous to acquire, and our supply is so exhausted that we can't run all the Shrikes we've built. We have a task force sailing out tomorrow to hunt for more. Unfortunately, we need all the help we can get on hunts like these, so I'll never pass up an opportunity to give the navy some extra hands. Join them and assist in acquiring us more pearls, and you can take these units and a generous supply of pearls and ammunition with you back to Kimori."

"Are they called leviathan pearls because they're huge?" Serena asked.

"Or because they must be ripped from the body of a giant sea-dwelling monster," Ivy said.

"Giant, sea-dwelling monster, of course!" The Shrike technicians said in unison, laughing as they set down their tools and turned to face the group. One male, one female, they had the striking similarity of features that could only mean a close familial relationship. Twins? Both had tan skin, dark hair pulled back in ponytails, and toned physiques that would be the envy of Kimori's finest gymnasts and acrobats. They looked to be around the same age as Serena and Ivy. Their Octari crawled to the edge of their walker's shoulders and jumped off, turning two-dimensional and flowing across their human's skin on impact.

"Meet Amara and Cole Morgan," Lordran said, "my eldest grandchildren. They'll be sailing with you on the *Lord Biga.*"

Z'han's war was going poorly. The Shrikes and the use of their own people as bait spelled that out nice and clear. And now the king offered his *grandchildren* for her use? Did he think they'd be safer away from the kingdom? "I'm honored and humbled by your offer of assistance, Your Highness, but are your grandchildren really the Shrike pilots you'd want to send back with us to Kimori? I can't in good faith promise it'll be a two-way trip," Annea said. Did he think they'd be safer away from the kingdom? If so, he hadn't listened to Serena or Ivy after all.

"They are the finest Shrike pilots in the kingdom," Lordran said. "They'll serve you well, and I want people I can trust reporting back to me on the true scope of this Vohr threat."

Amara and Cole exchanged a confused glance, not understanding what they'd been volunteered for.

Annea set aside her concern for Lordran's grandchildren and considered her more immediate problem. Should she take the king up on his offer? She'd seen the Shrikes in action. Each would be worth a thousand archers, if not more. Their firepower would be invaluable against swarms of manti. But could Z'han really spare even two of them?

What was the better use of their time? Humoring King Lordran and helping Z'han collect pearls, or calling this trip a loss and heading to the Nexus? She considered everything she knew about the Kroen and the Vohr and decided Z'han stood a better chance of survival without two Shrikes than Kimori did. They needed these weapons.

"Ivy's magic is plant-based, Serena is a pyromancer, and I specialize in melee combat. I'm not sure what assistance we can provide out at sea, but if you want us to join the hunt, we'll be there," Annea said.

"Excellent," Lordran said. "I'll have Captain Karrde meet with you at the docks tomorrow morning to give you a briefing before the ship departs." He turned to begin the trip back to the throne room. Everyone else fell in behind him.

"One more thing," Lordran said, pausing to tap Serena on the shoulder with his walking stick. "Your pyromancer will need to host an Octari for the entire trip. That's non-negotiable."

From Serena's expression, you'd think Lordran just slapped her. "You want me to play skin jockey to an Octari? Why?"

What was the matter? She'd been fascinated by them not that long ago. What changed?

"Don't take it personally," Lordran said. "Pyromancers have a reputation for leaving destruction in their wake."

"Indeed," Ivy agreed.

Serena scowled. "Don't help him."

"I will not accept the danger pyromancy could pose to the task force if not managed properly." Lordran resumed his slow walk back to the throne room. "Octari are masters of water magic. They'll keep her from blowing up the ship."

Serena glared daggers at the king's back, but said nothing.

"It'll be fine," Annea said, still caught off guard by Serena's change in attitude. "Octari are very nice. You'll probably enjoy the experience."

"I doubt it," Serena said.

"We'll discuss it in private." Annea didn't want to force Serena to cooperate, but would push it if she had to. Host an Octari, or be left behind. The king's stipulation wasn't unreasonable.

The real trial, as she saw it, would be figuring out how they'd contribute in a battle against a sea monster.

CHAPTER 20

A MEETING OF THE MINDS

The argument started the instant the door closed.

"I'm not doing it," Serena said, alone with Annea in one of the palace's guest quarters.

"May I ask why?" Annea leaned against a wall, arms crossed over her chest.

Flames danced across Serena's clenched fists. "Is it really such a mystery? Korahshka raped my mind in my sleep and you expect me to just cozy up to another being who can read my thoughts? I'm not doing it. You don't get to make that choice for me."

The idea of having an Octari draped over her body made her skin crawl. Her mind was her own, off limits to anyone else.

Annea blew out a breath and struck a conciliatory tone. "I'm sorry. I should have remembered. Coming back here has dredged up a lot of bad memories. I haven't been thinking as clearly as I need to."

"I don't care how rattled you are. You don't get to rent out my brain."

Annea's expression hardened. "You've seen what the Shrikes can do. You'd know even better than I how useful they'd be against manti. If the king wants you to host an Octari for a couple days, that's a price worth paying."

"You're not the one who has to pay it!" The flames coating Serena's fists shot up her arms. It took every ounce of self control she possessed to snuff them out before she incinerated another shirt, but she wasn't fast enough to prevent a few holes from appearing on her sleeves.

"Your fear springs from ignorance," Annea said.

"Have you ever hosted an Octari?" Serena asked.

"I haven't, but I've spoken to them mind-to-mind several times. They're nothing like Korahshka. Their relationship with their hosts is symbiotic, not parasitic. They're almost too kind and pure to be real."

"Fine, then you host one."

A knock at the door interrupted the argument. Annea opened the door to allow a woman inside. She looked to be in her late forties or early fifties. In typical Z'han fashion, she wore a band around her chest, leaving her midriff exposed and her Octari easy to see. "My name is Zalinda. You could say my partner and I work as matchmakers to establish successful pairings between human hosts and Octari partners. We've got the perfect partner picked out for you. He's very excited, and can meet with you now, if you're ready."

"I'm not doing it," Serena said.

"Why?" Zalinda stared at her with hurt in her eyes, like she'd been personally insulted. Like the refusal humiliated her in a way Serena couldn't even begin to understand.

"I'm not having this argument again. King Lordran asks for too much. If everyone onboard the ship is partnered with an Octari, why do I need one too? It sounds like the *Lord Biga* has more than enough people around to snuff out one pyromancer's accidents."

Annea sighed. "You don't know what you're turning down, Serena. But if you're determined to stand your ground on this, I'll speak with King Lordran in the morning and try to work something out."

"Tako's going to be devastated." Tears flowed down Zalinda's cheeks. She wiped them away, never breaking eye contact with Serena. "Would you at least talk to him before you make that decision? It would mean a lot to him. And me." Her Octari extended a limb to wipe away a rogue tear Zalinda missed.

That simple gesture made Serena reconsider. Everything she'd seen so far suggested a friendly relationship between the humans of Z'han and their Octari partners. Nobody seemed dissatisfied with the arrangement. If Octari manipulated people for their own sinister purposes, they were doing a masterful job of hiding it.

"Why do you care?" Serena hated the harshness in her voice. Zalinda hadn't done anything to her to deserve that. She tried again. "I can see you're upset. I don't understand why."

"The Octari we've chosen for you was my brother's partner," Zalinda said, a plea in her eyes.

Was. The past tense hung heavy in the air. Serena didn't want to pile onto whatever pain she was witnessing. This was personal. If she refused to meet this Octari, Zalinda would take it as an insult to her brother. Possibly as an indictment of her own professionalism too, acting as a matchmaker.

Silence dominated the room. Serena closed her eyes and fought to wrestle her anxiety under control and silence the part of her mind screaming DANGER, DANGER, DANGER. Did she trust in her ability to discern a genuine threat? Yes, she did. Did she think Annea treated people like tools to be used and discarded to get what she wanted? No, she didn't.

The ragged panic threatening to overpower her dimmed to a general unease. She could live with that. For now.

"Fine. I'll meet him. Lead the way," Serena said, agreeing mostly for Zalinda's sake. "But that doesn't mean I'll agree to be a host."

Zalinda flashed her a radiant smile. "You won't regret this. I promise."

Serena looked towards Annea, expecting some final admonishment to be a host and not jeopardize their mission. Annea just sat down on the bed and took off her boots, looking far too confident things would turn out the way she wanted.

Zalinda led Serena down a series of empty hallways, lit through a combination of candles and twilight sun filtering in through openings in the rough stone walls. The level of advancement Z'han showed with their weapon technologies didn't seem to carry over to their architecture.

They walked in silence for a few minutes before Serena couldn't take it any more. "What's it like to host an Octari?" She asked, falling into her standard routine when she felt nervous. Ask questions. Gather information. If she focused hard enough on that, she wouldn't have to think about anything else.

"It's difficult to describe," Zalinda pushed open a heavy wood door that led to a spiral staircase. She put one hand on a railing for balance as they worked their way down uneven steps. "The host and partner bond is the most emotionally intimate and fulfilling relationship there is. I've been married for over twenty five years. My husband is an empathetic, caring, wonderful man. We have three children together. But he'll never know me as well as Pachikaranokozinaya does."

"What do the Octari get out of the arrangement?" If they wanted to call it a partnership, then the Octari must benefit too.

"Torbakhal's oceans are violent and dangerous. Even with war raging, it's safer for Octari to spend the majority of their lives partnered with a human than it is to dwell below the waves. And believe it or not, they enjoy our company."

The staircase ended at an unadorned door leading outside. They picked their way across rocks to reach a dock that extended fifty feet into the ocean. Zalinda stopped short of the dock. "I'll wait for you here. Take all the time you need. Everyone's first conversation with an Octari is… intense. It's normal to experience big emotions. Don't fight it. Octari never violate someone's consent. He won't take your mind anywhere you're unwilling to go."

"He's here? I don't see anything." Serena said.

"You will. Go all the way to the end."

Half expecting she'd be dragged underwater the second she looked into the ocean, Serena did as asked. She walked past more than a dozen wooden pillars holding the dock in place, many of which showed signs of weathering. At least the planks under her feet felt solid. At the far end, she looked down, seeing only her own reflection on the dark water.

"Hello?" Talking to the ocean felt stupid.

Tempting fate, she got down on her stomach and put a hand in the water. When nothing grabbed it and yanked, she sloshed her hand around for a moment before pulling it out.

She damn near jumped off the dock when she felt the tap on her shoulder. The Octari had perched himself atop the last wooden pillar on the left, his skin color and texture matching the wood so perfectly it rendered him almost invisible. Had he been there the whole time? As if sensing her alarm, the Octari's skin shifted to a lemon yellow, making him far easier to see. He held out a tentacle, but didn't touch her again.

It was an invitation. She needed to meet him halfway. He wouldn't talk to her unless she wanted him to. Serena thought a prayer to the All-Mother and extended her hand. He wrapped a limb around her wrist firmly enough to hold his grip, but not so tight she couldn't free herself. He remained fully three-dimensional.

Suddenly, her mind wasn't hers alone anymore. She sensed a masculine presence that felt indescribably alien, but not hostile. Diffuse, as if parts of his mind existed in multiple places at once. Serena sensed happiness. Curiosity. Playfulness. His consciousness glided over the top of hers like soap bubbles over water. Her brain tingled.

"Hi there, hello! My name is Takoyakisobaramaki, but you can call me Tako." His voice managed to convey youthful exuberance and grandfatherly kindness at the same time. Like someone who had grown old, but never grown up. His presence swelled in her mind, then abruptly pulled back. *"You're terrified to be having his conversation."* He loosened his grip on her wrist.

"I am," Serena admitted. "This isn't the first time this week someone else accessed my mind. They weren't kind about it."

"How do you wish to proceed?" Tako asked. His skin rippled through a rapid succession of colors and patterns. Blue with green stripes. Green with yellow swirls. Yellow with black flecks. Black with pink dots. What did that mean? Was he nervous too?

"Tell me something about yourself?" Serena said. "If you're going to be attached to me for days, I think it's fair to know who I'd be dealing with."

"Certainly. What would you like to know?"

"For starters, why was Zalinda so upset when I told her I had no desire to partner with an Octari?"

"I was her brother Zedrick's partner for the final four years of his life. After his death, I returned to the ocean, awaiting my call for a new partner. Years later, it has never come. There are many more Octari available to serve as partners than there are human hosts. Most humans

don't want to start a new partner relationship with an old Octari. I've outlived both humans I've partnered with, which shouldn't happen. Most Octari have just one host their entire life. Perhaps I'm considered bad luck. Damaged goods." Tako's cheerful equanimity belied the sad weight of his words. He could have been discussing the weather.

"After Zedrick died, his wife couldn't bear to talk to me. My presence only brought her pain. And I'll be dead before their son is old enough to host. Zalinda is a good friend though. She still talks to me. I'd wager she thinks this is my last chance to ever partner with a human again. She may be right. Even if it's only for a few days, I would love to have that opportunity."

She had absolutely no sense he was trying to guilt her into hosting him. Just the opposite — she felt he'd much rather return to the ocean than partner with an unwilling host. Zalinda had said Tako would be devastated if she turned him down. That wasn't true. Any emotional manipulation happening here came from Zalinda, not Tako.

Serena's imagination conjured up images of dogs at an animal shelter, awaiting adoption. The cuter, younger dogs always got picked up first. Older dogs struggled to find loving homes. Her mental image shifted to that of a shady elder care facility, where grandparents were left to rot as their families moved on with their lives. Both metaphors felt appropriate in their own ways. How was Tako so calm about it?

"What happened to Zedrick?" Serena asked.

"Do you always ask people you've just met about the worst day of their lives?" Tako's voice held a note of gentle reproach.

Serena's face flushed. Every once in a while, her need to know things led to her putting her foot in her mouth. Of course he wouldn't want to talk about that. Just like she didn't want to keep explaining what happened to Alterra.

She apologized and tried a different tactic. "How about more open-ended questions? What's it like to be an Octari? What do you think is most important for a new host to know about you?"

Tako physically couldn't smile, but his presence in her mind brightened. His skin shifted color to a calming shade of purple.

"Much better questions. But to give you the best answer, I'll need to strengthen the connection of our minds. Would that be acceptable?"

Nothing he'd said or done thus far gave her bad vibes, so decided to take the risk. "Go ahead."

Tako wrapped up Serena's arm from wrist to elbow. The suckers on his tentacles massaged her skin for a moment before the limb flattened into a tattoo on her arm. *"You might want to sit down for this."*

Serena had just enough time to comply before the first image hit.

She was a larval Octari, floating along the surface of the ocean with more than a hundred thousand others. They fed on plankton, while many fish species fed on them. Adrenaline and fear coursed through her. She needed to eat, eat, eat. To survive, she had to grow as fast as possible. Larval Octari were ruthless, pushing each other out of the way as they competed for food. They shoved rivals into the paths of oncoming filter feeders. More developed Octari turned cannibal to eliminate competition.

"I'm showing you memories," Tako said. *"You'll see what I saw, enhanced with the knowledge of my present self."*

Serena struggled to reconcile the violence around her with the gentle mind layered over her own. "This is what childhood looks like for Octari?" She reached out with a pair of limbs and gouged out the eyes of a rival butting into her territory.

"No," Tako said. *"This decides who lives long enough to have one."*

The image shifted. Serena scuttled along the ocean floor. Maneuvering eight limbs at once felt effortless. Instinct propelled her towards a large opening in a coral reef. It opened up into a vast underwater cave. A dozen Octari drifted along near the entrance or clung to the rock. She felt a bond with a pair of Octari clinging to the ceiling and swam their way.

They reached out and touched her, pulled her close. She felt their minds merging with hers. Their happiness. Their pride. These Octari were her parents. They'd laid twenty-five thousand eggs, knowing at best one in a thousand of them would survive to return to civilization and receive a name. Mating was the last major act of an Octari's life. They'd die soon, entrusting others to raise their young as they had raised those of generations prior. But before they went, they would bless their children with all the knowledge and memories they'd accumulated.

Serena understood without asking that Tako returned home almost a year to the day after he'd hatched. His parents died a week later. "Do you miss them?" she asked, thinking of her own parents.

"Sometimes," Tako said. *"But with their memories, I feel like they're still with me. Their lives ran their full natural courses. They achieved everything they wanted to. I'm happy for them."*

What would it be like to have two lifetimes worth of knowledge deposited into her brain? "If parents can pass on their knowledge, does that mean Octari don't have schools? Don't need any education?"

"It takes a couple years for our minds to develop enough to understand all the information our parents share with us."

The image in her mind shifted again. She rested on the floor of an alcove of the underwater cave, surrounded by dozens of other young Octari. An adult perched on a rock nearby, instructing them on how to gradually draw forth the memories of their parents and incorporate them into their own consciousness without becoming overwhelmed. As this lesson required the students' full concentration, they didn't speak mind-to-mind, but rather used the Old Language. The teacher's skin changed colors several times a second. Every combination of colors, patterns, and skin textures represented a specific word or concept.

"While we're incorporating our parent's deeper knowledge into our minds, we're instructed in social etiquette amongst the Octari and the nuances of human civilization. Every Octari hopes to become a partner to a human someday, but we outnumber the humans five to one. Only the best of us are approved."

"What happens to everyone else?" Serena asked.

Rather than respond with words, Tako presented her a series of images. Octari hunting parties spreading out across coral reefs, killing fish and stuffing them into nets to be hauled home. Others manned stationary weapons designed to repel sharks, whales, and even more dangerous predators that preyed on them. In a cavernous chamber that could only be described as an underwater factory, Octari assembled weapons for the human war effort.

Unhosted Octari made contributions on shore too. She saw Octari scientists communicating mind-to-mind with humans to develop better medicines. Some tended human infants, allowing their parents a break. Octari provided extra limbs to hospital staff, prepared meals, managed logistical concerns for Z'han's navy… They all found ways to contribute to a greater good.

"Now that I've shared a bit about myself, may I ask you a question?" Tako asked.

"Go for it."

"Are you OK?"

The simple question shattered her. Though his consciousness still drifted along the outskirts of her own, she felt the depth of meaning in it. The concern for her emotional welfare. Lacking any context, he still felt something was broken in her and wanted to help fix it, if he could. He offered companionship and camaraderie in a way Annea and Ivy could never hope to.

"I'm not," Serena admitted. "And I don't want to talk about it. But if you can access my memories, I'll let you see for yourself."

"To do that, I would need to deepen our connection even further. Permission to come aboard, Captain?" Tako used a free limb to offer her a salute.

"Granted," Serena said, surprised at how much trust she felt for a being she'd barely met.

Tako's body flattened as he crawled up her arm. She felt him shifting position to sprawl across her back, the sensation like a hand brushing over her skin. Once he was satisfied, his presence swelled in her mind, momentarily overwhelming her own thoughts and sense of self. She felt him rooting around like a rock climber looking for the ideal handholds. She felt him sliding into the nooks and crannies of her brain. Making himself at home. Checking out the neighborhood. Assessing the kind of person he'd attached himself to.

From her perspective, it felt like having her mind wrapped in a warm blanket. Or a hug. Or being tackled and love bombed by a dozen puppies. Or reading a book and feeling like the author wrote it just for her. It couldn't be further from what Korahshka had done to her.

She understood now why every adult in Z'han had an Octari. If she could bottle up this feeling and sell it, she'd be the richest woman in the multiverse.

The euphoria faded as Tako created a metaphorical curtain between their minds. Her sense of him was still strong, but less distinct, fuzzier around the edges.

"A curtain is a good metaphor," Tako said, showing an ability to pick up on her thoughts in this state. *"Like a real curtain, both parties can talk to the person on the other side, but they cannot see through. This allows us to communicate and still maintain some privacy over our own thoughts. A dual, overlapping internal monologue would be a headache for us both. Like a curtain, it can be pulled back any time we wish to share deeper thoughts and memories. This barrier is permeable — some thoughts and emotions still drift through. There are times you'll know what I'm thinking without having to ask, and visa versa."*

"So, what now?" Serena thought, verifying Tako could hear thoughts intended for him.

He could. *"You offered me a look at your memories. May I?"*

"Go ahead. I won't think any less of you if you hurl yourself back into the ocean to escape me when you're done."

Serena braced herself for a cascade of images from across her life. For memories to be dredged forth without any effort on her part. To have to imagine yet again the deaths of everyone on Alterra. None of that happened. Instead, she felt like a librarian watching a patron roam through the shelves. She knew what selection of memories he was looking at, but she wasn't reading along with him. Tako said nothing as he rummaged around in her mind, reviewing memories with the same respectful care and attention she might if she held a particularly old, rare, and valuable book. He kept his attention on her recent history, staying away from the shelves she'd have labeled *Embarrassing Memories* and *Secrets That Die With Me.* She passed the time watching Zalinda and her Octari build a cairn from the rocks around the dock.

"Thank you for being willing to open up to me like this," Tako said. *"I understand now why that wasn't easy."* Korahshka's face flashed in her mind for an instant before disappearing. Oh, he definitely understood.

"Reconsidering partnering up with me?" The question wasn't a joke. She hadn't even wanted to meet him. Now she worried he'd reject her.

"Not at all. I think you're one of the strongest people I've ever met." His voice exuded warm sincerity.

"You can't possibly believe that." She knew he meant it, but couldn't fathom why.

"Zedrick was a soldier. I served with him on the front lines battling the Kroen. You're not in the mood to talk about the traumas you've endured. I'll spare you the sight of mine. I've lived long enough to know the kinds of horrors you've seen BREAK people. You're not only still functional, you're determined to fight back. I respect that resilience. I'd be honored to partner with you."

Serena laughed and closed her eyes as they misted up with tears. *"Hey now, I haven't decided if I'm keeping you yet."*

They both knew that was a lie.

CHAPTER 21
SETTING SAIL

"Don't say *I told you so.*" Serena pointed an accusing finger at Annea as the tall elf sauntered down the dock in her direction, Pik-Pik and Tik-Tik chattering to each other in her wake. Annea looked far too pleased with herself.

She spread her arms in a conciliatory gesture. "I would never. I'm glad you and Tako are able to work together. Zalinda was beside herself with joy when she told me you'd agreed to host. Did you sleep well?"

"Well enough." The words vastly undersold the experience. After returning to her guest room for the evening, she'd continued talking to Tako for hours. It was intoxicating speaking to someone who understood not only her words, but all the nuances of meaning behind them. Someone who understood what *wasn't* said just as much as what was. They'd stayed in safe getting-to-know-you territory. Z'han history. Books. Music. Past traumas and the upcoming mission were taboo. When she'd finally wanted to sleep, Tako just... turned her brain off? He insisted Octari could not manipulate human brain chemistry in any way, but he'd provided a sense of calm that felt like being enveloped in a weighted blanket, and consciousness melted away.

A warm ocean breeze sent Serena's auburn hair flying in every direction. Rather than try to reposition it, she turned to face into the wind so at least it flew behind her instead of around her face. They stood near the end of the largest pier in the kingdom, wide enough for four horse carts to travel side-by-side with room to spare. It served as the primary loading zone for supplies bound for Z'han's massive warships.

"You agreed to host," Ivy said. Serena hadn't heard the dryad's approach.

"What gave it away?" Serena asked, adjusting the band around her chest.

"I see an Octari draped across your back."

"I was being facetious," Serena said.

"I see."

She'd reluctantly agreed to dress in a similar fashion to the women of Z'han for the duration of the mission. The white chest band and black shorts were light, breathable, and surprisingly comfortable, but they left her showing almost as much skin as Ivy did. Leaving so much skin exposed allowed Octari partners plenty of room to hop off. They could see the world through their own senses instead of relying on their host's, and they could extend limbs to provide assistance with tasks. It was practical for both parties, and Serena understood the appeal of wearing less in the sweltering heat. That didn't mean she had to like it.

A series of footfalls against the deck signaled the arrival of newcomers. Serena turned away from the ocean and the three warships at rest to see the king's grandchildren following behind a man she didn't recognize. He stood just over six feet tall, with rich brown skin and dark hair pulled back into braids that ran halfway down his back. He had a well-kept goatee and a collar around his neck that must serve as a rank insignia, since he wore no shirt. An Octari tentacle served as his right arm from the elbow down, which gestured with such enthusiasm one would think he'd been born that way. All together, he looked like a man who'd be right at home in every pirate adventure novel she'd ever read.

"Good morning!" He bellowed. "It's a pleasure to meet our guests from other worlds. Especially you, Annea." He offered her a deep bow, sweeping his right arm in front of his chest. "I'm Julian Karrde, captain of the *Lord Biga*. You're here a bit early."

"We've been admiring your task force," Annea said.

"Beautiful ships, aren't they?" Karrde made a sweeping gesture to encompass the three ships anchored a half mile out from the pier. The largest of the three was at least twelve hundred feet long, double the size of the other two. Their hulls were were metallic. How Z'han got metal to float, Serena didn't know. Each had multiple rigs for black sails with a sparkling material woven into them, giving them the appearance of a slice of night sky shimmering with stars.

"The largest ship is, of course, the *Lord Biga*, where we will be stationed. The frigates are the *Duchess Elizabeth* and the *Von Spegman*, which have three turrets on each side, compared to the *Biga's* six, all capable of tracking targets above and below the waves. It's usually enough to deal with the leviathan's heads."

"Usually enough?" Ivy said.

"Heads, plural?" Serena asked.

Karrde raised an eyebrow. "You weren't briefed on leviathans?"

"I'm afraid not," Annea said. "We were told you'd give us a briefing."

"But you've been here before," Karrde pressed. "I'm well aware of your role in our kingdom's history."

"I was involved in the land campaign before the peace treaty was signed. You didn't have any technology powered by leviathan pearls back then. I always assumed leviathans were myths, or that sailors were playing a joke on me."

"Oh no, they're very real. The apex of the apex of predators that call the oceans of Torbakhal home. Before I carry on, don't you have any supplies we need to bring aboard?"

"They're all in the bag," Serena pointed to the enchanted satchel she'd set down near her feet. "It's bigger on the inside."

"An enchanted bag? I've always wanted one of those. That makes things easier, I suppose. We'll only need one boat." Karrde motioned for Amara and Cole to untie a rowboat from the side of the pier. "Shore leave ended for everyone else yesterday, and the ship's supplies are loaded, so we're clear to board now. I'll conduct a final inspection once we've boarded, then we'll be on our way."

"One moment." Annea stooped to stroke Pik-Pik and Tik-Tik's heads. "What's your mission while we're away?" She asked.

<Ask questions.>

<Learn about the last sixty years of Z'han history.>

<Learn about the new Kroen leader, Mother Superior.>

"You're both right," Annea beamed like a proud mother. "Don't pester sailors or soldiers going about their duties, OK? Make sure they're off duty, or talk to civilians. Zalinda agreed to escort you around when she's not working, so stick with her as much as possible. The citizens of Z'han aren't used to seeing ants your size. They may react better if there's a local with you."

<Yes, Mom.> The ants sounded just like human teenagers embarrassed at being smothered by an overprotective parent.

With her goodbyes complete, Annea joined the rest of them in the rowboat, settling in with far more grace than Serena or Ivy managed. Cole used one set of oars to push them away from the dock, then he and Amara started rowing the group towards the *Lord Biga*.

"You didn't want them with us?" Serena asked.

"They can't swim," Annea said. "And Z'han warships won't be built with them in mind. I'm sure they could help haul around materials, but... Let's just say I feel more comfortable with them sitting this one out and gathering information for me instead."

Karrde sat at the front of the boat, his back to the warship he commanded. At a nod from Annea, he began his briefing. "Leviathans are the lords of the deep sea, rarely ascending to shallow enough depths to harass our merchant vessels and navy, but they are a menace to fight when they do. You see, they have a long, extremely flexible body, with anywhere from twelve to twenty tentacles on one end, and an equal number of heads on the other. The heads have their own sub-brains so they can act independently, and they're all attached to their own rubbery, flexible necks. Fighting a leviathan requires keeping track of all of those heads while also fending off tentacles grabbing you from behind."

"It gets worse," Cole said. "The leviathans use their pearls to help enhance a nasty breath attack."

"And, to give you a sense of scale, leviathans are longer than the *Biga*," Amara added.

"This mission sounds unwise," Ivy said. "Perhaps we would turn back."

"You'll be fine. I've led expeditions for pearls several times now," Karrde said. "Leviathans are all fury and no brains. We've got hunting them down to a science."

Serena hoped Karrde was right. Torbakhal's leviathans sounded like the unholy lovechild of a kraken and a hydra. Even in her wildest daydreams she'd never imagined herself involved in a hunt for anything that colossal.

"I'll ask you the same thing I asked King Lordran," Annea said. "How do you expect the three of us to assist in this expedition?"

"As general labor, keeping our gunners supplied with ammunition. Severing any heads or tentacles that go after you or crew in the extremely unlikely event that our shields fail. We're always happy to have extra fighters onboard." Karrde cast appraising looks at Serena and Ivy. "Though I'll admit I see no obvious uses for pyromancy or a dryad's command of plant life."

A loud blast of expelled air to Serena's left made her jerk so hard she almost fell out of the boat. Annea placed a steadying hand on her shoulder. The sound repeated a dozen times over from every direction before Serena could get a look at the commotion.

A school of the weirdest fish she'd ever seen surrounded their boat. Twelve to eighteen feet long, their snouts were a gray which thinned out to a peppering against white skin further down their bodies. Straps wrapped around their bodies and fins, as well as the waist and legs of their human riders, linking the two together. The humans wore goggles and rubbery body suits that covered everything except for a hole in the back, where their Octari poked out in three-dimensional form like fleshy camel humps. Serena registered all of this distantly, because her mind couldn't get over the most important observation: The fish had *swords growing out of their heads.*

Each creature had a bastard sword sized blade protruding from their snouts, with lengths ranging from four to eight feet. The way the blades reflected sunlight confirmed they were metal, not bone, horn, or tusk.

"They're not fish," Tako said. *"They're Torbakhal's version of narwhals, a type of whale. They're the vanguard of our naval forces,*

harassing anything that threatens our ships. They also bait enemies into a ship's line of fire."

Serena chided herself for misidentifying the narwhals as fish. She hadn't seen any variant of whale before, but knew they needed to surface to breathe and didn't have gills. She should have noticed that. But they had swords. On their heads. Kind of distracting, that.

"Good morning, Captain Karrde," one of the riders said, snapping his right fist up to his left shoulder in the traditional Z'han greeting. "Captain Mansfield and Uproar Squadron reporting for duty. It's a good day to set off on a hunt. Any special orders, Captain?"

"Nothing now, thank you," Karrde said. "A standard deployment will be sufficient. Twelve of your number covering the *Biga*, and six each for the *Duchess Elizabeth* and *Von Spegman*. We'll be setting off within an hour or two."

Mansfield nodded and made a twirling motion with his hand. The narwhals clicked and whistled as they dived and headed for their positions around the ships.

"The body suits keep the narwhal riders warm. Their Octari partners use magic that allows them to breathe underwater," Tako said, answering questions Serena hadn't started to articulate in her mind yet.

"Don't be rude."

"I'm sorry?" Tako's presence radiated confusion.

"You knew I was going to ask about the narwhal riders and you supplied an answer before I could finish the thought. That feels like interrupting me. I don't appreciate having my thoughts disrupted."

"Apologies. I sensed your curiosity and guessed what you'd want to know. I didn't actually read your thoughts."

Serena felt a brief, warm flush in her mind, which she understood to represent embarrassment from her partner. *"I know you mean well. We just... we'll have to iron out our boundaries."* By which she meant *her* boundaries, but Tako would know what.

Sharing her brain with someone else felt so, so weird.

"Once we're aboard," Karrde said, oblivious to Serena's distraction, "I'd like you to tour the ship and get familiar with our weapons and defenses. I'll instruct the crew to make themselves available to answer any questions you have. You'll have several hours to review everything en route to our first stop," Karrde said.

"Why stop?" Annea asked. "Didn't you say the ships are fully supplied?"

"They are," Karrde agreed, "but to lure up a leviathan from the deep, one needs bait. Thus, we must sail north to a volcanic island chain and snag ourselves a magmadon." He gave Serena a knowing wink. "Magmadons are a species of shark that love to hang out near underwater volcanoes or volcanic islands. Such environments are saturated with fire-aspected energy, which they absorb. You'll love them."

"How big does a shark need to be to be appealing for a leviathan?" Serena asked.

"They're not that big," Karrde said. "Two hundred, three hundred feet long at most."

"In what universe is two hundred feet *not that big*?"

Karrde only smiled and whistled a jaunty tune as they closed in on the *Biga*.

CHAPTER 22

LAVA SHARK VERSUS THE NARWHAL SQUADRON

S erena's romantic notions of the thrill of an adventure at sea died a hard death over the next eight hours, in a torrent of tutorials on naval terminology and Z'han technology, weapon and shield operations drills, memorizing the ship's layout, and vomit. So, so much vomit.

"It'll get better with time," Annea said, rubbing Serena's back as she leaned over the side of the ship, caught in another fit of dry heaves. The elf didn't look much better. Sweat matted her dark hair against her scalp and drenched the drab, utilitarian shirt she wore, causing it to cling to her skin. Under the heat and relentless sunlight, she looked wilted and withered, more like an escaped prisoner than the ruler of a world.

Ivy, on the other hand, looked like the avatar of a nature goddess. Her skin almost seemed to glow. Soaking up so much sunlight had her radiating an invisible but potent aura of power that had the men of the ship (and a fair number of the women) turning to stare whenever she walked by. She looked calm, poised, and undisturbed by the rocking of the ship against the ocean's waves.

"I am as surprised as you are," Ivy told Serena, when asked about her radiant state. "I did not realize my body could store so much energy. Under the heavy forest canopy of Ataraxia, a dryad is not exposed to such intense sunlight. It is making me restless. I need to burn some of it off."

"I think the sailors have some ideas on how they could assist you with that," Serena said, waving to one whose gaze lingered too long.

"That would be helpful," Ivy said.

Serena and Annea roared with laughter as the joke sailed over the poor dryad's head — Serena's laughter cut short by another dash to the rail to heave.

"We have arrived at the target coordinates," Karrde's voice boomed across the deck from speakers built into the railing and masts, bringing Serena back to the present. "Commence chumming once all ships are in formation."

Four islands poked out from the ocean, a defiant line of calderas lording over heaps of volcanic rock. The land was barren and unadorned save for a coating of bird guano obvious even from a distance. The *Biga* came to a stop about a mile from the island chain, its starboard side parallel to the line of volcanoes, while the *Duchess Elizabeth* and *Von Spegman* moved in a half mile closer and turned so that the three ships came to rest in a triangular formation, their starboard sides facing their intended kill box in the middle.

Serena knew little about magic, but could tell this region was as saturated with fire energy as Karrde claimed. The ambient power made the hair on the back of her neck stand up. Her senses became hyper-focused. With a flick of her wrist, she had a fireball floating in the palm of her hand. It felt effortless — she didn't even need to get into the right emotional frame of mind. Satisfied with her test, she snuffed out the fireball by crushing it with her hand.

Small holes opened up on the side of each ship, pouring out fish blood stored in tanks on the lower decks. Along the main deck, sailors paired up to lift heavy deck plates, revealing storage compartments underneath, from which they lifted long, cloth-wrapped objects. The cloths unrolled as they held the ends over the railing, sending the corpses of Kroen tumbling sixty feet to the ocean below.

They're using Kroen corpses as bait? As vile as they might be, feeding their remains to a giant shark didn't sit well with her.

"Even in death, the Kroen work to destroy us," Tako said. *"Their bodies release toxic chemicals into the ground when buried, or the air when burned. Sharks find them perfectly edible. Burial at sea, where they can play a part in the natural cycle instead of corrupting it, has become our method for dealing with them."*

"Still, I feel like I'm watching a war crime."

"Do you have any other ideas?" Tako asked.

She did not.

One of the sailors went down to his knees to inspect the inside of one of the storage compartments. "This one's got a hole in it. Maintenance is skimping on repairs again."

"Kroen blood is corrosive, and we're dumping a much larger haul than usual. They'll claim the damage is new," his companion replied.

"I'm still reporting it when I get the chance. Gotta cover our asses, right?"

The sailors continued throwing bodies overboard until there were well over a hundred floating atop a crimson slick of blood.

Several minutes passed in silence, save for the ripple of the sails in the wind. All eyes scanned the waves, looking for the first sign of a disturbance. She felt the magmadon's presence before she saw it — a powerful concentration of fire energy was ascending from hundreds of feet below. The shark surfaced and swallowed a dozen Kroen with a streamlined efficiency that barely disturbed the normal wave pattern in the area. Instead of skin, the magmadon had a rocky outer carapace the same color and consistency as cooled magma, laced with veins of vibrant red and orange that pulsed like a heartbeat. Using the Kroen bodies for scale, she estimated the massive fish was a hundred and fifty feet long.

Up on the command tower's balcony, Karrde fired a flare to signal the narwhal riders hidden off the port side of each ship to dive and commence their attack. Meanwhile, tubes along all three ships fired hundreds of flares into the ocean. Enchanted to stay lit underwater, the flares made it easier to track the narwhals as they swarmed in from three directions to battle a creature more than ten times their size.

The narwhals used their smaller size and greater agility to evade the shark's every lunge. Their sword snouts punched into the magmadon's rocky exterior, leaving behind long cuts as they pulled free. Before long, the flares couldn't cut through the combined murk of fish and shark blood, making it impossible to see below the waves. She'd seen enough to know the narwhal squadron's "death by a thousand cuts" strategy seemed to be working flawlessly.

Gunners manned their posts on the ship's turrets, ready to take shots at the shark if it surfaced and provided them a clear opportunity. Sailors not manning turrets had their rifles trained on the water for the same reason. Everyone looked relaxed and unconcerned, as if this was just an ordinary day on the job. Could hunting giant sharks really be that easy?

Anxiety gnawed at her, a feeling distinct from the sea-sickness she'd been fighting all day. Something felt wrong here. *Just because your recent fights were pure chaos doesn't mean that's how it goes for everyone else,* she chided herself.

"It's fine, Serena," Tako said. *"You're watching highly trained professionals at work. Magmadons are big and scary, but they're not very smart. Narwhal riders can swim circles around one all day."*

"You don't sense it?"

"I sense you're not involved in the action, and it's driving you nuts."

He wasn't entirely wrong, but his misinterpretation of her concern showed her their mental connection was not flawless. She closed her eyes, opening herself up to her other senses. She sensed the magmadon below — not so much the shark itself, but the concentration of energy it held within it. After taking some time to familiarize herself with that sensation, she started looking for anything similar... and found it. Deep, deep below the surface, at the very edge of her perception, was another concentration of fire energy. One even more potent than the magmadon in view.

Tako's surprise rippled through her mind. *"Interesting,"* he said. *"I didn't realize it was possible to sense concentrations of similar magic like this."*

"There's a second shark!" Serena shouted. "Warn the narwhal riders!"

"I don't see nothin'," said a sailor to her side.

"How can you tell?" Ivy asked.

Serena ignored the question and sprinted across the deck towards the command tower, located at the front third of the ship. The ship's bridge at the summit was a glass walled room forty feet above the main deck, ringed by a balcony on three sides. It could only be accessed by a ladder on the stern-facing side, or via a winding staircase from the lower decks. She likewise ignored commands from sailors to not disturb the captain as she hauled herself up the ladder.

"Captain Karrde, there's a second shark in the deep," she paused to catch her breath. "You have to warn the narwhal riders." The bridge crew stared at her with looks that ranged from annoyed to outraged that a foreigner would disrupt their operation. Karrde stared at her like she'd spoken some unknown language.

"It'll go quicker if I handle this," Tako said. *"May I?"*

Understanding his intent, Serena gave her consent. Tako extended a tentacle towards the captain. Karrde took it in his hand, his eyes glazing over as the Octari relayed to him Serena's sensations. She felt him sending her memories into Karrde's mind with a mental sensation similar to sliding a piece of paper across a desk.

The captain's eyes snapped back into focus as he reached for the mouthpiece to the ship-wide communications unit. "Launch warning flares into the ocean," Karrde ordered. "Emergency retreat."

It was already too late.

Serena felt power surging up from the depths as the first flares hit the water. A second magmadon, double the length and triple the mass of the first, flung a narwhal and its rider into the air as it breached the surface. It swallowed another pair whole when it crashed back into the ocean with a deafening *ka-sploosh*. The tsunami created by the impact sent a surge of water over the *Biga's* railings, drenching sailors and knocking many of them to the deck.

"Fire at will!" Karrde shouted. The helmsman and navigator forgot Serena existed, turning to watch the carnage unfold outside. "Pick your shots carefully, don't hit our own!"

While the narwhal troops showed confidence and poise in evading the jaws of a single magmadon, that order dissolved into chaos when they had two targets to dodge. Their well-drilled formations and attack patterns didn't adapt well to the additional complexity of evading a second shark, and each other.

"This is unheard of," Tako said, alarm cutting through his perpetual state of calm. *"The blood of a magmadon acts as a repellent to others. Big as they are, magmadons are not the apex predators of our oceans. If one bleeds, others take it as a sign to stay well away."*

"Perhaps this huge one thinks it can take on any challengers."

Serena grabbed the sides of the ladder and slid down to the main deck. Her ears rang as the turrets of all three ships opened fire in short, controlled bursts, following Karrde's orders to only take clear shots to avoid friendly fire. Fortunately for the gunners, their targets were hard to miss. The turrets blew chunks of flesh out of the larger shark's sides, but didn't penetrate very deep through its rocky exterior. Energy beams from the sailor's rifles had no apparent effect at all.

The larger magmadon rammed the *Biga*, sending Serena sprawling. Annea wrapped her legs around the railing on the port side and grabbed a sailor before he tumbled overboard. After several fumbling attempts to regain her balance, Serena found her feet and dashed over to Ivy, who stared at her hands like she'd never seen them before.

"Ivy, what are you doing?" Serena asked.

"I have an idea of dubious merit."

"Dumb ideas are my favorite. What did you have in mind?"

"The Kroen showed it is possible to create an explosive blast of energy," Ivy said. "I wish to do the same with all the solar power coursing through my veins, but I do not know how."

Serena raised an eyebrow. Energy manipulation felt like the most basic component of pyromancy. She'd been doing it on instinct. It hadn't occurred to her that others might struggle with it. "Can you control the flow of magic in your body? You know, move power from one part of your body to another?"

"Yes, but not easily."

"Ok, so here's what you're going to do..." The ship's turrets resumed firing the moment they returned to an even keel, forcing Serena to shout to be heard. "Take all that energy and will it to flow into one of your arms. Keep the palm of your hand open."

Ivy's whole body tensed. She grimaced and closed her eyes as her right arm glowed with warm yellow light. "This is unpleasant." Her knees trembled. Her arm wavered. "I cannot control it."

"It's fine." Serena moved behind Ivy and placed her left hand between the dryad's shoulder blades. She grabbed Ivy's right arm with her free hand and aimed it at the larger magmadon. The shark surged towards a pair of narwhal riders hoping to use the *Duchess Elizabeth* as cover. They wouldn't make it. "Now, imagine your intended attack. Push that energy away from you, through the palm of your hand. Expel it from your body, as hard as you can, *right now.*"

Eyes still closed, Ivy obeyed. A continuous beam of concentrated sunlight erupted from the palm of her hand, punching a hole through the magmadon like it wasn't even there. Steam wafted up where water flash boiled as the beam continued on into the depths.

Ivy screamed.

Serena leaned into the dryad's back, using every ounce of strength she possessed to keep them both from flying backward. Ivy had no control whatsoever. Her arm wanted to pull up, forcing Serena to push down on it to keep the dryad's attack aimed where it wouldn't damage the *Duchess Elizabeth.* Goddess, the power was incredible. Ivy weighed less than Serena, but holding her steady felt like wresting a bear. Her muscles screamed in protest at the sudden abuse.

After several agonizing seconds, the beam dissipated. Ivy collapsed to the deck.

"Holy shit," Serena said.

"Did it work?" Ivy asked.

"See for yourself." Serena helped Ivy to her feet.

Ivy's attack struck the larger magmadon twenty feet in front of its dorsal fin, creating a hole wide enough for a narwhal rider to swim through. As her arm panned up, the beam continued slicing through the shark until it reached the gills on the right side. Red and orange light faded from the cracks in the magmadon's rocky exterior as it came to a rest alongside the *Duchess Elizabeth.* The narwhal riders they'd saved offered a wave of thanks before diving to join the survivors and finish off the smaller shark. *Biga*'s sailors greeted the carnage with cheers.

When both sharks were dead, Captain Karrde ordered everyone to stand down. "Uproar Squadron, secure tow lines on the larger carcass and connect it to the *Biga*," he said. "The *Von Spegman* can haul the smaller one as a backup. We'll hold here overnight and sail off with our prizes in the morning. I want the watches doubled in case we experience any further unusual shark behavior."

Karrde waited a few moments to make sure his orders were understood before issuing another. "Visitors from Kimori to the command deck, please."

"You good for the climb?" Serena asked.

"I am fine," Ivy said, not looking at her.

Serena didn't need Octari telepathy to know Ivy lied. "How can you store that much power without exploding?" She tried not to sound envious.

"I do not know," Ivy admitted. "Dryads are not exposed to such intense and direct sunlight on Ataraxia. It was an illuminating experience."

"Did you just make a pun? You might have a sense of humor after all. I'm proud of you." Serena patted Ivy on the back.

"Did I? That was not my intention."

Serena sighed. "Of course it wasn't."

"I'd like to thank you for your efforts today," Karrde told them when they reached the bridge. "We've never had a second magmadon show up after we've bloodied another, and that second shark was by far the largest I've seen. We lost some good people today, but things would have been much worse if not for your decisive intervention."

"Serena and Ivy are quite resourceful," Annea said. She sounded like a parent trying to put a positive spin on a situation in public, before scolding the children in private.

"That was an impressive display of power." Karrde bowed to Ivy. "Can you repeat it? That would make our battle against the leviathan much easier."

"I do not know," Ivy said. "I cannot control it. Had Serena not thought to aim my attack herself, I may have damaged the *Duchess Elizabeth*."

"I see," he said, keeping his expression neutral.

Karrde cast an appraising look at Serena. "Could I ask you to stay up with the first watch tonight to help them keep an eye out for more sharks? We've never had a pyromancer with us before. Your ability to sense magmadons is quite useful. With this much of their blood in the water, others should be scared off for at least a day, but I don't want to take any chances before we sail off for far more dangerous prey. One surprise was plenty for this voyage."

"No problem. The energy of this place has me so wired I won't be able to sleep any time soon."

"I'll join you," Annea said. "It's been a few days since our last one-on-one. We can use the time for another lesson," she cast an inquisitive gaze at the captain. "That is, if you don't mind me splitting her attention?"

"Not at all," Karrde said. "Whatever you think will help us in the coming fight, I support. Now, if you'll excuse me, I'd like to go supervise our cargo."

As they returned to the main deck, the trio accepted a hero's welcome from the assembled sailors. Ivy looked uncomfortable at the attention, a far cry from her obliviousness to the stares she'd been drawing all day. After a seemingly endless line of handshakes, they had a clear path to retreat to the lower decks to unwind before the first evening watch.

"Are you planning to beat me up again tonight?" Serena asked Annea, only half joking.

"Not this time. I'm thinking maybe if Tako and I work together, we can get you to a place where you don't almost kill yourself every time you use your power."

Well, that would be a nice change of pace...

CHAPTER 23

THE AFTER PARTY

After the surviving members of Uproar Squadron secured the magmadon carcasses for towing behind the *Lord Biga* and *Von Spegman*, they dismounted their narwhals and climbed aboard the ship, giving their animals free reign to feed while their handlers took a much needed break. That break took the form of an impromptu party in the ship's galley, where they could drink to their fallen companions. All of them wanted to thank Ivy for keeping their losses from being even worse.

Though Ivy bore the trademark look of awkward discomfort familiar to any introvert at a party where they didn't know the other guests, she made no attempt to escape. She even engaged in conversation, asking endless questions about the training and care of the narwhals. Their riders answered her questions in a way that suggested to Serena that they hoped to go on a different kind of ride later in the evening. They might as well have been talking to a potted plant for all their attempts at seduction accomplished. They took her disinterest in stride though and didn't get pushy or handsy, so Serena felt no need to intercede on the socially inept dryad's behalf.

She installed herself at a table nearest the cooking area, and over the next couple hours, proceeded to eat her own body weight in fried fish and steamed rice. At least, that's how it felt as the tower of emptied plates grew ever higher. Drinks flowed freely as she traded stories with a half dozen of the narwhal riders. Serena described her favorite hunts. The riders spoke of the Kroen getting over their generations-old fear of water to attack merfolk cities, bringing the reclusive ocean dwellers into the war.

Everyone kept Serena well supplied with a fruity cocktail. The taste of apples and strawberries completely masked the alcohol. She'd reached a state of buzzed, pleasant equanimity when Tako cut her off, pushing out limbs to shove aside every mug that got anywhere near her.

"You're drinking for two. That's enough alcohol," Tako said. She felt from him a sensation she could only describe as *Happy Little Brain Tingles.*

"What are you talking about? I'm not pregnant. You know how that works for humans, don't you?"

Tako laughed, the sound filling her mind with a kaleidoscope of colors. She realized he'd been referring to himself. He didn't have to say anything — understanding came though their bond. Octari siphoned off nutrients from their hosts to sustain themselves while connected. The process had no ill effect on the host as long as they ate and drank more to compensate. No wonder she'd wanted to eat so much.

"Wow. You've been stealing my buzz all night. You are a literal buzzkill. This crime shall not go unpunished."

Tako shifted his presence in her mind like a man leaning forward with a mischievous grin on his face. *"Yeah? What would you do?"*

"Bombard you with the memories of my awkward teenage attempts at flirting with boys."

The Octari recoiled in mock horror. *"My Lady, torture is illegal under Z'han law."*

If she had to share her brain, she was glad her roommate appreciated playful banter. *"Ok, but seriously, how drunk would I be right now without your intervention?"*

"You'd have passed out five drinks ago," Tako said, the mental equivalent of a hiccup tickling the edges of her skull. *"Don't worry, we won't get a hangover. Probably. Maybe. Octari are very good at metabolizing alcohol. Smoothing out the rough edges of our host's questionable life choices is all part of the host and partner relationship."*

"You could have said something sooner." Serena wobbled a bit as she stood.

"With the week you've had, you deserve to indulge and unwind a little. Especially —" he hiccupped again *"—before your session with Annea."*

"What about her?" Serena asked, casting her eyes about the cramped space for the elf. Come to think of it, she hadn't seen Annea at all throughout the party.

"You may not have noticed her reaction to the battle, but I did." He projected a series of images into her mind. Tako's eye level differed for each as he repositioned himself across her body. In every one, Annea looked like a woman straining to hold in her temper.

"Ivy and I saved the day. What's she mad about?" A ringing bell served as the five minute warning until the start of the first watch. *"Well, I guess we're about to find out."*

Annea was already on the top deck when she arrived, leaning against the main sail mast with her arms crossed, eyes closed as if deep in thought. The sun had set, and in its place hung a brilliant moon, casting soft light across the deck and surrounding ocean. In the sun's absence, the temperature had dropped considerably. Serena shivered as a gust of moist air ran over her skin.

They weren't alone. Twelve sailors manned assigned sections of the railing, six per side, spaced roughly two hundred feet apart. Some read books under the bright moonlight, while a few others sat on the deck, playing card games with their Octari. The sailors lacked the level of focus she would have expected, but to be fair, the arrival of giant sharks would be hard to miss.

"All hail our glorious hero," Annea said, knowing it was her without opening her eyes. "Enjoying the attention?"

"We saved at least two narwhal riders, so I'd call today a win. I doubt we'll be paying for drinks for the remainder of our time on Torbakhal. So why do I feel like I'm about to get lectured?"

"Because, once again, you did something stupid and impulsive which nearly resulted in disaster. Positive results don't give you a pass on poor judgment." She opened her eyes to give Serena a textbook *"I'm disappointed in you"* stare.

"The solar beam was Ivy's idea." She didn't mean to sell out Ivy, but she wasn't about to accept all the blame for their supposed mistake.

"I'll be having a chat with her too, but *you're* the one who walked her through how to do it. When dealing with power you don't understand and can't control, your first thought should not be *'Hell yeah! How can I weaponize this?'*" Annea delivered that last bit in a respectable impression of Serena's voice.

I don't understand it? I've known how to access my power for only a few days and I've already worked out how to to manipulate and concentrate energy. It's not hard. Don't patronize me.

It's possible the alcohol dampened her ability to restrain her temper. But at the moment, she just didn't want to. "What were we supposed to do?" Serena asked. "Pause and try to calculate how much power Ivy was packing? Conduct a cost and benefit analysis of the plan? Come up with three different options and weigh the pros and cons of each against the others? People were about to die. We had to make snap decisions. I thought you of all people would understand that."

"If you hadn't held Ivy's attack as steady as you did, it would have punched a hole through the *Duchess Elizabeth*. The ship sinks, sending over a hundred and fifty crew members scrambling for lifeboats or swimming in open water around rampaging sharks. I'm not saying you should let people die, but you have to be careful when your actions stand to do far more harm than good. Neither of you considered the repercussions of your actions. You could just as easily have killed the very narwhal riders you wanted to save."

Serena walked up to Annea until the two women almost touched. Close enough to smell old sweat and see faint hints of knives hidden in or under her clothes. Neither of them had rinsed off since the battle. The *Biga*'s sailors hadn't given Serena a chance with all the partying. She didn't even come up to the elf's collar bone, but she refused to be intimidated by the height difference. "Tako informs me I've had more than a few drinks tonight. So perhaps I haven't explained myself well. Let me try again. There. Was. No. Time. We trusted our instincts. You analyze tactics before or after a fight, not during it."

Annea's expression softened. She stepped to the side to buy herself some personal space. A conciliatory gesture, given how easily she could have knocked Serena on her ass. "I share responsibility too. These last few days have been chaotic, so I haven't been able to give you much guidance on magic. I've brought you along on this quest to seek aid for Kimori, thus placing you in dangerous situations where of course you'll react on instinct."

If Kimori's ruler wanted to take a portion of blame for mistakes that hadn't happened, Serena wouldn't stop her. But was Annea saying she thought bringing her to Torbakhal was a favor? Did she think she was the only one deciding how they'd fight the Vohr? Her friends and family were still alive. She hadn't lost everything. Serena was content to go it alone if she had to. If Annea's sanctimonious attitude held her back from doing what needed to be done...

Serena opened her mouth to make sure Annea was absolutely clear on where her priorities lay. Tako send her an image of herself with her mouth stitched shut. The image tripped her up the split second needed for a measure of rationality to reassert itself and keep her from escalating a pointless fight.

Annea sighed. "If I don't beat a little common sense and caution into that head of yours, you'll be dead in less than a week at the rate we've been going."

"Whatever," Serena said. "If you want to teach, *teach*. We've got the time."

"I don't enjoy being a killjoy, but at least one of us has to act like an adult in this group." Annea walked over to the railing to stare out at the ocean. "What did you know of magic, before you came to the Nexus? What was magic like on Alterra?"

"There wasn't much magic on my world." Serena choked up for a moment, realizing they'd both referred to Alterra in the past tense. She looked up to the moon, finding some comfort in its soft light, and forced herself to continue. "Maybe one in a thousand people displayed some form of magical aptitude. Entire kingdoms rarely had more than two or three people with enough power and skill to qualify as full mages. Since it was so rare, and I had no apparent magic, I never bothered studying it."

"Then let's start at the absolute beginning. Magic is everywhere. As invisible as air, but no less real. There is no inherently good or evil magic — it is a neutral energy which magic users draw into themselves to power their innate talents. Some beings can only use magic in one way, others are capable using it for a wide range of abilities, like the Octari. It can be bottled up and used as an energy source for various technologies, like what Z'han has done with their Shrikes. You'll see that a lot in the Nexus too. The nature of some places can imbue the surrounding magic with an elemental force, like the volcanoes here, which makes the energy more potent to people like you who are aligned to it, but much less useful to anyone else."

"How come Ivy could carry around so much energy all day no problem, but when I draw that kind of power, I'm falling apart in minutes?" Serena asked, then winced. *Worry about yourself. Stop being envious of Ivy.*

Annea raised an eyebrow, but answered the question. "The key word there is *draw*. Ivy absorbed her power passively, through natural processes in her body. She took what she could handle, no more, no less. We're not all created equal when it comes to magical aptitude and innate power tolerance. Alterra sounds like a reality at the 'low magic' end of the spectrum. I can tell you from experience Ataraxia is saturated with it, and beings from realms like that tend to have very high natural tolerances. Ivy is an outlier even for dryads, though I don't think she's realized that yet. Don't compare yourself to her."

Serena let it go, opting to ask another question that had been bothering her. "Why can I only use pyromancy when I'm angry? I'm a very easygoing person."

An image of an Octari with impossibly long tentacles appeared in her mind. They'd grown so unwieldy that they tangled up with each other in convoluted knots, to the point the Octari could no longer move. With the image came context — the fable of Makahnstalnokiio, an Octari who thought he could get what he wanted through lies and manipulation, rather than kindness and truth. As punishment, he was cursed, making his tentacles grow every time he told a lie. Unable to change his ways, he met his demise through his own machinations.

"You could have just called me a liar. No need to get all literary about it."

"I find humans respond better to pictures," Tako said.

Annea must have noticed Serena's drifting focus as she spoke with Tako. She waited a moment before continuing her lecture. "Some people have an innate grasp of their magical talents their whole lives. For others, like you, there is an inciting incident that triggers its emergence. This incident is usually some form of crisis. For emotionally activated people such as yourself, getting into the same emotional space you were in when it first appeared may be necessary to trigger it again."

"Are you saying I'm stuck like this? I'm going to have to be ready to go rage monster on a moment's notice for the rest of my life if I want to use magic?"

Annea shook her head. "Thankfully, no. It is possible to shift your emotional trigger to something else, or even eliminate it entirely. Such transformations take a lot of time, meditation, and practice. It's also possible some new crisis acts as a catalyst for a sudden change. That's not something I'll be able to help you with. Whatever the answer is for you, you'll have to find it on your own, unless Tako can help."

Tako shrugged. Well, his limbs rippled along her skin, but she knew what it meant. *"I probably could, but I don't think we'll have enough time on this voyage to see it through."*

"Introspection is key to any mage's control over their power," Serena said, echoing Annea's words from their first session. "Again with the *thinking*, not *doing*."

"Yes, well, you have a rare opportunity to make progress on that while you're hosting an Octari," Annea said. "Check your ego and let him help you. He's a neutral third party who can provide some outside perspective. Just don't expect anything to change overnight."

Serena saw her opening to avoid further lectures and latched onto it. "Tako's reminding me our time together is limited. Would you mind if I hit the showers then retired to my quarters for the night to do some soul searching with Tako?"

Tako sent her the image of Makahnstalnokiio again. *"We're going to bed and sleeping off the booze."*

"Annea doesn't need to know that."

"Go ahead. I think that'd be a smart use of your time," Annea said, oblivious to the byplay between her and Tako. The corner of her lip twisted into a smirk that suggested she suspected what Serena would actually be doing though. "You're in no condition for any physical training right now anyway. I'll cover your shift on deck. I'm sure you don't need to be up here to detect any sharks nearby."

"If I sense anything, I'll let someone know right away," Serena agreed. She said her goodnights and she headed for the stairs to the lower decks. She managed to walk in a straight line. Almost.

It had been a long day. She stank and was tired and tipsy. The fruity drinks more than countered the energy she got from being so close to active volcanoes. She needed sleep, a shower, and to relieve her tortured bladder. Not in that order. It was important to be functional tomorrow.

They had a leviathan to slay.

CHAPTER 24

IT DOESN'T WANT TO BE FED...

The next morning, Serena stood alone at the bow of the ship, watching the volcanoes recede into the distance. She yawned, then lifted her arms over her head and twisted side to side, trying to stretch out and sharpen her focus. Thanks to Tako's soothing nature, she'd fallen into a peaceful sleep the moment her head hit the pillow. But he hadn't quite been able to counteract the booze. She felt sluggish, and needed to shake that off before showtime.

"So... this is probably the last chance we're going to have to chat for a while," Tako said. He tried to sound casual, but he had something more serious in mind.

"You don't want to chat," Serena tucked a strand of hair behind an ear. The strong ocean breeze kept blowing it around. *"A chat is something simple and light, like discussing our favorite books. Or you could tell me about Torbakhal's merfolk. What you want to do is have A TALK — the kind where we dig deep into childhood traumas and diagnose everything that went wrong to make me the woman I am today."*

"You didn't have any major childhood traumas. But you do have a strong aversion to being emotionally vulnerable. You think it makes you appear weak."

"True," she said, running a hand along the starboard rail as she made her way aft. It felt good to finally have a sense of balance on the ocean. She wouldn't miss vomiting over the side a couple times an hour. Perhaps she should try to do some of the mindset work she'd claimed she'd do last night. Tako seemed willing enough to help. *"Tell me, Dr. Tako, why do I feel most alive when I'm furious? Why do I need that to manifest my talent?"* Annea seemed to think it was because she was enraged when her pyromancy first manifested.

That felt too simple. Serena thought the real explanation ran deeper than that. *"Being angry is easy, but I don't want to be like that all the time."*

She waved at Ivy, who stood at the center of the main deck. Long blades of grass grew from her arms, which she held out to catch the sun. Over Annea's objections, Ivy agreed to Karrde's request to store up as much energy as possible. She could unleash another solar attack if they needed it. If the dryad saw Serena at all amongst the bustle of sailors performing maintenance on the turrets, she gave no sign.

"Perhaps the first step would be to determine why anger is your trigger in the first place?" Tako asked.

"You don't already know?"

"We've been partners for less than two days. I've been getting to know you in the present, not digging deeper into your past. I could try to find the answer, but I'd rather you talked to me."

Serena found her mind wandering to old memories. In the quiet moments after her first session with Annea, she'd begun to have vague, half-formed notions of her own on the nature of her power, but had never focused on them enough to see if they rang true. Anger at the Vohr wasn't the only source she'd used to tap into her pyromancy in the last few days. *"Fine. Might as well go into battle with eyes wide open, right?"*

She recalled her thirteenth birthday. For months, she'd been taking archery lessons in secret with a couple local hunters. With a tailor and a librarian for parents, she'd just assumed they would never approve. One of them must have told her father about it, because for her birthday, he'd given her a bow and quiver of arrows. Her heart swelled at her father's tacit approval, but he clearly hadn't run it by her mom. *"Why would you give her that? She's no hunter, she'll hurt herself."* That afternoon, Serena snuck out of the house. She ventured out into the forest alone, shot two turkeys, and returned with her haul before her parents could form a search party. She'd never forget the look of pride on her father's face, and disbelief on her mother's.

Later in her teens, she'd taken to studying Korvahnese, the language of the far-eastern kingdom of Korvahn, based on an appreciation for their culture and folklore. Most people considered it a waste of her time since there weren't any Korvahnese people around to talk to. A year into her studies, a Korvhanese family moved into their neighborhood, fleeing an abusive relative. Her knowledge of their language and culture were instrumental in helping the family settle in and adapt to their new life.

She thought of the huge argument she'd had with her parents when she told them she'd taken a multi-year contract on the frontier. She wasn't ready, they'd said. It was too dangerous. She couldn't handle the dangerous animals or uncivilized men that dwelled so far from the capital. She'd spent years building her reputation, hoping word of her deeds would make it back to her parents.

"Sensing the theme?" Serena asked. *"Shall I keep going?"*

"You don't do well with people telling you what you're capable of. Nor do you like having your decisions questioned."

"That's an understatement. Condescension, assuming I'll fail, questioning my competence or intelligence… that stuff infuriates me. I have to prove the critics wrong. Even if it's my parents… ESPECIALLY if it's my parents. And don't —" Serena raised a finger in warning, an unnecessary gesture given their telepathic link. *"Don't give me some version of the 'they loved you and only had your best interests at heart' speech."*

"I wasn't going to," Tako said. *"Rather, I'd remind you that if you want Annea or anyone else to mentor you, get used to having your decisions questioned. I won't patronize you by replaying your greatest hits, but even you would admit you can be impulsive."*

Serena laughed. *"I appreciate someone who can call me out on my bullshit without being judgmental about it."*

"Perhaps the key to eliminating your emotional trigger is to learn you don't need anyone else's approval? To be content with your own assessment of your competence?"

"You make it sound easy. I'll reflect on that. Today, I'll settle for surviving a fight with a sea monster."

"Fair enough."

They sailed for several hours before reaching their destination — an unremarkable expanse of open water in the middle of nowhere.

Hundreds of enormous plants floated on the surface, bobbing with the ocean waves. They looked like mattress-sized lily pads, with six to eight pads connected to a central bundle of knotted stems and roots. Each pad looked thick and buoyant enough to support her weight, though she wouldn't want to test that theory.

After the *Lord Biga* came to a full stop, the crew inflated a giant balloon and tossed it overboard. Meanwhile, the narwhal riders tied weights onto the carcass of the magmadon until it sank. The carcass was connected by a long chain to a crane arm at the aft end of the boat, which hung out over the water like the world's largest fishing rod. Once the magmadon sank to the desired depth, the narwhal riders tied the balloon to the chain. When the leviathan took the bait and their makeshift bobber dipped below the surface, the crane team would reel it in, luring the leviathan to pursue. Serena left her bow and arrows nearby, figuring that area would be the best place to get some early shots in, though she was under no illusion arrows would do much to a creature the leviathan's size.

With the trap set, the crew of all three ships collectively stared at the balloon, waiting for their prey to arrive.

And they waited.

And they waited some more.

Serena's patience lasted an hour. "Does it always take this long?"

"It's a big ocean," a sailor said. "Nearest leviathan could be dozens of miles away, but we're right in the middle of a common migration route. One always finds the free meal within an hour or two."

"So, this really works?" A monster with a dozen heads and as many tentacles didn't strike her as the scavenging type.

Three hours later, the midday sun hung overhead. They'd seen no sign of interest in the magmadon carcass. Even the sailors' discipline was fading now. Someone brought up trays of sandwiches from below and delivered them to sailors so everyone could eat without leaving their stations. Boredom reigned supreme. Ivy did slow laps of the deck. Annea found a mat and ran her body through a series of complicated yoga poses Serena didn't recognize and couldn't replicate.

"The leviathan doesn't want to be fed," Serena said to nobody in particular. "It wants to hunt." She thought of the red and orange energy that pulsed through the magmadon's rocky skin while they lived, and the strong, detectable sense of fire they'd given off. What if those sensory cues were important to leviathans?

She had an idea. *"Hey Tako, buddy, pal. The narwhal rider's Octari help them breath underwater, right? Could you do the same for me?"*

"Yes," he said. He paused. She felt the moment he figured it out. The alarm he sent through their bond made her jump. *"Serena, you can't do that. That's madness."*

"Didn't we have a conversation about how I feel about doubters?" She turned to the sailors manning the crane controls. "Be ready to reel it in."

"What are you doing?" Annea asked.

"Something brilliant or stupid, I haven't decided which." Serena jumped over the side before anyone could grab her, keeping her feet pointed at the water and her arms locked at her sides. The frigid water knocked away any lingering sleepiness she had. When she surfaced, she swam for the balloon floating several hundred feet aft of the *Biga*.

"Serena, please turn back. I believe you CAN do this, but I reiterate, this is madness. What's your exit strategy?"

"Ride the chain up and hope the leviathan focuses on the big shark and ignores the tiny human." She reached the balloon and grabbed the chain that would guide her into the depths.

"Your entire plan hinges on my cooperation. What if I turn back?"

"If you were going to do that, you'd have already done so. You want to see if this will work too." That was an assumption on her part, but Tako didn't contradict her.

"Perhaps I'm determined to save you from yourself?" Tako sighed. *"I lack the words OR images to articulate how phenomenally stupid this plan is, but yes, I'm in. Let's do something the entire navy will talk about for years to come."*

Serena felt a tingle across her skin, then something like a glass dome appeared over her head. Her finger passed right through when she poked it. *"The dome you see is an illusion representing the magic allowing you to breathe underwater. You won't have to worry about inhaling the ocean,"* Tako said.

"Excellent." Serena dived under the waves and pulled herself down the chain. Wishing she had one of those rubbery body suits the narwhal riders used to keep warm, she experimented with her magic, devising a technique to spread power throughout her body in a way that kept her warm.

As the depth increased, the pressure mounted. Sunlight faded, then disappeared entirely. She couldn't even see the chain in her hands. She really hadn't thought this through. *"Got any tricks for this?"* Serena asked.

"I can help with the water pressure, but not the lighting."

Her skin hardened as Tako worked another of his magics. She lost some range of motion and flexibility, but not enough to hinder what she needed to do. Octari were such versatile beings. Telepathy. Shapeshifting. Powers that helped a human survive underwater. She'd miss this when they went their separate ways.

To calm her nerves, Serena hummed the bawdiest tune she could think of, a song about a mermaid with a magic touch and three princes who went to increasingly desperate and insane lengths to woo her. As she reached the third verse, flashes of light lit up the ocean all around her. Karrde must have ordered flares fired to the approximate depth of the magmadon. Had they worked out her plan? Whether they had or not, she appreciated the sudden visibility, which revealed they had another hundred feet to where the chain wrapped itself around the magmadon's carcass. Even dead, the shark's enormous bulk unnerved her.

Upon reaching her target, she debated settling for contact with the tail, but opted instead to pull herself along its body another hundred feet. Maybe her power would spread through it faster if she started from center mass. *"Time to see if this will work."* She thought of manti shrieking in pain as her flames roasted them. As power flowed into her, she pushed it into the magmadon, causing the cracks in its magma-like exterior nearest her hands to glow red and orange.

Yes! This would work. She could give the dead shark the appearance of life, but it would take more power than she'd anticipated.

She continued pouring energy into the corpse. Paying close attention to her own body, she kept the feed gradual and consistent, mindful to stop at the first sign of strain so she wouldn't overwhelm herself. Passing out several hundred feet below the surface sounded like a death sentence, even if a leviathan didn't show up to make a snack of her. Could Tako haul her back to the *Biga* if he had to?

Some questions were better left unanswered.

After another ten minutes of channeling power into the shark, it glowed almost as vibrantly as it had in life. Satisfied, she hauled herself back up the chain. She'd made it only twenty feet from the body when the magmadon thrashed beneath her, nearly giving her a heart attack. *"Is it supposed to do that?"* She asked, half afraid she'd somehow reanimated the damn thing.

"Its muscles are reacting to the power you poured into them, similar to how you'd react to a sudden shock. It's dead." Tako didn't know that for a fact. It sounded plausible though. He was pretty sure he was right. Ninety-nine percent positive.

Knowing the subtext behind someone's words wasn't always a blessing in human-Octari partnerships, Serena decided.

When the magmadon twitched a second time, she saw movement at the limit of the flare's illumination.

Descriptions of leviathans didn't even begin to do them justice. Serena lost all sense of herself in a fog of pure horror as a dozen heads emerged from the deep. The monster's necks and heads coiled together in a wedge formation to better slice through the water, but uncoiled as they closed in on the magmadon. They lashed out at lightning speed to tear whale-sized chunks of flesh off the giant shark. Her mind struggled to comprehend the scale of the beast. Each of its white scaled, crocodilian heads had to be sixty feet long, attached to necks so long they extended beyond the range of the flare's light.

If the leviathan attacked her, she'd be dead before she had a chance to react.

I really didn't think this through...

CHAPTER 25

...IT WANTS TO HUNT

With a violent jerk that almost made Serena lose her grip, the *Biga* started reeling in the chain. Giant shark and average-sized human rocketed towards the surface. Serena couldn't do anything but wrap her herself around the chain and mutter a prayer to the All-Mother. All eight of Tako's limbs danced furiously across her skin as he did everything in his power to keep her body from being torn apart by the rapid change in pressure. Serena kept her chin tucked to her chest, finding that put the experience on just the right side of bearable. It also gave her the ultimate view of the leviathan rending hunks of flesh off the shark's carcass as it gave chase.

Yes, enjoy the tasty shark. Ignore me. I'm not worth your time.

After thirty seconds that felt like as many years, her head broke the surface. She heard a series of clicks and whistles to her right. Something bumped her leg. She screamed.

"Hold on to these!" Someone from Uproar Squadron handed her a pair of straps. Relieved to see a friendly face, she relaxed and allowed him to position her on his narwhal's back. They raced for the *Biga*, weaving through or diving under giant lily pads along the surface.

A reptilian growl erupted from a dozen throats as the leviathan's heads surfaced behind them, the sound an even match for the roar of the capital ships' turrets as they opened fire. Surrounded by enemies, the leviathan forgot about its meal. Heads lashed out with whip-like speed to bludgeon the smaller ships. Blue light flashed with every impact, the ships' shields doing their job fending off the assault. *Wham. Wham. Wham.* Every failed attack enraged the leviathan further.

How long could their shields withstand that kind of pounding?

The narwhal stopped beside a set of rungs welded onto the side of the *Lord Biga.* "Up you go, quickly now, before the leviathan turns its attention on the *Biga,*" the narwhal rider said. As if to underscore his point, the ship rocked from a tentacle slap. He offered a final wave and left to rejoin his team. He must have sent a signal, for as soon as he was far enough away, blue light shimmered around the *Biga,* the capital ship activating its own shields. They'd left the ship vulnerable long enough to retrieve her? She'd have to thank Captain Karrde for that, after the battle.

The *Biga* released the chain holding the magmadon, retreated, then started a ponderous turn to reposition itself and join the fight. Serena climbed as fast as she could. Tako cancelled the magic that let her breathe underwater. The dome over her head popped like a bubble. He shared his vision, allowing her to see in her mind's eye the battle raging behind her. Blood dripped into the water from hundreds of holes in the leviathan's necks.

The beast didn't seem to care.

"Unless it's coming after us, I don't want to know." She shook her head as if that would cancel Tako's well-intentioned but unwanted distraction. It didn't, but he stopped transmitting his vision. She devoted all her energy to the climb, ignoring the sounds of battle as best she could.

A wet gurgle filled the air, followed by a sound that was part scream, part steaming hiss — the leviathan unleashing a breath attack. She resisted the impulse to let go of the rungs and cover her ears. It was deafening. Apocalyptic. The sort of sound her mind would be dredging up in nightmares decades from now.

We should never have agreed to join in this madness, Serena thought.

"Come on, Serena. Where's the irrational confidence that had you jumping into the ocean in the first place?" Tako asked. *"You're not in this fight alone. There are hundreds of trained professionals in this task force. FOCUS."*

She reached the top and flopped out on the deck, allowing herself a moment's rest. Even from her prone position, she had no trouble seeing the leviathan. *Stop shaking like a rabbit in an eagle's talons,* she ordered herself. *You are the hunter. Study your prey.* Each of the white-scaled heads moved as an independent entity, trying to bite into hull or bash the frigates. Every minute or so, one of the heads would unleash its breath attack, filling the air with the gurgle of the wind-up, then the scream-hiss of release. When they did, the pearls embedded at the top of their skulls glowed like stars trapped in glass. The oily blue and green flames the leviathan spewed splashed off the *Duchess Elizabeth* and *Von Spegman's* shields. For now.

Serena stood and looked out over the railing. *Where were the tentacles?* As she thought it, half a dozen of them appeared on the starboard side of the *Duchess Elizabeth,* trapping the ship between an assault from the tentacles on one side, and the heads on the other. The remaining six flailed around beneath the surface, engaged with their own battle against Uproar Squadron. While fighting the magmadon, the narwhal riders had employed a chaotic strategy of hit-and-fade attacks meant to confuse their prey. Here, they surged forward as a group, delivering concentrated stabs to render each tentacle immobile and useless as quickly as possible.

Studying the leviathan's moves helped walk her back from the ragged edge of a panic attack, but she still felt powerless and insignificant.

The monster changed tactics, suddenly giving its full attention to the *Duchess Elizabeth.* The blue bubble of energy surrounding the ship flared orange as the shields struggled to endure the abuse. A leviathan head went limp and slid down the shield, splashing into the ocean. The combined assault from turrets and energy rifles had cut deep enough into the neck to sever the nerves. In response, another head turned and *bit through the neck* of the injured one, severing it to shed the dead weight. It used a breath attack on itself to cauterize the wound.

"Do we have you to thank for our target showing up?" Annea asked, putting an arm around Serena's shoulder.

Serena nodded. "Do I have you to thank for the flares?"

"I thought your plan might work better if you could see what you were doing. Captain Karrde humored us." She sighed. "What *was* the plan?"

Serena never got a chance to explain. With a sound like a million glass jars shattering at once, the *Duchess Elizabeth's* shields broke. Leviathan strikes that previously bounced off now slammed into the deck, denting the metal more and more with each strike. The leviathan seemed dazed for a moment, then realized its prey was vulnerable and ramped up its assault. One head went for the bow of the ship, another the stern, each ripping out a chunk of the ship with the same ease she would have biting an apple.

"I will need your assistance in a moment, Serena," Ivy said, pointing her staff at the water below. The ubiquitous lily pads in the area bent into scoops, which Ivy compelled to paddle towards the leviathan. With multiple lily pads connected to a single mass of roots at their center, the whole procession looked like a horde of aquatic spiders crawling across the waves in perfect synchronicity toward their intended victim.

"What do you need?" Serena asked.

The *Biga* had finished its turn and surged forward to reinforce the *Duchess Elizabeth*. The smaller ship moved away in an attempt to extricate itself from the fight. With its main sail mast broken, and severe denting to the main deck and port side, the ship barely looked seaworthy.

"On my mark, light the lily pads on fire," Ivy said, the melancholy in her voice suggesting sorrow at harming plants. Her enchanted minions crawled up one of the leviathan's necks, towards a head in the middle of the formation. That particular neck shook with annoyance like a horse shooing a fly, unaware of the threat the lily pads represented.

"I don't think I can throw a fireball that far."

"Arrows," Ivy ground out, her face scrunched with effort.

Cursing her forgetfulness, Serena dashed to the aft of the ship and retrieved her bow and arrows. By the time she returned, the dryad had the first of the lily pads crawling into the leviathan's open mouth. The head thrashed about trying to dislodge the swarming plants. Neighboring heads roared with irritation at their flailing comrade. Ivy's target bit down, but its mouth was not designed for chewing. The plant mass soon became a choking hazard it could not swallow, either.

Serena found a rag, wrapped it around an arrowhead, then lit it on fire. Would her flames go out during the arrow's flight, or would they linger? She had no idea. *We'll just find out the hard way.*

"Now!"

Their chosen head froze over the *Duchess Elizabeth,* preparing to unleash a breath attack. Probably as much to clear its mouth as to damage the ship. Her arrow struck home and buried itself in the mass of green. They heard the scream-hiss...

The leviathan's head exploded from the inside out, showering the surviving sailors on the *Duchess Elizabeth's* main deck with blood, flesh, and fragments of bone. The remaining heads roared in mourning of their lost fellow, then one bit through the neck of the dead head and released a blast of flaming breath to cauterize the wound.

Serena sent a prayer of thanks to the All-Mother that the leviathan couldn't grow back severed heads like a hydra.

"Did you know that would happen?" Serena asked.

"I hoped," Ivy said. "I plugged the ducts in its mouth that emit flames."

Serena hadn't noticed that. "And my arrow?"

"Insurance. I hoped a fire in its mouth would force it to use its breath if the choking hazard was insufficient."

"Are there enough plants around here to try that again?"

"Yes," Ivy said. "But I will need a minute."

The deck beneath their feet rumbled. The *Biga* held a single Shrike in its cargo hold, to be deployed when the ship fully committed itself to the fight. That time was now. Karrde expected their superior weaponry would make them the leviathan's primary target the moment they let loose, so he'd wanted to keep them out of the action for as long as possible. But with the *Duchess Elizabeth* disabled so soon, they couldn't afford to hold back.

The elevator platform locked into place on the main deck, its lethal package delivered. "The Shrike may fire at will," Karrde said through the ship's speakers.

Cole sat in the Shrike's pilot seat. His Octari floated in the water tank above and behind him, each of their tentacles manning a lever to control one of the eight arms on the back of the unit. The pair opened up on the leviathan with everything they had. Cole maneuvered the two gun arms he controlled to spray a torrent of bullets across the base of the leviathan's necks, while the Octari took a more methodical approach, aiming all eight of its energy weapons at a single target. Each shot cut deep. After a few seconds, a neck slid into the ocean. The Shrike's lasers burned right through it. The salvo made it clear just how enormous of a leap forward the death machine was in the evolution of Z'han weaponry. It made the navy's ship-bound weapons look like children's toys in comparison. Having a couple of those on hand would be a major boon for Kimori's defenses.

Without a moment's hesitation, the Shrike pilots shifted their aim to rain death upon another neck, cutting though it faster than Serena could say *superweapon.*

Four heads down, eight to go...

Seated atop the Shrike's water tank like a ridiculous ornament, Amara maintained her balance despite the recoil of its weapons. She held a metallic tube that required both hands to keep steady and pointed at the leviathan. Her Octari pulled the trigger set near Amara's shoulder, launching a blast of light at the leviathan that looked like a miniature version of Ivy's solar beam. It burned a deep hole into the side of a leviathan neck, halfway between the head and body below the surface. Cole's Octari shifted their aim to finish that one off.

Karrde called it right. They had the leviathan's complete and undivided attention now. It gave up all attempts to chomp on the fleeing *Duchess Elizabeth* and turned its seven remaining heads towards the *Biga.* The *Von Spegman* moved aside so they could fire at will without fear of crossfire.

Fragments of metal shot out of the *Biga,* flashing against their shields before falling into the ocean. Serena registered the *boom* a moment later. Smoke billowed out of the side of the ship, pooling against the blue light of their shields.

Then the shields disappeared.

"Explosion in the generator room! Our shields are gone!" A sailor shouted.

"How is that possible?" Another asked. "We haven't even been hit yet!"

"How should I know?" The first sailor countered.

The *Biga* rocked from a blow to the port side, tipping the starboard side towards the ocean. Serena clung to the starboard railing as a half dozen tentacles slammed the deck, crushing several sailors. Other sailors slid into the railing so fast that they flipped over it and plummeted to the ocean below.

With grace Serena knew she'd never possess, Annea maintained her balance and jogged over to a storage box along the railing, where she retrieved a grappling hook and rope. She twirled the hook as if preparing to lasso a bull. "What do you plan to do with that?" Serena asked.

"I need to get into melee range." Annea made it sound like that should be obvious.

"You're going to swing yourself onto the leviathan?" It sounded like the kind of plan *she* would come up with, not the practical elf.

"It's focusing on the ship, not individuals. It won't notice me until it's too late." As the leviathan's heads closed in, Annea hurled the grappling hook. It wrapped itself around a neck several times before the hooks bit into scales. She backed up several paces, then dashed to the railing and jumped off, using her momentum to swing towards the monster.

Seven heads, six tentacles... Serena froze, crippled with indecision. With death looming from all sides, what could she do to make a difference?

Annea was wrong. The leviathan absolutely would target specific people. One of its tentacles slid along the deck on a direct line for Ivy. The dryad had wandered a hundred feet away and had her gaze lowered to the ocean, preparing to marshal another wave of lily pads into action.

As Annea swung towards the leviathan, another head moved to snatch her out of the air.

Both women faced imminent death.

She could only try to save one.

CHAPTER 26
DESPERATE MEASURES

Annea could handle herself.

"Ivy, watch out!" Serena shouted, tossing her bow aside. She dashed for the dryad.

Ivy looked up, abandoning her attempt to command more lily pads. She saw the leviathan head ready to snap Annea out of the air. An aura of sunlight glowed around her. She dropped her staff and extended an arm to unleash a solar beam.

Goddess, no... Ivy couldn't control it last time. Conditions were far worse now.

"Ivy, on your right!" She pointed emphatically at the tentacle snaking towards her.

Ivy either ignored her or didn't hear. She unleashed her solar beam without Serena's support. It severed the leviathan head targeting Annea an instant before the tentacle wrapped Ivy up and lifted her off the deck. Her aim went wild, cutting through Annea's rope, sending the elf plummeting into the ocean. An instant later, it decapitated the head she'd been swinging for in the first place. The tentacle lifted Ivy higher and twisted her to face down, sending the beam into the deck of the *Lord Biga* itself. Serena altered her path to stay clear of warping and melting deck plates.

An inarticulate cry of alarm from Tako was her only warning that Ivy's aim shifted again. She dived, rolling clear a second before solar energy melted the deck behind her. The skin on her back prickled. She'd been burned. Tako had it worse. *"You OK back there, buddy?"*

"I will survive," he said, downplaying his pain. She caught flashes of it through their mental bond, a sensation like a hundred needles

piercing leathery skin. He repositioned himself on her unburned chest and abdomen.

Ivy clearly couldn't stop the power she'd unleashed. The tentacle whipped around, sending her beam into the command tower. It cut halfway through the tower with a diagonal slash that carried on into the lower decks. Alarms wailed, signaling a hull breach. The *Biga* was taking on water by the time her attack dissipated.

Serena reached the leviathan's tentacle and pounced on it, clinging as tightly as she could. It wasn't easy — the limb was smooth skin, coated with a thin layer of slime that made it hard to keep her grip. It felt as cold as hugging a block of ice. *"Get ready to jump if you have to."* Could her power hurt him while he was attached? Flames coated her body for a moment before she could concentrate the power into her hands. Tako grunted at the brief touch of flame but made no move to leave.

She used her hands to burn through the tentacle. Not the most original idea, perhaps, but it was the best she could come up with while a battle raged all around them. The stench of burning flesh assaulted her nose. She had to be fast. If the leviathan decided to toss Ivy, the force of impact against water could be lethal. If it pulled Ivy underwater, she'd drown. Of course, it could just fling her into one of its remaining mouths like a piece of candy.

Tako pushed out his limbs, adding his grip strength to hers. As soon as he did, she learned something about Octari that Tako's memories hadn't made clear — the suckers on their limbs tasted everything they touched. He was too busy helping her hang on like a determined parasite to prevent those sensations from crossing over. Blend together bile, snot, pus, and urine, give it the consistency of molasses, and the resulting nightmare would probably taste like the thin layer of slime coating the tentacle. Tako wasn't enjoying it any more than she was.

Serena tried to take stock of the battle as a distraction from her gross work. The Shrike danced across the deck with agility she'd never expect in a bulky killing machine. Cole and his Octari had their hands full dodging five tentacles at once. They did as much damage as they could, but had to choose their shots with care to avoid friendly fire. Amara dropped her weapon and clung to a handle above the octari's water tank, sliding back and forth across it on her belly as she tried desperately to hang on. As the Shrike cut towards the port railing, she lost her grip and tumbled over the side.

That fall saved her life.

The leviathan was through with the Shrike's abuse. It grimaced and endured a flurry of bullets and energy beams to unleash a jet of oily fire at the construct from point-blank range. Cole strafed to the side and popped an emergency eject button, sending him and his Octari flying on parabolic arcs into the ocean below. The Shrike exploded a moment later, blowing up the attacking head and blasting a hole through the top three decks of the *Biga*. With the ship already sinking, the additional damage didn't matter. No crew were caught in the explosion.

Some sailors shot at the leviathan's tentacles, but most hacked at them with axes. Too often they had to step over the crushed bodies of their fellow sailors to do it. They were brave, but only faring slightly better than they would felling a century old oak tree with a butcher's knife. Lucky sailors got tossed overboard, where they might survive if they could tread water until a lifeboat found them. Unlucky sailors got smashed into the deck. The casualty rate was horrific.

Still four heads to go...

"Got any suggestions?" Serena asked. The tentacle she rode smashed into the command tower, bending it to the side. If not for Tako's superior grip strength, they would have gone flying. Still, Serena's body vibrated like a tuning fork.

"Cut faster," Tako said.

They slammed into the command tower a second time. Serena felt sure she'd have whiplash, but their grip held. She'd burned halfway through the flailing limb — it couldn't remain functional for long.

"All hands, abandon ship. I repeat, abandon ship." Karrde's orders blared from the few undamaged speakers. "The *Von Spegman* will go weapons free in two minutes."

Translation: The *Von Spegman* could fire at will on the leviathan, even if those shots risked injuring anyone still onboard the *Biga*.

Ivy hung limp in the tentacle's grip, unconscious or dead. It struck the command tower a third time. That blow proved fatal for both the command tower and the tentacle itself. The command tower toppled into the ocean. The tentacle ripped apart where Serena cut it. They lost their grip and tumbled twenty feet to slam into the deck, face down. If Tako hadn't repositioned his limbs to cushion her head, the impact might have knocked her out. Or worse.

I may have cracked ribs, Serena thought.

Metal groaned and squealed as the leviathan used tentacles to widen openings Ivy's beam created. Sensing an opportunity, the leviathan poked a snout into a tear in the ship and unleashed a torrent of flame. The rear third of the ship glowed orange as decking melted, then that chunk of the ship broke loose. Other leviathan heads culled their dead companions.

The *Biga's* bow pitched up. It wouldn't be long now before the whole ship went under. What sailors remained abandoned the fight and scrambled for lifeboats.

Ivy's body came free of the severed tentacle's grip amongst the chaos. She slid down the deck towards Serena. Rather than attempt to stand, Serena found it easier to use her arms and legs to push herself forward like she was climbing a steep hill. She rolled Ivy onto her back, placing two fingers to her neck to check for a pulse.

Nothing.

A sailor put a hand under Serena's shoulder to pull her upright, but she shrugged him off. "We have to get to the lifeboats!" he said.

"I'm not leaving Ivy behind!"

"You don't have to," he said, grabbing the dryad under the arms. "Grab her feet." Together, they lifted Ivy and set off for the nearest lifeboat. They'd gone only ten feet before they heard the growl.

One of the leviathan's remaining heads had them in its sights, eyes showing all the malice she'd expect from a wounded predator out for revenge. It opened its mouth, giving them an intimate view of its teeth, tongue, and the tube-like ducts that released flames. Its roar hit them with the force of a shove, knocking them to the deck. The starboard side of the ship tipped toward the ocean, causing Serena and Ivy to slide that way. The helpful sailor wasn't so fortunate. He hadn't slid, which kept him in range of the leviathan's jaws as it chomped down and ripped loose a segment of hull. Another couple inches, and the leviathan would have taken Serena's foot too.

"It's been a pleasure, Tako," Serena said aloud, rising to her feet to stand defiantly at the edge of the leviathan's bite marks. "It's time for you to hop off and save yourself. You wouldn't survive what I'm about to do." She sent him an image of herself as a blazing torch. She hoped to feed the leviathan a fireball, but if she couldn't, she intended to make her death as scorching and painful as possible for the monster.

"Our fight is not over yet," he said, not budging. *"You should duck."*

The leviathan opened its mouth wide again, but this time, its roar sounded pained. Purple lines of energy appeared at the back of its throat in a familiar pattern... She hit the deck and shielded Ivy's body with her own as the leviathan's head exploded in a blast of purple energy, showering the area in gore and bone fragments.

"Sorry about the lack of warning," Annea said, hopping off the leviathan's neck as it slid off the deck. She sheathed her kukris and offered Serena a hand. "Is Ivy OK?"

"I don't know. She's not moving." Serena grabbed Ivy's feet while Annea lifted her shoulders. The two of them shuffled downhill to the starboard rail, where a lifeboat dangled in open air.

"I don't think the winch will support all our weight as-is," Annea said, pointing to a bend in the pulley arms that lowered the boat to the surface. "Let's get Ivy in there, lower it, and jump." There was no graceful way to do it. They had to toss Ivy's body like a sack of grain across two feet of open air to get her into the lifeboat, then fight with the pulley system to lower it. At least they were able to work at it without interference. With all resistance from the *Lord Biga* and her sailors ended, the leviathan turned its attention elsewhere.

"How did you..." Serena trailed off and waved in the general direction of Annea's explosive entrance.

"I swam onto the leviathan and climbed up its neck. They're thicker and less sensitive to kukri stabbing than I'd expected. It never tried to throw me off." Annea jumped off the *Biga,* doing a front flip before plunging into the water. Under the circumstances, she couldn't be showing off. She just didn't know how to do anything without being acrobatic about it. "Come on Serena, get a move on."

"Just a second," Serena said. She felt they were forgetting something. Her bow and arrows weren't immediately visible, so she wrote them off as lost. Ivy's staff rested against the rail a dozen paces away, somehow not knocked into the water during the worst of the fighting. She grabbed it then threw herself overboard. Annea used those few seconds to haul herself into the lifeboat so she could offer Serena a hand getting in.

"You know more about dryads than I do," Serena said. "Is Ivy going to be alright? I didn't feel a pulse."

"Where did you check?" Annea asked. Serena demonstrated by placing two fingers against her left carotid artery. "Ah. The neck doesn't work for dryads. Their pulse is strongest in the wrists and ankles." She grabbed Ivy and held her ankle in a tight squeeze for several seconds. "She's alive."

Serena sagged with relief. Her efforts to save the dryad hadn't been in vain.

The leviathan let out a trio of roars from its remaining heads. It drifted towards the *Von Spegman*, but its movements were jerky and erratic, as if it struggled to keep its heads above water. Why didn't the beast flee? Where was the survival instinct? Nine of its twelve heads were gone. Even apex predators knew when to go lick their wounds and live to fight another day.

A group of narwhal breached the surface between their lifeboat and the leviathan, took a breath, then dived again. Of course. She'd forgotten about the separate battle happening underwater. Uproar Squadron's task was to cripple as many tentacles as possible. While that would reduce attacks against the ships, it would also make it difficult or impossible for the leviathan to get away. It probably thought it had no choice but to fight on. Or it was too enraged to think of anything but lashing out.

"Can you give me a hand here?" Annea asked, drawing her attention back to the boat. "Hold her down, I want to try something." She held out her index and middle fingers. An arc of purple electricity sparked between them. "This is a little trick I picked up during my Wandering Decade. It's meant as a stunning technique in hand-to-hand combat, but on someone who is unconscious, it can be a rather effective wake-up call."

Serena pressed down on Ivy's shoulders. Annea touched the electricity to Ivy's ankle where she'd felt a pulse. Ivy spasmed for a moment, then sat upright so fast she bashed her forehead against Serena's on the way up. "Ouch," they both said, rubbing their heads.

"Welcome back." Annea handed Ivy her staff.

The dryad looked around, taking in the scene, then pointed to sailors treading water nearby. "They require flotation devices." Apparently no worse for wear despite being knocked out, she aimed her staff at a nearby clump of lily pads. In short order, she had them swimming themselves up to the sailors, who stared at them as if expecting an attack.

"Climb on them!" Serena hollered. They took the hint when the lily pads spread out to look like floating mattresses, with a pad for each sailor. They really could support a human's weight.

"There must be something more we can do," Serena said, not enjoying the thought of riding out the end of the fight in a lifeboat.

"Against the leviathan? We've done enough. More than enough," Annea cast a disapproving look at Ivy, but refrained from voicing her displeasure. "We have room in here for more people. Let's grab who we can."

The last visible piece of the *Biga* surrendered itself to the ocean's depths. With it went the enchanted bag holding everything Serena had purchased or been given in the Nexus. She'd just lost everything she owned for the second time in a week.

Serena examined the motor at the rear of the boat, trying to recall the operating instructions she'd been given during their grand tour of the ship. The design was intentionally simple. A single button on top activated and deactivated the motor, with a lever to control speed and a stick for steering. She put the speed on its lowest setting and turned the stick side to side gradually to get a feel for how it handled. Once she felt comfortable she wouldn't run someone over, she set off for the nearest sailors treading water.

"No…" Despite the motor's rumble, the leviathan's roars, and unceasing gunfire from the *Von Spegman*, Ivy's pained exclamation reached Serena's ears. The dryad's face was a portrait of guilt, remorse, and shame. "I hurt you." She gestured to Serena's back, as if she could have forgotten about her burns and their associated blisters.

You also sunk a capital ship. Serena caught herself in time. Ivy would realize that soon enough. No point in drawing attention to it now. Ivy never should have unleashed that second solar beam. Serena couldn't argue with Annea on that point this time. But Ivy wouldn't have figured out how to do it without her help. She had a healthy share of blame for this too.

"I'm fine," Serena lied.

"Let me heal you," Ivy said.

"Later. After we've saved as many people as we can."

They worked in silence. Serena piloted the lifeboat. Annea grabbed sailors and hauled them in. Ivy tended to any visible cuts and bruises as best she could. She threw herself into the healing, as if every sealed wound would in some small way atone for the damage she'd caused. By the time they'd crammed two dozen sailors into the boat with them, the sound of gunfire ceased. The *Von Spegman* had finished the job, killing the leviathan's final three heads. Its blood coated the nearby lily pads. It stained the clothing of most of the people who'd had to tread water for a time. It spread out in every direction like an expanding oil slick.

The floating corpse of their vanquished nemesis stretched at least a thousand feet from the end of a head's snout to the tip of its tentacles. Severed heads and necks bobbed in the waves all around them. Dead sailors too. So much carnage, all to acquire the leviathan pearls needed to power Z'han's greatest death machines. Killing to be able to do more killing still. The industrial scale of it unnerved her. She couldn't put killing the leviathan in the same mental box she did hunting a deer for its fur and meat.

"War is ugly," Tako said, enveloping her mind in a warm hug. In that moment she felt like she was receiving a life lesson from a grandfather. *"The people of Z'han fight an enemy who would enslave them and make them breeding stock before finally killing them. The*

Kroen would drive the Octari into the ocean's depths to fend for ourselves, or kill us outright if they could. If you're serious about fighting back against the Vohr, this won't be the last time you'll participate in a fight like this. Our path is the one we believe results in the smallest loss of life in the long run."

"Even if that means wiping out the Kroen?"

"Isn't that what you wish to do to the Vohr? To Korahshka, and everyone associated with him?" How could she be so certain of the righteousness of the violence she wished to commit, then judge others for doing the same? Tako hadn't said it, but she could read between the lines.

With the battle over, Serena steered their lifeboat to the side of the *Von Spegman*, placing their boat in line to send people up the rungs on the side of the ship to reach the main deck. The ship used one of its own lifeboats to lift those too injured to climb, using it like a makeshift elevator platform. By the time Serena, Annea, and Ivy finally had their turn to climb aboard, the main deck was crowded. Medics patrolled the deck, tending to the wounded. Everyone found a patch of deck to sit or lay on until given orders.

To Serena's surprise, Captain Karrde had made it out of the *Biga's* command tower and must have been picked up by a lifeboat. He wandered the deck, helping the medics and offering words of encouragement everywhere he went. His efforts weren't well received. Bitter and hostile glares followed his every movement. Sailors cursed him under their breath. She'd been ready to defend Ivy from similar hostility, but the sailors' glances at the dryad were ambiguous, like they didn't know what to make of her. On the one hand, she was directly responsible for knocking out a quarter of the leviathan's heads. On the other, she'd dealt the killing blow to their flagship.

"This was supposed to be a routine hunt," one sailor said. "How'd it all go to shit so fast?"

"Someone screwed up royally. Probably several people," another said. "One of the Kroen corpses wasn't actually dead. She got into the *Biga* through an unfixed hole in one of the storage compartments. Shoddy maintenance. Of course, she could have made the hole, but nobody issued a security alert to sweep the ship.

Found her way into the shield generator room and blew herself up as soon as we'd engaged the leviathan, taking out our shield generator. Screwed us real good."

"How the hell does someone fail to notice a Kroen isn't dead?"

"Same way someone fails to ensure the Duchess Elizabeth's shields are fully charged. They never should have broken that fast. The war's been going on too long, man. A whole lot of dumbasses are getting sloppy."

The sailor's chatter helped Serena begin to form a picture of why everything went so poorly even before Ivy crippled the *Biga,* but she couldn't understand why everyone wanted to take it out on Karrde.

"Such is the burden of command," Tako said. *"The captain is accountable for the actions of his crew. Ultimately, he should have verified the holds for containing Kroen corpses were in good condition. He failed to make sure his ship and the others of his task force were properly maintained. He encouraged Ivy to harness power beyond what she could control, with devastating consequences. His debriefing with King Lordran will not be pleasant. Neither, I suspect, will ours."*

Over the next several hours, Uproar Squadron diced up the leviathan remains and pried loose pearls from the beast's heads, necks, and dorsal ridge. They carried them one at a time to large buckets tied to ropes that sailors on the main deck held just above the ocean's surface. Every time a bucket got half full, it was hauled up, emptied, and lowered back down. In the end, they harvested almost seventy, a total Tako said would keep the current inventory of shrikes powered up for over a year. Lifeboats searched the area, rescuing who they could, or carrying out the grim duty of retrieving the bodies of the fallen, knowing full well it'd be impossible to find them all. Their families deserved the opportunity to give them a proper funeral and burial.

Officially free of any responsibilities, Serena lay down on her stomach and let Ivy tend to her burns. She felt like a hundred needles pricked her skin over and over as Ivy ran her hands up and down her back. After a few seconds of agony, the sensation gave way to a calming, cool numbness. Ivy kept it up for several minutes without saying a word. She even took care of Tako's injuries. At last, she declared her work complete and took a seat near Serena's head.

Serena gave one of Ivy's hands a soft squeeze, hoping the dryad would understand she had no hard feelings over what happened. Ivy's posture relaxed a fraction, but she didn't break her silence.

As the moon rose in the evening sky, the narwhal riders climbed aboard and lay down on the deck, too exhausted to move any further. Their mounts were trained to follow Z'han ships even if they didn't have riders. There would be no after party tonight, Serena knew. Not with the *Biga* gone and the *Duchess Elizabeth* a useless, floating wreck. Not with so many sailors lost in the fight. The *Von Spegman* lacked the space to house the survivors of the other two ships, so most people rode out the trip back on the main deck, huddling close to each other for warmth.

Serena rolled onto her back and stared at the stars, wondering if the king would renege on their arrangement after learning of this debacle. She wondered where they'd turn next to find help for Kimori. She could sense Tako's mind thinking along similar vectors, but he kept his own counsel. For now. He wasn't a bad companion. Talking to him was really the only bright spot for her in this whole excursion to Torbakhal. She was going to miss him. Zalinda hadn't lied, no other type of relationship could compare to the understanding and acceptance of a human-Octari partnership. That symbiosis was something special.

"About us," Tako said, gently intruding into her thoughts. *"I've been thinking, and I have a proposal I'd like to discuss with you..."*

CHAPTER 27
THE DEBRIEFING

Serena couldn't decide if they faced a mission debriefing or the announcement of death sentences. Armed soldiers lined the conference room's stone walls. Their escorts pulled out chairs for Serena, Annea, and Ivy to sit opposite the king. Pik-Pik and Tik-Tik were allowed inside on the condition they remained silent. The locals had no patience for the duo's constant chatter and questions.

Karrde sat alone at the far end of the table, his usual charisma nowhere to be found. The braids that ran halfway down his back had been cropped up to the back of his neck in a ragged pattern, as if done in a hurry with no care for how the final result looked. For all she knew, that was a standard punishment for losing a ship. He looked more like a prisoner than a naval officer. How long had he been here before they'd been escorted in?

"Mr. Karrde told me some incredible things about your leviathan hunt," King Lordran said. "Things I'm finding hard to believe. And so, I want to confirm some details with you three directly."

"Are all these guards necessary?" Annea asked. "We are allies of Z'han, not your enemies."

"And what fine allies you are." Lordran didn't mask his sarcasm.

"We only participated in the leviathan hunt because you ordered us to."

"What a mistake that turned out to be." The king sat back in his chair. "When we're expecting three ships to return home and only get one, people start asking questions. Rumors spread like wildfire through the armed forces. There's no keeping what happened a secret. Not with a debacle of this magnitude. All these troops are here, Annea, so I have as many people as possible spreading the truth, not sensationalist gossip. Though there may be little difference between the two in this case."

Serena took the king at his word on that point, for now. Every human in this room, herself included, had an Octari partner. The more she thought about it, the more she couldn't imagine Octari allowing the execution of foreign dignitaries.

"Can we make this quick? Kimori could be invaded at any time," Annea said. "You have a war to fight. So do I. I'd like to take those Shrikes you promised me and be on my way."

Lordran scowled. "I keep my word. And I expect the same of you. Answer my questions honestly, and you'll leave with what you came for."

Annea nodded, conceding the point. They'd submit to this last demand.

"I ordered the pyromancer to host an Octari for the duration of the voyage. But the greatest threat to my fleet turned out to be a dryad of all things."

Ivy's expression remained blank and unreadable. Silence lingered.

"Was there a question in there?" Annea prodded.

"Mr. Karrde tells me she single-handedly killed a magmadon," Lordran said.

"That's correct," Annea kept her tone neutral.

"But I'm given to understand she could not control that ability."

"Serena helped aim the attack. Their collaboration saved Z'han lives." In private, Annea remained furious about what they'd done. It felt good to know she'd stand up for them against anyone else though.

"Yes, there was a happy ending the first time. The second time, she sank a capital ship."

"That's my fault," Karrde said, inserting himself into the conversation for the first time since their arrival. "Annea didn't want her trying it again. I insisted she store up the energy for it in case we needed it."

"He is correct," Ivy said. "As the commanding officer of the task force, I considered his orders the highest authority on the matter."

"Spoken like a warrior," Lordran said.

"I am not a warrior. I agreed with his logic and I did not wish to deny myself a means of self-defence. So I complied."

"And sank a capital ship."

"She single-handedly eliminated three of the leviathan's heads," Annea said. "The *Biga's* shields were gone, allowing the leviathan to hammer away at it. The ship was already crippled and on death's door. Ivy's attack only accelerated the process by a few minutes. Her attack weakened the leviathan enough for the *Von Spegman* to finish it off. Once again, her actions saved lives."

Lordran shook his head. "Have you ever considered becoming a public defender? You'd be fantastic at bullshitting on your client's behalf."

"Everything I've said is true."

"How did the *Biga* lose its shields? Mr. Karrde believes a Kroen faked her death to be brought onboard as magmadon bait, snuck inside through a hole in a storage panel, then waited and blew up the shield generators in a suicide attack once the ship fully committed to the fight."

Annea shrugged. "You'd know what Kroen can do better than me. But I'd say it's plausible. Perhaps they've developed a nonlethal version of *salamir* to put themselves in a state that mimics death. From what I caught of their assault on the kingdom when we arrived, I'd say they're not above suicide attacks any more."

"They never were," Lordran said. "The loss of the *Biga* couldn't have come at a worse time. We received word from the merfolk while you were away that the Kroen destroyed one of their island farming colonies. We cannot rule out attacks from the ocean anymore. Breaches in discipline will be dealt with harshly. All of our tactics must be reevaluated and overhauled."

It sounded like the beginnings of a speech, delivered for the benefit of the soldiers in the room.

"You have confirmed what I needed to know. Amara and Cole will meet you at the Planar Gate with their Shrikes and return with you to Kimori, as promised. You may go."

"Thank you, Your Highness." Annea bowed her head.

"All debts are paid Annea. If you come here seeking aid again, you will not find it."

"Understood."

It occurred to Serena that the king hadn't once referred to Karrde by rank. In fact, Karrde wore no rank insignia around his neck. "What's going to happen to the captain?" Serena asked.

"Julian Karrde is no longer a member of the Z'han navy. He and his Octari partner shall receive the same sentence as all capital ship captains who did not go down with their ships: exile, or execution. He has one day from the conclusion of this meeting to leave the city if he wants to live. If you were under my command, your fates would be the same. Consider yourselves fortunate."

Goddess, Serena wanted to get off this planet. She'd be just fine if she never saw an ocean again. These people had been at war for so long. She noted the soldiers' grim expressions. Their fatigue. The general air of hopelessness. What condition would they be in if they didn't have the Octari for emotional support?

"There is one last item we must discuss before we go," Annea said. "A request from Serena and Takoyakisobaramaki."

All eyes on the room turned to her. The intensity of it felt uncomfortable. *"Are you sure this is what you want?"* Serena asked. *"You've seen my memories. You know what we're up against. This is your last chance to back out."*

"This is YOUR last chance to back out," Tako said. *"Few Octari ever get the chance to leave Torbakhal. I want to see the multiverse! This will be so fun!"* He had the energy of a child about to rip open a birthday present, but sobered into a grandfatherly tone. *"But I'm just happy I had the chance to partner with a human one last time. I'll always cherish our time together, despite how the battle went. If this is goodbye, I'm content."*

He pulled open the curtain between their minds, giving her an unobstructed view into his psyche. He meant every word he said. No mind games. No attempts at emotional manipulation. If she wanted her mind all to herself again, he'd understand. This was a man at peace with how his life turned out, but not done seeking new adventures and experiences. Serena's eyes misted up at the power of his warmth and sincerity. It felt so strange to know *exactly* how someone else felt.

"Well?" King Lordran's voice forced her back into the moment. "Get on with it."

She'd made up her mind the minute Tako suggested this. She wanted it too. "I would like to remain Tako's host, and take him with me when we leave Torbakhal. He can be another set of eyes gathering information for your people about the Vohr threat."

"The Vohr are your problem, not ours," Lordran said. "We have enough problems as it is. Octari have the same rights and privileges as humans in our kingdom. If he wants to leave, he's free to go. There are far more Octari that want to be partners than there are available hosts anyway. It's not like anyone else wanted him, from what Zalinda tells me."

Tako's presence swelled in her mind, keeping her pinned to her seat as effectively as a firm hand on her shoulder. How dare the king belittle such a kind soul. She wanted to slap Lordran's smug face.

"We're getting what we wanted, Serena," Tako said. *"The rest is just noise. Let it go. Forgive his lack of courtesy. These are trying times for the kingdom."*

"Stop being nice!"

Tako laughed. *"I only know how to be myself."*

Annea and Lordran said their formal goodbyes, then a group of soldiers escorted them out the kingdom's main gate. They hadn't needed to pack, since they'd lost everything they'd brought except for Annea's kukris and Ivy's staff when the *Biga* sank. Their exit received mixed reactions from bystanders. Most of the survivors of the battle and their families hailed them as heroes, even Ivy. But just as many blamed them for everything that went wrong. Gossip and rumors really did spread fast. Tako prevented more than one hurled piece of fruit from hitting Serena in the head.

Pik-Pik and Tik-Tik had the good sense to wait until they'd left the kingdom to say anything.

<That king is a jerk!>

<You're much nicer than him, Annea.>

<Zalinda wouldn't let us explore anywhere.>

<We gave her the slip.>

<Multiple times.>

<She got quite exasperated with us.>

<We got kicked out of the palace three times while you were away.>

<They forgot ants can climb vertical surfaces. We got back in through open windows.>

<There were so many good smells coming out of the kitchen!>

<It would have been rude *not* to look.>

As always, Pik-Pik and Tik-Tik's banter was a rapid back-and-forth. Serena gave up trying to keep track of who said what.

Annea sighed. "Did you gather intel on Z'han's war like I asked you to?"

<Of course we did!>

<So much info.>

<Lots and lots and lots of info.>

"Good," Annea said. "When we get home, I'm going to open a bottle of wine and you can tell me all about it."

<Can we have some?>

"Maybe after you've shared what you learned. And only if you promise to behave. I haven't forgotten what happened last time you two had alcohol."

<Deal.>

They climbed the hill and entered the bamboo forest leading back to the Planar Gate in silence. The deeper into the forest they went, the more uncomfortable Ivy looked. Her pace slowed.

"Can we pause for a second?" Serena asked. "Ivy's looking constipated."

The dryad glared at Serena, but the sudden attention loosened her tongue. "Thank you, Annea," she said. Her posture relaxed, as if saying those words eased an anxiety eating away at her.

Annea looked as confused as Serena felt. "What for?"

"You disapproved of my actions. Yet you defended me against the king anyway."

"Of course I did. You're one of my people now, as far as I'm concerned. I'll always have your back in public. In private? If you thought our first training session was difficult, the next will be far worse."

"You do not understand. My actions showed I am a liability. A dryad would never do what you did. They would have left me behind. Or asked the king to execute me. Weakness cannot be tolerated. It must be pruned. It puts the safety of the group at risk."

"You're not weak, Ivy," Annea said, motioning for them to resume walking. "And you're not a liability either. Mistakes happen when you experiment with powers unfamiliar to you. Especially when they're as powerful as that solar beam. You'll learn." She paused, as if weighing whether or not to say anything else. "Did you ever witness your people pruning a weak link?"

"I did not," Ivy admitted.

Annea nodded. "I didn't think so," she said. She left it at that, leaving Serena and Ivy to ponder what she'd intended in asking that question.

True to King Lordran's word, Amara and Cole were already at the Planar Gate when they arrived. They sat on the ground between the legs of their bipedal death machines, eating sandwiches. Both offered lazy salutes to Annea. "We're ready to go when you are," Amara said.

"Thank you for coming. You'll have to park the Shrikes at the base of the world tree when we arrive. I'll have someone show you the fastest route back to them after we've all settled in."

After allowing the twins a minute to pack up the remnants of their lunch and climb into their Shrikes, Annea traced the eight symbols of Kimori's address in the air. The Gate popped to life. They all stepped through, with the Shrikes going last.

The time change threw Serena off again. They went from midday sun to sunrise in an instant. A burning pyre outside the ant colony's main entrance kept her gaze at ground level, instead of drifting up into the world tree's canopy like it wanted to. The pyre's shape looked lumpy. Inconsistent. Weren't the elves and ants both better at building things than that?

Curiosity spurred her forward. What fueled the fire? It took a half dozen paces for her brain to process what she saw. She knew what was burning.

Manti corpses.

CHAPTER 28

SINCE YOU'VE BEEN GONE

Annea stared at the pyre of manti bodies, struggling to form a coherent thought. *This is too fast. We've only been gone a few days. Are we already too late?*

Serena ran ahead, a fireball held tight in each hand. Her eyes scanned the skies, looking for something to fight.

Annea turned her attention to the heavens as well, expecting to see a rain of arrows, flying ants, or some other evidence of an ongoing fight. The skies were clear. No manti. No ants. Nothing. No drone army materialized in response to the Planar Gate's activation. To be fair, their enemy wouldn't be coming through the Gate. Even the usual bustle of ants bringing leaves and grasses back to the colony had ceased. Save for the manti piled up three high, the land between the Planar Gate and the ant colony was a dead zone.

"I think we can relax," Annea said. "It's way too quiet for there to be a battle going on."

"If Kimori had fallen, we would already know," Ivy agreed.

Serena snuffed out her fireballs. Pik-Pik and Tik-Tik's antennae ceased their nervous waving. Everyone relaxed. They still had time.

Annea turned her attention back to the pyre and had to laugh at the macabre absurdity of what she saw. Her two best friends sat on logs they'd placed around the pyre, roasting marshmallows over the burning corpses of their enemies. *Classic Inara and Pavi. Weirdos.*

"We can definitely relax," Annea said. "If my bodyguards feel content to let their guard down, it's safe." She ran ahead to give each of them a hug and a kiss on the forehead. As the rest of the group made their way towards the pyre, Amara and Cole hung back, the cockpits of their Shrikes sealed as if they still expected to be attacked.

"Former bodyguards," Inara said, poking at the tiara welded to Annea's skull. "We take a week off, and you go and quit your job. Or give yourself a promotion. I'm not sure what to call it. Either way, very rude. We don't know what to do with ourselves, now that we're not the queen's protectors anymore."

"I've been inconsolable." Pavi spoke with the light tone he always used when he meant the opposite of what he said. "I've had nothing to do but play with my son, make love to my wife, and murder killer bugs from another reality. It's been brutal, I tell you."

"He's right, because he's only good at two of those things."

"Don't lie to her. I'm great at killing bugs, thank you very much!" Pavi took the stick he'd been using to roast marshmallows and poked Inara in the side. She roared with laughter and smothered him with kisses.

Annea smiled and felt more tension ease from her shoulders. Monogamy was rare amongst Kimori's elves, but these two made it seem almost appealing. If her best friends could still be their weird and wonderful selves, then things couldn't be too bad. Yet.

Inara's expression turned serious. "Your new role will take some getting used to, oh great and mighty Sword of Kimori. We didn't expect to see you back so soon."

"We'll only be here long enough to get our allies from Z'han comfortable and get a status report on invasion preparations, then we're off to the Nexus," Annea said.

Pavi pointed his stick at the Shrikes. "Those look imposing." The machines stopped twenty feet behind the group and turned their backs to the world tree. They stood ready to take on any threat at a moment's notice. "But that can't be all the support we're getting from Z'han, is it?"

"Z'han is at war with the Kroen again. This is all they could spare," Annea said. "I've seen them in action, though. They're formidable." She reached into a pocket of Pavi's vest, fished out a marshmallow, and popped it into her mouth. She stole marshmallows from him, he stole roses from her bedroom whenever he and Inara came by to visit. She didn't remember how it started, but she took comfort in carrying on their weird tradition.

"Is it safe to be eating those?" Serena asked, wrinkling her nose at the smell of burning manti. Bile, with a hint of cinnamon.

"Pavi ate some manti. Roasting marshmallows over their remains can't be any worse." Inara poked her husband in the ribs.

"They wanted to eat us. Seemed fair to return the favor," he said. "For the record, they're edible, but I don't recommend it. Very bland taste. Far too chewy."

"What happened here?" Annea asked. Her relief at her world's continued survival transitioned into a need for more information.

"Everything was nice and quiet the first few days you were gone, but we've had a half dozen attacks in the last two days. All of them were small and poorly organized, but disconcerting nonetheless," Inara said. "Without you here to protect, Pavi and I volunteered for anti-Vohr patrol duties. This group of manti shredded one of the ant's food storage chambers before drones could get in there with Pavi and I to clear them out. Ants carried the bodies out here for us afterward. We've been replaced in the colony, so we just have to tend the blaze and keep our eyes open."

"Everyone is on edge," Pavi said. "If anyone doubted the reality of the threat before, nobody doubts it now. Vohr tunnels can appear anywhere. One opened up right in the middle of the market. Only one reaper came through, but it caused a panic. Bastard killed a dozen people before we stopped it. Hours later, a tunnel materialized in Ruta's hatchery chambers."

"We had a team in position for that, right?" Annea asked. "The queens are still alive?" As part of her war preparation instructions, she'd mandated they have elven teams posted at critical points in the ant colony at all times. The ants could fend for themselves just fine against whatever combat troops came through, but they'd need assistance finding any Vohr eyes conducting surveillance.

"Pavi and I were on hand for that one too," Inara said. "No combat troops came through, just a single eye. I shot it down. The *alucinatus* berries work like a charm." She swayed on her feet a bit as she gave Ivy a salute of appreciation.

"That's a relief," Annea said, looking her friend in the eyes. They had a dilated and out-of-focus appearance. "You're on them right now, aren't you?"

"I'm high as a kite and living my best life," Inara admitted. "It's my husband's turn to be the sober one."

Annea's eyebrows rose with realization. "You two were there for three of the six attacks?"

"Yeah. Some luck, right? I'm trying not to take it personally," Pavi said. "Hopefully we've taught them trying to tunnel into the ant colony or world tree is a waste of time." He unrolled a blanket he'd set next to a log, revealing a thin, curved claw as long as his arm. "This is one of the claws of the reaper from the market attack."

"Are you planning to make that a weapon?" Ivy asked. It looked better suited to puncturing and holding in place than slashing.

"I thought about it. Too heavy and unwieldy. I want to carve something into it and then hang it up over our bed. It would give the room a sexy, primal energy. What do you think?" Pavi asked, giving his wife a seductive smile.

"Do it. We promised Ryul a sibling. Your art could be... *inspirational.*" Inara stuffed an unroasted marshmallow into her husband's mouth.

"How is Ryul handling all of this?" Annea asked.

"As well as can be expected. Everything is changing so fast. We're building ballistae where statues of poets and philosophers once stood. His parents are taking turns eating the berries that showed him the *eye monster of doom*. It's a lot for a kid to take in."

"It's a lot for anyone to take in," Pavi said. "Kimori is experiencing cultural whiplash like you wouldn't believe. It's not easy to turn a society of artists, poets, writers, singers, farmers, and craftsman into warriors overnight. Our soldiers are doing their best, but, well... you'll see for yourself when you venture up the tree."

"Any news on how the selection process is going for my replacement?" Annea asked.

"It's done."

"Done?" She didn't know whether to feel relieved or offended that the Queens Emeritus replaced her so fast. She'd wanted it done quickly, but *four days?*

"She's probably in the royal chambers right now if you want to meet her. She's made a hell of a first impression. You'll like her," Inara said. She'd always been a quality judge of character, so if she thought so, it must be true.

Annea felt a faint but appreciated bit of relief as one of her many burdens slid away. Kimori had a new queen she should get along with. A power struggle or personality conflict would be a disaster when they had a war to fight. "Are you two on watch for much longer?"

"We're on duty for three more hours, and then we have a couple days off," Pavi said.

"Unless, of course, there's more trouble than the active teams can handle," Inara added.

Serena and Ivy had backed away from the pyre, not so far as to be rude, but enough to broadcast they wanted to be somewhere else. Given the smell, Annea couldn't blame them. "It was good to see you both." She wrapped up Inara and Pavi into a group hug. "I need to introduce our friends from Z'han to the people they'll be reporting to while I'm away. Then I'll meet the new queen. Stay safe, you two."

She had Amara and Cole put the Shrikes on standby. They were too big to walk through the ant colony, and too heavy to lift into the tree. They'd have to remain outside to deal with external Vohr attacks. Pik-Pik and Tik-Tik led the way up to the world tree through the ant colony, bombarding the royal twins with facts and trivia about Kimori the entire way. Their banter spared Annea having to hold a conversation, allowing her to think ahead to her inevitable meeting with her royal replacement.

Inara never steered her wrong, but she couldn't stop worrying. Kimori didn't have enough support to hold out against the scale of invasion she anticipated. She had to return to the Nexus to beg, borrow, or steal any additional weapons, personnel, or resources she could get. While she did, Kimori's new queen would have to be the glue holding their civilization together through a period of chaos not seen in thousands of years. In many ways, Annea thought she had the easier job, even with the threat hanging over her head that her power, and her life, would be forfeit the moment she lost the confidence of the ant queens, the Queens Emeritus, or the new queen herself.

Please, please let us get along…

CHAPTER 29

THE FRESH QUEEN OF KIMORI

Contrary to Inara's prediction, Kimori's new queen wasn't around when they arrived in the lodge for royal guests. To pass the time until the queen could meet with her, Annea introduced Amara and Cole to Kimori's military leadership. There weren't many people to talk to. Why keep a large standing army when you never thought you'd be attacked? Then they toured the world tree. The tour doubled as a chance for her to see their progress on fortifications. Serena and Ivy came along, wanting to see more of the elven city than they had in their initial visit.

The elves of Kimori moved with the grim purpose of a society that saw the proverbial axe dangling over their heads. They wanted to do everything they could to prepare themselves before it dropped. The largest hollow in the tree, which held fields for sporting events, now hosted soldiers running farmers through sword drills. Half of their art galleries were converted into archery ranges, with the art packed up and shipped down to the ant colony for storage. Schools were converted into field hospitals. The library, located near the center of the world tree, had its walls reinforced and armored to serve as a safe house to hide children and the elderly during an attack.

Nothing was spared some form of wartime conversion.

If she wasn't seeing it with her own eyes, she would not have believed it possible. Her people's ability to pivot into survival mode overnight was both inspiring and heartbreaking. Inara and Pavi had warned her, but nothing could prepare her for the site of the balcony where the statue of The Lovers once stood. The statue depicted two androgynous elves locked in a passionate kiss, meant to symbolize the universal nature of love. Their hands came together to form a heart, perfectly positioned to frame the setting sun. Now, the spot was an ammunition depot loaded with pallets of crates containing ballista bolts.

"Can you all manage without me for a while?" Annea asked, finding their tour surprisingly draining. She needed to return to the royal lodgings to rest, whether the new queen was available to talk or not.

"Sure," Serena said. "The rest of us can get something to eat. What's the name of that food that's slices of fish on top of rice?"

"Sushi."

"Right. We passed a restaurant serving it one level up. I'd like to try some."

"At this time of day?" Annea asked.

"It may be morning here, but my body says it's lunchtime," Serena said.

Amara and Cole exchanged a smug glance. "I doubt it's as good as Z'han sushi crafted by Octari masters, but it would be fun to see how elves do it," Amara said. "They don't serve octopus, do they?"

"They do not," Annea said. The royal twins sighed with relief. Their Octari no doubt frowned on their evolutionary relatives being used as a food source.

"I do not require sustenance at this time," Ivy said.

Serena took Ivy's hand in hers and started leading the dryad away. "Then you can dazzle us with your conversational skills while we stuff our faces. Come on." Pik-Pik and Tik-Tik fell in behind the two, babbling happily about which kinds of sushi they wanted to try.

Annea returned to the royal lodgings alone. She answered her people's questions as best she could or offered words of encouragement whenever someone stopped her, but she avoided conversation as much as possible without being rude about it.

The royal bedroom's decor hadn't changed. Perhaps its new owner had the same aesthetic tastes. More likely, she hadn't had time to change anything. Either way, Annea appreciated familiar surroundings while meeting the new queen — an event she'd not so long ago believed wouldn't be happening for another hundred and forty years. The door was open, but she knocked anyway, "May I come in?"

"You're back already? Come in." The queen lay on the bed, staring at the ceiling, but sat up at Annea's arrival. She couldn't be more than fifty years old, barely an adult by elven standards. The same age Annea had been when she set off on her Wandering Decade. Her dark hair flowed to her waist, laced with highlights in three different shades of green. She wore a simple gown of emerald silk with black accents. Like Annea, the woman had a preferred color scheme.

"Congratulations on your ascension to the throne, Your Highness," Annea bowed, affording the new queen the respect she'd earned. She didn't recognize the woman, but that wasn't surprising. Kimori's population was too large for her to know everyone, as much as she tried. "How are you settling into the role?"

The queen laughed. "I haven't been able to sleep since my trials began. I had a half hour to bathe and dress myself between the conclusion of my trials and my coronation. My first act as queen after my inaugural address was approving evacuation plans in the event the world tree falls and we have to evacuate survivors into the ant colony. I had a meeting with Queens Chibi and Ruta discussing drone deployments throughout the city, and where in the colony they want elven support. This is the first moment of peace I've had since you became the Sword of Kimori."

Annea winced. Every potential queen's trials were designed to push her to her breaking point. Even though most queens served their entire terms without dealing with a crisis, they had to be strong and resilient should desperate measures be necessary. Annea had the luxury of time to recover after her ordeal. This queen didn't. "I'm sorry. I can come back another time, if you'd prefer."

"No, please stay. I need someone to talk to, and I'm not about to open up to the Queens Emeritus right after four days of hell." The queen hopped off the bed and bowed. "My name is Jesserin Stoll. It's an honor to meet you."

"The feeling is mutual," she said, feeling some of her apprehension for this meeting melting away. "I hope you'll feel comfortable speaking your mind around me."

"Join me in the meditation chamber?"

Annea fell in behind the queen, keeping a respectful distance so she didn't tower over the younger woman. Annea was abnormally tall, but felt like an absolute giant next to the diminutive queen. "I hope you don't mind my asking, but I wasn't here to see it. What did they have you do for your trials?"

Every candidate for the crown who survived their Wandering Decade had to complete a series of trials upon their return. The trials were decided by the Queens Emeritus in consultation with one of the ant queens, and differed for each candidate. They would test each individual's strengths, weaknesses, and how they performed under extreme duress.

Jesserin grabbed a pillow and took a seat in the middle of the meditation chamber. "All of their tests related in some way to warfare and survival. Emeritus Kayloni brought me up to the medical ward, where dozens of elves lay on the beds with injuries simulated through illusion magic. She made me march up and down the ward for hours, looking at horrific injuries, triaging who would live, and who would die. We'd complete one circuit and the first person I'd seen would have a new injury to diagnose. I had no idea there were so many ways bodies could be broken. All the while, I was hounded with questions about the locations of critical supplies and how to triage our defenses as Kimori fell bit by bit to a simulated invasion."

"Emeritus Kayloni doesn't hold back," Annea said, taking a seat and casting her eyes at the lamps overhead. The candles Serena melted hadn't been replaced. "Most candidates who fail a trial fail whatever she's running."

"Out of a dozen candidates, I was the only one to get through her," Jesserin said. "Once I'd won Kayloni's approval, guards blindfolded me and a drone carried me into the deepest areas of the ant colony. I had to make my way back here without any assistance from the ants. I didn't get any time to rest between trials."

Annea had that same challenge during her own sequence of trials. The ant colony maintained slow, consistent growth for thousands of years, with underground tunnels stretching for miles in every direction. Most of its labyrinthine passages had never even been seen by elven eyes. Many weren't lit. She'd been told it was a test of an elf's sense of purpose and direction to find their way back to the tree, as well as a test of their knowledge of ant culture and architecture. If one understood the daily ebb and flow of drone life, that helped reduce the possibilities for where one was in the colony, shortening the amount of time spent searching for a path out. Candidates had three days to reach the world tree before failing the test. At that point, the ants could help the candidate. Annea passed with fifteen minutes to spare. She'd made a point of improving her understanding of the ants in the years since. That resolve led to Pik-Pik and Tik-Tik coming into her life, so she considered her near-failure one of the best things to ever happen to her.

"My condolences," Annea said. "That test is notoriously tough, even for candidates who can conjure up a light source."

"Oh no, that was easy. I'm a wayfinder," Jesserin said, referring to a rare form of magical aptitude that helped someone find the optimal path to their goal in any terrain or circumstance. "I just walked right out of there. No candidate has ever completed that trial faster."

"The Queens Emeritus didn't know you could do that, did they? There's no way they give you that test if they knew. You cheated." Candidates had to disclose their magical aptitudes, if they had any. It guaranteed trials were properly calibrated to each individual, so someone couldn't sail through one like Jesserin had.

"I took a calculated risk. Kimori needs a queen that can help us survive a war. In war, you never show the enemy your hand until it's too late for them to counter you. In their haste to move the process along as quickly as possible, the Queens Emeritus didn't make any of us provide disclosures. I saw an opportunity to make a point and hid my abilities from them. They didn't think I could use magic at all. Emeritus Flauren was furious and wanted me disqualified. I said if she couldn't recognize my powers and any potential threats I posed to Kimori, she couldn't be trusted to evaluate an enemy as diverse and alien as the Vohr."

Inara was right. The two of them would get along fabulously. "I would love to see a portrait of Flauren's face in that moment."

"I'll commission one when the war's over." Jesserin winked. "That stunt won me the approval of Queen Chibi. She wanted the trials discontinued and to have me crowned on the spot, but she didn't have enough votes. I had to do one last trial."

"What was their final test?"

"A scout ant flew me down through the opening at the top of the Forest in the Sky and set me down by the welded door. Then they planted a flag at Balor's feet. I had to reach the statue and retrieve the flag."

Annea's fists clenched so hard her fingernails almost pierced skin. She made no attempt to hide her anger. "Are the Queens Emeritus *insane*? If I didn't see you here, I'd call that a death sentence." She'd wanted a queen chosen quickly, not for the kingdom's best and brightest to be subjected to something like that. Forcing someone into the Forest in the Sky to reenact the legend of Balor's Game was madness. Pointless cruelty. It stank of insecurity, like the Queens Emeritus believed the people of Kimori wouldn't accept their new wartime queen unless she pulled off the unthinkable to prove her worthiness. "How —" Annea lost her voice.

"Did I survive?" Jesserin asked, finishing the sentence. "Balor's Sentinels inspire fear due to their numbers and their reach, but they're not very smart. I got them to bunch up, and then once I got around a tangle of them, it was an easy run to the finish line. Don't be too mad at the Queens Emeritus, okay? I think they only came up with that test because they were confident a wayfinder could handle it. You, Serena, and Ivy escaping may have led them to believe it's not as dangerous up there as we've always considered it to be."

Annea shook her head in disbelief. Jesserin was far nicer about it than she would have been.

"Oh! Just a second." Jesserin jumped up and ran back into the bedroom. Annea heard a dresser drawer slide open. A moment later, the queen returned holding a pair of kukris.

Jesserin offered Annea their hilts. "I believe you lost these."

Annea stared in disbelief. Jesserin held the kukris her father forged, which she'd assumed were lost forever. She took the blades and ran her thumbs over the rubies inlaid on the pommels, then set the weapons down and enveloped the smaller woman in a crushing hug. "I think you're insane to stop and pick up my kukris while dodging Sentinels, but I appreciate it more than I can say."

"It was no problem, really," Jesserin said, her voice coming out as a wheeze. Annea released her grip. "As soon as I got the flag, the scout ant picked me up and flew me out of there."

"I'd like to think I'm a good judge of character," Annea said. "You are going to make an incredible queen. You don't need my endorsement, but you have it anyway."

"I appreciate it!" Jesserin smiled. "Now you know how I earned the throne. I'm happy with how much Kimori has accomplished while I was going through all of that, but we are nowhere near as prepared for a full-scale invasion as I'd like. Please tell me help is coming."

"I'm working on it," Annea said. "We're venturing off to the Nexus by way of Torbakhal tomorrow. I'm going to demand to see the Sector Council. We will make them see reason. They can't continue to ignore the scope of the threat. We'll find the help we need. I swear it on my life."

"You already did," Jesserin said, tapping the tiara on Annea's head. Why did everyone want to touch it? "Now, would you like me to update you on those evacuation plans I mentioned earlier?"

"Hell no." Annea walked back into the bedroom to grab a bottle of wine and two glasses. "You can brief me on that when I return from the Nexus. You survived your trials. I survived a giant sea monster." She pulled a slender throwing knife from a holster at her thigh and stabbed it into the cork, then pulled the cork free. "No more official business. Now that I've met the queen, I want to meet Jesserin Stoll. What kind of music do you like? Who's your favorite author?"

"I'm an author myself," Jesserin said, swirling the wine in her glass. "I wrote almost four hundred pages last month, though I suppose that career will be on hiatus for the foreseeable future."

They became fast friends as the bottle of wine disappeared over the next two hours. Annea told tales of her travels across her

Wandering Decade. Jesserin read excerpts from her latest romance novel.

For a time, both women knew peace.

CHAPTER 30

MOONLIGHT RENDEZVOUS

Serena stared at the ceiling. Sleep eluded her. Perhaps she was cursed to never get a good night's sleep on Kimori. After all, she'd knocked herself out from overuse of magic twice here. She'd had her mind worked over by Korahshka. Losing consciousness on Kimori led to bad things.

Not even Tako could help her. He'd spent an hour trying before giving up. *"I can't make you fall asleep, Serena. Especially when a large part of you doesn't want to."* He'd finally gone to sleep on his own.

Her mind ran in circles for hours thinking about their return to the Nexus. Orlan's briefing on the Vohr inspired little hope that their sector's government would do anything about their plight.

She closed her eyes and focused on her breathing. She took a deep breath, exhaling slowly. Breathe in. Breathe out. If she focused only on her breathing, perhaps she could bore herself to sleep. It didn't work. A persistent headache didn't help.

She rolled out of bed and threw on a plain cloth shirt and pants she'd picked up from the marketplace several levels up, knowing Tako wouldn't mind an obstructed view while sleeping. If she couldn't sleep, she might as well go for a walk. The bioluminescent fungus lighting the lodge was dimmed for the late night hours, but provided just enough illumination for her to creep out without bumping into anything.

"Not much of a nightlife, is there?" She spoke to herself as she wandered deserted balconies and walkways throughout the world tree. As far as she knew, Kimori hadn't instituted a curfew. She'd expected a society of artists and poets would have an active nightlife, especially after spending an entire day in combat drills and other preparations. Instead, it felt like the whole population had disappeared. She walked through the cavernous hollow that served as a marketplace, running a finger across the counters of various booths. Except for the food vendors, all had their wares out on display, a tacit show of trust and lack of concern about theft. The lifelessness of the market gave her chills. She made haste to continue her wandering elsewhere.

She made her way to the amphitheater where Annea challenged Ivy to recreate plants from Ataraxia. Someone removed those plants while they'd been on Torbakhal, and the amphitheater now served as a briefing room. Bulletin boards filled the space between the stage and audience seating, holding duty schedules and supply projections. One board featured a graphic cartoon of an elf holding aloft the severed head of a manti, over the text *"We Shall Not Fall."* Moonlight poured into the vast, open space. She could have read a book in that light if she'd brought one.

"You couldn't sleep either?"

Serena jumped at the sound of the voice before recognizing it as Annea's. The elf sat five rows up, wearing only a bra and shorts that stopped well above the knee — not the sort of thing she'd expect one of the planet's rulers to wear out in public. Did Annea know the city would be a ghost town, or did she just not care who saw her like this? Serena swore the elf wasn't there when she'd arrived. Was Annea trying to be sneaky, or was fatigue impacting her senses that much?

"I can't stop thinking about tomorrow," Serena said. "You?"

"I'm worried about our new queen," Annea said, standing. "I fear the Queens Emeritus put too much emphasis on choosing someone quickly, and went with someone who won't be able to handle the stress and trauma of war."

"That's unfortunate," Serena said, frowning. All the buzz she'd heard during their tour of the city was overwhelmingly positive. But the general public lacked the perspective of someone who had lived the role. "Do you want to stay here a few days and mentor her?"

Annea shook her head. "We don't have time for that. How many more Vohr incursions can we survive before they start bringing serious pressure?"

"So we stick to the plan. How will you get the powers that be in the Nexus to actually do something?" Serena asked.

"No clue." Annea shrugged. "We start by getting the lay of the land, I suppose. See who on the Sector Council is most likely to support our cause, and go from there."

"That's it?" Serena said, making no effort to disguise her disappointment. "Just walk in and ask for a meeting, then hope for the best?"

"As opposed to what? Marching in there and demanding the strongest realms in our sector give us an extended loan on their militaries? I'm not sure there's anything we can do that will be good enough, or fast enough," Annea said. "It's a vast multiverse. The Vohr can't be everywhere. That truth makes it easy for many to see them as someone else's problem. I sometimes wonder if it wouldn't be better to save ourselves and make a new life in another realm in a different sector, or take up residence in some far-flung corner of the Nexus."

Serena didn't know what to say. Who was this Annea? She hadn't figured the elf she'd come to know over the last week was a quitter. Serena tapped her forehead, where Annea's tiara would be. "Wouldn't your fellow rulers kill you for desertion?"

"I've told you before, magic doesn't work across realities. The tiara is welded to my head for life, but the kill switch is an empty threat if I'm not on Kimori."

Serena took a deep breath, struggling to keep her temper in check. This whole conversation felt off in ways she couldn't explain. "Do what you want. I told you before, I'll go my own way against the Vohr if I have to. I didn't think you were a coward."

"Is it cowardice to step out of the way of certain death? That just seems smart to me. What makes Kimori more special than the three hundred worlds already destroyed? How arrogant are we to think we'll be the first to hold the Vohr at bay? Do you truly think you'd be able to make any difference against such a force on your own?" Annea said.

"If you really believed Kimori's defeat was inevitable, we'd have spent our time searching for worlds everyone could evacuate to."

Serena studied the elf carefully, trying to articulate the sense of wrongness threatening to overwhelm her.

She sent Tako a mental poke. She didn't want to wake him, but needed a second opinion. When she tried, she found the spot Tako occupied in her mind barren, as if she'd never hosted him at all.

She's naked, Serena realized, using Annea's term for anyone walking around unarmed. No kukris. No throwing knives strapped to her thighs. Not even a knife at her wrists or ankles. Annea never went *anywhere* without a weapon, ever. Serena coated her arms in flames as the truth dawned on her.

She'd fallen asleep after all.

"Your acting sucks," Serena said, hurling a fireball at the illusion wearing Annea's skin.

"Very good!" Annea's form shimmered and disappeared, leaving Korahshka standing in her place. He caught the fireball and crushed it as if it were no more threatening than a snowball. "It is very rare for anyone to notice one of my eyes. Rarer still for anyone to destroy my tunnels into their reality. And now you've recognized my dream manipulation. I'm impressed." Korahshka gave her a deep bow that managed to convey both respect and condescension at the same time. "It didn't take me too long to figure out which world I'd lost a connection to."

"Is that how you knew to recreate this dream version of Kimori?" Serena asked.

Korahshka shook his head. "Last time, I created dream realities inspired by fragments of your memories. This time, I opted to insert myself into a dream in progress. Every once in a while, subtlety accomplishes what brute force cannot. How's the headache? I've been learning from you this whole time."

Good thing she'd only been in an anxiety loop, instead of dwelling on anything worse for him to know about.

"I know what you are," Serena said, throwing another fireball. Korahshka swatted it into one of the bulletin boards, which exploded into a mess of wooden shrapnel. "Are you the only Davoh'rei terrorizing the multiverse, or am I going to need to hunt your friends down too?"

"We are legion," he said, smiling wide to showcase his multiple rows of shark teeth. At the snap of his fingers, the amphitheater was filled to capacity with Davoh'rei. The throng of purple skinned beings rose to their feet, offering their master a standing ovation.

Korahshka had to feel confident to engage in such theatrics. She tried her best not to be intimidated, but that was easier said than done. Despite knowing it all to be a dream, her senses told her she stood alone before thousands of the enemy. "It must be frustrating, attacking Kimori several times now with nothing to show for it," Serena said.

"This is mere foreplay, my dear. No world can remain in a state of vigilance forever. Balor's defeat marked the beginning of the end for the Luminous Ones. It's poetic that Kimori's fall will be a significant step towards restoring what was lost."

"Balor can't be that impressive. He got his ass kicked by elves and ants."

Korahshka laughed and waved a hand. The stage became quicksand beneath Serena's feet. She sank to her ribs before it hardened back into its original form, pinning her in place. Her arms were trapped somewhere beneath the stage, completely immobile. Korahshka took his time marching down to the stage to a chorus of cheers from his summoned companions. At a snap of his fingers, a chair appeared in front of her. Korahshka sat and studied her like a man who had all the time in the world.

"Pride comes before the fall. The Luminous Ones grew complacent. They underestimated the agents of chaos. For that error, they were sealed away, and the multiverse fell into an age of disarray. But it's impossible to contain gods forever. My master has had fifteen thousand years to learn from past mistakes. Once freed, he will restore order and reward us for our unwavering devotion." Korahshka twirled a hand. A skinning knife appeared in his grip.

Serena stared at the knife, panic rising. It may only be a dream, but she remembered the manti cutting her in half last time. The pain had been all too real. Could she force her way out of the dream again?

Korahshka removed the chair and sat cross-legged on the stage floor, grabbing the top of her head with the hand not holding the knife. Holding her head steady, he drew shallow cuts across both of her cheeks. Serena winced, then forced herself to maintain eye contact.

"Here's what's going to happen," Korahshka said, turning the knife so she could watch drops of her blood drip from the blade's edge. "You're going to go back to the Nexus, where you'll waste several days in a fruitless attempt to marshal support for this world. You'll come to realize that you stand alone. Nobody is going to save you. You'll put up a token resistance, and in the end, your power will be mine."

"Generous of you to give us a few more days," Serena said.

"I've grown bored, conquering worlds without resistance. I don't mind waiting for some proper entertainment. Besides, Kimori's conquest isn't the only thing I need to tend to."

"Keep going," Serena said. "I've always wanted to get talked to death."

Korahshka laughed. He cut above her eyebrows, sending blood trickling into her eyes.

She didn't make a sound. She wouldn't give him the satisfaction.

The bastard loved the sound of his own voice, droning on and on about the violence he'd inflict on Kimori. How the elves and ants deserved it. How the multiverse would be a better, more stable place without them in it. How he'd use her powers to make other rebellious worlds fall in line. He punctuated each point with another cut to Serena's face or the exposed portions of her arms. His grip remained rock solid on her head, as if he knew she'd try something reckless to force herself out of the dream if given the chance. Korahshka was the embodiment of the narcissistic villain from the adventure novels she liked to read, obsessed with his own supposed brilliance.

With every cut, her rage grew. *This is all fake. When I wake up, I'll be perfectly fine. But I will make sure Korahshka's death is very, very real.*

She focused her will, trying to make Korahshka's blood boil. Nothing happened. She tried to light his clothing on fire, but had no success there either. Was it because her powers didn't work that way, or were her failures a result of Korahshka's influence over the dream? She didn't know. Magic wasn't flowing into her the way it should. After throwing those first fireballs, tapping into magic felt like eating oatmeal by sucking it up through a straw. She kept trying. As Korahshka rambled on, finding her magic got progressively easier and easier.

Suddenly, the Davoh'rei jerked his hands back with a shout. The knife clattered to the stage floor. An aura of flame surrounded Serena, burning away the boards surrounding her until she could free her hands. She grabbed the skinning knife and stabbed Korahshka's leg, dragging the blade to widen the cut. He roared with pain and backhanded her to the face. He scooted backwards while she pulled herself free from the hole in the stage. Both pushed themselves to their feet and faced the other, Korahshka favoring his injured leg. His legion of imaginary friends had vanished, leaving them alone in the amphitheater.

Korahshka smiled. "Excellent," he said. Not the reaction she expected from a man with a long gash in his leg. "It's always more fun when the prey fights back."

"I'm not here to entertain you," Serena said, wiping blood away from her eyes.

Korahshka shrugged. "But you're doing such a good job of it. I'm looking forward to meeting face to face." The wound on his leg vanished as if he willed it out of existence. "But perhaps we've had enough fun for the night."

"Calling it quits already?" Serena did her best to project bravado she didn't feel. She really didn't want to have to fight right now, even if it might help her learn something about her enemy. "I thought we were just getting started."

"I wouldn't want you to oversleep," Korahshka said, faking concern. "Not when I've sent you a present. Consider it a taste of things to come."

Korahshka waved a hand.

The world went black.

The moment consciousness returned to her, Serena jumped to her feet and dressed in a rush. She left her room and banged on the neighboring doors. "Annea! Ivy! Wake up!" To Tako, she sent the mental equivalent of a series of rapid pokes.

"What's the matter?" Tako said, his voice groggy. *"I was in the middle of a lovely dream about having a tentacle massage at an Octari spa."*

Ivy stepped out of her room and pointed her staff at the fungus on the ceiling. The lodge's illumination grew to normal daytime levels. "What is so important that you would disturb my sleep?"

"Korahshka invaded my dreams again," Serena said. "Annea thought he needed an open Vohr tunnel to do that across realities, meaning —"

"Kimori is under attack, or will be soon," Annea finished, emerging from her room fully dressed and in the process of securing her kukris around her waist. She made her way up the stairs to what was now the new queen's bedroom. "I'll notify Queen Jesserin, then meet you outside."

Serena reached the doors leading up into the world tree as someone opened them from the outside, forcing her to spin out of the way to avoid getting hit in the face. A pair of flying ants hovered beyond the edge of the balcony outside, their wings filling the air with an electric buzz as they fluttered too fast for her eyes to follow.

"A pair of scout teams discovered a tunnel in the swamp to the south," the elf who opened the door said, his words coming out in a rush. "And something new came out of it. Something huge. These scouts can fly you there, if you're able to fight. We're rallying a force to take it out before it gets too close to the ant colony and world tree."

"We'll be there," Serena said, bracing herself to deal with Korahshka's parting gift.

CHAPTER 31
MOOGI

Ivy ran an appreciative hand along the thorax of the nearest scout ant. They were magnificent beings. The perfect balance of form and function. Triple the size of Pik-Pik or Tik-Tik, they looked like they could hover all day without tiring. Serena did not share her enthusiasm for the insects, keeping herself several paces away from the edge of the balcony. She did not display such anxiety around standard drones. Perhaps the thought of flying made her nervous.

Annea emerged from the lodge with a smaller elf in tow. The new queen, no doubt. "What do we know?" she asked.

"The scouts that spotted the tunnel are still hovering over it to observe," the soldier said. "They request reinforcements. Only one creature has come through so far. We didn't get much of a description. It's a quadruped, about twenty feet tall, forty feet long, and ten feet from shoulder to shoulder. A squadron of mounted scouts are mobilizing to intercept it. We have drones on standby if it gets too close to the world tree. These scouts can ferry you to the scene if you wish to see it for yourselves."

"Serena, Ivy, you two share one," Annea said. "Jesserin and I will take the other. We can get there ahead of the reinforcements and determine a plan of action for whatever this creature is." The second scout ant landed on the balcony and bent its knees, allowing the two elves to climb aboard. "Did Orlan's briefing cover any Vohr that might match that vague description?"

"It did not." Ivy studied the two elves. "Is it wise for Kimori's rulers to be flying into battle together?"

"We'll hang back and observe," Annea said. "If we're forced to fight, I'll dismount and send Jesserin back."

The ant at Ivy's side fluttered over her head and landed on the balcony. Serena backed away, her eyes wide with alarm. "Is there a problem?" Ivy asked.

"I've never flown before. We're just going to hop on, with no harness or anything?" Serena asked.

Ivy nodded, understanding. To her, insect transport was a normal part of life. Dryads rode butterflies from village to village to trade goods or visit family every day. Insects, in her experience, respected their riders and held to their objective. They did not engage in random maneuvers which might buck off an inexperienced rider. Serena must not know this. She required something to make her feel safe.

"I have a solution for your discomfort." Ivy created vines from her wrists as she had done to drag Serena and Annea away from the Forest in the Sky. When they were long enough, she snapped them off at the wrist, reabsorbing the remainder into her body. She fashioned them into a harness around Serena's waist and legs. With the ant's consent, she wrapped the other end of the vines around their body, careful to avoid interfering with the movement of their wings, then tied everything in place once Serena was mounted on their back. "This will keep you from falling to your death."

"Don't you want one of these too?" Serena asked.

"I do not."

With the group mounted and comfortable, the ants took to the skies, giving Ivy her best look yet at the territory surrounding the world tree. To the north, Kimori's Planar Gate stood at the edge of a field of prairie grass that stretched to the horizon. To the east was a vast lake. To the southwest, a wide river flowed down from a mountain range, losing steam as it meandered through a dense band of forest before losing definition as the forest transitioned to swamp.

They flew for miles in silence, their backs to the rising sun. Ivy found the flight a pleasant experience. Serena did not. She leaned forward, eyes closed, pressing herself against the ant, arms wrapped around their neck in a hug that did not appear to hinder them. Were all humans so distraught when not on solid ground?

"There it is!" Annea had to shout to be heard over the buzzing of wings. She pointed to the southeast, where the Vohr invader rampaged through the swamp, ramming into twisted trees and knocking them down like their presence offended it. Thick mud and knee-deep waters did little to slow the creature's trot towards the world tree. "Isn't that? No, that's impossible."

Ivy's skin paled. Her mind revolted against the reality of the monstrosity below. It was a perversion of everything dryads held dear. An inversion of the laws of nature that governed their existence. She knew what that creature had once been — an Ataraxian guardian beast.

Guardians resembled giant bears, with prairie grasses growing from their skin in place of fur. Those grasses, once a healthy blend of orange and yellow, were now brown, wilted, and shot through with flecks of purple. Patches of bare skin dotted its back and legs, showing dry, blackened skin riddled with sores. A mane of emerald-colored rose petals ringed its neck. They were the only thing on it that looked healthy. A guardian's mane represented a plant local to where they lived. Those roses were a rare breed which grew only one place on Ataraxia — the lands surrounding her family's village. They confirmed the identity of this guardian beyond any doubt.

Moogi, what have they done to you? Ivy's grip tightened on her staff.

Madness raged in the eyes of her village's guardian. It roared with anguish and pain. The giant bears were believed to be pieces of Ataraxia's soul given form, worshiped as avatars of the natural cycle of death and rebirth. Guardians only ate dead or dying animals and grasses, pruning decay and leaving behind land primed for fresh growth. Her favorite childhood memories involved playing with her sisters around the gentle giant while he slept, or climbing on his back to go for a ride. Moogi had guarded the region for a hundred years before she sprouted, and should have continued to do so for hundreds more after she returned to the soil.

His essence stank of rot and decay, but the blasphemy did not end there. At his shoulders above both front legs, the top half of female dryads were grafted onto his flesh, facing forward. The top half of a male dryad was grafted above his hindquarters, facing the rear. Most of their hair had fallen out. Their flesh was a sickly purple, their faces expressionless, eyes clouded over. They looked like zombies, denied the dignity of a true death and burial, where they could fertilize the soil new generations sprouted from. All three dryads waved their arms in chaotic patterns, using magic to make the vegetation around Moogi wither away.

Ivy squeezed her eyes shut and willed herself not to give in to despair. She did not know the three dryads grafted onto her guardian spirit. A small mercy.

"It was a guardian beast." She spoke for Serena's benefit, her voice hoarse. "Specifically, the one which guarded my village and my family." The one that snorted his approval when she conjured plants for the first time. The one who stood out in the lake and let her and her sisters fish from his back when they needed protein in their diets, for dryads could not live forever on sunlight alone. The one who sensed illness before anyone else could, saving dryad lives. "His name was Moogiderokhan."

This is not Moogi. Moogi is already dead.

"Oh Ivy, I'm so sorry," Serena said. "We'll make the Vohr pay for this."

"Yes, we shall." Ivy hardened her heart for what had to be done.

Annea maneuvered her ant to their side. "You can sit this fight out, Ivy. Nobody will think any less of you for it."

"No," Ivy said. "I will do what I must. Go destroy the tunnel. This abomination is mine."

"Wait for reinforcements!"

Ivy ignored her, ordering her ant to circle back and fly ahead of Moogi's path. They continued on past the edge of the swamp until they flew over forest again. When they had a minute of lead time on the guardian, they landed. Ivy's staff vibrated in her hand. It became an extension of her will, broadcasting her magic at a range she could never manage without it. A carpet of vines erupted from the forest floor along Moogi's expected path. She hopped off the ant and covered her body in the same emerald rose petals that ringed Moogi's neck — a trick she'd often used to get his attention.

"Ivy, what are we doing?" Serena asked, slipping free of her harness. She retrieved a bow and quiver of arrows from a large bag strapped to the ant's side.

"That should be obvious. We are correcting a crime against nature."

Not enough vines. She needed more. Her muscles trembled. She wavered on her feet as she pushed her power further out, turning the carpet of vines into a runway through the forest. Never had she attempted to conjure so many plants at once. It took everything she had to maintain them all.

Snapping wood and toppling trees heralded Moogi's impending arrival. As he stepped on her vines, they thickened into a tangled mass that threatened to trip him. Other vines wrapped themselves around his feet and chest, constricting as they worked to pull him to the ground. Moogi slashed through the first wave with ease. From their position on his shoulders, the zombified dryads fought to counter her magic. Vines turned brittle and snapped. Though their power paled in comparison to a healthy, living dryad, it might be sufficient to keep her from restraining Moogi.

She lacked the mental bandwidth to deal with them.

"Serena, kill the dryads." Ivy fell to one knee. Sweat dripped into her eyes. Or were those tears?

"Are you sure?" Serena asked, apprehension in her voice.

Moogi continued ripping his way through Ivy's vines, charging directly at them. Less than fifty yards separated them from a quick and violent death.

"They are already dead. Set their spirits free." Ivy sat down, crossed her legs, closed her eyes, and pointed her staff directly at Moogi. Her awareness shrank down to the vines alone. She sent a batch to restrain the bear's legs and collar his neck. As one wave grabbed on and squeezed, she sent another, and another still. Her muscles screamed in protest, her body begging her to cease using magic before she ripped herself apart.

Ivy ignored the pain. She would restrain Moogi. Or not, in which case Moogi would kill her, and the pain would not matter anymore.

A dim part of her mind heard Serena take three shots. Felt the ground vibrate beneath her as Moogi ran. Smelled his rot and decay in the morning breeze. Irrelevant details. She was the vines. Reaching. Grabbing. Constricting. Dragging Moogi back. Pulling him to the earth.

This is not Moogi. Moogi is dead. She would return his remains to the soil. She did not deserve to survive if she could not do right by her village's protector.

Moogi roared. She had him now. Vines ensnared his legs and chest in fifty or more places. Her will, manifested into a net to contain what was once one of the strongest creatures on Ataraxia.

The guardian collapsed two paces short of Ivy and Serena.

Withdrawing her focus from her conjured plants, Ivy opened her eyes to stare directly into Moogi's. There was only rage and pain in his glare, not a hint of recognition. The gentle giant who had once been her friend was truly gone. Moogi snarled and barked, trying in vain to dig his claws into the dirt and rise to his feet. With a flick of her wrist, fresh vines sprouted from the soil and wrapped themselves around Moogi's snout, sealing his mouth shut.

Ivy looked up to see the dryads grafted onto him slumped over, a single arrow through the forehead of each. Impressive marksmanship under pressure.

A flurry of arrows rained down on the guardian beast as reinforcements arrived. The attack did nothing but pincushion the dead dryads. Moogi did not appear to notice he had been shot.

"Hold your fire! This kill is mine!" Ivy roared in a voice that would tolerate no disobedience. Despite being a foreigner with no standing to give commands, the elves obeyed, holding position overhead on their scout ants as they waited for new orders.

"You don't have to do this," Annea said, placing a hand on Ivy's shoulder. When had she arrived? "I can do this. You don't have to shoulder every burden related to Ataraxia."

Ivy shook her head, pulling a kukri free from its sheath at Annea's hips. "I need to borrow this."

"Wait." Annea grabbed her hand. She touched the blade and channeled some of her energy into it, causing it to glow purple. "This will enhance the cut. Make it easier."

Ivy ignored the onlookers and their mournful silence. This was her responsibility. Ending Moogi's suffering was the last gift she could give him.

"From the soil we rise. To the soil we return," Ivy said, reciting the traditional funeral prayer. "This is but a temporary parting. What has died shall sprout again, for we are all links in the great chain of life. From now until the end of time."

Moogi continued to shake and twitch in a futile effort to break free. Ivy pressed the edge of the kukri into Moogi's neck, closed her eyes, and slashed in and up with all her strength. "Farewell. May you find the rest that you deserve."

Her voice broke. "...Thank you for being my friend."

She opened her eyes only long enough to verify her cut was true and lethal. Annea's energy traveled along the edges, widening it until it looked like a wound inflicted by a weapon four times the kukri's size. Ivy willed her feet to carry her away before she lost the will to ever move again.

"Do not speak to me," Ivy said, handing Annea the bloody kukri in passing. She could not pause to accept their condolences. If she did, the last fragile shreds of her composure would disintegrate. She had to keep moving, even if her body felt like a shriveled husk under a hot sun.

She sensed Moogi's struggling ease against her vines. When his breathing ceased, she released her magic. His restraints withered and disappeared.

"You are the best of us." Ivy recalled her final conversation with her sister Thistle before she set off to join the vanguard delaying the reaper advance. *"Your strength is unparalleled. And I am not just talking about your magic. We do not call you Unbreakable Ivy for nothing. If only one of us survives, it must be you. If there is any salvation to be found for our world, you will find it."*

Was there anything left to save? She did not think so. Moogi showed that anything Vohr did not kill outright suffered a far worse fate.

"Where are you going?" Serena asked.

Ivy passed their scout ant and did not stop. "I will meet you at the Planar Gate."

"You're *walking* back? That'll take hours."

"I know."

"Let her go, Serena," Annea said. "Everyone grieves in their own way."

As expected, the hike back to civilization lasted into the afternoon, but Annea and Jesserin respected her need for privacy. She made the trip without any ground escort or scout team monitoring her progress from above. She spent most of the trip walking blind, unable to see through her tears. She screamed until she tasted blood in her throat. She covered herself in bark armor, as if that could guard against the anguish ripping her apart.

Never stop moving. If you stop, you die. She'd thought as much on that fateful night, sprinting for the Planar Gate while monsters slaughtered everyone she loved. The advice seemed as appropriate now. Part of her wanted to lay down and die right there, to be free from the horrors she had seen and endured, and those she knew were coming.

Never stop moving.

The Vohr would not break her.

Never stop moving.

Ataraxia was gone. She was the last dryad. The Vohr had guaranteed her species' extinction.

She would return the favor.

Nature demands balance.

PART III
A MAP OF THE MULTIVERSE

CHAPTER 32

RETURN TO THE NEXUS

Serena sat on the ground beside the Planar Gate, eyes shut as she tried to comprehend her friend's grief. The way Annea explained it, dryads considered guardians pieces of the planet's soul given physical form. They were as loved and revered as any family member. They guarded orchards of gestation trees, and were one of the first things a child saw when their pod opened and released them into the world. "From the soil we rise" wasn't just a metaphor — at least part of the dryad reproductive process involved growing from the soil. Moogi had been a constant presence for Ivy's entire life.

If her mother or father had shown up in a similar mutated state, could she have done what Ivy did, and given them a true death? She wanted to think so, but prayed she'd never have to find out.

"It does you no good to dwell on such dark thoughts," Tako said. *"Ivy's pain is intense, but she's strong. The loss of fifteen sisters didn't break her. This won't either. You'll be there when she's ready to open up about it."* He didn't take the opportunity to chide her about her refusal to acknowledge her own grief. She appreciated that. *"For now, think about how we'll find aid for Kimori in the Nexus."*

"I'm hoping Annea has a plan for that," Serena said. "I still don't really understand how the Nexus works."

"Why not ask her about it? We've got time. And it'll stop your brooding."

"Fine."

Serena stood and twisted her back, feeling a satisfying crack. She'd been sitting too long. "Have you spent much time on the Nexus, Annea? What's the plan here?"

"I was there for a couple weeks at a time between each year of my Wandering Decade, only staying long enough to research and choose my next destination," Annea said. "Most of what I know comes from the general education every citizen of Kimori receives. It'll be enough to get by. As for what we do first, we should head to the N.E.S.T. for our sector. I'd like to have a chat with my former apprentice, then make decisions based on the information he provides."

"Former apprentice?" She felt like she should know who Annea meant. But after the torment of Korahshka invading her mind again, and witnessing Ivy's personal tragedy right after, she wasn't fully present at the moment.

"Orlan," Annea said, bending to pet Pik-Pik and Tik-Tik along their thoraxes. "He studied with me for three years before returning to the Nexus to join the Weavers. I haven't seen him face-to-face in almost twenty years." She sounded nostalgic, her words laced with a hint of loss. It suggested there had been more than a student and teacher relationship between them. "We exchange messages every time I send someone to the Nexus to gather news of the multiverse."

Annea's gaze shifted to the southeast, where Ivy emerged from the forest. It would take her several more minutes to make her way across grassland to their position. "Working for the N.E.S.T program requires Orlan to keep up with matters of importance, particularly any conflicts or problems which may result in people needing his help. If anyone can help us chart a course through the political landscape of the Nexus, it'll be him."

"I see," Serena said. It didn't sound like much of a plan.

"You don't approve?" Annea asked, sensing her dissatisfaction. "A good leader recognizes the limits of their knowledge and seeks additional information. The more we know, the smarter we can be about what we do next. I do us no favors pretending I have all the answers."

Serena sighed, surrendering to Annea's logic. As much as she wanted to kick down the doors of whatever served as government in the Nexus and demand action, such a move wouldn't win them any friends. They'd have to be deliberate, calculated, and methodical. She could handle that on a hunt. When dealing with other people? Not so much.

"I am ready to depart," Ivy said upon her arrival at the Planar Gate. The dryad leaned on her staff for support. Her skin from the neck down was covered by bark, except for the opening on her back that allowed her to breathe. If despair had a face, Ivy was wearing it. She had the slack expression and limp, apathetic body language of a woman too tired to keep fighting, but who forced herself to keep moving anyway. In her eyes shone the faintest flicker of anger, enough to tell Serena that Ivy wasn't lost to them yet.

"We're going to have to keep a close eye on her," Tako said. *"She's worse off than I feared."*

"You're a very calming influence, you know," Serena said, watching Annea trace out the eight sigils to take them to Torbakhal. *"Would it do any good if she hosted you for a few days?"* The Planar Gate activated and they stepped through.

"I'm afraid that's impossible," Tako said. *"I only bond with willing participants. If Ivy doesn't want it, I wouldn't do it. Besides, I can't change hosts as easily as you change shirts. At my age, it takes me several days to become detached enough from my last host to be ready for the next."*

"That's a shame," Serena turned her focus to Torbakhal's Planar Gate before Ivy could catch her staring. She wanted to wrap the dryad up in a hug, but imagined the woman's bark armor growing thorns and pricking her if she tried. *"We'll think of something."*

As soon as everyone was on Torbakhal and the Gate shut down, Annea traced an infinity symbol for the Nexus in the air. They stepped through the ribbon of light again and found themselves in the middle row of Gates in the transit cube. Against the opposite wall, she saw Kimori's Gate in the distance, more recognizable for its empty queue than the design of the Gate pillars themselves. Iridescent light from active Gates splashed across the walls, ceiling, and the bodies of the thousands of beings arriving in the Nexus or waiting to embark to different realms.

Serena kept herself entertained on the walk to the N.E.S.T by cataloging how many creatures from Alterran mythology were real. Goblins. Trolls. Centaurs. Harpies. The species she recognized made up only a fraction of the beings going about their business. Meanwhile, Pik-Pik and Tik-Tik narrated what they saw with the enthusiasm of children people-watching at a carnival.

<There's a goat-person riding a dog.>

<The dog has three eyes! Do you see the one on its forehead?>

<Is that a naga? I've never seen one of them before!>

<Their scales are so pretty!>

<Who are those people in the black robes?>

<I don't know, but if you have to hide your face in a hood, you're probably an asshole.> The two of them snickered at that.

When they arrived at the N.E.S.T, Serena had expected to see Estus floating around the lobby. The efreet had the air of a man who lived for his work, who wanted to make sure all guests felt welcome and cared for. Instead, the glass and gold doors opened up to an expansive rainforest rich in plants but devoid of people. Even the log counter in the back sat unmanned. The only sound they heard was the roar of the waterfall along the rear wall.

"Serena, Ivy, welcome back! I didn't think I'd see you again, to be honest."

The voice belonged to a man seated at a table tucked between three trees to their right, sufficiently obscured that they'd walked right by without seeing him. His left arm was flesh and blood, but his remaining limbs were prosthetics of obsidian-colored metal. Blue highlights accented his dark hair. His clothes had an unreasonable number of pockets. In his prosthetic hand, he held a translucent device twice the size of a deck of cards, but half as thick, which he tucked away into a pocket when he stood to greet them.

Serena's mind flailed for a moment before the memory returned to her. Her first visit to the N.E.S.T. already felt like a lifetime ago. "Hello, Cypher."

"How was your time on Kimori?" he asked.

"Chaotic," Ivy said.

"We've been blundering our way from one fight to the next," Serena said, elaborating slightly when Ivy didn't. "We discovered Kimori is next in line for a Vohr invasion, and we've come back to seek aid to stop it."

"I take it you've all met before?" Annea asked.

"Cypher's world was invaded by the Vohr about the same time as ours."

"I see. Why don't you two relax here and catch up. I'll find Orlan and meet up with you again after."

Cypher studied Annea, recognition blooming across his face. "You're Queen Annea, aren't you? You don't look anything like Orlan's photo."

Annea smiled. "So I've been told. Just Annea is fine. I don't put much stock in titles. Would you happen to know where Orlan is?"

Cypher pointed towards the hallway Orlan had taken the three of them down for their private briefing. "He's in the middle of an orientation class with another group of refugees. He'll be free in a half hour or so. In the meantime, would you be interested in grabbing something to eat? I think we have some *shared interests* we should discuss."

Given how little time they'd spent together, he could only mean one thing. If he had information about the Vohr he wanted to share, Serena wanted to hear it.

Annea looked ready to leave the three of them behind, as if she meant to pull Orlan from class early.

"We should eat," Ivy said, locking her gaze on Annea. "We may not have another opportunity for some time."

"I agree with Ivy," Serena said. They hadn't eaten anything all day. Ivy could subsist on light for a long time, but she'd collapse if they kept running around without a break.

Annea studied them both for a long moment before surrendering. "Very well. Lead the way," she said. They left Pik-Pik and Tik-Tik in the lobby to watch over their belongings and make arrangements for rooms for the night, should Estus or someone else on the N.E.S.T. staff come by.

Cypher led them to the left, down a cobblestone path though the rainforest. "I've kept myself busy since you left. I completed the training course about the Nexus and Planar Gates in two days."

"I thought that was supposed to take a week?" Serena said. "Or was it two weeks?"

"I'm a fast learner, and I read ahead." They reached the elevators and continued on down the hallway to the cafeteria. "Estus is letting me stay here while I figure out what I want to do next. Though with all the hush money they paid me, I won't have to get a job for quite a while."

"Hush money?" Ivy asked. "I do not understand. Money is an inanimate object. It does not make a sound. There is no need to silence it."

Serena and Cypher stared at the dryad. The Planar Gates' translation magic didn't always work quite right for her. She got confused sometimes by random idioms, phrases, and expressions, always assuming the most literal definition to be what someone meant. Maybe some concepts just didn't make sense to her, or her brain worked differently than the other species they'd interacted with so far.

Cypher opened and closed his mouth a few times, considering how to respond. He settled on moving ahead with his points. "I've been researching the Vohr on my own."

"How did you manage that?" Serena asked. "My Personal Encyclopedia wouldn't show anything about them when I asked it."

"The Nexus is a combination of magic and technology that's so advanced it might as well be magic. This sector has two data hubs. One is a gigantic crystal that I can't comprehend, but the other has a physical server structure similar to what we used on my homeworld, Mallozzi. I haven't come across any tech I can't bend to my will, given enough time." He lowered his voice to a whisper as they reached the cafeteria's double doors. "I hacked myself access to their restricted files."

She wasn't sure what he meant, but caught the conspiratorial tone. "Won't you get in trouble for that?"

"Perhaps, if anyone discovers what I did," Cypher said, holding open a door for the group. "But if I can trust anyone not to tattle, it's you three."

The cafeteria was mostly empty. A shirtless, grey-skinned being walked from station to station, stirring various pots and checking if anything needed a refill. Serena tried her best not to stare. He was twice her height, with the floppy ears and trunk of an elephant, plus the eye stalks of a hammerhead shark. Serving spoons looked tiny in his enormous hands.

"What do you recommend today, Carl?" Cypher asked the giant.

"The tuna steaks in row three. It's my own recipe," the elephant-shark rumbled. "Wild caught from the oceans of Tikkara."

Serena filled a big bowl with macaroni and cheese, another with grapes, and grabbed herself a brownie. Yes, she was eating like her five-year-old self. No, she didn't care. She needed the comfort food, thank you very much. They sat down at a table as far away from anyone else as possible to avoid being overheard. "Is his name really Carl?" she asked.

"Humans are one of the most common species across the multiverse," Cypher said. He'd taken Carl's advice and grabbed a tuna steak, as well as an apple. "A lot of other species take on human names if their native ones are too difficult for human and other humanoid species to pronounce. I tried saying his true name once. Almost choked to death."

Serena nodded, recalling that many Octari did the same thing.

Annea took the seat next to Serena. "Cypher, you were saying you've learned something about the Vohr?"

"She does eat, doesn't she?" Tako asked, mirroring Serena's thoughts. The elf had grabbed a piece of jerky and a granola bar. *"That's not a meal."*

Cypher grinned. "I learned just how tight a lid the sector government is keeping on all information Vohr related. Is that considered cannibalism?" He interrupted himself, pointing to the salad Ivy had paired with her own tuna steak. Under her blistering gaze, he shuffled his chair a few inches further away from her. "I can see that was inappropriate. I apologize." Ivy said nothing, but offered him a slight nod — as close to an "apology accepted" as she might be capable of right now.

He took a breath before resuming his thought. "All reports on Vohr activity get sent directly to the Sector Council, who just sit on them, as far as I can tell. Little information trickles down to the lower tiers of government or agencies that might act on it."

"What's a Sector Council?" Serena asked.

"The Nexus is too vast to centrally govern. There's no way one government body could address the needs of billions, maybe trillions, of different worlds, species, and cultures. Therefore, the Nexus is divided into sectors, each representing anywhere from one hundred to a couple thousand different worlds. Most realities tend to their own affairs, so sector governments handle diplomatic relationships, tourism concerns, interdimensional trade, and the operation of the cubes shared by their constituent realities. This sector has a senate, with one seat for every member world. However, because democracy across a thousand worlds is cumbersome and slow, the senate elected a smaller subset from within their ranks to serve as a Sector Council, with the power to made decisions and set policy in certain areas."

"And the Sector Council isn't sharing information," Annea said.

"Correct." Cypher nodded. "Some of them believe the Vohr aren't an issue for sector government, and that individual realities should handle the matter themselves. Others want to form a military coalition of the strongest realities in the sector to combat the problem. However, with no pattern found to Vohr attacks, such a move could be seen as the strong worlds banding together to conquer their neighbors. Orlan alluded to this a little, but they're also afraid knowledge of the Vohr will lead to panic, the spread of misinformation, and supply chain issues if people start hoarding critical goods. Until they have a solution they like, their strategy is to downplay, discredit, or deny any information that leaks to the public."

"Orlan did warn us not to speak of the Vohr," Ivy said.

"Oh, Orlan vastly undersold what could happen if you do. A couple men in black robes showed up at my door the night after you left, read me the riot act, and handed me a bag with enough currency inside to be able to afford an apartment in this sector for years. They called the money a 'resettlement grant,' but I know a bribe when I see one, especially after their threats. They had hoods over their heads and gloves on their hands. They're humanoid, but I have no idea what species. I took their bribe. Told them I understood. And then doubled down on my info gathering. Before you ask, no, I haven't figured out yet where the bribe money is coming from."

"Why would the N.E.S.T. give Vohr survivors *more information* if they plan to come down hard on anyone who talks?" Serena asked. She'd been too shaken up at the time to ponder that.

"Validation," Annea said after a pause. "If a lot of people have only a little information on the Vohr, they're more likely to talk with others about it to swap notes, as well as seek out others who might know something. Especially if they feel a government agency is hiding information from them. Providing a big briefing is a way to convince people the government knows what is going on, and that they're looking into it, so you don't have to worry anymore."

"Exactly," Cypher said. "Smile, take the money, and never speak of it again. The government will take care of everything."

Except that wasn't quite how it happened, was it? Orlan hadn't shied away from telling them the government wasn't doing anything. He'd made up Annea's offer of sanctuary to nudge them into meeting her. All signs pointed to him quietly resisting and subverting government policies. If not Orlan, who told the government who to bribe? A part of her didn't want to know. Cypher looked at her and nodded, as if he could follow her line of though as well as Tako could.

"What would you do in my position, Cypher?" Annea said, leaning forward with interest. "My world has been fighting off Vohr incursions for days now, and we need support. It's only a matter of time before they attack with overwhelming force. Most people are ignorant to the threat, and those who know are covering it up while they drag their feet with indecision. How would you proceed?"

"Is this a test?" Cypher asked, leaning away from the intensity of her gaze.

"Not at all. In my experience, most people would forget about the Vohr and move on with their lives after the kind of heavy-handed treatment you experienced. You kept digging. I respect that."

Cypher's posture relaxed. "You can't just go to the Sector Council and tell them Kimori is in danger. They'll demand proof. They'll have committee hearings and meetings. By the time they're ready to vote, the invasion will be over. The only way I see the Sector

Council taking immediate action is if someone can prove there is a pattern to Vohr attacks. Something that not only shows that Kimori will be attacked, but also what will happen from there.

"I've spent the last few days researching the nature of the multiverse in hopes of finding something. Unfortunately, the structure of the multiverse is not a popular field of study. But there is one scientist a couple sectors away who has books out on the subject, a Dr. Niles Venture. His theories could be the ticket to finding proof."

"Go on," Annea said.

"It's commonly accepted that the Nexus is a giant cube made up of smaller cubes, which is a bit of a misnomer since cubes are not all of a uniform size, and many are shaped more like giant rectangular shipping containers than cubes."

"Stay on target," Annea said, gently prodding Cypher back on topic like she would when Pik-Pik or Tik-Tik started rambling.

"Right. Sorry. If we accept that the Nexus is an artificial construction — and it's hard to believe it'd be anything else — then *where* is the Nexus? How does this place not fall apart under its own weight? I'm still wrapping my mind around magic, but the simple fact is this place is impossible under the laws of gravity and architecture as I understand them. The Nexus has trillions of cubes. Hollow out the Nexus, and entire planets would fit inside. Probably hundreds of them. This place defies comprehension, and yet here we are.

"Dr. Venture believes the Nexus floats in the center of what he calls an aetherial sea." Cypher held up his apple. "Imagine this is the Nexus." He emptied out a toothpick holder on the table and started jamming toothpicks into the fruit. "Now, imagine the tips of these toothpicks are different realities, with the toothpicks themselves representing the path a Planar Gate takes to bring someone from their reality to the Nexus. The aetherial sea is a vast expanse of magic energy that fills the void between worlds. Dr. Venture believes realities are fixed in their positions relative to the Nexus, like these toothpicks are in this apple. He's spent years charting their approximate distance from the Nexus, and from each other, in hopes of making a map of the multiverse."

"What's all that have to do with the Vohr?" Serena asked, not seeing where he was going with this.

"His full mapping research isn't public yet, but he released a list of the worlds he's studied so far. Part of the restricted data I obtained included a complete list of every world invaded by the Vohr, what sector they belonged to, and the date and time those worlds were quarantined from the Planar Gate network. Over eighty percent of those names Dr. Venture has positioning calculations for. I'm hoping his data combined with the Vohr invasion timeline will show enough of a pattern to move the Sector Council to action. Failing that, it might at least give us specific worlds to contact for support. I imagine those next in line would prefer a fight happens on Kimori rather than in their backyards."

"Do you know how to contact this doctor?" Annea asked. "Is he willing to talk to you?"

"Are you kidding? Finding his contact information was super easy, barely an inconvenience," Cypher said. "Academic types love talking about their work with interested parties, and Dr. Venture seemed particularly starved for attention." Cypher reached into a pocket and pulled out the transparent object he'd put away when they arrived. He tapped on it and glowing text appeared on its surface. "I messaged him expressing interest in his research, and indicated I'd like to show him some data of my own relevant to his findings. He texted me his address less than an hour later. I'm welcome to stop by his research laboratory any time I want."

The text disappeared, replaced by what looked like a three dimensional map. A red dot marked their position. A line weaved its way through a multitude of boxes she took for cubes, before ending at a star icon. "Since he lives a couple sectors over, we're in for some decent travel time, but it's nothing too difficult."

"Sounds like a plan worth pursuing," Annea said. "Do you mind if we join you?"

"I was hoping you would. The more the merrier."

"Orlan's class should be letting out about now, correct?"

Cypher nodded and gave her directions to the lecture hall.

"Let me speak with him, alone." An ominous expression settled over Annea's face. "Before we commit to this path, I'd like to get his sense of what kind of welcome we can expect when the time comes to deal with the Council. And will the Weavers be an ally, or another obstacle in our way?" She sighed, stood, and exited the cafeteria without another word.

"What's a Weaver?" Serena asked. "I get the feeling she's not talking about fabric."

Cypher and Ivy had no answer.

CHAPTER 33
UNOFFICIAL AID

Annea arrived at the lecture hall as Orlan dismissed his class. It was a far larger group than she'd anticipated. Fifty or more humans filed out of the lecture hall, all with the despondent body language of the recently displaced. Most of the refugees wore plain black clothing provided by the N.E.S.T, though a few had refused to part with their cultural garb, despite obvious bloodstains. The youngest among them clutched a dirty stuffed animal to her chest with one hand while she clung to the leg of her mother's pants with the other. Annea smiled and offered them words of hope. She took the seat near the door while the last few refugees staggered out.

Orlan didn't notice her as he gathered a collection of papers he'd spread across a table at the front of the hall. He wore the robe of the Weavers, a thick brown garment with white stitching reminiscent of a spider's web. *The years have been kind to him,* Annea thought. Under her tutelage, he'd grown from a nervous and twitchy young man into a calm, disciplined, and supremely confident scholar. She found him even more attractive now than she had in his youth.

With his papers collected, Orlan headed for the door, still ignorant of her presence. She wasn't trying to hide. She had at least six inches and twenty-five pounds on him, and was parked right by the door. You really had to *try* to be this oblivious. "Your situational awareness is slipping, Orlan," Annea said. "You're lucky I'm a friend and not an assassin."

Orlan jumped at the sound of her voice, sending his papers flying. As she'd expect from a former student, he recovered quickly. His momentary shock gave way to a heady aura of competence and composure. Annea smiled. Orlan's calming magic could make even his bloopers seem deliberate. "Annea?" He stared at her like a man seeing a memory from a past life. Twenty years meant a lot more to a human than it did an elf.

"Indeed, the one and only Annea Vantalos of Kimori." She jumped out of her seat and enveloped Orlan in a hug before he could make any move to resist. To her relief, he returned the gesture. "You're looking good. Keeping yourself in shape."

"I'd swear you haven't aged a day," Orlan said, pulling back from the embrace. "Forgive my surprise. You didn't write ahead. I didn't expect to ever see you again, unless I took a trip to Kimori. I didn't think queens could leave the planet during their tenure," he said, a hit of reproach in his voice.

"They can't." Annea tapped the tiara on her forehead. "I gave myself a wartime promotion."

"War? Who would attack Kimori?"

"The Vohr."

Orlan held up a finger, then poked his head out the door, checking to make sure nobody else was in earshot. He took that opportunity to scoop up the scattered papers. "Tell me everything."

Annea gave him a condensed walkthrough of the last week, from the Vohr eye and the discovery of the tunnel in the Forest in the Sky up to their battle with the mutated Ataraxian guardian. "Kimori has been successful in defending herself so far, but the attacks have been small. Tests of our defenses more than anything else. Sooner or later, they're going to send the kind of numbers that wiped out every other planet they've conquered. I don't think we can fight them off all on our own."

"I'm glad Kimori's held out this long, and I hope you're able to find the help you need. Unfortunately, asking nicely won't get you anywhere."

"That's why I've come to you. Between your connections with sector government and the Weavers, if anyone can paint a picture of how the multiverse is responding to the Vohr, it would be you. I'm not too proud to ask for advice."

"You flatter me." Orlan frowned and gazed off at nothing. She knew the look. He wasn't sure what he should say. He'd always been methodical in his speech, like he weighed his words two or three times in his head to judge their weight and potential impact before committing to speaking. She let him think without interruption.

"My position affords me access to all the reports the Sector Council receives on the Vohr," he said. "Hell, most of them I wrote myself, detailing first-hand accounts of survivors. I might as well be throwing those reports in the trash for all the good they're doing, since the Sector Council just sits on them."

"And bribes and threatens Vohr survivors into keeping their mouths shut," Annea said.

"What?" Orlan sounded outraged at the idea. "Where did you hear that? I will admit the government wants to downplay and discredit witnesses, but I've heard nothing about bribery or overt threats."

Either he was lying, or Cypher was. No, that didn't make sense. Orlan wouldn't lie to her, and Cypher had no apparent reason to. Her gut told her the bribes were real, and someone was going to great lengths to make sure Orlan stayed in the dark about it. He wouldn't willingly participate in something like that. Removing him from his post would draw unwanted attention. "I have to protect my sources," Annea said. "But I take it I shouldn't bank on any support from sector government?"

"No. Not without some extraordinary new information to prod them into action," Orlan said, his assessment of the government matching Cypher's.

"What about the Weavers? Have the greatest minds in the multiverse come up with any solutions?"

The Weavers were an ancient religious and scholastic order devoted to the preservation and expansion of knowledge. They operated from the Nexus, and saw it as their mission to weave together the fragmented flow of information between sectors into a more cohesive whole. Paradise to the Weavers was a multiverse where all realities had access to the sum total of knowledge from all of creation, not just the information they could obtain from within their home sectors or their neighbors. The Weavers operated independently of any government and answered to nobody. That aloof position won them respect and reverence from some, distrust and suspicion from others.

"The Weavers are even more divided than the Sector Council on how to handle the Vohr," Orlan said. "Some want them destroyed. Others want them contained for study. There's even a faction that believes the Vohr should be allowed to carry on unhindered."

"That's not funny."

"I'm serious." Orlan raised his hands in a *don't blame me* gesture. "Some Weavers believe the Vohr are agents of natural selection, culling weaker species and realities to blaze a path for richer future growth. Exterminating them would disrupt a vital natural process."

"If any of those fools ever saw the Vohr, they'd know there's nothing natural about those monsters," Annea said, imaging those callous scholars locked in a room with a reaper or two. That would change their attitude real quick.

"You'll get no argument from me. I've seen the suffering they leave in their wake. I'm not willing to watch people die for some mythical 'greater good.'" He sighed and took a seat in the lecture hall's front row, suddenly weary. "The Vohr's spread has been going on for at least ten years now, and our civility frays a little more with each fallen world. The divisions within the Weavers have us close to civil war, for lack of a better term. It's hard to make policy recommendations when you have multiple factions screaming at each other.

"My hands are even more bound than most, since the N.E.S.T. is a government organization. I have to straddle the politics of sector government and the Weavers both. If I'm seen to be taking a side, I have no idea what the fallout might look like, but I can guarantee it wouldn't help anyone."

"I'm sorry, Orlan," Annea said. He'd always wanted to be a force for good in the multiverse. Her heart broke to see politics hampering his ability to act. He'd never alluded to any of this in any of his letters, but she understood much better now why he'd wanted to send Serena and Ivy her way. "I don't want to put you in a compromising position. We'll carry on without support from the Weavers."

"I didn't say the Weavers won't help you. Just that *I* can't. Officially, I have no opinion on how to handle the Vohr. I humbly present the facts to survivors and help them find new lives, while staying out of the Council's closed-door arguments and Weaver infighting."

"And unofficially?"

"Kill the Vohr. Kill them all." Orlan reached into a pocket in his robe and pulled out a device similar to what she'd seen Cypher using. After spending a minute tapping on it, he handed it over to her. "Have you used a datapad before?"

"I have not. I try to avoid technology." On the datapad's screen, she saw pictures labeled *map, messages, sector database, contacts, camera, send / receive data, files,* and *other.* "This seems easy enough to use though," she said, experimenting with its touch controls to move through various menus.

"If anyone asks, you did not receive that from me. I didn't provide you a list of Weavers who favor military intervention. I would never compromise my position by suggesting you use that datapad to reach out to Patrick Evans, who will be attending a party thrown by Eldritch Augustus Blackwell two days from now. I certainly don't know that he's using the event as cover for a meeting with military leaders from Ankora and Chiroptera factions to discuss unsanctioned offensives against the Vohr. The Sector Council would be furious with me if I knew and didn't report it."

"Good thing you know nothing about it," Annea said, tucking the datapad away in a pocket. "It's a shame you couldn't help." She winked and she rubbed the smooth skin atop his head. "There's another lead we'll be investigating tomorrow. I'll spare you the details," she added when Orlan mimed plugging his ears.

"What about tonight?"

"Serena and Ivy have been through hell and are in desperate need of some diversion, so I'm planning to take them shopping. Serena has a habit of immolating her wardrobe, so we need to get her new clothes, preferably something fireproof. Ivy... I gave Ivy some space earlier today, but I'm afraid to let her spend any more time alone. That girl needs a hug. I don't think she'll let me give her one, so I'll call it a win if she'll let me buy her a professional massage. Frankly, we all need a little relaxation before the stress and anxiety break us."

"Well, after engaging in some well deserved retail therapy, why don't you all join my family for dinner?" Orlan said. They exited the lecture hall and started down the long hall back to the N.E.S.T. lobby. "It sounds like you all could use a home-cooked meal. Besides, I want to meet Pik-Pik and Tik-Tik. They sound fascinating."

"And I'd love to meet your wife and son," Annea said, giving him a playful poke in the ribs. "You're sure it won't be awkward having an ex over for dinner?"

"My wife feels like she owes you a debt of gratitude for hammering me into the man I am today."

Annea's grin turned mischievous. "As she should. She's the primary beneficiary of some of our *lessons.*" She paused. "Your wife is aware of our *complete* history, yes?"

Orlan's aura of composure cracked the tiniest bit. His cheeks flushed at old memories. "I keep no secrets from her."

"You're a wise man."

Orlan paused halfway between the lobby and the lecture hall at a nondescript door labeled *Administration.* "Take the elevator to the top floor in four hours. We live at the end of the hall. Until then, I'm afraid I have to take these survivor testimonies and turn them into reports the Sector Council will ignore." Orlan waved the papers in his hand.

Annea nodded and let him return to work, grateful to have a relaxing evening to look forward to, before the race to find aid for Kimori resumed in the morning.

CHAPTER 34
DR. VENTURE

Their journey to meet with Dr. Venture required passing through hundreds of cubes, representing the sector of the Nexus Kimori belonged to and two others. When they met with Cypher in the N.E.S.T. lobby the following morning and he pulled up their route on his datapad, Serena thought he was insane when he said they'd arrive around lunchtime. Covering that distance would take days on foot. Maybe weeks.

"Thankfully, whoever or whatever designed the Nexus included public transportation systems," Cypher said. "I take it neither of you have ridden a subway?"

"What kind of creature is a subway?" Ivy asked. "Please tell me it is not a bird."

Cypher looked ready to ask what she had against birds before thinking better of it. "It's not a bird," he said instead, motioning for the group to follow him.

They stepped onto the same elevator platform they used to reach the transit cube. Serena hit the button to send them up.

"Amazing," Cypher said. "Your tattoo is incredible, Serena. I've never seen anything so lifelike. I feel like it's watching me move."

"Thanks," Serena said. "I was nervous about getting it at first, but it has grown on me."

Tako snickered. *"You're not so bad yourself,"* he said. *"Thank you for being accommodating."*

Working out their fashion differences had been Serena's top priority during their Annea-funded shopping excursion. She didn't want to go traipsing across the multiverse in a chest band. Tako didn't want every inch of her skin covered so he felt confined. They'd found a shop that catered to pyromancers, efreet, phoenix-shifters, and all manner of fire-based beings, settling on a selection of tops that provided good coverage while still leaving a generous amount of her back exposed. Even better, the material could endure extreme heat for up to eight hours. She wouldn't burn these off if she had to fight. She felt happier no longer being so under-dressed, plus the arrangement allowed Tako to still watch her back at all times. They'd agreed to pretend he was a tattoo unless revealing his true nature became necessary.

Two levels above the transit cube, the elevator came to a stop. Here, the platform connected to a large, tiled floor that took up almost the entire cube. Along the wall to the left, vendors sold snack foods and reading materials from an eclectic mix of stalls. Some looked like ramshackle wood constructions, while others were sturdy metal carts on wheels that could be rolled away at their owner's convenience. There was a deep pit in the floor at the far right end of the cube, running parallel to the wall, with a tunnel at either end. Beings of a hundred different species milled about or sat on benches, clearly waiting for something.

Along the back wall stood a sapient apple tree, its roots stuffed into an enormous pot. It plucked apples from its own canopy using a pair of flexible branches that grew from the mid-point of its trunk, dipped the apples in a bucket of caramel, then sold them to an eager crowd of gnomes. As much as Serena wanted to satisfy her sweet tooth and try one for herself, there wasn't time. A giant metallic earthworm emerged from the closer tunnel opening, filling the pit in the floor. Not until it came to a complete stop did she realize it wasn't a living creature. Beings formed orderly lines near the doors, allowing space for passengers inside to disembark before stepping in themselves.

"This is a subway train," Cypher said, motioning for them to hurry and get in line so they wouldn't have to wait for the next one.

Serena and Ivy found seats behind a family of six rabbitfolk crammed together in seats meant for two human-sized beings. None of them stood taller than Serena's knees. They wore simple garments of blue and gold colored cloth draped over their shoulders like sheets. Turbans of matching colors around their heads had openings to let their ears pop free. Two of the rabbit children played a game of hand gestures that reminded Serena of Rock, Parchment, Shears. As if psychically linked, the two kept throwing the same symbol over and over again, their laughter over the unending deadlock growing more intense with each tie.

"I hope you're comfortable," Cypher said from the row behind Serena. "We're going to be on this line for about two hours before we need to transfer."

Serena closed her eyes and let the rabbit children's laughter wash over her like calming music. They knew nothing of the fear and suffering caused by the Vohr. She'd make sure those sweet, innocent souls never would. Her mind drifted to warm memories of their dinner the night before with Orlan and his family. It had felt awkward at first, with her, Ivy, and Annea sharing a table with Orlan, his wife Naya, and their son Damien, but it soon turned into the closest thing to a family gathering she'd had in years. Annea told stories of training Orlan. Damien wanted to hear of Serena's best hunts, so she regaled him with the tale of their battle against the leviathan. Ivy said little over the course of the night, but her posture relaxed. The look of despair on her face eased the tiniest bit. It was something. She was glad they hadn't let Ivy brood in solitude like she'd wanted.

Seated next to Cypher, Annea pulled out the datapad Orlan gave her and attempted to contact Patrick Evans. "He's not in range." She poked at the screen as if bludgeoning it enough would establish a connection to the Weaver.

"Is there a problem?" Cypher asked.

"I hope not," Annea said. "I'm trying to get myself into a very exclusive party." When Cypher raised an eyebrow, she added, "It's on-mission. There will be high ranking officials there representing forces receptive to fighting the Vohr. I don't suppose you know anything about Eldritch Augustus Blackwell?"

"Never heard of him."

"Neither have I. All I have is the location of Blackwell's party. No details on the host or the nature of the party itself."

Cypher spent the remainder of their travel time showing Annea the many uses of a datapad, including how to tap into a sector's public databanks for information. Pik-Pik and Tik-Tik babbled amongst themselves and to anyone they could rope into a conversation. Ivy practiced some form of dryad body meditation that involved growing, arranging, and then retracting tiny vines along her skin. Serena read a murder mystery she'd picked up during their shopping expedition.

"*It was General Steaksauce, on the plane of Likkola, with the barbed wire,*" Tako said.

"*That's what the author wants you to think,*" Serena said. "*But it's too obvious. They don't have the report about toxins in the victim's blood yet. It will prove the killer is Dr. Mango, who did it on the plane of Romakanti by poisoning the victim with Ataraxian death mushrooms. Remind me to ask Ivy if those are real. Also, what kind of an author names characters after foods? That's just weird.*"

"*I like it. The names are as colorful and memorable as the characters themselves.*"

After transferring trains twice, they stopped for a quick lunch before walking through a cube that served as a community park and garden. A heavy metal door at the far end marked their destination. Most doors between cubes opened automatically when they approached, or were just left open. This one had a button to the side with a sign over it reading *Push For Admittance*. When the door opened, they crossed the threshold and came to a sudden, confused stop. Cubes weren't all the same size, but this one was the largest they'd visited by a wide margin.

"Is this an aquarium? I thought we were going to a research facility." Annea said.

They stood on a wide walkway surrounding a tank so vast, they couldn't see to the other side, or even to the water's surface. A pod of whales drifted by, their songs loud enough to vibrate the glass. Coral grew along the bottom and sides of the tank, with thousands of different species swimming though or above the reef. There were eels more than twenty feet long. Crabs larger than Pik-Pik and Tik-Tik. A dozen species of squid. One large pipe in the floor appeared to lead into another cube. Unless Serena missed her guess, there was even a Planar Gate along the floor of the tank, with pillars set far enough apart that the whales could swim through it. The air was hot, humid, and smelled like the ocean.

Tako's sense of awe and wonder was even stronger than Serena's. If he had tear ducts, he'd be weeping tears of joy. *"The merfolk and the Octari are the only sapient marine life on Torbakhal,"* he said. *"I never imagined we had so much company across the multiverse."* He longed to get in there and swim with them, talk to them, learn everything about them. They both knew they didn't have time for that. She felt a twinge of sorrow on Tako's behalf. Her initial impression of him hadn't changed. He was equal parts calm, wise, kindly grandfather and goofy, inquisitive, playful child. Either way, totally adorable, and not someone she ever wanted to deny anything, if she could help it.

"Another time, buddy." She gave him a mental hug. His disappointment soon faded into his default equanimity.

Cypher pulled out his datapad and double-checked the map. "This is the right cube. Dr. Venture said to take a right and go around the corner to find the elevator, then take it as far down as it will go."

It was a long walk to the elevator. From the cube's entrance, they had to go a mile just to get to the edge of the tank, round the corner, then walk another half mile to the elevator itself. Every hundred yards or so they passed speaker boxes attached to the glass, presumably for land-dwelling beings to speak with those in the tank. Each speaker had a table and chair nearby if someone wanted to sit down. The place seemed designed for a crowd, yet they had the walkway to themselves.

"We're sure this is the place?" Annea asked again, voicing the uncertainty they all felt.

"We'll find out soon enough," Cypher said. He pushed a button labeled *M.* They rode the elevator platform in silence until it came to rest in front of an unimpressive wood door with the word *Maintenance* carved into it. The door had no handle, only a small round button along the right side, which Cypher pressed.

"Who is it?" The voice sounded muffled and garbled, as if coming from underwater. Serena couldn't pinpoint its source.

"Dr. Venture? It's Cypher. I'm here with some friends to discuss your multiverse positioning research."

"Oh. Yes. That." The voice sounded distracted. Perhaps distressed.

The door remained closed.

"Can we come in?" Cypher asked.

There was another pause, then the door retracted into the ceiling, revealing a damp, poorly lit cavern that smelled of chlorine and loneliness. A mess of pipes serving to circulate water filled much of the space, though it wasn't clear where the water came from in the first place. Sections of wall not taken up by pipe had racks of tools and spare parts for terrestrial species to service the plumbing.

Hovering in the middle of the cavern was a single being, encased in an ovoid glass tube filled with water. Four propellers kept it aloft, each anchored to an arm that pointed diagonally up and away from the front or rear of the tube. The being inside looked like a giant axolotl. His body was as long as Serena's torso, with a tail as long as her legs. He had the pale skin and red eyes of an albino, with a half-dozen feathery filaments protruding from the back of his head. His forelimbs manipulated tiny control sticks to maneuver himself.

Cypher stepped into the room first. "Dr. Venture?"

"That's me. So, you're Cypher. It's a pleasure to meet someone interested in my research. You're human. And male. And wearing a shirt. I wasn't expecting that." Venture's voice came from a horn at the base of the tube, set between two external manipulator arms. His voice warbled like a child holding a finger to their lips and moving it up and down rapidly while speaking.

"You're not what I was expecting either," Cypher said, his shrug to Serena suggesting he didn't understand the shirt comment any better than she did. "This is your lab?" He made an all-encompassing gesture to the area around them. Between the damp air and dim lighting, it felt more like a cave than a place where scientific discoveries were made.

"Yes. Well… Yes. My theories on the aethereal sea and the fixed position of realities in the multiverse are considered controversial by my colleagues. They refuse to give me the funding I deserve, so I sit here at the bottom of the Aqueous Collective, trying to create a whale-sized impact on scientific knowledge with a guppy of a budget."

Annea laughed, the kind of harsh bark someone lets out when the alternative is to scream. "This... This is the Aqueous Collective. The information critical to understanding the Vohr's spread throughout the multiverse... is in the hands of the Aqueous Collective." She buried her face in her hands.

"I don't understand," Serena said. "Is something wrong?"

"I'm so sorry Cypher, I really am. I wish I'd known sooner. I could have spared us this chameleosaur chase." Annea turned her attention to Serena. "The Aqueous Collective has a reputation for junk science so strong even isolationist worlds like Kimori know of it. Their most notorious publication stated that frequent Planar Gate travel weakens immune systems. Absolutely false and thoroughly debunked, but it had a chilling effect on trade for years. They were once contracted to do a population count on a species of fish on Ichthyo, and massively overestimated. The government of Ichthyo set quotas according to their figures, and that species went extinct five years later. We're wasting our time here."

"I am well aware of my organization's reputation," Dr. Venture said, floating over to a shelving unit along the back wall. With great care, he used a manipulator arm to open a small drawer in the center of hundreds of similar drawers. He extracted a bundle of envelopes tied together with string, then floated over to Annea and presented them to her. "I wish to show we *can* put out some quality science. My work could go a long way towards making aquatic species less of a joke in the scientific community. I'm tired of the Collective being derisively referred to as *'The Fish Tank.'*"

"What are these?" Annea asked, untying the string.

"Peer reviews of my upcoming papers outlining my theories and research methodology. You may not trust the Collective, but I bet you would trust some of these."

Annea pulled letters out of envelopes, gazing at the logos on the letterhead and skimming through the comments. "Statements of support from Lord Peter Styles, Loomis and Erger, Eagle Creek Quantitative Science... These are heavy hitters."

"Are you willing to accept the legitimacy of my research now?" Dr. Venture asked.

"It convinces me to give you the benefit of the doubt." Annea handed the letters back to the hovering axolotl. "With how serious the stakes are, we have to be sure we can trust the quality of the data."

"Hmm. Yes. The data." Dr. Venture sounded distracted.

"Is there a problem?" Cypher asked.

"Well, I'm afraid I don't have it right now. I believe my assistant borrowed it. Without consent."

"Borrowed without consent?" Serena said. "There's a euphemism for stealing if I've ever heard one."

"What makes you think your assistant took it?" Annea asked. She stepped around one of the support columns in the cavernous maintenance room and stopped before a desk littered with hand-written calculations, schematics for several different devices, and a sealed tub of earthworms.

"The data was here when I retired to my pond last night. When I arrived today, it was gone. My assistant, Lorelai Paulina Miriam Sinclair, has not shown up for work. Access logs show she entered the lab last night. There were no other entries," Dr. Venture said.

Cypher pinched his nose with his prosthetic hand in exasperation. "I could understand someone making an unauthorized copy of your research, but how could the data be *gone?* Are you telling us *all* of your research data exists in only *one* place, with no backups?"

"It's all stored on a crystalline computing matrix I had custom-built specifically to process all that data." Dr. Venture floated over to where Annea stood and pointed to the largest schematic on the desk. It depicted a large crystal in the center, slotted into a hexagonal housing. An intricate series of rods extended out from the points of the hexagon, each terminating with a smaller crystal. It reminded Serena of a snowflake. If the diagram was to scale, it was a foot long from end to end. "Once new positioning information came in, I downloaded it into the matrix and purged it from all other sources. Why have the data saved where someone could steal it?"

They let the stupidity of that statement hang in the air for a moment. Water leaked from a pipe in a distant corner of the maintenance cavern, splashing the floor with the staccato beat of a metronome. It was the only sound in the room other than the soft whir of the propellers keeping Dr. Venture in the air. The axolotl carefully pried the lid off the tub of earthworms and grabbed a handful. A circular hatch popped opened along the top of his water-filled capsule. He dropped the worms inside and sucked them down with the desperate urgency of a stress eater.

His snack consumed, Dr. Venture replaced the lid on his worms, then floated over to a safe built into the back wall. It looked like a black metal plate with no visible hinges or dials. When he poked it with a manipulator arm, the surface lit up to show an array of letters and numbers. "I stored the matrix in here. Lorelai Paulina Miriam Sinclair didn't have the password though, so I don't know how she got in."

"Is the password Venture One?" Cypher asked, staring up at the ceiling with a *'what did I do to deserve this?'* expression on his face.

Dr. Venture shook within his capsule. "How could you possibly know that?"

Cypher sighed, shifted the matrix schematic over a few inches, and pointed at a piece of paper that had been underneath it. **Venture1** was written on it in a thick black script.

"Oh. Yes. That. Doesn't everyone have a password reminder in case they forget?" Dr. Venture asked.

"You and I need to have an extensive conversation about data security," Cypher said.

"Why would Lorelai take the data without your consent?" Annea asked, clearly trying to move the conversation towards solving the problem. "What can you tell us about her?"

"Lorelai Paulina Miriam Sinclair," Dr. Venture corrected her. "In her culture, it's rude if you don't address someone by their full name."

"Yes, it would be terrible if we didn't show proper respect to the woman who stole your life's work," Serena said.

"Absolutely," Dr. Venture agreed, missing her sarcasm. "She's human. Roughly your age and height," he said, pointing at Serena.

"The most beautiful specimen of your species I have ever seen. She has straight black hair that runs halfway down her back. Black eyes too. She said it marked her as a member of the Vantoran royal bloodline."

"I see," Annea said, her expression mirroring Serena's skepticism that Lorelai was royalty. "I don't mean to sound rude, but why would someone of royal blood work as a research assistant in a laboratory crammed into a damp maintenance room?"

"Vantorans value scientific and academic achievement above all else. Lorelai Paulina Miriam Sinclair's parents unfairly called her a 'useless parasite,' kicked her out of the royal estate, and cut off her access to their funds until she 'got her act together.' She told me she found my theories fascinating, and felt assisting with something so groundbreaking would be her ticket back into her family's good graces. Lorelai Paulina Miriam Sinclair promised a substantial donation to our project as soon as she's mended her relationship with the Sinclairs — enough for us to rent out more appropriate facilities. She's amazing." Dr. Venture's warbling voice sounded almost wistful. Did the giant amphibian have a *crush* on her? "How could I turn down such an eager assistant with nowhere else to go?"

It sounded like a confidence game. Dr. Venture craved validation, as evidenced by how quickly he agreed to meet Cypher when he expressed interest in his research, and how defensive he became when Annea questioned his integrity. Lorelai crafted a backstory tailored to play well against that need, while also promising a solution to his funding problems.

"Dr. Venture is an easy mark," Tako agreed. *"I don't understand what makes this data worth the effort though."*

"There must be value in knowing where realities are positioned that we haven't considered," Serena said.

"How long has she been working for you?" Annea asked Dr. Venture.

"Nine months," the axolotl said. "In the beginning, Lorelai Paulina Miriam Sinclair took trips through Planar Gates with the equipment needed to take distance measurements. She helped me secure contracts with several multiverse trading companies at incredibly reasonable rates. They now include my measuring devices on packages they ship across realities, then send us the data, so field work isn't needed as often these days. She's been involved in every step of the data gathering and analysis process."

In other words, Serena thought, *she probably knows everything she needs to in order to continue the work without you.* "Did she leave any personal effects behind?"

"All of her textbooks are still here," Dr. Venture floated over to a desk tucked away in the back corner. It was piled high with books. "She spent a lot of time reading when not assisting with my work. It's my understanding that humans are a relatively endangered species, and she wanted to help research solutions to that problem. I gave her ample time to pursue her other scholarly ambitions when I didn't need her for mine."

Cypher and Serena shared a confused glance. Did Dr. Venture never leave his little research bubble? They'd seen humans *everywhere.*

A book lover herself, Serena examined Lorelai's collection. Yeah... they weren't scholarly materials. Most of the covers bore the image of a shirtless man. *Tempted by the Incubus King. My Guy Kai. Naughty in the Nexxxus. Knights in White Satin.* She failed to stifle a laugh. "This is all smut." She pocketed that last one. Couldn't hurt to have more reading material for the inevitable trip back to their home sector, right?

"Now I know why Dr. Venture was so surprised to see me wearing a shirt," Cypher said, grabbing *Naughty in the Nexxxus* and thumbing through it.

"What slander is this?" Dr. Venture said. "Lorelai Paulina Miriam Sinclair worked very hard on her studies!"

"You have been played for a fool," Ivy said.

"Sounds like being your assistant was a great job," Serena said. "Nine months of lodging paid for, and enough idle time to read a mountain of... literature."

Cypher snorted. "That's one word for it." He tossed the book back on the desk. "Pretty sure the scene I skimmed isn't anatomically possible."

Tucked between *Seven Suitors Seduce Susanna* and *Planar Gateway To Desire*, Serena found a handwritten note.

LPMS,

When EAB started the Seeker program, it was with moments like this in mind. Meet me at the appointed time, deliver the asset, and your participation in our lord's pageantry will be a mere formality. Welcome to the familiars.

It felt sloppy to leave behind evidence like this, but considering her employer, Serena could understand why Lorelai might not worry about it. The axolotl seemed smitten with her. He never once thought of questioning her motives. If they hadn't come along, it'd probably still be tucked between those covers a month from now. "Does this mean anything to you?" Serena handed it to Dr. Venture.

"There's only one thing this could mean." The perpetual smile plastered on the axolotl's face dimmed as the truth of Lorelai's betrayal sank in. "She's bringing my research to our local Akakami crime lord, Eldritch Augustus Blackwell."

"What's an Akakami?" Serena asked.

"You really don't know?" Dr. Venture asked. "Everybody knows the Akakami."

"We're new to the multiverse," Cypher said, pointing to himself, Ivy, and Serena in turn. "There's a lot we don't know."

Ivy opened her mouth, perhaps to remind him that Ataraxia had plenty of relations with the outside multiverse, but opted to remain silent.

Dr. Venture floated over to a freestanding metal tube placed halfway between Lorelai's desk and the one with the schematics. Using voice commands, he had it display the public biography of Eldritch Augustus Blackwell. The image projected in the air above the tube sent shivers down Serena's spine. He was humanoid, with skin the color of freshly spilled blood. Thick golden hair framed his face like a lion's mane. Blackwell's eyes were golden orbs devoid of any visible pupil or iris. A mask of rigid black material covered his mouth and extended out several inches, designed for obfuscation, not air filtration.

"The Akakami rule supreme in this sector, and Lord Blackwell stands above them all," Dr. Venture said. "Their wealth and power are limitless. They're above the law. Everyone knows Blackwell deals in drugs, information, and weapons. He has an entire division of poachers. His operation traffics beings. The government won't lift a finger to stop him, so this will go on forever, unless a rival takes him out. Akakami can be killed, but they're otherwise effectively immortal."

"How is that possible?" Annea asked.

"They have a unique method of sustaining themselves. Akakami siphon the life force from other beings."

"So they're vampires," Serena said.

"Never use that term in their presence!" Dr. Venture shook within his hovering tube. "They consider it derogatory. It will get you in a lot of unnecessary trouble."

"If they feed by sucking the life from others, why would anyone get near them? Wouldn't other beings fear for their lives around a predator species like that?" Cypher asked.

"The Akakami like to consider themselves refined and sophisticated. They don't have to hunt when their prey fight each other for a chance to be fed upon. The Akakami pay their victims — sorry, that's another term you're not allowed to use. They pay their *donors* a sum proportional to the amount of life they take. Would you give up a year of your life for an immediate payment of three years' salary? It is not uncommon to see beings let an Akakami rip at least ten, fifteen years of their life away in exchange for the funds to retire comfortably the moment they're done. Most of their volunteers are looking for a quick way out of tough financial situations."

Serena shook her head, disgusted. "They eat the poor. Such ideas are just allegories on my world."

"The Akakami can do more than take life force. They can also give some of their own to others, but they are stingy with this gift. A familiar who earns their favor can live many times their natural lifespan," Dr. Venture said. "Familiars are part executive assistant, part pet. Serving as avatars of their master's will, the political power they wield is considerable."

"So it looks like Lorelai is—" Annea started.

"Lorelai Paulina Miriam Sinclair."

"I'm not doing that," Annea snapped, losing patience with their amphibious host. She took a deep breath before continuing. "It looks like *she* is using your research to buy herself a place amongst Blackwell's familiars. What does this letter mean by *'our lord's pageantry?'* Is that related to the party he's throwing tomorrow?"

Dr. Venture had the projector bring up an entertainment broadcast. Two women in elegant ballroom dresses stood in the middle of a park. One wore red, the other black. Behind them, the back wall of the cube showed a giant mural depicting Blackwell, obvious even when out of focus. "We're here at Blackwell Plaza, a day away from the first familiar pageant Lord Blackwell has hosted in over a hundred years," Black Dress said.

"That's right," Red Dress agreed, brushing a strand of blond hair away from her eyes. "It's going to be an event that will be gossiped about for years to come. The confirmed guest list is packed with notable personalities, including members of several Sector Councils, royalty of a dozen worlds, some of the wealthiest business owners in the known multiverse, famous performers, and even a high-ranking Weaver or two."

"While the multiverse's elite mingle, a field of one hundred contestants will be fighting to impress Lord Blackwell across two phases of competition — the colorfully named Symphony of Lies, and the plainly named but no less important talent show."

"Lord Blackwell has kept the details of the Symphony of Lies secret. We have no information on it besides the name. What happens in that portion of the competition will not be made public. Those who advance will perform in the talent show, which will be broadcast across the sector, with the recording to be aired the following day on five hundred Akakami-governed worlds. Many of the contestants here hope that if they're not selected by Lord Blackwell himself, another Akakami will snap them up."

Dr. Venture killed the broadcast and looked at them expectantly, waiting to see their reaction.

"It sounds like Lorelai will be at that party," Serena said. "And finding her is our best hope for getting the data back."

"We can't just waltz in uninvited," Cypher said. "Blackwell is bound to have security we'd have to circumvent or neutralize."

"Is it worth the risk?" Annea asked. "Doctor Venture's research may have been peer reviewed favorably, but we don't know if it will be useful to us."

"Please," Dr. Venture's voice was awful in its desperation. "I've invested years into this project. I don't think I could bear to start over. Can you help me?"

Ivy spoke up before Serena could. "We must provide assistance. We have no other leads on information which could move sector governments to action."

"Lord Blackwell, or someone on his staff, obviously thinks this research is important enough to trade for a position as one of his familiars. Is it a good idea to let him have exclusive access to the multiverse data?" Cypher asked. "I agree with Ivy. We should try to help."

"I'll support any decision you three make," Annea said, "Just realize whatever you do, you're going to have to do it without me. I can help with your planning, but when the party starts, I'll be playing politics in the audience, assuming Patrick Evans can get me in. The opportunity to recruit a couple armies to our cause is too vital to pass up, no matter how important this data could be."

"And that's another reason we have to help Dr. Venture," Serena said. "If we don't get the data back, and you're not successful, we'll have wasted two days. Better to have two plans in motion than just one." *And,* she thought, *I really want to feel like I've done a good deed for someone. The poor guy needs us.* She knew too well what it felt like to need help and have those with the means to assist do nothing.

"Then we're all in agreement," Cypher said.

"Seems easy enough," Serena said, trying to lighten the mood. "Just infiltrate a party hosted by a wealthy crime lord, find Lorelai, grab the crystalline computer matrix, and get out. Nothing to it."

"Preferably without our faces being broadcast to billions of beings across the multiverse," Ivy added.

"We can totally pull off a heist," Serena said. "Right?"

CHAPTER 35

MEAN GIRLS

"This might be the dumbest thing we've done since we met," Serena said, watching their targets approach from the far side of Blackwell Plaza, their bodyguards following a discreet distance behind. "And that's saying something."

"I disagree," Ivy said. "I do not expect to be eaten if our deception goes poorly."

"Way to keep things in perspective."

After leaving Dr. Venture's lab, the group rented rooms at a nearby inn and got to work. They had less than a day to plan a heist, after all. Cypher and Annea spent time on their datapads, gleaning as much information as they could about Blackwell's party from public broadcasts and news feeds. Pik-Pik and Tik-Tik played the part of clueless tourists, meandering around the cube and peppering anyone who would talk to them with questions about the Akakami and his estate. They'd learned Blackwell loved employing rare, strange, or exotic species as servants, and managed to talk to the right people to get themselves hired on as additional catering staff for the event. Once Cypher verified which cubes Lord Blackwell owned outright, Serena and Ivy spent the remainder of the afternoon traveling around the sector, casing the exterior of his Nexus estate.

They hadn't found any way to sneak inside.

That meant that the only way in would be through the front door. Their focus shifted to evaluating the one hundred beings announced as contestants, learning how the invite process worked, and looking for any vulnerabilities they could exploit. Annea was the one who ultimately found their marks. Cypher, while giving Serena and Ivy a whirlwind crash course in common Nexus technologies unfamiliar to them, did the heavy lifting to arrange a meeting the following morning — the meeting now about to begin. Serena hoped she and Ivy had the acting skills to see it through.

"This will work," Serena said, trying to will away her stage fright.

"You've endured so much over the last few weeks, and THIS makes you nervous?" Tako laughed, his voice a warm, calming blanket over her unease.

Ivy said nothing. She'd fashioned for herself a dress of orchid petals in shades of pink and purple that really popped against her skin. She looked elegant, like a princess from some exotic, far-away kingdom only whispered of in fairy tales. Serena said as much when they left the inn. Ivy replied, "Beauty is irrelevant," but Serena caught the faintest hint of a smile.

Serena wore the earrings, slacks, open back blazer, and high-heeled shoes she'd purchased the night before to replicate the "professional woman" look that was in vogue in this sector. She carried the trendiest handbag. She hated all of it. Why would anyone in their right mind wear high heels voluntarily? She still half expected to roll an ankle and go sprawling across the pavement at any time.

As their prey closed in, Serena used the moment to study the two women. Olivia Lapierre was famous for being famous — her image was plastered across advertisements all over the sector, but she had no apparent skills or talents to justify her fame that they'd been able to find. When she wasn't making small fortunes in appearance fees visiting clubs and attending parties, she served as a personality on a vapid daytime talk show. She had the flawless skin of a fashion model, made possible by a moisturizing cream she advertised, a bottle of which cost more than Serena made in a month back in Valencia.

The other woman was Trish Abernathy, Olivia's half-sister. She ran the fashion division of their father's reality-spanning commercial empire, a division which had never turned a profit. Nepotism and daddy's deep pockets made her untouchable within the corporate ranks, allowing her to treat her share of the company more like a hobby than a business. Trish fancied herself a creative innovator, boldly releasing designs that looked indistinguishable from anything else they'd seen in dozens of clothing stores.

Neither of them were content with fame and wealth. They wanted the power only being a familiar to an Akakami could provide, and leveraged their money and connections into invites to Blackwell's party — invites Serena and Ivy intended to steal.

"Miss Lapierre, Miss Abernathy!" Serena said, affecting the bubbly enthusiasm of a die-hard fan. She extended a hand in greeting as she approached. "I'm Loretta Hildebrand, and this is my assistant, Rosemary Thyme. We're with *Dress to Thrill*." She thought the aliases were absurd, particularly Ivy's, but Cypher insisted both fit the conventions adopted by puff piece journalists in this sector and wouldn't merit a second thought to Olivia or Trish. "We're so grateful you could take time to meet with us on the day of Lord Blackwell's pageant."

"We don't usually concern ourselves with such small publications," Trish said, making it clear they considered this appearance, which Cypher had paid for with a quiet transfer of a small fortune of Kimori's funds, little more than charity work. He'd created and published their fictitious fashion and gossip publication onto the sector's public data network in the early hours of the morning, and filled it with a year's worth of backdated and plagiarized articles, many of which now sported bylines under Serena and Ivy's aliases. The phony publication wouldn't hold up to scrutiny if their quarry dug beneath the surface.

But Olivia and Trish were very surface-level people.

Serena nodded. "And that makes us all the more honored you would meet with us on such short notice. When Lord Blackwell names you as new familiars, this exclusive will put us on the map. It's genuinely a thrill to be able to speak with such distinguished personalities as you two."

Olivia ran a finger through her blond curls. "A rising tide shoots all the fish to the moon, they say."

Ivy looked ready to say something about the badly mixed and mangled metaphors, but held her tongue at a warning glance from Serena. *Please, Ivy,* Serena thought. *Don't break character, no matter how much you want to.*

Serena motioned for Olivia and Trish to follow her to *Lydia's Flour Garden*, a bakery at the opposite end of the plaza from this cube's entrance into Blackwell's domain. They'd scouted it out as the ideal location for their plan.

"Wow, that tattoo is detailed," Olivia said. "Whoever did it is brilliant."

"Thank you! That means a lot, coming from someone with such an eye for fashion as you," Serena said, her tone sticky sweet. "It's part of the culture of the Kingdom of Z'han. Everyone has one."

"How delightfully *ethnic.*" Trish spoke in the condescending and vaguely racist way only the super-rich could manage. She probably considered it a compliment.

Serena steered the group to a table in the back corner of the bakery's outdoor seating — outdoor being a relative term in the Nexus. She had the exterior wall of the bakery on her left and a half wall directly behind her and to her right, separating the bakery from a pedestrian walkway. A rectangular planter of rose bushes served as a privacy screen between tables. Ivy sat diagonally from Serena, close enough to the roses to surreptitiously coax them into growing wider and taller without needing her staff. Between the bakery's walls and Ivy's plant manipulation, nobody would be able to see under the table unless they got close and ducked down. Trish and Olivia's bodyguards took positions on the opposite side of the roses and turned away to keep an eye on pedestrian traffic around the plaza.

"We... understand you are about to... unveil a new floral perfume line." Ivy spoke with the halting, uncertain tone of a novice actress only half-remembering her line. "Can you share any information with us about it?"

"Of course!" Trish set her purse down on the table. As she opened it and rummaged around, Serena saw it for the briefest moment — the golden, envelope-sized engraved gold plate that served as an invitation to Lord Blackwell's party. Whoever handed one to the guards manning the door was allowed in. Who they were originally given to didn't matter, almost as if Blackwell *wanted* invite recipients to have to fight for their right to party. Their whole plan hinged on the assumption Trish and Olivia would carry their invites on them, rather than risk trusting them to anyone else. The invitation disappeared beneath other items in her bag: a silver comb, red nail polish, a clear bag containing some kind of leaf, and a copy of *Naughty in the Nexxxus*. With great fanfare, Trish pulled out a small glass bottle and handed it to Ivy.

Ivy stared at the bottle in her hands without comprehension. Crap. Serena hadn't thought of that. Why would a dryad know how to operate a perfume bottle, when they could produce hundreds of scents naturally whenever they wanted?

"Is something wrong?" Olivia asked.

"I am just... admiring the craftsmanship," Ivy said. Serena mimed taking the cap off the bottle, spraying her wrist, and sniffing, in a way she hoped Olivia and Trish wouldn't notice. Taking the hint, Ivy mimicked her gestures and took a whiff of the perfume. "This is certainly original. A fragrance without peer." Ivy returned the bottle to its owner. She did an admirable job feigning enthusiasm. Serena could tell she hated it.

"Right?" Trish beamed. She stuffed the bottle back into her purse, then slid it under the table. As she did, Tako pushed free from Serena's back and crawled slowly down the leg of her chair. "I'm thrilled we could bring this to market so quickly. We're capitalizing on a new opening in the market. One of our competitor's flagship lines ceased production. They can't source the flowers they used anymore. Apparently the world they grew on got cut off from the Nexus or something."

Tako reached the ground and lifted one of Serena's pant legs to wrap a tentacle around her ankle, restoring their connection so she could monitor his part of the mission.

"Nobody wanted that Ataraxian garbage anyway," Olivia said. "Your products are for a higher class of being."

Murderous intent flashed across Ivy's eyes. Serena offered her an exaggerated smile, praying the dryad wouldn't give voice to her anger. Olivia and Trish obviously didn't realize Ivy was Ataraxian, though such knowledge might not have had much impact on their behavior.

She needed to retake control of the conversation before Ivy lost her composure.

"How do you determine what materials to use for your perfumes?" Serena asked, making a show of opening a notebook and grabbing a pen to take notes. She did her best to nod and make approving noises as the right times, while in her mind's eye she watched Tako use a pair of limbs to open Trish's purse. He reached inside, gently sifting through her belongings, careful to make no sound while fishing for the invitation.

"Do you want me to take the leaves too? Could make for a fun after-party," Tako said.

"Stay on mission, old man. You're supposed to be the responsible one."

Tako used a third and fourth limb to hold items in position, then slowly pulled free the invitation. Given Blackwell's reputation, the metal plate which bore his likeness was probably real gold, not an imitation. Holding it aloft so it didn't clink against the ground, Tako opened Serena's bag and slipped it inside while closing Trish's purse with other limbs. He paused a moment, then slithered across the brick floor toward Olivia's bag. *"You're going to have to stall a bit,"* he said. *"This one has a latch I need to figure out."* Serena's fingers would have made short work of it, but Octari tentacles weren't as proficient at that fine level of detail.

Serena was about to ask another inane question about the perfume industry when Ivy cut in with a different question. "Thousands of beings wanted to compete at Lord Blackwell's event, yet only one hundred received invitations. How do you plan to win Lord Blackwell's favor amongst such stiff competition?"

"Well, we don't want to give away *all* of our secrets," Olivia said, then did just that. Serena kept her pen moving across the page, scribbling down lines that almost looked like words, her attention locked on Tako fiddling with Olivia's purse. He needed three tentacles to finally get it to open. He pulled back the flap, reached inside —

Pain shot through Serena's arm, a sympathetic reaction to the bite Tako had just taken. "Sorry, hand cramps." She set down the pen and massaged her forearm. "Please, keep going."

Perhaps sensing Serena's distraction, Ivy covered for her, asking the kinds of questions a star-struck reporter might ask of a celebrity and a fashion mogul. After a rocky start, she'd settled into the role of Rosemary Thyme.

"We have a problem," Tako said.

"No kidding. What was that?"

Tako opened the flap of Olivia's bag, careful to keep his limbs from going inside. Perched atop the hoard of junk Olivia hauled around with her sat a pink ball of fur, featureless except for a pair of comically large blue eyes along its equator. Its pupils tracked the movement of Tako's tentacle as he moved one back and forth along the opening of the bag. The creature looked adorable until it split near the bottom to reveal a lipless mouth filled with piranha-like teeth. No doubt they could strip flesh from bone in seconds if properly motivated. *"Fuzzball here needs to move if I'm going to have any hope of nabbing the second invite."*

"How fast do you think you could re-close the clasp?" Serena asked.

"It'd only take a second or two. That's a lot easier than opening it, why?"

Serena took advantage of their mental bond to imagine for him what she wanted. Tako wasn't thrilled but deferred to her judgment. He slapped the ball of fuzz, resealed the bag, then flattened himself onto Serena's leg as quickly as he could. Guilt radiated through their bond when the carnivorous ball of fur started to cry.

Olivia reacted with the frantic speed of a mother rushing into a burning building to save her child. Tako barely had the latch closed and his limbs clear before she hauled the purse up to the table. She brought the ball of fur out and clutched it to her breast like a newborn, rocking it back and forth.

"I'm not proud of that," Tako said.

"I'm not either, but you did no lasting harm, right? We're trying to save a planet here."

"Fuzzy McNibbles gets lonely sometimes if he hasn't been held in a while," Olivia said, transferring the creature to one hand while returning her purse to the floor under the table with the other. She left the bag open.

Tako waited a moment, watching the scene through Serena's eyes. Satisfied Olivia wouldn't be returning her pet to its leather prison in the immediate future, he squeezed out of Serena's pant leg and crawled back over to the purse. *"This is going to be a delicate operation."* Tako's eyes roamed over a cluttered mess of objects that wanted to make noise when touched. Coins of various shapes, sizes, and colors. Two glass bottles of the same perfume Trish carried. A dagger, its blade stored in a narrow leather sheath to keep it from cutting up everything else. Notes written on crumpled stationary. Three different kinds of lotion. Just visible at the bottom of all of it was the golden edge of one corner of the invitation.

"What was I talking about?" Olivia asked.

"How you will convince Lord Blackwell that allowing you to host a vocal competition series would drive revenue for his entertainment operations," Ivy said.

"No, that wasn't it. I was taking about how a singing show would make Blackwell money."

"That is what I just... My mistake. Please continue."

"I'm not going to be able to do this silently," Tako said. *"You'll need to cover for me."*

Serena slouched back in her chair, waited until Tako signaled his readiness, then kicked Olivia's purse. As the coins and perfume rattled against each other, Tako pulled the invitation free and dropped it into Serena's bag. He made another hasty retreat up her leg. "I'm so sorry," Serena said. "I was just trying to stretch my legs."

"You should be more careful!" Olivia said. "This purse costs more than your entire outfit." She put Fuzzy McNibbles away without looking inside, then closed the latch.

"I'm so sorry," Serena said again. She stood and made a show of stretching her torso and arms. "You've given us so much. We can't thank you enough." Both sentences were phrases meant to signal *mission accomplished.* Trish and Olivia wouldn't realize what they were truly thanking them for until it was too late.

"Yes," Ivy agreed. "We are in your debt."

They said their goodbyes and parted as quickly as politeness allowed, not wanting to arouse any suspicion.

Serena was all smiles when they arrived back at the inn. "I've got a golden ticket," she said, tossing one of the invites to Cypher. He'd done a significant amount of the research necessary to make their plan possible. It was only fair he get to inspect the fruits of their labor before she and Ivy cashed them in and began the next phase of their insane, half-baked plan.

"I did not enjoy that," Ivy said. "I do not enjoy pretending to be someone I am not."

"Well, then you're going to hate this next part even more," Cypher said. "I figured out what the Symphony of Lies entails."

CHAPTER 36

PRUNE EVERYTHING AWAY

"Welcoming Hall" is a poor name, Ivy thought, casting her gaze across the lobby of Eldritch Augustus Blackwell's Nexus estate. The vast chamber could fit a thousand beings milling about. The walls, the floors, the support columns, the stairs in the middle of the hall that led to the balcony level — everything was made from white marble. No art hung on the walls. No plants brought color or life to the space. Standing in an austere box of stone, Ivy feel more unwelcome than in any other home she had ever visited.

Halfway between the entrance door and the stairs, railings blocked beings from stepping onto an elevator platform designed to deliver something from the floor below. Probably food for guests.

Serena took Ivy's hand and led her to the base of the stairs, where they turned to watch other beings filing in. A week ago, she would not have allowed the human to touch her with such familiarity. Now, the gesture felt... tolerable. Maybe even trending towards *pleasant.*

They had arrived early in hopes of avoiding an encounter with Trish and Olivia. Contestants had to pass a security check by Blackwell's bodyguards to confirm they were unarmed and didn't have any communication devices on them before being allowed inside. As some of the first beings through, they turned in their golden invitations and were safely out of reach before Ivy caught a glimpse of the celebrities they had robbed. Both had a relaxed stride suggesting they would not realize their invitations were gone before reaching the security checkpoint.

The early arrival afforded them plenty of time to identify Lorelai Paulina Miriam Sinclair. What they did from there depended on if she had the multiverse data on her or not.

"Anything that calls for this much improvisation cannot be called a *plan*," Ivy said.

"It's not like we had much time to work out anything better. We're doing the best we can with the information we have. At least Cypher gave us some idea what to expect in here."

"Yes. A game of lies and deception." When a dryad chose to speak, they said what they meant, often with a level of candor that made other species uncomfortable. Modifying language to accommodate the delicate sensibilities of other species was difficult. To speak falsely and deceive harder still.

She would not enjoy Blackwell's game.

Most of the beings she saw passing through the gilded entry doors were human, or close enough she could not tell the difference. All had the same basic build. Two arms. Two legs. Little or no fur. Skin tones varied, but only within the range achievable by humans. Given the vast variety of life in the Nexus, the group filling the Welcoming Hall was shocking for its lack of diversity. Eldritch Augustus Blackwell had a specific mold he wanted his familiars to fit inside. It made Ivy feel even more out of place.

"Do you see Lorelai?" Serena asked.

"I do not." Ivy doubted she could identify the human with the limited information they had.

Several minutes later, her assumption proved incorrect. Among the last beings to clear security, Lorelai Paulina Miriam Sinclair turned out to be easy to recognize, with hair blacker than a night sky and eyes to match. No visible pupil or iris. She wore a red dress that hugged her outline, accentuating her bust and the curve of her hips. Males around the room could not look away once they saw her, marking her as a flower they very much wished to pollinate.

"She doesn't have the matrix on her," Serena said, watching Lorelai weave through the crowd towards them. "No place to hide it wearing that."

Serena did not have time to say more before Lorelai came to a stop at the base of the stairs, only a step or two outside Ivy's reach.

She ignored the lusting gazes of the men in attendance, focusing instead on the door at the the top of the stairs with an intensity that bordered on religious devotion.

Since Lorelai did not have the matrix on her, they would have to isolate her during the Symphony of Lies and somehow convince her to divulge its location. Ivy had a last-resort solution for that, one she had not shared with Serena. Her cheeks flushed with embarrassment that the idea even occurred to her. *We will find another way.*

"Attention everyone!" A human came down the stairs from the balcony level. He wore a black suit and tie, with dark glasses over his eyes, despite being indoors. A baton was strapped to his hip. "Please clear the stairway. The event is about to begin." His tone was courteous, but his expression suggested that would change in a hurry if they did not obey. Ivy and Serena stepped into the crowd, allowing the guard to position himself at the center of the bottom stair.

"Welcome, you fortunate few." The voice came from everywhere at once, like the disembodied voice of a god addressing his people. "What happens tonight will shape your destinies for decades, perhaps centuries. As my empire expands, I need more familiars. For the first time in a hundred years, I'm giving beings outside my organization an opportunity to prove your value to me, and ascend beyond your petty, common lives. But to be worthy of speaking to me directly, you must first pass a test."

Red and gold double doors opened at the top of the staircase, and through them stepped Eldritch Augustus Blackwell.

The image Dr. Venture showed them failed to capture the primal terror the Akakami's presence inspired. Ivy heard a collective gasp. Most of the crowd took reflexive steps backwards. They must not have ever seen an Akakami up close either. Lorelai smiled and held her ground. She cast an appraising look at Serena and Ivy. They had not moved either. Blackwell was not in the top five most terrifying things they had seen since losing their homeworlds.

The Akakami was flanked on both sides by human bodyguards wearing the same suit and glasses as the man at the bottom of the steps. Standing ten feet tall, Blackwell towered over both of them. He wore black slacks and a sleeveless vest, exposing muscles powerful enough to rip someone in half. His blood red skin seemed to swallow any light that touched it, offering no reflection. He wore the same mask he had in Dr. Venture's image, hiding his mouth.

"My enterprises span many industries across numerous realities. Some are public knowledge. Many are not," Blackwell continued, his voice still coming from everywhere at once. "Knowing when to speak the truth, and when and how to lie, is critical to be worthy of a seat at my table. And so, the trial you must pass is one I have dubbed the Symphony of Lies — a crucible which will weed out beings incapable of wearing many faces."

Everything Blackwell told them could have been explained by an underling. The man wanted to use his reputation and imposing presence to bring gravitas to the proceedings. He wanted the people below him humbled, nervous, and primed to make mistakes. Ivy would not allow herself to be intimidated.

The elevator platform in the middle of the hall rumbled. Ivy turned to see the metal roof of the elevator shaft slide away. A human woman appeared, standing next to a gilded cart with a golden box atop it. Blackwell clearly loved the gold aesthetic. The safety railings around the elevator shaft retracted into the floor as the platform came to rest in the hall.

The left and right sides of the Welcoming Hall each had five doors, all marked by golden numbers. "Each of you will draw a number, then enter your assigned door," Blackwell said. "Once everyone has entered their assigned rooms, you will be seen by my Reticulans in a random order."

All ten doors opened simultaneously. From each emerged a short, rail-thin being with gray skin. Their naked bodies lacked any apparent sexual characteristics. They had bulbous heads that seemed too large for their slender necks to support, with enormous black orbs for eyes. They had two small diagonal slits for a nose, a thin, lipless line of a mouth, and a small hole on each side of their head as an audio receptor.

"The Reticulans are masters of illusion magics, and will give you a new appearance," Blackwell continued. "Anonymity is essential for this trial to be conducted fairly. Once everyone has their new identity, our game will begin. The Reticulans will then roam the hall as judges. Think of them like reverse lie detectors. If they sense too much truth in how you present yourself, you will be escorted out of my domain and lose your opportunity to become a familiar."

Ivy exchanged glances with Serena. They knew to expect lies and deception, but not altered appearances. How would they identify Lorelai? How would they find each other? And where were Pik-Pik and Tik-Tik? The ants carried with them devices Serena and Ivy hoped would allow them to cheat, but they were nowhere to be found. They would have been in Blackwell's estate for almost three hours by now, serving as new additions to his catering staff. Hopefully food and drink would be offered during the masquerade.

"You may begin drawing door assignments," Blackwell said.

Ivy half-expected a rush on the box to draw numbers, but under Blackwell's intense gaze, everyone formed an orderly line to wait their turn. One by one, they withdrew fist-sized balls, each with a number printed onto them. The balls were different colors, with the color bearing no apparent connection to the number on the door. Ivy could not determine if that was significant before her turn to draw a number.

"Green seven," Serena said, showing Ivy.

"Red five." Ivy showed hers to Serena then headed for the appropriate door.

A counter ran along the wall to the right behind door number five. An enormous mirror took up the entire wall above it, save for lights placed near the ceiling. The room was small, no larger than the bedroom she slept in on Kimori. Did these rooms hold another purpose normally, or had they been specially built for the Symphony of Lies?

"Proceed through the door in the back." The gray-skinned being's mouth did not move, but Ivy had no doubt the words belonged to them. *"I will call beings in by color."* Their words felt like a harsh buzzing across the surface of her mind. Was this how it felt when Serena spoke with Tako? She would have to ask when she had a chance.

This waiting room had no exit other than the door she walked through. Ten stools lined the walls, each of a plain, unvarnished wood that stood in stark contrast to the opulence on display outside. Ivy ignored condescending glares from the five beings already occupying stools and selected one for herself. No doubt they considered her primitive, covered in nothing but a few patches of leaves, while they wore expensive formal attire intended to signify rank and prestige.

Their opinions were irrelevant.

Nobody spoke while the room filled. Why reveal anything which could potentially be used against them later? Sweat dripped from the brows of most of the people crammed into the tight space as their body heat warmed the room. A woman holding a blue ball stood and left, though Ivy had heard no signal to do so. Several minutes later, a man with a yellow ball exited.

"RED." The word filled Ivy's mind. She shuddered, disliking that a being could project their voice into her mind without seeing her. She exited the waiting room and set her ball on the counter.

"Blackwell called you Reticulan," Ivy said. "I am unfamiliar with that term."

"That is my species," the gray-skinned being said, gesturing for her to take a seat in front of the mirror. She caught her reflection in the Reticulan's disconcertingly huge eyes.

"What is your name?"

"You may address me as Zeta," they said, spinning her to face the mirror. Zeta's voice sounded neither identifiably male nor female. It carried a multi-tone quality to it, as if three individuals spoke in unison. Though the buzzing feeling that came with the telepathy felt uncomfortable, it seemed wiser to speak and obtain information than to be silent.

Zeta pointed to a diagram of a hexagon on the counter. Each point in the shape had a name associated with it. *"For the upcoming trial, you are a familiar of the Kraayen."* They pointed to the name on the graph. *"Your enemies are the Wendl and the Woj."* Those names were on the hexagon points adjacent to the Kraayen. Zeta then indicated the name directly across from Kraayen. A green line linked them. *"You may wish to represent yourself as a member of the Brinks, whom the Wendl and Woj are afraid of. You earn double the favor by unmasking members of your enemy factions. But you may accuse and eliminate members of any house, except for your fellow Kraayen or your Brinks allies. Make a false accusation, and you will be eliminated. Reveal someone as member of your house or your allies, and you will be eliminated. Be sure, or be silent."*

"Everyone is trying to identify members of two enemy factions, while pretending to be from a third, and actually belonging to a fourth," Ivy said. "Is this accurate?"

"You are correct," Zeta said. *"The goal here is survival. It is not necessary to eliminate anyone at all. But Blackwell does consider people's performance here in his decision making process. Passivity is unlikely to be rewarded. Non-participation results in elimination too, at our discretion. If we don't think you're playing the game, you're gone."*

"Are these designations supposed to mean something to me?" Anxiety fogged Ivy's thoughts. She felt like a sapling about to be knocked over by violent winds.

"They are ancient Akakami houses who wiped each other out in a war that predates the Lost Epoch. I will give you the information you need, from the Kraayen perspective. If you think carefully, you will notice the gaps which could get you in trouble." Zeta touched a finger to her temple. A hurricane of information assaulted her mind. She grabbed the counter to steady herself. Historical, cultural, economic, and political details blew by faster than her mind could latch onto them, yet when Zeta withdrew their finger, she felt like she had all the context she'd need to play the game.

It is too much. So many layers of lies. I will be exposed and eliminated the moment I open my mouth. The level of intrigue common in an Akakami's inner circle brought her to the ragged edge of panic. *I will fail.*

Zeta took a four-fingered hand and held it over her head. An aura of orange energy surrounded the being as they started their work. The grass on her head turned into thick, curly locks of black hair. Ivy's skin turned a deep brown. The color change poured down her skin from her head to her toes like falling water. Ivy felt like she was watching herself die. Everything that defined her was pruned away.

She had grown up with fifteen sisters. For her whole life, her sense of self and identity had been bound to her world and her family. She had only started figuring out who she was on her own terms when she had to slay Moogi. And now, days later, she had to completely erase herself and be someone else. To wear a false face, smile, and deceive a room full of beings all doing the same thing. Even in her most imaginative nightmares, she would never have dreamed up this scenario.

A single tear rolled down her cheek as her green eyes turned the same shade of brown as her skin. Her leafy coverings disappeared as the human skin tone spread across her chest and along her arms. The process accelerated as it went. Seconds later, Ivy stared at the reflection of a naked human female. She felt erased. Plain. Bland. Ordinary. Unexceptional. Then ashamed of herself for thinking of humans in such terms.

The orange energy surrounding Zeta faded as they stepped back to admire their work.

"Surely you do not expect me to step outside in this state," Ivy said. Even the sound of her voice had changed, now softer and higher pitched than before.

"Of course not," Zeta said. *"Flesh is the base layer of this magic. Next come the embellishments. Please stand."*

Ivy complied. Zeta's orange aura returned as they twirled a finger, creating a red ballroom dress on her body. It started much too large, but shrunk and reformed until the fit was right. A matching pair of high-heeled shoes appeared on the counter.

"No heels. Please," Ivy said. After seeing Serena struggle in them, she had no desire to try them herself.

Zeta stared at her, their wide, unblinking eyes revealing nothing. Did Reticulans feel emotions? They waved a hand over the heels, transforming them into ruby red slippers. *"Are these acceptable?"*

"Yes. Thank you, Zeta," Ivy said, putting them on. She ran a hand across her belly. The dress felt real, and responded like real silk as she moved it around, yet she could breathe as easily as if she wore nothing at all. She opened her pores, pulling in deep breaths. If she could not lower her heart rate, she would not be able to focus. There was too much at stake to allow anxiety to hobble her.

There could be no doubt Zeta was talented at their craft. Humans would probably consider this form beautiful. But it was not a dryad body. It was not *her*.

As she reentered the Welcoming Hall, she created a corsage bracelet of ivy around her left wrist, featuring an emerald rose. A small act of defiance against Blackwell and anyone else who would ever dare to erase her.

CHAPTER 37

A War with Many Fronts

"Who's ready to behold Lord Blackwell's first familiar pageant in over a hundred years?" Lorenzo, an elf with a distinctly non-elven name, paced back and forth in front of a large crowd of spectators. Receiving only half-assed applause and a single whoop, he shook his head in disapproval. "I thought the rich and famous knew how to party. I find your lack of enthusiasm disturbing. But it's fixable! Fear not, for we are" — he paused dramatically and clapped his hands, spreading his arms wide to encompass his partners on his left and right — "the Peril Dancers, and we will get you in a festive spirit!"

The three elves had sky blue skin not seen on the elves of Kimori. They wore loose-fitting pants and vests with a red and black checker pattern. Lorenzo wore a jaunty cap with a feather which made him look like a jester playing at being a pirate. The performers had set up on the street in front of one of the side entrances to Blackwell's Nexus estate. Since the Welcoming Hall was in use for the Symphony of Lies, Blackwell's VIP guests needed to use another entrance to get to the auditorium for the talent show. Annea couldn't determine if Blackwell hired the Peril Dancers to be pre-show entertainment, or if the performers were making an opportunistic appearance and bribed Blackwell's security not to haul them away.

We're all engaged in some theater today, Annea thought, looking over the crowd. *While Serena and Ivy play their roles, I must play mine.* This was the kind of event where the elite established connections, make backroom deals, and jockeyed for social prestige. Most of the humanoid species wore expensive-looking suits, dresses, or robes.

Annea, to her sorrow, also dressed the part, wearing a form-fitting black ballroom dress. No jewelry though. She had limits.

At least the Peril Dancers are honest about their act.

Lorenzo and his partners reached into a wooden chest and withdrew a pair of black rods, each as long as their forearms. They pushed buttons on the handles, sending a loud, angry electric buzz into the air. Satisfied the noise had drawn the crowd's attention, they deactivated the devices. "These rods give off enough energy to knock out an Elushan mammoth," Lorenzo said. "Getting struck by one makes for a Very Bad Day. Getting struck twice is lethal."

The crowd wisely took a couple steps back.

The buzz returned as Lorenzo's partners took up positions two paces away from him to either side and started passing the rods back and forth around him, each time missing him by a fraction of an inch. Never taking his eyes off the audience, Lorenzo tossed one of his rods to each of his companions. They added them into their pattern so Lorenzo had six potentially lethal objects making a circuit around him.

Where is he? Annea scanned the crowd for Patrick Evans for the hundredth time, trying not to get drawn into the Peril Dancers' antics and lose focus. *A Weaver's robes can't be that hard to find, right?*

"Annea Vantalos, my plus one for this evening's festivities. It's nice to meet you."

Annea jumped at the sound of the voice. She hadn't sensed any movement in the crowd around her. Either her focus was slipping, or the speaker was very, very good at stealth. Or both. Annea liked to think she had excellent situational awareness. People couldn't just sneak up on her. But he had.

The human was at least a foot shorter than her, which wasn't surprising. Few humans or elves were tall enough to meet her eye level. Gently curling brown hair ran past his shoulders, while a trimmed beard and mustache framed his face. His black robes featured web-like decorative stitching the color of lightning. She didn't know enough about the Weavers to know if the coloring signified a high rank, or if it was a unique affectation he'd chosen for himself. He looked to be in his early thirties, far younger than she'd expected. Seniority tended to influence ascension in the Weaver ranks more than knowledge or raw talent.

"Patrick Evans, I presume." Annea returned her attention to the street performance. Lorenzo spun out of the whirling pattern of electric rods, grabbed four more from their chest, then danced back into the pattern. The crackling noise in the air rose in volume as he activated them and started juggling. If Lorenzo's timing was off at all, his arms would pass into the path of a rod thrown by his companions. "I wish you would have responded to my messages." She couldn't suppress her irritation. She'd used Orlan's datapad to contact Patrick five times since her first attempt the day before. He'd never responded, leaving her no choice but to wait here and hope for the best.

"Forgive me," Patrick said. "I'm a very *wanted* man. Orlan sent me your photo with a report on why you've come to the Nexus. I'll be happy to introduce you to my contacts." He sounded weary, like he hadn't slept in days. His bloodshot eyes and pale skin reinforced that impression.

Annea didn't like the emphasis on *wanted*. "Expecting trouble?"

"In a perverse way, I'm looking forward to Blackwell's festivities," Patrick said, not answering the question. "We're about to watch rational, thinking beings compete for the chance to live in servitude to a vampire, in exchange for secondhand political power and the potential of an unnaturally long life. That's metal as hell. It'll be the closest thing to a break I've had in a long time."

"Metal?" Annea asked.

"Never mind." Patrick chuckled and waved her question away. The levity sounded forced. "It's a genre of music on my homeworld. Explanations on the finer points of Amarth culture will have to wait."

"Orlan told me the Weavers were on the verge of a civil war." Annea wouldn't let Patrick side-step her concerns. If she risked making enemies just for talking to him, she needed to know. She felt under-dressed without the comforting weight of her kukris on her hips. At least she had punch daggers hidden in the soles of her shoes.

Patrick sighed. "That war has already begun."

The crowd roared with approval as the Peril Dancers deactivated their electric rods and took a bow. One of Lorenzo's companions grabbed a cucumber from the chest, held it against an extended arm, then moved to stand before a wooden board. "Now, gentlebeings, I will show you how the Perils Dancers prepare toppings for our salads." With a level of accuracy Annea envied, Lorenzo took out a set of throwing knives and threw them with exceptional precision, making clean cuts through the vegetable without injuring his comrade.

"The multiverse is embroiled in a war with many fronts," Patrick said. "The Vohr invasions and the discord within the Weavers are just two lines of threat in a war so vast in scope that it almost drove me mad when I was shown the big picture. Few beings in the Nexus realize what's going on, but that ignorance won't last much longer."

"And who showed you this big picture?"

"The Cosmic Weaver herself, of course," Patrick said, as if that should be obvious.

Annea sighed. Claiming to receive visions from the Weaver's patron goddess meant he was even worse off than she'd feared. He'd been running without sleep so long hallucinations were setting in. Why had he done that to himself? "Let's focus on the here and now," she said. "Why didn't you answer my messages? Are we in danger here?"

"Not here, no. Public assassination isn't their style. They don't want to draw undue attention to themselves yet. There's no safer place for us to be than Blackwell's estate, surrounded by a crime lord's fans, lackeys, and security. They'll pounce though if I'm careless enough to separate myself from a crowd. They're here now. Look for the black robes."

Annea picked out a half-dozen robed figures scattered around the crowd that she hadn't noticed before. Had they been there the whole time? The thick robes came with a deep hood, making it impossible to determine the identity of the wearer. She couldn't even make out the species. Every bit of skin was hidden under robes, hoods, boots, or gloves. She recalled seeing similar beings from time to time as they moved about the Nexus. "Who are they?"

"Weavers. Though not wearing the official robes of our order."

"Explain," Annea said, her frustration rising. Were all scholars this difficult to work with? She grabbed Patrick by the shoulders and spun him to face her. A yellow aura enveloped him. An electric surge of power raced up her arms, paralyzing her muscles as if she'd wrapped her hands around a thunderbolt. As abruptly as it started, the sensation vanished, leaving her upper body numb. It took her several seconds to regain enough control to return her hands to her sides.

"Sorry about that," Patrick said, his aura fading. He looked ready to fall asleep on his feet, his eyes partially closed. "As you can see, I'm a bit uptight about my personal space. I am, after all, being hunted. I've been playing a game of fox-and-rabbit with my stalkers for five days now, keeping as many of them as possible focused on me so those I still trust can hide. It turns out favoring military intervention against the Vohr isn't good for your health. Four Weavers I consider friends have turned up dead, and another seven are missing. It'll be my turn soon, if I'm not careful."

"How do you know the people following you are Weavers?" Annea asked.

"It's a long story. They've entered facilities only a Weaver would know about. Two of my colleagues were found dead in one of our secure communication hubs. I'm sure our robed friends here are from the faction that wants the invasions to continue unimpeded."

Annea felt she owed it to Patrick to keep an eye on his stalkers and ensure he didn't come to harm. He was doing her a huge favor getting her into Blackwell's event and letting her take over the meeting to advance her agenda, even if it did overlap with his own. She'd never forgive herself if he got killed for it.

Another round of cheers and applause broke out as the Peril Dancers bowed, thanked the crowd, and held out sacks. Appreciative members of the crowd came forward to tip them coins in various shapes and colors. Behind them, a pair of human security officers opened a set of red and gold doors. Guests started filing in after first confirming their identities and passing a perfunctory check for concealed weapons.

"Have you ever met an Ankora or a Chiroptera?" Patrick asked, changing the subject.

"I have not." Annea said.

Patrick nodded almost imperceptibly. Annea followed his gaze to see a bipedal grizzly bear hanging near the back of the crowd. He wore a simple sheet of beige fabric with holes for his neck and arms. Five necklaces hung from his thick neck, each displaying the teeth of a different species of carnivore. "Our enormous furry friend over there is Kuma Wolfsbane, patriarch of a clan from the planet Yankari. The Ankora are a warrior species who have been at peace amongst themselves for over five hundred years. They love a noble fight, often taking work as peacekeepers and bodyguards. I consider them a very fair and egalitarian people with a strong sense of justice. They're not the type to pick a fight, but if you provoke them or offend their sense of honor, pray to your gods because they'll be the ones still standing in the end. The challenge with the Ankora won't be in recruiting them, but in seeing how many troops you can get them to commit."

"And the Chiroptera?"

Patrick pointed to a small being at the front of the crowd who wouldn't come up to her knees. He had the face of a fruit bat and the body of a lemur, though his size was closer to a chimpanzee's. He wore a gaudy vest loaded with buttons of various shapes, each made from a different metal. A pair of bat wings poked through holes in the back of the vest.

"The Chiroptera are shrewd businessmen and extraordinary blacksmiths. Don't be fooled by their size, they're terrifying in close-quarters combat. I've never seen a species faster and deadlier with a blade. Everything they do is motivated by profit — they tend to be either merchants or mercenaries. The Vohr have annihilated several worlds they had strong economic relationships with, so they're eager for some payback, even though they claim there's no profit in revenge. Appealing to their coin purse is critical if you want to enlist their aid."

"I can work with that," Annea said. "Anything else I should know?"

"Fair warning, the Chiroptera are irredeemably sexist. The Moon Doge won't be happy discussing military and business matters with a woman. Apologies in advance."

"Moon Doge?"

Patrick winced, then gave her an apologetic smile. "That's his title, and the only thing you may refer to him as if you wish to recruit his people. Amongst the Chiroptera, a person's worth and political power are both directly tied to their wealth. Since he's the richest of them all, he's considered the smartest and wisest, and thus will continue to rule until someone else's wealth exceeds his." His studiously neutral tone told her more about his feelings for the Chiroptera than his actual words did. It was the tone of a man who didn't have anything nice to say, but felt he had to say *something*.

She'd find a way to make it work. Kimori couldn't afford to be choosy about allies while facing imminent invasion.

Annea risked putting a hand on Patrick's back to keep him close and help steer him through the crowd as they approached the doors. This time, he didn't unleash any of his power on her. She took care to make sure they kept their distance from the black robed figures. Though she couldn't see into the hoods, she knew their eyes were on her. She wasn't hard to track, standing a head or more taller than most of the beings in the area.

"What does the title mean, though?" Annea asked.

"I didn't ask. I don't want to know."

It said a lot that a scholar would prefer ignorance.

CHAPTER 38

THE SYMPHONY OF LIES

Ivy assumed that since Zeta altered her appearance to look human, the other non-human species in attendance would receive similar treatment. She was mistaken. The glamored contestants represented a much greater diversity of species than they had before. She walked past a giant satyr, *giant* being a relative term, since they were the same height. One woman had snakes for hair, plus reptilian eyes. Everyone retained a humanoid body build.

As the Welcoming Hall continued to fill with contestants, Ivy scanned every face, hoping against all logic that she would recognize Serena or Lorelai in their new forms. Everyone spent the down time sizing each other up, studying posture, body language, and facial expressions. Deciding who to talk to first once the game began.

Nobody spoke.

She had enough self-awareness to know she struggled with the nuances of complex social dynamics. If she could identify Serena quickly enough, they could work the crowd as a team and cover for each other. She disliked idle conversation, and had little practice at deception. Serena might fare better, but they needed each other to make this work.

We are walking disasters, she thought. Gnarled vines of anxiety twisted up her abdomen, causing her thoughts to drift like a leaf in the breeze. She struggled to catch and hold any thought before it blew away.

On the balcony level, Blackwell paced the perimeter like a predator evaluating a herd of prey animals for weaknesses. Would she have to identify Lorelai's false form and coerce her into revealing the computing matrix's location while Blackwell watched? On an abstract level, Ivy knew she could. Every dryad had the means to compel truth from someone else, if they were willing to violate Ataraxian law.

"BEGIN." The Akakami's voice filled the room.

It is too soon. I am not ready.

A woman approached Ivy, her hair dyed the blue of tropical waters. "My name is Serena Lothal, director of the Vitae Reefs resort complex on Markona. You strike me as someone who could use a vacation."

Ivy almost broke character. *I am in a game of lies. My friend would not walk up to the first person she saw and use her real name.* Her friend. The truth of it still surprised her sometimes. Serena had showed her the error in making instant judgments of someone's character, and saved her life more than once. She was not the monster Ivy's upbringing led her to expect.

The dryad studied Fake Serena, uncertain how to reply. Thanks to Zeta, she felt like she had known the intricacies of ancient Akakami house politics her whole life. Markona was Rossum territory. If this Serena really was a Rossum, Ivy would not be her primary target. But the Rossums were allies to the Wendl, one of the two houses hostile to the Kraayen. If Fake Serena was pretending to be a Rossum to disguise being a Wendl, she needed to be careful. Fake Serena could also be a Woj, a mutual enemy to the Kraayen and the Rossums, pretending to be a Rossum to create a false sense of comradery. Ivy's head swam with possible implications and angles of deceit, and Fake Serena had only said two sentences.

"Hello? Did you hear me?" Fake Serena smiled the disingenuous smile of a woman attempting polite conversation while she decided where to stick a knife.

Ivy struggled to form a coherent response, chasing ideas but failing to pin them down.

"Say something," Fake Serena said, her tone harsh. "Or should I ask the Reticulans to eliminate you for non-participation?"

"I am sorry," Ivy said, her skin tingling with apprehension. "I have always wanted to visit the Vitae Reefs, but it is hard to afford that on a beast master's salary."

She intended to give the impression she was a low-ranking animal handler within the Curci family — allies to the Rossums, enemies of the Wendl. No family made more income from animal husbandry than the Curcis, yet they were notorious for underpaying their handlers, even those afforded familiar status. However, the statement also gave her a plausible connection to three other houses.

Fake Serena understood subtlety. An elf nearby did not. "Wow, you're terrible at this!" The eavesdropper pointed a finger at Ivy. "I name you as a Curci!"

Ivy did not have to reply. *"False accusation. Player eliminated."* The tri-tone Reticulan voice reverberated in her mind. One of the short, gray-skinned beings walked up to the elf and grabbed his hand. It was unclear if Reticulan telepathy broadcast to everyone, but Fake Serena and the elf clearly heard it too. Fake Serena looked at the elf with an amused grin as his jaw fell open.

Ivy took small comfort in the knowledge there was someone worse at this game than her.

"Bullshit! That's classic Curci!" the elf shouted, indignation in his voice. Conversation across the marble hall ground to a halt as he shook free of the Reticulan's grasp. He looked down on the small, naked being with contempt. "My accusation is true. You are wrong. That woman is a Curci."

"LEAVE." Blackwell said. "DO SO NOW, AND YOU MAY LEAVE WITH YOUR ANONIMITY INTACT. DEFY ME, AND THE RETICULANS WILL STRIP OFF THAT GLAMOUR RIGHT HERE IN THE HALL SO EVERYONE CAN SEE THE FAILURE WHO GOT HIMSELF ELIMINATED WITHIN THE FIRST TWO MINUTES."

The elf's skin paled. He shut his mouth and allowed the Reticulan to escort him out without further comment.

"That wasn't the result I expected," Fake Serena said, "but I'll take it. Run along now, *Curci*." She winked. "I think you need to warm up some more before you'll be any fun." Fake Serena bowed, then walked away to harass the satyr and a middle-aged human.

Ivy closed her eyes and attempted to center herself. The Welcoming Hall's artificial lighting tasted sterile and soulless against her skin. She longed for the sensation of wind running through her grass hair. She looked for the largest group she could find. The more people talking together, the less she would be expected to say. On the opposite end of the hall, a group of six stood in a circle. Careful not to look anyone in the eyes or make any move to draw attention to herself, Ivy advanced on them.

"The Akakami houses behaved far differently before the Lost Epoch than they do now," said someone with the appearance of a human male, dressed in a sharp black suit and red tie. A patch of gray hair amongst his thick black curls gave him a distinguished look. "Back then, it seems like they'd let almost *anyone* become a familiar." The group laughed.

One of the women in the group turned to face Ivy. She wore a lavender dress that sparkled in the light. "And who might you be?" she asked.

Ivy paused. Zeta had not given her a false name to use. "Loretta Hildebrand," she said, using Serena's alias from their morning heist. The first human name her mind could conjure up that was not Serena. *Humans have another step in their greeting rituals...* Ivy thrust a hand forward to be ready for the "hand shake." It hovered awkwardly in the space between them for several seconds.

"My name is Lyse," the woman said, not offering a family name. She did not shake Ivy's offered hand, so the dryad returned it to her side. "We were just discussing the differences between how Akakami cultivated familiars many millennia ago versus common practices today. Do you have any thoughts on the subject?"

I approached you to avoid talking. Of course you would make me speak. She had made a grave error. Rather than engage in one-on-one conversation, she now had six people ready to scrutinize her every word and pounce at the first mistake. "Twenty thousand years ago, the Akakami were vassals of a more powerful species," Ivy said, the historical trivia bubbling to the surface of her mind. It felt true, but there were gaps in the information the Reticulan granted her. She did not know the name of that species or the context of their relationship with the Akakami. "Perhaps familiars were offered as tributes to that species. Many were killed in feuds between houses, so higher numbers of them would be needed for operational consistency."

An older woman engaged in a private conversation nearby laughed, though Ivy could not determine if it was due to what she said, or the woman's own conversation.

The group stared at her, unable to speak. They wanted to stroke their egos and feel superior by mocking the past. Her logical answer denied them that satisfaction. Though it had not been her intent, it worked to her advantage. Nobody wished to hear any more of what she had to say. The conversation carried on without her for several minutes. Ivy understood less than half of it as she tried in vain to bring her anxiety under control.

Individual conversations became easier to pick out as the player population declined. At least a third of the players were gone when Ivy used a lull in the conversation to scan the room. After the elf's temper tantrum, those eliminated left the hall quietly, not wishing to draw Blackwell's ire. Had Serena been one of them?

A clock mounted above the entrance to the Welcoming Hall counted down the time remaining. Twenty minutes. She still had no idea where Serena or Lorelai were, or if they were still in the competition at all.

"What about you, Loretta?"

She had lost track of the conversation, and did not know who addressed her. "Could you repeat that?" Ivy asked, hoping her confusion came off as misunderstanding, not inattention.

"What is your opinion on the Kraayen monopolizing textile markets while cotton production was at its lowest levels in seven centuries?" Lyse asked.

They wanted to discuss ancient economics? The topic would have given her a headache even without the layers of lies and deceit the Symphony of Lies piled on top of it. The group stared at her intently. The pleasantries were over. Now, the knives came out. One misstep and these people would pounce.

She could not appear overly supportive of the Kraayen, or they would know she represented that house. Claiming to be a Curci would not work either — they had no business in textiles. The Brinks had done a lot of work behind closed doors to facilitate the Kraayen monopoly in exchange for deep discounts on the clothing and armor they produced. To imply the other houses were weak to allow such a monopoly to form would also make it easy to deduce her identity.

What is my lie? What do I say? The answer eluded her.

Ivy's hands shook. She would fail. Again. Like she failed to save her sisters. Like she failed Serena in the Forest in the Sky, where her panic attack almost killed them. Like she failed the sailors on the *Lord Biga*, crippling their ship with an attack she should never have unleashed.

"You are the best of us. Your strength is unparalleled. We do not call you Unbreakable Ivy for nothing." Her sister Sage's words rose in her mind as if summoned to mock her. They were false praise. Well-intentioned lies. She was weak. People put their trust in her, and she let them down every time. Serena needed her help to find Lorelai, and here she stood, unable to keep her emotions in check. Failing. Again.

Tears blurred Ivy's vision. Her game was over. All any of them had to do was signal a Reticulan and accuse her of non-participation. She would not resist.

"The Woj suffered greatly from that monopoly." The group turned to face a female of a species Ivy did not recognize. She had skin the color of strawberries, which looked radiant against her black dress. Dark, curly hair ran down to her waist. Curled ram's horns grew on both sides of her head. A thin tail wagged back and forth behind her. She inserted herself into the group as a Reticulan escorted the man she had been talking to before to the exit. Her confident body language marked her as someone used to being a commanding presence, even without a glamor. "Their inability to properly clothe themselves made them a laughingstock."

Lyse glared at the interloper. "I wasn't asking you, Ashlok. I asked this brainless lump of flesh." She pointed at Ivy.

"So uncivilized. Just like a Woj," the Ashlok said.

Lyse's expression went blank, but not fast enough. Even Ivy noticed the flicker of fear. "I didn't catch your name," she said.

"I didn't offer it, and you won't be needing it anyway. I formally name you a Woj."

The group did not require confirmation from a Reticulan. Lyse swore, flashed a rude gesture at everyone in the area, and marched herself out of the Welcoming Hall.

The interloper was not finished. She pointed to the man in the suit who felt the ancient Akakami were fools for having so many familiars. "I formally accuse you of being a Rossum. You portrayed their trademark arrogance very well, but this is a game of lies. Better luck next time." Like Lyse, the man swore and walked away. Pointing at the remaining members of the group in turn, Ivy's savior said four words. "Wendl, Brinks, Cursi, Woj."

"Is... is that an accusation?" One of them stammered. Their shocked expressions confirmed the Ashlok woman had them all pegged. They were at her mercy, and they knew it.

"My memory isn't what it used to be. Why don't you all scatter to different groups, and I might just forget everything about you."

The four nodded enthusiastically and wasted no time dispersing.

"What about me?" Ivy asked, wiping away tears. Her caution vanished in the shock of watching this woman, who had not even been a participant in the conversation, turn and go six-for-six in identifying the true identities of those around her.

"Why don't we have a talk over here?" The woman led her towards the side of the staircase jutting into the hall. "You're having a hard time with this, aren't you?"

"I will adapt," Ivy said, wishing she could find a dark corner to hide in. The marble hall's harsh, unnatural lighting offered up no such respite.

A few couches with plush white cushions flanked the staircase. The woman took a seat and patted the cushion next to her. As Ivy sat, her benefactor made a sweeping gesture, making a point of showing there were no other contestants or Reticulans within thirty feet of them. "This is as safe a place as you're going to find during the Symphony of Lies. You can speak honestly while you're with me. I'm untouchable in this competition. I'm just in here to thin the herd and have some fun."

Ivy stared into her companion's soulful blue eyes, hoping she did not reveal her surprise. "You are untouchable? Why is that?" She felt certain she already knew the answer.

"I have a prior arrangement with Lord Blackwell," the woman said, offering a hand for the human shaking gesture. "My name is Lorelai. Lorelai Paulina Miriam Sinclair."

Ivy took Lorelai's offered hand and shook it awkwardly. "I am… Loretta." She decided to stick with the name she had already used. "Why did you help me?"

"You looked like a scared lamb about to be ripped apart by hyenas," Lorelai said. "I have excellent hearing and a talent for tracking multiple conversations at once. I'd bet I heard and understood what they said better than you did. That group would not have granted you a quick, clean exit. They would have bullied and humiliated you first." She sighed. "I was on the receiving end of that a lot growing up. I refuse to allow anyone else to experience such abuse if I can do something about it."

"I see," Ivy said.

"You still look like a woman on the verge of an panic attack. Relax, I'm not your enemy. I didn't steal you away from a pack of bullies to prey on you myself."

Would you be so kind if you knew why I am here? Ivy thought. She asked, "Is my rescue an act of charity then? You are taking a risk. I thought this charade was meant to show one's worthiness to work with Lord Blackwell. Protecting me from consequences defies that goal."

"Let me worry about Blackwell," Lorelai said. "Haven't you noticed? He's not in here anymore. He's left to do a final check on the talent show. Besides, I'm already a familiar in all but name. My judgment carries a lot of weight with him."

"What makes you special? Why do you want to be a familiar to Lord Blackwell?" Ivy asked. How forthcoming with the truth would Lorelai be, if she felt untouchable?

Very forthcoming, apparently.

"Loretta, I need to become a familiar because I'm dying. I was an unwanted child. My parents poisoned me and left me to die on a pile of trash. The poison they used kills nine out of ten. Survivors find their eyes transformed into orbs of darkness. On a world as overpopulated as the one I grew up on, my fate is hardly unique. My eyes mark me as an abandoned child. A social pariah. A *ghoul*. Human garbage unworthy of any kindness or support." Lorelai's flat, matter-of-fact tone convinced Ivy she spoke the truth.

"The poison never fully leaves the system, so rather than a swift death as an infant, my reward for survival is slow bodily decay over thirty or so years. With Lord Blackwell sharing his life force, I can have a full life. Without it, I'll be dead within a year or two."

If Ivy had a year to live, would she be willing to sell herself into an Akakami's service for more time? Would she lie and steal to survive?

Was she not doing that right now?

Knowing more of Lorelai's background, Ivy understood the logic in the lies she told Dr. Venture. She had crafted a story of royal lineage, where her eyes no doubt marked her as someone special, reframing her condition as a blessing, not a curse. She needed validation as much as the axolotl did. Lorelai used her bitterness with her parents to add verisimilitude to her tale.

"I am sorry you have lived a hard life," Ivy said, trying to imagine what life would be like if she never had anyone she could rely on. "But is a life in service to an Akakami a better fate than death? Could you abandon your ethics to obey his every whim?"

Lorelai stared at her with an intensity that could melt ice. "That's an odd thing to say, since you're also here to become a familiar."

Ivy cursed herself. *Fool. Did you forget the entire point of this pageant?*

"Lord Blackwell was the first being to ever show me respect. He provided me an education and has invested heavily in mentors to train my unique talents. After years of loyal service, he gave me a final test — find and retrieve information or technology he could use to further his ambitions. If I returned with a valuable enough prize, I'd become a familiar and have a place in his inner circle of agents. I did it, but in doing so, I had to betray the *second* person to ever show me any measure of respect." Ivy did not expect the look of genuine regret on Lorelai's features. "I do what I must to survive."

She placed a hand on Ivy's shoulder. "The path I walk isn't for everyone, and I can see it's not for you. That you would question the gifts Lords Blackwell gives us shows you're not ready. You should leave."

"I too do what I must," Ivy said, feeling like pond scum. She would sacrifice her ethics for the sake of expediency. No other method was guaranteed to get the information they needed. "I am sorry."

"What for?" Lorelai asked, then coughed as Ivy thrust a wrist at her face and shot a jet of pollen up her nose. Her eyes lost focus. Her facial expression went slack, then euphoric. "What is this?"

Ataraxian dryads could produce a pollen-borne pheromone that temporarily altered brain chemistry, making the recipient extremely honest, compliant, and hypersensitive to physical sensations. Consenting partners used it as an aphrodisiac to enhance lovemaking. But the same chemicals that heightened pleasure could be used to force someone to give up secrets, coerce suggestible minds into doing another's bidding, or enhance pain. Therefore, strict laws and rituals governed the use of the pheromones so there could be no doubt about consent. By the standards of her village, Ivy just committed a crime worthy of exile. Not that she had a village to return to.

"Where is the crystalline computing matrix?" Ivy asked.

"How did you know about that?" Lorelai asked.

"I am here on behalf of Dr. Venture. Where is it?"

"I met with one of Blackwell's familiars and handed it off shortly before the Symphony of Lies. It will be in his private quarters deep within the estate. I gave him a high-level overview of the research, but we'll be reviewing the data with Blackwell himself after all the pageant festivities conclude."

"Tell me about the security surrounding his chambers," Ivy said.

Lorelai shook her head. "I haven't been there, but there shouldn't be any. Anybody who gets that deep into Blackwell's home has already gone through multiple security checks."

Under the influence of Ivy's pheromones, Lorelai could not lie. As far as she knew, there was no security there. That did not mean her assessment was accurate, however. Either Blackwell was arrogant enough to consider his security infallible, or Lorelai had not yet been trusted with that information.

Ivy coated the tip of her index finger with the sleep-inducing sap of a *kilora* tree, then traced a line down Lorelai's nose, mouth, and chin. Lorelai smiled like a lover being seduced. Another wave of guilt and shame washed over Ivy. Her sisters would be so disappointed to see her abusing dryad abilities in this fashion. She leaned Lorelai so her back lined up with the side of the staircase as she drifted off to sleep. If she estimated the dosages of pheromones and sap correctly, Lorelai would not remember their conversation. Or the crimes Ivy committed against her.

Time to find Serena...

CHAPTER 39

SISTERS

The clock above the entrance to the Welcoming Hall indicated ten minutes remained in the Symphony of Lies. Ivy had no energy or desire to stand up and begin a fresh round of lies and deception. Sitting next to the evidence of her crimes did not seem any wiser though, and she faced elimination if a Reticulan walked over and decided to eliminate her for non-participation.

As if reading her mind, one of the small, gray-skinned beings approached, an elderly human female at their side. It struck Ivy as odd that while the Reticulans made most beings look young and attractive, this woman looked like someone's grandmother, with silver and white hair pulled back into a tight, matronly bun. She walked with an ease that defied the elderly appearance.

"You have the right idea, my dear. All this double talk is exhausting. So is the standing. I need to rest my weary bones," the woman said.

Ivy nodded, accepting the roleplay, knowing the person would be at most half the age she appeared. The dryad sat upright and stiff as a tree, hoping to obscure Lorelai's condition from view. That effort was doomed before it began.

"I see I'm not the only one fatigued by this game of social deception." The woman gestured to Lorelai before taking a seat to Ivy's left.

Silence lingered. She expected Ivy to say something. "She... fainted."

"You're really not very good at lying, are you?"

"So everyone keeps telling me," Ivy said, confused by her new conversation partner's apparent lack of concern over Lorelai's condition.

"Call me Abbie. I suppose we need to have a chat. Wouldn't want my chaperone here to become displeased with us." Abbie nodded to the Reticulan staring at them.

"Must we? I have someone I need to find," Ivy said. She could not bring herself to move.

Silence.

"Has anyone told you that you have very sad eyes?" Abbie said. "You look like a woman who's lost much in her life."

"Indeed."

"Want to talk about it?"

Ivy snorted. "You expect me to share my pain with a stranger? I do not have time for this."

"And yet you make no move to leave. Maybe your heart's telling you something, and your head is too stupid to listen." Whatever the woman's true age, Abbie sounded remarkably like a disappointed grandmother. "Sometimes it feels good to unburden your troubles on a stranger. We've been doing it with pastors and barkeeps for millennia." When Ivy did not reply, she added, "Or, you could always walk back into that nest of vipers."

Roughly forty contestants remained, standing in groups of two to four. While they could not make out distinct words from where they sat, Ivy could tell the conversations amongst those who remained grew more intense and less civil with each passing minute. Abbie's gaze bored into Ivy, daring her to join them.

Ivy needed to find Serena, but felt rooted to the couch. Anxiety still ate away at her. She had violated her ethics so many times in the last day. For what? How were they supposed to reach Blackwell's inner sanctum? And if their heist succeeded, would the data tell them anything useful?

"I'm not your enemy, you can relax." Abbie said.

"People keep saying that to me too." Lorelai had said the same. So had Serena, back on Kimori. "It is irrelevant. I hurt everyone around me. You would not want to be my friend." Ivy closed her eyes, recalling the burns Serena suffered from her second solar beam.

"That's the worst lie you've told yet!" Abbie laughed. "You give off significant *'I want everyone to love me'* energy."

"Your ability to read people is even poorer than mine if you believe that."

"You're the compassionate sort. That woman passed out from the strain of the Symphony of Lies, and you're here risking elimination yourself to make sure she's OK."

Ivy clenched her fists, straining to beat back the rising tide of anger. Abbie wanted to frame her crimes against Lorelai as acts of *compassion*? "You said I lied about her condition earlier."

"I apologize. I misread you. I'm sure you're some pampered rich princess like most of the people here. You've never experienced a moment of pain or trauma your whole life. I wonder if Lord Blackwell is going to want someone with so little exposure to the darker parts of life."

The dam broke. Ivy's anxiety transformed into a purifying, righteous anger at having her traumas so casually dismissed. She stood and glared down at Abbie. The dim voice of reason in the back of her mind screamed that she was being baited, but she did not care. "I am the youngest of sixteen daughters. My mother was ambushed and devoured by predators when I was but a sprout. I have no memory of her. My father and sisters were ripped apart by reptilian monstrosities, sacrificing themselves to buy me time to escape the invasion that killed our world. My survival was a mistake. I am unworthy of their sacrifice. My family would be ashamed of me if they saw me now.

"I put those around me in danger unnecessarily. I hurt everyone who offers me friendship. I am weak. Indecisive. Useless." The truth spilled out of her, and she did not care. It felt good to unburden herself, and give voice to her pain. Ivy stared at her reflection in the Reticulan's enormous eyes. "And now I have failed again. Say it. Eliminate me."

"They can't." Abbie stood and placed a finger against Ivy's chin, turning her head until they made eye contact. "Much of what you just said is a lie."

"You are mistaken."

"I'm not. I know you, *Ivy*."

Ivy stared, disbelieving. "Serena?"

"Sorry you had to fend for yourself for so long," Serena said. "I had a hell of a time breaking loose from contestants trying to eliminate me. Everyone wanted to pick on the old lady."

Ivy had many questions. All she managed was, "How?"

"How did I recognize you? Your posture and gait are distinctive. Very elegant and regal. As upright and inflexible as a mighty oak — total giveaway you're a plant. Also, that corsage bracelet might as well be a calling card." Serena pointed at the emerald rose on Ivy's left wrist. "That was a smart move. Very subtle."

"You lied to me."

Serena raised her arms in a gesture of surrender. "It was Tako's idea. You looked wound up so tight you might explode. He deduced we have something in common — that the fastest way to tear down our emotional walls is to piss us off. We thought you needed to unload some of that tension, and wouldn't with someone you knew. So yes, I took advantage of the situation and lied to you."

"I see." Ivy's anger cooled as quickly as it flared up. Their assessment of her emotional state was accurate. They only wanted to help her. Because that is what friends do. "Everything I said was the truth."

"Bullshit. You've endured unimaginable loss and tragedy. I know you feel immense guilt about being the sole survivor of your family, but do you really think they'd want you putting all this pressure on yourself to be perfect? Please, please don't think you have to be the paragon of all dryads. You're more than good enough as just *Ivy*.

"I wish you saw yourself how I see you. You're amazing. You're not indecisive. You followed me after the Vohr eye with no hesitation. You saved narwhal riders from a magmadon. You..." Serena hesitated, but then plowed forward. "You made the hard call and did what had to be done with Moogi. Again, without hesitation. Our lives have been a whirlwind of misery and chaos, and somehow you manage to keep moving forward."

"So do you," Ivy said, uncomfortable receiving praise she did not feel she deserved.

"I have the multiverse's greatest therapist living in my head. You haven't had the same luxury." Tako risked poking a tentacle out of range of the Reticulan's magic to offer a brief wave. Serena tapped her temple. "Trust me, it's a mess in here. I'm surviving on a bizarre a cocktail of suppressed rage and Octari cheerfulness. You and I are battered, but we're not broken."

Serena closed the distance between them and enveloped Ivy in a tight embrace. "There's something else I need you to understand too. There are two kinds of family: the one you're born into, and the one you choose for yourself. You still have family."

"I do not. They are dead."

"You do, dummy. Two weeks ago, I'd never had a sibling. Now, I have a sister. And I'm very proud of her."

It took a moment for the meaning of Serena's words to register. When they did, Ivy fell apart again. She wrapped her arms around Serena, burying her face in the human's shoulder to muffle the sound of her sobs. Serena held her steady.

Sister. Serena considers me a sister?

Family was everything to dryads. Did Serena understand the implications of what she said? Would she wish to retract those words later? Did she have any sense of the duties and responsibilities that came with accepting someone else as kin? Family fought for each other. Died for each other, if it came to that. The only thing more important than the survival and prosperity of one's family was the health of Ataraxia herself. To claim a familial relationship with someone was the ultimate statement of commitment. Dryads never made such statements lightly.

Gratitude and shame warred within her. She had feared and hated Serena when they first met. She had put Serena's life in danger more than once. Yet she still claimed her as a sister. Why?

Cool, moist skin touched her arm. The suckers on one of Tako's limbs massaged her flesh. *"May I show you something?"* he asked. His voice was more pleasant in her mind than that of a Reticulan. Calming. Paternal. Warm, like a ray of sun filtering through the treetops. Simultaneously playful and serious. An old soul with youthful enthusiasm. She could understand why Serena liked him.

The dryad nodded, giving her consent. A flood of images poured into her mind. Herself in the fetal position on the floor of the transit cube. The time she made plants in Kimori's amphitheater. Her apology to Serena after their battle in the Forest in the Sky.

The moment she returned Moogi to the soil. In rapid succession, Ivy experienced all of those events from Serena's point of view, feeling Serena's emotions as if they were her own. She felt Serena's admiration and respect for her. How much Serena hoped they would become close. Her sincere desire that Ivy could find happiness and peace after losing her family and world. But she also noticed how Serena focused on her grief as a way of ignoring her own.

For a long moment, neither of them said anything. Nothing else needed to be said.

As her tears abated, Ivy withdrew from the embrace and turned to face the Reticulan observing their reunion. The being showed no hint of emotion. "Should we be speaking so freely with them watching us?"

"It's fine. Theta's on our side," Serena said.

"I will not eliminate either of you," the Reticulan agreed.

"I do not understand," Ivy said.

"Reticulans can detect truth and lies, making us ideal judges for this game," Theta said. *"Our ability to sense harmful intentions makes us a useful part of Lord Blackwell's security forces, as well. I observed two minds presenting as one person, both with ulterior motives."* They gestured at Serena. *"I called her aside first to determine her intent, speaking to her and the one called Takoyakisobaramaki. After consultation with my fellows, we have decided not to interfere with your actions, or allow either of you to be eliminated. Your success may in fact be good for Blackwell's long-term interests. But providing you an easier path through the Symphony of Lies is the most overt action we dare take. Blackwell's punishments are... extreme. You are on your own from here."*

"Why let us go?" Ivy asked, still confused.

"We serve our master in all things," Theta said, *"including protecting him from himself. Having such data on the multiverse in his sole possession would lead to conflicts with rival Akakami and acts of sabotage that he has not anticipated or prepared for. It is better you reclaim the data and release it through traditional scientific channels, when the time is right. Furthermore, a few of our operations were lost to Vohr invasion. If the data does help you defeat them, this too is good for Blackwell's interests."*

Serena shifted her focus back to the unconscious woman in their midst. "Is that who I think it is?"

"If you believe it is Lorelai, then yes," Ivy said.

"Were you able to find out anything?"

"She handed off the crystalline computing matrix before the Symphony of Lies started. It's in Blackwell's inner sanctum."

Serena swore. "That means we have to keep playing this game, doesn't it?"

"For now, yes," Ivy agreed, grateful Serena did not ask what she had done to Lorelai. She had suffered enough emotional duress for the day without confessing her crimes to her new *sister*. "Perhaps we will find an opportunity to sneak away later."

"That would be nice, but I doubt it's going to be that easy. We have to play to win. The only way to get close to the computing matrix may be to convince Blackwell to make one of us a familiar."

"I hope he needs a pyromancer," Ivy said.

"I hope he likes pretty flowers," Serena replied.

The sound of turning gears diverted their attention back towards the entrance of the Welcoming Hall, where the cover over the elevator platform slid away. As the countdown clock for the Symphony of Lies rolled under one minute, the guardrails around the platform's exterior retracted into the floor. The elevator from the lower levels arrived, bearing a single long table piled high with dozens of different fruits, meats, and pastries. Pik-Pik and Tik-Tik each stood at one of the far ends of it.

<Come one, come all, skillful liars!>

<Masters of deception!>

<Partake in these refreshments.>

<Enjoy a moment of relaxation before we move to the auditorium to prepare for the talent show.>

"It's about time they showed up," Serena said, leading the way over to the table. "I'll talk to the one on the left."

"You cannot tell them apart?" Ivy asked.

"I can't," Serena admitted.

How could Serena recognize her so quickly even while disguised, but not recognize which ant was which? "Pik-Pik has three black dots under each eye. Tik-Tik does not."

Conversations shifted towards discussing the food, the surviving contestants by unspoken but unanimous agreement opting not to snipe at each other in the last minute. Some questioned how sanitary the food could be if ants were serving it. Others noted Lord Blackwell's preference for exotic servants, and felt it would be in poor taste to question him or his staff's ability to vet the quality of the help. They were too absorbed in free food to pay any attention to Lorelai's prone form on the couch.

Ivy sat on the floor so she could look at Pik-Pik close to eye level. "I am Ivy," she whispered.

<I am glad to meet you,> Pik-Pik said, pretending not to know that name.

"Your translation device is fascinating," Ivy said, carrying out her part of their script. "May I examine it?"

<Of course.> Pik-Pik took a step to the side, allowing Ivy to examine the collar around their neck, which contained crystals that strobed as they translated and projected the insect's speech into a format non-insects could understand.

She ran a hand along Pik-Pik's collar and found the tiny crystal hooked onto it along the bottom, where it would be hard to see, and likely considered part of the collar even if it was observed. She pulled it and its wire free, turned her head so her right ear faced Pik-Pik's side, then wrapped the wire around her ear so the crystal dangled like an earring. These crystals could transmit a person's voice to a matched partner from as far as a sector away. They'd purchased them to be able to stay in touch with each other throughout the operation. Knowing they'd be searched and couldn't wear them through security, they'd hoped the ants would be able to smuggle them in.

At least that part of the plan worked as intended.

Ivy stood and snapped her fingers twice to activate the crystal, appreciating that it was less conspicuous than having to hold a finger to her ear. "Cypher, this is Ivy. Do you hear this?" She spoke softly, keeping her back to the crowd loading up plates.

"It's about time!" Cypher's voice was as clear in her ear as if he stood right beside her. "Nothing's being broadcast from in there. I've been worried sick about you two."

"That's sweet," Serena said, her own earring in place. "Our hopes of using these to cheat during the Symphony were dashed, but we've survived."

"Did you get the data matrix?" Cypher asked.

"We did not," Ivy said.

Serena piled up a plate with slices of meat and cheese, drawing surprised glances from those nearby. Her need for calories increased dramatically while bonded to an Octari, but her eating habits likely appeared gluttonous to most beings. She gave the crowd a smile that suggested she did not care what they thought of her. "We're going to have to participate in Blackwell's talent show while we figure out our next move. Got any suggestions?"

"How's your juggling?" Cypher asked.

CHAPTER 40

THE GREATEST SHOW IN THE MULTIVERSE

S erena stood on stage and stared out at a packed auditorium filled with beings of dozens of species. An enchanted curtain at the edge of the stage acted like a one-way window, allowing her to see them without them seeing her. Spotlights aimed at the stage made it difficult to distinguish individuals in the audience. Was Annea somewhere out there? What would she think when she saw her and Ivy performing?

At the center of the front row sat an ostentatious red and gold throne, no doubt intended for Blackwell himself. Their host was nowhere to be seen.

"I'm glad I'm not going first," Serena said, looking for the hundredth time at a small white ball in her hand, the number 13 stamped on it in gold lettering.

"Agreed," Ivy said. She was contestant number 17. They'd been restored to their natural appearances before leaving the Welcoming Hall. To Serena's eyes, the dryad seemed... lighter. Though she still carried a heavy weight on her shoulders, Ivy looked like she'd found a measure of confidence again. Good. They needed to be sharp while in enemy territory.

When the last remaining contestants had drawn their numbers, a voice boomed from the auditorium's public address system. "THE TALENT SHOW WILL BEGIN IN TEN MINUTES." The contestants returned their balls to the box they'd drawn from, then a human man rolled the cart offstage. A Reticulan followed behind, holding a clipboard with the list of contestants, their names, worlds of origin, and their order in the lineup.

Though the Reticulans wouldn't interfere with Serena and Ivy's mission, they refused to outright lie to their master. Their continued non-intervention was contingent on Serena and Ivy playing the part of real contestants, entering the talent show with their true names, and making a good-faith effort to win Blackwell's favor. No sneaking off into the rest of Blackwell's estate.

The survivors of the Symphony of Lies scattered to the wings on either side of the stage, which were set up to serve as both dressing rooms and prop storage. There were fifty stations per side, divided into two long aisles. Each station was marked with a contestant's name and held materials they'd shipped in for use during the talent show.

"Think there's anything in here we can use?" Serena asked, hoping to appropriate something from an eliminated contestant.

"Their belongings are irrelevant," Ivy twisted her wrist and conjured an emerald rose with uncharacteristically dramatic flair. "I do not need props."

"I'm thrilled for you." Serena stalked up and down the aisles like a cat on the prowl, focusing on the unmanned stations.

"What are we looking for?" Tako asked.

"In a perfect world, a bow, arrows, and some targets. I'll cobble together some kind of shooting demo and hope for the best." The nearest station had a stack of canvas, a folded easel, and a collection of paints. Another contained posters depicting charts and graphs on audience demand for singing competitions — Olivia's talent show materials. She walked by a table piled high with watermelons. A mallet so large Serena doubted she could lift it leaned against the side of the table. How were those supposed to impress an Akakami?

"Any particular reason you're ignoring pyromancy as an option?" Tako asked, nudging her back to the task at hand.

"I haven't had any stress-free moments to practice my magic, you know? Under pressure, I don't think my control is refined enough to put on a flashy display that doesn't end in nudity broadcast across the multiverse, no matter how fireproof the shop claims these clothes are."

Tako laughed. *"Fair point, but I wasn't around to help on those occasions. We can figure it out together."*

"You're not immune to my power," Serena said. *"I don't want to hurt you."*

"Your concern is noted and appreciated, but I'm not seeing other options."

Serena dashed across the stage to the opposite wing, the countdown timer in her head telling her she needed to find something fast. She took a wide path around a woman hurling knives at another woman, who caught them on their handles as they passed. A man played a golden, curved metallic instrument Tako identified as a saxophone. An elf stared at a series of metal bars placed on the table before him, which seemed to bend of their own accord. Up and down the aisles she went. No bows. No arrows.

Lorelai sat in a plush chair set near the curtain, reading yet another book with a shirtless man on the cover. She looked up as Serena drew close. "Hey, thanks again for waking me up. I can't believe I fell asleep in the middle of the competition."

"Don't mention it," Serena said, keeping her tone light but dismissive. Whatever Ivy had done to her, Lorelai didn't remember it. She felt she owed Serena a debt for not making a scene or trying to have her eliminated from the competition. She probably didn't want her fellow contestants knowing about her privileged position amongst them.

"Oh, I won't," Lorelai said. "I've barely slept in days. After all I've done to get here, I have no intention of risking my place at Lord Blackwell's side over a lapse in discipline like that."

Serena crossed the stage to return to Ivy's side. "You did not find what you wanted," the dryad said.

"I did not," Serena said. "I'll have to try not to burn this place down."

They stood silently in the wings as the curtain opened. One by one, contestants were called out to the stage to make their pitch to Blackwell. The talents on display filled Serena with awe and a sense of inadequacy. A burly man with a shaved head took two weapons reminiscent of Z'han's energy rifles, stripped them down to their component parts, reassembled them, then hit five targets circling in the air around him, all while blindfolded. Blackwell yawned and told the man he had a bright future in the world of gun assembly tutorials.

He eliminated a singer, a blacksmith, a chef, and the ladies with the knife-throwing routine. With such varied talents on display, Serena couldn't begin to guess the criteria Blackwell used to decide who he invited to compete. The Akakami was so brutal and unsparing in his criticism of each contestant that she half wondered if the whole pageant wasn't really an excuse to stroke his ego by harassing, mocking, and belittling anyone who dared to think themselves worthy of breathing the same air he did.

Of the first dozen contestants, only one met with Blackwell's approval. The tall, pale-skinned woman dyed her hair the blue of a summer sky and wore a dress to match. She called herself Siren, and claimed she had the ability to hypnotize anyone into doing her will. To demonstrate this, she had Blackwell pick four random members of the audience and invite them on stage. In under a minute, she had them braying like sheep as they undressed themselves. Blackwell ordered her to release them from her spell before they could fully disrobe. Audience reaction to that fell evenly between gratitude and disappointment.

"AND NOW, CONTESTANT THIRTEEN, HAILING FROM THE WORLD OF ALTERRA, SERENA EMBERS!"

Serena took a deep breath and marched out on stage, doing everything in her power to project confidence she didn't feel. *Well, Cypher, we're about to find out how well I can juggle.*

"Greetings, Serena," Blackwell said. "Congratulations on making it through the Symphony of Lies. You weren't on my guest list."

"Correct," Serena said. No point in lying about it.

Though his mouth was hidden behind his mask, Serena thought the Akakami smiled. "I respect the initiative. I was hoping someone would steal their way into these proceedings. I'm unfamiliar with Alterra."

Blackwell's admission surprised her. He didn't seem the type to admit to ignorance in anything, ever. "I would be shocked if you were. It's not in this sector, and until recently, nobody there knew Planar Gates existed." Not knowing how Blackwell or the audience would react to the mention of Vohr, she opted to say nothing of her world's annihilation.

"What skills will you be demonstrating for us today?"

"I'm a pyromancer, so I'll be showcasing control over fire."

"Your family name is Embers, and you're a pyromancer? That's a little on the nose, isn't it?" Blackwell laughed. The crowd followed his lead and joined in. "You expect me to believe that's truly your name?"

"It is."

Blackwell shrugged. "I'm not sure what use pyromancy would have in my operations. You'd be great at pest control. Cockroaches and spiders across the multiverse would fear you. If I travel somewhere cold, you could serve as a portable heater. I could use you as a living campfire. You could keep my coffee hot. Even better, you could keep the toilet seat warm for me." The crowd's mocking laughter grew with every trivial suggestion for her magic. He paused, making a show of looking thoughtful. "You'd do a fantastic job lighting my quarters, but I already have a lamp." He sighed, broadcasting that he expected to be bored. "Very well, Lamp. Show us what you can do."

That smug bastard. She'd thought watching twelve other contestants would prepare her for the verbal abuse. It had not. Her face flushed with embarrassment and humiliation. In that moment, pinned under the spotlights, she felt trapped. So much depended on winning Blackwell's approval, and he treated her like she was nothing, even after she'd taken the initiative to steal an invite and jump through the hoop that was the Symphony of Lies. Before she could stop herself, she'd channeled her anger to form a fireball the size of a watermelon. Gripping it with both hands, she lifted it over her head and hurled it directly at Blackwell.

You want to stay warm, asshole? See how you like this.

"Serena, have you lost your mind?" Cypher's voice shouted into her ear. She ignored him. He wasn't the one being humiliated in front of a crowd of thousands, as part of a talent show being broadcast to millions. He had no right to judge her from the safety of an inn room.

The Akakami held out his hands to catch her attack. The fireball evaporated into nothing before it got within arm's length of him.

Silence reigned in the auditorium, the crowd stunned anyone would dare attack Blackwell in his own domain.

Blackwell laughed. "You don't survive hundreds of assassination attempts without picking up a few tricks. More talented mages than you have tried, my dear."

"We're going to have to work on how you respond to rude behavior," Tako said, flooding her mind with images of peace and tranquility. She pushed back against his efforts to calm her down. He meant well, but anger fueled her power. Blackwell might be doing her a favor, in his own twisted way. If he wanted a show, she'd give him something to remember.

Security guards rushed the stage, batons held ready in each hand. Blackwell waved them off with a shooing gesture. "Go away. It's fine. Pyromancers are notoriously hotheaded and dimwitted. Lamp's just feeling sensitive today."

Serena forced herself to keep her mouth shut. He didn't have to like her, just be convinced enough of her usefulness to keep her around. She needed to show him something he hadn't seen before.

"You're not serious," Tako said, responding to mental images of Serena's plan.

"Can you do it, or not?" Serena asked. She softened her tone, not meaning to direct her anger at him. The plan asked a lot of him. *"I don't want to do this either. I know it'll suck for you, but I'm drawing a blank on anything better."*

"So am I," Tako admitted. *"We spent so much time looking for a way into Blackwell's estate that we didn't plan for the talent show."*

Blackwell stared at her, impatience clear from his narrowed gaze. "Lamp, if you wish to impress me, best get on with it."

She made three fireballs, each the size of an apple, and started juggling them. Boos rained down on her from the crowd, the masses unimpressed with such a basic display. "Not very impressive, is it?" Serena said, finding an ounce of showmanship as she caught the fireballs. "I guess I'll stop then." She tossed the fireballs lazily into the air, arcing them over her head. As they passed her shoulders, Tako reached out with three tentacles, each swatting one of the fireballs back up into the air. He held the tentacles out to the side so the audience would have a very clear view of their movements.

Serena made another fireball, and another still, tossing them over her shoulder for Tako to add into his pattern. The crowd gasped. She continued feeding Tako fireballs until he juggled one for each of his eight limbs. She felt his discomfort with each impact. Tako's water magics could mitigate the worst of the heat, but couldn't completely insulate his skin.

"Your tattoo is *alive?*" Cypher asked. She imagined he'd be choking on popcorn right about now, if he had any.

"I'm a little busy right now, Cypher," Serena muttered, wishing she'd thought to turn the earring off before stepping out on stage. "Please stop talking."

"Give me more," Tako said.

"But I'm hurting you."

"I agreed to this, so let's hold nothing back. Give me more."

Serena carried on until Tako juggled a dozen at once. It must have made for quite a sight, as the crowd's boos started shifting to cheers.

"More."

"Seriously? I don't want to kill you, old man."

"I'm just warming up." He split her fireballs into two groups of six. Using four tentacles per group, he soon had both groups of six moving in hypnotizing vertical circles.

Serena did as asked, tossing him more fireballs until he juggled sixteen. Then eighteen. Then twenty-four. He still wanted more. *"You're going to tell me when to stop, right?"*

"You'll know when," Tako assured her. Though every fireball impact against one of his limbs stung, he seemed to be enjoying himself immensely. He even hummed a little tune in their minds as he went.

Men, no matter their age or species, will try something stupid to impress a lady.

"I heard that." Tako laughed. *"I'm old, not DEAD. You didn't grow up in Z'han. Let me show you the agility Octari are capable of."* He moved at impossible speed, weaving her fireballs into complex circuits and orbits... and he *still* wanted more. Expecting their act to

crash and burn despite his assurances to the contrary, Serena kept going until Tako had thirty-two fruit-sized balls of flame under his control. Careful to alert Tako to her intentions so it didn't throw off his efforts, Serena slowly turned to present her back to the audience, allowing them an unobstructed view of Tako's tentacles erupting from her back like some eldritch horror. The crowd erupted into cheers as Tako had the air above the stage twinkling like a horde of fireflies. He varied the pattern, bringing fireballs into tight clusters, then flaring out his tentacles to show the full extent of his range.

"Consider me impressed," Serena said. *"I'm sure I won't be as spry in my old age."*

"Thank you, my dear. Now, for my last trick." Tako changed up the pattern so that he juggled everything off seven of his eight limbs, making a show of letting the last one dangle free at her side. In rapid succession, he let fireballs fall into the range of the free tentacle, which swatted them directly at Lord Blackwell. Like Serena's first attack, they evaporated into nothing a safe distance from the Akakami's face.

"Are you sure doubling down on my lapse in judgment is a good idea?" Serena asked.

"Absolutely, because now everyone knows there's no consequences for it."

The crowd roared with laughter at the bold display of contempt for power, knowing Blackwell wasn't in any danger. Serena turned to face a standing ovation, bowing on Tako's behalf. They'd won over the crowd.

Blackwell, however, was not amused. "I cannot deny you put on an impressive performance," he said. "If I ever expand into the carnival business, I could make a fortune with you. But I suspect you're not the real star of that show, Lamp. Though I don't know the nature of your tentacled friend, symbiotic pairings are not unknown to me. Together you'd make an exceptional candelabra, but I'm not interested in upgrading my decor at this time. You're dismissed."

Serena's face flushed with a fresh wave of anger and indignation. She felt Tako's pain in the back of her mind. Despite all his assurances, he'd overdone it. All of his limbs were sore and had minor to moderate burns along their length. He'd put his body on the line to help her succeed in this ridiculous stunt, all for nothing. She clenched her teeth and made no move to resist as a pair of Blackwell's guards escorted her off stage. She could walk out, or get thrown out. Making a scene wouldn't accomplish anything. She followed the guards up a flight of stairs and down a corridor that led back to the balcony level of the Welcoming Hall. Once there, they gave Serena more personal space as she showed herself out the front door.

Eliminated contestants didn't get to enjoy the rest of the show.

"Time for a new plan, Cypher," Serena said.

"Ivy hasn't performed yet. We still have a chance," Cypher said.

"That's not good enough. I'm not leaving her all alone in there." Serena ignored the line of reporters posted by the door, ready to pounce on eliminated contestants for an interview. They nipped at her heels like hungry jackals as she took a right, keeping the border of Blackwell's domain on that side as she marched towards one of the enormous doors marking the edge of the Blackwell Plaza cube. When one particularly insistent reporter reached for her shoulder to turn her around, Tako wrapped a tentacle around the man's wrist and spun him around. The group respected Serena's personal space after that.

"So," Cypher drew out the word to fill an entire breath. "How do you expect to get back inside?"

She thought about the insults Blackwell threw at her. The loose beginnings of an idea started to form. It relied on a lot of assumptions, but she'd find out soon enough if it could work or not. "Where are Pik-Pik and Tik-Tik?"

CHAPTER 41

BACKCHANNEL DIPLOMACY

Annea scanned the crowd, looking for black robed figures, but didn't see any. She didn't trust Patrick's assurances that rogue Weavers couldn't infiltrate the crowd. Any disruptions to her negotiations would be disastrous.

The auditorium was every bit as ostentatious and gaudy as she'd expected from Blackwell, based on his reputation. The seats of the auditorium were a plush red with gold edging, set in long rows that took up two thirds of the available floor space. The far left and right sides of the auditorium served as standing room for guests whose biology couldn't handle human and elf sized chairs. Along the wall to the left about halfway between the exit doors and the stage stood Kuma Wolfsbane. She didn't know if it was coincidence or design, but the Moon Doge dangled from a light fixture bolted to the wall several feet over the giant bear's head, behaving much like the bat-monkey hybrid he resembled.

"Let me make the introductions," Patrick said as they weaved through the crowd of standing guests to reach their intended targets. "They know to expect me, but we didn't discuss you."

Annea, used to being the tallest person in the room, didn't often have to look *up* to speak to someone. Kuma had at least three feet on her, and had to be five times her body weight. He stood with relaxed confidence, but she could tell he could spring into action in a heartbeat if he needed to.

"Greetings my friend," Patrick said. "I'm glad to see you arrived safely. The Ankora's quest for a righteous war is over. Allow me to introduce you to Annea Vantalos, the Sword of Kimori."

"That's a fancy title," Kuma said, appraising her. Apparently liking what he saw, he offered her the bow of one warrior acknowledging another.

"It marks me as the leader of my world's war efforts," Annea said. "The Vohr have been making incursions into Kimori for over a week now."

"And your world still lives? I thought worlds invaded by the Vohr were cut off from the Nexus." Kuma gave Patrick the wounded look of a man who'd been lied to. "The Sector Council and Weavers told us this repeatedly, while denying us the right to fight them."

"We've been using other worlds as intermediaries, rather than risk a lockout by travelling from Kimori to the Nexus directly. But you're saying you've been *seeking out a fight* with the Vohr? Why?" Annea asked.

"Because we are warriors. These days, our differences are resolved through non-lethal duels, with many rules and regulations in place to minimize injuries. Some Ankora take on mercenary work, serving as bodyguards for clients who meet our ethical standards. Others have joined private security firms serving righteous causes, like the Order of the Irwins, who protect animal sanctuaries from poachers.

"It's not enough. There is a restlessness within our culture. We haven't had a true war in generations. We're not savages — we only bring death to the deserving. When our leaders learned of the Vohr, we felt our blood sing for war. These monsters destroy everything they encounter without mercy. We make war to protect those who cannot protect themselves. That is our highest calling."

Annea smiled, feeling she'd met a kindred spirit. On a world of poets and artists, few understood the thrill she got from a good fight. She'd never have to explain herself to Kuma in that regard. "On behalf of the citizens of Kimori, I'd like to formally invite you to our world to join us in battle."

The auditorium lights dimmed, and Kuma bent low so the two of them could speak directly into each other's ears and carry on planning and negotiations over the noise of Blackwell's talent show. In her excitement to learn more of the Ankora's military capabilities and coordinate the details of their arrival on Kimori, she paid no attention at all to what happened on stage, until the voice on the public address system finally broke through her focus.

"AND NOW, CONTESTANT THIRTEEN, HAILING FROM THE WORLD OF ALTERRA, SERENA EMBERS!"

Annea watched the young woman saunter out onto the stage in an awkward, amateurish attempt at projecting confidence. *What in the world is she thinking? They were supposed to find Lorelai during the Symphony of Lies, get the crystalline computing matrix, and get out. Why go through the talent show?* She shook her head. *They haven't found it yet. I hope they have a plan.* She longed for one of the earrings they'd acquired to talk across long distances, but the merchant only had three, so she'd had to be the one to go without. *Serena has her job. I have mine. There's nothing I can do for her right now.*

Serena's face flushed as Blackwell mocked her before the entire crowd. She responded in peak Serena fashion, hurling a fireball at the face of one of the most powerful beings in this corner of the multiverse.

"Do you know her?" Kuma asked, noticing Annea's distraction.

"I do. She's a survivor of a Vohr invasion." Annea pinched her nose in frustration. "She's not supposed to be on stage. It's a long story." She marveled at Serena and Tako's double act. Was Tako immune to Serena's magic? She doubted it, but realized she'd never asked. A wave of regret washed over her. *I've been a horrible mentor to that poor girl.* She'd make it up to her when Kimori was safe, if they both survived.

"Well, if Blackwell doesn't want her as a candelabra, she can light up my bedroom any time," the Moon Doge said, dropping down from the light fixture on the wall to perch atop Kuma's broad shoulders like a trained bird. Kuma made no move to dislodge him, though his stiff body language conveyed he didn't enjoy being used as a perch.

Annea steeled herself for negotiations with the abrasive little creature. Orlan trusted Patrick. Patrick said the Chiroptera would be useful allies against the Vohr. She'd suffer indignity for the sake of her people, if she had to.

"Greetings, glorious Moon Doge." She bowed deeply. "I understand your business interests have suffered due to Vohr invasions. Kimori welcomes you to join us in battle if you'd like to get some payback."

It was the wrong thing to say. "Payback? There's no profit in revenge. Revenge is an emotional reaction. Exactly what I'd expect from a female." The Moon Doge's bat-like ears twitched with irritation. His breath smelled like dirty socks. He pointed an accusing finger at Patrick. "You expect me to ally with a world ruled by females? This is a gross waste of my time. How can any enlightened race allow their females to make decisions? That way leads to chaos and the breakdown of social order. Yes, we've lost valuable trading partners to the Vohr, but honestly, if they want Kimori, they can have it. Find me someone competent to speak with."

Patrick gestured for Annea to bend down so he could whisper into her ear as the next contestant in Blackwell's talent show took the stage. "I warned you the Chiroptera are sexist little assholes. Appeal to his greed."

Annea nodded and returned her attention to the Chiroptera. "I'm disappointed in you, Moon Doge," she said. If he wanted to play sexist games, she could too. "Patrick's been telling me all about your unrivaled business acumen. I assumed a man with your power and influence would take charge of the situation and try to leverage my vulnerability for maximum profit, not let his attitude towards women blind him to a golden opportunity."

"You can't bait me." The Moon Doge leaned in. His eyes widened and his breathing quickened. He flexed his wings and rubbed his hands together.

Annea stifled a laugh. She turned to Patrick. "I can't work with him. He's even more emotional than me. Find me a man rational enough to understand the value of an exclusive harvesting agreement."

The Moon Doge's eyes grew so wide they practically popped out of his head. "*Exclusive* harvesting rights?"

"If we can come to an agreement on the amount and nature of the military support you provide Kimori, we will grant you exclusive rights to the body parts and materials of our vanquished foes. Have you seen the blades of a manti? There's some excellent steel to be harvested there. What about the claws of Reapers? Those can be forged into weapons as well. I hear many Chiroptera are excellent blacksmiths. Who knows what other uses could be found for the Vohr? We are a peaceful people, and have no need for any of it. Since any world invaded by the Vohr gets cut off from the Nexus, these materials aren't common across the multiverse. Demand could be great, and you would control the entire supply."

The Moon Doge rocked back and forth on Kuma's shoulder like a crazed parrot. She imagined the words *exclusive* and *monopoly* popping off in his mind like fireworks. "See? This is why you don't let females run things. No business sense. Absolutely no financial sense at all. They stand to make a fortune, and she gives it all away."

"What assurances can you offer us that we would not find ourselves stranded on Kimori, if we come to your aid?" Kuma asked.

"None," Annea said. She wanted their help, but wouldn't lie to them to obtain it. "We're at war. Joining us in exile is a risk you'd be taking if you aid us. As I said, we've been using intermediaries to get from Kimori to the Nexus. We'd want you to travel to our world directly from your own, leaving the Nexus out of the loop until this invasion is over."

The Moon Doge appeared unconcerned, his mind visibly doing the calculus of potential riches. If the Vohr attacked in the numbers Serena had led her to expect, he'd soon make enough money to found his own kingdom on the world of his choice, even after paying his troops. "Very well, female. Let us negotiate terms."

Annea wanted to remind the Moon Doge that she had a name, but held her tongue. Before she could come to final terms with Kuma or the Moon Doge about troop commitments to Kimori, the public address system disrupted her focus a second time.

"UP NEXT, CONTESTANT SEVENTEEN, FROM THE WORLD OF ATARAXIA, LET OUT A CHEER FOR IVY!"

CHAPTER 42

PEST CONTROL

"**I** hope you know what you're doing," Cypher said.

"Just making it up as I go," Serena admitted, following the path towards the nearest elevator leading to other cubes. "It's something of an Embers family tradition." She was her father's daughter, she thought with a bittersweet smile. His life was full of spur-of-the-moment decisions that worked out far better than they had any right to — like proposing marriage to her mother an hour into their first date.

She choked down another wave of grief. It had been almost two weeks since the invasion of Alterra and the destruction of Valencia, and she'd had no time to properly grieve, running from one crisis to the next. Tako sent warm reassurance that he'd help her process it all when she was ready.

"The ants are probably still working in the kitchens," Cypher said. "Take the elevator down a level, and I'll direct you from there."

"I wish these earrings connected with Pik-Pik and Tik-Tik's collars so I could warn them I'm coming," Serena said. "I don't want them acting like they know me."

"They've already pretended not to know you once today."

"True, but I was glamored at the time, and the earring hand-off was planned." Serena maneuvered around a flock of talking penguins waddling their way towards the elevator.

"Pik-Pik and Tik-Tik seem perfectly capable of thinking on their feet. What's your plan?"

"One of Blackwell's insults actually gave me an idea. Have you ever had ants in your kitchen?" Serena asked. "It's a nightmare."

"I'll take your word for it," Cypher said. "On Mallozzi, we used food replicators. Nobody cooked."

Nobody cooked? Mallozzi must have been a strange world. Too bad she'd never see it. "I need to convince the kitchen staff that Pik-Pik and Tik-Tik are dangerous, so they'll be eager to release them into my care. Any suggestions for how I do that?"

Cypher obliged, putting words to concepts only half-understood by Alterran science. *Bacteria. Microbes. Genetic mutations. Zoonotic and communicable diseases.* He looked up and explained this sector's public health and safety regulations with the enthusiasm of a professor with a captive audience. She didn't understand half of it, but felt he'd given her enough she could bluff and bluster as needed.

The elevator platform reached her level and the safety rail along the front retracted into the floor. A centaur and a bird-person disembarked, leaving a bipedal turtle and a humanoid woman with glittery blue skin as the only occupants. The diversity of life across the multiverse continued to amaze her. Hopefully, she'd someday have the time to explore their worlds and learn about their cultures. She pressed the button to take the elevator down a level, but the turtle stepped on the safety railing as it started to ascend, triggering a safety mechanism that kept the elevator in place. "Not everyone is here yet," he said in explanation, pointing at the penguins still waddling towards them.

"Relax," Tako said, sensing Serena's mounting irritation. *"This slight delay isn't going to harm us."*

"Thank you, my reptilian friend," said the tallest of the penguins. The flock saluted the turtle with their flippers as they stepped onto the platform. "Our mission is on a delicate timeline."

"Silence, Private," barked a short, fat penguin. "Mission details are need-to-know, and not for civilians."

"Yes, Sir!" The tall penguin bowed his head, chastised.

"It's about to get hot. Last chance to eat for a while. Rations out," the fat penguin said. As one, a dozen penguins pulled out a fish from *somewhere.* Each swallowed their meal in a single noisy gulp.

Were they actually military? They didn't have any apparent weapons on them, and their appearance made them hard to take seriously as a fighting force. Perhaps that was just how their flock social dynamics translated.

A few moments later, Serena stepped off the elevator and into a residential cube, nearly tripping over a penguin in her haste to be on her way. Apartment buildings lined both sides of a wide boulevard, stretching almost all the way to the "sky." The cube's ceiling enchantments gave the impression of a starry night sky at this hour, with two moons tracing slow orbits.

"You're going to need to go almost all the way to the end of the cube, then take the last left," Cypher said.

Serena sprinted down the street, ignoring curious looks from beings of various species. She stopped when she spotted a discarded beverage container on the ground. Perfect. She channeled energy into her hands and picked it up. "How are things looking in the talent show?"

"The contestant after you was a comedian who spent his time roasting the host."

"That's a bold strategy. How'd it go?" She heated the thin metal can and crushed it into a flat disc. Anything heated through her own power remained safe for her to touch.

"About as well as you'd expect," Cypher replied. "Blackwell's clearly happy to dish out the verbal abuse, but he can't take any. His guards beat the guy up on stage for everyone to see. And people want to work for this guy? This sector of the Nexus is messed up. Lawless compared to our own. I... I think you're lucky Blackwell found your assault on him laughable. That could have been bad. The show's paused while they mop up the blood."

Serena shuddered, glad she hadn't been around to see that. With the metal can crushed and softened, she molded it into the shape of a shield. She took a finger and traced the letters SPCS into it. *"Mind cooling this down?"*

Tako extended a limb and sprayed her hand with water. The metal hissed and steamed as it cooled. *"Do you really expect that to work?"* he asked.

"We've seen how Blackwell treats people seeking powerful positions in his organization. Do you think he treats his kitchen staff any better? I'm counting on everyone being terrified of displeasing him. Most of his

security will be monitoring the main event, so if we can bully our way inside, we may have a pretty clear path to our goal."

"Your plan assumes Blackwell doesn't bribe people to prevent this sort of thing."

"And you're assuming Blackwell's kitchen staff would know about those kinds of arrangements, if they exist. We won't know until we try." Serena placed her fake badge of office in her left hand and turned down the street Cypher indicated. "Ok, now what?"

"Look for a large metal door on tracks to your right, about halfway to the back wall of the cube," Cypher said. "That's the service door where Blackwell's staff receive supply deliveries, and your best bet for getting back into his estate."

It wasn't hard to find — the door looked tall and wide enough for a half-dozen horses to walk through shoulder to shoulder. Serena pounded on it. "Health inspection, open up!" Not receiving a response, she continued to slam her fist against the door, using the gesture to work herself into character as an impatient and overworked government contractor. If Blackwell's staff were watching the talent show and recognized her, her ruse would be doomed. All she could do was commit to the act and hope for the best. "Open up! I'm paid by the job, not by the hour, so let's go!"

A slit in the heavy door opened wide enough to expose a set of eyes. "There are no inspections today. Do you live under a rock? It's Lord Blackwell's big party. Get lost," a man said.

"Serena's Pest Control Services." Serena flashed her improvised badge in front of the slit and pulled it back before the man had a chance to get a good look at it. "I'm Serena. The Sector Council contracted me, so let me in."

"It's Blackwell's big day. No inspections," he repeated. He showed no sign of recognizing her. Excellent.

Time to be a bully. "Don't give me that. Have you never heard of a *surprise inspection*? Why would the Council want me to check for pests at a time that's *convenient* for you, so you have time to hide the evidence? I'm here *because* of the party. Now open up, or get ready to explain to your boss that he'll be paying fines because you refused to cooperate."

The slot in the door closed. She realized fines might not mean much to Blackwell, given his obvious wealth and power. How could she escalate the threat? She'd give the man a ten count before banging on the door again. She got to seven before she heard the scraping of a metal bar being pulled loose, then the door rolled up on its tracks.

Her gatekeeper looked to be in his mid-fifties, wearing a white apron spattered with blood, sauce, or both. Behind him stood rows upon rows of shelves filled with boxes and canned foods. "Alright," he said, "show me the work order."

Was he calling her bluff, or was that a normal part of the process? "Look, I don't want to be here any more than you want me here, OK? This was a rush job. Typical bureaucratic incompetence, waiting until the last minute to make a decision. The Council wanted me here right away. The formal paperwork will be delivered tomorrow."

"Right," he snorted. "Typical Council bullshit. They give you a specific reason for this inspection, or are you just here to harass us?"

She saw the opening and took it. "There's rumors of an ant infestation."

"We don't have an ant problem."

At that moment, Pik-Pik entered the room, pushing through hanging strips of plastic that separated the receiving and storage area from the rest of the estate. They placed an enormous sack of rice they'd been carrying in their mandibles onto a shelf, then turned around to re-enter the kitchen, too focused on their task to notice Serena and the chef.

Serena let an awkward silence drag out. "So," she said at last. "What was that? Looked an awful lot like an ant to me."

"Well, about that..."

"Either everyone on your staff is blind to have missed a *giant ant in your kitchen*, or you're *employing it,*" Serena said, outraged. "Do you have its identification on file? Has anyone done a biological risk assessment on it?" The man opened his mouth to attempt a reply. She didn't give him a chance, piling on the questions. "Do you have any idea what kinds of bacteria that species harbors? Who interviewed it? Do you people take *any* precautions before bringing on insects? Or was the thought process '*Hey, giant ant. So exotic. Let's get one.*'"

She marched around the chef and pushed through the plastic strips to enter the kitchen. "Serena's Pest Control Services! This is a Council sanctioned health inspection!" Again, she waved her badge around with the air of someone who felt everyone should recognize it, not providing anyone a clear look at it before stuffing it into a pocket.

Pik-Pik and Tik-Tik stood in the center aisle of the kitchen. They had long rows of ovens and stovetops to either side. Both had been carefully picking up completed dishes and setting them on trays in preparation for delivery. They paused at the sound of her voice. "Who did a microbe check on those ants?" Serena shouted, thrusting an accusing finger at them.

A dozen beings of various humanoid species stared at her like she'd sprouted a second head. Pik-Pik and Tik-Tik tilted their heads in a gesture of confusion, but the notorious babble-boxes were smart enough to stay silent and let the situation develop. Thank the All-Mother for that. Nobody else said a word.

"I assure you, this isn't necessary," the chef who'd answered the door stammered.

"I assure you it is," Serena snapped back. "You'd better pray they come out clean from my tests, or I'll be forced to quarantine your whole staff, as well as any guests who came into contact with food they helped prepare."

"You wouldn't."

"I absolutely would. And that's just the start. If they've contaminated your food supplies..." She snapped her fingers. Fist-sized fireballs appeared in the air above her palms. "I'd have to sterilize everything."

Satisfied that bit of theater dampened anyone's desire to interrupt her "work," Serena snuffed out the fireballs and turned her attention to the ants. "You two, step outside." She pointed to a door leading deeper into Blackwell's estate. "Everyone else stays here until I say otherwise."

"*Did you have to lay it on so thick?*" Tako asked. "*These folks are only doing their jobs.*"

Serena cast a glance back at the door-answering chef on her way out the door. The poor man looked as if she'd struck him. *"These people live in fear of Blackwell's displeasure. They're less likely to question me if they think Blackwell's wrath would be worse than kicking me out."*

Though, when she paused for a moment, she could imagine Blackwell's very real wrath at letting a fake government contractor into his domain, then letting her run around unsupervised. Someone was going to lose their job for this. Possibly their head. A part of her had known that from the moment she banged on the door. If Dr. Venture's data saved Kimori, that was a fair trade, wasn't it? She'd still have the moral high ground, right?

Goddess, she didn't want to be making these kinds of decisions.

"Serena," Tako said. He loomed large in her mind, his tone that of a parent delivering tough love. *"You're not responsible for anything Blackwell does. The decision has been made. We're here. See it through."*

Serena clenched a fist and forced herself to focus. *"You're right."*

The area outside the kitchen was more utilitarian than she'd expected, all solid stone floors and plain white walls. Blackwell apparently didn't care about the service areas of his domain being aesthetically pleasing. Straight ahead was the elevator platform that led up to the Welcoming Hall. To the left was a long hallway with that led to a T-intersection where someone could go straight or take a right.

Serena motioned for the ants to follow her to that intersection. "The computing matrix is in Blackwell's private chambers," she said, once she was certain kitchen staff weren't following. "Have you two been able to explore at all? Any chance you know where we need to go?"

<We have been there.>

<We delivered him a meal an hour before the Symphony of Lies started.>

<Akakami can eat regular food too. Not just people.>

<He wanted to see the "exotic new hires.">

<He was quite mean.>

<Very inconsiderate.>

<He made sure we knew ants are a delicacy on many worlds.>

<He wanted to know if we'd rather be glazed in cinnamon or brown sugar.>

"That's horrible!" Serena said. She meant it, but she also needed to interrupt their flow and get them back on topic. "Can you show me the way to his room?"

<Of course.>

<You can't get in though.>

<There's a trap.>

Serena sighed. "Of course it is. Well, one problem at a time. I don't know how long we have until someone on the kitchen staff works up the nerve to check up on us, so lead the way."

She followed Pik-Pik and Tik-Tik down multiple hallways, losing all sense of their position after numerous turns. None of the rooms they passed featured any signage to indicate their purpose, nor did the hallway intersections offer any perspective on their position in the cube. She'd worried Blackwell may have security staff patrolling the hallways, but that wasn't the case. Nobody they encountered spared them a second glance as they rushed about whatever tasks they'd been assigned.

"This place is built like a maze," Serena said. "How do you know we're going the right way?"

The further they went, the fancier the decor became. Plush carpeting replaced bare stone. Plain white walls gave way to intricately patterned wallpaper with portraits of Akakami placed every ten feet. Blackwell's ancestors? Like him, every one of them had a solid black mask covering their faces from the nose down.

<Compared to navigating the ant colony, this is easy.>

<No vertical axis to consider. Just left, right, and straight.>

<Are you lost?>

<The path is quite simple.>

<Right, straight, left, right, straight until you've passed three corridors.>

<Then right, left, straight for four corridors, left, straight for two, right.>

<It's really very simple.>

"For you, perhaps. My sense of direction isn't great unless I'm under an open sky," Serena said.

"I didn't want to interrupt while you were busy intimidating the kitchen staff, but thought you should know that Ivy's about to perform," Cypher said. His tone suggested her earring transmitted everything she'd said. He sounded far too amused.

"Give me running commentary on her performance," Serena said. "I doubt it'll change my plans, but who knows? Ivy is full of surprises."

"As you wish."

At last, the ants led her around a corner and came to a stop. The hallway turned into a tunnel of steel on all sides, ending in a metal door in Blackwell's trademark red and gold. "I take it the walls and floor are a trap?" Serena asked.

<You are correct.>

<Blackwell disabled it from the inside.>

"I don't suppose anyone told you what the trap does?"

Tik-Tik bounced back and forth on their legs like an excited puppy. <It's a flame trap!>

<Serena is a pyromancer. This should be easy,> Pik-Pik agreed.

<That won't help with the door itself though.>

"I'm not sure it works that way," Serena said. "I'm immune to my own fire, but I haven't tested if other sources of fire can hurt me." Ivy's solar attack *had* burned her back, which didn't inspire confidence. This wasn't the time to test what flavors of magic she was or was not immune to. "Cypher, any chance you can disable a fire trap leading to Blackwell's inner sanctum? I'd prefer not to set it off any alarms."

"I'll see what I can do. No promises," Cypher said. "Ivy's taking the stage now."

Serena studied the bare steel, looking for buttons, switches, anything that might be used to deactivate the trap or open the door.

The lights overhead began a gentle strobe. A voice filled the air from no apparent source. *"Security alert. A suspicious human female is unaccounted for, last seen near the kitchens. She has red hair and a distinctive octopus tattoo along her back. She may be accompanied by two large red ants."*

So much for getting in without setting off alarms.

Did she dare have Tako hop off and risk intentionally springing the trap? If pyromancers were immune to *any* fire, she'd be fine. If not...

Better to not think about that.

CHAPTER 43

BREAKING AND ENTERING

Serena closed her eyes and took a deep breath, doing her best to ignore the security alert. One last door separated her from Dr. Venture's crystalline computing matrix and the answers it could provide about the Vohr invasion. She was *so close*.

Assuming she could get in without being incinerated first.

"Come on Cypher, give me something to work with here." Without stepping onto the metal floor, Serena felt along the walls, finding no uneven spots concealing pressure switches. She tried to remove the Akakami portraits, but they wouldn't budge.

"I'm doing the best I can here," Cypher said, tension in his voice. "The encryptions around that trap are orders of magnitude more complex that what they have protecting their security cameras."

"What about the talent show? Is Blackwell aware of the security alert down here?" Serena asked.

"Blackwell looks annoyed, but I think it's because Ivy is proving impervious to his efforts to insult her. The crowd loves her and she hasn't even done anything yet."

"Forget about disabling the trap. Keep an eye on Ivy. Let me know if Blackwell learns what's happening down here, or if you detect any security staff closing in on me."

"And what are you going to do?"

"More Embers family magic." She created a fireball the size of a watermelon and hurled it in a two-handed, overhead motion towards the door. It burst against the red and gold metal, doing no damage whatsoever. While the walls and ceiling showed no visible reaction, she heard the loud clicking of mechanisms changing position behind the walls. She tossed fist-sized fireballs into the floor, ceiling, and both walls, getting no response. She extended an arm over the steel floor and waved it around. Nothing happened.

"I'm starting to feel like this whole thing is a bluff," Serena said.

"The floor could be pressure sensitive," Tako said. *"In which case, nothing happens until you step onto it."*

"Why not just set it off? I can't be hurt by fire. Probably." She didn't know that for sure. Why did she bother trying to lie to Tako? She couldn't hide her anxiety from him when the barrier between their thoughts was so permeable.

He didn't dignify the comment with a response. Instead, he asked, *"And then what? Even if you're impervious to the fire, what's your plan for the door itself?"*

"I'll burn my way through it. Or maybe the ants can pry it open once the trap's disabled."

"How are you going to disable the trap?"

"Find components to melt? I won't know what I'm dealing with until it goes off."

"This isn't a plan, Serena. This is wishful thinking."

"I'll make it work!" Were they having their first argument? Tako hadn't dug in so hard about swimming down to the magmadon. But the ocean was his natural habitat. He'd had skills that could help. Here, trying to help would only get him killed, in all likelihood. *"We've got to take risks if we hope to succeed. I need to do this. For your own safety, I'm going to need you to hop off for this part."*

She felt Tako surfing the waves of her thoughts, looking for any angle he could use to dissuade her from being reckless. With a heartbreaking sigh, he pushed himself off her skin. *"Don't die on me."* He crawled off her back and onto Tik-Tik's head, where he looked like the multiverse's most bizarre hat. He wrapped a tentacle loosely around each of the ant's antennae for balance and let the others dangle off to the sides. Tik-Tik rocked back and forth on their feet, clearly delighted at the novelty of serving as a mount for an Octari.

Serena returned her focus to the door at the end of the hall. As she marched towards it, she imagined it crumpling in the face of a superpowered punch. Her magic responded to her emotions, her skin humming with a low level of power. She'd be ready to react to anything the trap threw at her.

She made it three paces before thick glass panels slid down from the ceiling, blocking off Blackwell's door... and her retreat. She pounded a fist against the glass. *That's dumb,* she thought. *Just melt it.* She placed one hand on the glass and channeled fire into it while keeping an eye out for fresh dangers.

The walls and ceiling irised open, revealing metallic cones. Rather than engulf her in fire, they blasted out water with such pressure Serena almost lost her footing.

"You said this was a flame trap!" Serena shouted, unsure if the ants could hear her through the barrier.

The ants looked mortified, bouncing back and forth on their legs with obvious agitation. Tik-Tik shook their head so hard they almost sent Tako flying. The collars around their necks strobed, but she couldn't hear whatever they said over the rush of water. The duo opened their mandibles wide and tried biting into the glass, but they couldn't even chip the barrier. Serena's flames made no difference either. The glass around her palm glowed orange but showed no signs of melting or shattering as she pounded against it.

Is this how I die? Separated by inches from the friend who could help me breathe underwater?

Tako slapped a tentacle against the glass. His voice burst into her head. *"Keep calm,"* he said. *"The water's only up to your knees. There's time to figure this out."*

"Easy for you to say!" Serena grabbed one of the nozzles and attempted to melt it shut to cut off the flow of water. Like the glass, it refused to submit to her will. *What is this stuff made of?*

Tako tapped the glass again. Serena realized she couldn't hear him. His voice returned as she placed her hand opposite his tentacle. *"...and the pressure should shatter the glass."*

"What?" She shouted.

"Why are you trying to blow my ears out? I didn't say anything," Cypher said.

She forgot her earring was transmitting. "Sorry Cypher, I need a minute." She snapped her fingers once to mute herself.

"I can't hear your speech. Think your words to me. Our bond is strong enough we can communicate from a few inches away," Tako said.

"Did you know we could do this?"

"Deeply bonded pairs can communicate from up to ten feet away. That's why human and Octari Shrike pilots can communicate even when they're not connected to each other. You and I haven't had cause to experiment with our range until now."

Magical theory would have been more fun if she wasn't about to drown. *"Can you hit me with another water breathing enchantment?"*

"Sadly, no. That still requires physical touch."

What had he been trying to say earlier? *"Did you say something about pressure?"*

"Boil the water. If those hoses continue to fill your prison cell, then that water, combined with the gas given off by boiling water, will put more and more pressure on the walls containing you, until they shatter."

"Brilliant theory, Tako, but I have some concerns." The water level now reached Serena's waist. *"How do we know boiling the water won't also boil me?"*

"Serena," Tako said her name like an exasperated teacher, but there was no mistaking the fear in it. *"You've held melted metal in your bare hands. You've established that anything heated through your own power won't hurt you. Besides, if it was going to injure you, I'm sure you'd feel that and know to stop."*

"Fair point." She forced herself to take a deep breath. Panic wasn't helping her think. *"How do we know the kind of pressure needed to shatter this is survivable?"*

"I don't know," Tako admitted. *"I'll let you know if anything else comes to me, but it's the best idea I have."*

Lacking any better ideas, Serena pressed her back against the glass, close enough to Tako she could still sense his barely suppressed panic. It did nothing to help her combat her own.

She closed her eyes and let rage consume her. Rage at Blackwell, because what kind of psychopath designed a trap to drown people right outside his private chambers? Rage at herself, for once again assuming she could blunder through a problem without consequences. Rage at Korahshka, for destroying her world and countless others with his legion of monsters.

The water around her bubbled, then boiled. She felt no pain. Tako was right, she couldn't boil herself. Her soaked clothes endured the heat as she vented energy into the water as fast as she could channel it.

Serena snapped her fingers again to unmute herself. "Hey Cypher, how's Ivy doing?" She needed a distraction while she waited to see if the rising pressure would free her or kill her.

"What's that background noise?" He asked.

How well did the earring pick up the roar of the water jets? "Don't worry about it."

"Ivy made a pair of trees sprout up from the stage. Their branches are growing out over the heads of the audience. The crowd's loving it. Ivy seems confused."

In spite of her circumstances, Serena laughed. "No surprise there. She doesn't know how to handle attention." Being just one of sixteen sisters, she probably never had much of a spotlight on her.

The water was up to her shoulders.

"How's the deliberately-setting-off-traps strategy working out?" Cypher asked.

"Fine. Delightful. Everything's going great, thanks for asking," Serena said. "I'm definitely not about to drown in a water tank."

"Did you throw around any fire before approaching the door? I wonder if the system has several modes to counter different methods of magical attack. If it knows you're a pyromancer, it may have shifted to water to counter you." Why did he have to sound so calm and rational about her potential demise? His theory did explain the mechanical sounds she'd heard in the walls though. "Do you have a way out?" Cypher asked, finally recognizing the peril.

"I'm working on it. And I changed my mind. Feel free to disable this trap if you can. How's Ivy doing?" Serena stood on the tips of her toes to keep her nose and mouth above water. Steam fogged up the glass and filled the air, making it impossible to see more than a few inches in any direction. She felt the mounting pressure squeezing her like a boa constrictor had her in its grasp.

"The tree Ivy grew over the audience is sprouting fruit, and she's telling them to try some."

Alucinatus berries? No, that plant was short, and Ivy wouldn't try that one again after what happened on Kimori.

"The crowd is going wild," Cypher said. The rising water level forced Serena to start treading. "I think she called them wine berries?"

"Why would people get so excited about grapes?" She knew she should stop talking, but she'd floated away from Tako and couldn't focus on reestablishing that connection right now. Cypher's voice was a lifeline keeping panic away enough to keep her boiling the water.

"Apparently the skin of the fruit covers a hollow core filled with wine. They're like wine shots, straight from the tree." He paused. "And now people are climbing over each other to strip the tree bare. Blackwell's security folks are stepping in to restore order. He's ordered Ivy to get rid of the tree. Can't tell with the mask, but I'd swear he's smiling."

"Having visions of all the money he can make off a woman who can spontaneously make wine, no doubt," Serena said, watching the ceiling draw uncomfortably close. *This glass better shatter before my eardrums do.* Goddess, it hurt now. Like being slowly crushed beneath the boot of an angry giant.

"Cypher, I'll be right back." She took a deep breath and dove below the surface, pouring everything she had into making the water boil. She stuffed fingers into her ears in an attempt to protect them from the intense pressure.

"Tako, buddy, can you hear me?" Serena pressed against what she thought was the correct wall. Boiling water tried to send her every which way.

"I can," Tako said.

"I think this is going to work. You all should back up. I wouldn't want you to get blasted by glass and boiling water when this thing goes."

"Indeed." He gave her a mental hug. *"Good luck. Don't die on me."* His presence vanished from her mind.

Serena kicked to the surface and found she still had room to breathe. Even with her ears plugged, she heard the glass cracking. She felt it in her bones. The odd crack here or there soon turned into a rapid drumbeat, like hailstones against windows. She felt the abrupt cessation of pressure as the glass to either side exploded outward. Serena fell, landed awkwardly on one ankle, lost her balance, and flopped onto her side against the steel floor. Water stopped flowing from the spouts around her — they must have sensed that there was no longer a tank to fill.

"Still alive, Cypher," Serena stood and limped up to Blackwell's door, water dripping off her sodden clothes. Tako and the ants would be back in a minute, once the water cooled enough that they felt safe to approach. In the meantime, she wanted to examine the door.

"Blackwell called off Ivy's performance because of the crowd's reaction. He's offered her a place in his ranks of familiars."

"That's good, I guess?" That *had* been the plan, though it seemed less relevant while she stood just outside their goal. She ran her hands along the door to Blackwell's sanctum, looking for any evidence of a hidden panel, button, knob, anything.

"Some troupe called the Peril Dancers are taking to the stage now. I think someone told Blackwell about the intruder alert. He's huddled up with a bunch of his security staff and new familiars in the wings, stage left. Ivy, Lorelai, and that woman who can control minds. Siren, wasn't it? You'd better hurry."

She prayed for time as Pik-Pik and Tik-Tik rounded a corner behind her.

<Serena will be so mad at us.>

<Blackwell doesn't have to barbeque us. She'll do it herself.>

<We told her it was a flame trap. And she almost drowned!>

<She'll never trust us again!>

"Relax, I'm not mad at you." Serena said, turning to face the ants. She crouched so she could look at them at eye level. The poor things quivered like they stood before Queen Ruta. She'd never given them cause to fear her, had she? "You told me the truth as you knew it. Nobody asked you to figure out the intricacies of Blackwell's security systems. I'm the one who went rushing in." She rubbed the tops of their heads between their antennae. As she did, Tako slithered off Tik-Tik's head and up her arm, his physical body rapidly dissolving into its two-dimensional tattoo appearance across her skin.

<You are very kind and forgiving.>

<Just like Annea.>

"Think you can do anything about this door?" Serena asked. It appeared to retract up into the ceiling, but she'd found no way to open it.

<We can do that.>

<It would be our pleasure.>

Serena stepped aside to give the ants room to work. Each of them took a position at a corner of the door, closed their mandibles, and poked at the floor, chipping and denting the steel as they worked to dig themselves a gap they could fit their mandibles under.

"Blackwell and company are on the move," Cypher said. "If they head directly for his private chambers, I'd guess they'll be on you in five minutes."

"Understood," Serena said.

The ants had the front few inches of their mandibles under the door and squatted low as they strained to lift it. Even though they could lift many times their body weight, she still wondered if the two of them working together could force their way through something so heavy.

Something cracked inside the door. It shot up several inches. Pik-Pik and Tik-Tik took advantage of the movement to get their mandibles further under the door and improve their leverage. As one, they lifted their heads and stood from their squatting positions until there was a gap large enough for Serena to roll under.

"Are you two going to need to hold the door?" Serena asked. In response, the ants looked down, then snapped their heads up, tossing the door into the ceiling, where it clicked into place.

"We don't have much time. Spread out." Serena crossed the threshold into Blackwell's sanctum. "Let me know if you find the computing matrix."

They needed to find it fast.

She wanted to be gone before the Akakami and his security arrived.

CHAPTER 44
BLACKWELL'S SANCTUM

Serena felt like she'd stepped into a museum, not a private residence. They found themselves in a vast, open room, with a ceiling thirty feet above their heads. The ceiling had a grid pattern that reminded her of a chess board. Every other panel provided artificial sunlight. There had to be hundreds of glass cases filling the space. Blackwell had huge collections of weapons, armors, and art pieces. There were taxidermied animals, including a reptilian creature suspended from the ceiling. It had a long, narrow beak and leathery wings which spanned almost forty feet from wingtip to wingtip. The creature looked like it could swallow a human as easily as a stork could gobble up a fish if it wanted to.

Straight ahead stood a mannequin wearing an ancient-looking suit of layered leather armor, sized appropriately for a being of Blackwell's stature. It was painted the same blood red as an Akakami's skin. The helmet featured a pair of antlers that reminded her of elder stags back home... or of Balor.

Pik-Pik maneuvered around her to the left, venturing down an aisle of cases displaying hundreds of varieties of edged weapons. Tik-Tik went right, following a wall dominated by an aquarium filled with fish she didn't recognize.

She opted to split the difference, following Tik-Tik's path until she reached the middle of the room, then turning left. The aisles were wider here, with additional, unnecessary lighting provided by an array of ornate lamps. Some blazed with magical fire that gave off no smoke. Others were lit by technological means. Lightbulbs, Cypher had called them.

A massive canopy bed was set in the middle of the back wall, the posts made of rich mahogany. She'd seen ponds smaller than that bed. Blackwell could fit himself and a dozen lovers on it at once if he wanted to. Flanking the bed on both sides were the mounted skeletons of bipedal creatures that stood ten to twelve feet tall, and were at least thirty feet long from snout to tail. Their arms looked too tiny to be practical for hunting, but their heads were huge and filled with sharp teeth, reminding her of the dragons in some of her favorite books. Clearly an apex predator.

The reflection of light off metal diverted her attention away from the intimidating carnivores. A single object rested on the crimson sheets of Blackwell's bed...

Serena dashed across the room, dripping water all over the Akakami's plush carpeting as she went. Shaped like a snowflake, the object had six small crystals at points around the exterior and a large one in the center. Dr. Venture's computing matrix. The repository of all his data on the positions of different realities, relative to the Nexus. The key to understanding if there was any pattern or logic to the Vohr invasion.

"I found it!" Serena shouted, seeing no reason for stealth. If Blackwell or his security forces were close enough to hear, they wouldn't have time to escape unobserved anyway.

"Serena, Blackwell's team is splitting up," Cypher said. "Guys in suits are working their way through the staff quarters now. I've lost sight of Blackwell and his familiars in the security feeds."

"We are in a narrow, secret passageway between sections of Blackwell's estate," Ivy said, her voice a barely perceptible whisper in Serena's ear. "We are on our way to Blackwell's private chamber. I am hanging as far back as I dare without arousing suspicion. I can say no more."

"The throne room of Z'han has two secret entrances the king can use to make a surprise appearance, or to escape." Tako said. *"I wonder if Blackwell designed something similar here?"*

"I wouldn't be surprised," Serena agreed. *"Someone paranoid enough to set up a lethal trap outside the door of his bedroom would also want to make sure that wasn't the only way in or out. You think they're setting up a pincer attack?"*

"Almost certainly."

"The suits are splitting up, Serena," Cypher said, confirming their fears. "Whatever you're going to do, do it now."

Pik-Pik and Tik-Tik arrived at her side. Serena motioned for them to follow her back the way they'd come, suppressing the urge to steal anything else on the way out as an extra *screw you* to the crime lord. "Lead me back to the kitchens. We'll bluff our way out from there if possible. Otherwise, I'm sure it'll be easier to push through cooks and dishwashers than armed security."

<You are soaking wet.>

<Is that part of the health inspection?>

"I said we'd bluff. Not that it'd be convincing." As long as they didn't have to fight their way out, she'd be happy. She may have overpowered the trap, but the effort left her stiff, sore, and exhausted.

"Serena, they're really close," Cypher's voice carried an edge of panic. "I can't follow everything across so many camera views. Tell me you're out of there."

"Almost." She picked her way around broken shards of glass along the slick steel floor outside Blackwell's sanctum, taking care not to slip.

As they approached the nearest intersection of hallways, three men from Blackwell's security team rounded a corner straight ahead. She looked to the left and right and saw three men approaching from those directions as well. Nowhere to go but back into Blackwell's suite.

"Serena's Pest Control Services!" Serena said, hiding the computing matrix behind her back with one hand while she reached into her pocket with the other and pulled out her improvised shield of office. "I was sent here to conduct a —" She stopped when the security guards reached into their suit coats and pulled out metallic objects that looked like miniature versions of Z'han energy rifles. "Yeah, I didn't expect that to work."

She retreated back into Blackwell's sanctum. The ants needed no warning to do the same. At the threshold, she slipped and flew forward. A beam of light sailed through the air where her head had been a moment before. She scrambled to her feet and spun around the corner, narrowly evading another two shots.

<We can't fight nine men with guns!>

<Close the door!>

"How am I supposed to do that?" Serena asked. An energy beam shattered the glass containing the ancient armor. Another hit one of Blackwell's weapon cases.

Pik-Pik lifted one of their front legs to point at a panel on the wall. A red button sat below a keypad. Below the button, the word "RESET" flashed in angry red letters. Serena slammed the button. For a moment, nothing happened. She heard a grinding in the ceiling as something fought against whatever damage the ants had done forcing the door open, then it crashed to the floor with the force of a guillotine.

"Hopefully that holds them off." Serena inspected the contents of the shattered weapons display case, selecting a machete-like blade the length of her forearm. It was lighter than she'd expected. If she had to fight, she'd prefer to do so without drawing on her magic. She'd used too much already freeing herself from the trap. She had no formal edged weapons training, but "slash them with the sharp end" seemed obvious enough.

"If I was so obscenely wealthy that I could own multiple cubes of Nexus real estate, where would I put my secret escape tunnel?" She scanned the floor, looking for any gaps in the carpeting, or rugs which might cover trap doors, but saw nothing.

She returned to Blackwell's bed, assuming he'd have at least one secret exit near where he slept. The huge carnivore skeletons flanking the bed stood atop platforms that could potentially slide away to reveal a staircase, but she didn't find any evidence of hidden buttons or switches. Bookshelves lined the rest of that wall in both directions. Serena set the computing matrix and her weapon on the bed, then ran to the closest shelf on the left and started yanking out heavy, leatherbound tomes, tossing them on the floor. She'd read a book once where the villain's lair was hidden behind a bookcase, and moving a specific book caused the bookcase to open like a door. Part of her winced at the casual disrespect she showed such lovingly crafted books.

Along the wall to her right, a grandfather clock chimed. Blackwell had a dozen of them lined up in a row. Like his lamps, no two looked alike. Each had the eight symbols of a Planar Gate address carved into them, with their time presumably set to match a location on those worlds.

With a loud whirring of gears, the chiming clock retracted into the floor, revealing an opening in the wall behind it. Through that opening stepped Lorelai, followed by Siren. They fanned out to make way for Blackwell and Ivy. As soon as they'd all stepped inside, the clock returned to its prior position, blocking off the secret passage.

"*Lamp?* You're the intruder who broke through my security?" Blackwell sounded equal parts outraged and disappointed, as if he'd expected a far stronger magic wielder to be the one to break in.

"My name is *Serena.* I just stopped by to retrieve stolen property." She picked up the computing matrix. "We'll be leaving now."

Blackwell glared at Lorelai. "Are you in on this?"

"Of course not!" Lorelai said. "Why bother bringing it here for someone else to take it?"

"She knew to find it here. That error is surely yours. Fix it. Kill her."

"Yes, sir." Lorelai braced herself before asking a question. "Do you have any blades nearby?" Blackwell made a lazy gesture to the weapons cases across the room. Lorelai took off running, giving Serena and the ants a wide berth. Her expression equal parts fear and anger.

Siren stepped forward, a predatory smile on her angular face. "Forget Lorelai. Allow me to deal with them, my Lord, to prove how wise you were to accept me into your service." Blackwell gave an almost imperceptible nod of approval.

"I've never tried this on ants before. Should be fun." Siren pointed an open palm at Pik-Pik and Tik-Tik. She spoke in a low tone of absolute command, "Kill the redhead."

The ants tilted their heads to the side, as if confused. For a moment, nothing happened.

As one, they turned to face Serena.

Shit. Serena snatched her pilfered blade from Blackwell's bed and slashed the air in front of her, trying to warn the ants off. "Don't do it, you two. I'm your friend."

<Kill the redhead.>

<Kill the redhead.>

They split apart, one circling to her left, the other to her right, allowing them to attack from two sides at once. She'd seen what their mandibles had done to the Kroen. They'd dismember her if she let them get too close.

"Tako, any ideas? I really don't want to kill my friends today."

The Octari let out an anxious, agonized whimper.

CHAPTER 45
BEDROOM BRAWL

Blackwell held up a hand. "Wait," he commanded. Siren ordered the ants to pause. Blackwell looked to the ceiling. "They've ruined the party of the century. I have hundreds of VIPs sitting around in the auditorium waiting for the talent show to resume, wondering what's going on. There will be reputational fallout from this. If my party can't proceed to plan, my consolation will be to have another one. Make her death entertaining."

The Akakami gestured like a conductor leading an orchestra with his left hand. Oppressively loud, pulsing music filled the room. Overhead, the lights dimmed and changed colors, going from sunlight to a chaotic assortment of reds, yellows, oranges, blues, greens, and violets, all strobing to the beat in different patterns. Was this his idea of a party atmosphere? It felt engineered to cause disorientation and migraines.

"Now you may proceed." Blackwell had to shout to be heard over his own music.

Siren reiterated her command to kill Serena. The ants inched closer.

"*I'll handle them,*" Tako said. "*Just focus on dodging their attacks.*"

"*Dodging?*"

"*To avoid something by a sudden quick movement.*"

"*I know what it means,*" Serena said. She should have been able to sense what he planned through their bond, but couldn't focus in these conditions.

She patted the air with what she hoped was a universal *calm down* gesture. Like Blackwell, she had to shout to be heard. "Pik-Pik, Tik-Tik, you don't want to do this. Annea would be really mad at you!"

They ignored her. Pik-Pik charged from her left, forcing her to jump back. A heartbeat later, Tik-Tik rushed to her new position. Tako extended four of his limbs, blasting each of them with twin jets of water to the face. With the ants blinded, Serena dodged their fumbling attempts to amputate her legs at the knee. Unfortunately, she couldn't get around them to attack Siren. Even blinded by the water, the ant's movements and clumsy attacks herded her away from the woman who'd stolen their free will.

Through it all, Ivy stood motionless along the wall of clocks. Serena wanted to scream at her to *do something,* but didn't. She didn't want to blow Ivy's cover if she had a surprise planned. Without her staff, Ivy could only manifest her power from her own body or immediate surroundings, limiting her options.

"Serena, what's happening?" Cypher asked. "Why am I hearing music? That track's a banger, but you need to get out of there!"

"Busy now! We'll talk later," Serena said, turning her earring off. He meant well, but Cypher's commentary was a distraction she didn't need at the moment.

It was only a matter of time before Lorelai joined the fray and she found herself on the wrong end of a three-on-one fight. Her legs felt like jelly after escaping Blackwell's trap. Every step was an act of concentrated willpower. She couldn't handle an extended fight.

Any time now, Ivy.

While she danced for her life, Ivy paced along the far wall, looking at Blackwell's collection of grandfather clocks like she was bored. She needn't have bothered with the act. Blackwell and Siren seemed to have forgotten she was even there. The dryad selected a long wooden chime from one of the clocks and unhooked it. She stepped forward and raised it over her head, preparing to bash Siren's head in.

With superhuman speed, Blackwell jumped to Ivy's side, grabbed her arm, and hurled her to the ground. "I had my suspicions," he snarled. "If Lamp is here to steal what's mine, what are the odds the only other contestant not on my guest list would be too?"

He straddled Ivy and wrapped his hands around her neck. Since dryads breathed through their skin, it wasn't an effective attack.

How long would it take him to figure that out and just snap her neck instead? Blackwell was almost twice Ivy's height and easily three times as heavy. He certainly had the strength for it.

Serena strafed around another blind charge from the ants. Her back struck a bookcase. No more room to retreat. The ants still had her covered from two angles.

Ivy created a smaller version of the purple dandelion head she'd conjured on Kimori. She jabbed the paint spores into Blackwell's eyes and slashed the plant across his face like a furious painter attacking a canvas. Blackwell roared with surprise and rage. He sat back and tried to wipe the paint from his eyes. Ivy grabbed the wooden clock chime. Using magic to lengthen it, she clubbed Siren on the head from her prone position on the floor. With the weight of the chime and her odd angle, she couldn't put enough force into the blow to knock the woman out.

"What the hell are you doing?" Siren turned and only now noticed Blackwell straddling Ivy on the floor. She grabbed the chime and tried to wrench it from Ivy's grasp.

Time to get aggressive. Sorry guys. Serena side-stepped Tik-Tik's latest change and kicked at the side of their head with all the strength she could put into her leaden legs. Disoriented, they staggered into Pik-Pik, giving her an opening.

Her foot caught on one of the books she'd thrown to the floor. Serena stumble-jogged forward, chopping down in desperation as she lost her battle to maintain her balance. The machete bit into the junction of Siren's neck and shoulders. An instant later, Serena fell into the woman's back, sending them both sprawling. Siren collided with Blackwell on the way down. More in surprise than from the force of the impact, Blackwell rolled off Ivy.

If Serena's attack hadn't been fatal, Ivy finished the job. She shortened the clock chime and swung for Siren's head hard enough the cracks of wood and bone could be heard over the music. Blood poured out onto Blackwell's expensive carpet. Siren wouldn't be getting up again.

Her hold over the ants evaporated.

<Serena kicked me!>

<You were trying to kill her, you idiot!>

<So were you!>

<Annea's going to be *furious* when she finds out about this!>

"Help Ivy!" Serena shouted at them.

Ivy got to her feet, heavy bruising visible on her neck despite the strobing, inconsistent lighting of the room. She rubbed her neck once, but didn't seem troubled by it. The ants took protective positions on either side of her, like loyal guard dogs. Unlike dogs, they didn't bark. They hurled insults and profanities at Blackwell so explicit and descriptive Serena marveled at their vocabulary. Still struggling with paint in his eyes, the Akakami staggered off towards his bed.

Serena risked turning her back on Blackwell, not wanting Lorelai to catch her by surprise. Good thing she did. Lorelai rounded the corner of a row of display cases with a dagger in hand. Her eyes widened at the sight of Siren, but she recovered her composure quickly. "I can't let you leave with that," she said, gesturing with her dagger to the computing matrix atop Blackwell's sheets.

"You can't stop me. Give it up. I don't want to hurt you," Serena said, stalling for time. She needed a weapon, but couldn't bring herself to yank the machete free of Siren's corpse. This should have been a violence-free heist. She hadn't wanted to kill anyone. Could it have been avoided if she hadn't been impulsive and charged into Blackwell's estate? Should she have just left it to Ivy to find a way to steal the matrix on her own?

"Escape now, question your decisions later," Tako said.

"You're going to have to. I won't back down. I'm dying, Serena." Lorelai sliced into her palm with the dagger. Her blood was a deep black that matched her eyes. "The poison used on me as a child tainted me. I'll be dead within a year without Blackwell's blessing." She ran both sides of the dagger against her palm, coating the blade in blood. "Being a ghoul isn't all bad though. The same poison that's killing me gave me the power to stand up for myself." Crimson energy radiated from the blood-slicked blade.

"The computing matrix could mean the difference between life and death for hundreds of worlds. It's coming with me."

Through Tako's eyes, Serena saw Ivy motion the ants to flank Blackwell as she marched towards him with purpose. She held the clock chime like a baton. Blackwell rubbed fistfuls of silk sheets against his face, using the expensive material to continue his efforts to clear his vision.

Lorelai stepped forward. Serena stepped back. The two circled, each wary of making the first move. Tako forced the issue, spraying Lorelai with the same tentacles he'd used against the ants. She held up her bloody hand to shield herself from the spray. As blood splashed away from her self-inflicted wound, crimson energy traveled against the flow of water, snaking into Tako.

Serena felt the Octari's suffering as if it were her own, collapsing to her knees as electric pain spasmed up and down her back. "What the hell was that?"

"Blood magic," Lorelai said, a smug smile spreading across her face. "Exposure to it sets pain receptors on fire. It took me years to learn how to inoculate myself from the effects. What you're feeling now was my every waking moment until my late teens. It's a wonder I'm not completely insane." Her smile turned apologetic. "I'm not a masochist though. I'll grant you a quick death."

Tako lacked the strength for coherent words, so he bombarded Serena with mental images instead. Two bulls butting heads. A hammer smashing fruit. The leviathan's tentacles bashing themselves against the ships of Z'han's navy. All pictures of direct, blunt-force violence. His normally serene demeanor was gone, replaced with grim resolve.

Message received and understood. Serena waited until Lorelai had almost reached her, then marshaled her strength and pounced. She plowed head-first into Lorelai's diaphragm, knocking them both to the floor. Lorelai's dagger flew from her hand. Before Serena could recover enough to throw a punch, Lorelai reached around with her bloody hand and pressed it into the exposed skin of Serena's back — directly on Tako.

The pain they'd felt before was a minor shock compared to the blinding agony overwhelming her now. Tako's scream filled her mind, his pain spreading into her, both physically and mentally. Through their bond, her pain flowed right back into him, creating a hellish feedback loop. Serena felt like she'd been struck by lightning a dozen times at once. Like something was peeling off her skin one layer at a time. Like a hundred thousand needles stabbed their way up and down her body.

Somehow, Tako still had the wherewithal to snag Lorelai's wrist before she could grab her dagger. He twisted her arm, then jerked his tentacle back. Lorelai screamed as her wrist snapped. With another limb, he slapped Lorelai across the face. The moves exhausted what remained of his reserve. Tako's consciousness faded from her mind, but his pain remained. His limbs shrunk back into tattoos on her skin.

Tako's actions bought her the time she needed to find the strength to dislodge Lorelai's bloody palm from her back. With that contact broken, the all-consuming pain faded away in moments. Serena screamed and punched Lorelai in the head, disorienting the woman. She pushed herself to her feet and backed into the center aisle of Blackwell's many glass display cases, looking for anything she could use as a weapon. Her eyes settled on a sturdy-looking wooden staff lying horizontally on a glass shelf. Like a museum, it had a small plaque describing it:

Walking Staff of Luminous One Annaceros the Benevolent
Claimed in battle by Yuriel Septimus Blackwell, approx. 60 P.L.E.

Walking staff? More like bo staff. It was longer than Serena was tall. Anyone using it for support would have to be twelve to fifteen feet tall. She grabbed one of Blackwell's nearby lamps and swung, using the heavy base to shatter the case. The walking staff vibrated in her grip when she retrieved it.

Lorelai grabbed her dagger with her uninjured hand and rose to her feet. "I won't let you ruin this for me!" She rushed forward, slashing wildly.

The walking staff moved of its own volition, placing itself in position to block or parry every one of Lorelai's attacks. Serena fought it the first few times, not understanding what was going on, and nearly lost a finger for it. Though she couldn't score a hit, Lorelai's aggression forced Serena backwards until her back pressed up against Blackwell's wall-spanning fish tank.

"Die!" Lorelai thrust and slashed with the dagger in her off hand. The staff parried her time and time again, but Serena couldn't escape the assault. A parry sent Lorelai's arm drifting low and away. Serena stepped forward, shoving her back to buy some space. She pointed the staff forward and drove the end into Lorelai's gut.

Lorelai grinned and pushed back. The other end of the staff punched into the fish tank. Serena let go and stepped to the side, allowing Lorelai's momentum to push her closer to the tank. The glass shattered, unleashing a wave of water that knocked them both down. Attracted to the smell of blood, two dwarf sharks, each about three feet long, bit down on Lorelai's arms. Her blood magic sent them into spasms of pain that made them latch on even harder.

The wave shoved Lorelai head-first into a display case, knocking her out. Serena stared in numb shock at the sharks, thrashing about like angry ticks in their death throes. Guilt pinned her in place. *I had no choice. She was going to kill me.* The rationalization did little to make her feel better.

"Serena, I require your assistance!" Ivy shouted. If she hadn't had the good fortune to speak in the brief gap between songs, Serena never would have heard it from across the room.

While she fought Lorelai, Ivy, Blackwell, and the ants had done their best to turn the Akakami's sanctum into a debris field. It looked like a tornado had torn through the room. The contents of a half dozen display cases littered the area around Blackwell's bed. Ivy's bare feet had to be tough to endure walking over shards of glass and pottery. Pik-Pik and Tik-Tik tried to bite into Blackwell's ankles whenever he got close, but he kicked them aside. He'd gotten his vision back and had Ivy scrambling to stay out of his reach.

Ivy used a fresh clock chime, this one made of metal, to smash every unbroken display case she passed. She'd grab whatever she could and hurl it at the Akakami before retreating again. Pottery. Bejeweled goblets. Knives. Blackwell dodged or swatted aside most of it. What hit him did no apparent damage. He kept pace with the dryad, seeming to enjoy her futile resistance.

"Leave her alone!" Serena screamed, tapping into her magic to hurl a fireball at Blackwell's face. He held up a hand, and the fireball evaporated into nothing before it got within an arm's reach of him.

"WAIT YOUR TURN." His voice came from everywhere at once, seemingly now tied into whatever system filled the room with "music." He ignored her to resume his lazy chase of Ivy.

Magic wasn't going to work on him directly. She didn't have the energy to keep trying and hoping for a different result. What could she do? Blackwell would annihilate her in hand-to-hand combat, no doubt about it. Only an idiot would go head-to-head with someone more than four feet taller and probably two hundred pounds heavier.

She needed to fight dirty.

Ivy's path took her closer to the center of the room, in the direction of the giant taxidermied flying reptile suspended from the ceiling. Her magic might not impact Blackwell, but it should work on *that*.

Praying to the All-Mother she had the timing right, she threw fireballs at the mounting brackets securing the creature in place. She could only reach the nearest two from where she stood. Both had the desired effect, blowing holes in the ceiling and dislodging the mounting brackets. The creature tipped forward, its entire weight now supported by only two points of contact.

They couldn't endure the strain.

The reptile broke loose from the ceiling, its hard, lengthy beak impaling Blackwell like a spear on the way down. It was so large its wings lay across the tops of numerous cases. Blackwell was driven to his knees, the beak going through his back below his right shoulder blade and coming out the other side as it was slender enough to fit between his ribs.

Blackwell made a conducting gesture again. The music filling the room died. The lighting returned to its prior sunlight configuration. "You stupid bitch. Do you have any idea how much that cost? How much everything in this room cost?" He held the beak steady with one hand, then chopped it with the other, snapping through it like it was the shaft of an arrow. He leaned forward to free himself. "I offered you power, prestige, an unnaturally long lifespan, and this is how you would thank me? By breaking into my private space to steal a worthless bauble?"

"The computing matrix isn't worthless, and you know it," Serena said. She picked up another of Blackwell's lamps, testing the weight. The top of this one branched out like a candelabra. "And you didn't offer me any of those things. I believe you said I wasn't good enough to be another lamp in your collection." She swung it before the Akakami could find his feet, smacking him in the face. His mask shattered.

She understood now why Akakami wore masks. Their mouths were pure, unadulterated nightmare fuel.

In place of lips, Blackwell had four tendrils surrounding his mouth opening — one at each corner. They were approximately four inches long and lined with teeth on the inner side. When they folded up, they'd cover his mouth. His mouth itself was a circular vortex of thousands of tiny, needle-like teeth.

Blackwell stood to his full imposing height, as if the bleeding hole in his chest was only a minor inconvenience.

"Tako, any ideas here?" Serena asked.

He remained unconscious.

This is it, Serena thought. *We're going to die. My skills are useless against him. Ivy doesn't have anything to work with either.* No, that wasn't true. There was at least one object made of wood in sight.

"Force him back to his bed!" Serena said.

"If I could have, I would have already done so," Ivy said.

Blackwell advanced, forcing Serena and Ivy to retreat. Serena's legs felt like tree trunks. If she wanted to walk away from this, the fight had to end. Now. The thought of using more magic in her weary state made her want to cry in frustration, but it was the only idea she had.

"Ivy, stay close to me." With the dryad behind her, Serena sprayed fire from the palms of her hands onto everything in sight, focusing the most on the carpet. They had enough separation she could get a decent blaze going before Blackwell reached them. She had to keep him pinned in the half of his room closest to the bed. The other half's carpet was too soaked from the broken fish tank to ignite.

As she'd hoped, Blackwell opted to go down a different aisle to reach them, rather than walk through flames. *He can't nullify magic in action AROUND him, only something targeting him directly. This can work!* Serena kept him boxed in, limping from one aisle to the next and getting a fire going before he could get to them. Blackwell skipped ahead several aisles to get ahead of her and circle back.

"Bed! Now!" Serena said. Ivy needed no encouragement to put distance between herself and the growing fire. Serena limped along behind, ducking around an aisle of cases and going prone. If Blackwell behaved as anticipated, he'd round the corner, see Ivy running for his bed, and focus on her.

"This won't stop me!" Blackwell shouted. "Activate fire suppression system!"

His words triggered something in the ceiling. Most of the panels that weren't lights slid open, revealing nozzles like the ones in the trap outside the room. Unlike that one, these sprayed a foam that battered and weakened her flames. When Blackwell passed, Serena waited a few seconds, then stood and ignited the carpet behind him, trapping them all in a small portion of the room. It wouldn't hold for long, but would have to be enough.

Where were Pik-Pik and Tik-Tik? She'd lost track of them in the chaos.

Ivy had the computing matrix in her hands and had scooted all the way to the headboard. Her gaze remained locked on Blackwell as the Akakami hopped onto the bed and crawled towards her.

Ivy didn't do anything about it.

Come on Ivy. Don't panic on me now. Surely, surely she understood why Serena wanted her near the most wooden thing in the room. She had to.

A sound like cracking rock came from the right side of the bed. Then another from the left. Pik-Pik and Tik-Tik each clung to the side of one of the giant carnivore skeletons. Both listed at an angle, tilting towards the bed.

<Take this, asshole!>

<Nobody hurts our friends!>

The ants finished biting through the legs of the skeletons, felling them with the precision of expert lumberjacks directly onto Blackwell, while avoiding Ivy completely. They'd calculated it so perfectly, the skeletons didn't even strike each other on the way down. Pik-Pik and Tik-Tik jumped clear at the last moment before impact. Ivy sprang to her feet. Vines erupted from the thick canopy bed posts and from the sides below the mattress, creating a net pinning Blackwell in place beneath the skeletons.

Ivy jumped up and down a couple times over Blackwell's pinned body. "It is secure," she said.

Blackwell roared with frustration. "In other circumstances, I'd be pretty aroused right now," he said, struggling in vain to free himself. "Wine and bondage games on demand. You could have been my favorite familiar."

"I must decline your generous offer," Ivy said. Her tone was neutral, but Serena *swore* she detected sarcasm. Perhaps Ivy had a sense of humor after all, in her own way. Too bad they didn't have more time to gloat over their victory.

Blackwell's fire suppression system had done its job, dousing Serena's flames. Vents in the ceiling pulled away the smoke. Ivy led them back to the clock that blocked the entrance to Blackwell's secret passage, which Pik-Pik and Tik-Tik then ripped apart with the enthusiasm of starving termites. Since Ivy had been in here before, she led the way out.

"Pik-Pik, Tik-Tik, you were great," Serena said. Both were shaking.

<We tried to kill you.>

<We didn't want to!>

<The mean lady made us do it!>

<We're so, so sorry!>

<We hate fighting!>

<Blackwell had to be stopped!>

"I'm not mad at you," Serena said. "That wasn't your fault. You were a big help with Blackwell." At that moment, her legs gave out on her. Serena leaned into the fall and rolled, coming to rest with her back against one of the passage's side walls. She tried to push herself to her feet, but her legs were done. Just absolutely done. They didn't care what she thought anymore, they weren't moving.

Ivy turned and helped Serena to a sitting position. Green energy radiated from her palms. "You overexerted yourself. Again. You must cease this habit. I may not always be around to save you."

Serena snorted. Ivy had indeed bailed her out a few times now. She'd helped Ivy in kind. Hopefully they never started keeping score. "Focus on my legs. I can't walk."

Ivy pressed her hands against Serena's legs, massaging the muscles while her magic worked its way into her tissues. It hurt and yet at the same time felt so, so good, like a troublesome cramp falling away into sweet, sweet relaxation.

Serena reactivated her earring. "Cypher, we have the matrix. We'll be heading out momentarily."

"You're still alive!" Cypher said. "I'm so relieved. You shouldn't have cut me off like that. I've been a wreck over here. Blackwell's party is falling apart. I think the audience can tell something's gone seriously wrong. Lots of restless energy. Annea must have concluded her business, because I can't see her in the crowd."

"Are we going to have any problems with security?"

"I doubt it," Cypher said. "I can't find any evidence Blackwell told his rank-and-file security forces about the hidden path you're in. Hurray for the paranoia of the rich, am I right? Half of his security forces are still tied up in the auditorium on crowd control, the other half spreading out through the staff areas of your cube, either locking things down, or working on opening Blackwell's bedroom door. You must have broken it pretty good. Guests are free to leave whenever they want, so as long as you're out of there before anyone finds Blackwell, you're home free. Find a crowd and try to blend in or look like you belong."

Serena sighed with relief. All the same, she hoped they didn't run into security on the other side of the hidden passage. She might still have Lorelai's blood on her back, and her clothes were still wet. She had no interest in trying to explain any of that. Ivy's magic was doing the job. In another minute or two, she'd be fine walking again. As soon as they got out of here, she'd see if Ivy could help Tako too. He was safe enough for now.

"Thanks for the update," she said. "If Annea gets back before we do, tell her I demand some sleep before we pay Dr. Venture a visit."

"Can do. I'll see you soon."

Satisfied their escape was as secure as it could be, Serena turned her attention to Tako, probing at him gently with her mind. Not hard enough to risk waking him, but enough to get a sense of his condition. He felt frail, battered, and weak. For the first time, Tako's comments about his age really struck home to her. He wanted to be her partner on adventures through the multiverse, but she'd get him killed if she wasn't more careful.

Thank you, Tako, for helping bail me out of a tough spot yet again. You've been a great partner. A calming influence went I needed one. A balm against the ragged edges of grief. I promise I'll be a better host to you, and that we never do anything this reckless again.

It felt like a promise she couldn't keep.

CHAPTER 46

WE NEED TO TALK

"This isn't bacon," Serena said, staring at the rectangular bars of lime green, gelatinous material on the paper plate Annea handed her. Each had a stick embedded in it to make it easier to pick up and eat while walking. "Bacon comes from pigs. I understand I don't know much about the greater multiverse, but there's no reality where this came from a pig." Her plate was piled as high as Annea's and Cypher's combined, given her need to eat extra to account for Tako. Ivy hadn't wanted any.

"Zentrakkian bacon is one of the best travel foods I've ever discovered," Annea said, taking a bite from one of her bars. Around the mouthful of food, she added, "It's filling, high in protein, and easy to prepare and store. There were times during my Wandering Decade that I was living on this stuff for weeks."

"I'll take your word for it," Serena said. "But this isn't bacon."

Annea handed the four-armed gorilla preparing and serving the "bacon" several coins in payment, then motioned for the group to follow her to the subway platform.

Serena and Ivy had escaped Blackwell's domain the night before without further incident, arriving back at the inn to discover Annea waiting for them in their room, pacing back and forth with barely contained nervous energy. Serena felt a sense of pride she'd managed to remain conscious long enough for them to swap notes. Kimori had pledges of support from the Ankora and the Chiroptera. Both had Kimori's Planar Gate address and would be sending their first batches of troops today. Annea escorted Patrick Evans to safety, avoiding battle with the rogue Weavers pursuing him. Serena and Ivy retrieved the computing matrix. Everyone survived their missions. Huzzah.

"Feeling alright back there?" Serena asked Tako. They'd both received healing from Ivy and slept the deep, dreamless sleep of the dead. She felt mostly recovered from their battle with the Akakami and his familiars.

Tako, however, was as sullen as he'd ever been. He had the aura of someone hungover and recovering from a bar fight. *"I'll be fine,"* he said. *"I'm just old. Very, very old. I can't recover as fast as I used to."*

"How old are you?" Serena asked, realizing she didn't know Tako's age.

"I'm almost twenty-one years old."

"That's not old! I'm older than you." He'd always felt like a grandfather figure to her. A weird, shapeshifting, mind-reading, cephalopod grandfather. Someone both old and wise and young at heart. She didn't know what to do with the knowledge she was older than him.

Tako sighed. For the first time in their relationship, Serena felt *she* needed to be the mental health counselor for *him*. Not how she'd prefer to start the morning, but she did right by her friends. *"Do you, you know, want to talk about it?"*

The Octari laughed, some equanimity returning to his presence in her mind. *"Oh my. What a mess I must be if it's role-reversal time. We do need to talk, but not now. We have a busy day ahead."*

"Wow, we really ARE in role-reversal mode. 'We'll talk about it later' is MY line." They had plenty of time to chat before they'd arrive at Dr. Venture's lab. If Tako wanted to put it off, he'd have to try a lot harder than that. *"I've learned if there's anyone in the multiverse I can talk to about anything, it's you. For once, let me return the favor."*

"Very well. I'm an old man, Serena," Tako said again. *"No Octari has ever lived more than twenty-five years. Most Octari my age have already retired to the sea to live out their days tending to children too young to bond. Some of us receive permission to take a mate and reproduce, while the rest eventually move into elder care facilities until we die.*

"I... I wasn't ready to bid goodbye to partnering with humans. I felt like I still had a good year or two left in me. King Lordran's insistence that you partner with an Octari represented my last, best chance to bond with someone. I'm so grateful to Zalinda for presenting me with the opportunity, and to you for agreeing to host me. After we came back with

the leviathan pearls, we were supposed to say our goodbyes and go our separate ways.

"As someone who's never been off Torbakhal, your mission provided me an opportunity to see other realities. You would be my vehicle for a grand adventure to explore places most Octari and their hosts only dream about. I thought the grief and despair you fight so hard to keep at bay would motivate you to keep me around. And so, I selfishly capitalized on your emotional state and asked you to take me offworld with you."

Remorse and shame radiated from Tako, filling her mind with a strong sense of regret. Did he genuinely believe he was using her? She didn't buy it. No way. He'd never manipulated her into anything. She enjoyed his company. She'd been happy to continue their partnership. At no point had she ever thought Tako was taking advantage of her or working against her best interests. This remorse had to be a smokescreen for something else. The curtain between their minds felt thicker than usual.

"Selfish? Come on. You've helped me so much. I'm grateful to have you with me," Serena said.

Whatever concern Tako was dancing around, it'd be nice if he just said it already. She'd gotten through the awkwardness and loss of privacy that came with him being attached to her skin *at all times.* She'd come to understand the symbiotic relationship between the humans of Z'han and their Octari partners. Not only did Tako have access to her memories, he had a front row seat to every thought she'd had since they met. The kind ones. The petty ones. The angry ones. The insecure ones. She'd never bothered trying to prevent thoughts from filtering through the curtain between their minds, and not once had he expressed discomfort over it or tried to mentally distance himself. He scrubbed the hard-to-reach places when she bathed, for Alainna's sake. After all that, how could any topic be too uncomfortable for him to handle?

Sensing Tako needed a moment, she worked up the nerve and took her first bite of the gelatinous Zentrakkian bacon. The texture was thicker and grainier than its appearance led her to expect, more like bread than gelatin. "This really *does* taste like bacon."

"Right?" Annea smiled. "Now eat up, we have a big day ahead of us."

"Yes, Mother." The disconnect between appearance, texture, and the taste would take some getting used to, but she'd eaten far worse.

Tako took the mental equivalent of a deep breath and carried on. *"If we survive the Vohr invasion of Kimori, I will be returning to Z'han with Amara and Cole."*

"What? Why?" Was she a bad host? Had he spent too much time in her head and couldn't take it anymore? She'd thought it impossible he could surprise her to any great degree, but the words felt like a punch. She choked down an unexpected swell of emotion. She would *not* be the woman crying for no apparent reason on a crowded subway platform.

Warm reassurance flooded her mind like sunshine over tranquil waters. *"You've been a good host and friend. I wouldn't have asked to hitch a ride if that wasn't the case."* Tako sighed — a deep, reluctant concession to the inevitable. *"Serena, I'm dying."*

"No, you're not. We got beat up, but you're going to be fine," Serena said.

Tako carried on like she hadn't spoken, his explanation clinical. *"As Octari age, our bodies become less efficient at absorbing nutrients from our hosts. You'd have to eat even more to sustain me, and a lot of that excess would be retained by your own body."*

"So I'll have to exercise more. Or maybe I put on a little weight for a while. Neither sounds great, but those are inconveniences I'm willing to live with."

"Octari cognition declines as we age. We begin to exhibit symptoms similar to dementia in humans. Those symptoms bleed over into the host, impairing their functioning too."

"Okay," Serena said, feeling her insides twist as she tried to digest all the implications of hosting an elderly Octari. *"So we'll have some rough patches. We're still two brains working towards one goal. I'm sure I can help pick up the slack."*

"There's more," Tako said, sounding embarrassed. *"Our bodies eventually start releasing toxins from our pores. In the ocean, this part of the aging process is harmless, since the water dilutes it. If attached to a host, that toxin builds up, causing nausea, vomiting, dizziness, and hallucinations. It can be fatal to a host."*

His comment about selfishness made sense now. He'd known all of this would be coming, but he hitched a ride with her anyway. *"Is any of what you just said happening already?"* Serena asked, her tone flat.

"I'm going to need you to eat all of that bacon," Tako said. *"Everything else is months away from being a problem. Maybe even a year. My mind is sharp. The dementia hasn't started. That would be the sure sign I need to return to Torbakhal's oceans."*

The bacon sat like a rock in her gut as she weighed all the good he'd done for her against a mounting sense that he'd been using her after all. He was an old man who felt cheated out of the time he should have had as a partner when his prior hosts met untimely ends. He'd been willing to risk her health to have one last adventure... *"You knew this whole time, and —"*

"I can't be the first elderly person you've ever met who made poor health choices," Tako interrupted. *"I was sure the onset of symptoms was a year or more away, not weeks or days. The stress of our recent fights has proven me wrong. I'm too frail. I'm not metabolizing food as well as I should. I never meant to expose you to this part of the Octari life cycle. I'm sorry. Genuinely. I need to go home before my presence does you real harm."*

The group waited silently for the subway to arrive, everyone seeming to understand without words that she was in the middle of something with Tako. When the train pulled into the station, she shuffled along behind the rest of the group as they packed into a car full to bursting with beings making their morning commutes. A station attendant stood outside the subway car doors, gently moving the arms, tentacles, wings, and other appendages of those near the doors to help ensure everyone fit inside and that the doors would close.

Tako's guilt and remorse made it clear he felt selfish for coming with her to the Nexus. That much was true, but their minds had been linked too long for her to believe that was the whole story. Tako would sacrifice himself for her in a heartbeat, if he had to. She was sure of that. It wasn't like he was stuck to her. He could hop off well before dementia disrupted her life, or toxins made her sick. This time, he really was trying to manipulate her, wasn't he? He wanted to create some distance between them, to make her hate him a little bit, to make their inevitable separation less painful.

He was still trying to protect her, even if it was from himself.

Serena wrapped an arm around a pole for balance while she ate her remaining bacon with joyless efficiency. She didn't even taste it. In place of the expected anger, she only felt pity for Tako. Was it so wrong to want one last grand adventure before succumbing to old age? To want to spend more time with a human partner when his last ones died too soon? Could she honestly say she'd have done things differently in his position? He'd been nothing but good to her, and now he wanted to rectify what he saw as a lapse in judgment before things got bad for both of them.

With Alterra now a Vohr-infested hellscape cut off from the Planar Gate network, Serena could count the number of friends she had on one hand. She wasn't about to give up on any of them easily.

"Tako, I need you to do a couple things for me," Serena said.

"Yes?"

"Keep me in the loop on how you're feeling, OK? No more surprises."

"Done," he agreed.

"Second: As your host, I have a say on when the side effects get to be too much. You don't get to make unilateral decisions about what my body can handle. Do you hear me?"

"Yes, but—"

"But nothing. It's less than a day's hike from the Torbakhal Planar Gate to the oceans of Z'han. It'll be easy to send you home if we need to."

"WHEN you need to," Tako insisted.

"The multiverse is vast, right? Billions, maybe trillions of realities? We can figure something out once Kimori is safe. A solution is out there."

"What do you want to do? Scour the multiverse for a cure for old age?" He sounded amused, not patronizing. *"The only people able to pull that off are the Akakami, and I think we pretty well burned our bridges with the only one we've met. I wouldn't want to live off someone else's lifeforce anyway."*

"That's a problem for another day," Serena said. *"Just promise you'll stick around long enough for us to at least try."*

"Very well," Tako said. *"I respect your right to make informed decisions about how much you can handle. Maybe a cure does exist. Wouldn't that be a discovery for the ages!"*

On their first day together, Serena might have believed him. Now, she could read his lie as easily as any of the neon signs along the storefronts of Blackwell Plaza. He thought she was naive and in denial. That searching for a way to stop his aging was an impossible dream.

If he really wanted to go home, could she do anything to stop him?

Did she have any right to try?

CHAPTER 47

AN UGLY TRUTH

Serena ran a hand along the giant tank of the Aqueous Collective, watching fish, crustaceans, and cephalopods go about their work. They conducted scientific research with technologies so alien to her they defied comprehension. She wanted to find a way into the tank to grant Tako his wish to talk to the aquatic species within, but they both knew there wasn't time.

"We can't pause to admire the Collective," Annea said, correctly guessing the gist of her thoughts. "Blackwell no doubt has a bounty out on you two by now. Let's get the information we need and then get even further from his sphere of influence."

"If Blackwell's after us, is Dr. Venture safe?" Serena asked. "He knows where the data came from. What's to stop him from sending Lorelai or another of his agents here?"

"Niles Venture will be fine." The voice was human. Male. Not one she recognized. He stood by the elevator leading to Dr. Venture's "laboratory." He wore black robes stitched with a yellow spider's web pattern. Though the coloring was wrong, its style mimicked Orlan's attire. Long, gently curling brown hair ran past his shoulders. A trimmed beard and mustache framed his face.

"Everyone, this is Patrick Evans." Annea said. "I didn't think I'd see you again, especially so soon."

"I took a risk to come here," Patrick said. "If your data combined with Dr. Venture's really does show a pattern in the Vohr's attacks, I need to know about it, so I can help distribute that information as widely as possible."

"How do you know Dr. Venture is going to be fine?" Serena asked, not willing to let the matter drop. She didn't want an innocent being worse off because of their actions. She already carried enough anxiety over what Blackwell might do to his kitchen staff.

"I've already talked with him. He'll be making the positioning data public as soon as your analysis is complete. Blackwell would be able to access it, but so will everyone else. Without the benefit of exclusive control over it, that data is much less valuable to him. Going after Dr. Venture would only make him look weak and petty in the eyes of rival Akakami. His reputation has taken enough of a hit with his big party turning into a fiasco. He won't compound the error by harming an academic."

Pik-Pik and Tik-Tik stayed behind to *ooh* and *ahh* at all the aquatic species at work in the massive tank. Everyone else rode the elevator down to meet with Dr. Venture. The giant axolotl hovered at the entrance inside his transparent, water-filled tube. He looked drunk, the feathery tendrils on his head flying off in all directions or twisting around each other. His body leaned at an odd angle, with his right shoulder floating several inches above his left.

"Are you OK, Dr. Venture?" Serena asked. "You don't look well."

Dr. Venture blinked rapidly. "I haven't slept in days. This isn't a dream, is it? I thought the Weaver was lying to me. I don't trust human males unless they're shirtless."

"What a strange view of humanity he's formed from exposure to Lorelai's books," Tako said.

"It is not a dream," Ivy said. "We have returned with the computing matrix and wish to collect our payment."

"Yes, of course." Dr. Venture turned and gestured with one of his manipulator arms towards a table littered with parchment. It was set on an open patch of floor, allowing everyone room to stand around it. "Set it there. I'll need to run a diagnostic to confirm the device is still in good working order and that my data isn't corrupted. Then we can input your data and run the calculations."

Cypher set down the matrix, then retrieved his datapad from one of his many pockets, as well as a cable to link it to a port at the bottom of the matrix's central hub.

One of Dr. Venture's manipulator arms spun and retracted into the base of his floating tube. A different tool emerged in its place, this one shaped like a tiny spatula. He waved it over each crystal in the matrix, one at a time. The crystals flashed a pattern of three staccato bursts while being examined.

"The matrix is in good working order," he said. He hovered closer to examine the metal latticework linking the crystals. "However, there is blood on it. Why is there blood on it? *Whose* blood is on it?"

She didn't actually know. There were several possible candidates. "Don't worry about it," Serena said, thinking of Lorelai's unconscious body lying on the plush carpet of Blackwell's sanctum, a small shark clamped onto each arm. She'd been alive when Serena last saw her, but she couldn't say if the woman had survived her injuries. Or Blackwell's inevitable fury.

The axolotl stared at her for so long, she worried he'd press the issue. He blinked several times. Cocked his head from side to side. The voice box affixed to his floating tube uttered a long sighing sound, but no words.

Dr. Venture regained his composure and pressed the tiny spatula down on a button alongside the center crystal, causing an image of a giant cube to spring to life in the air above it. "This is the Nexus, the center of all creation. A giant cube of unknown origin, made up of trillions of smaller, interconnected cubes. If anyone has successfully calculated the size of the Nexus or produced an accurate count on the number of cubes within it, I've never heard about it."

The Nexus shrank to a quarter of its original size. Five of the six sides of the cube had nothing around them. On the sixth side, a constellation of small pinpoints of light filled the air.

"My research thus far has focused on realities on the closest side of the Nexus, relative to the cube we're in now. I haven't been able to establish connections with researchers in cubes far enough away to be oriented towards the other sides," Dr. Venture continued. "Information dissemination across the Nexus is scattered and slow, a problem the Weavers have been trying to mitigate for centuries now. Anyway, you may input your data."

Cypher plugged into the matrix and tapped away on his datapad's screen for a few moments. "Alright, it's done. I've sent over all the data I obtained from our sector government on the names of the realities overrun by the Vohr, and the times their

Planar Gates were cut off from the rest of the network. If I did this right, your computing matrix will start from the beginning and draw a line from one reality to the next."

The group waited in expectant silence while the computer sorted through the new data. With a swirl of color, the Nexus disappeared. The image zoomed in on one specific world. The word *Chikandarr* appeared above it in a bold script.

"Chikandarr was the first known victim of Vohr invasion, lost over ten years ago," Cypher said. "After that, another world fell every week or two, until Mallozzi, Alterra, and Ataraxia fell together."

The image shifted again, moving the orb representing Chikandarr closer to where Cypher stood, while a new orb appeared in the middle of the image. As he'd intended, the system drew a line connecting the worlds. *Alayo.* The line moved towards Ivy. *Shavayy.* It cut towards Annea. *Makallah.* Individual worlds shrank and names became too small for Serena to read as the computing matrix continued to calculate the invasion path. The path zigged and zagged all over the place, jumping across the multiverse with no apparent sense of direction.

As the graph reached two dozen entries, Serena's frustration boiled over. "We wasted our time," she said, "the Sector Council was right, there is no pattern."

"We have almost three hundred points of data to consider," Cypher said. The intensity of his gaze on the gradually expanding map suggested he thought he saw something. "Give it more time."

When the invasion path reached its sixtieth world, Serena thought she saw it too. "It's an inefficient course, but the Vohr seem to be heading in one general direction."

Dr. Venture tapped another tiny button beside the central crystal. Grid lines appeared over the constellation of worlds. "The grid boxes represent the different operational sectors of the Nexus."

"Their path is deliberate," Ivy said, reaching up to trace the line of conquest from one world to another with a finger. It crossed through the lines representing different sectors of the Nexus every two to four data points. "They conquer the fewest worlds necessary to move from one sector to the next. Total conquest is not the goal."

She waved a hand through a cloud of many worlds in the general vicinity of the invasion path that hadn't been harmed.

"If their goal is somewhere specific, why take such a winding route, rather than go right for it?" As soon as she voiced the question, Serena knew the answer. "By spreading the pain across as many sectors as possible, they reduce the odds of any one sector considering them a big enough threat to band together to fight back."

"Easy enough for Sector Councils to dismiss the problem if the Vohr only attack a few of the worlds that make up their territory," Cypher agreed. "And once the Vohr move on to another sector, it becomes someone else's problem."

Dr. Venture's data wasn't public yet. The only way this invasion path worked was if Korahshka already knew where realities were positioned relative to each other and which sector of the Nexus they belonged to, or he had a way to figure that out as he went. How could he know?

They watched in silence as the invasion line grew longer and longer. The map of the multiverse zoomed out to keep the entire warpath in view. Dread twisted Serena's insides. It took a moment to realize the emotions were Tako's, not her own. *"What's wrong?"*

"I know where they're going," Tako said. *"The Nexus. They want to breach the Nexus."*

Serena didn't want to believe him, but the direction of the path was becoming clear. Her mind went into overdrive thinking through the implications. *"If they do, they can cripple the center of multiverse governance and trade —"*

"And have a beachhead from which to spread like a cancer, devouring any civilization they wish," Tako said, finishing her thought. *"Coordinating organized resistance against them would be much more difficult without the Nexus to serve as a hub."*

Cypher's already pale complexion grew even more so. Annea looked weary, but determined. Ivy clutched her staff so hard Serena expected it to snap. They'd all figured it out too.

Nobody wanted to be the one to speak the truth into existence.

Wordlessly, they watched as the Nexus appeared in the frame. The Vohr's path of death and despair wound ever closer. When the line branched into three, Cypher tapped a command to stop the sequence. He zoomed in on the targeted worlds. Alterra. Mallozzi. Ataraxia. Their homes formed three points of a squat triangle, with Ataraxia at the top. Compared to the rest of the multiverse, their little corner of it looked sparsely populated, with only three other worlds in view at their current zoom level.

"Were our worlds the last to fall?" Serena asked.

"Unfortunately, no," Cypher said. "Two other worlds were closed off from the Nexus between when you left for Kimori, and when we reconnected." The computing matrix traced a line from Alterra to one of the remaining worlds in view, and from Mallozzi to another. Only one other world hovered in the image, forming the bottom point of a hexagon.

Kimori.

"After their initial attacks against Kimori failed, they decided to spread out," Annea said. "When the true invasion starts, they could be tunnelling in from five directions at once."

"Why bother?" Serena asked. "They know we know how to detect and destroy their tunnels. Wouldn't the path of least resistance be to go around Kimori and attack someone else?"

In response, Cypher made a gesture on his datapad that zoomed out the view slightly. He rotated it, finding an angle that best showed Kimori's position and distance from the Nexus.

"This is the proof we needed," Annea said, understating it. "I'll arrange an emergency meeting of the Sector Council when we get back to our home sector. When they see this, the whole multiverse will rally to our defense."

They'd have to.

Nothing stood between Kimori and the Nexus.

The last, best hope for the multiverse was a world of farmers, hunters, artists, and the few allies they'd collected holding the line where more than three hundred other realities had not.

The implications of failure were too horrifying to contemplate.

"We'll win." Tako sounded like someone trying too hard to stay cheerful in the face of devastating news. *"Somehow, we will win."*

"How can you be sure?" Serena asked.

"Because you're too stubborn to die."

Serena felt a tear slide down her cheek as she laughed. His calming presence blunted the worst of the panic threatening to overwhelm her. Her friends looked at her with concern, but sensed she and Tako were having a moment and didn't intrude. *"Thank you for that."*

"As long as we live, there's hope," Tako said. *"Korahshka's used to wielding the Vohr against worlds fending for themselves. Worlds that had no advanced warning. He has no idea what it's like to face a united enemy, or one who's had time to prepare defenses. We have allies now. We'll have a whole lot more tomorrow. We know what's at stake if we lose. Korahshka probably thinks he can roll over Kimori with ease. He is mistaken."*

Tako's optimism assumed that the Vohr hadn't razed Kimori to a smoking ruin while they ran around seeking help. That Kimori still had a functioning Planar Gate and wasn't exiled from the rest of the multiverse. Korahshka had said they'd have a few days, but she knew better than to trust him, even if he claimed to want her there when it happened.

Serena couldn't shake the sense they were almost out of time.

CHAPTER 48
A VISION OF THE FUTURE

The remainder of the day blurred by as everyone tried to mitigate their anxiety in their own ways. Kimori's defense was no longer about protecting a single world — they were the last line of defense between the Vohr and the Nexus itself. Serena couldn't comprehend the number of souls depending on them to be the wall the Vohr broke against.

Every time that thought hit her, she wanted to vomit. She wanted payback for Alterra, but not like this. How could anyone function with the weight of the multiverse on their shoulders?

"It's not," Tako said, inserting himself into her train of thought. *"We're burdened with a grand cause, true, but it's not up to us alone. The Kingdom of Z'han provided us with the Shrikes they could spare. You saw what those are capable of. The Ankora and Chiroptera are sending armies. Let Annea worry about the big picture. She's been doing that for more than double your lifetime."*

When they reached their home sector, Annea only stuck around long enough to hand Serena and Ivy a small sack of coins before disappearing into the N.E.S.T. building to make the arrangements necessary for an emergency meeting with the Sector Council. She sent Pik-Pik and Tik-Tik back to Kimori to relay what they'd learned about the Vohr's invasion path.

Serena engaged in retail therapy, buying a few books she hoped she'd live long enough to read, and stuffing her face with anything that seemed tasty.

Ivy followed Serena around, saying little, buying nothing. For a woman who didn't seem particularly fond of physical touch, she stuck very close to Serena's side. She chose not to say anything about it, fearing calling attention to it would make Ivy self-conscious and pull away.

Cypher retreated to his room to do research, saying he felt most calm while in the pursuit of knowledge. "I want to figure out how the quarantine works," he'd said. "Who or what in the Nexus has the power to disconnect Planar Gates from the network? Can that process be reversed? Call me paranoid, but we're about to admit to the Sector Council that Kimori has a Vohr problem. If some bureaucrat decides to get overzealous, I'd love to be able to override them."

They reunited for a group dinner and made plans to meet in the N.E.S.T. lobby the following morning to head off for the Council meeting. After everything they'd been through, it almost felt like a normal afternoon and evening, but she'd been too rattled to truly enjoy it.

At 3am the following morning, Serena sat at a table in the rainforest lobby of the N.E.S.T building, people watching. She found herself simultaneously tired and wired, a combination that made sleep impossible. She'd gone to her room, changed clothes, and flopped down on the bed, staring at the ceiling for an hour before giving up on it and deciding she needed a change of scenery.

A family of four played a game involving kicking a fist-sized ball and keeping it up in the air. They all had dark pink skin and lavender hair. Short, rounded nubs of bone grew above each of their eyes. When they laughed, she caught a glimpse of two rows of teeth. The parents and children looked like they didn't have a care in the world, passing the ball back and forth while counting how many times they kicked it before someone missed and it fell to the ground.

They didn't know that the safety of the Nexus depended on one world fending off legions of monsters. They didn't know that if Serena and her friends failed, they'd be eviscerated at best, turned into corrupted monsters like Moogi at worst.

It'll be fine. She had to believe that. No rational beings could review the data they had and not be moved to aid Kimori. It explicitly served their own self-interest to do so. She didn't have to hope for any sudden attack of nobility from a group that seemed content to do nothing. Kimori just needed to hold out for one more day.

A buzzing sound from the marketplace outside the N.E.S.T. took her focus away from the family. She knew that sound. The drone of hundreds of wings beating at once, like a swarm of bees defending their hive. Manti.

Impossible. They couldn't be here already!

She sent a mental probe to Tako, finding the place he occupied in her mind empty. His absence actually filled her with relief. He wasn't around in her dreams. She must have fallen asleep after all, either in her room, or here in the N.E.S.T. lobby. And since magic didn't work across realities, this had to be a product of her own imagination.

Feeling greater confidence, she ventured outside the N.E.S.T building, finding the area unrecognizable. The floor and walls were coated with a mossy green and purple substance. Whatever enchantment powered the cube's artificial sky was gone, exposing a bare metallic ceiling. Manti prowled the floor, patrolling between egg clutches, each egg large enough to entomb an adult human in the fetal position. Other manti clung to the walls like horse-sized spiders. This group remained motionless, perhaps asleep.

Serena channeled energy to her palms to be ready if the manti wanted a fight, but the bugs only gave her a disinterested glance and returned to their patrols. The elevator platform at the end of the cube still worked, so Serena used it to explore. She couldn't articulate why, but she felt the need to check out the transit cube, as if the local hub of multiverse travel would also be the heart of the Vohr inclusion into the Nexus.

Every stop on the journey was another flavor of nightmare.

The cube that behaved like an arid desert was now a twisted maze of glass pillars, as if all the sand had been blasted by lightning at once. The next cube up still had humid air and pools of water everywhere, but where harmless looking amphibians had dwelled before, she saw giant snakes and frogs, all mutated into living weapons with poisonous quills and needle-like fangs. The aviary cube contained hundreds of eagles, each with purple-and-black feathers and dead eyes.

This is a hell of a stress dream, Serena thought. *I didn't think my imagination was strong enough to design Vohr monsters Orlan never mentioned in his briefing.*

The transit cube looked like a twisted parody of its former self. Vohr tunnels stood in place of Planar Gates, with legions of troops queued up for transit. She saw reapers, corrupted dryads, and dozens of monster species she hadn't encountered before. Like the manti in their nest, the monsters paid her no mind.

Serena pinched her nose shut against an overpowering stench of blood and rotting meat. Reapers crowded around a pile of bodies between a pair of tunnels, gorging themselves on the corpses of fallen humans, centaurs, and minotaurs. She dashed past them and through large double doors into another cube. Following an impulse she didn't understand, she meandered down a series of hallways until she arrived at a door marked SECTOR COUNCIL CHAMBER C.

As the seat of governance for a region of the multiverse that could contain a thousand worlds, she'd expected something far grander than the room she walked into. The council chamber reminded her of a courthouse, with an unadorned, elevated desk at the back of the room, wide enough for a panel of seven people. There were a hundred wooden chairs taking up the rest of the room, half of them filled with Davoh'rei. Korahshka sat alone at the elevated desk.

"I'm pleased with your progress so far, my friends. Once Kimori's conquest is complete, our focus going forward is twofold. We must locate and destroy all six cornerstones. If we don't, we won't be breaching the heart of the Nexus in our lifetimes. Derok'tar and Nergitsune's divisions will handle that. Xenosharr and Kalinandra's divisions will locate the heart of the Nexus so we're ready to storm it once its protections are gone." Korahshka paused when he noticed her standing in the shadows at the doorway. An unexpected expression flickered across his face: surprise.

"We'll cover the details later. You all know your duties. Dismissed." Korahshka waved a hand. The other Davoh'rei exploded into puffs of purple and black smoke. He glared at Serena.

"You're not supposed to be here." He waved a hand again, and the desk he'd been sitting at vanished.

"I could really do without these stress-induced dreams," Serena said.

Korahshka laughed. "You think this is your dream? No, Serena. It looks like when I summoned my agents for a report, you got swept up in the call. You're in *my* head this time."

"That's impossible," Serena said. "Magic doesn't operate across realities. You'd either need a Vohr tunnel leading into the Nexus already..."

"Which I don't have."

"...or be in the Nexus yourself." That couldn't be possible, right? If Nexus staff had standing orders to quarantine any world with a Vohr presence, sealing them off from the Planar Gate network, how could he get here?

Korahshka smiled. "The quarantines were never about keeping the Vohr out of the Nexus," he said. "The Planar Gates treat them as a biohazard, a sickness to be eradicated. Any Vohr I send through a Gate would be vaporized instantly. That's why we've had to tunnel our way across the multiverse for the last decade. No, the quarantines are about keeping anyone else from coming in. They're about protecting our flanks from reprisals and counterattacks."

"You're saying the quarantines were your idea?"

"Of course. Most intelligent beings across the multiverse are all too willing to enact burdensome, unnecessary, and ineffective measures for a perceived safety benefit. We've had no trouble getting sectors to go along with it, and recommending their neighbors do the same. We've been playing this game for a decade now. It works every time."

"But how did *you* get to the Nexus?"

Korahshka snorted. "The same way you have, I'm sure. Intermediaries. Every once in a while, at times of our choosing, the quarantine protocols experience brief... hiccups. I travel from a conquered world to somewhere else, and from there to the Nexus. Anyone looking into it here would never know a quarantined Gate was used."

While she couldn't be sure he spoke the truth, she had to assume the worst. Annea needed to know Davoh'rei operated freely in the Nexus. Some probably held positions of power, if they could set Planar Gate policy across whole sectors.

She had to wake up.

Serena pinched herself. When that didn't work, she slapped herself in the face as hard as she could. Then she tried jumping up and down. As she ran through her list of cliche actions that were supposed to help someone wake themselves from a dream, Korahshka watched, an amused expression on his face. He made no move to interfere.

"I told you; you're in my dream. My vision for the future of the Nexus. I decide when you get to leave. That stunt you pulled in our first meeting won't work again, but you're welcome to try it." He spread his arms wide, giving her the shark-toothed smile of a man satisfied his work was done. "You're going to miss your Council meeting, I'm afraid. How would you like to pass the time? Do we chat? Do you want to try to fight your way out of here? Entertain me."

CHAPTER 49

TAKO'S RUDE AWAKENING

Tako stretched as he woke, pushing his limbs free from Serena's back to twist through the air. With one tentacle, he gathered the sheet he'd knocked loose, pulling it up to cover the majority of Serena's back. With another, he slapped at the clock on the nightstand, triggering it to display the time in glittery gold numbers in the air.

Odd. Serena usually woke up before he did. She wasn't one to sleep in, especially on important days like this. But as he had the thought, he realized he had a problem.

Serena was *gone*.

Tako spent the majority of his life bonded to humans. He knew what it was like to be awake while his host slept. Serena's mind wasn't in a sleep state.

It wasn't there at all.

No. No no no. Not again. This can't be happening AGAIN. He felt a rare emotion overcome him: panic. His three hearts raced. He'd outlived two hosts already. That wasn't supposed to happen to an Octari. What horrible deeds had he done to deserve losing a third in one lifetime? Was he cursed? Was he a bad partner? Was this somehow his fault? Young women like Serena didn't just die in their sleep.

He knew their time together would be ending soon, but it couldn't end like *this*.

Tako extended all of his limbs and pushed hard against the mattress, rolling Serena from her stomach onto her back. One of her arms flopped over the side. He ignored everything his mental connection told him and checked her vitals. She had a strong pulse on her neck. Her chest rose and fell with regular breaths.

Serena was still alive.

Panic faded into dread. It wasn't much of an improvement, but at least he could think. Something of Serena's mind remained. Her body continued doing what it had to do to keep her alive, but her intellect, emotions, memories, and personality were gone. Their absence left him feeling like he was perched at the edge of a deep ocean chasm, surrounded by darkness and nothing else.

"Serena, wake up!" He shouted, knowing it would be useless. He bombarded her with every form of mental shake, slap, and tickle he could think of through their bond. He might as well have been flailing at empty air.

Nothing out of the ordinary had happened after their arrival at the N.E.S.T. They'd all checked into available rooms, formed their plan for today, said their goodnights, and gone to sleep. Serena had been fine through all of that. When did everything go wrong?

Tako closed his eyes and settled into a light meditation designed to boost memory recall. He recalled their entire time travelling through the Nexus subway system. He hadn't seen anyone casting strange spells or using abilities he didn't understand. Nobody had touched Serena beyond the incidental contact natural to over-crowded cars. He sifted through his parents' memories, as well as everything he'd ever learned about human and Octari partnerships. As far as he knew, no Octari had ever been partnered with someone whose mind went completely blank.

He needed help. Whatever this was, it was outside his experience. He needed someone more knowledgeable about magic in general. The Weaver, Patrick Evans. Or perhaps Annea encountered something similar in her journeys across the multiverse.

Tako crawled across Serena's skin, plopped down to the floor from her dangling arm, then headed for the door. Annea had a room two doors down the hall on this same floor. Since she was closest, he'd try her first.

Irritation manifested itself as rapidly shifting colors across his skin. The gap between the floor and the bottom of the door was only an inch. Octari had no bones. The only hard part of his body was his beak-like mouth. If he had to, he could flatten himself and squeeze through to the other side, but with that small a gap, the process would take longer than he wanted, and it'd leave him vulnerable. Who knew how someone would react if they came upon him oozing out from under the door? He could get hurt if someone thought him a dangerous monster.

Tako used his rear limbs to push his body up the door as high as possible, then reached for the doorknob. He could just touch it, but didn't have enough limb to wrap around it or get any traction.

You can do this, Tako. On the rare occasions where he felt stress, he liked to bombard himself with positive affirmations to get through it. *You are a good partner. Zalinda spent a long time seeking out another partner for you because she believes in you. Serena likes you. She likes you so much she thinks she'll find a cure for aging so you can spend more time together. You are smart. No door is going to defeat you. You will find help for Serena. YOU WILL.*

He looked about the room for anything he could use, feeling a flash of inspiration when he remembered the chair set beside the room's desk. Like Pik-Pik and Tik-Tik, he could lift more than his body weight. Dragging that chair across the room wouldn't be too difficult. If he placed it near the door and climbed it, he'd be able to reach the knob. He only needed to open the door a few inches to be able to get out with ease.

Tako scuttled across the floor, his skin again changing colors rapidly, but these were brighter hues signifying hope and determination. He wrapped a limb around a chair leg and tugged, careful to keep it upright so it wouldn't fall over. Trying to set it right again would be a pain. Getting squished wouldn't be any fun either.

He continued his litany of positive affirmations, not allowing himself a moment for self-doubt or negative thinking. *You are strong. A mere chair is nothing next to your might. No door can ever hold you back. You WILL find help. Serena will be OK.* The chair scraped its way six inches along the floor. Then a foot. Then two feet. Progress came more slowly than he'd expected, but the task was more awkward than difficult.

He switched limbs so he could move sideways and keep his eyes on Serena as he went. She had so much repressed anger. So much unprocessed grief. She possessed a classic volcanic temper. Serena buried the worst of the anger and hurt deep, letting the pressure build and build until she couldn't contain it anymore and she erupted. Yes, she'd gotten mad a few times recently. He'd seen her memories of her session in Annea's meditation chamber, and the battle in the Forest in the Sky. Those were small eruptions compared to the violence he knew she could unleash if she lost all sense of self-restraint. Blind rage awakened her pyromancy. He hoped she never went to that place again.

That won't happen, Tako assured himself, *not while she has me. We'll save Kimori and then finally process all those emotions. Together.*

He wanted more than anything for her to be happy and find peace. She had a good heart. How many other pyromancers could befriend a dryad? When she liked someone, she was all-in supporting them. She latched onto people *hard.* If anyone dared harm Ivy, Serena would tear them apart. She'd placed the dryad's needs above her own more than once already.

She's latched onto me too, he thought, *and deluded herself into thinking there's a cure for old age.* It was the denial phase of grief, of course. She'd have a very hard time letting go, when the time came. Hopefully, every friend she made would come to realize how lucky they were to have such a steadfast and loyal ally. He chuckled. *As long as they don't make her mad.*

Tako had the chair within two feet of the door when he heard a knock. "Serena, are you awake?" Annea asked. "We're leaving for our meeting with the Sector Council soon," she added when she didn't receive a response. "If you're not in the lobby in five minutes, I'm coming back."

Tako abandoned his plans for the chair and hurried back to Serena, using her dangling arm to climb back onto her skin. Relief washed over him. He didn't have to get help. Help would come to him. When Serena didn't show, Annea would know something was wrong. She'd have Estus open the door, then Tako could touch her and share what he knew of Serena's condition. No, that wasn't right. She'd probably kick the door down and pay for the damage, rather than spend time looking for the efreet, given their timetable and what was at stake.

Might as well try to learn as much as possible while waiting.

With Serena's consciousness gone, he found he could push forward into parts of her brain he shouldn't be able to access. Octari could share thoughts and memories, but had no ability to exert any control over a host's body.

Except now he could. His consciousness expanded outward, filling the abandoned spaces in her mind. Any time he came upon what felt like a lever to control some part of Serena's body, he grabbed it. Head. Neck. Arms. Torso. Legs. Feet. He felt like a puppeteer playing with an enormous marionette.

Conflicting emotions warred in his mind. Terror for Serena. The bizarre and unexpected thrill of realizing he could control her body in this state. The shame in knowing that doing such a thing was a deep betrayal of the bodily autonomy of his host. He hoped Serena wouldn't consider it a violation, given the circumstances. He only wanted to help. She would understand.

Tako spent several minutes working through the complicated mechanics of sitting her up at the edge of the bed. He understood the theory behind what he should do, but the human body was so alien to his own that actually executing the maneuver took all his concentration. After several false starts, he pulled it off.

Standing up was a whole different ordeal. Locomotion was so much easier with eight limbs. How did humans manage on two feet? It felt like they should be falling over all the time, yet they didn't. He swayed back and forth on wobbly legs like a sailor trying to right himself on rough seas. Overwhelmed with the task of maintaining his balance, Tako managed to sit Serena back down on the bed without falling over or bashing her head into a wall.

As he worked up the courage to try again, someone knocked on the door. "Come on, Serena, let's go," Annea said. "You know how important this is. What's with the delay?"

Talking! Words! Like everything else involving the human body, Tako's understanding was intellectual. A lifetime of observing humans talking to each other didn't mean he knew how to use a mouth to produce comprehensible language. *Annea, something terrible has happened to Serena. Her consciousness is gone.* He maneuvered Serena's mouth and tongue to produce the words.

The resulting gibberish sounded like the shrieks and cries of a dying cat.

"I know it's been a long few days. I wish I could sleep in too," Annea said, apparently interpreting the noises as Serena being grumpy, "but I need you to be alert for the presentation of our evidence."

Annea,   Serena   needs   our   help!
"Aaaaaaaaannnnnnnnneeeeeeeeeaaaaaaaaaaaa." This time, Serena's voice sounded like the wail of a tormented spirit. Progress! Moving lips, tongue, and mouth together was complex! How did humans do it and still have the mental bandwidth for anything else?

"Serena, are you okay in there?"

"H-H-Helllp. Help-p me-e. Help me." Despite the terrifying circumstances, Tako couldn't help but feel a swell of pride at starting to grasp mouth-sounds so quickly. His mind was still as sharp as an Octari half his age! He'd need all his focus today.

"I'm coming in," Annea said. As he'd expected, she broke through the door with two solid kicks. It knocked over the chair Tako had lugged across the room as it flew open. She walked in and stopped, clearly not expecting to see Serena sitting up on the bed, by all appearances perfectly healthy.

"Naught serene a," Tako said. "Sir Ina iz gaun. Thissss iz Tah Kou." He knew it sounded like drunken gibberish, with unnatural hitches and pauses between words, but he'd need time and practice to do better. They didn't have time. He didn't want practice. He wanted Serena back.

"I don't understand," Annea said, crossing over to the bed and crouching to be eye level with Serena.

Tako sighed, a gesture his host body replicated. He pushed out a tentacle and dangled it in the air between the two women. Annea would recognize it as a request to communicate with her mind-to-mind.

Annea took his tentacle in hand, and he pushed into her mind the memories of everything that happened since he'd woken up. Experiencing it from his perspective would be a far better explanation than trying to put it into words.

The elf gasped. She leaned forward to steady herself, placing a hand against the bed to Serena's left. "This is dream walker magic. It has Korahshka written all over it. But magic doesn't work across realities. He's got to be in the Nexus. How did he get here? Why attack Serena now? Does this mean Kimori has fallen in our absence?"

A single tear escaped Annea's best attempts at rigid emotional control. She wiped it away and stood, her bearing once again that of a wartime ruler — determined and regal. "No. Until we know Kimori is lost to us, we must assume it isn't. We should meet up with the others and figure out how we juggle helping you and Serena with getting the Council to aid Kimori."

Annea offered him a hand. Tako took it using Serena's hands, but wasn't ready for Annea to pull Serena to her feet. He wobbled, then fell forward into the elf's embrace. Annea carried Serena back to the bed. "I'm sorry," she said. "You showed me your memories, and I still thought you'd just know how to move a human body."

"Itz naht ee-zie. Not easy," Tako said, exploring the production of mouth-sounds while Annea pulled out a change of clothes for Serena, stuffing the rest into a bag. They'd come back for their belongings then return to Kimori as soon as they'd concluded their business with the Sector Council. He didn't know how Serena's absence would change that. "I donut un-der stained how yew ta-ta-tahk like thisss. Telly pathy iz butter."

"Yes, telepathy is better," Annea agreed, "but few people in the multiverse have such abilities." She stripped off Serena's pajamas and dressed her. Tako twisted and moved arms and legs to assist where he could, but Annea did most of the work, operating with the speed and detachment of someone dressing a bendable mannequin.

Tako ran a hand over the material of the shirt. It felt denser and heavier than cotton or wool, and was designed to survive the kind of heat Serena could generate. Could he access her pyromancy if he had to? He'd settle for just being able to walk.

"Ok, let's try this again," Annea said, pulling Tako to his feet more slowly this time. "It's time to teach you how to walk like a biped. I hope you're a quick study."

CHAPTER 50

STICKING TO THE PLAN

"**S**orry we're late," Annea said upon their arrival in the N.E.S.T. Lobby. "We have a new problem."

"Is she drunk?" Cypher asked, staring incredulously at Serena, who leaned heavily against Annea's side. The elf had an arm wrapped around Serena's waist to keep her steady. Tako knew how he must look, steering Serena around like she might vomit on someone at any moment. The uneven ground of the N.E.S.T's rainforest lobby didn't help matters. He'd be forever grateful he wasn't a biped.

"Naught Sir Ina," Tako said. He dragged a foot taking a step, causing Serena to pitch forward. Fast as lightning, Annea tightened her grip and helped him find his balance. She'd had to do that a lot over the mere ten minutes she'd allotted Tako for practice.

They had deadlines to meet, after all, and the Sector Council could not be kept waiting, no matter how much he wanted to pause everything until they had Serena back. The safety of an entire world took priority over one person, though he was sick with worry for his host. His friend.

"Serena's consciousness is gone," Annea said, explaining the situation so Tako wouldn't have to. "I suspect dream walker magic is to blame, considering it happened overnight. And we only know of one who would wish to harm Serena."

"Korahshka," Ivy said.

"Who?" Patrick Evans leaned against a tree just off the main path that ran from the N.E.S.T. entrance to its reception desk. He wore the same black robes shot through with yellowish webbing as the day before.

Annea gave Patrick and Orlan a quick summary of Serena's interactions with the mastermind of the Vohr invasion, his known capabilities, and his desire to add Serena's powers to his own. "During my Wandering Decade, I met a teacher who was a dream walker. She taught her students by pulling them into her dreams, where she could control every facet of the environment. She could show them moments from history as vividly as if they'd been there themselves. Her students were in a similar condition to this during the lessons. Alive, but seemingly braindead."

"There's a problem with your theory," Patrick said. "If Korahshka is indeed behind this, he'd have to be here in the Nexus."

"Or have tunneled in from Kimori," Ivy said.

"If that was the case, I'm sure we would have seen Vohr monsters by now, or at least signs of panic from the locals." Outside the N.E.S.T, they could see hundreds of beings going about their business, the same as any other day.

"Nough Pan Ick," Tako said.

"Let's say Korahshka's here," Patrick said. "How did he get here when every planet Vohr attack gets quarantined from the Planar Gate network?"

"An interesting question, but not our most pressing issue." Annea scooped up Serena and carried her to a nearby table. Tako was able to handle sitting down himself, though he would have knocked the chair over and tumbled backwards if Ivy hadn't been there to place a stabilizing hand on it. To Orlan and Patrick, she asked, "Do either of you know a way to forcibly extract Serena's consciousness from the dream and return it to her body?"

The two scholars looked at each other intently for a long moment, neither wanting to be the first to offer an opinion. Finally, Orlan broke the silence. "Taking her through a Planar Gate might resolve the issue."

"More likely it would kill her," Patrick said. "Traveling across realities would sever the magic that's called her soul away, leaving no way for it to return. If the body survived, I shudder to think where her soul would go. No, it's best she remains in the Nexus until she's been restored."

"From what I know of wraiths, Korahshka needs physical contact with Serena to take her powers. He can't do that while also holding her in a dream, which means the invasion of Kimori won't begin before Serena has returned to herself," Annea said.

"Perhaps he's holding her in this state to take her out of commission for the fight ahead," Cypher said. "He's attacked now to distract you and sideline her while someone else commands the Vohr during the battle."

"I suppose that's possible, but we don't have any evidence to suggest anyone else can command them."

"We don't have any evidence someone else can't, either," Cypher pressed.

"Fair enough, but from what Serena has told me, I don't think Korahshka's ego would allow him to step back and let someone else have the glory of conquering Kimori. The Davoh'rei have waited a long time for revenge after we kicked them and their master off our world many generations ago."

"You're making my arguments for me," Cypher said. "They're on the march to the Nexus, and Kimori is the last world in the way. It's wishful thinking to believe they'd pause for... whatever this is." He gestured with his prosthetic hand to Serena / Tako.

Annea shook her head. "It makes no sense to think Korahshka would sit out this battle to remove one human from the fight."

"He takes out Kimori's leader too, if you spend enough time trying to help her."

"Foe cuss!" Tako shouted, slamming a fist down on the table. His typical calm was nowhere to be found today. He'd never felt so wound up and anxious. He hated it. "No arrr gue. Fix." His host, his *final* host, needed their help. And they needed to convince the Sector Council to send military aid to Kimori. There wasn't time to debate what Serena's disappearance meant. They needed *actions*, not *words*.

That's a very Serena way of thinking, he thought. He wanted to be a good influence on her, and was chagrined to see that *she* was having an influence on *him*.

"Sorry," Cypher and Annea said, both looking chastised.

"There's another option," Patrick said. "I would bet my membership with the Weavers that this kind of magic leaves behind a signature that can be tracked, if you know what to look for. The Weavers have people skilled in that sort of thing. Perhaps they could help us follow the thread of magic back to Korahshka. Find and wake him, and Serena would be free."

"No doubt he is guarded," Ivy said.

"Nothing I can't handle." Electricity arced across Patrick's fingers.

"You're still being hunted yourself," Annea said. "Are you sure you'd want to be responsible for Serena's safety, as well?"

"Leave Serena and Tako with Orlan and me. The rest of you should get to your meeting with the Sector Council. We'll rendezvous afterwards."

"That won't be possible," Annea said. "As a stipulation for taking this meeting on such short notice, and considering the nature of my demands, the Sector Council insisted on testimony from the refugees under my protection. Serena and Ivy both have to speak."

I wish you'd told me that earlier! How was he supposed to impersonate Serena and tell her story, when he could barely walk or form words? The ruse would be doomed before it even began. They'd see something was off and start asking questions he wasn't sure he could or should answer. *"Well, counselors, it turns out the leader of the Vohr horde may already be in the Nexus..."* If they believed him, they'd probably look to save themselves at that point, and any hope of securing more troops for Kimori would vanish.

Ivy looked like she'd eaten something sour. "Must we?"

"If they ask you to speak, then I'm sorry, but yes. Ivy, you'll have to speak for Serena too, so Tako just has to nod and agree. Hopefully, the proof of the Vohr's invasion path will render such testimony unnecessary." Annea turned around, presenting Tako with her back as she bent over.

"Wat iz... this?" Tako asked.

"I believe it's commonly referred to as a 'piggyback ride.' We need to get moving, or we'll be late for our meeting," Annea said. "We can continue this conversation on the way. Lean against my back. I'll carry you."

Tako stood and followed Annea's instructions, wrapping Serena's arms around the elf while she held Serena's legs behind the knees. The Sword of Kimori returned to her full height and led the group toward the exit. Serena's weight didn't seem to inconvenience her at all.

"When this meeting is over, I'm returning to Kimori, regardless of the result or Serena's condition," Annea said. "With Ankora and Chiroptera troops arriving, I need to be there to organize what forces we have and update the queens on what happened here. Orlan, would you be willing to temporarily coordinate with the Sector Council on my behalf if they need any additional information before sending troops?"

"I'd be honored to. Does anyone stepping through the Planar Gate need a special pass phrase so the drones know they're friendly?" Orlan asked. Given the reception Serena and Ivy received when they first arrived on Kimori, it was a reasonable question.

"No need. Under the circumstances, the ants know to assume anyone and anything arriving through the Planar Gate is friendly unless they prove otherwise." The group reached the elevator that would take them to higher cubes. Annea pressed the button for the transit cube.

"Patrick, I'm entrusting you with Serena and Tako in my absence. Hopefully you're right, and the spell Serena's under can be traced back to its source."

"She's safe with me," Patrick said.

"I will stay with Serena," Ivy said. "I am not a warrior, but no harm will come to my sister while I still live."

The weight of that comment didn't register with the humans, distracted as they were with their own thoughts. Its significance wasn't lost on Tako. The bond those two formed with each other made him happy.

Annea understood as well. She greeted Ivy's statement with a nod. "She's lucky to have you."

"Indeed," Ivy said.

Annea asked Patrick questions about who he would contact about magic tracing, talking about Serena and Tako as if they weren't riding on her back. He didn't enjoy that, but didn't know what he could say to advocate for himself. He didn't know much about magic other than his own, but he wanted to contribute. He needed to feel useful right now. Annea must have a lot of trust in the Weavers in general, and Patrick in particular, to entrust his and Serena's fate to a man evading his own enemies.

Unless, of course, her judgment was clouded. Was she so tunnel-visioned on protecting Kimori that it blinded her to other threats? Assuming Korahshka was indeed the cause of Serena's problems, that meant the enemy's leader was right here, in the Nexus. Yet Annea treated it as a secondary concern to proving Kimori needed military support from other realities. Wouldn't it be better to drop everything and go chop the head off the snake, right here, right now?

Lost in his thoughts, he didn't realize they'd passed through the transit cube and into a government administration cube until they stood before a thick set of wooden double doors, stained to look aged and distinctive. A sign to the right of the door read *Sector Council - Main Chamber.* Two men stood on each side of the door, all wearing layered leather armor. They had swords slung over their backs and some kind of pistol strapped to their hips. Whether they fired projectiles or energy bursts, Tako couldn't say.

Besides their party and the guards, the hallway was deserted. Suspiciously so. Rich tapestries depicting different worlds in the sector decorated the walls between each set of chamber doors. Tako had never known such art to be wasted in low traffic areas. Where were the bureaucrats running about on business, or local reporters documenting the happenings of government?

"They wanted to see you in the main chamber?" Patrick asked, his glances around the empty hallway mirroring Tako's misgivings. "That's an awfully big space to house a meeting for three people — six, if you include Cypher, Orlan, and myself."

A native of Z'han wouldn't have forgotten to include an Octari in the count. Tako took the omission as an oversight, not an insult.

Responding to a signal Tako couldn't perceive, one guard on each side of the double doors moved to open them. "The Council will see you now," one of them said, motioning the group inside.

Before they could cross the threshold though, the other guards stepped into their path. "You'll need to leave your weapons outside."

From his position on Annea's back, Tako couldn't see her expression, for which he considered himself fortunate. "I'm here to request aid for my world. Why would I want to harm the Council?"

"No weapons allowed inside, ma'am. I don't make the rules." As the guard stepped forward and reached for one of the kukris at Annea's waist, Tako prepared to be dropped to the ground, fully expecting the elf to break the man's wrist before letting him touch her weapons.

Instead, Annea twisted away from his reach with a dancer's grace. "I come with the support of two members of the Weavers. Do you mean to impeach the honor of their organization, which has done a lot of work for this Council over the centuries, by implying they would associate with an assassin?"

"No weapons in the Council Chamber. No exceptions."

A voice shouted from inside the chamber. "If she wanted me dead, it would have happened a long time ago. Let her keep her damn weapons!"

Ashen faced and chastised, the guard stepped aside to allow them admittance. Two of the guards followed a discreet distance behind them. The other two pulled the doors closed and remained outside.

The Sector Council's main chamber reminded Tako of the courtrooms of the Z'han navy, full of wood paneling on the walls and a hardwood floor. Nine beings sat behind an elevated desk, each wearing red robes that struck Tako as more religious than judicial. Three were human, the other six a mix of species he'd never seen before.

Jury boxes sat along both the left and right wall, each composed of three benches, with their own doors leading out of the chamber. Annea led them down a wide aisle that parted a sea of uncomfortable-looking metal chairs. At capacity, a thousand or more beings could fit in here.

At present, the entire population of the chamber consisted of the nine counselors, the two guards, and their group. He wasn't sure what kind of reception he'd expected, but it certainly wasn't this.

"Hold this for me," Cypher said, handing his datapad to Orlan. He grabbed his prosthetic wrist with his organic hand and twisted it. The motion released a small puff of gas from his wrist and elbow.

"What was that?" Orlan asked.

"Nothing," Cypher said softly, taking back the datapad. "Because we're going to have a nice, civil, *productive* chat with some of the most powerful people in this corner of the multiverse, and then we'll be on our way, safe and sound."

Tako hoped time proved Cypher correct.

For some reason, he doubted it.

CHAPTER 51
AN ANNOUNCEMENT

"**A**nnea Vantalos, it's wonderful to see you again. It's a shame it's not under better circumstances." The speaker was Valon D'Laris, a tan-skinned human who compensated for his bald head with a beard that extended to his waist. He looked younger and more vibrant than she'd expected, considering he had to be in his nineties. He'd been the one to say they could keep their weapons. Valon's smile was that of a politician at his warmest and friendliest, but Annea saw malice lingering in his eyes.

Valon was correct. If she'd planned on killing him, he'd have been dead decades ago.

That didn't mean she liked him.

"Valon D'Laris, I must admit I'm surprised to see you. But I could never forget a voice as stentorian as yours, nor your distinctive nose." His nose was long, thin, and as crooked as ever. She knew he hated it. "You're moving up in the multiverse, I see. How's the weather on Valaris this time of year?"

Valon schooled his emotions well, but Annea saw the twitch. "Balmy, no doubt. I represent Kalix now. The climate suits me better."

Translation: The people of Kalix weren't sick enough of his grift yet to do something about it.

Annea spent a year on Valaris as part of her Wandering Decade, and considered that year the most instructive on how *not* to rule a civilization. As she returned to the Nexus to choose her next destination, Valon's palace was burning to the ground while rioters looted everything they could carry. She'd always assumed the mob had hunted him down and executed him. While she'd had nothing to do with his downfall, she'd been a vocal opponent of his policies.

Kimori historically didn't engage in multiverse politics. They didn't even send a representative to fill the seat they were entitled to in this sector's senate. Annea had never bothered to learn who sat on the Council. She regretted that oversight now. Valon D'Laris ranked near the bottom of people she would want to have a say in Kimori's fate, but his aggressive brand of self interest might work to their advantage here.

Another of the counselors, a middle-aged human woman, pointed at Serena, still riding on Annea's back. "Is she well?"

"Serena's fine," Annea said, bending over to allow Tako to dismount. "She injured an ankle, so I've been carrying her around so she doesn't have to walk on it. Why don't you take a seat." She helped Tako sit down before returning her attention to the counselors.

"You wished to speak to us about the Vohr?" Valon asked, putting an end to any further small talk.

Prepared speeches weren't Annea's style. She thought through what she wanted to say, then went for it. "The commonly accepted view is that Vohr invasions are impossible to predict. They attack randomly, with no clear plan or motive. Despite more than three hundred worlds falling to the monsters and those worlds being sealed off from the Planar Gate network, there has been little collective will to study, contain, or eliminate the threat. That ends today.

"For more than a decade, the Vohr have been systematically marching across the multiverse with direction and intent. Every fallen world has brought them one step closer to their intended target: the Nexus itself."

"We assume you have proof for this sensational claim," said another of the council, a hairless elderly woman of a species Annea didn't recognize. She had pink skin lined with black tiger stripes. A nameplate before her identified her simply as Valathea.

"We do, counselors." Annea motioned for Cypher to step forward. "We met with an independent researcher of multiverse cartography. He's working to pinpoint every world's location in the aetherial sea relative to the Nexus. When we cross-referenced his data with the list of worlds sealed off from the Planar Gate network, the pattern became clear."

One of the counselors, a bipedal moose-like being named Grakk, shook his head in irritation. "That data hasn't been made public, in order to avoid inciting a panic. How do you know your data is legitimate? And if it is real, how did you come into possession of it?"

"That data's not hard to find if you know how to look," Cypher said. "Multiple sectors were involved, after all. You're not the only folks gathering information."

Annea smiled. It was a much better answer than *I hacked into your databases and stole it.*

"If this pattern is so clear, why haven't we seen it ourselves?" Valon asked.

"Multiverse cartography is a fringe field," Valathea scoffed. "Believing every reality has a fixed position in a cosmic soup of magic is absurd. Who is your source?"

Annea considered trying to keep Dr. Venture anonymous, but there'd be no point. He'd made it clear he planned to move forward with publishing his research on his own, even if he had to do it without the blessing of his organization. "The research comes from Dr. Niles Venture."

"Of what institute?" Valathea pressed.

Annea coughed. "The Aqueous Collective."

Four of the counselors laughed. The rest looked unamused. "You would have us make policy decisions that impact the nine hundred eighty-six worlds of our sector based on data from the laughingstock of the scientific community?" Asked another of the human counselors.

"The data checks out," Cypher said. He reached into a satchel at his side and pulled out a stack of papers clipped together. "I'm holding a hard copy of the invasion data. If you inspect it, I'm sure you'll see it matches your own. Dr. Venture also provided us with a briefing on his positioning research methodology, so you can see for yourselves how he figured it out. If that's not enough, we have peer reviews of his findings."

Annea prayed they wouldn't demand to have those documents studied by their own hand-picked group of scholars. There wasn't time.

"I've taken the liberty of reviewing it myself," Patrick said. He'd done no such thing, she was sure, but Annea appreciated the scholar's intervention. A Weaver's backing would lend their claims additional weight. "It's genuinely a breakthrough in our understanding of the multiverse. I anticipate a whole new discipline emerging in the Weavers to expand upon Dr. Venture's work."

"Dr. Venture is still preparing copies for dissemination through traditional means," Cypher said. "But for now, I have a copy we made during out last meeting with him."

"Very well. Show us what you have."

Cypher stepped closer to the Council bench and touched something on his datapad. It projected a hologram into the air, replaying the invasion path. He ran the playback at triple speed until they reached the final ten worlds. From there, he toggled forward through the data one entry at a time.

"As you can see," Annea said when the playback reached its conclusion, "the Vohr have been weaving their way across the multiverse, spreading out in such a way as to minimize the damage to any individual sector, in order to best avoid raising the alarm and provoking an organized response. But the time for subtlety has ended. The last five worlds to fall have all been in this sector. As far as I know, you're looking at the only survivors from Alterra, Mallozzi, and Ataraxia," she gestured to Serena, Cypher, and Ivy in turn. "Kimori is their last stop on the way to the Nexus. If we fail to drive them back, you'll be dealing with them yourselves soon after."

Silence greeted Annea's pronouncement. The Counselors exchanged nervous glances amongst themselves. What did that mean? She'd expected shock and horror, perhaps grim resolve. Instead, they looked awkward and uncomfortable, as if she'd suggested this meeting would proceed more smoothly if everyone disrobed. A silent conversation played out before her eyes. Subtle nods. Nervous ticks. Retracting postures. Accusing glares. Not the body language of a group of beings preparing themselves for a war.

"Before this body can commit to a course of action," Valon said, the first of the group to recover himself, "I'd like to hear more from the Vohr survivors, to learn more about the enemy you'd ask us to face."

Orlan was having none of that. "Do none of you read my reports?" he asked. He'd never match an Octari's level of equanimity, but he didn't lose his temper easily. He looked livid now. The Council's muted reaction to an impending apocalypse clearly destroyed the last of his patience with them. "I have been interviewing survivors for months. I've sent you hundreds of pages of testimony from displaced souls who were lucky enough to get through a Gate before the quarantine protocol kicked in. I've sent you dossiers on more than a dozen species of Vohr monstrosity, including those that destroyed Cypher, Serena, and Ivy's worlds. What information could they give you which you wouldn't already know, if you were paying attention?"

A few members of the Sector Council had the decency to look shamefaced. Valon looked indignant. "We oversee the affairs of almost a thousand worlds. You can't expect us to read every report from an emergency services officer."

"I sure can, when those reports deal with the literal deaths of those worlds."

While she shared Orlan's indignation, excoriating their incompetence wouldn't produce the result she wanted. If they had to dance to the Council's tune for a little while, so be it. They'd do the right thing in the end.

Nobody could be stupid enough to disregard a threat of this magnitude staring them in the face.

"If you wish me to speak of the Vohr, then listen well," Ivy said, stepping forward to take Cypher's place before the counselors. At some point since they'd entered the chamber, she'd replaced her leafy coverings with bark armor, the physical manifestation of her anxiety. Cypher got out of her way and took a seat next to Tako.

"I am the youngest of sixteen children, all daughters. My family lived deep in the rainforest, a mile from two trees we named the

Lovers. Their trunks twisted together as they grew, leaving a gap between. We were a village unto ourselves. My father had hoped some of us would take mates and expand the village with the next generation, but it was not to be.

"One day, two warriors arrived in our village upon the back of a guardian beast. They warned of villages to the north being attacked by reptilian monsters unlike anything they had seen before." Ivy described the reapers and their vicious claws. "My eldest four sisters rode off to aid those women in battle. I never saw them again.

"Less than two days later, my sister Rose returned from a flower gathering expedition, clutching the bleeding stump of a severed arm. She warned us reapers were coming, and died minutes later.

"My eldest remaining sisters, Sage, Lily, Lotus, and Ash took our own guardian beast and spent hours constructing defensive rings around our village of dense hedges laced with poisoned thorns. The reapers cut through them in two minutes.

"Magic is ineffective against reapers. Sage tried confusing them with hallucinogenic spores, which did nothing. Lily conjured acid-spitting flowers. The acid rolled off their scales like rain. Lotus and Ash tried to pin the reapers to the ground with grasping vines. The reapers slashed through them as fast as my sisters could make them. I stood by like a coward and did nothing as Lotus and Ash were beheaded, ripped apart, and devoured." Ivy's voice broke. "I am not a warrior. I was unprepared. I shall not make that mistake again."

A tear rolled down Annea's cheek as Ivy told her tale. Until now, Ivy had refused to elaborate on the deaths of her sisters. She suspected Serena had made strides on getting her to open up a little. In Annea's presence, Ivy remained quiet and dedicated to the mission. Getting multiple sentences out of her was a rare event. The young dryad should be sharing this story with a therapist, or with her or Serena in private, not with a group of dispassionate counselors. But for the sake of Kimori, Ivy ripped open the wound for all to see.

Your sisters would be so proud of you if they could see you now.

"Thank you for your brave testimony. I think we've heard enough," Valon said, gesturing to Serena. He had the air of a man trying with only moderate success to hold down his breakfast. "Why don't we hear what she has to say?"

"I am not finished," Ivy said, her tone a command. "When it was clear we could not defend ourselves, my father ordered everyone left to flee to the Lovers. We intended to climb the trees and pray for divine intervention from Ataraxia herself. As we ran, my father and remaining sisters died protecting me, the youngest of us, the coward too terrified to fight back. I lost sight of our guardian beast and assumed the reapers killed him too. Once the reapers breached the hedge wall, everyone I had ever known or loved died violent, bloody deaths in less time than it takes to peel an orange.

"None of us knew the Lovers was a Planar Gate, but it activated Emergency Recall as I drew close. The last thing I saw before stepping through the Gate was my sister Vera impaling a reaper with a shaft of sharpened bamboo through its jaw and into its brain. It disemboweled her with its blades before dying.

"This same horror is coming for Kimori, and will be visited upon other worlds a thousand times over if we do not annihilate them." Ivy stepped back and retreated into herself, visibly exhausted from reliving that horror.

Annea took Ivy's hand and gave it a gentle squeeze, leaning close to whisper in her ear, "I have met many cowards in my lifetime. You are not one of them."

Ivy nodded — acknowledgement of what she'd said, not agreement.

"We have no way of knowing how much time Kimori has before the Vohr invasion begins," Annea said, regaining control of the conversation before the counselors could make another attempt at questioning Serena. She could tell at a glance Tako remained in control of her. Serena looked awkward, self-conscious, and withdrawn in a way she attributed to Tako's discomfort at being a puppeteer. "In light of that, I must return to my world to help finalize our defensive preparations. I would ask this distinguished body to urge the worlds of our sector to send us any troops, weapons, and provisions they can spare, immediately."

A couple counselors looked inclined to reluctantly agree, but most had sour faces like they'd sucked on a lemon. They looked back and forth amongst themselves as if arguing over who would have to be the one to deliver bad news.

How could there be any hesitation or need for debate? Could they really not see it would be in everyone's interest to help her win the fight in her backyard, before the war arrived at their doorsteps?

"We should take a recess and discuss this amongst ourselves," said Grakk, running a hand along one of his moose antlers.

"Good members of the Council, that will not be necessary. This meeting has gone on long enough." The deep, rumbling voice came from Annea's left, where a tall, black-robed figure stood in one of the jury boxes. His face was hidden by the deep hood, while long gloves covered his hands. She didn't have enough information to guess his species.

They'd seen black robed figures like him frequently in their travels through the Nexus. She'd never thought anything of them until she'd met Patrick outside Blackwell's estate.

How did he get in without any of us seeing or hearing it?

"Do you think he's one of the people hunting you?" Annea asked Patrick.

"He is, I'm sure of it."

The doors to the boxes on both sides of the council chamber opened, admitting more of the robed beings. The large wooden doors behind them creaked open. Another contingent of robed men took positions just inside, blocking their exit. In total, the robed men outnumbered Annea's party by at least five to one.

"I'm sorry," Valon said. "We've made a grave mistake."

"Nonsense," the robed speaker said. "Grakk and Valathea saw the natural and inevitable course of history and placed themselves on the side that would allow them to survive. And you all took our bribes to keep quiet and let us deal with the *Vohr issue,* which we have, in our own way. You never asked for details on *how* we'd do that." He and his followers pulled back their hoods, allowing Annea to see their faces.

Davoh'rei. Every single one of them. Two of them blocking the exit stepped forward and slit the throats of the guards who'd come inside with Annea's party.

"While the Vohr worked their way across the multiverse, we've been here, keeping sector governments distracted. Downplaying the threat. Buying favor." He offered a shark-toothed grin. "This sector was cheaper than most."

"You can't silence the truth by killing us," Cypher said. "The data has been copied and will be disseminated before you can track it all down. People will find out what's going on."

The Davoh'rei chuckled. "That's fine. It's too late to do anything about it now. You did catch us by surprise figuring out the invasion path though. Very clever. It's forced us to come out of the shadows a couple days ahead of schedule." At the wave of a hand, his troops reached into their robes and withdrew hidden swords.

"Valathea and Grakk are collaborators and not to be harmed. They're our witnesses. Leave the red-haired human alive too. Korahshka wants her. Kill everyone else." He turned his black, soulless eyes on Annea. "Your deaths are an announcement. Submit, or be destroyed. Until we've restored the Luminous Ones to glory, the Davoh'rei rule the multiverse."

CHAPTER 52

BROKEN DREAMS

Serena stared at Korahshka's shark-toothed grin, wishing she could knock those teeth out. What was the smart play here? Based on past experience, death in a dream had no impact on reality, so she could go all-out fighting him without consequences. It would provide more insights into his capabilities. On the other hand, how reliable would any information be when obtained in an environment where Korahshka could alter the rules of reality on a whim? Worse, she risked showing him what she could and couldn't do.

No, slugging it out wasn't the play. She made a token effort to eject herself from the dream despite his warning. Slapping herself in the face as hard as she could hurt like hell, but didn't accomplish anything. Nor did doing burpees until she wanted to puke. Korahshka wouldn't let her burn the council chamber down around them. Every time she ignited something, he snuffed it out. It felt pointless to try anything more dramatic.

Unless she came up with some novel new idea, it appeared she really was stuck here.

Korahshka loved the sound of his own voice. Perhaps she'd learn something useful if she got him talking.

"So, what's the grand plan?" Serena asked. "Let's say you're right. Kimori falls, giving you a direct line to the Nexus. You've killed me and absorbed my power into yourself. Where do you go from there?"

"You expect me to give out my secrets because you asked?"

She did, actually. He'd been the gloating type in all their interactions so far. "What's the harm if I'll be dead soon? Besides, haven't you been seeking revenge for more than a decade now?"

Korahshka laughed. "Try fifteen thousand years. The Davoh'rei have sought to restore balance since the dawn of the Lost Epoch. I'll be the one who finally succeeds."

"Lost Epoch?" She'd heard that term a couple times, but never gotten an explanation.

"After the Luminous Ones were sealed away, the Planar Gates stopped working for ten thousand years. Then, a little over five thousand years ago, they started working again. The first beings to figure that out discovered an empty, abandoned Nexus. It took hundreds of generations for multiverse travel and trade to reach the levels they're at now. Many worlds still don't know what Planar Gates are or how they work. Alterra was one such example."

She shouldn't have asked. His explanation had her mind spinning with more questions. Why were the Luminous Ones sealed away, but not the Davoh'rei? Why did the Gates stop working? What changed to make them functional again? Was the Nexus evacuated before it happened, or had people been trapped here and died out? How did anyone relearn how to use the Planar Gates after ten thousand years? How did they repopulate the Nexus? How much of the Nexus she'd seen so far was how it had always been, and what had changed since its rediscovery?

Focus. None of that information is relevant to your current problem.

"You have a captive audience. Literally. According to you, I'm a dead woman walking. So come on, enlighten me. What's all this for?" Serena left the room, trusting Korahshka would follow her.

"You know more than you think," he said, falling in behind her. He sounded like a teacher prodding her to find the answer for herself.

She mulled over the problem while they returned to the nightmare hellscape that was the Vohr-infested transit cube. Korahshka wanted to free beings he called Luminous Ones. Balor, the dragon who once enslaved Kimori, was one of them. He'd said the Planar Gates destroyed any Vohr trying to pass through them, so they tunnelled from one reality to the next instead. The Davoh'rei would have figured out how to do that about a decade or so ago, given the invasion timeline. She doubted they'd wait to utilize an ability like that once they had it. They needed to get to the

Nexus. There was something here they wanted. Vohr would help the Davoh'rei crush any resistance while they looked for it.

"What's the heart of the Nexus?" She asked, recalling the conversation between Korahshka and his minions that she'd stumbled into. He'd said something about stones too. Cornerstones. In context, they sounded like keys. "Is that where the Luminous Ones are sealed away?" That... didn't feel right. Why would whatever god, species, or civilization that created the Nexus want to house such evil in the de-facto hub of the entire multiverse?

She came to a stop in front of a reaper queued to walk through a tunnel to some unknown world. The long line of reapers stood at attention, unmoving, completely uninterested in Serena's presence.

"If only it were that simple," Korahshka said. "I'm not looking for the prison. I'm looking for the warden." He tapped the reaper on the arm. The massive reptile got on all fours and lowered itself so he could sit on it like a living park bench.

"Meaning?"

"It'd take more time to explain that than you've got."

Fine. If he wouldn't share, she'd ask something else. "How do you make your monsters?" She took advantage of the reaper's disinterest to study the beast up close. If she ever got this close to one again, she'd probably be dead. Best to utilize the opportunity for research when it presented itself.

"Davoh'rei have been masters of genetic manipulation for millennia," Korahshka said. "Such knowledge was the first gift given to us by the Luminous Ones. We take what exists in nature, recombine it, and enhance it to a state of perfection. The reapers are an amalgamation of Thalossian river crocodiles, Kassak monitor lizards, and an ancient beast allegedly known as Therizinosaurus. I've never been able to track one of those down to get fresh source material, so I can't be sure. We've had reapers for a long time."

"Your ancestors didn't leave notes?" Crocodile genetics suggested a strong bite, but weaker muscles for opening the jaw. If someone could manage to avoid getting skewered by the arm blades, it might be possible to bind its mouth shut. If it behaved like a lizard, it wouldn't like cold climates. The Theri-xeno-thing must have provided the blades.

"Fifteen thousand years is a long time. Knowledge gets lost. The Lost Epoch did us no favors."

"I don't think you can call your monsters perfect if the Gates consider them a biohazard."

She crossed over to the next aisle of Vohr tunnels, where a corrupted dryad leaned against the far wall. Her skin was a pale, sickly green riddled with dark purple bruises. Half of her hair had fallen out, and she had sunken, dead eyes. "How is this an improvement on nature?"

Rather than stand, Korahshka tapped the reaper he sat on. It crawled across the floor towards her, its blades leaving gouges in the floor in its wake. "The dryads of Ataraxia are a recent acquisition. We're still studying them to determine their best use. In the meantime, we experiment."

"Like grafting them onto the back of Ataraxian guardian beasts. Did you know the one you sent to Kimori protected Ivy's village? She loved Moogi, and because of you, she had to kill him."

Korahshka shrugged. "That animal was a useful test subject. Am I supposed to feel remorse?"

"I wouldn't expect it from you. Don't underestimate Ivy. If you cross paths with her, she will kill you."

"She's welcome to try. Is this how you wish to pass the time, then? Offering critiques on our inventory of improved creatures? Each is a tool with a specific purpose. Perhaps you can offer your thoughts on the manti? They're one of our most common, expendable units, designed to soften up worlds in advance of occupation forces. They made such short work of Alterra."

Serena ignored the barb and gestured broadly to encompass the entire corrupted transit cube. "Is everything here accurate? This is your dream, after all. There aren't any... embellishments or anything?

"All the Vohr you see are a true and accurate representation of the real thing."

"And the decor around the Nexus, is this all your imagination too?" Aside from the corruption he'd brought to the place, his representation of each cube of the Nexus matched her memory. He had to have been through the area before, but what about the N.E.S.T building?

"Everything here is a product of my mind. Where are you going with this?" Korahshka asked.

"Interesting. Follow me." Without looking back, Serena headed to the elevator to leave the transit cube. One thing she'd seen made no sense compared to anything else. His reaction might be revealing.

In the N.E.S.T's lobby, she'd seen a happy family of pink-skinned beings playing a game before she observed the manti nest outside. Had they merely been the last thing she remembered before falling asleep, or were they another manifestation from the Davoh'rei's mind? If they were still there, what did their presence mean?

They were still there when Serena returned to the lobby — a mother, father, and two kids, all still keeping a fist-sized ball aloft without using their hands. Whenever one of them would miss, they'd laugh, pick up the ball, and try again.

"If everything in this dream is a product of your mind, who are they?" Serena asked, turning around to face her tormentor.

"What have you done?" Korahshka's purple skin paled. His dark eyes went wide. He was afraid! Shame she couldn't take credit for inspiring it.

Serena offered him her sweetest, most sarcastic smile. "I haven't done anything. You insisted that everything I'm seeing around here is your glorious handiwork. So, I'll ask again, who or what are they?"

Like the manti and the reapers, the family seemed disinterested in her presence, passing the ball amongst themselves without regard for how close Serena got to any of them. There was a repeating pattern to their movements. Once she had it figured out, she moved into the center of the circle and danced out of the way of the ball whenever one of the family members passed it through the middle.

Korahshka said nothing, just continued staring with an expression that betrayed a terrified sense of incomprehension at what he saw. Her own face might have looked similar as the manti descended upon Valencia.

As Serena danced around another pass, she paid attention to the details she'd caught in passing when she first saw them. The deep pink of their skin. The bony nubs above their eyes. The two rows of teeth.

"We take what exists in nature, recombine it, and then enhance it to a state of perfection."

She had an epiphany. There were leaps of logic involved, but it felt right. "I'll tell you what they are. They're the repressed memory of what you *used to be*. Your monsters are nothing but obscene attempts to replicate what the Luminous Ones did to you."

"You know nothing." Korahshka dug his fingernails into the palms of his hands hard enough to pierce the skin. Blood dripped onto the floor to be absorbed into the soil of the N.E.S.T's rainforest lobby.

Nobody, especially egotistical, genocidal maniacs, liked learning they weren't as special as they thought they were. Was this a product of his subconscious mind? She didn't know how or why this ancient bit of Davoh'rei history would manifest itself here and now, but she wasn't going to waste the opportunity.

"The Luminous Ones twisted and corrupted you to suit their purposes," Serena said. "You didn't create the Vohr. You're just the first species in the menagerie. But whatever the secret sauce is, the Luminous Ones were the only ones to do it right, since you can still go through Planar Gates. Everything you've made is a pale imitation of their craft."

"We are the chosen race to restore the Luminous Ones to glory." Korahshka's words sounded rote, forced. His reactions convinced her she had it right.

"You're pawns. Tools. Your glorious purpose is nothing but ancient programming. The Luminous Ones ruined you, and you carry on ruining everything you touch. But somewhere, deep down inside, you haven't completely forgotten what you used to be. What you're *supposed* to be." Serena spun out of the family's circle and placed a hand on the mother's shoulder.

Korahshka fell to his knees, clutching his head like it would split in two. Serena didn't relent. This was the way out. If she hammered him with the cognitive dissonance between what he believed and reality, she might disturb him enough to end the dream.

Whatever pain he felt right now, he deserved it. And so, so much more.

"You speak lies," Korahshka said. He dragged his fingernails across his face, leaving shallow cuts down his cheeks. He looked more like a panicked animal now than a cruel, confident general.

"Your gods don't care about you. You're nothing to them. This family was happy. They represent everything the Luminous Ones took from you." She'd consider herself cruel if she spoke this way to anyone else. But she couldn't find it within her to feel empathy or pity for a destroyer of worlds.

Korahshka roared, surging forward. "I will not listen to this slander and blasphemy!" He bit the mother's neck and tore her throat out. Blood sprayed all over him, fueling his frenzy. The rest of the family acted like nothing happened, continuing their looped actions until he fell upon them too.

The floor rumbled like an earthquake, though those didn't seem possible in the Nexus. Cracks formed in the dirt beneath her feet. Then holes opened up in the floor, swallowing up the lobby's trees. The ceiling caved in outside the N.E.S.T. building, crushing the manti out there under rubble.

"My friends and I are going to grind you and your army of horrors to dust," Serena said. "And when you turn to your gods for salvation, they won't answer."

Korahshka screamed with incoherent rage. Serena's vision blurred. She felt a disorienting sensation, like she was being tied up and dragged away from the scene.

As her sense of her surroundings faded, she smiled. Korahshka thought himself invincible in his own mind, but she'd won this round.

With the All-Mother as her witness, she'd win the next one too.

CHAPTER 53
FIGHT AND FLIGHT

Tako's perception of time slowed. He pushed his senses to the limit accessing the situation. There were thirty-six Davoh'rei in the Council chamber, split into three groups of twelve. What he thought of as jury boxes along the left and right walls each contained a group, while the remaining dozen blocked their exit. If they made a hard push for the doors they might be able to break through, but they'd have a lot of enemies chasing them.

Where could they go? With Serena's soul still off Who Knew Where, they couldn't risk using a Planar Gate to escape. Yet, this might be their only chance to flee back to Kimori. How many more Davoh'rei might arrive to hunt them down, if given time?

"Suggestions?" Annea asked, unsheathing her kukris.

"You, Cypher, and Ivy go to Kimori," Patrick said. Electricity crackled up and down his body, causing his hair to stand up at random angles. "Leave Serena with me and Orlan. We'll track down the dream walker and return Serena to you as soon as possible."

"I'm staying with you," Cypher said. The group of Davoh'rei to their left began vaulting over the waist-high wall of their jury box. "I've been researching the Planar Gate quarantine system. If Kimori gets sealed off, my best chance of fixing it is if I'm here."

Ivy pointed her staff at the enemies approaching from their right. "We have a more immediate problem." Vines sprouted from the wooden flooring and wrapped themselves around five Davoh'rei. The vines killed their momentum, keeping three within their jury box, while the other two spilled over and landed on their faces. Another wave of vines emerged to ensnare those two and keep them pinned to the floor.

The dryad didn't stop there. She conjured a riot of vines, ferns, and shrubs, single-handedly frustrating the advance of that entire group. They hacked through her plants, filling the air with the scents of pollen, sap, and cut grass. They were fast. She was faster. Still, the distraction wouldn't work indefinitely.

"I don't love these odds," Cypher said. With a subtle whirring of gears, his prosthetic hand collapsed on itself, twisting and reconfiguring until it looked like the barrel of a rifle. "Why don't we take this conversation elsewhere?"

"I'll take Serena and Tako," Orlan said, presenting his back to Tako so he could climb on for a piggyback ride.

Lightning erupted from Patrick's fingers, catching the leading attacker to their left square in the chest, knocking him into the rest of the group. The energy arced from him into his companions. Two others collapsed, their bodies blackened and smoking, but the effect diminished across the rest of the group. Survivors twitched for a moment before recovering and resuming their advance.

Patrick looked at his fingers like they'd betrayed him. "Bad time to be out of practice. We should push for the door."

"We can't leave this many enemies behind us." Annea surged forward to meet the remainder of the left group head-on. She blocked a sword slash with each kukri, then did a front flip over a thrust meant to impale her. She landed behind the group, decapitating two Davoh'rei and slashing two others before they could turn.

Tako marveled at Annea's agility. Hope swelled within him. The average Davoh'rei was no magical powerhouse like Korahshka appeared to be. They'd underestimated the skill of his companions. *We can survive this. No. We WILL survive this.*

The councilors, rather than aid those who'd warned them of impending danger, fled out a pair of doors in the rear of the room. Several Davoh'rei changed course to pursue them.

While Patrick and Annea worked on their group of enemies, the rest of the party retreated towards the team blocking their exit. That group held their position for the moment. Ivy walked backwards, never taking her eyes off her conjured plants. Sweat coated her forehead. Her staff shook in her grip. She wouldn't be able to mass produce plants for much longer.

Free of the need to move Serena, Tako considered how he could contribute to the fight. Serena would toss fireballs into Ivy's mess of vegetation, creating an inferno to roast the Davoh'rei before they could escape. Could he tap into her magic to do the same?

Anger fueled Serena's power. Octari understood that emotion on an intellectual level. He'd certainly felt it from Serena through their bond. Creating the emotion himself was another matter entirely. Asking an Octari to get enraged would be like asking an alligator to write a sonnet, or expecting a sparrow to herd cattle.

Figure it out, old man. Get angry!

Two shots rang out. A pair of Davoh'rei guarding the exit had new holes in their foreheads. "I'm going to need some help here," Cypher said. That rear group now decided staying put and waiting was a bad strategy and instead joined the fray. "I don't have enough ammo for all of them."

"Help them!" Annea shouted to Patrick. "I've got this."

Patrick fired off one last blast of lightning from his fingertips then joined Cypher. The survivors weren't slouches with edged weapons. Annea jumped, spun, and parried, looking more like a dancer than a warrior. Every movement was calculated and methodical. A diving roll under a slash left her in position to slice through the back of her assailant's knees. She twisted away from one Davoh'rei's overhead slash to bury a kukri into the neck of another. Annea dodged more attacks than she made, but when she lashed out, her strikes hit home with lethal efficiency. That look of smug confidence on their leader's face transformed to shock as Annea cut him down.

"My magic is failing," Ivy said, her matter-of-fact tone at odds with her exhaustion. The second jury box contained its own miniature rainforest, with a density of plantlife thicker than anything Tako had seen in nature. She'd held them at bay for as long as she could, but they'd break free any second now. Her bushes and trees wilted like they'd been left too long under a desert sun.

Tako tried to channel Serena's magic. *I am angry! The Davoh'rei will kill my friends unless I stop them first. They are evil and must burn!*

Kill, kill, kill! Arrrr! He felt like an actor reading a poorly-written script translated into three languages before being returned to its native tongue. The words failed to invoke the desired emotional response. He felt determination and resolve, but no anger. He could poke at the source of Serena's power, but not activate it.

Well, that didn't work. I'll have to settle for my own talents. Tako extended an arm from Serena's back, blasting a jet of water into the face of a Davoh'rei vaulting chairs to flank the group. Caught off guard, the purple-skinned man slipped and bashed his head into the back of the next row of seats. Cypher spun and shot him before he had the chance to get up.

"That's helpful," Cypher said. "Keep doing that."

He heeded that advice, maintaining just enough concentration on Serena's body to keep her from letting go of Orlan. The rest of his attention he devoted to harassing the enemy. He unleashed jets of water. He made his skin ripple through rapid color changes. He grabbed and repositioned chairs. Anything he could think of to annoy, confuse, or distract, he did.

Cypher aimed his arm at two Davoh'rei still blocking the door. They dived out of the way. Three shots rang out. One shot hit, the others missed. Cypher pressed a piece of metal on his wrist. His arm from the elbow down twisted and reconfigured itself into a miniature crossbow, with a walnut-sized orb loaded and ready to fire.

"Did everyone on Mallozzi have such elaborate prosthetics?" Orlan asked.

"This was done *to* me, not *for* me," Cypher said.

Tako, Orlan, and Patrick settled into a three-man combo. Orlan positioned himself to give Tako the easiest lines of fire with his limbs. Patrick blasted Korahshka's freshly soaked minions with enough electricity to render them unconscious or dead.

Annea took a spare second to cut down the last two Davoh'rei in the immediate area on the way out. Ivy released her magic and dashed to catch up with the rest of the group. Cypher's crossbow fired with a twang, launching its payload into the floor outside the Council chamber. Pores opened across the surface of the orb, filling the air with dark, oily smoke. They sprinted through it and didn't slow down until they'd arrived in the crowded transit cube.

"We can't go back to the N.E.S.T," Orlan said. "If they've been tracking your movements at all, that will be the first place they look for us."

"You assume we have shaken them," Ivy said. "We have not."

At first, Tako thought she referred to the ones freeing themselves from her plants. Then he picked out what she'd seen. Dozens of black-robed figures milled about the transit cube, with many guarding the queues leading to various Planar Gates. *Of course*, he thought. *If you're making a play for control of the Nexus, one of your first actions would be to monitor the flow of traffic.*

With a unity that gave Tako chills, the robed figures turned their attention in the group's general direction. *They know their ambush failed to eliminate us.* Serena, Ivy, and Cypher had been able to maintain communication over a distance with special earrings. It didn't surprise him that someone else would have the means to achieve a similar effect.

It was mighty inconvenient though.

"This is where we part ways," Patrick told Annea. "We'll bully our way to a Planar Gate. Jump through to a different world, then go to Kimori. We'll keep Serena and hunt down Korahshka."

"Orlan's not getting away from them while giving Serena a piggyback ride," Annea said. They walked into the thickest groups of beings they could find, as far from any Davoh'rei as possible. "We're all stuck in the Nexus until we have Serena back."

"We'll manage it," Cypher said, raising his crossbow arm to fire three smoke bombs into the transit cube. As soon as one launched, another emerged from an opening in his arm and slotted itself into firing position. He took a fourth orb and lobbed it with his organic arm to land twenty feet away, in the middle of the nearest aisle of Gates. "The smoke's non-toxic. Innocent bystanders will be fine."

Chaos erupted across the transit cube. Beings of dozens of species screamed, shouted, roared, chirped, or hissed with panic. Believing themselves under attack and not knowing the source, crowds fled through the nearest Planar Gate or dispersed in random directions, often colliding with each other. The stampede forced most of the Davoh'rei to stand their ground and weather the storm, rather than seek them out.

Tako's vision blurred. A wave of nausea overwhelmed him. *The smoke may be non-toxic to humans, but did Cypher ever test it on anyone else?* The transit cube spun around him. He lost his grip on Orlan. Without intending to, Tako leaned back. The sudden shift in weight caused Orlan to lose his grip too. Serena's body tumbled to the floor.

Tako felt like a giant hand was stuffing him into a tiny box. Whether it was a reaction to the smoke or a new kind of Davoh'rei attack, he couldn't let it incapacitate him. He had to help Serena while she couldn't help herself. But the more he struggled, the greater the pressure grew. Pathways to controlling Serena's body closed off to him like a series of doors slamming in his face.

Then a familiar presence returned to his mind. He stopped struggling.

"That was not a pleasant way to wake up," Serena said.

"Welcome back," Tako said. *"Sorry to dump this on you. No time to explain."* He flooded Serena's mind with memories. His flailing efforts to stand and walk. His broken speech. The ambush in the Council chamber.

"You did what you had to. I'm not upset," Serena said, responding to the undercurrent of shame attached to the memories. No Octari wanted that kind of power over their host. She sent him her own flashes of memory. Korahshka's desire to find the heart of the Nexus, whatever that meant. The happy family whose mere existence shattered something in his mind.

Telepathy is so much better than speech!

Serena pushed herself to her feet and coated her arms in flames, presenting an obvious target to any Davoh'rei who could push through the crowd and smoke to reach them. Tako moved to his customary position on Serena's back. After a moment of mental recalibration, he could once again see through her eyes as a passive observer, as it should be.

"Serena, is that you?" Annea asked.

"I'm back. Looks like I broke free just in time."

"Then take that Gate and get out of here," Orlan pointed to an inactive Gate nearby. Through the smoke, it was impossible to tell which world it normally serviced. But an inactive Gate could be used to reach any world in the network if you knew the address, so it'd serve as well as any other.

"I'm staying with you," Cypher told Orlan. A trio of Davoh'rei emerged from the smoke, swords in hand. He stepped forward, ducked under a sword slash, and delivered a kick strong enough to send his assailant flying back into the haze. What sorts of technology did he have packed into those legs?

"I must stay too," Patrick said, shooting lightning into the other two. The streams of electricity looked only half as thick as his initial bursts. He had to be getting tired too. "The Weavers need to learn how deep corruption has spread."

"Good luck," Annea spoke with a gravity that suggested she understood Orlan, Cypher, and Patrick might be sacrificing themselves by declining this chance to escape. "This is farewell for now, but not goodbye. I'll be back when Kimori's safety is assured."

With the speed of much practice, Annea traced the eight sigils for Kimori in the air in front of the Planar Gate. She risked sealing Kimori off from the rest of the Gate network right now if there were Vohr on the other side. Perhaps she considered that an acceptable risk.

The Gate popped to life. Ivy ran through the shimmering ribbon of light without a backward glance, Annea right behind her. Serena stopped at the threshold and turned back, wanting to offer some parting words to the men covering their exit.

Annea reached back through the Gate, grabbed Serena's wrist, and dragged her out of the Nexus. As soon as they stood fully on Kimori soil, the Gate shut down.

Hopefully, not for the last time.

PART IV
THE BATTLE OF KIMORI

CHAPTER 54

THE WAR COUNCIL

They'd only been gone a few days, but in that time, Kimori had continued its rapid transformation in their absence. Weapon emplacements stood out on the world tree's branches, placed every thirty yards or so. Most were gigantic crossbows, while others were a type of weapon Serena didn't recognize. All she could see from their angle were what looked like eight rifle barrels welded to a wheel. Some kind of high-speed projectile weapon?

The exterior of the ant colony buzzed with bodies. Scout ants flew out for patrols from new openings scattered around the colony's exterior. Thousands more held positions on the steep incline of the colony's surface, ready to take off the moment enemies appeared. She'd been under the impression that scouts were a small, niche caste. How many of these ants were born in the last couple weeks?

They shouldn't have returned. Not yet. She felt like a traitor abandoning Cypher, Orlan, and Patrick to the Davoh'rei. She'd woken up in the middle of a battle. It all happened so fast. They could have done more. "We have to go back. We left them behind!" Annea grabbed her hand before she could trace the infinity symbol representing the Nexus.

"We did no such thing," Annea said. "They chose to stay behind. They have their battle, and we have ours. Going back now would only compromise their efforts. We are needed here."

"She's right," Tako said. *"We did the best we could. They're all capable of taking care of themselves."*

Serena swore. She had to believe Cypher, Orlan, and Patrick hadn't sacrificed themselves to cover their retreat. But then what? Would they be fugitives, always on the run? How tight a grip did the Davoh'rei have over Nexus infrastructure? What about Orlan's family? Were they at risk because of his actions? It pissed her off knowing there was a fight going on that she couldn't help with.

"Focus on what you can control, Serena. Worry about the rest after our battle's won." Tako gave her the mental equivalent of a shoulder squeeze.

The Ankora had a well-organized tent city set up between the Planar Gate and the main entrance to the ant colony. Men and women were equally represented in their ranks, with no evidence of any gendered division of labor. Women mended clothes and ran combat drills. Men tended cooking pots and sharpened blades. All of them carried knives long enough to qualify as a short sword in Serena's hands, plus a larger sword or pair of hand axes. Given Kimori's imminent future as a warzone, she was glad she didn't see any children running around.

As they walked through the Anokra camp, the bearfolk stopped what they were doing to give Annea crisp salutes. Clearly, they'd been given Annea's description and briefed on her role in Kimori society. She waved and nodded politely, her body language conveying respect and appreciation, but also that she didn't have time to stop and chat.

Serena once again appreciated having a guide through the ant colony. The tunnels curved and connected in ways that confused her, without a right angle to be found anywhere. If someone dropped her in the middle of the colony, she'd never find her way out without help. Like the tree above, it looked much different than the last time they'd walked through it. New cubby holes were dug into the sides of earthen walls at irregular intervals, each just large enough for a single drone to hide in. Through new holes in the ceiling, she could see into other tunnels overhead. The ants wanted to ensure they could get from point A to point B as quickly as possible. It made sense, as they couldn't know what direction the Vohr might come from.

As was often the case with Pik-Pik and Tik-Tik, Serena heard the ants before she saw them.

<What will happen to us? Will we have to fight?>

<Queen Ruta doesn't want us in the colony. We'll be up the tree, carrying ammo to help gunners reload.>

<Any drone could do that. We shall be Annea's bodyguards.>

<Annea is a peerless warrior. You ran screaming from chameleosaurs.>

<I helped defeat Blackwell!>

<She won't want us facing the Vohr. We'll be in the vault keeping the children entertained.>

The pair faced the warm glow of a fireplace, their backs to the group as they entered the lodging space connected to the royal reception chamber. At the sound of their footsteps, Pik-Pik and Tik-Tik raced to Annea with the boundless enthusiasm of puppies overjoyed at their owner's return.

Annea went down on her knees to stroke them both on the head between their antennae, which waved with happiness. "I missed you too," she said, cutting into their babbled greetings. "We'll have time to chat later. Right now I need you two to round up Jesserin and the Queens Emeritus. Have them meet us in the Grand Chamber of Rule in two hours."

<What about the Ankora?>

<And the Chiroptera?>

<...and Mother?> Tik-Tik tilted their head and backed up a couple paces. Their legs wobbled with obvious apprehension at the idea of spending any time near Queen Ruta.

"Ask Jesserin to send runners to bring the leaders of our allies. Dispatch one to confer with the ant queens, as well. I won't make you talk to them."

Both ants sighed with obvious relief, then ventured out to see to their duties.

Serena, Annea, and Ivy grabbed food from the lodge's pantry and ate in silence, each grappling with their own thoughts. They took turns bathing and changing clothes. For Ivy, this whole routine amounted to eating a handful of strawberries, soaking in a tub for two minutes, and then going outside to photosynthesize.

Two hours later, they reunited in the Grand Chamber of Rule, which had been converted into a war room. A round table dominated the center of the chamber, its circumference wide enough that if Serena and Ivy lay down on opposite sides and reached for each other, they'd just barely touch. At its center stood an incredibly accurate representation of the anthill and world tree that constituted Kimori's civilization, which also showed the surrounding terrain for miles in every direction. A young elf stood at the edge of the table, moving his fingers like an artist holding a paintbrush, creating new elements before her eyes. The Ankora's neat tent city popped into existence, followed moments later by a haphazard splattering of figures near the swamps to the south that could only be the Chiroptera.

At the back of the chamber, queens Chibi and Ruta stood before the doors to their respective domains within the ant colony. Their height allowed them to see the table without difficulty. Pik-Pik and Tik-Tik posted up on either side of the Grand Chamber's other entrance, as far from the ant queens as they could be without leaving.

When the Queens Emeritus arrived, Serena backed away from the table to find a place near Pik-Pik and Tik-Tik. She felt out of place at a war council. What right did she have to be here? A month ago, she hadn't known she had magic, or that a vast multiverse existed. There were generals and queens in this room. She was a nobody.

Kuma and the Moon Doge arrived last. Annea gestured for them to stand next to her at the table. Kuma did so, but the Chiroptera ignored her, circling away from Annea, Jesserin, and Kimori's former queens to stand next to a pair of male generals.

"I return from the Nexus bearing ill tidings," Annea said without preamble. "Davoh'rei have compromised our sector of the Nexus." She held up a hand and gestured for quiet as the chamber erupted with exclamations and obscenities. Some elves turned their gaze reflexively to the mural along the back wall. "Our ancient enemy has worked in the shadows for years, downplaying the threat the Vohr represent." She summarized their meetings with Dr. Niles Venture, the infiltration of Blackwell's estate, the retrieval of the crystalline computing matrix, and what they learned of the Vohr's invasion path.

"When the babbling ants told us of the invasion before your return, we thought it a joke. Dark humor to rile us up for a fight," Kuma said. "But you're serious, aren't you? If Kimori falls, the Vohr have a direct path to the Nexus."

"Correct," Annea said.

Kuma laughed. Elves cast nervous glances at each other, uncertain what to make of the enormous bear's genuine mirth. "Annea, our meeting may be the happiest event in my tribe's history. We have long sought a glorious battle where we could put our skills to use for the greatest good. This is the kind of battle that will be sung about until the end of time."

I'm glad SOMEONE is happy, Serena thought.

"When we presented this information to the Sector Council, the Davoh'rei ambushed us, hoping to silence us and destroy the data," Annea said. "They failed. Dr. Venture and our allies in the Weavers will be distributing the invasion data. They'll also be building a resistance movement within the Nexus." She couldn't know that part. Not for sure. Was it wishful thinking, or simply telling everyone what they needed to hear?

"Unfortunately," Annea continued, drawing herself up to her full height, "such a public ambush shows they no longer feel the need to hide. The attack on Kimori could begin at any time. Nobody else is coming to help us. The forces we have now are all we're going to get, so it's time to finalize our plans accordingly."

Annea yielded the floor to Jesserin, who, together with a pair of elven generals, walked everyone through the map on the table, pointing out troop positions and their intended zones of coverage. Serena did her best to pay attention, not knowing what scrap of information might prove important to her in the heat of battle. Her attention drifted as the topics moved on to ammunition counts, food supplies, cache locations, retreat corridors, and chokepoints. They even had depth charts for who would replenish losses on the stationary weapons. Then the ant queens chimed in with information on troop counts for each caste and their intended roles in the battle. While Serena and friends had been looking for help, Jesserin, her generals, and the ant queens had all done a depressingly thorough job of planning around what they had. For them, Annea's bad news didn't change anything.

Nothing they discussed involved Serena or Ivy. What were the two of them supposed to do during the fight? Just stick close to Annea?

Jesserin stood on the tips of her toes and tried to point to a specific door on the side of the world tree, but even on tiptoes and leaning forward, she couldn't get her finger close, so she asked Ivy to create a stick she could use as a pointer. "The school chambers have had their walls and doors hardened into a vault." She tapped the door she meant with her stick. "Children and the elderly will be sealed inside until victory is assured."

Or until we're all dead, Serena thought.

"What's with the sudden defeatism?" Tako asked. *"I expected you to be eager to be part of the Vohr's downfall."* He knew her feelings. Emotions were highly permeable through their bond. They didn't need to have this conversation. But having Tako in her head was like being attached to a therapist all day, every day.

He wanted her to talk about it.

"I'm terrified. Korahshka won't be holding anything back. I still barely know how my power works. I can't be counted on to use it for any extended period of time without hurting myself, and I have to be extra careful not to burn you. What are the two of us supposed to do to turn the tide in a battle on this scale?" She recalled how much she'd struggled to kill just one manti. They'd be facing thousands soon enough.

"You'll do what you always do. You'll survive."

While the two of them talked, Kuma and the Moon Doge each had a turn explaining the capabilities of their forces and their planned tactics.

Images flashed through Serena's mind as Tako served her highlights from her own memories. Her victory over a dire bear early in her tenure on the Alterran frontier. Her escape to the Nexus. Driving back Balor's Sentinels in the Forest in the Sky. Saving Ivy from the leviathan's clutches. The fight in Blackwell's sanctum.

Tako knew how to give a heck of a pep talk while hardly saying a word, she had to give him that. *"And what about Korahshka? You know he'll be seeking me out."*

"You're right, so use that knowledge against him."

"I doubt I can defeat him alone."

Tako uttered a long-suffering sigh. *"Now you're just TRYING to be difficult. Why would you have to fight him alone? Everyone on Kimori would help you with that fight. And you have a plan for him."*

"I do?" Skepticism turned to shock. He was right. A dozen scattered, disparate thoughts fit themselves together like puzzle pieces in her mind. She knew now why she was in the room. What she could do to contribute to victory.

"I'm sorry to interrupt," Serena said, stepping around a pair of elves to join the conversation at the table. "But there's a gap in your plans. Korahshka."

"What about him?" Annea asked.

"He's commanding the Vohr," Serena said. "I have reason to believe taking him out will break their will to fight."

"He's proven he can invade your dreams across realities through Vohr tunnels," Annea said. "What makes you think he doesn't command his troops that way as well? He'd be safely out of our reach."

You know damn well he won't do that. Not here. Not now. She choked down the reflexive outburst. Annea wasn't undermining her. She played devil's advocate on purpose, offering her an avenue to explain the situation and sell her plan to everyone else, who didn't know the whole story yet. Korahshka wanted her power for himself. He considered victory inevitable. He'd command from the front and treat Kimori's defenders like minor nuisances until proven otherwise.

She told everyone so. "...and when he shows himself, this is how we'll take him down." She outlined her plan, crude as it was. As she did, some of the elven generals offered tips and suggestions to address logistical concerns.

Annea laughed. "This is risky, but I like it." She gave Serena a pat on the back. "Definitely the kind of plan you would come up with."

Serena chose to take that as a compliment, given that nobody had objected. Their easy buy-in filled her with confidence that they might actually pull it off. Then again, all of the risk fell on the shoulders of just a handful of people.

"I want scouts on constant patrols of the fifty miles surrounding the city," Annea said. "Everyone else should rest up or see to any last-minute preparations. Be ready to report to your stations the moment anyone reports Vohr sightings. If they're kind enough to let us sleep, everyone knows their assignments for the morning. Dismissed."

CHAPTER 55
ON THE EVE OF BATTLE

"I 'm bored," Serena said. She lay on her back on the dining table of the lodge outside the queen's chambers, staring up at the ceiling. Her feet ached from hours spent running around the tree and ant colony, helping with final preparations for the battle. Anyone who wanted her to move would have to pick her up and carry her. Ivy sat on a bench to her right, near her head. Serena continued to be surprised the normally touch-averse dryad would place herself in such close proximity. Or was this a normal family dynamic, now that she'd accepted Serena as a sister?

"Do you regret declining Annea's invitation?" Ivy asked.

"Nope. Everyone prepares for battle in their own way. I don't think the traditional elven methods would work for me."

The elven way, as Annea described it, involved dancing, drinking, and taking a man or woman to bed to cuddle for hours. Or both, because *why choose.* Considering the source, *cuddling* was certainly a euphemism, but Annea wasn't an outlier. Most of the elves wanted to get one last "cuddle" in before the fighting (and the dying) started. From Annea's point of view, Serena and Ivy finding themselves elven partners would simply be "participating in local culture." Neither woman felt pressured to participate, and Annea hadn't been disappointed when they went their own way.

My only regret in skipping the elven party is that I won't get to watch Pik-Pik and Tik-Tik interacting with a crowd of horny and terrified elves. Anyone who doesn't keep their eyes on their drinks will probably lose them. I'd bet those two are hilarious if you get them drunk.

With their duties tended to, Serena and Ivy had no formal responsibilities until dawn. Unless, of course, the Vohr attacked first. Serena wanted to make sure Ivy didn't spend that time alone, so she couldn't get lost in negative thoughts or dwell on her lost sisters. She didn't have the advantage of an Octari in her head, providing constant emotional support. Ivy needed camaraderie. She needed a sister. If nothing else, Serena could be that for her right now.

And worrying about Ivy kept her distracted from the roiling chaos of her own emotions. Even with Tako, she felt the best way to deal with the fear and anxiety around an upcoming battle was to ignore them. "Do you understand what Annea's invitation entailed?" Serena asked.

"Partially. I do not understand the appeal in pairing off and engaging in sustained rhythmic movements," Ivy said.

"Yeah, I've never been much of a dancer either."

"I refer to how Annea intends to conclude her evening."

"Oh," Serena paused. Ivy seemed too old for nobody in her family to have given her "The Talk." Maybe things worked differently for dryads? They were basically plants, after all. It would explain why she'd been oblivious to numerous advances from Z'han's sailors. "It'll make sense when you're older."

"I am fully mature."

Serena rolled on her side to face away from Ivy, stifling a laugh. "Sorry, it's a joke. Something my parents used to say." As amusing as it might be to become Professor Embers and offer Ivy a lecture on sexuality amongst elves and other non-dryad species, that wasn't how she wanted to spend their time together.

"Do you know any games we could play?" Serena asked. What did dryads do for fun? They had to understand the concept of fun, right? There was so much she didn't know about Ivy or her people. "I forgot to buy a deck of cards when we went shopping. I didn't think to ask Pik-Pik or Tik-Tik if they have anything similar around here before they took off with Annea."

"I know a game," Ivy said. "I will need you to move."

Serena sat up and hopped off the table. Vines sprouted from the wood, wrapping the middle two-thirds of the table with seven bands. The vines then branched out and interlaced until they formed a seven-by-seven grid. Ivy spread her arms wide and placed a palm at either end of the table. A miniature *alucinatus* tree sprung up in front of her right hand, its branches loaded with berries. A tiny seed-laden sunflower grew next to her left hand.

"Which would you prefer to represent you?" Ivy asked. "Seeds or berries?"

"Does it matter?" Serena asked, taking a seat across from Ivy.

"It is irrelevant. They are merely to distinguish us."

"I'll be the seeds." Though she'd held *alucinatus* berries before without incident, she didn't want to risk them having a strange effect on her so close to a battle.

"Very well." Ivy twisted the head off the sunflower and scraped out the seeds. With the seeds removed, the flower shriveled out of existence.

The dryad placed the seeds in a pile near Serena's right hand, then pointed to the end of the table where the sunflower had been. "This side of the table will represent the bottom. We each take turns placing our token in one of the open grid spaces. You must start at the bottom, and may not place a token on the next row up unless one of us has placed a token in the space directly below it. The goal is to be the first one to create a line of four consecutive tokens, either vertically, horizontally, or diagonally."

"Sounds simple enough," Serena said. "I take it you played this with your sisters?"

"I still do," Ivy replied. Serena's heart swelled. "It has been at least a year since my last game, however. I played with Vera and Sage the most. Both grew tired of losing."

"Challenge accepted." Serena picked up a few of the seeds. "So, who goes first?"

"You may choose."

"I'll go first then," Serena said, placing a seed in the middle of the bottom row, leaving three open spaces to either side. "May I ask you a personal question?" The threat of imminent death notwithstanding, Serena longed to understand Ivy better, if the dryad would open up.

"Only if I may ask you one first," Ivy said, placing one of her berries at the far left of the game grid.

"Go for it." Serena placed a seed to the left of her first one.

"During the Symphony of Lies, you said there are two kinds of family; the one you are born to, and the one you choose for yourself." Ivy placed a berry to the right of Serena's seeds, blocking her from making a line of four in the first row. "You called me your sister. Did you mean what you said? Do you understand what family means to dryads?"

Serena couldn't blame Ivy for having lingering doubts. How could anyone be sure of anything said in an environment where everyone lied to survive? "To your first question, yes, I absolutely meant it. We've been through hell and endured a lot together in a short period of time. Those kinds of bonds are hard to break. To your second question..." She paused to place her third seed directly above her first. "I have to admit I still know very little about dryads."

Ivy nodded. "Then allow me to educate you. Family is sacred to us. Family prosperity, in a holistic sense, matters more than the happiness of any specific individual. The collective comes first, the individual second. In that regard, we may not be so different from Kimori's ants. Before the Vohr invasion, I rarely had to concern myself with functioning on my own, only contributing to the group. Thinking and acting as an individual has been... difficult. I am not good at it."

"Under the circumstances, I'd say you're doing great," Serena said.

"It is kind of you to say so." Ivy placed a berry on top of Serena's most recent seed. "I am unused to privacy. My sisters and I shared everything with each other. There were no secrets between us. We slept in the same room."

"All sixteen of you?" Serena placed another seed.

"It was a large room." Ivy paused, considering the game grid between them, then placed another berry. "My point is this: There is absolute candor between members of a dryad family. In accepting you as a sister, I am giving you my absolute trust that I can tell you anything."

"And I'll never do anything to betray that, I promise."

"It means I expect absolute candor from you, as well."

Where was Ivy going with this? "I'm sharing my brain with a shapeshifting cephalopod," Serena said, placing a seed so she had a stack of three. "My thoughts are an open book to Tako. I have no problem bringing you into the circle of trust."

"Good. Then you can explain to me why we are here, playing this game." Ivy placed a seed in the space above Serena's, preventing her from winning on her next turn.

"Aren't you having fun?" Serena picked up a seed, intending to place it on top of one of Ivy's berries to create a diagonal line of three. Before she could, Tako wrapped a tentacle around her wrist and gently dragged her hand away from the game grid. He then picked up one of the seeds and placed it on the bottom row, one space in from the far right of the grid. Serena didn't catch it until his tentacle retracted onto her back. If he hadn't placed the seed there, Ivy would have won on her next turn. Tako said nothing. The teasing sense of satisfaction he radiated through their bond said everything. She'd let Ivy's comment distract her.

Ivy raised an eyebrow. "I did not realize I faced two opponents." She popped one of the *alucinatus* berries into her mouth.

Weren't those berries supposed to improve concentration and memory in dryads? "That's cheating," Serena said, not meaning it.

"Blame Tako for escalating matters. I merely seek to maintain competitive parity." Ivy placed a berry so she had her own vertical stack of three. "You did not answer my question. Why are we here?"

Serena placed a seed on top of Ivy's berry, cutting off the dryad's victory without Tako's help this time. She took a deep breath. Time to find out how serious Ivy was about absolute candor between sisters. "I have a lot of reasons for not partying with the elves, but the primary one is I didn't want you to be alone tonight. I was afraid if you were left with nothing to do but think, you'd dwell on your lost sisters, fall into a bout of despair, and be unable to fight when we need you most."

"Good." Ivy nodded approvingly.

"Good?" Of all the ways Ivy could have reacted, Serena hadn't expected that.

"You answered honestly. I would have been offended if you had not." Ivy placed a berry at the far right of the bottom row.

"You're not mad at me?"

"I am not. I appreciate your concern. I declined Annea's invitation for a similar reason."

"I thought it was because you didn't understand the appeal."

"I actually do, but pretending not to served my purpose," Ivy said. "I knew if I declined, you would too. You would feel the need to be protective of me. You use action and taking care of others as ways to avoid dealing with your own emotional duress. Korahshka seeks your power, and your plan to deal with him places you at great risk. You need distractions because you do not wish to think about that."

Tako laughed. *"Wow, Ivy's got you pegged."*

Serena needed a moment to digest that. "You're saying you offered yourself up as a distraction so I would have someone to take care of, so I wouldn't dwell on negative thoughts. You're doing the same thing for me that I thought I was doing for you."

"Correct," Ivy said, a mischievous smile spreading across her face.

Serena couldn't help but stare. The entire time she'd known Ivy, her facial expressions had come in four flavors: impassive, angry, frightened, or sad. She never smiled. This felt like her first glimpse of the real Ivy, when she felt comfortable enough to shed her emotional walls.

"Well, I think this proves we're definitely sisters." Serena grinned in turn, placing a seed in the last open space on the bottom row. She didn't care if the move made any strategic sense. Tako's presence in the back of her mind radiated happiness and contentment — the psychic equivalent of a cat curled up in her lap.

"You wished to ask me a personal question earlier?" Ivy asked, placing a berry on the far left of the grid, second row from the bottom.

"I was going to ask what it was like to have such a large family, but you kind of answered that," Serena placed a seed next to the berry Ivy just played. "So let me ask you something else. What does a happy ending look like for you? We've driven the Vohr off Kimori. Korahshka's dead. Then what?"

Ivy's eyes lost focus as she turned her gaze inward. "I do not know," she admitted. "I have not considered the matter." She placed a berry, creating a vertical column of three on the left edge of the game grid.

Serena countered Ivy with her next move. "I don't have a grand plan either. But when Amara and Cole take their Shrikes back to Z'han, I'll be going with them. Tako doesn't think it's safe to be partners for much longer. He thinks his aging will harm me, so he wants to return to his own kind."

"You do not wish him to leave," Ivy said, seeing through Serena's poor attempt at nonchalance.

"I don't. With so many worlds out there, someone must have a way to cure the harmful side effects of Octari aging. Maybe even lengthen their lifespans. I want to at least try to find those remedies. Tako doesn't."

"The Davoh'rei have infiltrated sector governments in the Nexus. They can be counted on to continue expanding and tightening their grip." Tako said. *"Even with Korahshka gone and the Vohr diminished, the fight to prevent them from releasing Balor and the rest of his kind is not over. There are more important things at stake than the life of one aging Octari."*

"When did it become my job to save the multiverse? That's on the schedule for tomorrow. I should get some time off before doing it again." Serena took a deep breath. Her irritation faded. Tako was right, and she knew it. It wasn't in her nature to look away and do nothing. If she did, she'd be no better than the Sector Council. But she'd feel better about that fight with Tako around.

"Let's not have this argument again tonight. Relax. Enjoy your time with Ivy. You can yell at me all you want when Kimori is safe. It'll mean we won, and that we survived."

Ivy said nothing, watching with a concerned expression. They'd all learned how to tell when she was having a telepathic conversation.

"Whose turn is it?" Serena asked, forcing a smile as a single tear rolled down her cheek. She wiped it away and clamped down on her emotions. These might be the last quiet moments of relaxation they ever had. It would be a shame to waste them with arguments and negativity.

"Still mine," Ivy said, filling a gap in the grid Serena would have exploited to win on her next turn.

"Tako made a good point just now," Serena said, studying the state of the game. "The fight's not over for me while I know the Davoh'rei work to free the Luminous Ones. I'd wager Annea will retain her title as Sword of Kimori and be the person spearheading Kimori's war efforts offworld while Queen Jesserin keeps things running at home." Serena placed a seed where she could win on a diagonal line on her next turn.

Green magic swirled around Ivy's fingers as she plucked another berry from her miniature *alucinatus* tree. "Then you will need a healer to keep you alive."

"Probably. Do you know one?" Serena asked.

"I am aware of one," Ivy said, matching Serena's tone. "She is proficient in the basics, and will no doubt have plenty of opportunity to practice while following you around." Ivy placed a berry to set herself up for a win on the next turn. She'd missed Serena's setup.

"I win." Serena placed a seed five rows up, five spaces in from the left edge, completing a diagonal line of four.

Ivy stared at the table for a long moment, shocked. She could have won on her prior turn. They'd both missed it while talking. "You were correct to keep me company tonight. I am clearly not myself."

"Beginner's luck. Want to play best out of three?"

"Yes."

It turned into a best of five. Then best of seven. Then best of nine. Each of them wanted to continue the series, until they both had to concede the hour was late and they should try to get some sleep before the insanity started. Ivy, to Serena's chagrin, did emerge the ultimate winner. She had a competitive streak Serena hadn't expected. Probably a byproduct of being the youngest of sixteen children.

Serena hadn't thought it would be possible to sleep, but she managed it, picturing Ivy's smile as a dreamless sleep claimed her.

CHAPTER 56

TOURING THE FRONT LINES

An hour after sunrise, Serena met up with the Ankoran leader, Kuma, outside the main ground-level entrance to the ant colony. Despite carrying a spear in his hands, a broadsword on his back, and a pair of axes at his hips, the enormous bearfolk looked friendly and relaxed as he bowed in greeting.

"Good morning, Lady Pyromancer," Kuma said. "Today is a wonderful day. The air sings with the anticipation of glorious battle. We are ready and eager to fight."

"I love the enthusiasm," Serena said. She meant it. For now, she had the worst of her apprehension, anxiety, and dread under control. She felt as comfortable about this battle as she could be, knowing she'd start it behind a line of massive bears genuinely excited about the peril facing them all. For most species, she'd consider their attitude a product of ignorance or arrogance, but with the Ankora, it looked like absolute faith in themselves and their abilities. "I'm afraid I lack your vigor at the moment."

"Ah, don't you worry about that," Kuma grinned. "Our secret weapon will perk you right up, you'll see. But we'll get to that. As our foes have yet to grace us with their presence, I thought I would take this time to familiarize you with the layout of our forces. It is one thing to see troop deployments on a map. Quite another to be amongst them at ground level. In the heat of battle, it's important to know where everyone should be."

"You're right," Serena said, noting the Ankora had taken down their tents and piled up everything they didn't need for battle against the exterior of the ant colony. Where a tent city stood the day before, the ground for at least a quarter mile surrounding the world tree was nothing but barren dirt. The Ankora intended to engage the Vohr further away from the tree, leaving the immediate vicinity an open kill box for the elves to shoot into from the branches above, should anything fly over the Ankoran line.

"I don't recall seeing those yesterday." She pointed at behemoths posted at regular intervals along the rear of the Ankoran battle line. The creatures faced away from them, staring off into the open fields to the north.

"We had our toro-akabi hunting in the forests and swamps to the south yesterday," Kuma explained. "We wanted to give them one last quality meal before the fighting started."

Kuma put fingers to his lips and let out three quick, shrill whistles. The creature to the far left of the line turned and trotted towards them. It was fifteen feet tall, and more than forty feet long from snout to tail. Turquoise scales covered its body. Sharp quills protruded from the back of its head. Its head shape landed somewhere between the long and thin shape of a crocodile's and the more robust carnivore skulls in Blackwell's sanctum. Despite its reptilian appearance, its stride reminded Serena of wolves. Its tongue lolled out from between serrated teeth as long as her hand, further enhancing the canine aspect.

It's just an enormous, reptilian puppy, Serena told herself as it stopped to sniff Kuma's outstretched hand. *With very, very sharp teeth... and claws.* The toro-akabi's feet had four toes, each ending with a curved claw longer than Annea's kukris. Probably designed for climbing, or pinning and holding down prey.

"Let her get your scent," Kuma said. He tapped the beast's nose twice, then pointed at Serena.

She fought to keep her balance when the toro-akabi looked at her and yawned, allowing her to inspect its many, many teeth from within arm's reach. It could easily swallow her whole if it wanted to. The stench of rotting meat in its breath assaulted her like a shove. Serena's instincts screamed for her to run. She closed her eyes and held her ground, forcing herself to trust that the Ankora trained their animals well. This thing was a natural predator. Fleeing might make it see her as prey and give chase. It closed its mouth and pressed its nose into her chest, taking a series of deep sniffs.

"It doesn't have to be that close to do this, does it?" Serena asked, mustering the courage to look the beast in the eyes. Its front-facing eyes were looking right back into hers.

"You are correct. She had your scent from the moment you stepped out of the ant colony. But toro-akabi only allow the fearless to ride them."

"Fearless? I nearly peed myself."

"Hmm. Perhaps it's better to say they respect courage and show deference to beings who won't back down."

As Serena's heart rate slowly returned to normal, her brain caught up to what Kuma had said. "Wait, *ride them?* You want me to mount this beast?"

"Why not? It'll make it faster and easier to survey the battle lines," Kuma said. "You'll have to hop off when the fighting starts though. It's dangerous to ride a toro-akabi into battle without extensive training. And protective gear." Kuma whistled again, a long tone followed by two staccato blasts. The toro-akabi presented its side to them, then lay flat on the ground. Even in that position, Serena would need a ladder to reach the saddle situated between its shoulder blades.

"Protective gear?" Serena asked.

"You'll see." Kuma stepped onto the creature's left front leg, using it like a stepladder to reach the quills on the back of its head. Grabbing onto them, he leapt into the saddle with ease, then reached down to offer Serena a hand. He hoisted her onto the saddle as if she weighed no more than a pillow.

It took her a few minutes to get used to how they swayed in the saddle while the massive reptile walked, but once she adjusted to it, she was able to settle in and enjoy the unique view of the Ankoran army.

Three thousand bearfolk soldiers stood at attention a quarter mile to the north of the world tree, arranged in groups of one hundred. They were deployed in a wide arc that stretched over three miles, covering the "northern hemisphere" if you considered the world tree the equator of a map. Each group had their own toro-akabi behind them. Like Kuma, the rank-and-file soldiers held spears, and carried a sword, axes, or both. As imposing as the

Ankora were, Serena's stomach knotted at the thought of them wading into combat against swarms of manti and other potential horrors with nothing but melee weapons. Sure, they had covering fire from elves in the world tree's branches overhead, but still, it felt insufficient.

"You're forgetting about the ants," Tako said.

"You're right. Where are they?" Serena asked. Everyone had their zones of responsibility. The Chiroptera would cover the land to the south of Kimori, the Ankora the north. The elves would protect the tree from its branches. The ants... The ants were supposed to be *everywhere.*

"They'll be here," Tako spoke like a teacher chastising a student for nodding off during an important lecture. She'd done her best to follow along, but yes, her focus drifted off several times during the lengthy battle planning session. She learned better from books.

If he thought ignorance would jeopardize her safety, Tako would have told her, which meant he was teasing her and wanted to see her reaction when she figured it out. She considered seeing if she could look into Tako's memories like he could hers and getting the answer that way, but decided not to. *Let Tako have his fun.* They both had to find amusement where they could.

Kuma marched them to the west end of the Ankoran formation, then they rode east, marching in front of the first rank of troops. He waved to the soldiers and shouted encouragement the whole time. At the midpoint, he brought their mount to a stop and gestured to the rider of the nearest group's toro-akabi. "Golgari, the Lady Pyromancer would like a demonstration."

"No problem," Golgari said, his voice a bass rumble. "Am I targeting something?" He wore the same rubbery gray suit she'd seen on all the toro-akabi riders, which came in four pieces – pants, coat, boots, and gloves. Combined, they effectively sealed in an Ankora from the neck down. Given the bear's thick coats of fur, she had to imagine the suits were stiflingly hot and uncomfortable. Nothing she'd want to fight in.

"Full charge only, no release," Kuma said.

"You're the boss." Golgari kicked the toro-akabi's flanks with his boots and tugged a pair of quills at the back of the beast's head. It responded by shaking back and forth like a wet dog drying itself. The quills along its body started to glow a dim yellow. Electricity crackled down the toro-akabi's spine like a tightly contained thunderstorm, pooling at its tail. A ball of lightning formed on the flat, paddle-like tail, which reminded her more of beavers than anything she'd seen on a reptile. That ball of lightning was large enough that she could have stood inside it.

After a few seconds, the electricity discharged into the air. The hair of the nearest Ankoran soldiers stood out at random angles, but nothing else happened. Serena would have gone flying off the toro-akabi with all its shaking. Golgari looked as relaxed as a man just awoken from a nice nap.

"In the wild, toro-akabi hunt by clinging to the sides of trees, waiting to ambush prey," Kuma said. "They use electricity to stun their victims, then pounce for the kill. For our needs, they are siege weapons, cavalry, and combatants all in one."

The rubbery suits the riders wore made a whole lot more sense now. Must be some sort of protection against electricity. It wouldn't do to get fried by your mount in the middle of a battle, would it?

Their tour concluded near the Planar Gate, where Serena would be stationed for the first phase of the fight. "We come at last upon the greatest weapon of the Ankora."

Beside the Gate, five ancient-looking bearfolk stood on a stage that was nothing more than a group of logs lashed together and hastily sanded down to be level. The musicians' stooped posture, tentative movements, and graying, almost white fur suggested their fighting days were well behind them. They had an eclectic mix of instruments, including a guitar, some kind of flute, and many kinds of drums arranged into two distinct sets. The last bear, no doubt their vocalist, hummed softly to himself as he paced in front of the others. Two hundred Ankoran soldiers surrounded the stage as a last line of defense to protect the musicians.

"They're the secret weapon you've been hyping up?" Serena asked. "I love music as much as anyone else, but it's not what I think of when someone says *weapon*."

"Music is a universal language. It can convey feelings and emotions without words. It can enhance pleasure, relaxation, grief, anger, and so many other feelings, depending on the song and the context. The Bards have learned how to infuse their music with magic, amplifying its power a thousand-fold. You'll see soon enough. When this battle's won, the musicians of Kimori will be begging The Bards for lessons."

She'd read about music's use in battles, like tales of noble knights marching to war to the sound of regal battle marches, or trumpeters using specific songs to relay orders over the noise and confusion of battle. Now, she'd have a chance to see the concept in action. No doubt such signalling would help, but how were these old bears a *weapon?*

"They are also the ones we have entrusted to deliver your signal when the time comes," Kuma said. When Korahshka arrived on the battlefield, Annea and Ivy needed to be told so they could get into position. It'd be too obvious something was up if Serena sent the signal herself.

Behind the stage and its defenders, Amara sat in the cockpit of her Shrike with the hood open, snacking on fried fish. Her Octari offered Serena and Tako a wave from within their tank above and behind her, a gesture Tako returned.

Without warning, the Planar Gate popped to life. Serena was in the act of dismounting and almost stumbled at the sight of the unexpected ribbon of light. *"We weren't expecting any more reinforcements, were we?"* Serena asked.

"No. Everyone's here," Tako said. *"Look at where it's coming from."*

Above the Gate floated the infinity symbol representing the Nexus.

After a few seconds, the ribbon of light disappeared with a pop. The infinity symbol in the air faded away. Nothing came through.

A shiver ran up Serena's spine. Fearing the worst, she traced the eight symbols for Torbakhal in the air, praying to the All-Mother it would work.

Nothing happened. No golden light appeared at her fingertip. No symbols hovered in the air.

The Davoh'rei quarantined Kimori.

Cypher failed.

They'd just been denied any hope of escape. They'd either defeat the Vohr, or they'd die.

She wasn't given time to dwell on it. A screaming whistle pierced the air, followed by a pop. Purple light filtered down through the many branches of the world-tree overhead. It was the warning that scouts detected Vohr troops.

It marked the start of a battle that would determine the fate of the multiverse.

"Don't think like that," Tako said. *"Dwelling on stakes that big would drive anyone mad. Focus on the here and now. Survive the next minute, then the one after that."*

The Bards' drummers beat out a martial cadence. The guitar and flute joined in, giving the song the feeling of an ancient battle march. Their vocalist screamed and bellowed lyrics laced with primal aggression and righteous fury in a language she couldn't understand. Did the Planar Gate's translation magic not apply to music? She'd ask about that if they survived.

Her eyes went wide when the music's power took hold. She felt lighter, as if Kimori's gravity dropped by a third in an instant. She felt invigorated. Rejuvenated. Stronger than she'd ever been. Like she could punch a hole through a Z'han battleship if she wanted to. Like she could run ten miles without breaking a sweat.

Tako vibrated against her skin as if dancing to the beat. A quick check through their bond confirmed yes, that's *exactly* what he was doing. She didn't need to see him to know his skin was cycling through different colors and patterns in time to the music. *"This is incredible! I FEEL AMAZING!!!"* The Octari radiated pure, childlike joy.

"Now you begin to understand why we call this a weapon," Kuma said in response to Serena's undisguised grin. "Our music helps us transcend normal limits, and there have never been better practitioners of this art than the men before you."

Nobody showed the transformative power of the music more than the musicians themselves. Immersed in their performance, The Bards moved with the speed and vigor of men a quarter of their age.

"I must join my people now," Kuma said. "I wish you good fortune with your hunt, Lady Pyromancer. Chop off the demon's head. We shall deal with his minions." Flashing her a savage smile at odds with his calm demeanor, Kuma turned and jogged back to the Ankoran battle line, his toro-abaki matching pace at his side.

Serena marched herself to an empty patch of ground at least a hundred yards away from anyone else. Nothing to do now but wait for the enemy to descend upon them.

And pray her plan worked.

CHAPTER 57

THE BRAWL IN THE SWAMP

I vy stood at the edge of the swamp alongside a scout ant, enjoying the damp scent of stagnant water and rotting plant matter. It reminded her of the mangrove forest an hour's walk from her family's village. It was the scent of happier times.

Warm sunlight filtered down through the world tree's branches overhead, enough to nourish her and the forest surrounding her, but not enough to let her produce the kind of solar beam she had on Torbakhal. She did not mind. Holding in so much power had not been pleasant.

When the signal came, the scout ant would fly her back to the world tree as fast as possible. Until then, she would use her magic to distract, delay, suppress, and contain the Vohr as best she could, making it easier for the Chiroptera to cut them down.

Despite the high probability she would return to the soil today, Ivy felt calmer than she had at any point since arriving in the Nexus for the first time. Her sisters had given their lives so she could survive, and for a while, that seemed a useless sacrifice. What purpose was living when everything that gave it meaning had died? Why carry on when she could never again bury her feet in Ataraxian soil? In those first days, her family's sacrifice felt more like a curse than a gift.

But she was not alone anymore. She had a new sister. A human. A *pyromancer*. Never had she thought she would feel affection towards someone using magic her people considered evil. Serena taught her to see beyond assumptions and stereotypes, and to begin to understand her own value as an individual. She mattered for more than what she contributed to a group.

She had purpose again.

I am not a warrior, but I will still fight, in my own way. She could not match Annea's speed or ruthless killing efficiency. Nor could she compete with Serena's ability to channel power into herself. Nature was her weapon; every tree, flower, and bush hers to command. Her talents would help keep the Vohr from breaching the Nexus. She would make her sisters proud.

At the moment, however, she would have preferred better company.

"This waiting is stupid," rasped a Chiroptera to her left, a finger buried to the second knuckle up his nose. He rooted around in there, fishing out a wad of mucus that seemed too large to fit inside his nasal cavity. He flicked it at a tree, where it stuck. "These swamps cover miles. Why are we allowing the Vohr so much uncontested terrain?"

"If you wish to fight in the swamp, I will not stop you," Ivy said, irritated that the small mammal pulled her from her thoughts.

"Just like a woman to sit back and let the men take care of business," another Chiroptera said. Several of his companions nodded in agreement.

Ivy ignored the remark, wondering what happened in the simian, batlike creature's history to make them so persistently hostile towards females. Though the Chiroptera only fought for profit, they were still here, willing to fight, when so many others would not. That earned them a small measure of respect in her eyes, even if she found them repulsive. Annea made clear their welcome on Kimori post-battle would only last as long as it took them to handle their dead according to their customs, collect their spoils, and depart.

She could endure them that long.

"The swamps are the hunting grounds of chameleosaurs — an invasive species of predators that can make themselves almost invisible," Ivy said, suspecting the rank-and-file Chiroptera had not been briefed beyond where to deploy. Perhaps additional information would make them less irritating. "Annea intends to let the Vohr march through the swamps in hopes those two problems cancel each other out."

"Smart thinking," said a third Chiroptera, leaving *"for a woman"* implied.

Eager to have something to do, Ivy stepped into the swamp and pointed her staff at the nearest trees, coaxing them into twisting and entwining their branches in ways that would slow approaching forces. She lifted roots to position them above the soil but below the surface of the water, creating a hidden nightmare of trip hazards that extended a hundred yards into the swamp. Altering what already existed required much less effort than producing new plants, and she wanted her stamina to last as long as possible.

She sloshed through knee-deep brown water, working her way west. Her eyes darted left and right, keeping an eye out for the faint shimmer of camouflaged chameleosaurs. All the while, she used her staff as a conduit to extend the range of her magic, transforming the swamp into what she needed it to be. She stayed within fifty feet of the water's edge. Close enough she could sprint back to the forest if she spotted predators. Or so she hoped. Her insect companion hovered twenty feet overhead, never saying a word.

The Chiroptera watched her from the relative safety of the shore. None offered to follow along as bodyguards. No surprise there.

Satisfied she had made the transition between swamp and forest as hazardous as possible, Ivy returned to dry land. She mounted the scout ant to survey the scene one last time from the air. Two thousand Chiroptera hid in the forest below, most perched on the upper branches of trees. They carried blades made from an obsidian-colored metal she did not recognize. The Chiroptera insisted the primitive-looking weapons could slice through any known material. With their speed and agility, they would perform coordinated hit-and-fade attacks against the enemy, diving down from tree branches for a slash or two before disengaging.

A shriek filled the air, followed by a pop. Purple light filtered down through the world tree's branches. The invasion had begun.

After several minutes of silence, Ivy asked her mount, "How far away were the scouts?"

<They're coming into view now,> the ant replied. They gained altitude and zipped to the left to avoid one of the world tree's branches.

The Chiroptera deployed further away from the world tree than the Ankora had. This far out from the world tree's trunk, its branches were either unpopulated or partially hollowed out and filled with dirt to serve as farming terraces. Ivy could just glimpse tiny specks of more scout ants in the distance. All flew straight towards them.

"The Vohr are close," Ivy said.

<Indeed. We will be fighting soon. Do you wish to return to the ground?>

"Only if we see flying Vohr. If the sky remains uncontested, keep us ten feet over the canopy. I will work my magic from above." In retrospect, that is what she should have been doing the whole time. There was never any need to wade into the swamp and risk a chameleosaur attack. *Make better decisions,* she chided herself. "Take us a quarter mile into the swamp. I wish to see the enemy's advance before they reach the Chiroptera forces. An aerial view will help me see where we are needed."

And allow for rapid retreat when the signal comes.

The pair hovered in tense silence as the scouts passed by. One paused to give Ivy an update. <We saw three tunnels, each about a mile apart. They are guarded by amphibians that spray poison into the air. Some kind of giant frog. We couldn't get close. We'll need major reinforcements to attack the tunnels.>

"How many troops?" Ivy asked.

<Of the Vohr? Many, all from species not known to us. They poured out of the tunnels and massed up before setting off this way.>

"Describe the creatures you saw. Please," Ivy added, recalling the ants were not hers to command. They deserved courtesy.

<We could not get close enough to get a good view. But amongst them was a pair of very large monsters. I must report to Queen Chibi,> they said, soaring off abruptly.

For now, Ivy had the sky to herself. Several minutes passed in silence before she saw movement at the limit of her vision.

Hundreds of hairless, gray-skinned canines with spikes all over their bodies dashed through the brackish water, with ten times as many tan-skinned deer not far behind. The canines she recognized from Orlan's briefing. He'd called them shredders. The deer were Ataraxian, and should have had a pseudo-fur of red and orange leaves.

These must be disposable shock troops, meant to soften up resistance before more dangerous Vohr arrive. Her stomach twisted seeing more fauna from her world corrupted into mindless killing machines.

Streaks formed in the water below. She could not see what caused them, meaning the chameleosaurs had arrived to defend their territory.

The dinosaurs waited for the invaders to pass before ambushing them from behind. A dozen deer fell in seconds when the pack pounced. Blood sprayed from severed arteries. Some of it splashed onto the attackers, rendering them partially visible. The chameleosaurs had a *kill now, eat later* mentality, moving on to new targets after delivering mortal wounds.

The shredders spun at the deer's cries of distress. Hunting by smell more than sight, they showed no confusion fighting targets Ivy could not see.

The swamp water ran red with blood.

Roars, growls, howls, and yelps filled the air. The noise drew in additional packs of invasive dinosaurs, who attacked stragglers at the edges of the melee.

The corrupted deer delivered their share of carnage too. With hooves transformed into spikes, they reared up and stabbed down into their opposition. They missed more often than not, but there were so many of them that blind flailing still killed dozens of dinosaurs. It also resulted in many deaths on their own side. They did not seem to care.

Within minutes, so many corpses clogged this shallow section of swamp that combatants walked on the dead more often than through water.

Ivy bore silent witness to the perverse mockery of nature playing out below her. She made no move to assist either side. *So much unnecessary death. The Davoh'rei will pay for this.*

In the end, the dinosaurs were outnumbered and overmatched by the invaders. The few survivors yelped with rage and pain before retreating deeper into the swamp. Annea's plan to concede the swamps to the Vohr had borne some fruit, at least. The dinosaurs slayed ten mutated beasts for every chameleosaur killed. They were fearsome predators. However, most of the Vohr remained.

A pair of deeper roars forced her to look away from the carnage below. On the horizon, trees swayed. Others bent or snapped as something rammed through them.

Does the desecration of Ataraxia have no limit? Ivy's fingers tightened around her staff.

Two guardian beasts came into view. The bearlike creatures stood twenty feet tall and looked like more refined versions of the monstrosity Moogi had become. They showed no signs of Moogi's madness. Like her village's guardian beast, both had the top halves of dryads grafted onto their shoulders and another above their rear legs — three former dryads each. These dryads' skin was closer to their natural shades of green and orange, but looked far too pale and sickly. Their eyes were sewn shut or gouged out. Despite the visual impairment, the dryads at the front of each beast looked skyward.

They stared at Ivy.

She felt certain they would hunt her to the exclusion of anything else until she died, or they did.

CHAPTER 58
THE OBVIOUS TARGET

Serena bounced back and forth on her feet, savoring the sense of strength and power brought on by the music of The Bards. The elderly Ankora flowed from one song to the next without pause. All of them were fast paced, aggressive pieces that spoke to her on a primal level. Her fear and anxiety slid away, replaced by determination and a persistent sense of righteous anger. She'd never felt more ready for a fight. That was, she assumed, the whole point of their performance.

The Vohr didn't keep them waiting long. Less than ten minutes after the signal flare, the harbingers of death appeared on the horizon. Thousands of manti filled the skies; a swirling, ever-shifting cloud of simple-minded malice flying their way at top speed. Sunlight reflected and bounced off their bladed arms with an intensity that made the swarm difficult to look at. She might have found the sparkling reflections pretty, if she didn't know what she was looking at.

Amara broke away from The Bards to position her Shrike behind the main Anokran battle line. As soon as the manti were in range, she opened up with the Z'han death machine's arm guns, sending a torrent of bullets down range. Her Octari joined in from the water-filled compartment behind her, maneuvering each of the eight multi-jointed arms on the Shrike's back independently to spray the manti with beams of concentrated energy. Every hit blew a fist-sized hole into the overgrown insects. Green blood and severed body parts filled the air. The duo racked up dozens of kills in half as many seconds. The manti, each the size of a horse, created quite the mess when their bodies splatted into the ground. Amara and her partner would need to watch their fire soon if they didn't want to drop a bug on someone's head.

If only the king of Z'han had let them borrow more than two of the things…

How can the Octari keep track of eight different weapons at once? Serena thought. In human terms, that felt like asking your hands, elbows, feet, and knees to act independently of each other, each with minds of their own.

"That's more or less how it is," Tako said. *"Octari brains are decentralized. Each of our limbs has its own sub-brain with the ability to independently make decisions when we want it to. An Octari simply has to give a generalized command, like 'shoot the manti' and then allow their limbs to take control and make their own decisions about how they do it. It makes shooting eight targets at once much less complicated than it appears."*

The buzzing in the air intensified as scout ants zipped by to join the fight. They flew low, barely high enough to clear the top of the Planar Gate or The Bards. They would be a big help in the battle for aerial dominance, but the manti seriously outnumbered them.

"That can't be all the ants. I thought the queens said they had plenty of troops for this fight."

Tako snickered. *"You'll see. Any second now."*

As the manti closed in, the swarm split. Some soared into the world tree's branches above. The scout ants pursued them, drawing some of the enemy into dogfights. Elven weapons sprang into action. Ballista bolts punched through three or four manti before slowing too much to penetrate their exoskeletons. The elves' other stationary weapons were rapid-fire projectile weapons similar to the Shrike's arm guns, though not as powerful. Still, bullets were like arrows — if you put enough of them into an enemy, they tended to die.

The elves were deliberate in the placement of their weapons, situating them to minimize the potential for crossfire into another tree branch. They still had to pick their shots with care so they didn't fire into the Ankora. Most of their shots went into manti safely clear of the battle line.

The majority of the bugs focused on the Ankora. The bears had their spears pointing up, ready to counter attacks from above. Apparently recognizing this, manti landed in the open fields to the north of the line and formed up for a charge.

The ground rumbled beneath Serena's feet.

"Here it comes!" Tako said.

Dirt exploded into the air. Hundreds, perhaps thousands of holes opened up in the ground in the manti's midst. Drones erupted from the openings to dismember and disembowel the invaders. Mandibles bit through manti legs. They ripped open gashes in manti flanks. They severed arms. Drones climbed over each other to get high enough to decapitate their enemies. Some ants clung to their enemy's sides, using their weight to slow the monsters down so others could swarm and rip the enemy apart.

One moment, thousands of manti had the fields north of the Ankoran line to themselves. Seconds later, they were outnumbered at least ten-to-one. Any manti that slipped and fell in the blood and gore coating the ground got buried under a surge of furious drones.

Goddess, Serena thought. *If the ants ever turned on the elves, the elves wouldn't survive a day.*

It looked like war between insect tribes on a grand scale. Drones threw themselves at the manti with no regard for their own lives. Scythe-like blades flashed like lightning, every strike cutting a drone in two. At least six ants died for every manti they killed. The ants didn't care. They poured out of their underground tunnels faster than the manti could kill them.

While the ants took the bulk of the early losses, the Ankora held the line, ducking under slashes and impaling manti with spears. One of them dodged a swipe and ripped that arm off bare handed. Another leapt over a pair of slashes and decapitated two manti on his way down. Their toro-akabi charged up and flung balls of lightning into the air, using their tails like catapults. Each sphere of concentrated electricity burst on contact with a manti, sending bolts of lightning chaining into another two or three before dissipating.

Amara dashed up and down the rear of the Ankoran line, the Shrike raining death upon the manti with incredible precision.

She'd shifted her focus to ground-level targets to avoid splattering ants or Ankora under falling Vohr. She had an incredible eye for spotting bearfolk in distress. Any time one fell out of position or was about to get flanked, the Shrike was there to provide covering fire.

Serena watched it all with the hyper-focus of a woman expecting death to descend upon her at any moment. Her plan depended on it, in fact. *"This is it, my friend. It's time for us to do our part."*

Tako bunched himself up as low on her body as he could, spreading himself across her legs and butt. He didn't even make a joke about it, though she knew he wanted to. He kept enough of himself above the waistline of her pants that he could continue to watch her back.

With her upper body clear and Tako as safe as he could be, Serena coated her arms, shoulders, and head in flames. She pushed them out as far as she thought she could without overly straining herself. She needed to save her strength for the real fight. The goal here was flashiness, not high heat.

Serena's Grand Plan to Save the Multiverse, Step One: Make yourself a big, obvious target for the man who wants to kill you.

She created weak, snowball-sized fireballs and hurled them at low-flying manti battling scout ants. They moved too fast to accurately target. Most of her attacks fizzled out in the air or exploded harmlessly on open ground. She scored a few lucky hits, but they did no real damage to the manti.

Killing them wasn't the point. This was all about drawing attention to herself.

If Korahshka wanted her so bad, he could come and get her.

The onslaught of manti forced the Ankoran line slowly but inexorably backwards. The bearfolk guarding The Bards would have no choice but to join the fray soon. The manti's numbers seemed as limitless as the ants. Despite dying in huge numbers, there always seemed to be more. A second wave landed while she'd had her attention skyward. A contingent of them pounced over the Ankora to land on open ground behind the line.

As one, they charged Serena.

Amara saw it. She maneuvered her Shrike to spray bullets into the advancing mob, but soon found herself unable to assist as a second, larger group went after her, forcing her to pivot to self defense. For every airborne manti Amara dropped, two made it through the hail of fire free and clear.

She'd assumed Korahshka would come for her himself, not send minions. *You know what they say about assumptions...* Serena forced herself to take a deep breath. Korahshka needed her alive to steal her magic. The manti wouldn't kill her.

A dozen of the bugs encircled her. At a distance of ten feet, they gave her more space to maneuver than they could have. She stood still, not daring to make a move. The manti didn't either, as if awaiting fresh orders. What if they tried to carry her off?

Korahshka needing her *alive* didn't mean he needed her *unharmed*.

If the manti got violent, she'd have to blast her way clear, sprint for the ant colony, and figure out a different way to get Korahshka to show himself.

"Are we just going to stand around staring at each other?" Serena asked. "Go fetch your boss. He and I have a score to settle."

The manti advanced with unnaturally perfect coordination.

Serena charged at the one directly ahead of her. Jets of flame erupted from her hands. With any luck, she'd burn or blind it. As she closed in, she slid, expecting the manti to slice high like the one she'd encountered on Jonah's farm a lifetime ago. It flapped its arms awkwardly, as if attempting to strike her with the flat of its blades. A scythe tip missed her forehead by less than an inch. She rolled to her feet clear of the circle of monsters and sprayed fire at the closest two.

"I can roast your bugs all day!" Serena roared, putting all the bravado she could into the lie. She didn't want to be using this much magic so early in the battle. The Bard's music helped, but she couldn't afford to rely on it. "Korahshka! Man up and fight me!"

The nearest manti collapsed, writhing in agony as they cooked inside their exoskeletons. The others fanned out to stay clear of her flames, positioning themselves between her and the entrance to the ant colony.

Ten manti in front of me. Thousands behind me. No sign of Korahshka. Fantastic. Serena backed up and risked peeking at Tako's vision. She needed to know what was happening behind her.

The Anokran troops were still losing ground to the invaders. Serena was now closer than she'd wanted to be to the battle line. Corpses carpeted the ground, many partially crushed under the feet of manti, Ankora, and toro-akabi. All the spilled blood turned the ground soft and muddy. Drones were still emerging from their holes to join the meat grinder. Amara's Shrike was knocked over. Five manti crawled over it, trying to pry open the cockpits. A third of the elven weapons in the branches above had stopped firing, their operators presumably dead.

We're losing. So much death…

In a flash of desperate inspiration, Serena pulled her dagger from its sheath at her hip. She held the blade to her throat.

"Serena!" Tako radiated alarm. Then he understood.

"Korahshka!" Serena shouted. "If you want my power, you're going to have to fight me yourself! I'm not going to stand here and let your manti soften me up like this is some royal's stag hunt. You don't get to just swoop in and deliver the final blow. I'd end myself before making it easy for you."

She'd do no such thing. She'd fight to her dying breath, but hoped Korahshka didn't feel like calling her bluff. He wouldn't want to risk losing his prize, would he?

Shouts and the screams of the dying accompanied The Bard's songs of righteous rage. The air hummed with the electric crackle of toro-akabi lightning attacks. The fight was close enough now to hear the cracking and crunching of manti and ant exoskeletons. The untranslatable *thrum* of drone war cries.

She still had no sign that Korahshka heard her and was on his way.

The manti facing her remained still as statues.

Would she have to cut herself as a show of sincerity to get him to arrive? Given his enormous ego, she hadn't expected to have to wait. Then a new sound reached her ears, a buzzing of wings deeper than the others.

"Stop being melodramatic," Korahshka said. He rode a variant of manti different from the others she'd seen. It was more than twice the size of the others, with four bladed arms instead of two. It landed behind the ten manti standing between her and the ant colony. Regular manti swirled around him overhead, harassing elven gunners to keep them from shooting at their master. "Do you have any idea how complicated it is to coordinate the simultaneous opening of so many tunnels? To keep thousands of troops dancing to the same tune?" He gestured dismissively towards The Bards, as if to say *You call that music?* "I've been a bit busy. No need to be so impatient. You'll get your turn."

The Bards' drummers switched to playing one-handed and bent over to pick up the flare guns at their feet. With a flourish that made it look like part of their act, they sent red flares streaking into the sky. The signal would be mirrored by observers throughout the branches above, until everyone knew Korahshka had been sighted.

"I'm sorry our resistance has been so inconvenient for you." Serena killed the flames coating her arms, shoulders, and head. They'd served their purpose.

"This hardly qualifies as an inconvenience. The fight will be over in an hour or two." Korashka dismounted the super-sized manti. He wore the same black leather he had in her dreams, with a sword over his shoulder and daggers at his hips. He pointed at the Ankoran battle line, and his mount took off to join the fray. "Now then, since you're in such a hurry to die, it'd be rude to keep you waiting."

The ten manti before Korahshka moved aside to give him a clear path to Serena, then surrounded her again.

"If you need to keep manti around for moral support, it's only fair I get to call in friends too," Serena said. She couldn't let herself be surrounded. Their duel couldn't happen here. Through Tako's eyes, she saw a couple Ankora nearby she thought she recognized. "Kuma! Golgari! Can I borrow you for a minute?" She called over her shoulder.

The Ankoran elder and the toro-akabi rider turned to face her. Thanks to the mural in the Grand Chamber of Rule, both would know what a Davoh'rei looked like, and knew to assume if they saw one, it was Korahshka. They reacted very differently. Golgari roared a command Serena didn't understand and jumped off his enormous reptilian mount. Kuma took off in what seemed like the completely wrong direction.

Korahshka drew his sword and charged.

Golgari ran between manti and hurled himself at Serena, wrapping her up in a flying tackle. He twisted to take the brunt of the impact with the ground, then rolled to pin her beneath him. "Stay down," he said, moving his gloved hands to shield his face.

Serena understood a second later, when a deafening thunderclap exploded overhead. Golgari had ordered his toro-akabi to fire *at her,* using her as the focal point for the deadly discharge of electricity. If not for Golgari shielding her with his rubber-suited body, the attack would have killed her.

Bold. Reckless. I love it.

Golgari stood and pulled Serena to her feet. Eight of the nearest manti were charred corpses. The other two spasmed but remained upright. Kuma came at them from behind and beheaded each with his axes. *He stayed out of the blast radius so he could flank any survivors. They've pulled a stunt like that before.*

"You lived. A pity," Kuma said, addressing Korahshka. The Davoh'rei picked up the sword he'd dropped, flexing his hands as if worried he'd suffered nerve damage. He didn't appear injured.

Walk away guys. I have a clear path now. You know the plan. Serena suspected asking an Ankora to stand down would go as well as asking the sun not to rise in the morning. She couldn't say anything without arousing suspicion anyway.

"That tickled," Korahshka said. He snapped his fingers twice with his free hand, then pointed at Golgari's toro-akabi. His special manti leaped clear of the main battle to dive for the beast. Golgari ran back to aid his mount.

Korahshka offered Kuma a mockery of a salute, then rushed him. Kuma made no effort to disengage. *He wants his shot at chopping the head off the snake.* The two slashed at each other, parried, and spun with such speed and violence that Serena didn't dare add fireballs into the mix. She was as likely to hit Kuma as Korahshka.

The Ankora fought valiantly, but it was soon clear Korahshka was toying with his opponent.

"Leave him alone! I thought you were after me?" Serena threw caution to the wind and hurled a fireball at Korahshka. He swatted it aside with the flat of his blade.

Kuma stepped forward with a heavy downward slash. He overcommitted to the attack. Korahshka sidestepped it, repositioned his sword, and ran the bearfolk elder through.

"It's not all about you, Serena." Korahshka flicked blood off his sword. He stepped away from Kuma, content to let his adversary bleed out on the ground. "I'll play with anyone who's eager to die." Behind him, Korahshka's oversized manti feasted on a dead toro-akabi. Golgari's corpse was impaled on one of its blades.

With supreme effort, Serena clamped down on her rage. *Enjoy your last moments Korahshka. Because I will kill you.*

But not yet.

Kuma and Golgari's deaths helped sell what she needed to do next. It was a critical step. One that went against her instincts.

She fled the battle, running away as fast as her legs would take her.

CHAPTER 59

AN UNPLANNED DESCENT

Annea stood at the edge of a railing, looking down on the world below. She'd chosen this spot strategically. She was on the eastern side of the tree, where a lack of branches nearby afforded her a clear view of the terrain. It was near the base of the tree, so she could get to where Serena needed her to be quickly when the signal came. Though "near the bottom of the tree" still meant over three hundred feet above ground level. She couldn't see all of the conflicts raging to the north and south, but saw enough to have a fair idea how the battle was going.

Worse than she'd hoped. Not as bad as she'd feared.

They'd left the east undefended, not anticipating a Vohr attack from the direction dominated by a large lake. None of the information Orlan provided indicated the Vohr had aquatic creatures. Therefore, this walkway lacked any of the defenses built onto the outlying branches. The branches above had been evacuated. Any manti landing up there would have the run of the place until they tried to get inside the tree itself. Then they'd run into barricaded doors, traps, and squads of armed troops if they broke through.

She paced back and forth, needing the movement as an outlet for her restless energy. She longed to be in the thick of the action on one of the two fronts, but this was a fight where her talents were better utilized elsewhere. Her moment would come. Nobody expected the Ankora or Chiroptera to keep the Vohr away from the ant colony and world tree forever. They had fallback plans.

Queen Jesserin had direct command over the tree's defense throughout the battle. All Annea had to do was wait.

She couldn't stand it. As the Sword of Kimori, it was her duty to lead Kimori's war efforts. This felt like cowardice. The minute her part in Serena's plan was complete, she'd run up the tree and support her people any way she could.

Movement drew her attention away from the battle to the north. A half mile to the east, the lake's surface rippled. Swarms of jellyfish-like creatures breached the surface and soared into the air on puffs of gas. Their flight made them look like living balloons. They deflated as they zipped forward. Each would drop for a moment as they refilled themselves with air, then they'd jet forward again. Light shimmered off them in shades of blue, yellow, and pink.

We may have made a huge mistake leaving the east undefended, she thought.

Without needing a command, Annea's honor guard of six archers nocked arrows, but waited to draw until the strange creatures came within range. She hadn't wanted any troops with her, feeling they'd be better utilized elsewhere. Who needed an honor guard while holding ground nobody expected to be attacked? Jesserin demanded she take a dozen archers with her. The six were a compromise.

"What do you think they do?" Annea addressed the question to everyone and no one. It would be a few minutes before the jellyfish drifted into bow range.

"Maybe they latch onto your face and suffocate you," one archer offered, a young man barely of adult age.

"Probably poison," said another. "They float by, sting you, and drift away while your flesh melts off your bones."

"You're both half right," said a third. "They latch onto your head, then inject you with a chemical that allows them to control your brain. Once under their spell, they'll have us fighting and killing each other."

Everyone laughed. Better to enjoy gallows humor than fall into despair. "Very creative theories," Annea said, studying the jellyfish formation. "The Vohr would be much scarier if you were the ones creating them."

Several hundred of the creatures drifted in the air now, with more emerging from the lake every minute. There had to be a tunnel down there. That one would be a pain in the ass to destroy, assuming they survived long enough to mount a counter-offensive.

Annea didn't like the way the jellyfish maintained a minimum level of distance from each other. If any drifted too close to each other, they'd break off with their next expulsion of air. She turned to the opening into the world tree, where her stewards stood at the ready, each uncharacteristically quiet. "Tik-Tik, run down to the colony and ask Queen Ruta to divert some scouts to the east." At the ant's crestfallen expression, she added, "This is important. I promise she'll be too busy to harass you."

Tik-Tik nodded their head in reluctant understanding and took off.

<Should I go as well?> Pik-Pik asked.

What answer would Pik-Pik prefer? The ants were terrified of their mother, but also experienced separation anxiety from each other. Most days, that wasn't a problem while running basic errands.

Today was not most days.

"No," Annea knelt and stroked Pik-Pik's head. "I may need you to head up the tree with a message for our archers, but I'd prefer not to divert any of them unless we absolutely have to."

"Fire!" One of the archers shouted. The group loosed their first volley into the approaching swarm. Their flight patterns were easy to predict. They inflated, jetted forward in a straight line, paused to reinflate, then repeated the process. They'd shown no ability to make evasive maneuvers.

Every arrow found a target.

Each jellyfish exploded into a ball of fire matching their color.

That's why they keep their distance from each other. They don't want to take each other out when they explode. Annea drew her kukris. The blades glowed purple as she channeled energy into them. She slashed, whirled, and twisted, leaving a lattice of energy in the air where her blades had been. One by one, she gave those slashes a mental push, launching her attacks at the enemy.

The archers loosed arrows as fast as they could, now firing at will rather than waiting for a combined volley. Dozens of jellyfish exploded in the air harmlessly, but it soon became apparent they'd be overrun.

"Fighting retreat!" Annea shouted, drawing two quick slashes through the air and sending the resulting energy at the nearest targets. "Swing south and take the ramp to higher ground!"

The jellyfish weren't interested in living targets. In fact, they didn't seem to know or care that many of them had been destroyed. One group puffed higher into the air, aiming for the first tier of branches overhead. Another group went low and plowed into the ant colony.

They're not trying to kill us. This is about softening us up for something else.

Annea risked a look over the railing. The jellyfish concentrated their attacks on a fifty-foot section of the colony's exterior. As soon as one wave of jellyfish hit the wall and detonated, the next would jet in.

The vantage point allowed her to see another detail she'd missed. Reapers emerged from the lake's waters and advanced towards the ant colony on the same path as the jellyfish. They punched into the colony with the long blades between their knuckles, creating handholds for themselves as they climbed towards the growing hole in the colony a hundred and fifty feet above the ground.

Tik-Tik won't reach the queen in time. Not with the Vohr creating a much more direct route. I'll have to take a detour.

"Carry on without me!" Annea shouted to her men. "Have Jesserin send archers to the eastern branches. I'm making my way to Serena's rendezvous point!"

She traced another series of slashes in the air, calculating where to aim them. If she wanted to do this and live, she needed to create a hole in the jellyfish ranks. "Pik-Pik, get to the rendezvous point, I'll meet you there." She unleashed her energy against the nearest wave of enemies. They exploded harmlessly a couple hundred feet from their destination.

<I want to stay with you, Mom. Please don't leave me,> Pik-Pik said.

The ants were so good about calling her by name. But when scared, they sometimes fell back on titles. It warmed her heart that *Mom* was what they defaulted to for her.

Annea made a snap decision. This stunt would be easier for Pik-Pik than it would be for her, anyway. "Alright. Stay close to me. We're entering the ant colony through that new hole below us. We'll have to warn Queen Ruta ourselves." After launching another wave of slashes at the jellyfish, she sheathed her kukris. She jumped up onto the railing, then turned around to face the tree. With a small hop, she jumped over the side, grabbing the edge of the railing.

Dangling over three hundred feet above the ground, with another wave of explosive jellyfish incoming, she had to move fast. She swung forward and back, building up momentum, then launched herself forward, directly at the section of tree beneath the exterior walkway. While in midair, Annea unsheathed her kukris, intending to stab into the side of the tree to arrest her momentum. From there, she'd climb down the side of the tree, then slide down the slope of the colony to reach her destination. She'd climbed up and down the exterior of the world tree plenty of times as a form of exercise. It was often a faster, if much more difficult, way to get from point A to point B in the tree-city.

Faster, but not risk-free.

The hard exterior of the world tree shrugged off Annea's attempt to stab into it. She slammed into a wall of bark, almost losing her grip on her weapons as she spun into a free fall.

CHAPTER 60
FALLEN GUARDIANS

The Ataraxian guardians stared at Ivy. She stared back. Under normal circumstances, she would have no hope of overpowering a single mature guardian beast, let alone two. Had Moogi been able to think clearly, she could not have restrained him. The finest warriors of Ataraxia occasionally sparred with the beasts as a way to test the limits of their strength and magic. Sometimes, they even won.

I am not a warrior, Ivy thought. But she wasn't alone, either. She would not allow this to become a —

Her scout ant zipped to the left an instant before a tree branch would have impaled them. Ivy held on tight as the ant went through a flurry of evasive dips and rolls. Kimori's world tree was not impacted, but every other tree in the area came alive like a nest of snakes. Their branches magically twisted and extended as they thrust up like spears to skewer Ivy and her ant or swat them from the sky.

Ivy held out her staff, exerting her own will on the branches around them. She could do no more than deflect attacks by a few degrees. It made the difference between survival and a sudden death. Ivy felt a breeze against her skin with every near miss.

She did not dare armor herself in bark. It would add to her weight, slowing down her mount.

"We must lure them back to the Chiroptera," Ivy said. "Let them swarm with numbers."

<Is that wise?> The ant asked, swooping under the canopy. Closer to the ground, fewer trees had a shot at them at the same time. Their trunks and branches would interfere with each other. They dived under two swinging branches. The branches smashed

into each other, shattering both and sending splinters flying in every direction.

"They will follow me all the way back to the world tree if we allow it. I am certain of this." Ivy held on tight as the ant whipped around in a rapid U-turn. "The guardians must be defeated here, now." She did not know if they would have the power to exert influence over Kimori's world tree if they got closer to the trunk. She did not wish to find out.

The ant flew straight at the guardians. As it did, the attacks against them eased up. The guardians were smart enough not to risk having their own magic used against them. As soon as they zoomed past, the assault resumed.

As Ivy hoped, the beasts followed. Perhaps their magic had a limited range. Perhaps they wished to be in close proximity to watch her die. Either way, their fixation on her served her purpose.

"Kill the guardians following me!" Ivy shouted to any Chiroptera in the area. "They are the most dangerous threat."

The scout ant came to an abrupt halt, nearly throwing Ivy. A tree branch swung down in front of them, sending swamp water flying everywhere on impact. It would have been a fatal blow had they not stopped. The ant took off before nearby trees could try again.

They had been fortunate so far that the guardians left plenty of space between themselves and the Vohr's shredders and mutated Ataraxian deer. They only had to worry about trees trying to kill them. That would change soon.

Ivy acted on instinct, pointing her staff at anything that looked threatening. A swiping branch bent up and over her head. She swung her arm right. An impaling thrust curved back on itself by a few inches to skewer ground. They were over dry land now. Right in the heart of the chaos.

A shredder pounced. Her ant shot up, evading the spiny, hairless monster and a thrusting tree branch. The branch impaled the shredder before embedding itself in a neighboring tree. Another shredder caught her ant's rear right leg in its jaws. They lost precious speed and altitude. The ant screamed. Ivy diverted a swiping tree branch so it hit the shredder, knocking the hairless canine free.

Closer to the bulk of the Vohr forces, staying low was no longer safer than flying above the canopy. "Take us up," Ivy said. The ant complied.

Ivy had no idea how she could break away or fight if the Chiroptera did not lend their support. It felt like a thousand spears targeted them at once. The corrupted dryads on each guardian's back bent nature to their will. Tapping into the guardians' strength, their ability to exert influence over plantlife dwarfed her own.

They lacked the time or stamina for an extended fight. The guardians needed to die quickly. But all they had managed to do was dodge.

Then, as suddenly as it started, the attacks against her and her mount ceased. They turned so they could see the action below.

The Chiroptera were executing their plan with terrifying precision. Ivy only caught brief flashes of movement as they pounced on a target, decapitated it in a single swing, and jumped off their victim's back to return to the trees. She estimated an individual Chiroptera killed one Vohr every four seconds. Bodies piled up to the point the Vohr had to jump over their own dead to advance.

Even killing that fast, more than half of the monsters would have survived the ambush to make a break for the world tree.

The guardians changed the equation. Branches narrowed and became whiplike, wrapping themselves around Chiroptera and flinging them into the Vohr horde. Shredders tore off the wings of their unlucky victims or crushed skulls. Mutant deer impaled them with their hooves. Some tree branches slammed into each other like clapping hands, crushing Chiroptera between them.

"Kill the creatures with dryads on their backs!" Ivy shouted. "That will stop the trees."

She had to act now, while they were distracted. Ivy issued instructions to her mount. They dived right at a guardian. It did not notice until her ant hovered over its back and bit off a dryad's head. Some trees in the area went still.

The guardians' muscles tensed like they planned to run. She could not allow that. Vines erupted from the ground where Ivy pointed her staff, wrapping themselves around their forelegs, pinning the beasts in place.

Chiroptera rained from the trees, landing by the dozens on each guardian's back. The beasts went into an enraged panic, using the forest for defense. Branches grabbed and crushed the small mammals. They knocked others loose. But the mercenaries would not be deterred. Ivy did what she could to keep the guardians ensnared while her allies cut down the dryads. Every one that fell reduced the number of trees attacking them.

The shredders and deer continued their mindless race to the world tree, not stopping to aid the guardians. If they had, their numbers may have made victory impossible. When the last of the trees returned to normal, the Chiroptera swarmed like fleas, jumping onto a beast, drawing blood, and jumping off. Speed mattered more than precision.

Ivy tightened and retracted her vines, dragging the guardians to the ground. The beasts roared with rage. They tried to push themselves to their feet, but the Chiroptera would not allow it, risking jumps close to the ground to sever tendons in their legs.

"Take us higher," Ivy said. Her mount obeyed.

The guardians snarled and roared in their death throes as Chirpotera kept pouncing on and off them and slashing away. Individuals moved too fast to track, but collectively there were so many small bodies on the guardians at any one time that they reminded her of ants swarming prey. These kills were not glorious. They gave her no sense of satisfaction. But they were necessary.

Loud pops filled the air. Ivy looked skyward and saw the red light of flares filtering down through the world tree's branches. Korahshka had been sighted. She needed to get into position.

She would leave. In a moment. Her world's most sacred creatures deserved their funeral rites.

"From the soil we rise. To the soil we return." Guardian blood soaked the ground. One had already stopped moving. The other would soon. "This is but a temporary parting. What has died shall sprout again, for we are all links in the great chain of life. From now until the end of time."

She prayed the words were true, that Ataraxia would somehow give her avatars another chance at life. It was a dim hope while the Vohr occupied her world, but nature had a way of enduring. The Cleansing Flame could not destroy Ataraxia. Perhaps the Vohr would fail too. Perhaps, even now, Ataraxia fought to cleanse herself.

Hope was hard to hold onto as thousands of monsters raced for the world tree, with only a single Shrike somewhere back there to thin their numbers before they reached the ant colony.

Ivy shook her head. She could not afford to think of her homeworld now. She had another battle to survive.

"Take us back to the world tree," Ivy said. "I must be in place when Serena needs me."

CHAPTER 61
ON THE RUN

"Why are we running?" Korahshka asked, keeping pace with Serena as she sprinted for the entrance to the ant colony. "You seemed so eager to fight a few minutes ago."

"If you want my power, you'll have to work for it," Serena said. She hugged the right wall upon entering the colony. She'd never memorize all the turns needed to reach her destination, but had made a point of remembering the first. It took her eyes a moment to adjust from daylight to the perpetual twilight of the colony's interior. Running full speed, she'd have blown right by Ivy's first marker.

Serena's Grand Plan to Save the Multiverse, Step Two: When Korahshka shows himself, lure him away from his troops.

Yesterday, before settling in to relax, Serena and Ivy had Pik-Pik and Tik-Tik lead them through the ant colony, from where it connected to the world tree all the way back to the main entrance at ground-level. At every intersection, Ivy created a bioluminescent mushroom along the wall of the path leading back. Though the species was native to Ataraxia, they looked enough like the local varieties already illuminating these tunnels that they doubted Korahshka would notice a difference. The lime green light they put out was a subtle contrast to the soft yellow of the others, but different enough Serena would recognize it under pressure.

She couldn't afford to get lost.

"You like to talk tough, but you're just a coward when pressed, aren't you?" Korahshka sneered. The acoustics of the colony's tunnels amplified his voice. Even with a hundred-foot lead, she heard him fine.

"For someone who can steal the power of others, I'm surprised you run so slow," Serena said, noticing she'd widened her lead on him as the chase went on. "You call me a coward, but you're the one letting your minions do all your work for you."

Assaulting his ego seemed the best tactic to keep him focused on her. She couldn't let him question why he'd followed her into the ant colony. She took a left turn, briefly taking her out of Korahshka's sight. This phase of the plan was a balancing act. If she got too far out in front of him, she might lose him in the maze of tunnels. Who knew what he'd do then?

But if he got too close, she'd be dead.

When Korahshka rounded the corner behind her, all hell broke loose. Passages that seemed deserted swarmed with drones. Ants erupted from holes cut into the sides of the walls. They dropped from openings in the ceiling. They charged Korahshka from behind, having waited in holes by the entrance for him to pass.

"You may lead him through our domain," Queen Ruta had said when Serena outlined her plan. *"But only if I can give our would-be-conqueror the welcome he deserves."*

Serena made it a life goal to never piss off Ruta.

He's outnumbered at least a hundred to one, Serena thought, clinging to hope. *Maybe Ruta was right. She could end the arrogant bastard here. Maybe I won't have to fight after all.*

Korahshka smiled. He swung his sword in wide arcs, slicing through drone legs and severing heads. As he stabbed one, he kicked another away. He punched a drone with enough force to break through the exoskeleton, then used the poor insect like a club to bludgeon their companions to death while still slashing away with the sword in his other hand. When the drone's body finally broke apart from the abuse, Korahshka muttered in disgust and shook the gore off his hand.

Drones swarmed up Korahshka's legs. When one tried to bite into his neck, a concussive blast erupted from the Davoh'rei's body, sending every ant in a ten-foot radius flying into the walls with crushing force. Exoskeletons cracked. Blood splattered the walls. None of the ants stood again.

He'd killed every drone in sight in less than a minute.

"Cute little ambush," Korahshka said, flinging blood off his sword. "I hope you have more lined up. This is much more fun than I expected it to be."

Serena resumed running. If nothing else, the ants bought her a moment to catch her breath. Doubt invaded her thoughts as she took another turn. *I'm not baiting Korahshka into traps because of his ego. He expected to be ambushed in here. He just doesn't care.*

If Korahshka felt confident enough to walk right into the heart of his enemy's territory and not even flinch, did they have the strength to defeat him?

One of us is going to die today. I'm starting to think it might be me.

CHAPTER 62
THE HATCHERY

Acting on instincts honed from thousands of hours of training, Annea relaxed her body, preparing it to roll with the inevitable impact. She raised her arms over her head like a diver, kukris pointed up and away so she wouldn't stab herself. She slammed into the exterior wall of the ant colony, rolling several times before she could use her weapons as brakes to dig in and control her descent down the steep slope.

<I'm coming, Mom! I'll save you!> Pik-Pik shouted.

"I'm fine!" Annea lied, wincing as her shoulders almost popped from their sockets at the sudden deceleration. Her tactics worked, but didn't stop her from slamming into the colony repeatedly on the way down. She'd have some spectacular bruises when all of this was over.

While she struggled and flailed, Pik-Pik walked along the underside of the exterior walkway, onto the side of the world tree, then down to her position without effort. Gravity was optional to an ant when they had something stable to walk on.

I'm not going to make the opening before the next wave of jellyfish arrives, Annea realized. She dug in with her blades and feet, creating as much friction as possible against the ant colony. After several tense moments, she came to a stop. She pulled one of the blades free, then reached down to embed it in the colony wall at waist level. Clutching the other kukri tight, she pulled herself up until she could set her feet on the handle of the lower one. She pressed down, putting more and more of her weight on it. Satisfied it wouldn't break loose, she stood on the handle, then spun to place her back against the wall. She was still over two hundred feet above the ground.

Explosions filled the air. One of Z'han's Shrikes came into view far below. The Octari co-pilot fired with pinpoint precision into the clouds of enemies in the air, taking out those closest to Annea and the colony first.

That must be Cole's Shrike, Annea thought. *Very timely assistance. I hope the battle to the south is going well enough they could spare him.*

While the Shrike removed the threat of imminent death by explosion, she still had reapers to contend with. She'd lost any lead she'd have over them. If she jumped down now, the first pair would arrive at the opening at the same time she did. They paid her no mind, their attention seemingly locked on the colony's new and unwanted side entrance.

Annea lowered herself until she hung down from the kukri she'd used as a temporary foothold. She wiggled it up and down until she could wrench it free from the wall, then slid thirty feet. She jumped the rest of the way, planting her feet squarely into the crown of a reaper's head. Using it as a springboard, she backflipped into the colony. The impact didn't jar the reaper loose, but stunned it long enough that the next nearest reaper arrived at the opening alone, allowing her to face it one-on-one.

A gurgling, crocodilian growl rumbled from the monster's throat. It slashed down at her. Annea ducked under the swipe and stepped towards it before the reaper could reposition itself. She thrust a kukri up through the soft flesh where the base of its jaw connected with its neck. Blood painted the walls as Annea cut sideways to free her blade. The reaper staggered forward two steps before collapsing to the floor.

They may be resistant to magic, but conventional weapons work just fine.

Pik-Pik raced through the hole in the wall and stopped a safe distance behind her, along the tunnel that would lead them to Ruta's hatchery.

The ant queens kept separate chambers on the same floor, but at opposite ends of the colony. It was an ancient defense strategy going back thousands of years, intended to prevent invaders killing both queens at once. If one queen died, the other could assume total control of the ant population, if given enough time. The modern justification was that Ruta and Chibi couldn't stand each other. The separation helped them focus on their own areas of responsibility and spheres of influence within the colony, keeping each from biting the other's head off.

If the Vohr conduct a similar attack to the west, Chibi will have to figure that out on her own. I don't have time to check in with both of them.

Annea backed away from the fallen reaper and created a fresh mesh of energy slashes in the air. As soon as the second reaper appeared at the opening, she launched them all at once. Angry purple streaks of power slammed into its skin and dissipated with no apparent effect. As she'd feared, that trick wouldn't work against their magic resistance.

Reapers may be powerful and strong, but they'd never match her speed. Annea dashed forward and slashed through the reaper's wrists as it tried to impale her. She dove between its legs, slashing the tendons in its ankles. No longer able to control its hands or feet, the monster collapsed in a heap. She finished it with a stab through the back of its neck, severing its spine.

<Mom! You can't fight them all,> Pik-Pik said. <We must run!>

Annea wasn't convinced. She held the high ground and a chokepoint. She could fight reapers one-on-one all day. Their own bodies would become a barrier blocking entrance to the colony. *But I don't have all day,* Annea reminded herself. *Serena needs my help.* She risked leaning out through the opening to survey the area. The Shrike's bullets tore through many of the advancing reapers, but at least a hundred were still climbing the exterior of the colony toward her position. As if to reiterate the urgency, red flares exploded in the air.

Korahshka had arrived on the battlefield.

I'll still be able to warn Ruta and get into position in time, but it'll be close.

<Mom!>

"I'm coming," Annea said, "but this opening has to go." Together, they retreated a dozen paces down the corridor, then Annea turned back. Once more, she channeled energy into her blades and slashed the air, leaving jagged ribbons of purple hovering in the blade's wake. Each one packed far more power than the ones she'd thrown at the jellyfish.

"Ruta's going to be very unhappy with me, but she'd like the alternative less." Annea made a pushing gesture, launching the energy into the walls and ceiling nearby. Her attacks exploded on impact, shattering the ceiling and triggering a cave-in of the surrounding area. She'd needed to aim carefully to keep the exterior wall from opening further. The pile of rubble would slow the reaper's advance, but not by much. Dissatisfied, Annea repeated the attack, destroying a chunk of the colony two levels up. When the dust settled, debris plugged everything but the top couple feet of the opening. The reapers would either have to clear the rubble before entering, or crawl over it one at a time. It would have to do.

She followed Pik-Pik through a series of twists and turns down passages lit only by bioluminescent moss and fungus growing on the walls. This section of the colony saw little foot traffic even under normal circumstances. With the drones deployed elsewhere for the battle, it felt like a cave. Or a crypt.

"Stop," Annea said. Though she couldn't detect the pheromones and other subtle signals ants used to communicate orders and mark positions the way Pik-Pik could, she had enough spatial awareness to know Pik-Pik's turn led the wrong way, back up towards elven territory. Was it an unconscious act to head home, or a deliberate move to avoid talking to their biological mother? "We came down here to warn the queen, we can't go back yet."

<I... I can't do it.> Pik-Pik didn't move. Their whole body quivered with fear. <I'm sorry, Mom. I'm weak. I'm useless. I'm a mistake, just like Mother always said.>

Annea's anger flared. Not towards Pik-Pik, but towards their mother. The psychological damage Ruta's harassment inflicted upon her most unique children was unconscionable. She had no use for drones who could think for themselves and had a sense of self-preservation.

Despite the need to hurry, Annea sat down beside Pik-Pik and ran a hand up and down their thorax. "You're not weak, or useless. Those are Queen Ruta's lies. Who do you trust more, Ruta, or me?"

<You,> Pik-Pik said without hesitation.

"And what do I say about you?"

<That I am special. That you enjoy my company and that I'm very helpful. I make you laugh. Also I talk too much.>

Annea laughed. "I do need quiet sometimes. But if it wasn't an emergency, have I ever told you or Tik-Tik to be quiet?"

<No.>

"And that's because I adore your babble, even if it wears me out sometimes. Have I ever lied to you?"

<No.>

"Then it must be true. You are very special. You're irreplaceable to me." Pik-Pik's shaking eased. She could tell the fear remained, but Pik-Pik had it under control again.

Someday, sweet thing, I hope you'll learn how to ignore your mother's cruelty. And you won't need my words to shore you up, because you'll know your own worth.

Time to get them focused on the task at hand.

"You knew what our goal was when we came down here," Annea said, her voice gentle and without reproach. "We have to let Queen Ruta know the colony has an exposed flank so she can divert troops. If she dies, there will be chaos before Queen Chibi can assume command over all the castes." She sighed. "You can wait outside her chamber when we get there. She won't even see you."

That got Pik-Pik moving again. <Ok. Fine. I'll take you to Mother. You can say "Hey! Look out!" Then we'll get into position so you can kick the bad guy's ass!> Annea smiled at the sudden, childlike enthusiasm.

They spent another five minutes winding their way through narrow, empty corridors before the pathways widened out. One final turn brought them to a wide hallway sloping down into the vast chamber where Ruta laid eggs. Pik-Pik waited out of sight as Annea strode into the queen's sanctum.

Ruta lay on a raised dais, a steady line of drones at her rear, each grabbing an egg the moment she laid it, then transporting it away to one of the nurseries. Even in the midst of battle, while commanding many thousands of drones through a combination of telepathic commands, pheromones, and spoken orders, she still carried on as a one-woman factory, cranking out a new generation of ants to replace her no-doubt staggering losses outside.

"Annea? What are you doing here?" A dozen paces before the queen, Inara and Pavi stood ready for battle with weapons drawn — a heavy compound bow of her own design for Inara, a standard shortsword for Pavi.

"Why are you here?" Annea asked, surprised to see her friends.

"Ruta invited us here," Inara said. "I know. Shocking, right? After our assistance snuffing out earlier incursions into the colony, she wanted someone she could trust watching her back while she commands her troops."

Annea eyed the elephant-sized soldier ants stationed at the queen's sides. "They weren't sufficient?"

Inara lowered her voice. "There are only a dozen soldier ants. Extras didn't hatch in time for the invasion. The existing stock is spread thin protecting key areas of the colony. Besides, Ruta wanted protection from someone who can act independently. Can you imagine the mental strain of commanding so many troops? Apparently it creates lag time in processing what's happening around her, so she wants someone who can respond in an instant to threats without an order."

"That's us," Pavi said. "Ready to explode into action at a moment's notice. One. Two. It's finished," he said, thrusting his sword dramatically.

"Are you talking about the battlefield or the bedroom, my dear?" Inara asked.

"I regret my phrasing," Pavi said.

Proving Inara's point about delayed reactions, Ruta shook her head as if waking from a troubled sleep. <Sword of Kimori. I didn't invite you here. Don't you have a battle to fight? State your business and be gone.>

"It's always a pleasure to be in your presence," Annea said, unable to mask her disdain. She wasted no further time on pleasantries or preamble, outlining for Ruta the threat coming from their eastern flank.

<Typical elven overconfidence. Because nobody has seen them open a tunnel underwater, that must mean it can't be done! Let's

leave one side of the colony and world tree completely exposed!> Her translation collar rendered a sound that was half sigh, half snarl. <This will be the last time I follow elven tactical advice. Very well, I'll divert thousands of the drones I allocated to dying in the north to dying in the east instead. Thank you for the warning. You're dismissed.> Ruta's eyes glazed over as her focus returned to commanding her troops.

With great effort, Annea held her tongue. How could any mother be so callous about the lives she brought into the world? *She doesn't see any of them as individuals,* she reminded herself. *Drones are just cogs in the machine that is the colony. Disposable, and easily replaced. The queen's survival is the colony's survival.*

"Have fun Inara, Pavi. I hope this is an easy assignment for you." Selfishly, she hoped her best friends would be safe here. Ryul was a good kid. She'd hate to have to tell him he'd lost one or both parents. Too many children would be getting that news soon, no matter how well the battle went.

Not everyone survives a war.

Annea turned for the exit, not bothering to remind Ruta that in naming her Sword of Kimori, she'd given Annea absolute power over the handling of the war effort. Ruta could not dismiss her like some inept royal guard in her first week on the job.

<Mom! Look out!>

<Behind you!>

Pik-Pik and Tik-Tik dashed into the hatchery chamber, the latter no doubt relieved to see their sibling upon arrival and learn they wouldn't have to speak to Ruta directly. Only a threat to Annea's life could motivate the pair to rush into their least favorite place on the planet.

"Well, darling, I hope this is indeed a *one, two, it's finished* situation," Inara said.

"Yes. It would be bad if these monsters had staying power," Pavi agreed.

"Now you're doing it on purpose."

Dread and determination warred in Annea's mind. Thirty feet above and behind Ruta, a Vohr tunnel emerged from the wall of the hatchery chamber. Manti crawled out of the fleshy pathway between universes and positioned themselves on the ceiling to get their bearings. A half dozen reapers followed and fell unceremoniously to the floor behind Ruta.

The hatchery transformed from a quiet sanctum into a bloodbath in an instant.

Drones in line to receive eggs from the queen dogpiled the reapers, trying to rip them apart before they could regain their footing.

Ruta's soldier ants unleashed jets of concentrated acid at the manti overhead.

Inara loosed arrows into the tunnel's opening to no apparent effect.

Pik-Pik and Tik-Tik came to a stop behind Annea. They wouldn't be able to shelter there for long.

"Pavi, toss me!" Annea shouted, sprinting directly at him. As children, they'd made a game of seeing how high into the air Pavi could throw her. Despite the chaos, he understood what she wanted, dropping into a sturdy stance and cupping his hands together into a step. They hadn't performed the maneuver in years, but each fell into their role without hesitation. Pavi lifted and tossed Annea over his head. She timed her jump for the moment his hands reached their apex. The move sent Annea soaring right at the Vohr tunnel opening.

She tuned out the noise and chaos below and poured energy into her kukris. She stabbed into the fleshy edge of the tunnel, using her kukris like climbing picks to haul herself deeper inside. Once she'd fully crossed the threshold, the tunnel had its own gravity holding her to the floor. She stood and twisted to the side, evading a slash from an oncoming manti. It exited the tunnel, diving for the motionless ant queen below. Annea swiped at its wings, but missed.

The tunnel pulsed and vibrated beneath her feet. Another manti charged her. In the narrow space, the manti and reapers only had enough room to advance in a single file line. Their Davoh'rei masters probably never thought they'd have to fight in these things. The bug slashed at her head. Annea parried with one kukri, then severed its arm with the other. She buried her weapons in the bug's neck and decapitated it before it could strike again.

The dead insect's body now blocked the tunnel, keeping other Vohr from advancing. A reaper ran it through with its claws. Before it could rip the manti apart enough to get through to Annea, she sliced into the organic tunnel walls, pouring energy through her blades and into the cuts.

She jumped out of the tunnel, spinning in midair to face the battle raging below. The Vohr tunnel exploded behind her. The concussive force of the blast slammed Annea to the ground. Her bruises were going to have their own bruises.

<Mom!> Pik-Pik and Tik-Tik shouted in unison, rushing to her side.

"Follow me," Annea said, backing away from the melee so she could assess the situation.

Three reapers lay dead at Ruta's feet, each surrounded by the corpses of a dozen or more ants. The other three faced off against the few remaining drones. Some drones died in their efforts to knock down the reapers, or pin their arms. Others died for no other reason than to force the reapers a few feet further away from their queen. Inara, Pavi, and the soldier ants were bogged down fighting manti and couldn't assist.

Annea told Pik-Pik and Tik-Tik to stay put. Deciding the flying insects were the greater threat, she sprinted at Pavi. He dropped his sword and gave her another toss into the skies — directly at a manti holding position on the wall overhead. She saw her reflection in its multifaceted eyes. It readied its blades to dice her to pieces as soon as she entered melee range.

It died before she got that close. Annea flung streaks of energy off her kukris towards the manti. It lacked the intelligence to comprehend the purple ribbons of light spelled its doom. It never tried to dodge or block them. Annea hit the wall a second after the explosion blew it apart, then pushed off to return to the floor in a spot clear of blood or random body parts.

Two manti remained. One fell to the ground as a combined blast of acid from the soldier ants ate through its wings. Inara put an arrow through each of its eyes. As it flailed around blindly, Pavi came at it from the side, beheading it with a downward stroke.

The final manti attempted a diving attack at Ruta. It pushed off from the ceiling on the far side of the hatchery, as far from the queen as anything could be in here. The distance gave the soldier ants enough time to line up their aim. Their acid reduced it to a puddle of steaming goo before it covered half the distance to the queen.

With the manti gone, Annea looked for the reapers. Only one remained. It marched over the broken bodies of the last of Ruta's drones, heading directly for the queen. The soldier ants were too far away to reach it in time. Annea's ranged energy attacks wouldn't harm it.

Ruta had her head turned to the sky as if in prayer, seemingly oblivious to her surroundings.

"Ruta! You're under attack!" Annea shouted, hoping she could return her focus to the here-and-now in time to defend herself.

In the whole chamber, only two beings had any hope of intercepting the reaper in time: Pik-Pik and Tik-Tik.

The two looked at each other. They knew it too. And they knew how crippling it would be for Kimori's defenses if either of the ant queens died. Their bodies shook with terror as they nodded to each other. Without a word, the duo charged the reaper with courage Annea hadn't known them to possess.

"Ruta! Look out!" Annea raced toward the impending carnage, knowing she'd arrive too late to do anything but clean up the aftermath. The babbling ants she loved shouldn't have to sacrifice themselves for a mother who resented their very existence.

Ruta didn't deserve them.

Pik-Pik and Tik-Tik came at the reaper from behind. Focused on the queen, the reaper didn't notice them coming. Each ant bit into one of its ankles, halting its advance. Before it could stab them, they'd succeeded in chewing through its legs. It collapsed to the ground and crawled towards the queen, almost close enough to thrust its knuckle-blades into her exposed neck.

The twins shifted focus and bit down on the reaper's arms, pulling back and shaking their heads like wolves prying meat off a fresh kill. The reaper's pace slowed further, but it continued its single-minded push for the queen, dragging Pik-Pik and Tik-Tik with it. Had it taken a moment to roll onto its back and attack, the ants would be dead. Its arms, thick with dense muscle, did not give as easily as its ankles.

The reaper reached its target and rolled into position to strike. Pik-Pik and Tik-Tik had to release their mandibles to maintain their balance. They surged forward, biting into the reaper's arms violently, repeatedly, their mandibles like cleavers slamming into a cut of beef. The reaper couldn't lift its arms to attack them or the queen in the face of their furious last stand. It roared in rage and pain as Pik-Pik and Tik-Tik dismembered it.

<What's going on?> Ruta demanded, coming to her senses and backing up a step in time to see Pik-Pik bite into the reaper's head and lift it from the ground. It took Tik-Tik three bites to chew through its neck. Pik-Pik dropped the severed reaper head like it was hot.

Their foe vanquished, Pik-Pik and Tik-Tik raced back to Annea's side. She bent over to stroke their heads and offer them reassurance. Both shook uncontrollably. Such violence didn't come naturally to them. They weren't warriors. The queens had no power over them, so they couldn't be sent into a killing frenzy like regular drones. They'd killed on their own volition.

And they'd just kept Kimori's hopes alive a little longer.

Ruta stared at Pik-Pik and Tik-Tik. Ant faces were not expressive, but Annea swore she saw surprise in the queen's body language. And calculation. Ruta always had been one to view beings through the lens of what they could do for her.

<It appears I've misjudged you,> Ruta said. That came as close to an apology as anyone could expect from her.

No shit, Annea thought.

"You will never speak ill of them again," she said, making it clear she'd tolerate no argument.

Ruta nodded her assent. <Thank you Tik-Tik, Pik-Pik.>

Acknowledgement? The actual use of their names? The twins were too stunned to speak.

"Your hatchery is secure, for now," Annea said. "As much as I don't like it, I'd suggest pulling back some troops for internal defense. They baited us, waiting until we'd committed our forces outside before striking from within."

<Death approaches from the north, south, and east, and now I have to wonder which of our colony's thousands of corridors might erupt with Vohr at any moment. Delightful.>

Annea pulled Inara and Pavi into brief hugs. "We must be going. Even now, Serena marches Korahshka into our trap."

<I know. He's slaughtering everyone I've left behind to greet him,> Ruta said. <Annea.>

"Yes?" She paused at the threshold of the hatchery.

<Kill him fast. We can't hold out for much longer.>

CHAPTER 63

SHOWDOWN

Serena's calves burned from running for so long on a constant incline. She was out of range of The Bard's musical strength and stamina enhancements. How many different turns had she taken? Thirty? Forty? She didn't know. Time had no meaning. She'd been running for fifteen minutes. Or maybe it was an hour. Both options seemed equally likely.

Along the way, drones ambushed Korahshka at least ten different times. She couldn't bear to watch anymore, but couldn't prevent herself from hearing their untranslatable war cries or the crunching of exoskeletons as they died. Their sacrifices amounted to a mere handful of small scrapes and cuts to his arms, plus a few tears in his pants.

Her whole world shrank to controlling her breathing and keeping her feet moving. Even tired, she ran faster than Korahshka. She wouldn't have to worry about him chasing her down.

At least, not until she wanted him to.

She rounded one last corner, sighing with relief when her destination came into view. The Grand Chamber of Rule. Their final trap. A pair of Ivy's mushrooms stood proudly to either side of the wide-open entrance, her signal that everyone else was in position. Serena ran to the back of the chamber, stopping before the wall-spanning mural of Kimori's ancient battle against the dragon Balor.

Save for the mural, nothing else in the chamber looked like it usually did. At the conclusion of their war council, they'd cleared out the room.

Then Ivy got to work.

If the redesigned chamber were an art piece, Serena would call it *Painful Ways to Die on Ataraxia*. Pitcher plants grew from the chamber's support columns, each filled with the flesh-dissolving acids they used to digest the insects they lured inside. Snake vines criss-crossed each other on the ceiling, named for their ability to strike like vipers at their intended prey. Most lethal of all were the spike-covered trees growing near each of the chamber's corners.

Despite Ivy's numerous and varied warnings, Serena couldn't wait to introduce Korahshka to that species of Ataraxian flora.

"Blasphemy." Korahshka's voice dripped with disgust. As expected, his eyes locked on the mural of his god's downfall upon entering the chamber. "This is the work of uneducated peasants, glorifying their defiance of the natural order of the multiverse." He paid no attention to the plant life around him as he marched to the center of the chamber.

"You invade and destroy worlds with artificially created monsters," Serena said. "You have no right to talk about the natural order of anything."

"Did you think bringing me here would upset me, or give you some kind of edge? I don't care where I harvest your power. This room is as good as any other. Once Kimori has fallen, I'll paint over that mural with the blood of the queens. You expended a lot of energy just to die alone, so far away from the action."

"I'm not alone," Serena said, gesturing back to the entrance.

Serena's Grand Plan to Save the Multiverse, Step Three: Trap Korahshka in our chosen battlefield.

Pik-Pik and Tik-Tik each hid behind one of the Grand Chamber's heavy doors, and took her words as their cue to push them closed. As they closed, they revealed Annea standing behind one, Ivy the other. The dryad covered herself in bark armor.

The ants scrambled up the doors to slide a series of freshly installed bolts into place, locking them shut. With the doors leading to the ant queens' domains sealed off from their sides, Korahshka could not easily escape.

Neither could they.

Only the winners of this fight would walk out alive.

With their work complete, the ants split up and hid behind Ivy's spike-covered trees.

"I see. This final trap was the plan all along. Adorable." Korahshka clapped his hands together like he'd been delivered a gift he cherished. "You must think you're so clever. Is this the part where you scream at me for destroying your insignificant worlds? Or vow to avenge insignificant lives?"

"Words are unnecessary," Ivy said. "We just need you to die."

Annea unsheathed her kukris and charged, not giving Korahshka time to respond. As their best fighter, she'd keep him busy while Serena and Ivy harassed him with their own abilities every chance they had.

Korahshka slashed at Annea. She jumped over the blade, flipping and twisting in the air to land behind him. He threw his head back, headbutting her in the nose. Blood trickled down her face. He kicked back a leg and tripped her. She rolled away before he could turn and skewer her to the floor.

Ivy unleashed the snake vines while Annea regained her feet. They shot down from the ceiling and wrapped themselves around Korahshka's arms, then drew back, lifting him off the ground. He maintained his grip on his sword. Annea thrust for his exposed gut. He kicked the attack aside, then started cutting the vines.

Annea's follow-up attack sliced into the black leather protecting his back, but didn't cut through. Korahshka freed his sword arm and hung awkwardly, spinning to keep the weapon pointed at Annea.

Seeing an opening, Serena hurled a fireball at his exposed back. Big mistake. The explosion didn't harm him, but it blacked and weakened the remaining vines holding him in place, allowing him to shake himself loose. Annea kicked him square in the chest, knocking him back into several of Ivy's pitcher plants. Korahshka's weight crushed them, spilling acid all over his shoulders and back.

Though they primarily ate insects, Ivy said this species could consume rats and other small mammals. Its acid dissolved bones. Korahshka roared with pain as it dissolved leather and ate into exposed skin.

"Those were my sister Rose's favorite plant," Ivy said. "Like her, their unassuming appearance belied hidden lethality."

"Not enough to save her from reapers, I'm sure," Korahshka said. He held a palm out to Annea and hit her with the same kind of concussive blast he'd used to knock away drones. She leaned back and rolled to the side to avoid hitting a different set of pitcher plants. Korahshka used the opening to drop his sword and strip off his leather vest before the acid ate all the way through it.

Korahshka retrieved his sword, which had landed in acid when he dropped it. In that brief period of time, the acid already created pock marks and corrosion in the metal.

That stuff is seriously potent. Ivy's going to take her own allies out with that if we're not careful. Too bad his flesh was holding up better than his weapon and armor. Was that some kind of mutation he'd given himself? Another of his stolen magical powers?

The Davoh'rei frowned at his ruined blade. "This is worthless now. Good for only one thing." He hurled it at Ivy.

Ivy raised her hands in a futile attempt to shield herself. The sudden movement excited the remnants of her snake vines, which lashed out to strike the flying blade. It clattered to the ground, coming to rest between her legs.

Korahshka didn't dwell on the failed attack. He had daggers out and ready for Annea's next charge. They traded thrusts, feints, and parries, both moving at speeds Serena struggled to track. Neither landed a blow on the other. Annea imbued her blades with magic, making them glow purple.

If we survive this, I need Annea to teach me how to fight like that.

"If?" Tako said. "I'd say the fight is going well, all things considered."

"I wish I shared your optimism," Serena said. Despite some acid burns to his shoulders, the Davoh'rei looked fighting fit.

Annea repositioned herself between Korahshka and Ivy to protect the dryad. Korahshka moved with her, exposing his back to Serena. Seeing her chance, she hurled a fireball at him. The resulting explosion knocked him towards Annea's waiting blades. He parried one of Annea's slashes. The other achieved a shallow cut across his left arm.

Seriously, what is his skin made of? She'd scored a direct hit, but he wasn't burned at all. She thought she'd seen a flash of blue light when her attack landed. Some kind of shield?

Ivy waved to get Serena's attention, then pointed to one of the spiked trees. Serena was on the opposite end of the chamber from Ivy, so she jogged to her nearest tree. Careful to avoid touching the spikes, she reached up and plucked a couple fruits from its branches, recalling Ivy's explanation of how they worked.

"We call these trees Spoiled Children," Ivy said, *"because they throw tantrums to get what they want."*

"I don't get it," Serena said.

Ivy plucked one of the pinecone-shaped fruit from the tree's branches. "Spoiled Children have a unique method of seed dispersal. When the fruits are sufficiently dry, they explode, launching flat, sharp seeds in every direction. It can be quite lethal to anyone caught in the blast radius. We leave warnings around the trees to prevent unintentional exposure."

"That's quite the tantrum. Should you be holding that then?"

"We have known how to weaponize these for millennia. I will show you."

The fruit of the Spoiled Children changed color in a predictable manner as they dried, dulling from a bright orange to a deep brown. *When you see brown, get down.* Dryads primed the fruit for detonation by absorbing its moisture into themselves. Serena achieved a similar result by treating it to a low-intensity heat in her hand. By keeping the base of the fruit pointed in her direction and throwing it like a spear, she could ensure most of the seeds went flying where she aimed when it exploded.

"Incoming!" Serena shouted, lobbing her fruit at Korahshka's feet. Ivy aimed higher, likely trying to time hers to explode in the air. Annea sprinted across the chamber to dive behind a support column. Serena ducked behind another, not sure where Ivy ended up.

Four thunderous bangs reverberated through the Grand Chamber of Rule.

Korahshka screamed.

<Again! Hit him again!> Pik-Pik and Tik-Tik called from their positions of relative safety behind the Spoiled Children closest to the entrance.

Serena obeyed, lobbing two more at Korahshka's last known position. Again, deafening bangs reverberated through the sealed chamber. She stepped out of cover to assess the damage.

Korahshka stood ten feet from one of the Spoiled Children. The flurry of explosions caused him to drop his daggers, which lay far enough apart he couldn't grab both at once. His black leather pants were in tatters. He bled from numerous little holes across his chest, back, and legs where seeds punctured skin. Despite the damage, he stood tall.

That's not the posture of a man with a punctured lung. Damn.

"Still having fun, Korahshka?" Serena asked.

"Absolutely."

"Liar."

Ivy used the distraction to emerge from behind the tree closest to Korahshka and run away. He lunged for her, snagging a handful of her grassy hair. He yanked it, sending her sprawling on the ground.

Serena hurled fireballs at his face to divert his attention. Now that she knew to look for it, she noticed the flashes of blue light every time one of her attacks landed. *Whatever that shield is, I'll need to find a way to nullify it. Or overwhelm it.* It protected Korahshka from magic, but hadn't helped him against physical threats.

Pik-Pik and Tik-Tik ran out from behind the Spoiled Children, each grabbing one of Korahshka's daggers in their mandibles before retreating to their hiding places. Serena continued pelting him with fireballs. If nothing else, she wanted to make it too hard for him to see his surroundings to hurt Ivy. Annea dashed in to rejoin the fight.

As Annea closed in and Ivy regained her feet to flee, Korahshka unleashed another concussive blast. Annea was ready for it and maintained her balance. Ivy smashed into a wall and crumpled to the floor. The Davoh'rei focused on Annea, pointedly ignoring Serena's attacks.

We were so sure we could collectively take down one man. He's not all ego after all. Just how badly did we underestimate him?

Annea danced and rolled, using her superior agility to entrap Korahshka in a cage of purple energy slashes she left hanging in the air. She clapped her kukris together, sending all of that energy flying at him. His body shook from the force of the impacts. Blue light flashed in time with most of the hits. A few got through, slicing into his muscular torso.

His defenses CAN be overwhelmed. Serena felt a fresh wave of hope.

"I have an idea," Tako said. *"It's a bit of a mixed bag though."*

"I'm listening."

"Juggling." He filled her mind with images of his intent.

He was right. It was a mixed bag. She loved the concept, but it would hurt him even more than the last time they'd tried it.

Annea jumped back, buying herself space to prepare another wave of energy slashes. Korahshka didn't allow her a moment's rest. He surged forward and chopped one of her wrists, stunning her nerves and forcing her to drop a kukri. She tried a horizontal slash with her other blade to drive him back, but Korahshka caught her wrist and dragged her towards him. With a sharp twist, her wrist snapped. Her other kukri dropped to the floor. With his free hand, Korahshka grabbed the tiara crowning her head and tried to rip it off.

"So, the legends were true," Korahshka said, whipping Annea's head back and forth. Welded to her skull, the tiara wasn't going anywhere. Annea struggled in vain to break his grip on her wrist or her head. "The Sword of Kimori exists. The world's chosen war master. Supposedly able to draw energy from the world tree itself for a limitless supply of stamina and magical power. I am not impressed."

Annea went limp, dragging Korahshka's arms down. She grabbed a kukri with her good hand and slashed deeply into the wrist holding her head. Korahshka roared with pain. Never releasing his grip, Korahshka dragged her to the nearest wall and bashed her head into it three times.

When Annea went limp this time, it wasn't a ploy. Pik-Pik and Tik-Tik cried out but remained hidden behind Spoiled Children.

"Juggling," Tako insisted. *"Juggling juggling juggling."*

"I don't want to hurt you." Serena felt her rage building. Her friends were injured or dead. She had to finish the fight.

"DEATH WOULD BE WORSE!" Tako sounded as close to anger as an Octari could get. *"Now give me some fireballs."* Without waiting for agreement, Tako fanned out his limbs behind her back.

"What is that?" Korahshka asked, bending over to retrieve Annea's kukris.

"Another friend of mine," Serena said.

Korahshka tucked the weapons into the waistband of his pants. Serena caught a glimpse of bone before he pressed a palm against his slashed wrist. Dark energy flowed into the wound. When he withdrew his hand it was sealed, as if cauterized. He repeated the process on the gashes across his chest.

"Ok, Tako. Fine. Juggling time." Serena produced volleyball-sized fireballs and tossed them into the air.

Korahshka spread his arms wide, mocking them with an open invitation to hit him with everything they had.

They obliged him.

Tako swatted fireballs at the Davoh'rei as fast as Serena could produce them. Korahshka just stood there and took the abuse. A dozen fireballs scored direct hits without any effect, each shot met with a blue flash of light.

Then one broke through.

And another.

And another.

Blisters welled up on Korahshka's chest. His smile faded. *Didn't think we had that in us, huh?* Serena thought. *There's plenty more where that came from.*

Korahshka drew Annea's kukris and advanced, now ducking and spinning to dodge their attacks. At first, Serena walked backwards, keeping distance while feeding Tako fireballs. *No. Let Tako be your eyes.* She turned and dashed for the mural at the other end of the chamber, lobbing fireballs over her shoulders as she went. They hadn't practiced fast-moving cooperative fireball flinging. Their timing was off. Tako missed every third fireball. The ones he did hit lacked their typical accuracy. He was slowing down, his pain clouding both their minds.

Turning her back on the enemy was a mistake.

Octari minds could juggle multiple tasks at once. Hers could not. Creating and tossing fireballs. Ignoring Tako's pain. Sprinting on legs already worn down from the long climb through the ant colony. Avoiding puddles of acid on the floor.

It was too much.

They'd broken Korahshka's shield. Skin blackened and flaked off after enduring multiple strikes. But they were worn down and he knew it. Serena stumbled but found her balance before falling. It gave Korahshka the opening to push through their increasingly sporadic attacks and run her down.

The Davoh'rei slashed down with an attack that could have severed both of Serena's arms near the shoulders. Tako slapped his arms away. Korahshka retaliated, dropping the kukris and grabbing Tako's limbs. He kicked Serena in the back, sending her flying into the mural along the back wall.

Tako's presence abruptly left her mind. Serena whirled, desperate to see what happened to him.

Korahshka held the Octari in his hands.

Though ripped from his host, Tako never stopped fighting. His limbs stretched to the max, trying to wrap themselves around the Davoh'rei's throat. His skin cycled through rapid and disorienting changes in color and texture.

"What a disgusting creature," Korahshka said. He grabbed Tako by his bulbous mantle and hurled him into the wall near Annea's prone form. Tako hit with enough force to shatter bones, if he'd had any. Blue blood splattered the wall, leaving a streak as he tumbled to the floor.

Time stopped.

She couldn't look away from the blood running down the wall. She couldn't unsee Tako's crumpled, motionless body. He'd become such a large presence in her life, but now he looked tiny. Insubstantial. Broken.

Any sense of self-restraint she had vanished. She surrendered herself to pure, blinding rage, drawing power into herself without reservation. Flames engulfed her. The rush of power almost knocked her off her feet. It was intoxicating. Pure euphoria.

She felt like the avatar of a vengeful god.

She reveled in the darkest, most violent forms of retribution her imagination could produce. She'd rip the horns off Korahshka's head and gouge his eyes out with them. Then pry out his shark teeth and jab them into the ritualistic scars covering his body. She'd hang him from the world tree's branches with a rope made of his own intestines. No torture she could inflict on him would equal even a fraction of the misery he'd inflicted upon the multiverse, but she vowed to balance the scales as much as possible before her own magic consumed her.

It didn't matter if she died, so long as he died first.

"Where has this energy been the whole time?" Korahshka asked. "You've been holding out on me."

She didn't reply. The air rippled with heat as she pressed the heels of her palms together and sent a jet of flame at him. Her prior efforts were like a flickering candle compared to the torrent of flame she unleashed upon him now.

Korahshka jumped back, eyes wide. Surprise? No, fear. A feral smile spread across her face. Fear looked very good on him.

She switched to fireballs, aiming to keep him from picking up Annea's kukris. Though smaller, her new fireballs were more condensed, each stuffed with as much power as she could pack into them. They glowed like miniature stars in her hand. She held nothing back, unloading on him with the elegance of a hammer slamming a particularly stubborn nail.

Korahshka strafed, spun, jumped, and dived, proving damnably elusive when he didn't feel like taking a hit. The wood of Kimori's world tree remained immune to Serena's assault, but the temperature in the chamber rose significantly.

Not every attack missed. She scored hits to Korahshka's legs, slowing him enough that she landed a headshot. His defensive powers couldn't withstand the abuse. His pants were gone below the knee, the skin in that area a blackened ruin. His face looked like melted wax. Despite all the punishment inflicted upon him, he still stood.

All too soon, Serena's body failed her. Her knees wobbled, then buckled, sending her to the floor. Her aura of flame vanished. *No.*

Not yet. That bastard has to die! She pounded a fist against the ground, unable to hold back tears of frustration. *It can't end like this.*

"What incredible power you have! It shouldn't be squandered in such amateur hands. I'll make better use of it." Korahshka kicked her onto her back, then grabbed her by the neck and lifted her off the ground.

She felt the skin on the palm of his hand split apart against her throat. There was pressure, then a sharp stab of pain as something like teeth bit into her. Then an intense cold.

This is it. It's over. We failed. Power drained out of her through her neck and into his arm, as if a giant mosquito sucked her life away. Her rage abandoned her, replaced by heavy fatigue. She felt like her weight doubled.

Everyone was counting on us, and we let them down.

Her eyes drifted to the crumpled form of Ivy. She recalled that rare glimpse of a smile as the two played games together. Ivy was no longer the standoffish and broken woman she'd been when they first met. They were sisters now.

She looked at Annea, the warrior spearheading action against the Vohr when nobody else cared. The woman who'd offered her and Ivy sanctuary without hesitation. The woman who'd opened her eyes to the nature of her pyromancy.

Were either of them still alive? Did it matter? If they were, they wouldn't be for long.

She couldn't bring herself to look at Tako again.

The cold sensation spread across her chest.

You all deserved to live. I'm sorry I couldn't end this.

Korahshka grinned. He created a fireball in his free hand. "Pyromancy will make a fantastic addition to my collection."

Serena's eyelids grew heavy. She wanted to sleep. She had, every other time she'd used more power than she could handle. *Power. Using too much power...* Her eyes shot open with a flash of insight. She might have a way out.

Hey, Korahshka. Want my magic? You can have it. Choke on it, asshole.

She thought of all the atrocities he'd committed, all the lives he'd ruined. The citizens of Valencia, butchered and devoured by manti.

Ivy, reduced to an inconsolable puddle of tears at the beauty of the transit cube, knowing her sisters would never see it.

The haggard looks on Cypher and Orlan's faces when they'd ordered her to leave them behind and flee to Kimori.

Kind, noble Kuma, who charged into battle to save a world full of people he'd just met, only to be left bleeding out by an opponent too cruel to finish him off.

Tako's blood streaking down a wall nearby.

Her rage had plenty of fuel.

She fought her fatigue, summoning all the power she could. As soon as she had it, she channeled it through her link into Korahshka. She turned herself into a conduit of magical energy, force-feeding him all her rage, frustration, and grief. When the energy flowed through her that fast, it didn't seem to cause her any further harm.

This might be the only thing keeping me alive, she thought. As long as power flowed through her, he couldn't drain her completely. Maybe. Hopefully.

"Magic is a bit like breathing," Annea once said. *"Like air, magic is all around us. Like air, we draw that energy into ourselves."*

Korahshka grew taller before her eyes. His muscles bulged with stolen power. An aura of flame danced across his upper body. "How? How were you able to draw so much power?" Greed fueled the question, not concern. He drank in the energy with reckless abandon, never pausing to question how she could endure it for so long.

"However, lungs have a finite capacity — you can only inhale so much before you must exhale."

She understood the drunken euphoria Korahshka had to be feeling at this point. His appetite had no limit. That much magic would have killed her several times over if he wasn't taking it as fast as it came in.

"With magic, it is possible to keep inhaling and inhaling until your body breaks down from the strain."

Her existence became nothing but the cold sensation suffusing her body and the rage she stoked with every ounce of willpower she had left.

"You possess a rare talent for channeling large amounts of power quickly, but seem to lack any natural feedback on what you can handle. That's a dangerous combination."

She'd bet her life that weakness was a part of her power. Part of whatever Korahshka meant calling her "more than a pyromancer." Which meant her problem became *his goddess-damned problem* when he stole her magic.

After what felt like an eternity, Korahshka released his grip on her neck and stepped back. Serena collapsed to the floor, unable to stand. Korahshka wavered on his feet before falling to his knees beside her. "What have you done?" he asked. His usual expression of smug superiority was gone, replaced with naked shock.

It worked. Praise the All-Mother, it actually worked.

"I gave you what you wanted," Serena said. "You got my magic. Turns out it comes with unfortunate side effects. I'd say I'm sorry about that, but I'm really, really not."

Korahshka's swollen muscles contracted and spasmed. Blood leaked from his eyes, nose, and ears. She heard bones snap as they became too brittle to support his weight. He fell facedown on the floor. Unable to endure the vast amounts of power he'd taken in, Korashka's body ripped itself apart before her eyes. He extended an arm, reaching for the mural on the back wall as if begging for Balor to save him.

Should she use her dagger and finish him off? Nah. She'd show him the same mercy he'd given Alterra, Ataraxia, Mallozzi, and over three hundred other worlds — none whatsoever.

She didn't consider herself a cruel person.

He'd earned this.

Serena's Grand Plan to Save the Multiverse, Step Four: Kill the Bastard.

She crawled across the hard dirt floor to Annea and Tako. She felt hollow, as if Korahshka's attack had reached inside her, scooped something out, and thrown it away. What did that mean? It was a problem for later.

She heard movement and looked over to see Ivy shaking herself awake. The dryad ran towards Serena, green energy glowing around her hands. "Don't worry about me," Serena said, though she clung to consciousness through willpower and stubbornness alone. "Check on them."

Ivy obeyed, crouching down to inspect Annea and Tako. "Both will survive," she said. "Annea has a broken wrist and fractured skull. Tako has a bleeding head wound and severe burns to his limbs. All of this I can heal, with time. I will start with their head wounds."

"Thank you."

"There is more," Ivy said, tension in her voice. "Both have concussions. Tako's in particular is... severe."

"Can you heal that too?" Serena asked.

"I cannot. Using magic on someone's brain is extremely dangerous. Only master healers would dare attempt it. Their concussions must heal naturally."

Serena said a silent prayer of thanks that they'd all survived.

Under Ivy's ministrations, the wound on Tako's head closed. He woke up and untangled himself from the awkward jumble he'd landed in.

She reached out for Tako, eager to rejoin their minds. He slapped her arm away. "Tako, what's wrong? Talk to me." She offered him her hand. Again, he slapped it away.

When Serena persisted, Tako touched the tip of a limb to her skin with obvious reluctance. His presence appeared at the edge of her consciousness, tucked away behind the thickest mental curtain he'd ever created. *"I've broken every bone in my body,"* he said, his voice dim and distant. He sent her an image of his body and limbs wrapped in a cast. It looked like a child's drawing.

"You have no bones."

"I know!"

Serena chuckled. It wasn't a great attempt at humor, but if he was trying to bring a smile to her face, it couldn't be that bad, right? *"Come on, buddy. Climb aboard and let's see if we can sneak our way up to an infirmary."*

Tako flashed through a rapid series of color changes. Pink. Yellow. Purple. Black. His body spasmed. Black ink spread out in a puddle around him as if he'd wet himself. The heavy curtain between their minds disappeared in an instant. Dizziness and nausea overwhelmed her. *"NOT SAFE. NO BOND. TIL HEALED."*

The words were maddeningly loud in her head, like he'd screamed into her brain because he didn't know what a normal speaking voice sounded like anymore. The nausea crescendoed into a tension headache that left her feeling like her brain would drill a hole through her skull above her right eye and flee. She crawled a few feet away before vomiting all over the floor.

Her heart broke, understanding now how much pain Tako was in.

She crawled away from her mess to returned to Tako's side, setting her back against the wall. Some of his ink stained her skin and clothes. She didn't care. He'd survived. They'd all survived. Many brave people outside this room wouldn't be so fortunate.

"Is Korahshka dead?" she asked Ivy.

Pik-Pik and Tik-Tik answered. She hadn't even noticed them emerge from behind the Spoiled Children. <He's dead.>

<Extremely dead.>

<I didn't know a body could liquify like that.>

<It's very disgusting.>

<I don't envy whoever has to clean that up.> Pik-Pik and Tik-Tik ended their inspection of Korahshka's remains and parked themselves at Annea's feet.

"What happened to him?" Ivy asked.

"He stole my magic," Serena said, too exhausted to elaborate. Finding an infirmary had been a flight of fancy. She had no energy left for that. She needed sleep. "I hope everyone can finish the fight without us. I have nothing left."

"We have done our part. Kimori's defenders will do theirs," Ivy said. She'd finished attending to the worst of Annea's injuries and shifted her attention to Tako's burns.

Serena closed her eyes. "Rest up, sister," Ivy's words had the soothing tone of a lullaby. And with a dose of optimism so surprising Serena thought she might already be dreaming, Ivy added, "All will be well."

CHAPTER 64

AFTERMATH

"Few things bring people together like mourning the dead," Serena said, her mood dark despite the abundant sunshine filtering down through the world tree's branches. She stood beside Ivy on one of the many walkways ringing the exterior of the world tree, watching the grim post-battle cleanup playing out down below. From their vantage point, they had an unobstructed view of ant drones carrying Ankoran dead and laying them respectfully upon communal pyres built from the trees of the surrounding forests. When each pyre ran out of room, it was set alight.

When the breeze shifted in the proper direction, it carried with it the sounds of funeral hymns sung by the bearfolk and elves who'd made the trip to ground level to pay their respects.

Though they still didn't understand how it worked, their suspicion had been proven right. Korahshka's control over the Vohr functioned much like how the ant queens controlled their drones, or how Siren had controlled her victims. It didn't work without him. Upon his death, the Vohr became listless and confused. Many manti stopped in their tracks, not even trying to defend themselves as Kimori's defenders hacked them apart. Mass assaults disintegrated into disorganized and half-hearted attacks. Within hours, the battle shifted from inevitable defeat into decisive victory. The smartest of the Vohr used their tunnels to flee back to wherever they'd come from before Kimori's defenders destroyed them. Others scattered into the wilderness — a problem they'd have to deal with later, lest they endanger Kimori's native wildlife.

"We have won a great victory, Serena," Ivy said. She had her eyes closed and her face pointed towards the sun. "It is only right and proper to pay respects to those who returned to the soil helping us achieve it." If she picked up on Serena's mood, she showed no sign of it.

"And, if you're the Chiroptera, make a nice profit for services rendered," Serena added, shifting her gaze to watch a convoy of drones carry Vohr corpses to the Chiroptera, who harvested manti arm blades and any other monster pieces they thought they could use or sell. Other drones carried away what remained to be burned in pits dug for the purpose on the other side of the tree, out of view of the Ankoran funerals.

Ivy said nothing. Tako would have picked up on her attitude and said something wise and calming by now. Goddess, she missed him. They hadn't even been apart a day yet.

She needed to take a more direct approach. "We did it, Ivy. We saved the world. Maybe *all* the worlds. So why do I feel so bad?"

In all the adventure novels she'd read, this would be the part where the heroes celebrated their successes. Poems and songs were crafted in their honor. Their heart's desires were fulfilled. Everyone basked in the afterglow of a job well done.

Serena just felt hollow.

"The battle happened yesterday. Eighteen hours of sleep is not enough time to recover from your physical traumas," Ivy said. "You drew in too much magic. Again. You have small muscle tears and soreness across your entire body. Your bones are weakened and brittle. Until I can provide you further healing, you should consume bovine lactose to strengthen them. That is a human custom, is it not?"

Serena laughed, then grimaced as her ribs tried to burst through her chest. "Milk, Ivy. We call that milk. And that's not what I meant."

"Oh. You were speaking of emotions." Ivy turned to face the world tree. Their walkway connected to a hospital facility, one much larger than the clinic they'd visited before. It overflowed with wounded, leaving many less critically injured elves sitting on the balcony or laying on stretchers as they waited to be seen by healers. "I have been sealing wounds and mending broken bones all morning. My mind still dwells on injuries."

"I get it. How are you holding up?"

"I am exhausted, but functional. I will resume healing in an hour or two, but I must absorb more sunlight first to have the energy for it." Ivy paused, realizing she'd missed the point again. "You meant my mental state."

"Yes," Serena said. She'd once found Ivy's social awkwardness and emotional blind spots off-putting, but now they felt weirdly endearing. When Ivy showed feeling, you knew she meant it.

"It may surprise you to know that I am doing well. With Korahshka gone, I feel my sister's souls can be at peace. My talents are valued by the people of Kimori. I have a sense of purpose again."

"I'm happy for you."

Ivy nodded in acknowledgement. Then her face wrinkled with concern. She'd finally figured it out. "You are troubled."

"It's complicated." How could she articulate it to someone who couldn't read her mind? This conversation would've been so much easier with Tako, but he wasn't available. Ivy was all she had at the moment. "I imagined killing Korahshka so many times. I thought I'd be thrilled that he's gone, but I just feel empty."

Ivy wrapped Serena up in a hug. "You did what had to be done," Ivy said. "Survival matters. Protecting others matters. Whether it felt satisfying or not is irrelevant. Chasing heroism and glory is for fools."

"I won't tell the Ankora you said that."

"Many beings get to live because of your actions. You achieved your goal. Now move on and make another."

Count on Ivy to deliver blunt, direct advice. "You're right," Serena said. She had some thoughts on that next goal, but couldn't do anything about it with Kimori quarantined from the rest of the Planar Gate network.

"Serena?" Serena withdrew from Ivy's embrace to greet an elven nurse. The man looked like he hadn't slept since the invasion started. His skin was sallow, and he had dark circles under his eyes. "We set up Tako's recuperation tank last night. At his request, we sedated him to help him rest and recover. He's still unconscious, but you can visit him if you'd like."

As much as she'd come to enjoy Ivy's company, visiting Tako was her primary reason for lingering outside the hospital. If the staff were ready to let her in, she couldn't say no.

"Go," Ivy said. "We can talk again later."

Serena followed the nurse through wide hallways lined with wounded. Every recovery room was loaded to triple the intended capacity. The hospital staff all looked as ragged as her escort, but they held their heads high, pride evident in their work. As overwhelmed as they were, it had to help knowing Kimori won the battle. There wouldn't be more wounded coming. Everyone could eventually move on from the horror of the day before.

The nurse led her into a large room intended for irregular cases. It was an open design without privacy curtains, though the patients in the room all looked too injured to care. Most of the dozens of beds had Ankora or Chiroptera survivors airlifted from the battlefield by teams of scout ants. The citizens of Kimori did right by their allies.

A few tables held ant drones. A golden paste covered cracks in their exoskeletons, reminding her of Alterran artists who fixed broken ceramics with a lacquer mixed with powdered gold, creating something new and beautiful instead of hiding the cracks and imperfections. Given how cavalierly they'd thrown themselves into battle, Serena hadn't thought anyone would bother giving drone survivors treatment. She was glad to be wrong.

Tako's rectangular tank rested on a table in a poorly lit back corner of the room, as if he'd been set aside and forgotten about. "I know how it looks," the nurse said, sensing her agitation. "With so many people coming and going, we wanted to put him somewhere where he wouldn't get bumped into or disturbed. It was difficult to get care instructions from him given his condition, but he was able to write down his desire for low light and sleep. I promise you, he approved of this setup before we sedated him."

The nurse pointed to a bell with a wooden handle inside the tank. "If he wakes up and needs assistance, he'll lift the bell above the water and ring for us. We will continue with written communication until he's ready to resume telepathy. He just needs rest now."

"Thank you for taking care of him," Serena said, her voice cracking. "He... He means a lot to me. How long will he be in there?"

"None of us have worked with an Octari before," the nurse said. "I don't know their natural recovery speed. When an elf has a concussion as severe as his, we keep them here for two days. Full recovery takes two to four weeks."

"Can't you use magic to speed that up?" Serena asked.

The nurse shook his head. "We don't dare use healing magic on someone's brain unless it's a life-or-death situation. Too many things can go wrong. We especially wouldn't want to do it on a species we're unfamiliar with. Tako was clear he considered his situation painful but not life-threatening."

Serena said nothing, just stared at the tank. Two to four weeks. She might be alone in her head for two to four weeks. Weird how that felt like an eternity.

"I'll leave you two alone." The nurse bowed and took his leave.

Serena grabbed a nearby stool and sat down beside the tank. He wouldn't hear her, but in a way, that didn't matter. As soon as they reconnected, he'd be able to access her memory of this moment.

This would be so much easier if we were connected, so you could just understand how I feel, implicitly. So I don't have to put it into words. He wanted her to be more open about her emotions. She owed it to him to try.

"If you wanted a break from me, you know you just needed to ask, right?" Serena stopped herself. No attempting humor to dance around her anxieties and insecurities. This wasn't the time for that. Not with him.

"I'm glad you're alive. I know that's an obvious statement, but when Korahshka hurled you into the wall, something broke inside me. I lost all sense of restraint. All I wanted to do was cause pain. I defeated him by surrendering completely to feral, animalistic rage. By reveling in the darkest fantasies I could imagine. Rage is how I access magic, and I've come to hate that. I don't want to be like that anymore."

Annea had told her that it was possible for people whose emotions fueled their magic to shift their emotional trigger. She hoped she could figure out how to do so.

"I know you want to go home once you've recovered, but like it or not, you're stuck with me for a while. Nobody knows how long Kimori's Planar Gate will be inoperable, or if it's even possible to fix. It's impossible to return to Z'han. I wouldn't want you to, anyway. I'm not ready to say goodbye.

"I appreciate your concern for my welfare, and wanting to spare me the effects of your aging, but we haven't experienced any of that yet. We've seen only a tiny fraction of what's out there in the multiverse. Surely, amongst billions of worlds, someone knows how to counter your cognitive decline. Or extend your lifespan to more closely match what remains of mine. Or reverse aging entirely. Who knows? I just don't want you to give up before we've even tried to find a solution."

Was she being selfish, wanting him to stay with her more than for him to live out his last years amongst his own kind? Was it delusional to seek what amounted to a cure for old age? Tako was family. The weird, kind, humorous, empathetic, telepathic, shapeshifting cephalopod grandfather figure she'd never imagined she'd want — and now couldn't live without. It felt so quiet and lonely being the only voice in her head. She missed his soothing presence. Was it so wrong to want that to continue?

As Ivy said, she needed to set a new goal. If she wanted to convince Tako to stick with her, they needed a shared purpose, a goal he could believe in too. "We have more work to do, Tako. The Davoh'rei aren't going to stop their schemes because we killed a ton of their pet monsters. They're building power in the Nexus. Left unchecked, they'll keep going until they unleash something even more evil than they are. I just... I don't want anyone else to suffer like Ivy and I have. To have their whole world destroyed. Or worse, see it twisted into some unnatural abomination.

"If we're ever able to leave Kimori, I have to fight this battle. With you, or without you. I wouldn't be able to live with myself if I walked away and left the job unfinished. I'd feel better if I had you along for the ride."

A sense of peace settled over her. She felt lighter for having spoken her mind. *Tako's a great sounding board. Even when he's asleep.*

Serena stood and twisted, cracking her back. She took a finger and traced a heart on the condensation outside Tako's tank. "I'm going to be okay, and you will too. Rest up, old man. Get well soon. We've got work to do."

EPILOGUE
TWO DAYS LATER

"You can't have your bedroom back," Jesserin said, poking Annea in the chest to drive her point home. Given the size difference between the two, she had to reach over her head to do it, rendering the gesture more comical than intimidating. "Those are the queen's chambers, and I remain the queen."

"We could share it," Annea said, gently grabbing Jesserin's hand and bending over to kiss it.

"NO. MINE." Jesserin grinned. She didn't pull her hand away. "But if you want to stop by sometimes to talk, you'd be welcome."

"*Talk?* My queen, you write romance. Two characters forced to share one bed is a popular trope, isn't it? *Anything* could happen. Where's your sense of adventure?"

Jesserin blushed. "I had my fill of it keeping my head attached to my neck while manti swarmed us, thank you very much."

Serena leaned on the railing of the walkway outside the entrance to the queen's lodgings, guest rooms, and the royal reception chamber. She kept a discreet distance from the elves, waiting to be noticed. Should she come back later?

Annea had been in constant motion the last few days, inspiring her people and helping to organize recovery and rebuilding efforts. All while suffering a concussion of her own.

The Sword of Kimori had plenty of things she still needed to figure out as the planet's wartime leader. Elven forces destroyed all the Vohr tunnels, but nobody knew when or if a new leader would rise to lead the monsters for another attack on Kimori. Could they endure another fight of that scale with no hope of resupply or reinforcement from other worlds? Would they even need to? They had no way to know if they were truly safe, or if they still had the threat of annihilation hanging over them.

I didn't expect sleeping arrangements would be the topic I'd walk in on when Annea asked to see me, Serena thought. She cleared her throat to alert the elves to her presence before Annea could advance her unsubtle desire to create the planet's ultimate power couple.

"Are they really going to stay out there?" Serena asked, stepping forward to join the elves when Annea waved her over. From their vantage point, the three of them were ideally situated between branches to have an unblocked view of the grounds surrounding the Planar Gate. The Chiroptera had a tent city surrounding it for a half mile or more in every direction. Manti and reaper blades were piled up in carts, ready for transit offworld as soon as the Gate worked again.

"They insist on it," Jesserin said.

"If we cannot leave Kimori, I'm grateful to have the Chiroptera camped out around the Gate," Annea said.

"It's better than having them in the tree amongst us." Jesserin shivered with disgust.

"I'd remind you they fought and died for us," Annea said. "That's earned them a measure of respect."

"They're mercenaries who saw an opportunity. They only fought to line their own pockets. And they've been miserable company."

"The incorrigible misogynists aren't behaving well on a world ruled by women? I'm shocked," Serena said.

"That's exactly why I'm happy to have them around," Annea said, drawing raised eyebrows from her companions. "Historically, Kimori has been an isolationist world. The loss of multiverse travel means little to the average daily life of our citizens. Without the Chiroptera, many would see restoring the Gate as an academic problem with no particular urgency, especially with all the rebuilding we have to do. With them here, elven scholars are working around the clock trying to fix the Gate so the Chiroptera will go away."

That... actually made a twisted kind of sense. "Have they made any progress?" Serena asked.

"It's slow going. We've never bothered studying the Gate, for fear of breaking it. We have no knowledge base to work from. Hopefully Cypher can figure it out from his end."

"If he's still alive," Serena said. They had no way to know if he'd escaped or been killed.

"Have hope. If we survived our fight, it's entirely possible he survived his. If there's a way to lift the quarantine, Cypher will figure it out."

She wished she shared Annea's optimism. Cypher was a smart man. He'd proven himself more comfortable and skilled with advanced technologies than she thought she'd ever be. But her gut told her the situation with the Planar Gate wouldn't be an easy fix. Who or what controlled the quarantine protocol responsible for isolating worlds from the rest of the Gate network? The practice continued across multiple sectors of the Nexus for years. The Davoh'rei had shown their hand. They had agents at work in sector governments, and perhaps even controlled some outright. Asking them nicely to remove the quarantine wouldn't be an option.

Serena shook her head, clearing away negativity. Tako wouldn't want her dwelling on things she couldn't control. She moved the conversation away from the battle's aftermath. "You asked to see me?"

"We both wanted to see you," Jesserin said, "to share with you some news before it becomes public. In light of their courage and valor on the battlefield, the ruling powers have voted unanimously to grant the Ankora full Kimori citizenship. Unlike the Chiroptera, we're quite happy to have them around. They don't wish to dwell high above the ground in a tree, so we've granted them wide tracts of land to the north to use as they please. Regardless of whether our Planar Gate works or not, they will always be welcome to reside amongst us."

"That's awesome." Serena felt happy for them, but didn't see how the news led to her being summoned here.

"As you know, we're not big on government on Kimori," Annea said, picking up where Jesserin left off. "The less involved leaders have to be, the better. The Ankora will have full autonomy to live as they please, so long as they live in harmony with the environment.

From what we know of them so far, we have no concerns in that regard. Nonetheless, we need someone to serve as an ambassador facilitating communication and cultural exchange between the elves and the Ankora."

Serena didn't like where this was going. "You want *me* to be that person?" Nobody would ever make the mistake of calling her a diplomat. Patience and tact weren't her strong suits.

"Actually, the Ankora do." Jesserin had a mischievous grin on her face. "They specifically asked for the Lady Pyromancer. They may not know you well, but they trust you. We agree with their choice."

"Why? I'm not qualified for inter-species diplomacy. Surely you can see that."

Annea ignored the question. "You spent some time with them before the battle. What is your impression of the Ankora?"

Serena grinned. "They're pretty badass. I wouldn't want one as an enemy. They seem noble and honorable."

"So you like them?"

"Sure, as well as can be expected from the limited time I've been around them."

"And they like you. You're a hero in their eyes for slaying Korahshka. Mutual respect is all it takes to start building a meaningful relationship with someone," Annea said.

Technically, Korahshka killed himself, Serena thought. *I just helped him douse himself in oil and light a match.*

Perhaps sensing Serena's hesitancy, Annea added, "It's a very informal role, I promise. Besides, leadership on Kimori is ninety-five percent cheerleading your people to live their best lives, four percent arbitrating petty disputes, and one percent soul-crushingly-difficult life-and-death decision making. You'll be fine!

"We'd want you to spend some time amongst them, learning more about their culture and values while helping them build new permanent homes. But nobody's asking you to do anything until Tako's recovered and back with you."

Her reflexive answer was *hell no*, but she checked that impulse. She needed something to do. How would she rather spend her days, if not doing this? It could be fun seeing what the Ankora's warrior ethos looked like in daily life when they didn't have enemies to fight. They could train her to be more proficient with edged weapons. She doubted they'd be mad if she said her goodbyes to join any resistance against the Davoh'rei in the Nexus if the Gate started working again. They might even want to join her.

Calm settled over her as certainty set in. This was the right decision. "I'm in," Serena said. "There's one small problem though."

"Whatever it is, I'm sure we can work it out," Jesserin said.

When she'd talked to Ivy about feeling empty, it hadn't been entirely about emotions. She still felt a physical hollowness inside her, like something had been scooped away. It hadn't taken much experimentation to figure out what that meant.

"I may be the Lady Pyromancer to the Ankora, but my pyromancy is gone. I think Korahshka really did steal it all before he died. I can't light a candle right now if my life depended on it." For a brief time, she'd had magic. Fire was hers to command. She'd relished that sense of power. It would be handy for the battles to come. She didn't want to be an ordinary human again.

"Your magic may be in remission, but it's not gone," Annea said. "A person's magic is bound to their very essence. It's a part of your soul. As long as you live, it will be there. Given the trauma Korahshka subjected you to, that part of you may need more time to heal. Something significant may need to happen to awaken it again. But it's there. I promise you it's still there."

Serena nodded. She didn't believe it, but saw no reason to argue. It was easy to promise the magic would return when you weren't the one feeling the gaping hole of its absence.

"From what we've learned of the Ankora so far," Jesserin said, "your situation may enhance your standing amongst them even more. *We bow our heads in acknowledgement of the Lady Pyromancer, she who sacrificed her power to slay the demon who would have unleashed evil gods upon the multiverse.*" She spoke as if reciting an epic poem.

Leave it to the novelist to make it sound as epic as possible, Serena thought. *As if I'd planned it that way from the start.*

"Last question," Serena said. "Can Ivy join me?"

"Ivy is free to do whatever she'd like," Jesserin said. "If she wants to go with you, we won't stop her. I'm sure the Ankora wouldn't mind having a dryad around when they start cultivating crops."

"I'm glad we got this settled," Annea said, disengaging herself from the group. "I need to head out for another important matter. Pik-Pik and Tik-Tik have a meeting with Queen Ruta, and I want to be there for it. I'm not quite ready to leave them alone with her yet."

"They're going voluntarily?" Serena asked.

"With all the chaos of the last few days, I'm not surprised you hadn't heard. Pik-Pik and Tik-Tik saved Ruta's life during the battle," Annea said. "Speaking from personal experience, surviving a near brush with death can change a person. Ruta can be a hard, mean bitch, but she's not a liar. She wants to get to know the two unique drones she'd cast aside, and I believe her interest is genuine. She's seeing the value in drones who can think for themselves. Those two may be the template for a whole new caste of ants in the near future.

"Pik-Pik and Tik-Tik are sponges for affection. They want to be loved by everyone. They're nervous, for understandable reasons, but they want to explore this opportunity to finally have a good relationship with their biological mother. I'm going to be a supportive mom and do all I can to help make it a success. Ruta can't make up for a lifetime of hostility in a few days, but as long as she's serious about making an effort, I'll support her."

Serena's heart lightened. Pik-Pik and Tik-Tik deserved their mother's love. Hopefully Ruta would do right by them.

"This battle has changed us all," Jesserin said. "Kimori will never be the same. Based on how everyone has handled themselves in the aftermath of the invasion, I'm confident we'll come back stronger than ever. This is the dawn of a new era for Kimori. I can't wait to see what we become."

THE SAGA CONTINUES...

Serena, Annea, and Ivy's adventures have only just begun! Want to be amongst the first people to read the sequel? For early access to chapters of the next book in the series as they're completed, please visit planargates.nategillick.com, or stop by www.nategillick.com for details.

All books in the *Planar Gates* series will be released in other formats, including but not limited to ebooks and paperbacks, when they're complete.

Get FREE deleted scenes and behind-the-scenes info on Welcome to the Nexus by signing up for my newsletter at: subscribepage.io/NVRCX1

Chat with the author and other fans of the series on Reddit at /r/PlanarGates/

Lastly, if you enjoyed this book, please consider giving it a review! Reviews are social proof that people are reading a book and give potential new readers an idea of what they have to look forward to. Thank you for your support!

Acknowledgments

While it's true the process of writing a book involves a lot of solitary time in front of a computer screen plucking away at a keyboard, publishing a book isn't a solo venture. There's a lot of advice out there for folks who want to write a book. One tip I don't see often enough is this: surround yourself with people who want to see you succeed. Meeting and making friends with other authors pushed me from "I've always wanted to write a book," to "I've finished one and am working on others." I'm grateful to everyone who has provided advice, encouragement, and support along the way.

First and foremost, I want to thank my parents. They've always celebrated my creativity and encouraged me to keep going. I was never made to feel like writing was a waste of time. Having talked to hundreds of authors over the last few years, I've come to appreciate how uncommon that is. I cannot articulate how grateful I am to my parents for their unwavering support of my desire to write books.

I'd like to thank Scott Kelly for believing in me and giving me time and space when I needed to push hard to complete some major milestones on the road to publishing. I could not ask for a more supportive boss. Laterpress isn't just a great place to publish books or serialize stories, it's a great company to work for.

Let it be known that my friend Stefan is my biggest fan. He was almost always the first person to read new chapters as they were released while I serialized the initial draft. His positive feedback gassed me up and motivated me to keep going. He'd lead you to believe I walk on water and am The Best Author Ever. I know better, but still, I wish every author starting out had a hype man like Stefan in their corner.

When an author intentionally names a character after someone they know in real life, and then kills that character off in a brutal way, it means one of two things: Either the author hates that person and is exacting a measure of petty revenge, or they're tight and that person is in on the joke. The real-life Jonah falls into that second category. Unlike fictional Jonah, real Jonah is one of the strongest, most resilient men I've ever met. It was an honor to kill you off. (I'll do it again.)

Some authors I also wish to thank:

L.P.M. Sinclair was an invaluable sounding board while working on the book, helping to make sure my ideas passed the "smell test" and didn't seem ridiculous or logically inconsistent. If you enjoyed *Welcome to the Nexus*, you'd probably like L.P.M. Sinclair's *Crimson Steel* series too.

Shana Brooke has excellent taste in memes and made me laugh plenty of times while working on this book. I like to think we kept each other motivated and in high spirits. The song Serena hums to herself in chapter 24 is a subtle nod to Shana's *Queen of Tridents* series. She's three books deep into that series as I write this, and clearly the winner of our short-lived "word count war." I'll catch up... eventually.

Dale Roberts is a wellspring of knowledge when it comes to publishing. He's been a valuable resource for news, resources, networking, and more. I'm better as both an author and a publishing professional thanks to everything he does.

Thank you as well to authors E.A. Blackwell, Jessica Erin, and Christine Daigle for support and encouragement throughout the writing process. Even early on, you saw what I wanted to achieve and pushed me to keep at it. That support helped me get to a place where I feel confident in my ability to write and publish a big fantasy novel. On to the next one!

About the Author

In 1997, young Nate Gillick had his mind blown during the theatrical Special Edition release of *Star Wars*. All the strange aliens in the Mos Eisley Cantina filled him with a sense of awe and wonder he's been trying to replicate ever since. The first story he ever wrote involved "The Scary Scwad" hunting a refrigerator that came to life and ate people. It's safe to assume his writing and spelling have improved since then. Nate graduated from the University of Wisconsin, Eau Claire, with degrees in English (Creative Writing) and Sociology. He resides in Minnesota.

Welcome to the Nexus is Nate's debut novel.

www.ingramcontent.com/pod-product-compliance
Lightning Source LLC
Chambersburg PA
CBHW020650010826
48969CB00012B/30